POWER!

A novel by Michael F. Chenoweth

Lulu Publication 2008

Cover Credits:

Cover design by Maggie McClellan (www.maggiemcclellan.com)

Earth at Night Photo: NASA; C. Mayhew & R. Simmon (NASA/GSFC), NOAA/ NGDC, DMSP Digital Archive

Aerospatiale SA-341 "Gazelle" photo courtesy of photographer Miroslav Bozovic.

(Helicopter in photo produced in Yugoslavia under license from Aerospatiale as SOKO SA-341 "Partizan." Photo from www.airliners.net.)

Prometheus Statue Photo: Elena Valadimirovna Filatova (www.elenafilatova.com)

(The statue of Prometheus stealing fire from the Gods and giving it to the humans once stood in the middle of the town of Chernobyl. After the nuclear accident on April 25, 1986, the statue was moved to the nuclear plant.)

Mitsubishi MU-2 aircraft photo by the author.

Photo of author by Linda Howard Bittner

ISBN: 978-0-6152-0241-9

PROLOGUE

Prometheus was a Greek God who stole fire from Mt. Olympus and gave it to man. Men (and presumably women too) thereafter had intellect and knowledge which fire symbolized, but which Zeus had not intended them to possess. Zeus was so infuriated that he ordered Prometheus chained to Mt. Caucasus to be the eternal prey of a vulture, which would eat his liver through all time.

Project Prometheus has changed the world. This is a chronicle of the high points as they happened.

D.S.

CHAPTER 1

Suppose you could change the world. What would you do? What problems would you address first? War? Global warming? Overpopulation? Famine? Pollution? Energy shortages?

Or you might look at problems that are more local. Health care? Education?

What if there was a way to make a difference – a big difference – in all of these?

What if ...?

****

Everything is political.

Danielle had forgotten that and it nearly killed her. When she smelled exhaust gas in the pressurized cabin of her airplane, her reactions were nearly automatic; grab an oxygen mask, turn off the air-conditioning, turn on the auto-pilot and reset the altitude for a flight level where there is breathable air. Everything was going pretty well until she passed out.

But let's go back to the beginning.

It was after midnight on January 6. Danielle Simones switched off the computer, pushed her chair back, opened the French doors, and walked from the library out of the house, turning out lights as she went. The lounge at the end of the terrace was very comfortable, and she tried to relax after a long day spent writing a complex article for an economic journal on the impacts of current population trends on the world economy. It was a very sobering article.

She had collected all of the projections on petroleum reserves written during the previous fifty years, back to the end of World War II. Over the years, both academic scientists and petroleum industry geologists had estimated the total amount of petroleum in the Earth's crust. Over time, the estimates had varied higher and lower as the science of geology had refined its methods. Industry geologists tended to have higher estimates of the remaining supply than the academics, but all of the estimates, adjusted for those refinements, were surprisingly consistent. She had also collected the figures on estimated global production up to the present date. It was clear from the figures that a large fraction of the original total known supply of geological petroleum had been consumed during the preceding century. It was also clear that global rates of consumption were increasing dramatically, faster than the Earth's exploding population, because many countries with primitive industrial bases were struggling to increase their industrial production, and consumption of energy, to match the most industrial western economies. During the preceding five years, the world had consumed as much petroleum as had been consumed during the

1

first half of the century. At the increasing rate of petroleum consumption, if all energy were produced from oil and gas, the global supply would be exhausted in less than thirty years.

There were, however, several other factors in the equation. A minor fraction of the world's energy demand was being provided by nuclear power or hydroelectric dams. Another larger portion was being provided by coal and coal-like minerals, including lignite. Her research indicated that there was enough coal and lignite to provide a few more years of energy supply. This was contrary to the predictions of many so-called "experts" who claimed that the world had 400 years of energy supply from lignite. Their predictions were based on a single report from the 1970s which stated that, at the then-current rate of consumption, there was enough coal and lignite in the earth's crust to last for four hundred years. The experts had conveniently disregarded the fact that, at the time the report was written, only part of the world's energy was being produced from coal. As a result, with the rate of consumption of energy many times that of coal, the supply of coal would have lasted only a few years if it had been the sole source of energy at the time the report was written. Now, however, the world's appetite for energy was several times as great as had been the case in the 1970s, and at current rates of consumption, all the coal and lignite would rapidly be exhausted in just a few years. The reality was that neither coal nor lignite could be mined fast enough to meet the demand.

Her conclusion was that, including nuclear energy, Earth had an energy supply that would last perhaps forty to fifty years. Even if her estimates were off by a large factor, it was beyond question that the energy supply was finite and running out. Even with a shift to hydrogen and other alternative forms of energy, most of them depended on one of the sources that were running out. The many nuclear plants in the world were aging and there was no coherent effort to build replacements, nor was there a reliable method of handling the radioactive wastes. If the Earth ran out of abundant energy, the global economy, and society generally, would collapse. There were still many thousands of nuclear warheads that could be detonated if they fell into irresponsible hands as society disintegrated. Albert Einstein said he didn't know how World War 3 would be fought, but World War 4 would be fought with sticks and rocks. Danielle tried to imagine how mankind could cope with such a condition, but it was impossible to conceive. It meant a return to a pre-industrial culture, if any culture survived at all.

She closed her eyes and as she re-opened them, they were slowly adapting to the darkness. The evening sea breeze was mild, for January, and the sky was clear. The ancient granite house, an almost invisible presence behind her, sat in the darkness as it had for over five hundred years.

She looked upward. St. Peter Port, the nearest village on Guernsey, had lights that were too few and far away to ruin her view of the night sky. She scanned the stars. There were friends she had known since childhood: Ursa Major, the Crown of Ariadne, and Orion, always Orion. The Milky Way was bright. Idly, she wondered what it was like up there. Lying back on the lounge and desperately hungry for relief from the depressing research, she began to play her favorite game. She called it the "what ifs". 'What if X? What if Y? What if ... ?'

Many years earlier, when she had been a child visiting with her Uncle Bob, who babysat her while her parents were out of town, he used to play the game with her for hours on end. He would invent a problem and she had to invent a solution. She didn't realize it then, but he taught her about the power of the human imagination, and about how to analyze a situation and develop creative solutions to any problem. She had used those lessons many times since then. Now, however, she was grown, and thought about more serious questions than she had as a child.

Suddenly, she sat up. It couldn't be that simple! There must be a reason why it hadn't already been done.

Rushing into the pitch-black library, she turned on the lights and took down a tattered NASA design study from 1977. It discussed the possibility of using orbiting satellites to collect solar energy, which would be converted to electricity and beamed as microwave energy to the Earth's surface. Danielle had read it many times before, and all the pages were loose from the binding, but she had never given it this much serious consideration. What if ...?!

It was 1 AM in the Channel Islands west of France. She picked up the phone and called her travel agent in Miami. Marilyn vanDuser was working nights and answered on the first ring. "Neverland Travel." The voice was cheerful. An uninformed caller would not suspect that Marilyn's travel agency was a cellular telephone in her purse. Marilyn worked part-time for several Miami law firms and sold travel services on the side. She thought of it as working full-time for Marilyn. Her other employers didn't mind her occasional reservations call; she was still more productive than their other employees.

"Marilyn, it's Danielle."

"Dee!" Marilyn said. "How are you? How's Guernsey? I wanted to get over last month but so many things were going on here, I couldn't get away."

"I can imagine. I used to have the same problem. Let me tell you why I'm calling. I need a ticket from Paris-Orly to New York tonight. Wait ... I'd better get the time straight. It's 1 AM here. I want to fly out of Paris on the first flight for Newark that leaves after 6 AM, Paris time. That should put me in New York by Noon. From Newark, I want a flight leaving at 6 PM, Eastern USA time for Melbourne, Florida, and hotel reservations there for tomorrow and the next night. Got that?"

"Paris to Newark on the first flight that leaves five hours from now. Newark to Melbourne, Florida at 6 PM, New York time. Reservations in Melbourne for two days. Then what?"

"I'll call you from Melbourne, but be checking on connections to Santa Cruz, California."

"Okay. Your itinerary and tickets will be waiting for you at the Omnisphere counter at Orly. If there are any glitches, I'll call you right back."

"Don't worry about glitches. Get me the best routing you can, but I need to be in New York as long as possible and make it to Melbourne by 2200 tomorrow. I trust your judgment and I'll take whatever you have waiting for me at Orly. I'm leaving here in a few minutes." After putting the phone back in its cradle, she switched on the computer again.

An office number for Andy Brown was answered by his answering service. Danielle hung up and typed an e-mail. "Andy. I'm coming to Florida tomorrow evening. I need you to meet with me in Melbourne day after tomorrow to talk about space stations and how to build an airplane that can fly to them. I will call you when

I get to New York tomorrow. Plan on meeting me at about 0900. I will let you know where."

She then called friends at Ames Research Center and Stanford University as well as a private firm in Cambridge, Massachusetts, and left similar messages.

Danielle debated, then called a number in Paris. In French, she said "Maurice, darling. I'm so sorry to wake you in the middle of the night, but something urgent has come up....

"No, I'm fine. I need you to meet with me, and some friends, day after tomorrow, in the morning, in Melbourne, Florida. My secretary will arrange your ticket for you, if you will call him in the morning. And Maurice, thank you. It's very important. Please give Sophie my love. Good night, dear, go back to sleep."

Maurice d'Orleans was the best and brightest aircraft systems engineer in the industry and had been her right-hand-man two years earlier. She called her London office and left a message for her secretary with the night answering service. Bill would take care of Maurice's reservations through Marilyn.

Guernsey airport answered on the second ring. "Herbert, this is Danielle Simones. Please prepare my airplane for departure in one-half hour."

Finally, she called her flight planning service. "Account zero six seven alpha. IFR, Guernsey to Orly."

She gave them her "estimated time of departure or 'ETD' of 2:30 AM Greenwich Time. "Echo Tango Delta zero two three zero Zulu today. Aircraft registration - 'G-L-O-B-E, that's Golf, Lima, Oscar, Bravo, Echo'. Use my standard flight plan. Fax it to Guernsey Flight Services and file it with Paris Center." The service already had the rest in their files. She grabbed an overnight bag, wrote a quick note for Mrs. Nelson, the housekeeper, and locked the house. Across the gravel drive, the old stable and coach house now served as a garage. She tossed the bag into the passenger seat, started the car and drove out onto the deserted highway.

The airport office was quiet and the ringing telephone startled the mechanic on duty. Danielle Simones was well-known at the airport as fussy, and as a pretty good pilot. The mechanic answered, listened, said "Yes, Ma'am." and hung up. He hurried to her hangar, unlocked the door and switched on the lights. There was a loud thump as a solenoid powered up the sodium-vapor lights suspended from the ceiling. Transformers hummed and the lights began to glow, rapidly becoming intensely bright and brilliantly illuminating the hangar. The gray epoxy-covered hangar floor was spotless, its waxed surface glistening in the bright lights. He pushed another button, and a motor began to lift the sixty-foot-wide door. Light from the brilliant lamps inside the hangar flowed through the open door onto the pavement outside.

The white and blue Mitsubishi MU-2 turboprop was fueled and waiting. Although it was twenty years old, the MU-2 was an exceptional propeller-driven personal aircraft. Danielle had this one equipped with state-of-the-art engines and avionics. From the flight bag next to the left pilot seat, Herbert removed the exterior and interior preflight checklists and began a meticulous examination of the aircraft.

By the time Danielle arrived he had finished. She drove her Aston Martin into the hangar and parked it on the left side of the aircraft.

"Everything is fine, Miss. It's ready when you are."

"Thanks, Herbert. Let's recheck it together, if you have time." They made another circuit around the aircraft, opening inspection panels, peering into the dark interior of compartments with a flashlight, then snapping the panels shut. Props, Engine Intakes, Engine Condition, Tires, Brakes, Spoilers, Flaps, Skin, Vertical Stabilizer, Horizontal Stabilizer, ... Check, Check, Check. The list seemed endless, but was finally complete.

Carefully, he attached the electric tug to the plane's nose wheel, removed the wheel chocks, and pulled the MU-2 from the hangar into the glare of the outside floodlights.

She looked around. The airport was quiet in the night. The rotating beacon flashed out its green and white code. Nothing else was moving. "Busy tonight?" she asked.

"No, Miss. Hasn't been anyone here all evening."

"Help me do the checklists up to taxi?"

"Yes, Ma'am!" He grinned. He enjoyed working or flying with her, and he had told her so. He was sorry he couldn't volunteer to fly tonight as he had in the past, but he was by himself in the office. They sat in the cockpit and he read the checklists while Danielle verified each item.

When the pre-taxi checklist was finished, he climbed out of the co-pilot's seat and exited the aircraft, the propwash and exhaust of the port engine buffeting him, and closed the door securely. A warning light on the panel blinked out as the door latch closed.

Danielle released the brakes, pushed the prop levers very slightly forward from their flat pitch neutral position and the airplane began to roll toward the taxiway. All the instruments were indicating in the green. In a few moments, the plane was climbing into the night sky, with only the flashing strobes on its wingtips to mark its presence among the stars.

Two years earlier she had made this same flight almost every day, when she was CEO at Global Aeronautique Internationale in Paris. When Global ran into financial trouble several years before that, Danielle had been 24 years old and a minor shareholder in the company. Her godfather, Bob MacDonald, had owned a controlling interest in the stock. He arranged for her to be appointed to run the company, and she had revolutionized Global's operations, moving it rapidly into the lead in the design and manufacturing of composite aerospace structures. Once the crisis was past and that company was running smoothly, she had taken indefinite leave, turned over management to her assistant, and gone back to her law practice and writing. She was comfortably wealthy and didn't need more.

Almost unconsciously, as Guernsey dropped behind the MU-2, with the lights of the French coast visible ahead and those of Jersey out the right windows, her thumb touched the small transmit button on the control yoke. She called the French air traffic controllers, identifying the aircraft by its British registration, "G-LOBE". "Paris Center, MU-2 Golf Lima Oscar Bravo Echo. Departing Guernsey."

The voice on the radio came back immediately. The controllers gave her a transponder code to identify her aircraft. They identified the blip on their radar screens and approved the flight plan, including a climb to twenty thousand-feet. They would follow its progress on radar for the remainder of the flight.

Danielle set the transponder code and called back, "Roger, Paris. Out of six thousand for flight level two zero zero. Golf Lima Oscar Bravo Echo." She was about to enter French airspace.

Soon the English Channel was far behind and the lights of Paris were visible in the distance ahead. She eased the power levers back, set the flaps for descent, notified air traffic control, and began the approach to Orly Field.

January 7

Thirty-six hours later she was in Florida. Near a small airport on Merritt Island by the Intracoastal Waterway, some amateur airplane builders were having breakfast at a local restaurant. The group included several former employees of the USA's National Aeronautics and Space Administration.

Andy Brown was a tall, white-haired man, retired from NASA, with bright blue eyes and a thinning flat-top haircut. He had met Danielle a few years earlier at an aviation convention in Wisconsin, and he was the hub of the Merritt Island group. As she entered the restaurant he got up from his chair to greet her. Taking him aside, she outlined her idea, and asked who he knew with the desire and talent to be part of the design team. He listed several names, including his own.

The rest of the day was spent meeting with Andy Brown, Maurice d'Orleans, a physicist from Stanford University, an electronics engineer from NASA, and another physicist from Massachusetts, in a hotel room, hastily making notes, lists of experts and drawings of possible structures. They all knew Danielle from many aerospace conferences they had attended together. Scattered across the beds were many technical papers that the men in the room had brought with them.

January 8

Bob MacDonald had retired to a small ranch near Santa Cruz after selling his real estate business. After a full life in the business world, he had made a lot of money, but his fortune didn't help ease the boredom.

Although he was past seventy, he still felt full of energy, and often wished he were still meeting new people and working on deals every day. His doctor told him to get out of the real estate business, or it would kill him, so he had retired. Now, while he often enjoyed a peaceful horseback ride alone in the mountains, from time to time he wished he had more company. The other people his age in the neighborhood were all golfers or card players, and he never had any interest in either.

When the phone rang a day earlier, the caller was his goddaughter, former lawyer and good friend - Danielle. She said she was coming to visit, and at first he thought she merely wanted to come for some riding, since he kept her mare at his ranch along with his own horses.

Something about her tone, though, told him there was more, although she wouldn't discuss it on the telephone.

He was many years her senior, but they thoroughly enjoyed each other's company whenever she could get to the ranch. Bob MacDonald and Danielle's father had been in college together at Purdue after the war, and Bob had briefly dated Elizabeth Owens, the woman who would become Danielle's mother, but Elizabeth had not been interested in him. When she met Archibald Simones, however, there was magic in the air, and MacDonald ended up as 'Bob MacDonald - best man at the wedding' of a couple who would become Danielle's parents. While he had gone into real estate and marketing, Arch had gone into telecommunications and Liz had raised the children. They had been a wonderful, happy couple for many years, but now Arch was gone and Liz was remarried. MacDonald was as close as Danielle had to a father.

She arrived early the following morning and had not yet eaten breakfast, so he took her out onto the terrace. Millie, the housekeeper, brought out fresh fruit, pancakes, eggs, grits, home fries, and homemade biscuits, but Danielle didn't eat.

Uncharacteristically, she jumped to her feet and blurted out, "I've had the craziest idea, and I want you to spend a fortune on it. It all came to me a few days ago. It seemed crazy, but I've spoken to several experts in the field and they tell me it can be done and without too much difficulty, just a lot of expense." She was striding back and forth in front of him like a mad woman.

"Dee, sweetheart," he said, "I love you like my own child, but you haven't yet told me what your crazy idea is."

"Listen, Uncle Bob. If I told you right out what it is, you'd have me locked up. Let me lead into it gradually, okay?"

"Okay by me."

"Let's start with the big obstacle, money. I want you to bankroll me in this scheme. It will take a hell of a lot of money."

"That's all right, honey. I have a hell of a lot of money."

"No, I mean really a hell of a lot of money. What you have will only be a drop in the bucket and will only get us started."

He considered her statement. He knew she knew he was rich. He wasn't sure she knew exactly how rich, but she was quick to dispel his doubts.

"You were reported in Forbes to be worth six and a half billion dollars since you sold your business to Waste World. I want you to loan me a billion dollars, without any real collateral. There's no way you can spend all that money yourself in several lifetimes anyway, and I think this project will be more fun for you than anything else you could buy with twice your fortune."

He said, "You're serious, aren't you, gal? Hmmm, ... You better tell me more." He couldn't imagine what she might have dreamed up.

"Yesterday," she said, "I met with several of the brightest engineers and physicists in the world. I outlined my idea to them. They say it'll work, and they say it can be done in just a few years."

"Well, what is it?"

"I've figured out how to end the energy shortage, probably forever. It involves building a city in space and a series of satellites to beam energy from the Sun to the surface of the Earth. I know it'll work!"

MacDonald was a little shocked. "Sit down, dear. Why are you so confident you can do what several national space programs haven't been able to do?"

"I'm confident because I know how to do it, and I want to do it. Those national space programs have never really had the full support of their governments, which had competing military and domestic programs, and as a result those programs have always been enmeshed in all kinds of politics and bureaucracies that dragged them down. I don't, and won't, have those limitations.

"Uncle Bob, I need more than your money. I'll need your influence with many important business and political leaders. I'll need you to negotiate important parts of this plan for me, without ever disclosing the plan itself.

"It'll cost a lot to get started. I think a billion will get it rolling. Then it'll cost at least forty or fifty billion more to complete."

"Dear," he said, "even I don't have that much money, as you pointed out."

"I know that, but I intend to pool funds from investors from all over the world. All the world's wealthiest people will be paying for the privilege of being part of this project. It can work ... it *will* work. I know it."

"Yes, dear. Tell me more about it. And eat your breakfast." He was already hooked.

Looking back later, Bob MacDonald never was sure whether it was her enthusiasm, or his fondness for her, that made him so willing to go along with the plan, but it didn't seem important to him at the time to know which, and never did later.

CHAPTER 2

January 9

Danielle returned home with her work cut out for her, and started immediately. Sitting at the computer, she called up files of corporate documents. Delaware, California, Florida, New York, Oregon, Texas, Washington, Isle of Man, Switzerland, Cayman Islands, Panama, Liechtenstein and more. She would need them all.

She rapidly punched numbers into the telephone. A familiar voice answered. "Neverland Travel."

"Marilyn, its Dee. Do you still want to have your own travel agency?"

"Yes. Sure."

"How soon can you give notice to those law firms you work for?"

"Are you serious?"

"I've never been more serious."

"Why?"

"I need you to have a fully operational 24-hour travel service. It won't be just for me, but for many people, maybe thousands of people. If it goes as I expect it to, you won't have time for legal work."

"I need to give my employers at least two weeks."

"In two weeks you may be working thirty-six hours a day on travel business."

"Still, I have to give my employers two weeks notice. I may have to miss this opportunity if it means dropping these people, Dee. They have been really good to me."

"Okay. Give them two weeks. We'll manage somehow. I'm going to send you a business manager. He'll help you staff up an office to handle the travel business. Maybe it would be easier to buy an already running travel agency and merge it with your own travel corporation. That way you won't feel quite as pressured to leave the law offices, and you can still handle the travel side too. I don't want anyone else to have my travel business. Got to go now." Danielle called her secretary and had him arrange for her firm's business manager to go from New York to Miami.

Two days later, she was in Liechtenstein. An agent there had the papers for a blind trust ready for her signature and they were filed that day. On January 12, she landed at the airport on the Isle of Man and when she left, there were several new corporations registered.

Ten days passed, and many Swiss bank accounts and more business entities were created around the world. Their stock was owned by many other corporations, but ultimately, everything was owned by the Liechtenstein blind trust.

A week later she began meetings in Seattle contacting a group of Boeing employees; then to Southern California, speaking with a group of former employees of Kelly Johnson's Lockheed 'Skunk Works'. She had her design team, as well as the foundation for the production team.

An hour after her flight touched down in Atlanta on the morning of February 27, she was in Ted Harrison's law office.

His instructions from her were clear: Buy an entire office building with at least 100,000 square feet of floor space. It had to be finished and ready to move into immediately, with carpets down and all utilities in place. It had to be functional, but she wouldn't spend a cent extra for "pretty". This would be a "bare-bones" project from start to finish, if she was to stay within the budget. She was not willing to accept any delays, knew the clock was running on the project, and as the numbers of personnel working on the project grew, the money would run out at increasing rates. Even a billion dollars was a tight budget for what she had to do. Harrison had a week to find a suitable building and a second week to close, in an all-cash deal. The owner would be an out-of-state accounting firm, Lone Star Financial Consultants, Inc., and Harrison would sign any required documents, as he was now an officer of the firm. The building would then be leased to a Texas engineering company, Harvard Design Consultants, Inc., which had been incorporated two days earlier, as had the accounting firm. The engineering firm had one customer. Danielle.

Harrison also had to insure absolute security for the building, including security guards, identification systems, and secure communications facilities. No one should be able to get in or out without being pre-approved. There would be no cleaning staff from the outside. All building maintenance would be by the company's own maintenance personnel, and there would be areas which even they would not be permitted to enter. Elevators would not operate without an access code. Access to individual offices was to be by individual identification cards only, with fingerprint verification. Many public and private entities could upset the schedule if word of the project leaked out too early.

Harrison was to hire a complete administrative staff to handle payrolls, insurance, bookkeeping, travel payments, etc. The administrative staff also had to be in the secure building. Funds would be forwarded from Texas. The project's engineers didn't need to concern themselves with administrative details, but Danielle needed to know that they would get paid on time, every time.

Harrison estimated the cost of the building and security arrangements, added a cushion for safety and told her. Danielle told him he would have available the amount he had estimated, but not to spend anything not absolutely necessary.

From Atlanta, she went directly to Tallahassee, where Clifford Kelly served as Chief Justice of the Florida Supreme Court. In addition to having served as a college professor and as head of the controversial state land management agency, as a private lawyer he had represented everyone from developers to environmental groups. His integrity and ability were admired by lawyers and legal scholars across the country and around the world, including Danielle. They met for lunch at a quiet Asian restaurant. After lunch, Kelly returned to his office and dictated a resignation letter.

On the morning of March 1, she arrived in New York City to meet Kenneth Morgan, head of a large public relations firm. Morgan welcomed her into the firm's main conference room. The room had glass walls on three sides, and windows looking down on Central Park. The large table was a single sheet of inch-thick glass, supported on two black granite columns, and was surrounded by tall black leather chairs.

Beginning slowly by explaining her perception of the global energy situation, Danielle outlined the plan. Finally, after an hour of background, she explained the need for the world's space powers to cooperate with her space program.

Morgan listened carefully, then proposed an alternative.

"Suppose the U.S., China, Russia, and Japan too, were to abandon their space programs. What impact would that have on your plans?"

She carefully considered his question before replying. "There are two major problems with the existing space programs, as they relate to the program I'm planning," Danielle said. "First, I need freedom to operate in space without interference, but the continued presence of the U.S. and Russian programs in space creates a constant potential for conflict. Second, I can't secure financing for this project without the assurance that our satellites will not be confiscated by one of the great national space powers flexing its muscles."

Morgan said, "What you need is for public opinion in these countries, and perhaps even around the world, to oppose continued national expenditures in space. I suggest a campaign to alter public opinion. You might think of it as dis-information, but what it really is, is empowering people who already have those opinions and informing others so they can form those opinions for themselves."

"Dis-information?" she asked apprehensively. "What do you mean by that? Propaganda?"

"Not if you mean am I proposing we lie to people," he answered. He paused, "Let me explain. We can begin a campaign to change public opinion away from space programs. While there are always going to be people who feel putting man in space is a good idea, there are also those who sincerely believe the space program is a misuse of public funds more urgently needed for domestic programs.

"In order to change national policy, we have to create a vocal minority, and make government leaders sensitive to the criticism that would result from acting contrary to that vocal minority."

She pushed her chair back from the table, stood and walked to the window. The sky was overcast and a light mist was falling. Central Park was dark and gray in the morning overcast. Most of the trees held barren branches skyward, except for a scattering of evergreens. A few patches of grass had retained their greenness over the winter. She leaned on the windowsill and watched the people on the street far below scurrying along in raincoats and under umbrellas, hurrying to reach protection from the soft cold rain. She paused, thought of New York City without electricity, then turned back to Morgan.

"Mr. Morgan," she said, quietly, but a little annoyed, "I came here today because I need a favorable climate for my project, but as you describe it, I'm really concerned about the ethics of your proposal. How can *my* company ethically support a program to stop the financing of the U.S. space program, while I believe so fervently that going into space is the thing to do? The destiny of mankind is in the stars. It *must* be done! ... I'm sorry. I'm sure there's an answer that I should know, but I'm really tired from travelling, and I'm afraid public relations isn't an area where I'm very familiar with the ethical issues."

"I understand your concern, Miss Simones," Morgan answered, carefully, "and if, in my opinion, you were justified in a moral or ethical concern, I would recommend that you obtain a different consultant. But if you'll let me ask you a few questions, perhaps you'll understand what I'm proposing more clearly, and why there's no moral or ethical problem.

Danielle returned to a chair and sat down. She looked at Morgan and leaned back in the chair. "Go on."

"First," Morgan began, "you're concerned because you're in favor of the development of space, but the program which I've proposed is an 'anti-space' program, isn't that right?"

She said, "I guess so. ... Yes."

Morgan continued, "Well, that's your first logical error. What I'm proposing is *not* an "anti-space" program. I want you to think about that. To put it in better focus, let me ask you the second question. Is the U.S. space program going to accomplish any serious beneficial use of space anytime in the foreseeable future?"

Danielle responded, "Not if they continue the way they've been going since the end of the Apollo program."

"Good," Morgan went on. "Next question. Is there any likelihood, based on your better-than-average knowledge of the forces acting on the U.S. decision-making process, that the U.S. program will change from the way it has been going?"

"I don't think so."

"Good," he said. "Now we're getting somewhere. Next question. What's the program with the greatest likelihood of moving mankind into space in the shortest time and for the least cost?"

"I'm surprised you ask," she answered. "You know from what I've told you that my company's program is the only program with any chance of success at this time. But I think I see where you're going."

"Now the final question," Morgan asked quietly, "If your program is the only one with a chance of success, isn't the expenditure of U.S. funds on its failing space program a waste of those funds, provided your program is there to fill the void?"

She said, "Well, yes, I guess so, if you put it that way. You mean that there really isn't a moral dilemma if what we are trying to do actually *does* urge the government to spend its money in a more effective way?"

Morgan banged his fist on the table for emphasis. "You've got it. That's exactly what we're proposing. Your contributions will enable people who *correctly* believe that government expenditures on space are not well spent, or should be spent elsewhere, to have an effective voice with their government. Remember, we're not going to pay citizens to change their views. We're merely giving them organization and an outlet, plus additional information to educate them on the degree to which U.S. space expenditures are wasted. And it will help get an effective space program - yours - going sooner.

"Beyond that," he continued, "it would help immeasurably if Congressmen in the U.S. and leaders in Europe, Russia, China and Japan were contacted by their campaign contributors or influential supporters and asked to put other programs on higher priorities than the space effort. Their reasons could be as simple as their desire to reduce their taxes, or to get more immediate returns from their tax payments."

"I can handle the second part," she said. "I know just how to approach it. But the first part – I wouldn't know where to begin."

"My firm has the ability to handle the entire first part of the public opinion campaign, Miss Simones, if you can handle the second part. But you should know right up front, this campaign will be very expensive. You also need to know there's a risk that it might backfire and produce public opposition to your own project."

"I'm prepared to take that risk, Mr. Morgan, but I need to have a number. How much will it cost?"

"At least 10 million dollars," he answered. "We need to establish several groups to focus the attention of politicians on spending funds on programs other than space. There will have to be many contributions to those groups from many sources. I hope that figure's not beyond your budget."

Danielle said, "No, No. That figure is one we can live with. If we set up an account for your expenses and pay you a ten percent fee on top of your direct expenses, will that be satisfactory?"

"Very. Should we bill you?" he asked.

"No. You'll be able to draw directly on the account. My attorneys will contact you regarding our need for periodic reports and accounting for the funds used, and will provide you with the necessary information to access the account."

"All right," Morgan said. "My staff and I will start to develop the detailed plan beginning this afternoon, and we'll furnish your attorney a copy of the draft plan at our first meeting along with an engagement letter setting out our agreement. If there's any portion of the plan which bothers you at that time, we can still change all or part of it, or you can withdraw the entire plan and only be liable for our expenses to the date you cancel. Does that seem fair?"

"Very fair," she answered. "I feel a lot better now, but I have to be moving on. I have a plane to catch. Thank you." She picked up her briefcase and walked out. Morgan went directly to work.

CHAPTER 3

March 2

Bob MacDonald was in his stable, currycombing one of the horses, when the early morning silence was interrupted by the phone on the paddock wall. Danielle asked him to meet her at Oakland Airport at 2:30 that afternoon. He put Danielle's mare back in her stall and moved to the next horse, which nodded its head vigorously at the prospect of getting a rubdown and maybe a carrot. It nuzzled the jacket pocket where it knew he kept the supply of carrots. By noon, Uncle Bob was in his car, on the way to the Oakland airport.

They found each other in the crowded main concourse of the terminal. Danielle gave him a hug and a peck on the cheek. "Let's find somewhere quiet to talk," she said. "We haven't much time. My next flight leaves in an hour."

The airport had a coffee shop on the lower level. It wasn't a good location for a coffee shop, as it was away from the main flow of passengers, so it had been through a series of operators, none of whom could make it pay. But it was perfect for this meeting. It was deserted. They found a booth in the corner and ordered lunch. The coffee was good.

"I spoke this morning with Kenneth Morgan, of Morgan, Friedman and Tinker, the big public relations firm in New York. He suggested the framework for a plan to induce the major space powers to pull out of the space exploration business. I've given it a lot of thought during my flight here, and realize he's right. He's initiating a campaign to get the public to pressure Congress to spend its money on domestic programs, rather than the on-again, off-again space program it has funded for the last few years. I told him I'd work on getting business leaders and big contributors to the political parties to start agitating, both personally and through their lobbyists, for the U.S. and other countries to stop spending money in space. He suggested the tax angle; that they feel their taxes are being wasted and that they don't want to continue paying taxes for a do-nothing program which has only produced failures and disappointments, particularly when there are so many urgent domestic issues at home that need funding.

"Uncle Bob, I'd like you to contact your old business cronies and start them calling their senators and representatives, as well as party leaders. I know they all carefully maintain their associations with both major political parties for their own reasons. Now's a good time to make those connections pay off.

"One angle they can push is that those funds should be spent on job retraining programs to make the American work-force more productive. A lot of workers can be trained for the cost of one shuttle launch. Can you do that?"

"Piece of cake," he answered. "What else?"

"Suggest to your wealthiest friends that they should begin watching the classified section of the Wall Street Journal in about eight or ten months. Tell them the key words will be 'One Hundred Million Dollars,' and that they will need that much to play. Don't tell them anything more.

"Oh, and maybe you could start a non-profit group of businessmen, organized for the purpose of producing a more competitive work-force. It would need to have its headquarters in Washington, D.C. And it needs to be immediately heard on Capitol Hill.

"Then there's another aspect that Morgan suggested. Would it be possible to get the Russians and Japanese to abandon their programs as well? Morgan's going to work on public opinion in those countries, but some inside pressure would help. Do you know any European, Russian or Japanese political power-brokers, Uncle Bob?"

"I sure do!" he said. "Leave that to me. Russia will be easier, if anything, than the United States, because their power structure hasn't had time to become as diverse as ours. But the United States will have to take the lead. The Russians and Japanese won't quit unless the U.S. has. You know, there are several joint launches planned. But I don't think Russia can afford an independent space program any more, economic conditions in Russia being what they are. They've had a very hard winter. And funding for the U.S.-Russian joint space station program is in big trouble in Congress. The Japanese may be harder because they are just starting on their own space program and it hasn't had time to form an entrenched bureaucracy, but," he paused and thought about it for a second, "there may be some angles there, too. I don't think you should expect any of them to stop launching the usual communication and weather satellites, though."

"I don't. We just need to eliminate the budget for expansion and research-in-space activities. It will be terrific if you can do that. There's just one more thing. Uncle Bob, did you ever hear of the Law of the Sea Treaty?"

"Sure. That's the one that Reagan wouldn't sign. The old fool. His refusal to sign prevented American companies from getting in on marine exploration. Some of that was a smokescreen for a top-secret Navy salvage project, but there were real opportunities the US missed because of not being a party to the treaty. As a result, many companies that would have operated from the United States and employed American workers, and used American ships and equipment, instead set up foreign subsidiaries to explore the sea-beds. All because Reagan's shortsightedness has effectively prevented American companies from getting clear financing."

She nodded. "The Law of the Sea Treaty was premised on the deep sea beds being 'the common heritage of mankind'. That was the basis of Reagan's opposition, because that declaration required companies mining the deep-sea bed to 'share' technology with the third-world countries, which would also have the right to mine the seabed. He viewed the 'common heritage' declaration as some kind of communism, which he opposed. He didn't think of the consequences. It has driven American businesses to set up foreign companies to exploit ocean resources."

"I remember hearing something to that effect, although it wasn't very well covered in the media," he said.

Danielle continued, "The importance of the Law of the Sea Treaty and the U.N. declaration on the deep-sea-bed, to us, is that there are similar U.N. declarations and treaties relating to Space. I realized while thinking about getting the big space powers out of my way in Space, that we also need to foreclose the U.N.'s ability to come in after the fact and declare our work to be 'the common heritage of mankind'.

"We need the U.N. to *sell* us all of the rights of mankind to space, forever, to preclude future interference in our activities, and to enable me to provide our investors with assurances that their money won't be lost to an arbitrary action of the

U.N. No single nation can convey those rights, so what we need is a U.N. action, approved unanimously by the General Assembly and Security Council, conveying them to us. Then on top of that, we need a 'Deed' to Space, actually signed by the appropriate head of state of each and every country, deeding the rights in Space of its citizens to us.

"You weren't born yesterday," she continued, "and you surely realize that this 'Deed to Space' business is all a fiction, since there's no reason for the U.N. or any country to seriously think it has any rights to any part of outer space. It's a throwback to the 'Man is the center of the Universe' concept. The fiction of man's rights to Space is born as a result of centuries of common law, and the pathetic efforts of lawyers to justify their claims to Space based on prior law concerning claims to land, which are obviously entirely different.

"A country can at least occupy and defend a piece of land from invaders or others who would attempt to take it away from them. No country on Earth has the ability today to do any of that in Space. The whole thing is sort of like a medieval monarch standing up to his ankles in the Atlantic Ocean and claiming all of the lands on the far side.

"Uncle Bob, do you have any ideas how we can get the U.N. to sell us Space, and can you handle it without letting the cat out of the bag?"

He answered, "I think I can, honey. I know where the power-brokers are in most of the countries in Europe and South America, and in some of the countries in Africa and Asia. That knowledge was necessary to make my old real estate business work. Why, I haven't felt so excited since the first time I kissed your mother. ... That was before she met your father, of course."

"You old lecher. Just think, if she had married you, I'd be calling you 'Daddy' instead of 'Uncle Bob'."

"I've often thought of that, dear, but honestly, I couldn't be more proud of you if you were my own daughter."

"Why, you sweetie. I'm proud of you too, and we're going to have a lot of fun with this, aren't we?"

"I don't know about you, but I'm having fun already," he said. "Listen, you better get trucking, or you'll miss your plane. And I have to get going myself. I certainly have my work cut out for me, don't I? To hell with doctors."

MacDonald threw a twenty-dollar bill down on the table for the uneaten lunch, gave her a hug, and watched as she hurried out into the terminal corridor.

After checking in at the boarding gate for her next flight, Danielle went to a pay phone and called the office in London. Her secretary, Bill Townsend, answered, "Simones Associates."

"Bill, its Danielle. I need you to call Jean Claude Lebec. You remember, he retired from Global last year, right after I left. His number is in my address book file on the central file server's 'H' Drive. I want him to take charge of managing the logistics of this project. Ask him if he will do it for me. Tell him the following things from me, and be sure he knows to call you if there are any questions. I'll be checking in and I'll help with any rough spots he runs into.

"First. He's to hire seven of the best managers he can find. Use seven of the paper corporations that I set up last week in the U.S., but not Harvard Design Consultants. I have a special job for them, and I'm setting up the management of that company myself. For the others, put one manager in charge of each corporation. They'll each need an experienced purchasing staff.

"Second. Each company is to buy a small, say 30,000 square foot office building, in a nice but not too pretentious part of the largest city within a few minutes drive of the major aerospace corporation in that state. It'll be obvious to him which corporation fits this description. The office also should be within a few minutes drive to the largest airport in town, and must have a loading dock and ample storage facilities for merchandise, let's say ten thousand additional square feet. Perhaps it would be good to buy an office-warehouse combination. Let Jean Claude handle that decision. Try not to spend more than a million for each building. I'm transmitting ten million for each company from a foreign corporation.

"Third, Jean Claude will soon receive a list, broken into seven sections, of computer and office equipment. He's to assign one section to each corporation to purchase. I'll let him know what to do with it later.

"Fourth, Lone Star Financial Consultants, Inc., in Houston, is to be our accounting firm. It is one of the seven, and needs to be fully staffed with top-notch economists, financial analysts and accountants. Jean Claude needs to work out the personnel needs with our personnel firm.

"That brings me to the fifth item. I incorporated Omega Personnel Industries in Indiana. It's going to be our personnel agent. They need to be fully staffed and operating by the end of next month. They're also one of the seven. They're to be used to staff the other corporations.

"Tell Jean Claude to hit hard on the best accounting and personnel firms for the management and employees for Lone Star Financial Consultants and Omega Personnel Industries. We want the absolute best people we can find, and will pay competitive salaries, but the connection of each company to anything else has to be kept secret. Only the managers should know Jean Claude, and they should not be aware that there are other corporations, or that Jean Claude is not actually the owner of the parent corporation.

"Next, I want Jean Claude to find out who made the space suits used by NASA and the Russians for their space programs. I need to know how much it will cost to buy a space suit for a man, average size, to wear in space, doing construction work. It has to have some protection against accidental punctures, and enable several hours, say four hours of work in space on its internal supplies of air and water. When we get a price for one suit, find out how much they would want to make a thousand suits, assorted different sizes and sexes, because we'll also need them for females. Check out both the U.S. and Russian manufacturers. We reserve the right to require a standard set of connections for air, electrical, whatever. Get me full spec's and prices.

"Finally, I want Jean Claude to do some research. He can call it industrial espionage, if he likes, but I need some very specific information. He's to find out which company has the best photovoltaic cells, which company has the largest photovoltaic production capacity, and which company or other entity has the most promising new approaches to photovoltaics. He's to find out how much it would cost to buy each of them. He's to find out who the brightest people in the field are. I need the information two weeks from today.

"There *are* some strings. The information must be obtained without doing anything illegal. That means it must be done by searching technical literature and personal contacts, but I don't want anyone to suspect that we're looking for both space suits and photovoltaics.

This project *must* be top secret from here on. Be sure Jean Claude understands. If I learn that anyone has obtained any information illegally or disclosed our internal information, they'll get sacked. Please pass that on."

"I will. Anything else?"

"Nope. Got to run. I'll call you from Japan." She hung up. The station agents were announcing the flight. She had a billion dollars at her disposal but was flying coach class, to save money.

CHAPTER 4

The flight to Japan was packed. Danielle had reserved a window seat, just behind the wing on the starboard side. As one of the last passengers to board, when she stepped through the door into the cabin she wondered if she'd made a mistake. Unlike most overseas flights, the plane was not a wide-body. It was an old stretched DC-8. She hoped the maintenance was up to date.

The passengers in the aisle were totally disorganized. Many were trying to load bags, which obviously belonged in the cargo compartment in the airplane's belly, into overhead compartments entirely too small to hold them. Others were pushing and shoving, trying to get past those standing in the aisle. Still others were trying to get flight attendants to attend to some unimportant personal whim, while the flight attendants were struggling to get the unruly crowd organized and into its seats, so that they could present their safety briefing, then get on with the flight. Those passengers demanding service would have to wait, as the flight attendants could no more move around the aircraft now than could the passengers who were still trying to get to their seats.

Reminded of many years of aircraft safety training, Danielle wondered idly, *'if the plane were to catch fire right now, how many would die?'* The aircraft was still parked at the gate. There was an exit to the jetway only a few feet away. And no one, except herself, and maybe the flight attendants, had any idea of the necessary procedures to evacuate the aircraft. Perhaps a better question was, would any survive? *'I would,'* she told herself. *'We'll see how well the cabin crew establishes its authority as soon as everyone is in their seats,'* she thought.

After a seemingly endless time, the melee in the aisle settled down, and there were only a half-dozen people who seemed unable to decide whether they wanted to sit or stand for the entire flight. They were like 'jack-in-the-boxes', sitting down, then jumping up to stow some item in the overhead compartment, then sitting down again, then jumping up again to shed some too-warm outer garment, then sitting down again, then jumping up again to look for a pillow or blanket, which they would not need for quite a while yet. It was only 4 o'clock in the afternoon, and the plane would be following the Sun westward at Mach .82. They had at least eight more hours of daylight if not twelve. She pitied the cabin crew. They'd have to endure these passengers for a very long flight.

Deciding she could make it to her seat, Danielle walked slowly toward the rear of the aircraft, locating the emergency exits and safety equipment. When she reached the seat, there was a very large woman sitting in it.

"Excuse me," Danielle said, "but you're in my seat."

The woman said, "Oh, no. This is my seat."

Danielle rechecked her boarding pass. It said seat 33-F, which was where the woman was sitting. "I'm sorry but you're in my seat. Seat 33-F. See, here's my boarding pass. Please check yours and you'll see you've made a mistake."

"Well," the woman said, "I'm *sure* this is the correct seat."

Danielle repeated, "Please check your boarding pass."

19

The woman grudgingly reached into her purse, a giant overflowing carpet bag which would in no way fit under the seat in front of her, as was required for carry-on luggage. "Oh, my goodness," she said, "my pass says seat 30-D. Someone has made a mistake."

Danielle thought to herself, 'I know who,' but didn't say anything. Instead she said, in her most friendly voice, "Oh yes, your seat is three rows forward. Up there. That empty seat."

The woman looked forward indifferently, as if she already knew what that seat looked like and said, "I'm already comfortable here. Why don't you sit up there?"

Danielle considered it for a half-second, then realized why the woman was in her seat. Seat 30-D was in front of the over-wing exit, and an aisle seat beside. She spoke with a voice developed overseeing an uncooperative board of directors some years previously. "This is my seat, and I'm going to sit in it. If you don't move now, I will have no alternative but to have you moved."

The woman realized her effort to improve her seating location had failed. She began to get up, complaining bitterly at the inequities of the system, the lack of charity of people, etc. This meant the passengers between the window seat and the aisle also had to stand and move into the aisle so the woman could move out of the seat from which she had just been evicted.

Danielle located a half-filled overhead compartment and placed her jacket and travel bag in it. She kept the briefcase, which contained a laptop computer. Finally sitting down, she pulled the seat belts from under the seat cushion where the woman had shoved them, and latched them across her lap. Wondering if the woman she'd evicted had planned to wear the seat belt at all, she gave the loose belt-end an extra tug for good measure.

Next to her was a youngish but balding man wearing wire-rimmed glasses and a blue pin-striped suit. He was smiling and chuckling to himself. Finally he spoke. "That was worth seeing. You did a great job on that lady."

Danielle thought to herself, 'That was no lady.' and wondered what kind of person she was seated next to. Most people on aircraft were so shy, or snobbish, or afraid of offending, that they would ride ten thousand miles and never say 'hello.' This guy certainly didn't fit that description. She said, "What do you mean?"

"I was almost the first person on the plane. She came in, tried that seat she had the boarding pass for, then came back here. I thought she might be in the wrong seat and asked her. She said it didn't matter, that all the seats were alike. Then the plane filled up and you arrived."

"I suspected that she was avoiding that seat," Danielle said. "It's on the row in front of the over-wing emergency exit, so it doesn't recline. And it's not a window seat."

"So that's what it was. I knew there was some reason she came back here." He smiled. Danielle thought it was a nice smile.

He stuck out his right hand, awkwardly because Danielle was sitting shoulder-to-shoulder with him on his right and both of them were belted in.

"I'm Eric Savage."

Danielle tried to shake his hand, which was also awkward for her because she still had the briefcase on her lap. They both laughed at their predicament. She said, "I'm very pleased to meet you, Mr. Savage. I'm Danielle Simones. But I'm sorry I had to make such an issue over the seat."

"Doesn't bother me. I get really ticked-off when rude people pull stunts like that. I think she should have to walk to Japan." Then he smiled again and laughed a half-laugh.

Danielle opened her computer. She had just begun a memo regarding hiring criteria for employees when the flight attendants began their safety briefing. It was excellent, all business and very authoritative.

She wondered if the flight attendants were even told anymore that it was so important to give a sober and official-sounding safety briefing because in the event of an emergency, the flight attendants had to be recognized as THE figures of authority, to control panic, and to get as many passengers as possible to safety. Most passengers thought cabin crews were there to bring them drinks, or in-flight meals, or a pillow or blanket. Danielle knew from years of working with airlines that cabin service was only window dressing to keep the cabin crew visible during the flight, after they had established themselves as the authority figures in the cabin. Of course, if any little emergencies came up, they would also deal with those problems. Now she had to stow her briefcase under the seat in front of her, which was nearly impossible.

It *would* fit. She knew that. But the side of the fuselage curved inward near the floor, her legs were in the way, and it seemed there was no way to move her legs aside and simultaneously reach to the bottom of the seat in front of her while maintaining her feminine dignity.

Savage noticed the dilemma, smiled, and said, "May I take that and put it over here?"

Danielle handed him the briefcase, thanked him, and thought, 'There's that smile again.' He easily reached the space in front of his feet and then sat up. 'How did he do that so easily?' she wondered. Then she leaned back to enjoy the acceleration of take-off. Silently, she counted to see how long it took the big jet to get the mains off the ground. 38 seconds, which was what she expected with the new, more powerful, high-bypass engines. She could hear the clunk as the gear extended to its stops and the sound of the gear doors opening and reclosing.

They had been off the ground only a few seconds, and the plane was already beginning a noise-abatement power reduction and a steep turn to the right. She estimated the altitude between 2,000 and 3,000 feet, and the right wingtip seemed pointed directly at the ground. As she watched the baseball fields, shopping centers, and apartment houses speeding by and growing ever smaller, she wondered whether anything she was doing would ever make a difference for the people down there. She turned her attention back to the interior of the aircraft.

The smiling man next to her was no longer smiling. He was tightly gripping the arms of his seat. "What's wrong?" she asked.

"Nothing," he said.

The airplane slowly began to come out of the turn, leveling the wings in the process. Looking out of the window, it took an effort to see the ground, or rather San Francisco Bay, which was now beneath the airplane. On the opposite side of the airplane, she could see through the windows that the horizon was again visible. As the aircraft leveled, the man next to her seemed to relax. Finally, he said, "I always wonder why they do that."

Danielle thought an improbable thought, of airplanes trying to turn without banking, then said, "Have you ever flown an airplane - as the pilot, I mean?"

"Me? No."

"Maybe some day I could show you why the airplane does that. I fly a little myself from time to time. Could you hand me my briefcase, please." She had work to do.

CHAPTER 5

March 4

The flight arrived in Tokyo just at sunrise, after making a passenger and refueling stop in Hawaii. The view during the landing approach was spectacular, as the Sun was illuminating the Eastern slopes of the mountains of Japan and seemed to focus a spotlight on the tiny yards and homes on the mountainside. The view was a picture of perfection, and Danielle could see directly down into the yard of each house as the aircraft descended only a few hundred feet above the mountain slope toward the airport at the base of the mountain.

A taxi took her to her hotel, where she checked in and slept until late in the afternoon, when she was awakened by the phone. It was the office of Tomasuko Oribati, with whom she had an appointment the following morning. Oribati was one of the most wealthy and influential men in Japan, and an expert in his own right on electronic switching systems. Their appointment needed to be moved because of some problem with his schedule. Danielle told the secretary that ten was fine, then rolled over and tried to go back to sleep. It was no use. At 5:30, she got out of bed, took a shower and was just about to leave the room when the phone rang again.

"Hello?"

"Miss Simones, it's Bill Townsend." The caller was her secretary, calling from London.

"Hello, Bill. Where are you? Isn't it sort of early there?"

Townsend laughed. "It's seven in the morning, and I came in a few minutes early to try to get ahead of the boss while she's away. Didn't do me any good. Your fan club is after you."

Danielle was puzzled. "What do you mean?"

"There's a guy named Eric Savage holding on the other line. He's calling from Tokyo, and says he met you on the plane. He wanted your number in Tokyo and I didn't know if it was important, and wasn't about to give it to him, so I thought I'd check with you."

"Bill, can you get his number? Tell him you're talking to me on the other line and I'll call him as soon as we finish our conversation. I'll hold." There were a few moments of silence then Bill was back on the line and gave her the number. She thanked him and hung up.

'Eric Savage?' she wondered. She dialed the number, and he answered immediately.

"Hello?"

"Mr. Savage? It's Danielle Simones."

"Please. Call me 'Eric.' I'm so glad I was able to locate you. You're probably wondering why I'm calling."

"Yes, as a matter of fact, I am."

"I was hoping you'd be free to have dinner with me this evening. If you don't have other plans already?"

She thought for a second, then answered, "No, Eric, I don't have other plans, and I'd love to have dinner with you. I was expecting to eat alone. I do it so

23

frequently that I hadn't really considered any alternative. Did you have a place in mind?"

"I know a wonderful restaurant, but it depends on where you're staying. It might be too far."

She told him which hotel she was in and he said, "Perfect. It's about a half-hour drive to the restaurant from there. Would it be all right if I met you at your hotel at seven? We can eat at about eight."

"That's fine with me, Eric. I'll be waiting."

"Bring a good appetite, this place has the best food in Japan."

She wondered idly whether it could top some of the fine restaurants she already knew, or even if it was one of those. She spread some notes on the desk and turned on the computer to review her meeting objectives for the following morning.

At six forty-five she refreshed her makeup, then turned out the light and left the room. She sat in the hotel lobby for a few minutes before Eric Savage came through the entrance toward the front desk. He looked taller than she remembered, then she realized during most of her experience with him on the flight he had been sitting down.

Savage had a car and driver waiting in front of the hotel and they were soon on their way northeastward out of downtown Tokyo. Eric turned to her and said, "I was concerned that I might not be able to locate you. I'm glad I was successful."

"I'm surprised that you were able to. How did you manage it?"

"I remembered the phone number and name on the tag on your briefcase. I didn't really expect to be able to get anyone in England so early in the day, though. I expected to get an answering machine."

"I won't use a machine to answer the phone. It can malfunction and if it does, I can't fire it," she said, then added, "that's supposed to be a joke."

"Listen, I believe it. The gentleman who answered the phone was really tough. Even after I reached a person, I didn't think he was going to tell me anything."

"That's my secretary. Tell me, did he tell you anything?"

"Now that you mention it, no, he didn't. He got my number from me, and told me nothing."

She laughed. "That's his job. Get all the information I need and release nothing about me. He's pretty good at it, and has been doing it for some years. And he knows what I want before I ask for it. I'll give you one of my business cards so you can call in the future without straining your eyes to read my luggage tags."

"Thank you. My old eyes aren't as good as they used to be. Tell me, Ms. Simones, if you don't mind me asking, what's your line?"

"No," she replied, "I don't mind you asking. But it's easier to ask than to answer, and please call me 'Danielle'. I used to know a simple answer, but as time passes the answer gets more difficult. A few years ago, I was a lawyer. Since then, well, I guess I've become sort of a business consultant. Most of my work involves aviation. But I also do other things."

"Other things? Like what?"

"Well, I teach at a couple of universities, and I write a lot of articles on law and economics."

"You sound like a renaissance woman to me. Is there a Mr. Simones?"

Danielle smiled, and thought, '*There* was the question.' "No, there isn't," she answered. "I had a husband once, but our careers evolved until they didn't harmonize, so we went our separate ways. Since then, I've been on my own, and I love it. What about yourself? What do you do for a living? Is there a Mrs. Savage?" 'We'll play the game for a while,' she thought.

"I'm in the defense and security business. I work for myself, selling weapons and advising my clients about their self-protection needs. And no, there isn't a Mrs. Savage."

Danielle hesitated, "That's a very interesting occupation. It immediately makes me think of drug dealers and crime-lords."

"That's a common reaction, but I won't have anything to do with anyone whom I even suspect of criminal connections. There is a surprisingly large number of very wealthy, and honest, people in the world, and I charge them a lot of money for advice on their personal and corporate security arrangements. Some of them just need an alarm system for their home, others want to protect corporations with thousands of employees."

"How'd you ever get started in the security business? Were you in the police?" she asked.

"No, although I've worked with many police agencies over the years and I'm a consultant to several with unusual problems. I was an officer in the U.S. Army in Vietnam. My expertise was special weapons, explosives and booby traps. I developed a knowledge of electronic surveillance equipment through my association with my friends in the Army Signal Corps. When I got out of the Army, I realized my military training would be useful in protecting people from burglaries. It developed into the security business for corporations and individuals that I have today."

The conversation sagged for a few minutes, as they sat watching the scenery pass by. It was rapidly becoming almost too dark to see. Finally, she spoke. "Eric?"

"Yes?"

"Have you ever considered working full-time for someone else?"

"No one can afford to hire me full-time. A couple of companies have tried, but they couldn't pay me enough to keep me interested in their business. Once the basic situation is under control, it gets dull fast. I usually do an annual security inspection for each of my big customers, and we fine-tune their arrangements to fit the changing situation. Of course, if a corporation opens a new office, or one of my individual customers moves to a new house, I make a special inspection and charge an extra fee."

"What if there was an employer with a dynamic and diverse global business, which required constant re-inspection and amendment of security procedures? Would you consider working for such a corporation?" she asked.

"Maybe, but I'd probably be too expensive for any single employer."

Danielle persisted. "What if the job was more exciting than anything you had done before, and presented new and unprecedented security challenges? Do you think you might be willing to reduce your salary expectations somewhat under those circumstances? It might require you to run an entirely separate corporation with the security mission."

"I'd be interested in hearing about it," he said. "Whether I'd be willing to work for less than my current consulting fee would depend on the specifics of the situation."

She said, "You might have skills some of my clients could use. I'm not at liberty to discuss their business right now, but from what you've told me so far, I think it might interest you. Do you have a card?"

"Here." He squirmed around in the seat of the car and removed his billfold from a back pocket. He dug out a business card, a little dog-eared, and handed it to her - and then laughed, "I *do* have a answering machine."

Danielle examined the card. It said, 'ERIC SAVAGE SECURITY - Gastonia, North Carolina.' and the phone number. There was a drawing of a snarling Alsatian dog at one side. She put it in her purse.

The car pulled off the road into a tree-lined parking lot. Eric said, "We're here." As the car stopped, he got out and came around to open her door. He reached out his hand and helped her from the car.

On one side of the parking lot was a wooden fence with an ancient-appearing gate in the center. At the gate, an old man, dressed in a simple garment, bowed deeply and welcomed them. They stopped there and exchanged their shoes for sandals. They thanked the gatekeeper and were directed inside.

Danielle gasped. Inside the fence was a formal Japanese garden, illuminated by many small lanterns, each strategically placed to provide the exact amount of light needed in exactly the correct location. It was as close to perfection as Danielle could imagine and took her breath away.

"I know," he said softly, "it affected me the same way the first time I saw it."

They walked around the small compound for almost half an hour. It seemed like only a few minutes until a woman in a kimono slid open a door and came out of the building toward them, bowed and spoke to Eric. Danielle was surprised when he answered in Japanese. The woman turned back toward the door, kneeled and slid the door open for them to enter. Leaving their sandals outside the door, they stepped inside. The hostess followed them through the door and closed it behind them.

The dinner *was* indeed wonderful. Danielle tried to find a superlative adequate to describe it and failed. They talked about their youth, and school, and childhood dreams. It was the best evening Danielle could remember, a trip to another world, and was over too soon.

The drive home brought Danielle back to reality. As they cruised toward her hotel, several other cars weaving through the heavy traffic cut them off, and their driver had to take violent evasive maneuvers. They grabbed the hand-holds in the rear seat, and waited for the crash, which never came. The other cars sped away, and Eric's driver accelerated the car back into the flow of traffic.

"Let me introduce you to Yoshi," said Eric. The driver raised one hand from the wheel and waved. The hand was immediately back on the wheel. "Yoshi was trained at a special school for police pursuit and security drivers. He works for one of my clients. Whenever I'm in Tokyo I won't let anyone else drive me."

"His responses to those other cars were certainly quick. I feel better knowing I'm in his care. Thank you, Eric."

"How much longer are you going to be in Tokyo?" he asked.

"Another day. Maybe two."

"I'll arrange for Yoshi to be your driver for as long as you're here. Say you'll let me do that."

"But who'll drive you? You're here on business too."

"I finished my business today and I'm leaving on a 1 AM flight. What time do you have to go out in the morning?"

"My only appointment is at 10 AM, at an office in Musashino. But I can take a taxi," she protested.

"You could, but why do it when Yoshi is available? *I* won't take a taxi when I can get Yoshi, and I'm not an unaccompanied female." The car pulled up to the steps of the hotel and stopped.

"Eric, I don't want to mislead you. I appreciate your offer, but I don't want to be indebted to anyone. I can't afford to be."

"You weren't reluctant to have dinner. How do you explain that?"

"You invited me. I accepted. I assume my company was what you wanted, and you got it for dinner. I enjoyed myself, too, and really appreciate your asking me, truly I do, Eric. But Yoshi works for someone else, and even if he worked for you, it is much too complex."

"Suppose *you* hire Yoshi the same way I do. Would that be acceptable?"

"I guess so. How much does it cost?"

"I'm paying four hundred dollars, U.S., a day for him and the car. Does that sound reasonable?"

"Here? Yes." She paused. "Okay, who do I pay for Yoshi's services, and how long can I keep him?"

"I'll arrange for them to bill you, and you can keep him as long as you like. Is that acceptable?"

"Yes. How early do you think I need to leave to make my morning appointment on time?" She already knew the answer.

He told her eight-thirty, which agreed with her own estimate.

"All right," she said. "Have him pick me up then."

"He's working for you. You tell him."

Danielle struggled to think of the correct Japanese expression. After a long silence, Yoshi turned around and looked at her. "Would you like me to pick you up at eight-thirty, Miss Simones?"

She regained her composure, "Thank you, Yoshi. That will be just fine."

Eric walked her to her room, and didn't try for a goodnight kiss. She sort of wished he had.

The meeting with Tomasuko Oribati began promptly at ten, and Danielle got straight to the point. "Tom, I know you're a genius with electronic switching. I need to know how to build a sophisticated, but simple, switching apparatus.

"What kind of a system is it going to be switching?"

"Imagine a tree with a million leaves, with each leaf generating electricity. I need a system to cut each leaf out of the circuit if it stops producing electricity, or falls below a certain output, and that will also enable the system to command any one or more, up to all of the leaves, to be remotely disconnected or reconnected, as the demand on the system decreases or increases. It has to maintain a very high constant output voltage, with the current varying according to demand. It has to be all solid state, and totally reliable."

27

"What do you mean, 'totally reliable'?" he asked.

"I mean I'm going to put the thing where no one can work on it. It has to be totally reliable. That's all."

"All right, totally reliable. How much power will each of these 'leaves' be producing?"

"I don't know. Somewhere between one hundred and a thousand watts. I suspect it should have at least a one hundred percent safety factor, maybe more. It mustn't burn out, ever."

"How many of these 'leaves' are you really expecting to have on this system, Danielle? A hundred? A thousand?"

"Actually, about two hundred and twenty million."

"What's the joke, Danielle? Seriously, now. How many?"

"I told you. Two hundred and twenty million."

"Danielle! That's twenty-two gigawatts minimum, upwards to two hundred twenty gigawatts, according to your figures. Recheck your numbers."

"Can it be done, Tom?"

"I'm sure it can, but I'm not sure how. What are you planning, anyway?"

She said, "I can't tell you right now, but I need the basic design for the system which I just described, and right away. And it needs to be absolutely hush-hush. Understand?"

Oribati answered, "As if anyone would believe me if I told them."

"How long will it take for you to prepare me a rough outline of a system to do this?" she asked. "I need it yesterday."

"What kind of an arrangement do we have on this?" he asked. "Am I working by the hour, or by the job, or what?"

"Tom, I'm picking your brain. For now, let's say this is a single job, and you're doing it on a per job basis. I know the number of units is only important to size the components, and that as soon as you have the basic concept down the rest will fall in place, so I'll pay you by the job. What's your price?"

Oribati replied quickly, "A million dollars, U.S."

"Cheap at twice the price," she said. "I'll have the money transferred today. How soon can it be done? Yesterday? Oh, and I want to have draft designs sent to me as we go. There may be revisions in the basic requirements. I'll forward any technical information on the 'leaves' as we develop them. We're at a very preliminary stage right now."

Oribati laughed mockingly, "Ha. Ha. How about a month? Maybe a month and a half."

"Not that long, surely," she said, somewhat surprised.

"Yes," he said. "That long. Not counting any revisions you may cause with your changes to the specs. Those will run the cost way up. Now what's this all about? What's the real plan here? *This is a switching system for a solar power satellite.*"

"I suppose that's what it looks like, Tom, but I can't tell you right now. I'll tell you as soon as I can, if that's good enough. When the entire plan is in place, I'm hoping you'll invest in it."

"If you're involved, I just might. Who's doing the microwave system?" he asked.

Danielle asked, "What microwave system? What makes you think there would be a microwave system? I told you I was planning a tree."

"Danielle, you know the Japanese government's planning a solar power system? I've worked on some of its components."

"Yes, I know. But what they propose to do in fifty years, I can do in fifteen. What do you know about microwave that would be useful to me?"

"That'll cost you a lot more. How do you figure you can do what the Japanese government is proposing in thirty percent of the time?"

"I don't have their limitations. Do you really want to be a part of this? If it all works out as I'm expecting it to, I'll need you to work closely with my design team, both on switching and on microwave, and to be a big investor. You'll be paid for your design work up front, and your investment will take a long time to pay back, but then it'll pay very well."

"Yes," he said. "On both counts. I want to be in on the design, and I want to be in on the investment."

"Good. Be prepared for a really big investment, though."

"I will," he said.

"Tom, I can't tell you how glad I am to have you working with me on this. Now, I have to get on the road. Call my office as soon as the first draft of the design is on paper. And don't tell anyone. The safety of your investment depends on secrecy."

She left the building, and found Yoshi waiting, who drove her directly to the airport, where she boarded a plane bound for Manila, then caught another plane for Koror and Babeldaob.

CHAPTER 6

March 6

Danielle checked through Belau customs and collected her suitcase. She was travelling light, but the weather was much warmer than Tokyo and clothes for Japan were too hot for Belau. She stopped in a shop and bought a blouse and skirt appropriate for the climate, and a very light business suit. It was still before noon, so she registered at the small hotel in the heart of town, and went out to learn more about the island nation and its government.

A block from the hotel was a large white building, with the American and Belau flags flying in front of it, red tiles on the overhanging roof, and the impressive designation "UNITED STATES OF AMERICA - GOVERNMENT HOUSE. There was no activity visible, and she walked on by.

A small, noisy restaurant and an adjoining watering hole was at the end of the block-long waterfront, and they both had obviously targeted the island's small tourist industry. The bar was full of neon lights, loud music, plastic furniture and affluent plastic tourists wearing too much jewelry, each trying to look more important than the next. She looked into each of the places, but went on past.

Near the waterfront, but a block off the main street, she found a small and shabby bar, and went in. It was quiet and the decor looked at least fifty years old. Upholstery on the furniture was threadbare, and Danielle wondered if the place had ever been painted. The walls were adorned with faded photographs of World War II Navy, Marine and Army aviation crews, held in place by rusty thumbtacks. One customer sat in a corner.

Danielle sat down at the bar and ordered a beer. The afternoon passed slowly, and the bartender replaced empty beer bottles several times. He didn't get many single female tourists; he couldn't even remember the last one, and he had been tending bar here for a long time. She told him she had come to Belau because she wanted to take it easy; too many pressures in her hometown. She hoped it would be a little more relaxed here. She told him about a lot of her problems with the local government in her hometown, not many of which were true.

Eventually the bartender began to tell her about his town and its people. There were only about twenty thousand people in the entire country. Yes, they were pretty laid-back. There wasn't much crime; if someone did something out of line, most of the town would know who it was before the police chief arrested them. Most serious crimes in the past had been committed by tourists, robbing or trying to murder one another.

Koror was the capital of the small island nation, but it was a relatively meaningless capital, since the United States had run Belau from Government House, and Washington, D.C., for over fifty years. Government House was in fact the office for the United States Administrator. The real local government, such as it was, consisted of the popularly elected President, whose family had been leaders of the island as long as anyone could remember, but who had no meaningful legal authority under the Trusteeship.

Whenever there was a dispute, the American Administrator would make a pronouncement from his lofty position of authority, which all the citizens would ignore, and the President of Belau would quietly decide what the outcome would be, and that was it. The Administrator was an imposed authority, while Belau's President had the respect of the citizens. The United States had used its position as 'trustee', as well as the Belauans' need for public services, as a lever to coerce the Belau government into an agreement, called the 'Compact of Free Association,' under which the citizens of Belau would be anything but free. It provided their so-called 'independence,' in exchange for a long-term occupation by the Americans in the form of a huge military base. The Americans had lost their bases in the Philippines and needed a fall-back position to anchor their influence in the Western Pacific. Belau and the Belauans were the solution, or victims, depending on one's point of view. Beginning in 1983, the population had repeatedly rejected the agreement, because it violated their constitutional prohibition on nuclear weapons. Belau was, by the terms of its Constitution, a 'nuclear-free zone' and the population had been unwilling to give the agreement the seventy-five percent majority approval their Constitution required. The first 1983 vote was sixty-six percent for the agreement and the ninth vote, in 1990, voting on an amended agreement, had only sixty and a half percent for approval. Seeing the agreement consistently unable to gain the needed seventy-five percent approval, the Americans had suggested an alternative – amend the constitution, which would require only a majority vote. The seventy-five percent requirement was replaced with a simple majority, and the agreement was finally approved. Belau was set for token independence – at a price. It had to sell its soul.

Danielle sat at the bar for a long time, ate at least two delicious fish sandwiches, and drank – well, she lost track of how many beers. Finally, she carefully got down from the barstool, thanked the bartender for making her feel welcome, and slightly unsteadily made her way back to the hotel. The bartender had given her many important insights into the workings of the little nation's hidden power structure.

Danielle spent the entire next day visiting shops and businesses which few, if any, tourists ever visited. They were all run by local community leaders, most of them women, and she spoke with them in ways they never expected from a tourist. It was obvious she was in no hurry, and neither were they. They told her things they would not have believed they could tell a tourist, or that a tourist would take the time to hear.

They talked about their homes, and families, and their love of their islands and their traditional way of life. They spoke about the impact tourists had on their young people; how the children were influenced by the affluence to which they were exposed. The children were losing their respect for the old ways. Many of the children went to university in the United States, Asia or Europe, and many didn't come back. The people with whom she spoke explained to her, in ways she understood better than they, why they were unhappy with their situation. They appreciated the tourist revenue, which brought them advantages such as education and health care, but they didn't want the increasing degeneration of the old customs, which was becoming more evident as time passed. They were afraid of the American military base, and didn't trust American promises to exclude nuclear and biological weapons from their country.

31

On the morning of the third day on the island, she toured the big island of Babeldaob, looking at maps she had brought with her and comparing them to the topography of the island. That afternoon, she walked into a small law office on the main street. The friendly receptionist asked how she could help. Danielle wanted an appointment with the attorney and handed the receptionist her card. The girl read, "DANIELLE SIMONES – Legal and Economic Counselor – London, England", and took the card into the adjoining room. A few moments later, a short, thirtyish, smiling, brown-skinned man came out of the office. He was wearing a loose-fitting short-sleeved shirt, tan slacks, and boat shoes without socks. He stuck out his hand, and said, "How do you do. I'm Bertram Allen. I hear you want to meet with me?"

Danielle shook his hand and introduced herself. "Mr. President, I was hoping I could arrange a time when we could sit down and talk at length about some issues which might interest you. I want to make it clear, I'm not seeking your assistance as an attorney, I want to speak with you in your capacity as the leader of this community. I'm sure you're busy, but I think you'll find it worth your while."

The President looked her over again. What could she have that would interest him? Why had she been all over town talking to people about themselves? He already knew most of the details of her activities the previous day. "Miss Simones, my calendar is open all day. My practice here is a little more casual than you probably see in England. Do you want to sit in the office and talk, or walk on the beach and talk? I can do either equally well."

"Sir, I've been here for two and a half days, and haven't seen the beach yet. If it's all right with you, I'd love to walk on the beach."

The President held the front door open for her, and they strolled down the street to the water, turned right, and headed up the beach. The fresh breeze from the lagoon rattled the palm fronds. Frigate birds soared on updrafts near the island. They walked beneath the palms, and past the already noisy bar facing the beach. Gentle surf lapped at the sand. Far out in the lagoon, the occupants of several boats were pulling in fish for the evening meal. Nearer shore, tourists on jet-skis were racing around in circles, with no discernable purpose except to make noise and see how close they could come to a collision with each other, or other boats or docks, without actually doing so.

As they passed the end of the town, the number of homes along the beachfront decreased significantly. The only sounds were the gentle surf at the shoreline, the wind in the trees, and the crying of sea birds. Danielle had already removed her shoes and jacket, and was struggling to carry both. The President noticed her difficulty and took them from her. Carefully folding the jacket, he put the shoes and jacket at the top of the beach, beneath a palm tree. "We'll pick them up on the way back," he said, kicking off his own shoes and leaving them also.

He stuck out his elbow and Danielle took his arm. "Now, Miss, what was it that you wanted to talk about?"

She looked around; the beach, the water, the palm trees, the boats. It was a placidly beautiful place. In the clear water beyond the surf, silvery fish were racing back and forth, apparently harassing schools of smaller fish. Sea grasses and sponges were indistinct dark shapes beneath the gentle waves. She began, "Mister President, ..."

He interrupted her. "Please, ... 'Bert.' I have the dubious pleasure of having been named for a fiberglass boat. But I vastly prefer it to 'Mr. President'." He smiled warmly.

"Bert, then. I'm so glad to be here. I've heard about your country, but have never been here before. The first time I heard of this place, there were oil companies who wanted to make this into a refinery island. There was quite a rhubarb, as I recall, about the potential for polluting the ocean around your island. Anyway, I wondered what all the fuss was about, and now I know. It really *is* a special place."

"Actually," he said, "there *is* a small refinery on the far side of the big island, on the deep water side, but nothing like what was proposed in the 1980s. We've been very fortunate in that regard. We get a little income from the rent for the refinery site, but it hasn't been as good for the island as we had hoped."

"I think I may look like another oil refinery coming at you, Bert," she said. "I've looked all over the world for sites for an industry that I want to establish. I've considered a hundred different variables. Every time I reexamine the site selection criteria, I end up back here.

"The rest of the world is being threatened with pollution, just as your refinery threatens you, just as the proposal in the 1980s threatened you. Oil is driving economies all over the world. Everyone wants it, everyone needs it. As the demand for oil increases and the supply diminishes, there will be more and more short-cuts in safety procedures, and serious oil spills are virtually inevitable. The only real question is where and when they will occur.

"I have a plan for a new kind of clean power. My system will collect solar power in space and beam it to Earth where it will be converted to electricity. Eventually, it will mean the end of oil and nuclear energy. It will mean an end to the pollution of our planet by fossil fuels, oil spills, and nuclear accidents. But in order for it to work, I need a special airport. I need a runway six kilometers long, and a place to assemble some very special equipment. I need a place to build a space-port. I need a very large piece of land, about ten square miles, just like the part of the big island, Babeldaob, between Pkulngril and Ngardmau, where the Americans want to build their new base. It has to be oriented properly to the prevailing winds, and should have reliable constant wind straight down the runway. It needs to be within ten degrees of the equator. It needs to be in a country where the government can be relied on not to interfere with our operations. Every time I look for places suitable for the space port, I end up with Belau.

"My problem is that I don't want this project to be like the oil refinery which was proposed here or like the American military base. I don't want my project to damage your islands as the oil companies would have done or to violate your non-nuclear principles as the military base surely will. But I can't guarantee that it won't have negative impacts, despite my good intentions."

"Don't you have another problem?" Bert asked. You need a government you can rely on to stay out of your way – to be a help rather than a hindrance. The American Administrator is, very frankly, an idiot. We would never have had that debacle with the oil refinery, except the Administrator saw it as a way to increase his personal prestige. That was the prior Administrator - this one's worse. If we don't let the Americans build their base here, we violate the agreement for independence, the Compact, and the trusteeship will continue."

"Bert, I spent the last day and a half visiting people in your town and trying to figure out what they want and need, *really* need. I think I've figured it out."

"Well? What did you learn?"

"You need to get rid of the tourists, AND the Americans."

"That's impossible! The United States is hanging onto us like a leech. *Fifty years* since World War II, and we're still part of the Trusteeship! And the military base will continue our status as a puppet of the Americans. As for the tourists, our people don't really appreciate them..."

"I noticed."

"But, we can't get rid of them. The Americans insist we pay a percentage of the costs of the Trusteeship. They say it's for the medical facilities, and other costs of government we use, but it keeps us in servitude. Then there's the power plant. Our leaders were persuaded to agree to the construction of a huge power plant with capacity many times our requirements and Belau is a hundred million dollars in debt as a result. Even the rent from the refinery isn't enough to pay our obligations. We need the tourist revenue, and if the Trusteeship were ended, we'd still have those expenses, because our people do need those services, all but the power plant, which we never needed. That's the biggest reason for agreeing to the military base."

"Suppose we developed an industry that produced revenue that looked like your tourist income or the income from the military base, but didn't have the negative impacts? Enough for your island to pay for its own medical program? And your own educational program, without the Administrator or the base."

"We'd still have the Americans, and the pressure from the United States for us to be a tourist spot for its tour operators will continue."

"Suppose I could get rid of the Americans. What then?"

"Impossible!"

"Maybe ... maybe not. Hypothetically, what would happen?

"Tell me more about your idea and then I'll tell you what would happen."

They walked a long way down the beach before turning back toward town. They had a working agreement, but it had at least one big contingency. It required the United States to give Belau its full and complete independence, without the Compact and imposition of the military base. The President was extremely skeptical, and although she talked a good talk, she didn't look to him like she could deliver on her plan. He wondered who she really was.

When they reached the main street, they turned and started walking toward his office. Danielle said, "I'll send you a copy of the site plan for the space port, and the documents for independence, as well as a draft of the contract with my company. You look them over, make any changes you think are necessary, and send them back to me. We can keep that up until we have documents we agree on. I'll try to do what I can, and we'll see what happens. Okay?"

"It's a deal, if you can manage the independence."

She stopped. "Bert, it's been a pleasure meeting you. Here's my hotel. If I'm going to make it happen, I have to get back to that other world where the money is. I hate to leave, but I must." She shook his hand.

He clasped both her hands in his. "Good luck. And thanks."

Danielle turned and went into the hotel. Three hours later she was on a plane headed for Manila and London.

CHAPTER 7

March 18

When Jean Claude LeBec reported back, his research revealed three important positions in the photovoltaic industry. One, Power-chip, Inc., in Ohio, was highly automated, and out-produced all the rest combined, but was still growing solid silicon crystals, slicing thin, fragile wafers from them and soldering wires onto the wafers. It was the oldest and best-established technology, but rapidly becoming obsolete. Another company, Nordic Power, Inc., in Minnesota, had the leading process for thin-film, amorphous photovoltaic technology. There were some experts who felt the thin-film technology was going to overtake the old crystal-based photocells. The most promising new approach was that of a young inventor located in Oregon, who had developed a new material promising higher efficiencies than either of the companies with photo-cells in production.

The Minnesota company could be purchased for 22 million dollars. The Ohio company could be purchased for somewhere between 58 and 65 million; Jean Claude couldn't get a more precise number. The independent inventor was virtually unemployed, but had appeared interested by an offer of thirty thousand dollars a year to work for a small electrical engineering firm.

Danielle instructed Jean Claude to buy both companies, with the condition that the key personnel must remain on-board for at least four years. She immediately ordered 90 million dollars transferred into a special account for this purpose. The companies continued their operations uninterrupted, but there was a merging of their technologies, and enhanced security at each location. The independent inventor was placed under contract, for 45 thousand dollars per year, and provided with assistants and a well-equipped laboratory for research and development. If her photovoltaic invention could be developed and used, she would rapidly become one of the world's wealthiest people.

CHAPTER 8

March 29

The first design teams had arrived in Atlanta. Most of their office equipment was waiting for them in the receiving area, still in its boxes. All of the computer equipment, supplies and software had been sold first to other companies, then reshipped to the building. No supplier could know that here in an otherwise ordinary office building was the most sophisticated assemblage of computers, computer design and drafting equipment, software and professional staff in the world. It was all being paid for with Bob MacDonald's billion dollars.

The design teams set immediately to work installing the computers and other equipment. They were more than just engineers. They included all of the usual engineering disciplines, structural, mechanical, electrical, hydraulic, aeronautical, space, plus project managers. But that was only the beginning, as the teams included physicists, biologists, medical doctors, and several scientists who had been researching such exotic subjects as ceramic structures and nano-polymers. The former NASA, Russian, and Japanese employees were very excited at being able to move forward without the bureaucratic restrictions they had endured at their former employment. Here they only had to satisfy their supervisors' desire to design excellence into a finished product and have it flying as soon as possible. The top supervisor was reporting progress daily to Danielle.

Team A's task was simple: design an aircraft to take off and land like an ordinary aircraft, reach an orbital altitude of 500 kilometers without external booster rockets, carry 100,000 kilos of cargo or 200 passengers to the orbital location and transfer them to another vehicle, and do it with existing technology, on a daily basis. When the design was complete, this team would supervise the contractors manufacturing components, then supervise the assembly of the space plane itself.

Team B was to design a satellite for low earth orbit, to serve as a transfer station for personnel and materials and have needed life-support provisions for personnel brought up by the Team-A aircraft as well as living quarters for the satellite's crew.

Team C was to design a satellite-supply shuttle to carry and return cargo and passengers from the low-earth satellite to a satellite in geo-synchronous orbit, 22,400 miles above the Earth's surface.

Team D was to design a solar power-collecting satellite having a nominal power output in excess of 90 gigawatts. Team D also included the scientists who were to design the power transmission system, to move power from geo-synchronous orbit to the surface of the Earth, and from receiving stations to the local distribution network. The output of the Earth-located receiving antennas would be at least five gigawatts each. Transmitter antennas would focus power on at least six receiving antennas at a time. Receiving arrays had to be designed for relatively simple installation on the surface of the Earth. The single most important requirement for power transmission was that it be harmless to Earth's environment.

Team E was to design the living quarters for satellite construction crews and the permanent Space Station to be located at each Solar Power Collecting

Satellite. This facility would become the living quarters for the operators of the Solar Power Collecting Satellite.

Team F was to design a Lunar mining facility and the equipment for moving lunar ores into orbit. Moving construction materials from the surface of the Earth would require lifting every pound out of Earth's deep gravity well, which was necessary for the first several satellites, but as soon as the first few were operating, production of structural metals for constructing later parts of the project would be done on the Moon or in orbit, using lunar materials, because the Moon's gravity well was only a shallow one, and there was no dense atmosphere for the materials to punch through in order to achieve orbit. It would cut production cost for later satellites by as much as thirty percent.

Expertise regarding human needs for other design teams came from Team G, to insure that each component for the project would include optimum safety and health provisions for the occupants.

Team H was responsible for developing the design and specifications for the Earth Base, including the runways and taxiways, road network, office buildings, hangars, residential buildings and all the support buildings and facilities.

Team I was responsible for preparing standard operating procedures and all the needed documentation for every aspect of the operation.

All of the design teams coordinated their activities constantly, so that each step meshed smoothly with the next. Overseeing the entire operation were Andy Brown and Maurice de Orleans. If anyone could make all these disciplines work together, Danielle knew these two were the ones.

CHAPTER 9

April 1

It was a fine spring day in Washington, D.C. Danielle's Uncle Bob had been busy contacting his old real-estate friends and political contacts. Things were beginning to warm up in the nation's capitol. Senator Preston 'Stoney' Parker (Republican, Iowa), Chairman of the Senate Finance Committee, was just starting his second cup of coffee when his private telephone rang. The caller was the head of the Iowa Republican Party.

"Stoney," he said, "the natives are getting restless out here. The Feds responsible for assistance to farmers hit by soil erosion, nutrient depletion and pesticide pollution of their drinking water are claiming they haven't the funds to pay the usual subsidies for our voters to stop doing these things to themselves. I got a call from the President of the Iowa Farmers' PAC a few minutes ago informing me that unless they get some cash, fast, they'll not be able to afford support for your next campaign. This is urgent business and you need to take care of it."

"Now, Ben," complained the Senator, "you know how tight the federal budget is these days. There just isn't an ounce of fat to be shifted anywhere. Every program has suffered significant cuts because of the push to balance the budget."

"Well, how about cutting that space stuff. I guarantee you, the voters in Iowa don't appreciate it. We spent billions – I don't know how many billions, but billions – on putting Americans on the Moon, just so the Ruskies wouldn't get there first, and all we got from it was some moon rocks. Those moon rocks haven't done you any good, Stoney. They don't vote. And another thing – all of the space stuff that has occurred recently has been a big flop anyway, and out here we're getting embarrassed that you keep voting for it. You can do something about it, in your committee, and the voters are noticing that you keep spending money in Florida, but aren't doing what they need in Iowa."

"I certainly understand how they feel, Ben. I'll see what I can do."

"You do that. Remember, moon rocks don't vote, and you're dead meat if these folks don't get some more money out here."

"Thanks for the advice, Ben. I'll work on it." He hung up.

An hour later, in another part of the Old Senate Office Building, an aide stepped into the office of Senator J. Ricardo 'Dick' Pinata (Democrat, Florida), and said, "Mr. Piper is calling you on line four. Shall I put him through?"

"Of course." Senator Pinata picked up the phone.

"Hullo, Pete. How are you?" Pedro "Pete" Piper was the owner of the 200,000 acre sugar farm next door to Senator Pinata's own sugar farm, and was also the largest grower and packer of vegetables in the entire Everglades Agricultural Area, on the south side of Lake Okeechobee.

"Not well, Dick. These enviro-freaks are running us ragged, wanting us to obey the law and everything. We need you to step in and do something to help level the playing field a little."

"What did you have in mind?" Pinata asked, "We don't have the votes to change the environmental laws."

"How about some money for the Corps of Engineers to build a huge plant to clean up the pollution from the water we pump off our farm fields and into the Everglades. You know we can't do it all by ourselves and still continue to make the profits we're accustomed to getting every year. You know, the ones that pay for your campaigns?"

"I know, Pete, but where do you propose we get the funds to cover such a project? The federal treasury is empty."

"How about that space program? The money spent on that up in Brevard County doesn't pay for your campaigns, Dick. We do. And those voters up there usually vote against you anyway. You know, your last campaign was more than fifty percent paid for by us sugar growers, through our various channels. Take care of this situation and we can maybe raise a little more. What do you say?"

"Okay, Pete, I'll look into it. Thanks for your call." He was thinking about how he could get more federal funds for his sugar-growing buddies, when another aide popped into his office.

"Senator, Mr. Rubenstein is on line two. Would you like me to give the call to an aide?" Ezra Rubenstein was a powerful political activist and was the President of the Florida League of Retired People (F.L.R.P.). The Senator decided to answer the call himself.

"Hullo, Mr. Rubenstein, this is Senator Pinata speaking. What can I do for you today?" He tried to sound interested.

"Senator, you're probably aware of the crisis that currently exists in Florida and is of great concern to the older people of the state?"

Senator Pinata didn't have the foggiest idea what the caller was talking about. "Of course, Mr. Rubenstein, but perhaps you can give me some details to bring me up to date on the problem?"

"We can't go on like this anymore, Senator. We're being forced to *walk*! Our people insist on public transportation *and* bus benches in their neighborhoods. The bus service in our neighborhoods is terrible. We never would have put up with such terrible service in Brooklyn, I'll tell you, Sir. It's time you, our Senator, did something about it."

"What did you have in mind, Mr. Rubenstein?"

"We need a new federal program to assist older Floridians in getting around. We have carefully evaluated the needs, and the distribution of the population, and the cost of providing the service, and we believe it could be done for only six billion dollars each year."

"Well, Mr. Rubenstein, you certainly have done your homework. I appreciate your interest in this. I hope you'll send me the facts and figures so I can read them over. Have you considered where that money might come from? The federal budget is pretty thin right now, you know."

"We know right where it can come from. Close down that useless space program on the East Coast. There aren't any old people working in that program anyway, and we need the money for really important programs for retirees on the West Coast, around Tampa. Besides, we paid for that program, and we're still paying our taxes for it, and we're tired of being drained for a program that doesn't address our needs. If it doesn't benefit seniors, it can't be very important anyway."

"Well, thank you, Mr. Rubenstein. I certainly am glad you called. I wasn't aware that your group's needs had become so urgent, and I do appreciate you bringing it to my attention, um, that is, reminding me of how urgent it is. I will definitely see what can be done about it. Thank you for your call. Goodbye." He hung up and began wondering how many of 'his' voters were working in the space program. Perhaps the nation's priorities would be better served if the country got out of the space business entirely, except perhaps for the occasional launch of a weather satellite, or some other Earth-centered satellite.

Around the U.S. Capitol, all the other Senators and Representatives were receiving similar calls. Simultaneously, Bob MacDonald and some of his friends were working to kill Congressional funding for the military base at Belau.

On June 1, before declaring a summer recess, the United States Congress took one final action. Bowing to a new groundswell of public sentiment, and recognizing an opportunity to show great fiscal responsibility in an election year, the members adopted a resolution withdrawing funding from the American space station program, and declared it to be the policy of the United States to focus on the needs of its citizens at the Earth's surface. Most instrumental were legislators from Florida, Texas and California, homes to the US space program, whose private polls indicated that more people favored spending those funds on domestic rather than space projects. Pleased that the decision would enable more funds to be spent on his domestic policy programs, the President signed the bill into law the following day, June 2. It was Uncle Bob's present to Danielle on her birthday.

The Russian Assembly of Delegates and Duma, recognizing that continuation of their space program was dependent on the ability to share technology and launch capabilities with the United States program, and realizing the other members of the Commonwealth of Independent States had withdrawn their financial support, followed suit three days later, with the strong urging of the President of Russia.

Governments of France, Suriname, China and Japan, which had previously sponsored ambitious space programs, suddenly were the subject of widespread internal criticism for expending so much of their national funds on programs similar to those which the world's major space powers had abandoned. In each country, the legislative body, with the concurrence of the executive, expressed its unwillingness to go further with space programs.

Behind the scenes in each of these countries, as well as in all of the major countries and most of the smaller countries around the world, a carefully orchestrated campaign to change public opinion was being carried out, at the public level by Morgan and his personnel, and at the political level by Bob MacDonald's friends and business associates.

There were whisperings that space programs were taking the food from babies, that space was only for dreamers, even that space programs were somehow contrary to "God's plan," with selected biblical references to support the arguments. Citizens' groups, such as the Earth Now Society, the Margaret Schweitzer Society, and the International Association for the Advancement of the Earth, "sprang up" almost overnight, dedicated for the "good of society" to the emphasis of domestic social programs over space programs.

Some were surprisingly well funded, considering no one had heard of them six months earlier. Many pre-existing organizations, seeing an opportunity to enhance their membership with a new issue, had jumped in to support the effort to divert funds to their own pet earth-bound projects. The fledgling organizations had received contributions from many sources, few of which were what they really seemed. They were all receiving pieces of Uncle Bob's initial billion dollar investment.

At the same time, some of the most influential lobbyists in many other countries that previously had small space research projects in the U.S. or Russian programs had been telling political leaders and staffers that they objected to paying taxes to participate in unproductive foreign space programs. They insisted that the funds being spent on those programs could be better applied elsewhere in their own national budgets.

In the United Nations, delegates from around the world were receiving messages from their heads of state indicating their countries had tired of involvement in the space race. Someone, no one knew quite whom, had started the idea that perhaps it would be better if space exploration were a private enterprise, although there was no suggestion as to who would be so foolish as to spend their own money on that kind of risky venture.

"Market forces," it was said, should control such efforts. No one publicly expressed a belief that there actually were any "market forces" which would make such a private effort desirable.

Chapter 10

August 17

Atlanta was oppressively hot in August and a layer of smoggy haze hung low over the city. Joggers in Piedmont Park seemed to be moving in slow motion, trying to exercise without getting any hotter. A few blocks away, in the characterless office building on West Peachtree Street, design work was progressing rapidly. Andy Brown called and invited Danielle to come for a visit. Three days later, she arrived, accompanied by Bob MacDonald and several other key staff members.

The senior engineers were assembled in the small conference room on the first floor. Andy stepped to the front of the room and looked around. In the front row were the primary design team leaders and a group of visitors, including Danielle. Behind them were a dozen other staff members and their primary assistants. Andy cleared his throat and the numerous conversations around the room began to subside. They were an unruly bunch, as creative people tend to be.

When it was quiet, he began, "Good morning. We've gathered here to review our progress to date, and to share the information with some important visitors. I'd like to begin by introducing our visitors to you, if they'll stand up and turn around, then we'll go around the room and introduce the design teams to the visitors." Half of the front row stood up and faced the back of the room.

"At the far end," Andy said, gesturing to his left, "is Clifford Kelly. Cliff is the legal advisor for the principals behind the design project.

"Next to Cliff is Jean Claude LeBec. Jean Claude is the President of a group of companies which will be producing components and sub-assemblies for the satellites.

"On Jean Claude's right is Eric Savage. Eric is the President of Savage Security, which is our consultant for security matters.

"On Eric's right is Danielle Simones. Danielle is a management consultant who is assisting the various companies as they proceed through the design and production process."

Danielle had decided from the beginning to keep her role in the project secret from all employees except for the top tier of managers. The reasons for this decision were based on her belief that the bottom-level employees would be more candid with her if they believed she was one of them, rather than a supervisor. During her experience as CEO at Global Aeronautique, she was often distressed at the cleansing which occurred in status reports between the shop floor and her office. She had discussed this strategy with the top managers, and they endorsed it. Each of them knew he had her unquestioned support, and each of them had either worked for her previously or knew her through professional connections in the past.

"On Danielle's right," Andy said, "is Robert MacDonald. Bob is also a consultant to the various manufacturing companies working on the project.

"That takes care of the visitors. We'll introduce each of the design team leaders as they come up to speak. But before we start, let me review for our visitors the design process that we're using. It's what we call Integrated Design and

Production, or 'IDP.' Our design teams are multi-disciplinary groups of engineers, scientists and cost evaluators. These teams have developed the designs that you will see today, based on the needs of the overall project. We have many meetings between the several teams to insure that each team fully understands the requirements and limitations of the designs that the other teams are developing. As a result, we expect the final products for which we're producing the designs to be on schedule and at or under budget. This system makes the entire team responsible for the successful completion of their project. Each of them is a project manager, and each of them can stop the process if he or she sees a potential problem. When production begins on the parts that have been designed, the team members will be working at various contractors' plants to insure that all questions that come up during the manufacturing process are answered immediately and correctly."

The several team leaders then came to the front of the room. Using various visual aids, each described, in considerable detail, the space plane, the solar power satellite, the low earth orbit satellites, the shuttles for moving people and materials between the satellites, and the Earth Base, all of which they had designed during the preceding months. Each design was focused on creating a simple and relatively inexpensive product, unlike many earlier NASA designs for space equipment, which had been extremely complex and astronomically expensive. By comparison, the space hardware they were designing was dirt-cheap. The goal was to produce electric power at a cost of less than one cent per kilowatt hour, a fraction of the cost of any competing technology. It appeared the design would meet this goal.

The penalty for the simplicity in these designs was weight. All of the components were marginally heavier than earlier equivalent NASA or Soviet space equipment. The differences in weight increased the amount of mass that would have to be boosted into orbit. The simplicity of the systems however, allowed the launches to be very much less expensive, and Danielle's original concept, which involved making the fuselage do the majority of the lifting through aerodynamics, rather than using the brute force of rockets producing vertical thrust, made it possible. The design combined NASA's earlier plans for an aerospace plane with the Burnelli concepts from the 1930s, flying wing technology from the 1940s and modern composite materials technology. It had occurred to Danielle that the aerodynamics of a very large lifting body would result in lift much greater than that produced by any aircraft of conventional size.

The space plane would be huge, nearly seven hundred feet long. Its cargo compartment would be larger than that of any existing aircraft and designed to carry a load ten meters square and one hundred meters long, weighing a hundred metric tonnes. It looked unlike any airplane anyone outside the project had ever seen before, with a giant scoop on its underside to capture thin air at extremely high altitudes. The trapped air would then be compressed by the very high speed of the plane, mixed with fuel and ignited to produce thrust.

The power satellite design was equally outlandish, a six-spoked wheel twenty miles in diameter, with large numbers of antennas rotating at the ends of the top and bottom spokes. The spokes were connected with hundreds of parallel diagonal struts, onto which the photovoltaic cells would be attached. The whole structure resembled nothing more than a spider's web. It was anticipated that impacts from the various-sized meteors in the orbital path would damage the solar cells on the satellite, so long-legged machines which the design teams called "spiders" would move around on the satellite and replace damaged photovoltaic cells with new ones. The designers called the satellite "The Web." The short axle through the hub of the "wheel" had a pressurized space station attached by a single cable to the end away from the Sun. The end toward the sun had a space ship, called a "tug" attached to it to tow the entire station and satellite toward the sun whenever it was necessary to counteract the pressure of the sunlight on the huge surface of the station. The station and satellite would be constructed from ordinary aircraft-grade sheet aluminum, for ease of fabrication and cost saving.

Andy Brown returned to the front of the room. "As you can see, these designs have come a long way in a very short time. As we proceed into the construction phase, most of the design team members will be traveling as teams to work with the contractors selected to build the components.

"Some teams are farther ahead than others, and we're working already on new phases in the project. We don't know at this time when construction contracts will be awarded. Until then, we'll proceed to complete the current design missions, then begin looking at the design of parts of the project farther down the road. When all the design work on the Web is completed, for example, the satellite designers will be starting on the design of a smaller solar collector to power the lunar production facility. Others will be designing the lunar facility itself, and we will be adding some new expertise to develop ways to refine metals on the surface of the Moon and to launch the finished parts into lunar orbit, then move them to other geo-synchronous satellite locations.

"I'm very satisfied with our progress to date, and expect our designers to be busy for at least eight months, completing the current design missions. After that, we expect to be fully involved in the production of various components, and working on-site with the selected contractors. That concludes this meeting, unless there are any final questions."

The engineers left the back of the room and the visitors began talking with the team leaders.

"Well?" asked Andy. "What do you think?"

Jean Claude LeBec was the first to speak. "How soon will we be ready with contract drawings?" He paused. "Seriously."

Andy replied, "For the space plane, the end of the year, although my hunch is that the manufacturing fixture designs will require a little more time than the troops here are projecting. For the satellite, Thanksgiving. The rest should be entirely finished by mid-April." It was a great schedule, if they could keep it.

Danielle shook Andy's hand. "You're doing great, Andy. Just keep us on schedule. Now, I'd like to take a tour through the design and engineering offices, unless someone else has another idea, then have some lunch."

CHAPTER 11

October 12

At the international level, Uncle Bob's friends had been working on many governments. The Ambassador from Belize to the United Nations General Assembly made a motion to the effect that a search should be started for a private entity that would actually pay money for the rights to Space. The Vatican delegate suggested very politely that the Ambassador from Belize had slipped over the edge. The Chairman called for order.

The Ambassador from Uruguay seconded the Belize motion to allow discussion.

Sudan asked what would be the advantage to third-world countries of such an arrangement. The Ambassador from Belize said that, since Space had been found by the big space powers to be so worthless, if there were actual money which could be obtained from the sale of Earth's "rights" to it, why not take whatever some fool could be talked into paying for those rights, and split it among the third-world countries, which, of course, were the most needy countries and could put it to the best use.

The representative from Ethiopia inquired how much might the U.N. expect to realize from such a sale. The Ambassador from the United States, not wishing to be left out of the discussion, suggested that such a sale should bring not less than 100 million dollars. This seemed to some like a very large amount for such a useless commodity.

The Chinese Ambassador inquired whether each country would receive an equal share of the proceeds, or whether the distribution would be apportioned according to the population of each of the member countries. The Peruvian Minister requested that the matter be tabled to enable the delegates to take the idea back to their respective heads of state to determine how their nations viewed the proposal. The Chairman instructed the ambassadors to return in six weeks with positions from their countries on this issue.

Six weeks later, the General Assembly again took up the sale of ... what? It could hardly be called "real" estate. Was it 'imaginary' estate? Lithuania had prepared and presented a proposed contract and deed, which purported to grant to the purchaser, on behalf of all the countries and peoples on Earth, all rights in perpetuity to the "use and exploitation of all of Outer Space beyond the Earth's troposphere, including all planets, asteroids, and any other object, without limitation."

The Lithuanian Ambassador asserted that this language had been examined for legal sufficiency by the Attorney General of Lithuania, and by the U.N. legal ministry, therefore it was certainly proper. Actually, Danielle's legal staff had drafted the entire document. Nigeria asked the chairman to poll the delegates to determine a consensus regarding distribution of proceeds from such a sale.

The Russian Ambassador announced that Russia, for the good of the third-world nations, would relinquish its share of the sale proceeds for distribution among third-world nations on the basis of population. Ukraine seconded the Russian initiative, and proposed that all of the industrial nations should do likewise, in the interest of global harmony.

The United States called for a conference of the industrialized nations to determine whether they would all agree to such a plan, and asked the chairman to table the item again for a week while the industrial nations conferred.

One week later the item was again being considered on the floor of the General Assembly. The industrial nations, except China, had agreed on distribution of the proceeds of such a sale to the third world nations. China wanted distribution on the basis of population, and it also claimed to be a third-world nation, a theory which neither the industrial nations nor the third-world nations accepted.

The chairman appointed a committee to consider the distribution, and again tabled the issue. No one questioned the fact that there was no buyer in sight for these "space rights."

Likewise, no one questioned whether the amount, 100 million dollars, to which they had agreed by default, would be of any measurable benefit to even one of their countries.

The General Assembly adjourned for the Christmas holiday.

CHAPTER 12

December 22

The Christmas tree in the living room of Danielle's house in St. Andrew on the island of Guernsey was an excellent specimen. The house was fragrant with pine odors from the tree. Strings of tiny lights extended among the branches. She was sitting on the floor, back to the wall, busily installing ornaments on the back of the tree. Sunlight was streaming in through the living room windows.

Uncle Bob shouted from the front door. "Someone give me a hug!"

She wiggled out from behind the tree and jumped to her feet. "Uncle Bob!" She called, "I didn't expect you for three days." She ran to the front door and gave him a big hug, and a kiss for good measure.

"I had a chance to get away a few days early," he said, "and took it. Glad I did, too. My choice was to spend three days with the horses, or come here and be with you and enjoy Mrs. Benson's cooking. It was an easy decision."

Danielle took his hand. "I really *am* glad you're here. I need to talk with you about strategy." They walked together into the kitchen and she made two cups of hot tea.

"In what kind of strategy are you interested?" he asked.

"In about three or four months," she said, "I have to start selling investors on this project, and I need some professional direction. I can direct a business to turn it around from loss to profit, but you're the marketing genius, and I think that's what I need. I'm going to be asking each investor to sink a hundred million dollars in this project, and I haven't a clue how to close that sale."

"Sweetheart," he replied, "you need a 'hook.' The biggest problem you have right now is your own attitude. You're thinking of these folks as somehow better than you, because they're unusually rich. That's wrong. They're still marks, and you have to sell them just the same as if they were the neighbors to whom you sold Girl Scout cookies when you were a child.

"You have something of value to offer to them. Remember that. You're giving them a chance to have a piece of the action, and that's a valuable opportunity. If you think your job is to 'convince' them to participate, you won't succeed. They have to believe there's something there worth being part of. Then they'll convince themselves."

"Hmmm. So what do I do to plant that idea in their minds?" she asked.

"Well, for starters," he told her, "your presentation has to be really different. It has to be so full of confidence that there's no opportunity for them to doubt the success of the project. Maybe it should be even a little arrogant. You almost have to dare them *not* to be part of the project, but not quite. That should get their attention."

"You know," she said, "I never would have looked at it that way. I've argued cases in court, and negotiated with boards of directors and shareholders, but there I only had to present the law and the facts, and sometimes, policy and economic arguments. My mind doesn't work that way."

"I think there's another consideration you need to look at," he said. "After you run your ad, how many people do you expect to respond?"

"Well, ... I've spent a lot of time during the last six months trying to figure that out. The economists tell me there are just under 1,000 people in the world who can be expected to have the ability to raise and invest 100 million dollars."

"How did you reach the hundred million number?" he asked.

"I came to that almost at the beginning. We need 50 or 60 billion to reach completion on the project in a reasonable time. I figured that about 500 people was the maximum number I could reasonably reach and interact with. If there are more investors than that, all my time would be spent just dealing with investors and there wouldn't be enough time for operating the business."

"Hmmm, yes, that assumes everyone puts in the same amount of money?"

"Yes. Isn't that reasonable?""

"No, it's not. Your investors must have at least 100 million minimum. But there must be a curve there somewhere. Some investors will want to invest more, and get more control."

"I'm not going to give any of them any control."

Uncle Bob's jaw dropped. "What? You're not? Is that wise? Or possible?"

"It's essential. If I have to give up control, or even share it, the project can't succeed. The big problem with past space programs was that they diluted their energy with politics and 'P.R.' The only way for it to work is to totally focus on the job at hand. If we have to stop and argue about anything, the project fails. Almost none of the people whom I expect to invest know anything about the science behind the project, so there is no valid reason to give them a voice in its direction. It's essential for the project to keep moving, because our overhead is the big part of the budget. As long as we keep on schedule, we allocate overhead to each phase of the project. But if we stop, the overhead continues without any production, and we immediately go into the hole. Oh, I *have* planned for some unavoidable delays for weather, or materials delays, but I know first-hand how a shareholders' dispute can screw up a production schedule. If we have any internal disagreements about the technical aspects, they ultimately get decided by me. It was I who borrowed your money."

"Okay. So you don't give up control. How many eligible investors do you expect to respond to your ad?"

"Actual responses? I expect probably fifty to seventy-five," she said.

He started mentally reviewing the numbers. "All right. We start with fifty prospects, with the actual financial ability to invest. That's only five billion, plus you already have my billion. How are you planning to get ten times that many investors involved? How do you get the other forty-five or fifty-five billion?"

"That's why I wanted to confer with you," she said. "I need your opinion on whether my sales plan will work. I intend to challenge each early investor to become the head of a 'syndicate', and each syndicate will be required to raise two billion dollars from twenty investors. I'll provide some special benefits for the heads of the syndicates."

He thought for a few seconds then said, "You need another gimmick to insure that the word gets out, beside your syndicate heads."

"I do?"

"Yep. And I know what you need to do, but you have to promise not to get mad at me."

"I beg your pardon?"

"Sweety, there's an old canard in the States about how to get the news out, about anything, the fastest way."

"There is?" she asked.

"Yes."

"Well, what is it?"

"*You tell a woman it's a secret.*"

"What?!"

"You heard me."

"What does it mean," she asked.

"It means you're going to get them to spread the word for you, to all of their wealthy friends, by impressing on them how top-secret it is. People love to have a secret they can share with their friends. What we have to do is choreograph the presentation of information in order to plant firmly the need for secrecy."

"But, Uncle Bob, what we are doing is hardly secret at all. Well, it *is* secret that we are doing it right now, but the technology is almost all *old* technology. Why should we care if someone talks about it?"

"We don't care. We *want* them to talk about it. But in order to emphasize how valuable the information is, we're going to hit them with secrecy over and over. How are you going to advertise for investors?"

"I thought a news article about the project, followed by a full page ad in the big financial papers."

"No article. You put a small classified ad in those papers. All it says is 'Invest one hundred million dollars. Big risk.'"

"You're joking."

"Nope. I'm dead serious. Then when anyone responds to the ad who can really make the investment, not cranks, you send them a very uninformative letter asking to meet personally with them. But it will have your name on it. Anyone with that much money will certainly check you out. Your credentials are impeccable and their curiosity will force them to find out more. Then, when you have your personal interview with them, you tell them only the bare minimum, and make them sweat it out of you, *after* you swear them to secrecy. Don't give them anything technical. Make them pay for the technical stuff. You and I know it's all mostly public domain, but you can hint that you have some other razzle-dazzle that you can't tell them even then. Do it right, and you'll have to fight them off."

"Uncle Bob, you *are* the most devious person I ever met."

"Yes, dear. That's why I have billions of dollars and can give a billion of it to my best girl to play with on her space project. It's also why I'm going to have the most fun and make more money with this program than I ever did in real estate."

He was about to start counting future profits when Mrs. Benson announced that lunch was ready.

YEAR TWO

CHAPTER 13

January 6

The committee on the sale of Space reported back to the U.N. General Assembly that there was an impasse with China, and requested that the matter be referred to the Security Council for resolution. The Chairman instructed the committee to prepare a statement expressing the specifics of the impasse, then forwarded the statement to the Security Council.

In the Security Council, China was severely criticized by Brazil for creating dis-harmony in the world organization. The Brazilian delegate then proposed that a compromise would pay two-thirds of the proceeds into the treasury of the United Nations to be divided among the third-world nations, then the remainder among the other nations, with China receiving one-half the amount it would receive if the balance of the funds were apportioned according to population. China accepted that formula. A motion was passed unanimously by the Security Council, with much self-congratulation that the group had been able to so cleverly resolve this thorny issue. The matter was referred back to the General Assembly for further action. No prospective buyer for the rights to Space had yet appeared.

February 20

The Honorable Charles Hazenhurst, Secretary General of the United Nations, welcomed Robert MacDonald, retired real-estate tycoon, into his office. His secretary had concluded that this old man was just another VIP visitor. MacDonald was pretty well known as an eccentric, but harmless and extremely wealthy, retired businessman.

MacDonald had made a very large fortune locating and selling sites for garbage dumps, which were euphemistically called "landfills," as if the land were empty without the garbage. His land deals always seemed to work out to his advantage.

His acquaintance with Hazenhurst had started in Surrey, England, where Hazenhurst had represented MacDonald in one of his real estate ventures, before Hazenhurst entered politics. The last time they had seen one another was a year earlier during a vacation to California, when Hazenhurst had stayed at MacDonald's ranch for a few days.

They exchanged some pleasant conversation, then Bob began, "Charlie, we've known each other for many years, and you know I've had many dreams which I've not been able to accomplish.

"I don't have many years left, but there *is* one thing I'd like to do, and I believe I can afford it. I know it's only an old man's dream, but maybe you can understand.

"Since I was a young lad, I have been reading stories of space travel. One of my favorites was by Robert Heinlein, about a man who bought the rights to the Moon. I still have a copy of that book in my library.

"I've heard the U.N. has been talking about selling the rights to Space. I want to buy Space from the U.N. All of it."

"You're not really serious are you?" Hazenhurst asked. "How are you proposing to do it? And what will you do with it after you buy it? Are you going to be Bob MacDonald, owner of Blackacre and Mars?"

Bob chuckled. "Well, ... Yes and No. I have a corporation in mind that would receive the deed from the U.N. Does that sound too impractical? Am I crazy?"

The Secretary General thought seriously about the question, then said soberly, "Bob, I do *not* think you're crazy. You *are* eccentric, but you know that. In all my years, I've never known you to make a bad land deal. I don't know what you're up to, but I want in on it."

"Ha! Ha! Charlie, how can you think such a thing? This is just an eccentric old man's dream. I can't spend my money as fast as it accumulates now, why shouldn't I have some fun with it?"

"So you say, you crafty old schemer. Well, I'll push it through for you. The General Assembly and Security Council are certainly primed for a deal. How much do you plan to pay for this "worthless" Space?"

"I've given that some thought. I'd like to pay five dollars or a peppercorn for it, but I know the Assembly has a hundred million dollars stuck in its mind. I'm agreeable to the hundred million. I have enough that I won't miss it. And I have a formal written proposal prepared for consideration."

"Okay. I'll convey your proposal. After you get this deal, promise me you'll let me in on it."

"I'll let you know if anything develops, that's for sure. If it does, though, be prepared to put in some really big bucks."

Hazenhurst said, "I can't wait. Stick around for a few days. This shouldn't take long."

It didn't. Three days later, on February 23, Robert MacDonald had a piece of paper, signed by the Secretary General and every country's ambassador to the U.N., giving an Isle of Man limited partnership the perpetual and fully transferrable title to all of Space and everything it contains. The United States and Russia reserved an easement for their military, navigation and earth-sensing satellites. By June 17, he would have formal signatures on his "deed" from every major country and most minor countries. All the others would sign it within the year.

CHAPTER 14

March 8
　　The small ad ran first in the back pages of the <u>Wall Street Journal</u>. Two days later it appeared in the financial newspapers of London, Hong Kong, Tokyo, Paris, Berlin, Moscow, Beijing, Sydney, Melbourne, Johannesburg, Cairo, Riyad, Tel Aviv, Rome, and Delhi. It said,
"Serious Investors Sought. Extremely High Risk, High-Tech Project. Minimum Investment One Hundred Million Dollars US. Reply to Danielle Simones, P.O. Box 1268, Wall Street Station, New York."
　　There were more than fourteen thousand replies to the ad. Over thirteen thousand were from the curious who had no ability whatsoever to invest. The remaining replies were carefully examined. Danielle already knew who the people were with the financial resources to be involved. Her primary "hot" list had the name of every person in the world believed to have access to 100 million dollars. It was a very carefully researched list of nine hundred fifty-three names. For three weeks, she matched the responses from the ad with the names on her list, and decided in what order she should contact the responders.
　　The whole scheme sounded impossible. Similar ideas had been considered and rejected by the largest and wealthiest countries in the world. Why would it work now for her? Of course, that was the question that she would have to answer for each of the potential investors. Fortunately, she knew the answers.
　　The preceding ten years had been years of dramatic political upheaval around the world. Germany was reunited. The Soviet Union had collapsed. South Africa had eliminated apartheid. Israel and the Palestinians had reached a peaceful resolution of their differences. Ireland, Northern Ireland, England and the Irish Republican Army were working together to establish a peaceful reunification of Ireland.
　　Conditions no longer required nations to maintain huge national defense forces to counter military threats from their neighbors. The situation seemed optimal for nations that had been spending hundreds of billions of dollars each year on military forces to shift their priorities to scientific advancement.
　　Instead, lacking clear opponents, all of the major countries had withdrawn into themselves. They had begun to focus on their internal problems, most of which were due to stagnation and lack of imagination, and in response to those problems the countries seemed to alternately spend excessive amounts on those problems, and then withdraw all funding from those problems, as if they would solve themselves.
　　The United States Congress had killed its greatest research project, the superconducting super collider, on the altar of budget cutting. It had similarly cut back plans for a space station until the final design failed to meet any of the goals originally planned for it, then had pulled out all funding from the program.
　　The Russian government, heir to the Soviet Union's space program, had abandoned its manned space program. The total space capability of the former great space powers was reduced to maintenance of earth-centered information-gathering, navigation and communication satellites.

Meanwhile, unemployment around the world was increasing, supplies of fossil fuels were declining, farm lands continued to erode away to the sea, and more people in more countries were starving to death each year as drought and famine grew more common.

Danielle was working on the design for the electrical switching system for the power satellite with Tomasuko Oribati. He had come to Atlanta to confer with the designers of the satellite on the interconnections between the photovoltaic cells and the wiring of the satellite. While in Atlanta, Danielle showed him the designs for the space plane.

Oribati said, "Is there somewhere we can speak privately?"

She thanked the designers who were explaining the space plane, then she and Oribati stepped into Andy Brown's office.

Tom did not waste any time before getting to the point. "Will this airplane actually fly?" he asked.

"I believe it will. The computers say it will. And the wind-tunnel tests make us think it will. But Tom," she paused, "there isn't a wind tunnel in the world that can duplicate its flight regime. The best empirical data we have is from Soviet scramjet research, which only gets into the Mach 7 to Mach 10 speed range. This plane should come near Mach 25. And there are no airfoils this large flying anywhere. I can't say without qualification that it will fly, but I believe it will."

Oribati considered the implications of the unique plane. "How much money do you have to develop it?"

"A billion. And I've spent about a third of that already. I might be able to get another billion where the first billion came from, but I haven't asked."

"Your godfather." It was a statement, not a question.

"Yes."

"How much will the entire project cost?"

"At least fifty billion; not more than sixty for the first phase."

"How much to build the first space plane?"

"Somewhat less than four billion. We calculate later ones will cost less than a billion a copy. The first one is so expensive because we have to build the tooling to make the parts. That is basically a one-time cost."

"What if you don't raise as much as you need for the whole project?"

"I'll have to go public. I don't like it, but it will be the only way if I can't raise that much money from private investors within the next year."

"Suppose I make you a loan? Would that help?"

"What are you proposing, Tom? You don't have enough to pay fifty billion. Neither does Bob MacDonald. And I don't want to borrow your money. If you want to invest it in this project, I'd love for you to participate, but I can't promise you'd ever see your money again. It would have to be an investment, not a loan." She described the funding plan, with its syndicates of investors and told him about her "deed" to Space.

"Danielle, I want to make a special business arrangement with you. I'm prepared to put three billion dollars into your project almost immediately. But I don't want the security for my investment dependent on whether you can raise fifty billion, or so, more. If you don't find a way to raise that large figure, I'll invest three billion in the first space plane for a piece of the action. Call me your first syndicate if you wish. I'm confident I can round up some more investors. Once the word gets out about your space plane design, if you don't build it, someone else will. If they do, your deed to Space will just be a very expensive piece of paper. You have to be there first and I'd like to help make sure you are."

April 10

She was tense as she prepared for the first investor meeting. Felix O'Brian's offices were on the Penthouse level of the Transco Tower in Houston. He had made a large fortune in real estate and oil. As the time for the meeting approached, Felix O'Brian was also wondering. 'What is this woman really like, who is asking some of the world's most wealthy people to commit a hundred million dollars each to some hare-brained idea?'

She was bold enough to get his attention, that was for sure, and he would give her a chance to present her proposal.

The written answer to his response to her Wall Street Journal ad had been tantalizingly uninformative. "I am developing an enterprise the likes of which the world has never before seen. If you would like to learn more about it or to participate, we have to meet in person, at your office, at which time I will give you some details of the nature of the project. Please contact my office to set up an appointment." The telephone number for her office was in London, but the letter had been expressed to him from Australia, where she had stopped on return from a trip to Belau to confer with Bertram Allen.

Upon receipt of the letter, he had contacted his attorneys and asked them to run a complete investigation of her.

Their results were most interesting.

DANIELLE SIMONES;
Born: Danielle Marie Elizabeth Margaret Simones, Age: 29
Height: 5'4"/162 cm.
Weight: 120-lbs/55 kg.
Education:	*AA, Sacramento Community College*
	BS & MBA, Stanford University
	Majors: Business & Political Science
	JD, Tulane University
	LLM, University of Miami
	Major: International and Ocean Law
Residence:	*St. Andrew, Guernsey, Channel Islands*
Occupation:	*Industrial management and investment counseling*

Adjunct professor: Harvard School of Law (International Law) and Wharton Business School (International Investment Policy)

Author of numerous articles on economics for Forbes, Fortune, and other financial magazines, both in the U.S. and Europe, as well as numerous law review and legal journal articles, mostly on the subjects of aviation law, international law and legal ethics. Occasional articles in <u>Aviation Week and Space Technology</u> magazine.

Prior employment:
CEO of Global Aeronautique Internationale, Ltd., French manufacturer of advanced composite aircraft and aviation components. Appointed in 1989 when company was in bankruptcy. Left in 1993 on extended leave after making company most successful in aviation industry.

54

Financial: *Estimated net worth in excess of ten million dollars US. Believed to be major shareholder in Global Aeronautique Internationale, Ltd.*

Hobbies: *Horseback riding, gardening, reading (science fiction), flying: holds commercial, instrument and instructor pilot ratings in sailplane, single and multi-engine aircraft, and rotorcraft. Type rated for Boeing 757. Instructor rated in MIG-29.*

Marital Status: *Divorced from Elliot Wilson, New York tax attorney. No children. No known current involvements.*

Family: *Father: William Archibald Simones, deceased.*

Mother: Maryellen Elizabeth Stevens, retired, lives in Southern California with her third husband, Roger Stevens.

Siblings: Brother, David, single, teaches philosophy at Boston College. Sisters, Alice, homemaker, married to a pig farmer in Illinois; and Phyllis, homemaker, married to a dentist in Birmingham, Alabama.

O'Brian finished reading the report and called Danielle's office for an appointment.

They met in his conference room. Danielle stuck out her hand, "Hello, I'm Danielle Simones."

O'Brian began with formal pleasantries normal to the beginning of a meeting with a stranger, but she interrupted.

"Mr. O'Brian, I know you're busy, and so am I. I appreciate your courtesy and politeness, but we must get to the meat of this matter. First, I must have your word that what I'm about to tell you will not leave this room. If you agree I can begin to explain this project. Do you agree?"

"Of course. Please proceed."

She began slowly, "A little over a year ago I realized that there was a need developing in the world and that no one was positioned to address it, and further, that no one was making any serious effort to position themselves to be able to address it in the future.

"Since that time, I've assembled a group of scientists and engineers uniquely qualified to address this need. After extensive discussions with this design team, they've confirmed that my basic concept is valid.

"They have begun design work on this project, and they've convinced me that we have the technology available, using designs which they have developed, to carry out the project.

"This project will revolutionize life on earth as we know it. It will provide a means of addressing the most difficult problems confronting humankind.

"You're a Texas oil man and understand the energy industry. You know how much the cost of developing an oil or gas well has increased during the last decade. You know that these cost increases reflect the decreasing untapped reserves of fossil energy, and the difficulty of proving new wells, as well as the increasing demand for energy.

"You know the problems, which have impacted the nuclear energy industry around the world. From Cherynobyl to Three Mile Island to Rocky Flats to Iraq to North Korea to India to you-name-it, there have been constant reminders of the dangers of nuclear energy.

"Because of public perceptions, whether correct or not, about dangers of radioactivity, waste disposal, cancer and threat of accidents, it's simply not cost-effective at this time, and therefore not practical, to develop the kinds of nuclear power plants that we've used in the past. The only plants still under construction in the United States have increased in cost to nearly ten billion dollars each.

"Nevertheless, the demand for energy is increasing. As third-world nations strive to attain the resource consumption level of the industrialized world, their demand for energy is exploding. The hunger of the United States for ever-increasing amounts of energy is obvious in the amount of imported oil reflected in the U.S. national debt. We are currently *importing* 21 million barrels per day and are using about a third of the world's total oil production.

"More and more countries are competing for a diminishing supply of fossil energy. Even the current short-term over-supplies due to boosts in production haven't changed the overall trend toward eventual fuel shortages.

"We know from experience that increased productivity and economic growth occurs when energy is cheap and plentiful, yet each of us intuitively realizes that the easier it is to get cheap fossil energy today, the less there will be for the future needs of mankind. We can easily envision the time when fossil fuels are neither cheap nor plentiful. That prospect suggests the future economy may be much worse than today.

"I presume you're already aware of this situation. Have I over-stated it?"

"Yes," he replied, "I *am* aware of the situation. The oil industry has made many projections about the amount of oil and gas reserves remaining. The most pessimistic of these studies have been closely guarded secrets."

"I know those studies," she said. "The only studies which don't predict a catastrophic collapse due to exhaustion of petroleum supplies are those which anticipate undiscovered new technology or premise their predictions on strip mining and burning the low-grade deposits of coal-like lignite minerals in the southwest U.S. and elsewhere. Some of them intentionally mis-interpret old supply projections to reach an optimistic result. Unfortunately, while disregarding environmental impacts, those reports also fail to disclose that the energy produced by lignite is likely to be less than the energy required to dig it from the ground. India's experiment with lignite is failing, as it costs more energy to produce than it generates."

"Plus, no one knows when or if new technology will appear," he volunteered. "And *No*, you have *not* overstated the problem. The only disagreement in the industry is *when* the collapse will occur."

"All right," she said. "We have a starting point. You may also be aware that our dependence on petroleum-based energy has dramatically and adversely impacted our atmosphere and that conventional methods of generating electricity, with steam, waste about two to three times as much energy as they produce. Although politicians and interest groups, including the fossil-fuel industry, argue about who's responsible or about the degree of the problem, the reality of acid rain, smog, and other forms of air pollution cannot be denied."

"Why should I care?" he asked.

"Because it has the potential to profoundly impact your economic position, and that of your family, one way or the other. Some scientists link the use of petroleum fuels to the apparent degradation of the ozone layer and climatic change. In other areas, the need for energy and farmable land is resulting in destruction of rain forests and resulting damage of unknown dimensions to the living resources of those forests. Again, experts disagree only about the degree of the damage.

"Many of the problems relating to consumption and exhaustion of the world's resources are the result of over-population. Those population-related issues must be addressed by the world's political and religious leaders. Frankly, I have neither the talent nor the ability to do anything about them in any direct way.

"However, I can do something about them indirectly and, in the process, provide a business opportunity of unprecedented proportions for a number of alert investors, *if* the investors are willing to accept the risks involved. That is why you should care – because it is an opportunity that you can take advantage of.

"The competition for the remaining sources of energy has produced an environment in which energy is an increasingly valuable asset. What I'm proposing is to construct, in increments, the largest electric power generating plants ever built. They'll be large enough to power entire countries, or even entire continents. They'll produce and distribute electric power, at low cost, to local distribution utilities worldwide, and will produce environmentally benign power and fuels for vehicles of all kinds. If this project works according to my predictions, oil wells will become historical artifacts. Existing nuclear plants will be unnecessary and will be dismantled. You are heavily invested in these energy sources. I know. That should make you care quite a lot.

"If you decide you're interested in being a part of this venture, I must advise you that the minimum investment will be one hundred million dollars, as my ad said, although I expect some investors to put in much more than that amount. The initial cost of this venture will be many billions of dollars, and it'll be some years before there's any return on the initial investment.

"If we're successful, and as I've said, I have every reason to think we will be, the eventual return on the investment should be very good.

"However, I must reemphasize the risks involved. We'll be operating in a strange environment, and there will certainly be setbacks from time to time. I don't want to paint you too rosy a picture.

"Furthermore, I control the corporations developing this project. You're undoubtedly familiar with boards of directors that argue interminably about minutiae, and decide nothing. I certainly have had to deal with such boards in the past, but I don't intend to ever again. I'll be in complete control. Only me. I'll have many assistants, any one of whom will be competent to take over in my absence or upon my death, but I won't have a board of directors second-guessing my decisions.

"Therefore, if you choose to invest, you'll get no vote in the operation of the business.

"Each investor will be a beneficiary of an investment trust of which I am the trustee. If you invest, you, like other investors, will get a personal note from me which will promise you a significant return on your investment, approximately twenty percent per year, after a ten-year delay, provided the corporation succeeds in its venture. Payments to investors, when they occur, will be made to accounts in a country with no income tax. How the investors get those funds to other locations will be up to them.

"The investors will have the kinds of benefits from their investments that owners of a corporation normally expect, except control. And there will be provisions for continuity of the corporation and continued payment to the investors, in case anything happens to me." She looked him straight in the eyes. "What do you think so far?"

He started to speak, then hesitated, which was unusual for him. It was rare that he met a woman who was so direct. He had never met anyone who would suggest such a large investment. And on top of that she had bluntly said that investors would have no control over the corporation. He was surprised to realize he was actually considering the proposal. He could easily raise a hundred million, although he would have to sell some of his favorite properties to do it.

"Your plan sounds intriguing, Miss Simones, but you have left out some important details. Like where and how you propose to build such power plants. The permitting requirements in any industrial country would be prohibitive and, without petroleum, you're still dependent on nuclear power to produce the amount of power you propose, and that has many drawbacks.

"Still, this is a very interesting proposal, and my primary business is energy. If you can convince me it's workable, I'd like very much to be part of it. But pardon me if I'm skeptical. I don't see how you're going to overcome the political obstacles."

Danielle smiled. "I'm glad you see the problems, Mr. O'Brian. Let me give you some more background – you're right that dependence on petroleum is impossible. But there *is* a source of nuclear power that is available, clean, and relatively pollution-free. And while the power plants will be *very* expensive to build, the fuel will be free." She waited, watching his eyes and letting his curiosity increase.

"I've heard of the experiments with fusion at Lawrence Livermore and elsewhere," he said. "But they haven't managed to sustain any reaction for more than a fraction of a second. And their fuel – I believe they're using deuterium or tritium – certainly isn't free."

"Our fuel *will* be free," she repeated. "And we'll not be operating our plants with any technology as uncertain as Livermore's nuclear fusion. We already *have* that new technology people have been anticipating." She paused again.

"Mr. O'Brian, you're certainly aware that the Earth is constantly bathed in energy from the Sun. The potential solar energy reaching the surface of the Earth with the Sun directly overhead is approximately 747 watts for each square meter of the Earth's surface. ... We're going to use solar power.

"The Arizona desert, or west Texas, could produce immense quantities of energy, if the area were dedicated to solar collectors. We're going to use the Sun as our power source. It *is* the ultimate fusion generator, and free." She waited again for his predictable response.

It came quickly. "Yes, but that's all been considered before. First, the Sun only shines during the daytime. Even if you get clear weather during the daytime, much of the demand is at night. Plus, the Sun is seldom directly overhead, usually it's at an angle and thus less energy is received at the surface. Then there are storms, which block out the Sun and, even when there are no storms, it can be overcast, blocking out most of the sun's energy.

"Then finally, there are the tree-huggers to contend with. Dedicating a large amount of desert to solar production would bring every environmental group from Earth First! to the Sierra Club down on your neck. You'd never get out of the first permit process." He caught his breath, thinking he had destroyed her premise.

She smiled at him and said, "I know all that. That's why we're not building our plant in the desert of either Arizona or Texas.

"I have examined the permit problem. The obstacles there are indeed insurmountable. Instead of a permit from any country, our solar collector sites will be acquired from all of the countries, and will be dependent on none of them for permits. And we don't worry about weather or nighttime. The Sun shines almost 24 hours a day at our plant sites, Mr. O'Brian, at an intensity of almost fourteen hundred watts per square meter.

"We are going to build dozens of multi-GigaWatt plants, *and* a city, in Space."

O'Brian's jaw dropped, then he composed himself. This was no normal investment proposal. That was for sure. Could it work? Was it feasible? If it was, why hadn't it been done before?

After a moment, he asked, "You can't be serious, Miss Simones. Congress has already looked at a space station and concluded that the United States couldn't afford it. The Russians couldn't afford it. How can you be so naïve as to think you can accomplish what the greatest industrial powers in the history of the world cannot do?"

"The answer to your question requires some explanation," she replied. "First, the United States cannot put up a successful space station because it lacks the will to do so. That's the only reason it can't. When it decided, with an imaginative leader, and with competition from the Soviet Union to urge it along, to put a man on the Moon, it did so, although it wasted a lot of energy getting there. The technology to put a man on the Moon was available twenty years earlier.

"Second, the United States is *not* the greatest industrial power in the history of the world, or at least the United States government is not. What I'm proposing is an enterprise which *will* be an industrial power, multinational, and of sufficient magnitude to accomplish this project. We won't have to answer to Congress or to voters, or to any national government. I will personally have the obligation to make it pay for the investors, and the managers will answer to me. We'll have the strong support and encouragement of national governments all over the world, which we will obtain for a kiss and a smile, plus the promise of cheap energy to help fuel their desire to realize national objectives for growth and development.

"You need to remember that the most important technological accomplishments in history have been the result of work of individuals, not of governments. Think about that.

"The telephone, the electric light, the airplane. All were done by individuals. Government's primary functions these days are to pay for public programs too large for individuals to afford and to protect us from one another. No government, not the United States, nor Russia, nor Japan nor any other country, can do what I'm proposing because they can't escape their own bureaucracies and entanglements with one another. It's precisely for that reason that I alone will control this project. Any other approach would result in unacceptable delays and resulting failure.

"What this project can and will do is focus all of our energy on the construction of very large space facilities, which will generate electric power and deliver it back to Earth.

"Exactly how we propose to do that is proprietary information, but you *can* buy a ticket to a technical briefing at which we will describe that process in detail.

"In the process of constructing our facility, we're going to revolutionize several other industries, and we'll have more to sell when we're done than we started out to produce. We can't know for sure what kinds of things we'll have at that time, because they'll be discoveries made as we go along, but history tells us that we'll surely learn a lot as we go. Look at the American space program and see how many industries have been spin-offs from it.

"What we're offering to our investors is a piece of the action. Being in on the ground floor, our investors will also automatically be set up to receive some of the profits from the industries which we're able to spin off from the primary project. They'll also be in a good position to make related investments in areas helped by our project.

"Our space facility will also provide a center for research on new technologies, which the United States and other national governments have so far only been able to dream about.

"We'll provide a site, with unlimited space for expansion, for the fabrication of unique products in low or zero-gravity conditions. We're going to lease space, probably initially to governments, but very soon to other industries, new industries who will need the facilities and environment, including zero-gravity and near-perfect vacuum, which will be available at our site and nowhere else.

"Your ticket to the technical briefing will cost you a million dollars, Mr. O'Brian, which will be applied to your hundred million investment in the project, if you decide to go on. I could as easily make the admission to the briefing free, if I wanted, but the million-dollar tag is to eliminate folks who are not seriously interested. We *will* expect you to keep all information presented in strict confidence, of course.

"The briefing hasn't yet been scheduled, because I have a number of other potential investors with whom I must discuss the plan before the briefing.

"If you want to attend the briefing, you may place your million dollar deposit for your ticket in escrow with Mr. Seymour, my attorney here in Houston. Here's his card. You'll receive interest on your deposit at the prime rate until the date of the briefing, and if you decide to back out before the briefing, we'll return your deposit." She stopped, and waited.

"Well, you certainly have caught my attention. I don't need time to decide on the million-dollar ticket. I want to attend your briefing and find out the details. I'll send a check to your attorney this afternoon."

"There's a further aspect of this which you may want to know", she continued, "and since you *are* interested enough to attend the briefing, I want to explain it to you.

"Our budget for Phase 1 of the project is on the order of 50 billion dollars. Financing for the project will be through a number of syndicates, each of which will have to raise at least two billion US dollars from at least 20 investors. This is primarily because, as you can understand, once this project gets rolling, I won't be able to personally consult with all of the investors, and will need some intermediaries. There will be a special staff to keep investors informed of project status, as well as periodic, probably annual, investors' meetings.

"If you want to head up a syndicate, in other words, if you think you can find at least nineteen other investors willing to kick in 100 million dollars each, and want to maintain direct communication with me, please let me know.

"There *will* be some special compensation for the syndicate heads, although with these numbers, many of the syndicate heads may be satisfied with the position for its own sake. If you elect to participate with at least 100 million dollars, but don't let me know you want to head a syndicate at the time you deposit your 100 million, I'll assign you to someone else's syndicate, and you'll not have direct access to me.

"If you try to raise the two billion as a syndicate head and fail, or fail to get 19 other investors, within a reasonable time-frame that you and I will have agreed to, I'll assign you and any investors whom you have recruited to another syndicate, and you'll still not have direct access to me. I want to be sure you're clear on this."

"Thanks for your candor," he replied. "I can appreciate that you'll have a special need for your time. We'll see whether I go beyond the first million *after* I've seen your technical briefing."

She turned and closed her portfolio. "Very well. I have to get back to the airport and get to three more meetings with potential investors today. I'll hear from Mr. Seymour when he gets your check and will notify you of the briefing date. Thanks for your time."

O'Brian escorted her to the door and closed it after her. He walked back to his office, wondering and humming to himself. She hadn't disappointed him. This was going to be very interesting.

CHAPTER 15

June 18

Briefing packages, in express envelopes, arrived simultaneously at offices around the world. Each package contained a single first-class round-trip airplane ticket between the nearest airport and Bangkok, an identification card, and a set of instructions. The I.D. card had the picture of the person to whom the envelope was addressed, and his or her thumbprint, but a different name.

The instructions read:

"A room is reserved for you in the name on the enclosed identification at the Royal Thai Sheraton for July 5, 6, and 7. You will be met at the hotel at 0800 hours local time on the morning of July 6 by a representative of the corporation.

"The briefing will begin that morning, and will last two days. The enclosed identification card must be presented to attend the briefing. This admission is non-transferrable.

"You are reminded that the briefing is strictly confidential. No cameras, tape recorders or other recording devices are permitted. You will be provided notepaper and pencils. Bring nothing with you other than the enclosed identification card. Wear casual clothing. Special attire will be provided at the site for your wear during the briefing."

At 0800 on July 6, a group of large tour buses drove into the parking lot of the Royal Thai Sheraton. Minutes later, 200 people were escorted onto the buses, which immediately departed the hotel. After a few minutes in the congested traffic of Bangkok, the buses turned into the campus of Chulalongkorn University, closed at that time between class sessions.

The passengers exited from the buses and followed their guides into a meeting room, where they were informed that they were to go to one of several locker rooms and change into special uniforms for the briefing.

One man objected to the uniform. He was offered a refund of his admission fee, but reconsidered and went into the locker room. Each guest was asked to provide a thumbprint, which was compared by a computer to the thumbprint on the identification card, and to another print in the computer's memory. After the guest's identification was verified, each was provided a white jumpsuit or other similar attire appropriate to the guest's culture, with his or her name embroidered on the left breast and an embroidered logo on the right breast.

From the locker rooms, the members of the group were led into a large lecture hall. At the front of the hall, dressed also in a white jumpsuit, was a short, slender, dark-haired woman – Danielle. They had all met her previously. She was the reason they were there. Bob MacDonald sat near the back of the room, with Maurice d'Orleans, Jean Claude LeBec, Cliff Kelly and Eric Savage.

The microphone clipped to her collar transmitted her voice to all who were present. Some who did not understand English had been provided special headsets, from which her words were heard, but in their native languages. Danielle's image, projected on a screen six meters high, appeared on the wall behind her. Next to the projected image, her real self seemed tiny.

"Welcome to Thailand," she began. "And welcome to Project Prometheus. My name is Danielle Simones. I have met each of you during the past two months and promised you a briefing on the technical details of our project. Your special uniforms are our way of insuring that our meeting is totally confidential. The uniforms are yours to keep, and you are required to wear them each day of our meeting. There will be a fresh uniform for tomorrow waiting for you in your room this evening. Please feel free to take any notes you wish using the paper provided. If you require more paper or pencils, there are assistants around the room to help you.

"There is a package at your table with your name on it. In it is important information which you are to take with you from this meeting, and we ask you to keep it confidential. The most interesting portions of this information are our projections for return on your investments. Do not attempt to read it now. You will have ample time to do so later."

"You have each made a significant commitment to be present here today. Those of us who have been working on this project up to now appreciate your confidence. I'm sure both your confidence and your expectations for this briefing and our project will be satisfied.

"We will proceed as follows: First, I'll outline the overall project to you and introduce to you the leaders of the project teams. Then I'll turn over the podium to each of them in turn and they will discuss their particular area or discipline.

"At lunch today, we'll dine informally together in a nearby dining room and you may talk freely with our experts. Following lunch, we'll reconvene here for continued briefings from other leaders of the project teams.

"This format will be used through tomorrow morning, and then again during lunch you may speak with our personnel. There will be a question-and-answer session for the remainder of tomorrow afternoon. I'm sure you will have many questions, and we want to answer them all. Please write them down as they occur to you during the briefing today and tomorrow.

"Tonight we'll serve dinner in the hotel's penthouse, and we hope everyone here will attend. We'll be available after dinner for any questions or clarification you wish to obtain from me or the team leaders at that time.

"Tomorrow evening, after the question-and-answer session here, we'll also serve dinner at the hotel penthouse, and will take time afterward for any who wish to commit to their full participation in the project to do so. On the day after tomorrow, we'll be meeting here again with those who have made the commitment to the full one hundred million-dollar investment. At that meeting, we'll discuss confidential financial aspects of the program. Now, I'd like to introduce some of our key personnel.

"First, our aircraft design team leader, Glenn Skinner." Skinner's picture appeared on the huge screen.

"Mr. Skinner is a specialist in design and construction of unconventional aircraft. He has been involved in several successful space-probe projects and formerly worked for McDonnell Douglas Aircraft and NASA.

"Next, our spacecraft design team leader, Richard O'Donnell. Mr. O'Donnell was head of spacecraft design at the NASA program prior to his retirement.

"Third, our solar power design team leader, Aaron Parrish, who was previously head of thin-film and amorphous silicon power generation research at the Massachusetts Institute of Technology.

"Fourth, our power transmission team leader, Tetsu Nakamura, who was previously chief of electrical power transmission systems at Matsushita Electric Co.

"Fifth, our structural design team leader, Bill McLaughlin. He was previously Dean of the Engineering School at Ohio State University, and before that headed NASA's Office of Outer Space Structures. Bill is a specialist in ceramic structures.

"And last but by no means the least important technical area, our bio-medical team leader, Yuri Petrosky. Mr. Petrosky was previously chief of the space medicine department for the Soviet and Russian space programs.

"Following the technical briefings, we'll hear from our lead economist, Arthur Peterson, formerly Director of the Wilson Corporation for Economic and Public Policy, who will explain the method used to project return on investments in this program, including the rationale for cash flow and reinvestment strategies; the secondary benefits which investors are expected to realize from technologies which we will develop; and the economic side-effects in the general economy, which we are anticipating.

"You may have been hesitant about spending the ticket price for this briefing. I assure you that, if you will pay attention, take good notes, and then invest in the industries for which our project will produce secondary benefits, Mr. Peterson will tell you enough during today's briefing to enable you to recoup your investment many times over.

"We'll first look at the overall concept. Fundamental to our concept is the principle that we are using existing technology wherever possible. I'll elaborate on that in a moment.

"We expect to develop some new approaches to various parts of the program, and have included funds in our budget for limited research along those lines, but we don't require any breakthroughs for the basic overall project to be completely operational.

"Our Earth Base will be in a small country located near the Equator." The screen displayed an artist's rendering showing an aerial view of a runway with numerous large buildings nearby.

"We have selected the site for the Earth Base, and are also interested in offers which any other interested country might make for supporting facilities. The project will make significant contributions to the economy of any country where facilities are located.

"At our Earth Base, we are building a large airfield, from which our aircraft will depart for space. Our aircraft will take off as an airplane, boost into orbit as a rocket, then re-enter the Earth's atmosphere and land again as a powered airplane. We refer to our new aircraft as 'the space plane.' Unlike NASA's space shuttle orbiter, which is really a very bad glider, our plane can return from space, set up an approach to land at an airport, then abort its landing and fly to another airport hundreds of miles away." A three-view drawing of the space plane appeared on the screen. Some recognized the logo on their uniforms as a stylized drawing of the space plane.

"These aircraft will take off and climb to a very high altitude and very high speed as winged airplanes. At a certain altitude, being above most of the earth's atmosphere, there is simply too little air for the wings to produce lift, so the space plane will ignite internal rocket-like engines, and rendezvous with orbiting satellites like a rocket. We will have a small fleet of these space planes constantly carrying supplies into space.

"American and Russian space shuttles use large booster rockets for launch and use air friction to slow their re-entry into the atmosphere. Our aircraft will not require boosters to achieve orbit, and will utilize a less-demanding reentry, which will use braking rockets to dramatically reduce the velocity of the space plane as it enters the atmosphere. The system that present launch vehicles use is equivalent to climbing a wall or a rope, straight up. It uses a lot of energy to get through the dense part of the atmosphere. Our launch will use that atmosphere and dynamic lift to lift our spaceplane above the dense air. It is like walking up a ramp instead of climbing a rope. We will use less energy, but it will take a little longer. The energy we will save at launch will enable us to carry the fuel we need for reentry braking and to avoid the reentry problems caused by high kinetic energy of orbital speed during the descent into the upper atmosphere. Our aircraft will enter the atmosphere at much slower speeds than spacecraft used previously. Our aircraft will then be able to fly and land normally and will be able to land easily at alternate airports in case our primary field is unavailable, then take off and come back to our field under their own power. Also unlike the American space shuttles, our space plane will have a turn-around time of hours, rather than the weeks of the space shuttle.

"The design for this aircraft was completed seven months ago and we have been negotiating with several of the world's top aerospace companies for construction of the many space plane components, which we will assemble into complete aircraft at our own facility. We're now ready to issue the construction contracts for those components. We expect to spend about three billion dollars to build the first plane, and about one and one-half billion for the second and following planes.

"This aircraft will revolutionize long-distance travel and will be the first spin-off of the program. We envision a space plane production program, for aircraft leased to international airline companies. We will not be selling the space planes, because in that way we can insure that we retain control of their use.

"Satellites in low earth orbit will unload supplies from the space plane for transshipment to our power stations. From the low earth orbital satellites, we will go directly to one of several geostationary power satellites, using a system of shuttles between satellites. Thus, we will have a network of three satellites in orbit during the initial construction phase: two low earth orbit satellites and the first geostationary power satellite, to be followed by two additional power satellites in phase one. The initial construction phase will use materials brought up from Earth in the space plane. Later, we will construct a main station complex, which I will explain when I describe Phase Two.

"At each geostationary satellite there will be a solar collector array and a power transmission antenna array, as well as a construction field office and living quarters for any maintenance personnel.

"The construction of the power stations will proceed to the point that the solar power collector arrays are complete, while building simultaneously the mechanism for transmitting power via microwave from our geostationary satellites to Earth.

"Microwave transmission will require large-area receiving antennas on the Earth's surface, approximately ten kilometers in diameter – preferably in areas characterized by arid climate, low population density and predominantly clear skies – which will then be connected to transformers and land transmission lines to consumers. Initial sites under consideration are deserts or other large, relatively flat areas within 30 degrees of the equator.

"We plan on locating the first antennas in Africa, for several reasons. Africa contains countries with some of the worst economic conditions in the world. To us, this means the greatest opportunities for economic growth and development, and therefore, the greatest opportunities for profit. We intend to have the first antenna receiving power within five years from the starting date of our project, which is today.

"We've also considered the potential for present adverse economic conditions in Africa, if unchecked, to develop into internal and external conflicts which would require wasteful dedication of resources from developed countries in attempts to halt those conflicts. We've seen those conditions repeatedly in recent years in South Africa, Sudan, Somalia and other African countries and they seem to benefit only the armament manufacturers.

"Our projections indicate these events will become worse if a fundamental change does not occur, and that such events would adversely impact the return on many of your existing investments around the world.

"By providing new sources of electric power to African countries, we'll give those countries new reasons to work cooperatively, resources to develop jobs necessary for productive economies, and the ability generally to improve living conditions for their people in ways each country finds appropriate, which will then create significant opportunities for profit in many industries beside ours.

"After Africa, we intend to offer receiving antennas to the countries of the Middle East and Southern Asia, then to Latin America, and last to the developed countries. Our ability to serve additional countries will depend on the rate at which we can build more power-generating satellites.

"As we approach each country for authorization to construct our receiving antennas within its borders, we will need you, our investors in that country, to 'assist' the local government in seeing the wisdom of having our electrical generating stations.

"The completion of the first group of African microwave transmission systems will signify the completion of Phase One of the project. We estimate this will take approximately ten years. Transmission of power from receiving antennas to the commercial power grid for each country will usually be by existing utility companies. Where links between countries exist, we will use them. Where they do not exist, we will build them. We will control the distribution of power between countries on the grid, through remotely controlled switching facilities, as a means of insuring compliance by each country with their agreements with us.

"Phase Two is the construction of a highly developed main space station, housing thousands of people, at which we will build more solar power satellites using materials from the Moon. Phases One and Two will actually proceed simultaneously, but because of the potential for immediate returns on our investments and secondary benefits once the first satellites are producing power, Phase One will be the focus of our initial efforts.

"The importance of Phase Two is that it will dramatically reduce our cost of placing construction materials at the solar power satellites. The main space station will include a factory, at which solar power satellites will be built for deployment around Earth, and around the Moon. Solar power satellites in lunar orbit will enable rapid and economical development of industrial and scientific facilities on the Moon, which we expect to develop rapidly into a new community. The main space station will also provide almost Earth-like recreational and residential facilities for employees of the corporation, including personnel from the power stations.

"Phase Three involves leasing space at the main station complex to third-party users for research or production of space-oriented materials. This facility will be expanded, as circumstances permit, to provide enhanced quarters for scientific and industrial tenants.

"Phase Four is a concurrent phase with all of the other phases. It involves developing and exploiting, for other uses, the technologies developed for the project. One of these technologies is the use of the earth-to-orbit aircraft for commercial passenger and cargo service between points on Earth. This will enable flights from London to Auckland, New Zealand, for example, in about one and one-half hours.

"Because of our superior space launch capability, we will also be able to provide service to existing satellites of various governments and industries, at a fraction of the cost of their existing transportation systems and, for this reason, we expect to dominate the satellite placement and repair business.

"Other commercial enterprises are anticipated, but, due to uncertainty regarding technical developments, we don't wish to suggest that any of them are sure things.

"We also expect to have subsidiary enterprises producing devices to use the abundant power that we will be furnishing, for example, in electric or other alternate energy vehicles.

"I told you a few minutes ago that I would elaborate on the use of existing technology. The degree of risk in a project like this one depends to a large degree on how much of the project is dependent on untested technology. What we are going to carry out is basically a solar power satellite system that was proposed by a United States National Aeronautics and Space Administration study years ago, in 1977. Most of it was technologically possible then. Our contribution is the space plane, which will dramatically lower the cost of placing material in orbit, the most difficult and therefore the most costly part of the project. However, even the space plane is not entirely new. It is actually a refinement and expansion on a prior United States design, called the X-30 "National Aerospace Plane," which was proposed in the 1980s. We have refined the design, and made it several times larger than the United States envisioned, but it is basically the same concept. The concept is public domain information. The Americans recently declassified the X-30 design and testing information, and we have combined their data with known technology from the Lockheed SR-71 Blackbird, the XB-70 Valkyrie, the Concorde, the American SST, scramjet technology research of the former Soviet Union, and the American and Russian space shuttle programs, plus aeronautical experience with the Burnelli family of aircraft, the Northrup flying wings and American studies into lifting body design, into an entirely new design in which we have a significant proprietary contribution, and there are many elements for which we will be obtaining patents. It is this space plane which makes our project possible, and we expect to be flying this plane within two years.

"What we've added to prior designs is the imagination and creativity of engineers and designers whom we released from the constraints of old-fashioned national space programs. When the Americans and Russians recently announced the cancellation of their space program, we hired many of their top people, and we now have unquestionably the best aerospace design team ever assembled.

"The remainder of the system, beyond the space plane, is basically straight from the 1977 NASA concept, but incorporating technological and materials improvements that have occurred since then. What we have now, which the Americans lacked then and still lack now, is the determination to focus our efforts on this mission. We have thousands of engineers, scientists and other employees working on our program as we speak today, and we are going to build the space plane no matter whether we build the solar energy stations or not.

"Therefore, even without the investments which I have invited you to make, we are proceeding with the space plane, which I expect to have flying soon. We do not need additional financing to complete this aircraft. Once the space plane exists, others will realize its potential for space exploitation.

"We need your investments, however, to proceed with the Prometheus solar energy program and we have brought you together today because we believe that a fundamental change in the energy supply of this planet is necessary and possible, and we know it will be very expensive to put it in place. You and the other people in this room have the ability to make it happen, and to benefit from that event.

"Keeping a project as large as this one a secret is very difficult, if not impossible. With as many people as there are in this room, that difficulty increases significantly. Nevertheless, each of you, by the time we are finished with our briefing tomorrow, will recognize the potential our project has to provide a significant return from your investment. We ask you to keep confidential this project, for as long as possible. As news of our efforts begin to leak out to the rest of the world, we will be announcing that we are developing a revolutionary aircraft. The solar power satellite program will not be disclosed until someone outside learns what we are doing and we are no longer able to credibly deny it.

"I would now like to introduce Glenn Skinner, the leader of our aircraft design team, who will explain some of the details and considerations which went into the design of our space plane."

The briefings continued through the morning, and into the afternoon.

As the afternoon session was concluding the second day, Danielle again came to the center of the raised platform and said, "During the last two days you've seen the tip of the iceberg. But, before we adjourn for dinner, I want to give each of you something to think about.

"Technological change occurs when people realize it is possible. History is full of inventions or discoveries which occurred virtually simultaneously at more than one location, sometimes on opposite sides of the world.

"What we are proposing is very feasible, but it will require at least fifty billion dollars to accomplish. We know that in this room is a group with the ability to raise that amount and more. Whether you decide to be a part of this endeavor may determine whether Project Prometheus will be able to carry the solar power project through to completion. We have to raise at least fifteen billion dollars today in order to proceed with that part of the program.

"But regardless of whether we succeed with the energy program or not, it is clear that *someone* will do it, because we now know it *can* be done and *how* to do it.

"Many of you are already in the energy business. Whether you sell oil, gas, uranium, or wood, the handwriting is on the wall for your industry. Petroleum will continue to be important for the production of lubricants and in chemical processes, but as an energy source, it is soon going to be as dead as the market for whale oil.

"We're offering you today an opportunity to be part of mankind's new energy industry. This is a bold step. And there *are* risks.

"You are all gamblers in some respect, or you would not have gambled a million dollars each to be here yesterday and today to learn exactly what we are proposing to do and how. You each understand, as successful businessmen and businesswomen, that sometimes it *is* necessary to accept risks, in order to achieve success.

"But there is another risk which you may have overlooked, beside that of investing one hundred million dollars in this project and I want to be sure you understand what that risk is. That risk is the risk of *not* being part of this enterprise. Once our program becomes public knowledge, there will be many who will want to become part of it. Without adequate private financing, we could be forced to spin off a public company, in which you would not have the advantages now offered.

"You will have an advantage over those who get in later, both economically and politically, by being part of this project from the beginning.

"This program will be operated as a trust. I am the initial trustee. You who contribute the principal to the trust will be the beneficiaries, and as your information materials package explains, distributions from the trust will be made in countries which do not have taxes on those distributions. As early investors, your benefits will also be superior to any who might invest later. Your information package discusses some of the advantages for being in early, and we will discuss those advantages and more tomorrow with those who commit to the 100 million dollar minimum.

"There is a second factor of which you should be aware. Early this year, the United Nations transferred perpetual, unconditional and unlimited rights for development and exploitation of Outer Space and all it contains to a private entity. Every nation in the world has concurred in that transfer.

"Project Prometheus owns those rights. We consider this ownership essential to enable us to move smoothly forward with our program."

A murmur went through the room and many pencils, already worn-out, were busily writing notes.

"After dinner this evening, which will be held at 8 PM in the Penthouse of the hotel, representatives will be available for those of you who are ready to commit to the 100 million dollars minimum. If you do want to make that commitment, please see me and I will introduce you to one of our staff members who will handle the details.

"Dinner this evening will also be the time for you to tell us if you want to head an investors' syndicate. Every investor will be in a syndicate. We plan to have at least twenty such syndicates, each with a minimum goal of two billion dollars and twenty investors. Only syndicate heads will have direct access to me, while other investors will be required to communicate through their syndicate leader, although we will have a special office to keep all of our investors informed.

"Whatever you decide, thank you again for being here today. We sincerely look forward to working with you very soon.

"If there are no further questions, the buses are waiting in front of the building to return you to the hotel. I look forward to seeing you at dinner."

As Danielle stepped down from the podium, a small mob of people in white enveloped her, all trying to get to the head of the line. She smiled at them and raised her hands. "Please, one at a time. We have a representative here who will assist each of you." She reached out and took the hand of a short, slender, elderly woman with long dark hair, wearing a white sari. "You're first." Project Prometheus was begun.

CHAPTER 16

July 9

It was Independence Day. The President of the United States of America, convinced by his political advisors in the State Department that it was a propitious time for a magnanimous act, demonstrated for the world that the United States had absolutely no colonial agenda. The ideal way to accomplish that was by setting free a little-known island chain, which had been under American administration as part of the Trust Territories of the Pacific Islands for fifty years, and by abandoning the plans for an American military base there. The President's political and military advisors said the foreign policy of the United States didn't need the little island group any longer. Congress, which was busily closing bases around the United States, had enthusiastically embraced the idea and passed enabling legislation. It had also refused to authorize funding for the military base. The name of the island chain was Belau.

American President Johnathan DeWitt sat on the reviewing stand on the main street of the Belau 'business district.' It seemed to him that there were few 'real' buildings and the heat was blistering, even though a brisk breeze was blowing from the lagoon. A brisk breeze always blew from the lagoon, which was fortunate, as many of the buildings didn't have air conditioning. The President couldn't wait for the ceremony to end so he could escape back into his jet, which was sitting at the airport waiting for him, with its auxiliary power unit running and the air conditioning on.

The Belauans were very happy. There were men and women in grass skirts, and men and women in formal evening attire, including tuxedos with long coattails. The President wondered if someone was playing a joke on him. 'No one here really dresses that way anymore, do they?' he thought. There were also people dressed in everything in between. Everyone was celebrating.

The President's aircraft had brought an American military band and the international press corps. The military band had started the ceremony by marching past the reviewing stand, leading the parade and carrying the American Flag, followed by the Belau High School Band carrying the yellow and blue Belau Flag, and the President had felt very proud.

The President of the United States sat with the President of Belau and the U.S. Administrator of the Trust Territory of the Pacific Islands, which had been reduced in size until the only remaining islands were those of Belau. The small parade went to the end of the street, did an about-face, and stopped, waiting.

The President of the United States stood and stepped forward to the microphone. A hush fell over the small crowd of Belauans and international press assembled before the reviewing stand as he began to speak.

"My friends. It is with great pleasure that I am here today to represent the people of the United States of America on this important occasion. For fifty years, the United States has provided Belau the shelter of its all-encompassing umbrella of protection, under the Trust Territories of the Pacific Islands. Today Belau joins the world community of independent nations. It is my great privilege to be able to

71

participate in this ceremony and celebrate this happy day with the people of Belau. I will now sign the Certificate of Independence for Belau, which recognizes its independence and absolute autonomy, forever."

The President leaned forward and with a grand flourish, signed his name to a document that already bore many other signatures. He was followed by the U.S. Administrator, who by this action became the U.S. Ambassador, and by the President of Belau, who with independence became its chief executive officer in fact as well as name.

The signal for which the leaders of the parade had been waiting was given when the President of Belau held up the large document and the parade, now with the Belauan High School Band leading and holding proudly aloft the blue and yellow Flag of Belau, began marching back down the street past the reviewing stand. This time the person in charge on the reviewing stand was the young President of Belau, Bertram Allen.

With the ceremony over, the President of the United States shook hands again with everyone on the reviewing stand, then immediately departed for his aircraft where he would rest in the cool until the celebratory dinner scheduled for that evening.

Danielle had watched the entire ceremony from across the street. When it was over, there had been twenty minutes of hand-shaking and back-slapping, then the new Belauan President came across the street to her.

"I believe we have some business to transact, don't we Miss Simones? Please come with me."

His small law office was in the building directly behind the reviewing stand. On a table in the library was a small pile of carefully drafted documents. They amounted to an agreement with P.I.M. Investing Pty., Ltd., an Isle of Man limited partnership, for the use of a significant portion of real estate on Belau to construct a new airport having a very long runway, offices and residential buildings, and an industrial complex.

The documents were signed one after another by both the President and by Jean Claude LeBec, who represented the Isle of Man partnership. Clifford Kelly, the attorney for the partnership, and Danielle watched as the documents were executed. Half-way through signing the pile of documents, the meeting was interrupted by a secretary who opened the conference room door. "This was just received from the Assembly." The new Belauan Legislature, only minutes old, had passed an act establishing a Belau Aviation Ministry, and authorizing that Ministry to certify the manufacture, sale and use of flying machines.

When all of the documents were completed, the new President shook the hands of everyone in the room and pronounced, "This is a big day for Belau." Everyone agreed.

The international press corps was in the street, photographing pretty Belauan women and children, and interviewing dignitaries. They never suspected that the real international story was taking place in a quiet office only a few feet away.

PART II - FLIGHT

CHAPTER 17

July 14

Six days had passed since the technical briefing in Bangkok. The International Council of Energy Producing Industries and Countries ("ICEPIC") was holding an emergency meeting at its headquarters in Zurich. Of the forty-five members, thirty-nine were present, an unprecedented high number. Usually only about twenty-five members showed up for meetings. Considering that three members – one country and two corporations – were currently on suspension for being involved in an unsuccessful military action against another member, it meant that only three of the members who could have attended were absent.

The chairman, Gilbert Smith, President of Inter-Nuclear Technologies, called the meeting to order. "Please. Gentlemen. Let's get down to business. This situation requires our full attention. Felix, rather than me doing all the talking, how about you giving us a summary of what happened in Bangkok?"

Nine of those present, including the chairman and Felix O'Brian, had been in attendance at the Bangkok technical briefing. Felix summarized the plan for the satellite power system. The eight others who had been present in Bangkok added details that they felt were significant. Some of those listening to the report were extremely agitated.

Carlos Hernandez-Guerra, from Venezuela, interrupted. "But is this possible? Can this woman carry it off?"

"Her experts were certainly impressive." said Ali Ibn Faud, from Saudi Arabia. "And she could hardly have a better number-cruncher for the economic side than Peterson. But still I wonder whether it is possible for her to do what she claims, considering that the big space powers couldn't."

O'Brian spoke. "I checked out this woman, as I suppose some of you also have. If your information agrees with mine, then I'm sure you realize that she has the ability to do it, if it can be done. Her technical staff is excellent. She understands the aerospace business. And, she *owns* Space. Six months ago, if someone had described this situation to me, I would have laughed in their face, but now I'm not so certain. I think she just might do it."

"What are we going to do about it?" Hernandez-Guerra insisted on knowing. "If she's successful, it will ruin us."

O'Brian responded. "I don't know about you, Carlos, but I've already pledged my 100 million and my lawyers are transferring the funds today. And I've asked to head up a syndicate. I may even up the ante, and go for another hundred million or two. If you want in, see me and you can be in my syndicate, if you like. If she succeeds, I don't want to miss out on the opportunity. This won't be a business that an outsider can break into by simply spending a few bucks. You'll have to be in it from the git-go."

"Pardón?"

"I mean you have to be in it from the beginning. It looks to me like, if it's successful, it'll be self-sustaining and not require additional investors over time.

73

Those who make the original investment may be the first *and last* investors. So you better get in now if you're ever going to want in."

The Saudi member was extremely unhappy. "Our entire economy is dependent on the oil market. This threatens our very survival as a nation. If we can't sell oil, my country will be back to raising sheep and goats in the desert."

"I don't think it's quite that bleak, Ali," said O'Brian. "Remember her plan is to make this a gradual process starting with the less developed countries and moving to the most developed countries last. The big boys are your main customers. You might not even be alive when the market for oil dries up. Also, she's only proposing to produce electricity. People can't run cars and planes on electricity – yet. And the fluctuations in demand over a day's time can't be accommodated by the huge base-load plants she's proposing. Everyone will still need peaking capacity, and petroleum-fueled generators are best for that anyway."

"But if what you say is correct, she also plans to convert a lot of fossil fuel industries to electricity," the Saudi added.

Dieter Juergens, who sat on the Council for the largest manufacturing conglomerate in Europe, jumped into the discussion. "The briefers do *expect* to develop an entire new technology based on electric vehicles. They didn't say that right out, but it was between the lines. There will be significant opportunities for large profits in these new industries. You're right, Ali, your industry is doomed, eventually. But, tell me this: What were you going to do when you run out of oil, even if this new technology didn't appear?"

Ali didn't answer. He just sat, brooding.

The Libyan member of the Council, who had been quietly absorbing the conversation, spoke quietly, "Can she be stopped?"

"If you mean, can she be persuaded not to make the effort, I think the answer to your question must be an unqualified negative," said Juergens. "She appears fully committed to the project, and she already seems to have significant financial backing, including both Felix and myself. If you mean could some kind of dirty tricks or sabotage cause her project to fail, I suppose so, but I'm not going to be part of anything like that."

The Libyan didn't say anything more.

O'Brian leaned toward the chairman, "Gil, you're the one whose fat is really in the fire. If she succeeds, I believe the first plants which will immediately be obsolete are the nuclear ones, for two reasons; a) they're all base load plants, unsuited for anything else, and b) they're the continual focus of unmitigated bad publicity because of their various accidents, unplanned shut-downs, radioactive releases, thermal pollution, waste disposal problems, etc. You're the ones with the big potential loss."

Smith protested. "The shut-downs that have occurred only prove that our safety systems work."

"Save it for the public, Gil," answered O'Brian. "The issues here are bigger than that. I think, if we're smart, all of us will jump into this new venture with both feet. We all can afford to, perhaps more easily than any other group. And we can cover our backsides at the same time, just in case she manages to do what she says she's going to do. I don't see any alternative."

The Iranian member, silent until then, lashed out. "You! O'Brian! *You* are the problem. You accept this *woman*," he almost spat the last word, "as a credible person. You would write off accomplishments that have taken generations of sacrifice to bring about. This is just another western scheme to oppress the peoples of the Middle East! I denounce it! My people will not stand for it." He exchanged glances with the Libyan.

Following more seemingly endless discussion, it was finally decided to appoint a committee to study the situation more fully. Some of the members quietly decided to restructure their investment portfolio to include a new aerospace venture, and sought out Felix O'Brian after the meeting.

Another group, not appointed by the Council, began planning another kind of action in response to the events in Bangkok.

CHAPTER 18

July 14

In other places around the world, representatives from a dozen companies, all of which no one had ever heard two years earlier because they didn't exist, began executing contracts with major aerospace manufacturers for components of the space plane and other parts of the program.

Robinson Aluminum, one of the largest producers of aluminum in North America, received a contract for fabrication of nearly 100 thousand extremely large aluminum panels with many fasteners along the sides and ends. They were not told what the panels were intended to do, although they concluded the panels could be attached to one another to form a very large tube. They didn't realize the panels eventually would be assembled into the main spokes of the Web.

Other contracts were signed, by a dozen apparently unrelated corporations, and with General Electric, Philips, Furuno, Matsushita Electric, Grumman, Hitachi, Northrup and McDonnell Douglas. None knew what the components they were building were designed to do. They were actually being given contracts to produce parts for both the transmitting and receiving antennas, as well as switching equipment, connectors for attaching solar panels into the satellites' structural grids, and components of the low earth satellite. It was all top-secret and there were no explanations.

Two weeks later, on August 2, more contracts were executed – with Global Aeronautique Internationale, Boeing, Aerospatiale, Gulfstream, Pratt and Whitney, Ilyushin Aviation Industries, and a host of smaller contractors – for components for the space planes, shuttles and low earth satellites. Global Aeronautique Internationale handled all of the contracting. Construction also began that day at Belau on the runway, main hangar, and the Belau Aviation headquarters building, following completion of the fences around the site.

The August 24 issue of Aviation Week and Space Technology reported that several aircraft manufacturers recently had landed large aerospace contracts. The details were sketchy, but it appeared that an unidentified independent airline was building a very large supersonic plane, apparently designed to compete with the Concorde on international flights. The stories promised more information as it became available. The same issue carried an editorial questioning the wisdom of competing against the Concorde when the Concorde had been such a dismal failure economically. Its infrequent flights were more to bolster English and French nationalism than to generate revenue. The "industry rumors" section of the magazine reported that Global Aeronautique Internationale was being purchased by a corporation headquartered in Panama. Calls from Aviation Week to Global's offices had not been returned, and the Chairman of Global, caught between planes in the terminal at Dallas-Fort Worth, said "no comment" when asked about the rumor. The sources of the rumor were unable to furnish the name of the Panamanian corporation.

Siberian producers of titanium received a proposal to buy, at a price somewhat below the current market, a year's production of titanium. They agreed immediately, since the world market for titanium had fallen sharply with the end of the cold war, and they were in deep financial trouble.

CHAPTER 19

September 5

The crowd pressed up to the edge of the stage at the front of the main hall in the Tampa Convention Center. The speaker leaned closer to the microphone on the podium. "Ladies and gentlemen. Please take a seat and we will begin. Please, take your seats."

A few people began sitting down at the tables in the giant convention hall. The speaker repeated his request. More people sat, but many continued to mill around in the aisles, and others still were on the stage near the speaker.

The speaker motioned to several assistants who began directing people from the stage to the tables on the convention floor in front of the speaker. Slowly, the crowd in the front of the room began to settle down, although there was still considerable disruption from the middle to the rear, where there were indistinguishable voices discussing something.

The speaker turned to the woman on his right. "How many?"

She shrugged. "Neil said there were three thousand who had signed in when they closed the doors. There were probably that many more who were turned away."

"We'll get to them all eventually. I hope we don't have a riot before we finish." He saw that the last few rows of seats were beginning to be filled and again turned on the microphone.

"Ladies and gentlemen, please finish finding a seat and we will be able to begin. First, let me thank you for responding to our advertisement and introduce myself, and my teammates.

"We're delighted to have such an enthusiastic response to our ad. We know we cannot hire everyone here, but you can be sure your application will receive careful consideration.

"My name is Joe Mason. My teammates and I are here from Omega Personnel Industries. Our assistants are now starting to hand out the application forms. On your tables are pencils for you to use.

"While they pass out the forms, I want to tell you something about the forms and how to complete them, as well as a little about the company we represent and the jobs for which these applications will be considered.

"This is probably the longest job application you will ever encounter. We expect it will take you most of today to complete it. If you want to take a lunch break at noon, please feel free to do so. There are many decent fast-food places near the convention center.

"Your information will remain confidential, and the application may not be taken from this room. You will be able to leave your partially completed application with one of the attendants at the door and pick it up when you return from lunch. Each attendant station has a large number behind it. Be sure to remember which station you leave your application with.

"If you want to take a break to go to the restroom, please go ahead. If you do so, please leave your application with one of the attendants at the tables in the back of the room. You will have until five PM this afternoon to complete the application, but it must be completed by then. Each question has a suggestion at the beginning for how much time to spend answering it.

"This application is not a test, although you may think it looks like one. There are no right or wrong answers. It is designed to enable us to get a complete picture of you as a potential future employee. The only requirement is to complete the application by five PM.

"Some parts are multiple choice questions; some parts require you to write a few lines about yourself and your experiences, and some parts may make no sense to you at all.

"All of the parts are important, so be sure your answers are as accurate as you can make them, and be sure to answer all of the questions.

"We have many attendants located around the room. You can identify them by their red jackets, and their job is to help you understand the questions. If you do not understand any question, please take the application to one of the attendants at a table near you. There are no 'trick' questions.

"Many people have asked us about the jobs for which we are seeking employees. I can't tell you much about them except this: First, these jobs will be with a new company working on a major construction project. There will be positions for many disciplines: cooks and farmers, engineers and airline pilots, miners and teachers, machinists and laborers.

"Second, many of the jobs will be very dangerous, which is why we are particularly seeking single people without children for those positions. One activity this company is considering is mining the deep sea bed, at depths over ten thousand feet, which is certainly a dangerous and hostile environment.

"However, there is no assurance that the corporation will actually hire anyone from today's group for that plan.

"There also are some positions which do not involve a high degree of risk, and for those positions we welcome persons with families. We will do all we can to treat everyone fairly. Just be sure to answer every question. We are an equal opportunity employer and everyone will get fair consideration.

"Third, our minimum standards for all employees are quite strict: Each employee must read, speak and write clear English, and have no drug, alcohol or tobacco dependencies. If you don't meet that test, you can leave now. If you are addicted to caffeine and are hired, we may require you to give up coffee, tea, or soft drinks, whatever your caffeine source is. Educational and physical requirements will vary depending on the position.

"The company will require strict discipline among its employees, who may be living in close quarters for long periods of time, and there will be many rules which must be observed. It will be a lot like being in the military, at least during the early phases of the project. If you don't think you could fit into such a regime, you can leave now. We don't want to waste your time filling out an application for a position in which you wouldn't be happy.

"Many, if not most positions, will involve extensive travel, and many will be far from here, probably in foreign countries. We will provide the usual health and other benefits, as well as some other unusual opportunities, such as an educational program for those interested in self-improvement.

"The pay will vary depending on the position. The work, and the company's activities, will be very exciting and many of the employees will visit places where few other humans have ever been. Please begin filling out the application now."

The ad had run in the employment opportunities sections of many newspapers around the country. A typical ad read:

"Multinational corporation looking for talented applicants with diverse experiences in all fields for major construction project. Many different positions available. Preference for single applicants without dependents, because of dangerous working conditions. Work may involve significant risk to life and very extensive travel. Fluent English required. Drug, alcohol and tobacco-free personnel only. Apply only in person at the Tampa Convention Center on April 4 at 7 AM local time. Applicants will be required to remain at application site until 5 PM on that date. Applications will be taken on following days from any who are present but cannot apply on that date due to site space limitations and number of applicants."

Response to the ad had been excellent. In ten major U.S. cities, a total of 50,000 people responded. In Chicago, the applications continued for five days.

Jose Roberto Olivero Garcia-Diaz looked at the application. It was a thick booklet which reminded him of the instructions for the federal income tax return. He printed his name, address, phone number and social security number in the appropriate places on the cover, then opened it to the first page. The first question read, "Describe in detail your hobbies." There followed a half page, blank except for lines to guide the applicant's answer. It was the strangest job application Jose had ever seen.

Ali Ben Muhamet tried to think of hobbies. Hobbies? Perhaps walking on the beach with his sister's kids counted as a hobby. Then there was astronomy. His ancestors had invented astronomy to navigate the deserts of Arabia and he had once been a guide at a small community planetarium. He wrote it down. The next question was equally unusual. It read, "List all of the different kinds of occupations and recreational activities you have ever engaged in. We want to know how diverse your talents are. For example, if you have repaired cars or boats or airplanes, if you have been a cook or a pianist or a sky-diver, if you have been a typist or a social worker, we want to know about it. You need not list any experiences which you did not enjoy, as we are trying to match people with positions which they will enjoy, and don't expect everyone to have had experience in the specific jobs which we have to fill." There was nearly a full page provided for the answers to the question. He thought a while, then began writing.

Scott Moore listed his numerous experiences and activities and turned to page 2. The third question said, "Have you any experience with SCUBA diving or spelunking? Describe your experiences." The blank space was only about a quarter of a page. He decided to write very small.

CHAPTER 20

September 15

Both General Motors and Daimler Benz received contracts from Global Aeronautique Internationale to construct components of the living quarters at the power collector construction sites. Both also received, from another company, a contract to build a strange eight-legged machine, designed to remove and replace extremely thin, flat, triangular objects, exchanging them for new ones from a supply it kept in a rack on its side. The machine was huge. Its pressurized "body" was the size of a large car, and the spindly legs were each over 100 meters long. The purchaser called the machine a "spider" but could not explain what purpose was served by its bizarre configuration. If the prototype worked as planned, the purchaser had said there was a possibility that hundreds more of these machines could be needed. They cost many millions of dollars each.

On September 25, the first shipment of titanium-carbon-carbon-ceramic composite sheets for the skin of the first space plane arrived at Boeing and Aerospatiale.

On October 3, Motorola, Furuno, Philips and Westinghouse all received contracts for construction of microwave antenna components. Each was told that their different customers were building a communications network with thousands of remote locations. Actually, all of the components were for the first receiving antenna.

The world market for business aircraft was in a slump and Lockheed, Rockwell, Gulfstream and Messerschmidt were about to issue lay-off notices to their employees, when they received contracts to build components for the Station Supply Shuttles, the tugboats of the solar power project. Lockheed would build the command module; Gulfstream would build the structural framework, and Messerschmidt would build the main engine of the shuttles, in cooperation with Rockwell.

CHAPTER 21

December 8

John F. "Jomo" Williams walked carefully along the icy sidewalk of the Indiana University Law School at Indianapolis and opened one of the heavy front doors. His spirits were nearing an all-time low. He had graduated two months earlier in the academic dead center of his class. He had not at the time realized that his job-finding potential was equally dead, because he had not graduated in the top ten percent of his class.

So far, he had sent out over two hundred resumes and letters to law firms across the country requesting an interview, and he had a grand total of three rejection letters which were short and sweet, indicating they were looking for new associates with "other qualifications." Jomo had not been able to determine from the letters what those necessary qualifications were.

Jomo had spent several years working after his graduation from Engineering School and prior to Law School, supporting himself and saving his money for further education. He had spent two years in the Peace Corps in Africa, then returned to the United States where he had been a successful partner in a real estate agency while in Engineering School. He envisioned himself as a developer's attorney, working on land use, planning, zoning, and permitting. His daily trips to the Dean of Student's Job Placement Office were becoming increasingly depressing, now that the excitement of preparing for and taking the Bar Exam was behind him. Nevertheless, he knew that new job notices were posted on the Dean's Bulletin Board each day at 10 AM, and he was determined to be the first to apply, if a job appeared for which he felt qualified.

Naturally, there were a number of hopeful notices from public service agencies and non-profit groups, looking for a new lawyer willing to work for nothing but the glory of starving slowly while protecting high ideals for their group. He couldn't afford the luxury of donating his time. He had exhausted his savings and had begun working part-time at night as a secretary for a temporary office-services agency, in order to be able to pay the rent on his apartment while he awaited his scores on the Bar Exam. The scores had finally arrived, and he had been sworn in as a member of the Indiana Bar, but he still didn't have a job.

As he turned the corner into the hallway in front of the Dean's office, he saw the clerk lock the glass door on the notice case and go back into the office. He hurried to read any new postings. There was only one:

"International corporation seeks recent law school graduates. Knowledge of Arabic, Swahili or Bantu languages required. Salary commensurate with experience. Send resume to Omega Personnel Industries, P. O. Box A, Indianapolis, Indiana 46203."

Two hours later he delivered his resume to the clerk in the Post Office, paid the postage and walked out, a bit more optimistic than he had been that morning. Maybe he didn't want to work for a big law firm anyway.

The initial interview three days later was less painful than he had expected. The company was "head-hunting". They were under contract to some big corporation that needed lawyers to represent them in Africa. He met the criteria provided by the corporation and the interviewers thought he would be just right for one of the positions. It seemed there were six fresh new lawyers being hired for the corporation's program, although the interviewer wasn't quite clear what that program was.

Actually, the interviewer knew fairly well what the program was, but the young lawyer didn't need to know that yet, so he wasn't told.

The interviewer gave Jomo an envelope containing a plane ticket in his name, departing the next day, from Indianapolis to Nassau, Bahamas. It also contained two thousand dollars in cash; and instructions to pay his rent two months in advance and plan not to return to Indianapolis for that length of time. Jomo signed a receipt for the envelope and left.

He went home, packed a small bag, paid two months rent as directed, and started preparing dinner, still in a daze from the lightning change which had occurred in his life. He had forgotten to ask how much the job paid. He called his mother.

"Mom, … I've got a job ... I think."

"What do you mean, 'I think'," his mother retorted. "Do you or don't you?"

"Well. I'm pretty sure I do. But I was so excited that I forgot to ask about the pay, and they didn't say, and I don't know yet what the job involves. But, Mom, they gave me two thousand dollars in advance, and a ticket to the Bahamas for tomorrow morning, and said to expect to be gone for two months."

"Oh my!" she exclaimed. "Ohmyohmyohmy. Johnny, that sounds like drug dealers. I don't want you involved with drug dealers."

"Mother! Please! Drug dealers don't advertise their jobs in the Law School Job Placement Office. I'm sure it's okay. And Mom, I think it may let me go back to Africa again. They did say they were an international company, and the only requirement in the notice was that the applicant must speak Arabic, Swahili or Bantu. No drug dealer is going to require a foreign language, and besides, just about everyone in Africa speaks English or French anyhow. I just haven't been able to figure out what it's all about."

At 4:30 PM the next day, Jomo checked into the Paradise Island Hotel in Nassau, Bahamas. A young and very pretty desk clerk gave him a smile, his room key and an envelope. Her eyes crinkled as she said "Enjoy your stay with us."

He smiled back and tore the end from the envelope. There was a typed note inside. It read, "There will be a dinner and briefing at 6:30 PM. Meet your escort then at the front desk. Dress is slacks, golf shirt and boat shoes. If you didn't bring these items with you, stop now in the Hotel Men's Shop and buy them. Charge them to your room number." He asked the desk clerk for directions to the Men's Shop and more puzzled by the note than ever, moved off in the direction indicated.

6:30 found him and several others standing before the pretty desk clerk. As he was about to ask her if she knew whom he was to meet, he heard someone behind him clear his throat. A short man in cutoff blue jeans and a blue cowboy shirt, with a grizzly salt and pepper beard, 'Captain Jack' embroidered on his shirt pocket, and wearing a black baseball cap which had military-looking 'scrambled eggs' on the bill and 'TOP GUN' embroidered on the front, was speaking. "Howdy.

I've been instructed to be your escort. My name is Captain Jack Darlington. Now let me see if we have everyone. Miss Mayhew? Check. Mrs. Overmeyer? Check. Mr. Ekhart? Check. Mr. Schwartz? Check. Mr. Thompson? Check. Mr. Williams?"

Jomo nodded his head and said, "Here."

"Check. Okay, that's everybody. Please follow me." Captain Jack turned and walked out of the hotel's rear entrance at a fast pace without looking back. If anyone had hesitated, they would have been left. None hesitated. The path they followed circled the swimming pool and several 'Tiki bars' under the palm trees and headed for the marina. The exotic smells of the sea, outboard motor exhaust, swimming pool chlorine and cocoa-butter suntan oil combined to give Jomo the sense of being in another world. He followed Captain Jack in a daze, as did the others. Captain Jack strode down the dock, turned down a finger pier between two boats, and stepped aboard a very large yacht, tied in a boat slip with its bow toward the dock. Jomo had never seen such a large boat.

"Welcome aboard!" the Captain announced. They all carefully stepped over the gap between the boat and the dock, still following their leader as he led them into the pilothouse. As the third guest crossed from the dock to the boat, bells in the pilothouse began to ring and a throaty rumble came from the rear of the boat, followed quickly by a cloud of blue diesel exhaust smoke. A few seconds later, the bell rang again and the noise and smoke repeated as the other engine came to life. The last guest stepped into the pilothouse.

"Cast off forward," said Captain Jack. A crewman on the forward deck tossed several ropes to someone standing on the dock in front of the boat. "Cast off aft," said the Captain. Two crewmen with boathooks at the rear of the boat removed the mooring lines from metal cleats on the rear corners of the boat and hung them on the large pilings at the side of the boat slip. The boat backed from the slip, turned, and then began moving forward.

As the boat turned from the marina into the channel leading to the ocean, a door opened at the front of the pilothouse, revealing a spiral stairway down about four feet into what appeared to be a living room. A middle-aged man with light brown hair stood in the door. "Will y'all please come below and have a seat," he said, his Southern accent obvious even in the short sentence. He turned around and went down the stairs. Jomo and the others assumed 'below' meant wherever the man was taking them and followed.

The salon of the yacht had seats for probably twenty or more persons, but there was a conference table at one end and their new host was standing behind a chair at the head of the table. There were three chairs on each side of the table and none at the opposite end. The guests went to the table and each selected a chair. "Please sit down and relax," their host said. "Welcome to the *Imperator*. My name is Clifford Kelly, and I work for a law firm in London. Our client is the corporation that brought you here today.

"Let's introduce everyone. First the ladies. Elizabeth Mayhew is a recent graduate from the University of Miami Law School. She has a Bachelor of Science in Botany and a Masters in Oceanography. Next is Helen Overmeyer. Mrs. Overmeyer has recently graduated from the University of Chicago Law School. She has an Bachelor of Arts in Elementary Education, a Master's in Political Science, and a Ph.D. in Economics.

"Now the gentlemen. Phil Ekhart recently graduated from Washington University Law School. He has a Bachelor of Science in Electrical Engineering and a Masters in Physics. Steven Schwartz recently graduated from Stanford University Law School. He has a Bachelor of Arts in Music and a Masters in Special Education. Samuel Thompson is a recent graduate from Harvard University Law School. He has a Bachelor of Arts in Journalism and a Masters in Political Science. John Williams is a recent graduate of the Indiana University Law School and has a Bachelor of Science in Mechanical Engineering and a Masters in Geology. That's everyone.

"I want to use this opportunity to give you some preliminary information about the positions for which you are being considered.

"Yes, I said 'being considered'. None of you has definitely been hired; however, we do want to hire all of you, provided you're willing to work for us under the conditions of the job.

"If you decide you don't want to work under those conditions, none of us will think ill of you. We'll merely allow anyone feeling that way to ride in a different part of the boat during our cruise, while the rest of us talk business. If you want out, you can keep the advance you were provided, keep any clothes you bought for this meeting, and stay for three more days as our guest at the Paradise Island Hotel. We'll pay those expenses and furnish you a ticket home. The rest of us will be leaving for London first thing in the morning. Is that clear?"

All of the heads around the table nodded their assent.

"First, this meeting is strictly confidential. We consider the advance we furnished you to be a retainer, and for the purpose of this meeting, the corporation is your client and each of you is our attorney. Information that I'll provide you today contains proprietary trade secrets. If the information were to be released prematurely, our client's business position could be badly, perhaps irreparably, damaged. If any of you has a problem keeping that confidentiality, please say so now, and you can leave.

"Good. We've done some checking on each of you, and didn't expect any problems regarding your protection of our confidences.

"Second, both the corporation and our law firm are very strictly run. In many ways it is more like the military than a civilian company, but it nevertheless is a civilian operation, and its purposes are strictly legal and peaceful. We receive orders from time to time from our client and we follow them, so long as our ethical obligations as attorneys are not compromised. If we find an ethical conflict, we confer and attempt to resolve it, usually by restructuring our client's activities, but if we can't resolve it in a way we feel satisfies our personal ethical standards, we are each free to resign.

"I say 'we are free to resign' because I also am an attorney, and will be your supervisor if you stay with us. I resigned, about a year and a half ago, from my former position as Chief Justice of the Florida Supreme Court to accept this position. That may give you some idea of how I value this opportunity, but each of you has to make your own decisions.

"You may be required to travel to the other side of the world on a moment's notice. You may then be told your move is permanent, and that your possessions, family, whatever, will be moved by the corporation. You will only have one choice to make if such an order is sent to you: Accept it or quit. If you're worried about arbitrariness, let me tell you that employees will be usually, and I emphasize *usually* be asked beforehand whether they would be agreeable to such transfers, but sometimes there will not be time. The business of the corporation is such that it cannot afford to wait while an employee ponders such questions for an extended period. We are on a critical schedule.

"We have strict dress and behavior codes. Everyone is expected to dress and act like a professional. We expect all employees to comply with those codes while they're in our employ.

"The primary rule, however, is one of secrecy; not to talk about the business of the corporation with anyone inside the corporation who does not need the information, or anyone at all outside of the corporation, not even your true love. Our need for secrecy is the reason we brought you here; the reason we are on a boat far from land. The punishment for violation of the secrecy rule is to be fired, and possibly to be subject to a suit for damages for harm done to the corporation by your disclosures.

"Does anyone here feel that they can't live with this level of regimentation? If so, I strongly urge you to say so and leave now. I repeat, there will be no penalty for doing so, except that you'll miss this opportunity, and there will be no hard feelings."

No one said a word.

"I need an affirmative confirmation from each of you to our conditions. Mrs. Overmeyer?"

"I accept the conditions."

"Miss Mayhew?"

"I'm in."

"Mr. Eckhart?"

"Don't we have to sign a loyalty oath, or something?"

"I thought someone might ask something like that. I want each of you to understand that we have made inquiries about you. We believe your word is as good assurance of your intention to keep our secrets secret as any piece of paper you might sign. If you violate our secrets, it may not matter if you have signed a piece of paper anyway, as any breach of security could be devastating to the business of the corporation. If we can't trust your word, why should we believe what you write on paper? So no, you don't have to sign anything. Are you in or out?"

"I'm with you."

"Mr. Schwartz?"

"I want to be part of it, whatever it is."

"Mr. Thompson?"

"OK for me."

"Mr. Williams?"

"I'm in."

"Great! That confirms my belief in each of you. From here on out, you're all on the payroll. I'm not going to go into your pay now, as it's not simply a number, but a package of pay and benefits which defies quick explanation, but let me assure you, you'll be most satisfied with it, and as you learn more about our company, you may feel you would have been willing to work for much less, just to be part of it. You'll each be receiving the same pay, in case you are wondering.

"Now, let's get down to the nitty-gritty. You certainly must be wondering, "What's the name of this corporation? What does it do? Have I ever heard of it? Let me answer those in reverse order.

"You have never heard of this corporation. Its name is 'Stellar Power Corporation.' It's a solar energy company.

"'Well,' you say, 'Solar energy companies have been around for a very long time. Why all the secrecy?'

"The answer is that the means by which we are going to produce energy from the Sun is unlike any in use today, and we need your skills to help us make it work and we need to keep it secret until we're ready to begin production.

"Let me give you a little simple physics lesson, which you may already know. The radiance from the Sun striking the disk of the Earth produces a potential energy of 747 watts of energy per square meter. If that energy were harnessed, all of the present energy demands of the entire world could be provided by the energy striking a relatively small area.

"However, there are numerous technical problems. Solar collectors to date have either operated on heat production, such as solar water heaters, or by photovoltaic action on inefficient crystal wafers that convert sunlight into electricity. Because the Sun's light strikes the Earth's surface at odd angles, and because half of the Earth is always in darkness, there are serious limitations to those processes.

"We have another process. It involves the construction of large antennas or 'power transformers' in remote areas that will receive the energy of the Sun twenty-four hours a day in the form of microwaves and convert it into electricity. When I say 'large,' I am speaking of antenna arrays approximately six miles in diameter. I'm not going into all of the details of this process now, only enough to let you perform the job you need to accomplish. In time, the details will become public knowledge. We can't avoid that. You'll be given additional information, as you need it, but not earlier. You can expect much more detail very soon, beyond the very little which I have told you so far.

"You each have graduated from law school during the past year. You may think you're hot stuff; that you know it all. You aren't and you don't. But what *we're* going to do with you will make you more competent in more disciplines than you've ever thought possible. Most importantly, during the next several months, you'll receive training that will prepare you for the real world of business. You'll be negotiating with African leaders the most important business deals in the history of the world and you will have to be able to confer with them both formally and informally in their native languages.

"We're going to train you in every aspect for your assignment. At the same time, we'll be teaching you every detail of the power system that we are planning to build. We'll be teaching each of you about all of the political, social and economic factors that are relevant to our project in each African country.

"We'll start with your language skills. You each already speak some African language. We know. We've checked and confirmed it. You'll all be getting refresher and further intensive courses in your present languages and training in additional languages that you may need later. You're going to learn those languages and their various dialects to a level of detail you never would have believed possible. You'll learn vocabulary, grammar and syntax as well as all the formal and colloquial usages and phrases.

"You'll learn all about the cultures of the countries where you will be meeting people including the traditions of their tribes.

"You'll learn about the personal background of all of the leaders of the countries in your area of responsibility.

"You'll have your English polished. Some English-speakers in other countries are more conscious of correct English grammar than you would believe, and when we're done with you, you'll never again split an infinitive or dangle a participle in formal conversation. That goes for French as well.

"You'll be receiving a refresher course on table manners and all other kinds of polite social behavior, in many cultures.

"You're going to be representing our client, so we want you to make a good impression every time. When we're done with you, you'll be able to visit, talk or dine with royalty or commoners, and everyone in between, in any country, without any self-consciousness or even awareness of your social skills. It'll all be automatic to you.

"Then, when we're done with your training, each of you'll be sent with one of our engineers to brief the leaders of certain African countries about our project, and to sell them on being part of it, so yours will be a uniquely responsible task. There are many locations in Africa where we want to have our power grid, and our goal is to convince each of those countries to be an enthusiastic participant in the project. Their rewards for participation are economic benefits for their countries, both through payments to them of a royalty for each kilowatt produced by the power station in their country, but also through enhanced development opportunities because of new supplies of less expensive electrical energy. We are going to provide clean electrical power to the entire African continent.

"They'll also be rewarded by the ability to have a pollution-free country, a condition impossible now.

"We intend to further boost their economies by buying, at a minimum price, their obsolete power plants, after our grid is operating. This will insure that protection against pollution is maintained, and also that a new level of international cooperation exists throughout the African continent, because the countries will be required to buy and sell electric power cooperatively from and to each other, impossible if they are not allies.

"The construction of these power stations will provide new job skills and training for millions of people. Many of these skills will be transferable to new industries that will arise with the conversion to this power source. Others will be required to maintain the power stations, which will provide additional jobs.

"Overall, we expect a dramatic change for the better in the overall economic health of all African nations. Are there any questions so far?"

Six hands were raised simultaneously. Kelly pondered whose question to take first.

"I'll tell you what; let's eat dinner first, then we'll have a question and answer session for another hour, then we'll just go up on deck and enjoy our cruise back to the hotel.

"If you'll now go through that companionway into the dining salon, you'll see that the chef has dinner ready."

YEAR THREE

CHAPTER 22

January 6

Construction work progressed rapidly at Belau. By mid-November, the huge main hangar, a half mile square, had been completed and the Belau Aviation Headquarters Building had been enclosed and air conditioned. The interiors were only begun, however, and all energies were focused on completing the executive suite so Danielle could move in.

Her office, as well as much of the top floor, was completed on December 30, and work shifted to completion of the remainder of the interior. Furniture began to arrive for the office building and was stored temporarily, wrapped in plastic, in the empty main hangar. On New Year's Eve crews began moving furniture to the top floor.

A week later, she was in her new office. She stood at the soundproof window looking out onto the airfield. Construction equipment was moving busily, carrying soil from one area to another, contouring it, compacting it, and covering it with thick layers of concrete. The runway was about half done. The far end could be seen beyond the hangar, the new concrete blinding white in the tropical mid-day sun. Runway construction had begun at the most distant, and down-wind, end to enable the Hangar and Office Building to be built without so much dust on the job-site. The coral and volcanic dust was everywhere. It blanketed the hangar floor and seemed intent on getting into the office building. The building's designers had done a good job of dust control however, and the office was free of the gritty substance. A gas-turbine electrical generator the size of a railroad car, which powered the office building and other facilities, was behind the hangar. Danielle realized she would have to be sure it was carefully maintained, or the dust would ruin it. Other machines were building the network of roads connecting all of the buildings, while crews of local laborers were planting trees, shrubs and grass. When the landscaping was completed, the dust would cease to be a problem, or so she hoped.

It was two years to the day since she had come up with this wild idea, and look where it had brought her. 'I'd better get back to work,' she thought to herself, and turned away from the window.

CHAPTER 23

June 8

    The receptionist in the Kenya Interior Ministry rose from her desk and walked into the adjoining waiting area. Two men were seated there, reviewing their papers. "The Minister will see you now, gentlemen," she said. The men closed their briefcases, stood, and followed the receptionist through the ornately carved doors of the Minister's office. In five other African countries, similar meetings were beginning simultaneously.

    The Minister, Joseph Kotali, a short, overweight man, remained seated at his desk, a clear and rude display of his disdain for foreigners. John "Jomo" Williams spoke a few words of Kiswahili to the Minister, a formal greeting which required an equally formal, and standing, response. The Minister, realizing that his guest was not an ordinary foreign businessman, but was instead a person of culture and education, immediately jumped to his feet. He responded with the formal phrase appropriate to the situation and paused before continuing.

    "Mr. Williams. I am so glad to have the opportunity to meet you. I'd like very much to hear what you have to say." A few days earlier, the Minister had received a letter indicating that the ministry would be very much benefited by hearing Williams' proposition. The letter had been from Elias Kenyatta, president of the largest corporation in Kenya. It told the Minister, in terms that could not be misunderstood, that he was to listen carefully to whatever this young stranger had to say, then carefully check out the information. After checking it out, he was to call Mr. Kenyatta, and tell him what he had learned.

    Instructions such as these were not to be disregarded. Kenyatta's recommendation to the Prime Minister had been necessary for Kotali's appointment to his present position. The Minister realized that his position depended upon the continued good will of the man responsible for his appointment. He would listen carefully to this young man.

    Jomo spoke. "Mr. Minister. Thank you for your time. If you don't mind, I would prefer to use English." Hearing no objection, he continued. "My employer, Stellar Power Corporation, is planning a network of power stations to be located throughout Africa. We want to build at least one of the first ones here in Kenya. We want Kenyan industry, and the government of Kenya, to participate in this project and benefit from it.

    "We believe that participation in this project will be the most important action in Kenya's history; perhaps even more important than its independence. This project will make Kenya independent of foreign energy producers on whom Kenya is now becoming increasingly dependent. On the other hand, if Kenya misses this opportunity, it will slip into a second-class status compared to its neighbors, whom we expect to participate actively in this project."

    Kotali listened intently, without interrupting, knowing his longtime relationship with Kenyatta was somehow connected to this brash young man's presentation.

"I have brought with me Ivan Roberts, who is an engineer with our company. He will answer any technical questions you have that I am unable to answer." Kotali reached across the desk to shake hands with Roberts.

Jomo went on, "Our system will include an electrical distribution grid connecting Kenya to its neighbors, to the extent that such a grid does not already exist. It will enable the rapid and inexpensive transfer of electricity to and from Kenya. To this grid will be connected power stations – at least one, perhaps more – producing significantly greater generating capacity than currently exists in-country. Larger, in fact, than any in the world.

"The power stations we are planning are unlike any you have ever seen before. These stations are going to convert energy from the Sun into electricity. You may be aware that the Earth receives enormous amounts of energy each day from the Sun, much of which is simply radiated back into Space. We are going to optimize the Solar output and convert the Sun's energy into electricity much more efficiently than ever before, using a new system of energy conversion and collection.

"You are probably aware that the Sun produces energy through a wide spectrum, from thermal radiation to radio waves. As a result, the Earth is continuously surrounded in energy. While former collectors used either photovoltaic or thermal collectors, operated in the visible and heating portions of the spectrum, and collected energy only during the daytime, our new design will receive energy twenty-four hours a day in an entirely different part of the electromagnetic spectrum.

"Each power station will consist of an antenna grid, approximately ten kilometers in diameter, suspended about fifteen meters above the ground, and wiring to connect the antennas to the power distribution system.

"We know how protective Kenya is of its environment, and we share those concerns. Every effort has been made to avoid adverse impacts. The antenna is designed to minimize impacts on the environment at the site, through a design which allows the sun to shine through the antenna itself, minimizing shading, except from the supporting poles.

"The most significant negative effect will be the visual impact of the antenna, which we believe can be minimized if the antenna is located in an area which is rarely visited by Kenya's tourists. We have identified several such potential sites in Kenya.

"Conversely, there will be many benefits to Kenya, both direct and indirect. Unlike other programs you may have seen in the past, in which most of the labor force has been composed of foreign workers, the first benefit of our project will be employment of many presently unemployed Kenyans. We will train them for the construction of the power stations and the grid connecting Kenya to its neighbors.

"We will utilize your Kenyan power company for construction of the connecting lines, transformer sub-stations, and electrical distribution grid, if they choose to participate. This will be a temporary benefit, but the training will help Kenyan citizens obtain other positions as the Kenyan economy develops after the stations come on line.

"The second benefit will be new permanent jobs in maintenance of the power station. We will be employing these workers ourselves, and again, they will be Kenyan residents, not foreigners. Many of these may currently be employed in the existing Kenya power-generating plants, and will be displaced by the new generating system when it goes on line.

"The largest benefit, though, will be to the Kenyan government, in the form of a royalty paid for each kilowatt of power generated. This royalty will be fifteen percent of the price for which we sell power to your present electric company, in lieu of taxes on revenues made by our company. There will be no interruption in the business of the present company, or of its revenues. It will simply be a change in the source of its power, from the present expensive, unreliable, polluting, fossil fuels to a clean, reliable, affordable power source. We expect your power company's cost of electricity to be less, not more, over time, as a result of our power stations.

"We propose to begin construction within a few months. It will take about five years for our plants to begin coming on-line. Then there will be a period of limited output while we test each antenna array."

"During the transition period from present power plants to the new power stations, our personnel will operate the new stations in parallel with the present plants. This will be the proof for your government that this technology works, although I assure you that my employer would not consider spending the many millions required for this construction if it were not proven.

"After an initial demonstration of the new stations' reliability, we will change over to operating the new power stations on a full-time basis, removing the load from your present power plants, which will be maintained on standby during a second test period.

"During that second period, we will assume the expense of all payrolls for the former power plant employees, and begin the transition for those employees to operation of the new power station as employees of our company.

"When the new power stations pass their final performance tests, proving to you their effectiveness, the old power plants will be closed and dismantled, removing permanently these serious sources of pollution from Kenya.

"While our company will pay the entire cost of building the new power stations, labor costs, and purchase of the existing power plants, we want you to clearly understand that any government now using nuclear power will be required to participate and cooperate fully in disassembly and final storage of any nuclear waste from its present nuclear power plants. And while you are being asked to contribute land both for the power stations, distribution system, and any required nuclear waste disposal sites, I want to reemphasize that your government will not have to come up with any other money for this project.

"We will purchase all the present plants from your power company, at a fraction of their present value, of course, but as we are insuring that Kenya's present power company is an active participant under the new system, this will not represent a loss to the power company. The ultimate rate that your citizens pay for this abundant electric power will, as now, be decided by the Kenyan rate-setting agency, in the same way as you currently regulate your present company's profit, but we expect that rate to drop, at least over time.

"Sir, you are an educated, intelligent man. I am sure that you recognize this program will give our company an effective monopoly on the production of electric power in Kenya, just as your present company has now. We are not attempting to conceal this fact. Our proposal includes a three-party contract with your government and the Kenyan Power Company, to sell electricity to the power company at a predetermined rate, in exchange for your government's consent and cooperation for the construction and operation of our power stations.

"Other questions may occur to you, such as 'What if someone else can produce the same power at a lower price?' or 'What if we simply decide not to participate?'

"With regard to the first question, we welcome competition but, frankly, we know for a certainty that no other company can offer anything similar to the arrangement we are offering. You are welcome to look for another source. You will not find any. Our technology is unique and no other company can reproduce it.

"With regard to the second question, not participating, I must candidly tell you I believe such a decision would be economic and political suicide for Kenya and its present government. This technology will soon be in wide use, if not by Kenya, then by other African countries. Representatives of my employer are in other African countries today, making this same proposal to their governments. If only one other country accepts our offer, it will have such a competitive advantage that other African countries will have to follow suit or fall hopelessly behind.

"If it retains its present dependence on petroleum-generated power, Kenya will find itself at an increasingly large competitive disadvantage with its neighbors. Your citizens will not accept having Kenya as a 'third-world' country while the remainder of Africa moves into a period of economic prosperity without the energy restrictions of the past. We are planning to install our power stations in the sequence that national governments agree to participate, so there is an advantage if your country signs up early. If you delay, years may pass before we can get an installation here, because other countries will have been scheduled ahead of you. We expect to take five years for the first plants to go on-line. If you wait, even a few days, you could delay the installation of the Kenyan power stations for ten or fifteen years. We realize you might think we are trying to pressure you into agreeing to our proposal. We assure you that we are not. We are merely offering Kenya an opportunity that it is entirely free to ignore. It is we who are under pressure, and we must determine which countries will be the sites of our first plants within the next week. All we ask is that you carefully examine the materials that explain our project.

"Our company has prepared a package that covers the information I have given you. You are free to verify any facts therein. However, because much of the technology can only be explained by my employer, we are available to you to answer any questions you have during your review.

"Mr. Roberts and I will be at the Nairobi Hilton, solely to be available to the Kenyan government.

"What we want from you is to arrange a meeting for us with the President of Kenya within the next three days, and we want your personal endorsement of our project to the President. Our sources have advised us that he is in country and available.

"If we have convinced you of the benefits of this program, we will plan on meeting the President and presenting essentially the same briefing you have just received, after which we will remain an additional three days to answer the President's questions.

"If we have not convinced you, we will leave Kenya four days from now to present our program to another nation.

"However, if the President endorses our plan, we will furnish him enabling legislation, which we already have prepared, to be introduced in the Parliament when the Spring Session opens at the end of next week. This legislation will authorize acquisition of necessary land to be set aside for our power plants, and authorize additional actions necessary to make the conversion possible. Do you have any questions?"

The Minister, realizing that what had been laid before him was beyond his expertise and that, *if* he asked a technical question, he would likely not understand the answer, demurred.

"I will review your information package, Mr. Williams, and ask my staff to examine it. They will call you at the Hilton if they have any questions."

Jomo said, "Thank you, Sir. We'll be glad to come right over or meet anywhere in the Nairobi area with your experts."

The Minister led the visitors to the doors and shook their hands. "Thank you for bringing this to me." He closed the door behind them, sat down, picked up the package, opened it, and turned slowly through the pages.

It set out precisely the program that Williams had outlined. Each page had a schematic drawing of some element of the power stations or the connecting network, or a chart or graph showing present power consumption, cost and projections for demand.

One of the most interesting was a graph that plotted the increasing cost of energy, over time, against the primary economic indicators for Kenya. The conclusion was inescapable – that current trends would result in financial collapse of the national economy within a few years, with even modest increases in the cost of conventional energy.

The next graph showed the projected international cost of energy for the next ten years, based on demand, availability, and increased effort to locate new reserves, plotted against the ability of the Kenyan economy to pay for such energy. That ability fell below the cost of energy in only three years.

The charts also showed that revenue from the construction of the new power stations would give Kenya's economy a significant boost, even before they began operation.

The Minister doubted the accuracy of the numbers and punched his intercom. "Call Mr. Murang'a and Mr. Nguni. See how soon they can come over." Murang'a and Nguni were the Ministers for Energy and Finance, respectively.

He took a breath, composed himself, and picked up his private telephone. Quickly, he punched in the code for his influential patron's home. The phone was answered by a servant. After a short wait, Elias Kenyatta came on the line.

"Hello?"

"They just left my office. Did you know what they are proposing?"

"Yes."

"It seems most unlikely that what they say could be true. Their story is too wild to believe."

"Believe it."

"Are you sure? I mean, have you seen their numbers on the economy?"

"I did say believe it, didn't I? What do they want from you?"

"They want to see the President and make their presentation to him within three days. They want my endorsement of their plan."

"What happens if they don't see him?"

"They leave and offer this to another country."

"What are you going to do?"

"I called Murang'a and Nguni to come here. To verify the numbers in these statistics."

"Do you really believe the company hasn't done its homework on such simple facts? How much are they proposing to spend?"

"Millions and millions. I guess they probably have checked these out. Thanks."

"Call me anytime. I want to know any developments on this, immediately, as they happen. No delays! Understand?" There was a click as the patron hung up. Kotali leaned back in his chair and stared at the ceiling for a moment; he noticed a spider building a web in the corner. He leaned forward and dialed the President's number.

CHAPTER 24

Jomo Williams and Ivan Roberts had just returned to their hotel room when the telephone rang. Roberts answered. "Hello ... No. Just a moment." He turned to Jomo. "It's for you."

As he took the handset from Ivan, Jomo wondered who could be calling so early in the day. "Hello. This is John Williams."

"Mr. Williams, this is Minister Kotali. You and Mr. Roberts have an appointment to brief the President at nine o'clock tomorrow morning at the Presidential Palace."

"Yes sir! We'll be there. Thank you sir." Jomo hung up the phone and turned to Ivan.

"We did it! That was the Interior Minister and he already has an appointment for us tomorrow morning with the President. We're on our way!"

"You have to call London," Ivan reminded him.

"Right. Call London."

"Don't forget the scrambler."

"Right. Let's see. I have it here in my suitcase." Jomo placed the telephone handset in the cradle on the scrambler and closed the cover, then picked up the scrambler's handset. Everything he said would be digitally encrypted and transmitted as undecipherable noise to a phone in London, where another similar device would make his voice intelligible. He dialed the number, asked for Clifford Kelly, then switched on the scrambler. He quickly outlined the results of the meeting with the Interior Minister and explained that he had an appointment for the next day. Kelly congratulated them both but reminded them that the Interior Minister was just the first step. They still had to sell the President and the Legislature on the project. Jomo acknowledged the work yet to do, and signed off.

The next morning at nine, Jomo and Ivan were in the waiting area outside the President's office. A receptionist escorted them into the office and invited them to sit. Already present was the Interior Minister, with whom they had met the previous day. They greeted one another formally and sat awaiting the arrival of the President. After a few minutes, the door at the side of the office opened. The Interior Minister leaped to his feet, startling both Jomo and Ivan, who also stood, although not as explosively. Beaming, the President entered the office and exchanged formal greetings in both Kiswahili and English, with introductions by the Interior Minister and handshakes all around. He went directly to the subject of the meeting. "Minister Kotali tells me that I need to hear the presentation you gave him yesterday. Something about a power plant, I understand." He had also been told by Elias Kenyatta that this project could be very beneficial to Kenya as a country, and, if he played his cards properly, to himself personally.

"Yes, Sir. We represent Stellar Power Corporation, which is proposing to build one power plant here in Kenya initially, with the possibility of more later. However, these are not ordinary power plants. They are power plants of unprecedented size. One of them would be much larger than the combined generating capacity of all of the power plants now in Kenya, and once they are operating, they will make all existing power plants obsolete."

The President was immediately alarmed. He was a major shareholder in the Kenyan electric company, along with his friend, Kenyatta. "If I understand you correctly, your plant could cause serious losses to the owners of the present power plants. I'm very bothered at that prospect."

'I'll bet you are,' Jomo thought to himself. He already knew exactly how extensive the President's power company holdings were. What he did say was, "Mr. President, we understand the financing mechanisms of the existing power companies and are committed to insuring that the investors in those companies are fully protected. As you may know, most large power plants are built with borrowed money. While our plants are under construction, the existing plants will continue to operate just as they do today. Once our first plant is on-line, existing plants will begin to be phased out and, as they are phased out, they will be purchased by our company from the present power company. In that process, we will be paying considerably less than what the plants cost to build, simply because the plants will then be worthless.

"Your electrical rates, however, will remain unchanged. Kenya Power will continue to pay the interest and principal payments on the outstanding construction bonds for their present plants from the revenues which sale of power provides, just as it does today. This approach provides continuity of cash flow to lenders through the power company. What we will also be doing at the same time, which may be of considerable interest to the power company, is relieving them of the maintenance and operation costs of the phased-out plants, and substituting a reasonable and stable charge for electricity, which they will thereafter buy from Stellar Power Corporation. The power company will continue to sell power. The only difference will be the source of its power.

"What will change, and what *must* change if Kenya is to be a healthy and economically viable nation in the future, is that Kenya must move away from traditional fuels for its power plants, which means in the future Kenya can not be dependent on either fossil or nuclear fuels. The old plants represent a continuing threat to Kenya's environment, which is a critical resource for Kenya's people. It is critical both because Kenya is deeply committed to its tourist industry, but also because the people of Kenya are culturally tied to the land and its resources in ways which are threatened by continued dependence on traditional fuel sources.

"Let me elaborate on that. If Kenya does not change its present path, the cost of both domestic and imported fuels will continue to climb as worldwide demand for energy increases. We know that such demand is increasing, not only because there are a hundred thousand more persons in the world each day requiring fuel for their lives, but also because many nations are striving to raise their standard of living, which virtually guarantees higher per-capita energy consumption.

"As those costs climb, which they *will* do with your present energy sources, the ability of Kenya to pay the increased cost must either climb also, or the amount of available energy will be reduced. We know Kenya, like other countries, is trying to *raise* its standard of living, which means its consumption, which means consumption of energy. But its ability to pay increased energy costs is not growing at the rate the cost of energy is growing. This is an inherent and unavoidable conflict, using present energy sources. If that effort to increase the standard of living of your upper class continues, the rising cost of energy must necessarily mean that the lower socio-economic groups will be forced into worse living conditions. Their need for energy for cooking alone, even with novel approaches such as solar cookers, will mean that the countryside will be stripped of all its vegetation. As Kenya's natural resources gradually disappear, the populations which are dependent on it will become increasingly agitated and severe social and political disorder will necessarily follow.

"Your wildlife is totally dependent on that vegetation. Injure the vegetation and you injure your wildlife. Destroy it and you destroy your wildlife. What happens to the vegetation in Kenya therefore happens to your tourism economy, because the tourists come to see the wildlife. Intuitively you know I am correct, but we have furnished Minister Kotali documentation of this effect, and your economists are welcome to check out our facts and projections. If your experts have any questions, all our economists and economic consultants are at your disposal; you have only to ask.

"Let me tell you a little about the plants that we propose to build. These plants use power from the Sun." He continued to make the same presentation which he had given Minister Kotali a day earlier. When he mentioned the power stations in other African countries, the President interrupted.

"Other countries? Which other countries?"

Jomo said, "Sir, as I explained to Minister Kotali, other representatives of our company are meeting as we speak with other governments. I can't tell you which ones, but I can tell you we want Kenya to be the first country with an operational power antenna. Eventually, we hope to have receiving antennas in virtually every African country where we can obtain a site. As we explained to Minister Kotali, our economists believe failure to participate in the Stellar Power program would be economically disastrous to Kenya, because other African countries who do choose to participate in the program will thereby have a significant competitive advantage over any country, including Kenya, which does not have this technology.

"Even if Kenya buys power generated in a neighboring country, it will lose the benefit of the royalty which it would receive from power generated here. I'm sure you realize fifteen percent of even very low-priced electricity is a lot of money, if it is fifteen percent of the value of all the power generated. If you do not have plants here, you will buy your power from a neighbor, and we are certain you will do that, because unlike your present power, which uses fuel that is constantly increasing in cost, the fuel for our power - the Sun - is free. Therefore, your cost of conventional fuel will continue to increase and increase indefinitely, so energy from our system should always be less expensive.

"If you decide Kenya should participate, we will provide a package of legislation for adoption by the Kenya Assembly. These laws will authorize acquisition of land for our power plants and supporting facilities, duty-free importation of materials for the plants, duty-free importation and exportation of electricity after the plants are in operation, and tax-free status for our company. All of these provisions are in consideration of the fifteen percent royalty, which Kenya will receive when the power begins coming from the plant.

"We also pointed out to Minister Kotali that because of employment and secondary economic impacts resulting from the construction of the power plant antenna array, the power grid, and associated structures, the benefits to Kenya will begin long before the plant actually starts operation, which is expected to take five years."

"Yes, Mr. Kotali mentioned that."

"It should be very good for Kenya, and the revenue should start flowing into your country quite soon, but the proposal which we are offering to Kenya is non-negotiable. We believe it offers Kenya unmatchable advantages, but we are making similar offers to other countries in Africa. If you refuse this offer, we will certainly find some of those other countries will accept. We must have your decision within three days. I apologize to you for being so rushed. I assure you we would allow more time for you to decide if we could; however the financing on this program is of unprecedented size for a private project, and we must begin as soon as possible or the interest on our funds could put us out of business before we start. If I have done a proper job explaining the project and Kenya's possible participation, I hope you realize that Kenya can keep its options open until the plant is operating, then see if our representations are correct. If at that time Kenya can produce power more inexpensively than we can sell it to you, we wouldn't blame you if you kept on using your existing source of power, but we would of course still sell the power from our plant to others.

"If you agree to our requirements, we will furnish the legislation I just described, for introduction in the Assembly next week. It must be approved by the Assembly and signed by yourself within two weeks from now. If it is not approved by then, we will take our offer to another country. This offer puts Kenya at the top of the line for first installation of one of our power stations. If you do not take it now, Kenya will be placed at the bottom of the list of African countries, and will only be offered a power station again after all other countries in Africa have been offered a station and have either accepted or rejected that offer. We expect that to take about ten years, after which about five years would be required for construction. Whether Kenya can stand to wait fifteen years before obtaining this new power source is a policy decision that only you and the Assembly can make, Mr. President.

"Mr. Roberts and I will wait at our hotel for three days for your response. Do you have any questions?"

The President ran his hand over his forehead, wiping away perspiration that was forming despite the air conditioning. He knew this decision was an important, perhaps critical one for Kenya, and for himself. He thought about his friend Elias Kenyatta, with whom he had spoken just before the Americans arrived. He said, "Mr. Williams. How to start? First, let me say that your company's direct approach is most unusual." Without Kenyatta's recommendation, the proposal might have been taken as an insult.

"Yes, sir, I understand how you may feel that way, but please understand that our company is on a very restricted schedule and cannot expend the amounts of money involved in this program, amounting to many billions of dollars, and accept any delays."

"Yes. I can understand that. Therefore, let me go straight to the finish. I don't need three days to decide. You have my unqualified support. Bring your proposed legislation to my office this afternoon. I will review it, then meet with the leaders of the Assembly in the morning. If they have any questions, may I assume that you will be available to answer them?"

"Of course, sir. Mr. Roberts and I will be standing by at the Hilton."

"Very well. You may deliver the legislation to my receptionist this afternoon."

"Sir, if you would like it now, I have it right here.

"Please."

Jomo handed the President an envelope.

The President thanked Jomo and Ivan again and they departed for their hotel. Roberts would buy dinner.

CHAPTER 25

June 28

Morocco, Western Sahara, Mauritania, Mali, Niger, Chad, Egypt, Sudan, Ethiopia, Somalia, Kenya, Tanzania, Zambia, Mozambique, South Africa, Botswana, Namibia, Nigeria, and Ghana had agreed to full participation in the program. Zimbabwe, Angola, Central African Republic, and Malawi wanted to see what happened to other countries before making a decision and remained undecided. All of the West African countries, except Nigeria and Ghana, as well as Uganda, Libya, Algeria and Zaire, summarily rejected the plan as either not credible or politically incorrect.

By July 1, survey crews arrived in Kenya, Morocco and Namibia to prepare the first three power station sites for the beginning of construction. Other crews were examining existing high-tension power transmission lines for compatibility with the 10,000 kilometer-long direct-current power grid that would reach from Egypt to Morocco and on to South Africa. Materials would begin to arrive within the month. A year had passed since the technical briefing in Bangkok, and 17 syndicates had so far raised over 40 billion dollars. Uncle Bob's billion *was* just a drop in the bucket, and the project was moving forward.

CHAPTER 26

August 1
    Production of the space plane was ahead of schedule. In less than eleven months, a speed unprecedented in aerospace history, Boeing and Aerospatiale had completed the major wing and fuselage components for the first space plane. The plane was being called 'the shovel,' because of its long, wide nose, and to distract people from its actual purpose. Aviation Week and Space Technology writers had actually been able to look at some of the components, but were only able to say that they were very large, whatever they were, as the components would not be assembled into anything resembling an aircraft until they reached Belau. After careful inspection and packing, the components were loaded on chartered Antonov AN-124 cargo aircraft and flown to Belau, where the new runway had just been completed. They arrived on July 10.
    By August 25, all the design staff had been moved from the Atlanta office to Belau. Employee housing had been built on the installation, and although the apartments were still somewhat Spartan, none of the design or production team members complained. Everyone involved in the project understood the importance of the project, and all of them were excited to be in Belau at the new Earth Port.

CHAPTER 27

September 6

Danielle's white and blue MU-2 had been towed from a hangar and was waiting for her on the parking apron at the Marrakech airport where she had left it a few days earlier. Her visit to the Moroccan antenna site had been very informative and construction was on schedule, but only just barely. The timetable had a number of weather-delay days built in, but those had been used up by problems getting materials to the site. The first hang-up had been the customs office.

'Old habits die hard,' she thought. Morocco was one of the first African countries scheduled to have a power station installation, started after Kenya and before Namibia. The contract between the Moroccan government and Stellar Power Corporation clearly provided that materials and equipment for the power station and all repair parts were to enter the country duty-free.

The trouble began almost immediately when, on July 15, the airport's chief customs officer had announced that Stellar Power's contractor's trucks and tools were not specifically mentioned in the agreement, so when the huge Galaxy and Antonov transport aircraft containing trucks full of materials for the project had landed at the airport, the customs office had demanded payment of the usual 150% duty on the trucks.

After a day of unproductive arguments with the customs director, the superintendent called London for backup. Helen Overmeyer had negotiated the agreement with Morocco and within two hours she was on an Air France flight to Rabat. The next morning, after a detailed telephone interview with the company's Morocco superintendent, she went directly to the Interior Minister's Office as it opened and identified herself. The Minister's male receptionist stiffly asked if she had an appointment. Helen said she did not. The receptionist was "soo verry sorry, but the Minister has a full calendar and cannot be disturbed, so please come back tomorrow and I-will-see-if-I-can-work-you-in-thank-you-very-much."

Helen's job didn't include arguing with minor functionaries, and it was against company policy to do so, so she returned to her hotel and called back to the office. When the Stellar Power operator answered, she asked to speak to Clifford Kelly, then switched on a scrambler. After quickly summarizing her findings, she was told by Kelly to stand by, that he would call her back. She called room service for lunch and waited.

In London, Kelly was immediately on the secure line to Belau. The Belau Aviation operator answered.

There was a short pause, and Danielle answered. "Hello, Cliff. What do you need?"

"We have a problem in Marrakech. The customs people have had our equipment tied up at the airport for the last twenty-four hours, and are demanding payment of duties on all the trucks and tools. Helen Overmeyer is there to deal with the situation, but couldn't get in to see the Minister for Interior because of a hard-headed receptionist. She's waiting at Hotel Sahara in Rabat for instructions."

"I'll call you right back."

Danielle touched a button on the intercom. "Bill, get me the biggest investor from Morocco on the line."

"Yes, Ma'am. That would be Mr. Sorachi. I'll get him."

She returned to her paperwork. A moment later, the intercom buzzed and her secretary spoke. "Mr. Sorachi on line two."

She picked up the handset. "Jeffrey, how are you?'

"I am fine, Miss Simones. To what do I owe the pleasure of your call?" It was very unusual for Sorachi to speak to the chief of the space corporation. He had only invested 150 million, and was not a syndicate head.

"We are having some difficulty obtaining cooperation from the Moroccan government. The materials to begin the Atlas-site antenna arrived yesterday at the Marrakech airport, and have been stuck there because they insist we pay duties on our trucks and tools. We sent an officer to meet with our friend the Interior Minister, but she was blocked by an obstinate receptionist."

"Where is your officer now?'

"At the Hotel Sahara, in Rabat."

"Very well, I will send my car for him."

"Her."

"Her. And I will personally see that the materials are released today."

"Thank you, Jeff. I appreciate your help."

"Any time. And Danielle?"

"Yes?"

"How about having dinner with me in London the next time you are there?"

"What a nice idea! I'm not sure when I'll be able to do that, but if I'm planning a trip to London in the near future, I'll call and see if you're available. Thanks for the invitation. Do you need anything from me to help handle the authorities in Marrakech or Rabat?"

"Don't worry about that. I grew up in this country. Just tell your officer to be ready to go with me in thirty minutes."

"All right. And thanks, Jeff. Goodbye." She switched off and touched the intercom. "Bill, get Kelly for me."

In a moment Kelly was on the line. She told him that the situation in Marrakech should be resolved by the end of the day, and to have Overmeyer ready to be picked up at the hotel within fifteen minutes.

Helen Overmeyer sat in the living room of her suite in the hotel. She was reviewing a new contract for materials for the Nigerian power station. Her phone rang. It was the desk clerk telling her that her driver had arrived. She locked the room and rode the elevator to the lobby. Near the front desk was a tall, fortyish gentleman wearing a djellaba.

She recognized him as Jeffrey Sorachi, a friend of the company. His Mercedes was waiting at the curb in a no-parking zone. The driver opened the rear door for them, then drove directly to the King's palace. They stepped out of the car and were escorted into the King's private office.

The conversation that followed was mostly in Arabic with a little bit of French. Overmeyer didn't say a word although she could speak both languages fluently. Sorachi introduced her, then managed to simultaneously be infuriated and ingratiatingly polite with the King. The King made one telephone call, and informed the person on the other end of the conversation in Arabic that they "were unworthy of their office, and if they held up this project, or allowed a representative of the power station company to be turned away from their office again, they wouldn't be able to get an appointment as street sweeper. Was that clear?"

The King then turned back to Overmeyer and smiled. He said, in perfect English. "Miss Overmeyer, your equipment will be released within the hour. Here is my private number. If you have any further difficulty with anyone in Morocco, please call me and I will take personal care of the situation." Overmeyer and Sorachi thanked him and left.

That had been over a month earlier. Since then, work had proceeded without customs delays, but other things had cropped up. There had been labor disagreements. Half the Berber work force had threatened to quit because they felt their tribe had not been treated as well as members of another tribe also working on the project. There were demonstrations, a work slowdown, and the threat of a strike. Stellar Power consulted with a local religious leader, who met with the factions involved and told them to go back to work. Work resumed, but six days had been lost.

Then there had been problems with the quality of the concrete. The locally manufactured Portland cement didn't produce concrete with sufficient compressive strength to meet the specifications for the antenna's support foundations and anchors.

Stellar Power retained an expert in cement manufacturing and provided him to the local cement factory. It cost a few hundred thousand for some new equipment, but Stellar Power made a loan to the factory to buy the equipment, and negotiated a reduction in the price of the cement. By the time the contract was completed, the equipment would be paid for, the concrete would meet the required specs, and Morocco would have a better grade of cement available in-country for future construction projects of all kinds.

But it had taken nearly a month to resolve, during which little could be done but surveying and digging excavations for the foundations for the antenna's thousands of supports.

Danielle's visit to the antenna site was somewhat reassuring. At least the delays had not been completely wasted time. Virtually all of the excavations for the foundations were completed and many had the reinforcing steel installed and were ready for the concrete, which had begun to arrive. With a little help, the slippage that had occurred so far in the schedule might be recovered through more efficient handling of the concrete deliveries. The foundations had to be poured, and cured, before the masts started arriving. She didn't want the masts damaged by being stacked on their sides while awaiting installation, and she had seen stranger things happen during her many years in business. Still, there was hope of getting back on schedule yet, and she left the antenna site a little more optimistic than when she had arrived.

The cockpit of the MU-2 was suffocatingly hot in the mid-day sun as she prepared to leave Marrakech. She finished the exterior inspection and, after completing the initial cockpit checks, started the starboard - number 2 - engine. She still had the cabin door open on the port side but wanted the air-conditioning. When the starboard engine was running, she closed the cabin door, started the port engine and the temperature in the airplane very slowly became bearable. Ready to roll, she called the tower and received clearance to taxi to the active runway, then to take off.

The approved flight plan was Marrakech to Casablanca at 19,000 feet, then overwater to Lisbon at 23,000 feet, then direct to Guernsey at 21,000 feet. The first leg went smoothly. The flight director and autopilot were turned off and she was enjoying hand-flying the airplane. She didn't have to fly it that way; the custom-built Collins flight director/autopilot computer system could fly the airplane without a pilot if it was programmed properly. She had seen to it that this MU-2 was equipped with the most sophisticated systems when she was CEO at Global. There was no other aircraft equipped like it in the world.

She had just turned the plane onto the heading for Lisbon when she realized something was wrong. The airplane was flying smoothly at 23,000 feet, but she suddenly smelled kerosene exhaust in the cabin. Her reaction was almost automatic. She turned off the air-conditioning system and reached with her left hand to the hook over her left shoulder, grabbed the oxygen mask hanging there and held it over her mouth and nose. She couldn't fasten the mask without taking off her headset, which she didn't take time to do. She reached over the empty co-pilot seat next to her and turned on the oxygen pressure regulator under the right armrest. The gas automatically began to flow into her mask from cylinders stowed on the airplane's aft bulkhead. Inhaling deeply, and struggling to focus on the increasingly difficult task of flying the airplane, she switched on the autopilot and flight director and reprogrammed the flight director's selected altitude from 21,000 to 2,000 feet.

The flight director's auto-throttle, linked to the engines' power levers, reduced the power to provide the appropriate descent rate. Still flying 280 knots, the turboprop began to descend at 6,000 feet per minute under the control of the flight director-autopilot. Danielle fought to stay conscious while holding the oxygen mask over her mouth and nose and inhaling deeply. Reaching across with her right hand while her left hand held the oxygen mask, she managed to open a four-inch-square vent door in the fuselage side below the left cockpit window. There was a rush of air outward through the vent door as the aircraft depressurized. The cabin pressure warning system activated in response to the loss of cabin pressure and the 'Cabin Low Pressure' light on the instrument panel began flashing. The Master Caution light flashed in the center of the panel and the Master Caution warning horn howled. The noise would continue until its reset button was depressed.

She struggled to focus her mind on flying the aircraft as she switched to the guard channel, 121.5 MHz, pressed the transmit button on the control yoke and spoke weakly into the microphone in the oxygen mask, "MAYDAY! MAYDAY! Golf-Lima-Oscar-Bravo- ...,". Then she passed out.

The airplane continued its rapid descent. As she slumped forward against the shoulder belts, her left hand, still holding the oxygen mask, fell to her side.

300 miles from Lisbon over the Atlantic, the airplane reached an altitude of 2,000 feet. In the cockpit, Danielle slumped in her seat. The flight director eased the throttles forward to maintain the altitude and speed selected. The MU-2's groundspeed, set by the navigation computer, was the same at 2,000 feet as it had been at 23,000 feet, 280 knots, 320 miles per hour. The powerful turboprop engines strained to maintain the high airspeed in the dense air of the lower altitude.

In the radar room at Lisbon Center, the controller on the Atlantic approach screen was alerted to the approaching aircraft by a special computer program that monitored aircraft displayed on his radar screen. The aircraft had descended to only 2,000 feet and was flying in excess of the airspeed permitted at that altitude. The intruder alert, designed to detect hostile jet aircraft, was marking the MU-2 as a possible attacking threat aircraft. The identification tag accompanying the blip on the screen, however, identified it as a civilian MU-2, British registry 'G-L-O-B-E,' which according to its flight plan was supposed to be at 23,000 feet. The air-traffic controller punched a button connecting him to the Air Defense Force. "Do you guys see this MU-2 200 miles southeast of Lisbon at 2,000 feet? I think there's some problem. It shouldn't be there and fits the intruder profile."

"Affirmative. We just picked it up. There was part of a mayday on the radio a few minutes ago, but we couldn't get a fix on it. It started Golf-Lima- then quit."

"Don't suppose you might have an interceptor in that area?"

"Our guys are scheduled for some training anyway. We'll scramble a flight and check it out."

"Roger. We'll monitor the frequency."

72 seconds later, two NATO F-5 fighters were in the air, headed out over the Atlantic at 8,000 feet and 400 miles per hour. Within minutes, they saw the white MU-2 approach them, then flash beneath their wings at a closing speed of over 700 miles per hour.

The pilots exchanged signals and, with the two aircraft wing-tip to wing-tip and moving as one, they rolled inverted and dived toward the deck, reversing their course as they hauled back on the control sticks. Contrails spiraled from the wingtips as abused air was compressed then re-expanded as it rolled out from under the ends of the wings. Pushing their aircraft into full afterburner, they began rapidly to close the interval between themselves and the MU-2.

As they came within the last mile behind the MU-2, one F-5 deployed its speed brakes and took up its station above and to the rear, while the second one took up a formation position near and just ahead of the MU-2's left wingtip. The pilot of the wing interceptor peered across the space between the two aircraft, then keyed his microphone. He could see the pilot's head slumped forward. "On position on left wing of bogie. Aircraft is confirmed golf-lima-oscar-bravo-echo. Turboprop, high-wing, white with blue trim. Pilot is either asleep or dead."

In the cockpit, fresh, dense, oxygen-rich air had been pumping in through the open vent door, and the Master Caution warning horn was still blaring. Danielle began to regain consciousness. Over the noise of the alarm and the air rushing past the cockpit vent window, there was another sound. It was a voice in her headphones.

"Golf-Lima-Oscar-Bravo-Echo. Golf-Lima-Oscar-Bravo-Echo. Do you read me? Golf-Lima-Oscar-Bravo-Echo. This is NATO Air Force F-5." The message repeated several times.

She began to hear something. Where was she? She looked around. She was in her airplane and there was a warning horn. Master Caution. What was it warning? She saw the Cabin Low Pressure light flashing. Cabin Pressure. That's it! Something was wrong with the cabin pressure.

She also heard a voice, but couldn't understand it. She thought, 'Fly the airplane. Got to fly the airplane. Wish that voice would go away. First thing. Fly the airplane.' She scanned the panel. 'Altimeter steady at 2,000 feet. Airspeed, my God,

280 knots.' At 2,000 feet she didn't need cabin pressure so she pushed the button to reset the Master Caution warning. The horn stopped, but the screaming sound of air rushing past the open vent window at 320 miles per hour would have been deafening but for the electronic noise-canceling headsets. She reached over and turned off the oxygen valve. Then she heard the voice again in her headphones.

"Golf-Lima-Oscar-Bravo-Echo. Golf-Lima-Oscar-Bravo-Echo. Do you read me? Golf-Lima-Oscar-Bravo-Echo. This is NATO Air Force F-5."

She touched the push-to-talk button on the control yoke, "NATO Air Force. This is Golf-Lima-Oscar-Bravo-Echo, Go ahead."

"Bravo Echo, you have been out of contact with ground control for some time. What is your status?"

She tried to remember. What had happened? She remembered something. She remembered opening the tiny vent door. Nothing else. No, she remembered she was going home.

"Air Force, I'm not sure what my status is. Where are you calling from?"

"Look out your left window. We're right here."

She looked to her left and saw the nearby jet fighter. "Okay, Air Force. I need to slow down. We're over the redline. I'm coming back on the power." She reached up to the switch panel above the windshield and turned off the flight director, then placed her right hand on the engine power levers and slowly began pulling them back.

"Roger that." The speed brakes on the side of the F-5 began to deploy, maintaining its position relative to the MU-2, as the speed bled off. The F-5 was now flying a little nose-high.

"Air Force, where are we anyway? I think I must have passed out."

"We're just south of Lisbon, and you better start climbing or change course. Another few miles and you'll be in the mountains."

"Air Force, I'd like to land somewhere and check out my aircraft. Can you arrange that?"

"Roger. Wait one." The Air Force pilot switched to another frequency and then came back. "Bravo-Echo, Lisbon Approach Control is waiting for your call. Contact Lisbon Approach, one one niner point one."

"Thank you, Air Force. Golf-Lima-Oscar-Bravo-Echo switching to one one niner point one."

She changed the radio frequency selector to 119.1 MHz and pushed the transmit button. "Lisbon Approach. MU-2 Golf-Lima-Oscar-Bravo-Echo."

Lisbon Approach Control was waiting. "Golf-Lima-Oscar-Bravo-Echo. Lisbon Approach."

"Lisbon Approach, Bravo-Echo requests radar vectors to Lisbon Airport and clearance to land."

"Roger Golf-Lima-Oscar-Bravo-Echo. Lisbon Approach. Do you wish to declare an emergency?"

"Negative emergency. I just want to get on the ground and inspect my aircraft."

"Roger. Bravo-Echo, squawk one three three six."

Danielle dialed 1-3-3-6 into the transponder, which now sent that code back to any radar receiver tracking the aircraft.

Lisbon Approach came right back. "Contact, Golf Lima Oscar Bravo Echo, you are cleared to Caridad N.D.B. Frequency three eight niner megahertz. Turn right to zero eight zero degrees. Climb and maintain 4,000 feet. Hold at Caridad N.D.B. and contact Lisbon Tower, one one eight point niner."

She altered the plane's course to 080 degrees, began a climb to 4,000 feet, set the radio's standby frequency at 118.9 Mhz, set the Automatic Direction Finder's frequency at 389 Mhz and reached into her flight bag. Pulling out the binder that held the Jeppesen charts for Europe, she leafed through the charts until the binder was open at Lisbon. The Lisbon chart showed the approach to Lisbon Airport was from the Caridad non-directional beacon, then descending to the runway, either on a straight-in approach to runway 03 or over the river on a downwind leg then turning left as the plane descended to the base leg of the pattern then to final approach to land 347 feet above sea level on runway 21. Which approach the tower would give her would depend on the wind direction.

As she flew over the Beacon, she heard the International Morse Code for 'C' 'D' in the headphones, the identification for the Caridad Beacon. She began circling, changed radio frequencies and called Lisbon Tower.

"Lisbon Tower, Golf Lima Oscar Bravo Echo at Caridad. Landing."

Lisbon Tower answered immediately. "Golf Lima Oscar Bravo Echo, you are cleared to land. Make left traffic for runway two one. Wind one niner zero at one zero gusting to one five. Barometer one zero one two. Turn right heading zero niner zero, descend to pattern altitude, one two hundred feet."

The airport was there, in the distance to the right. She initiated the turn to 090 degrees and began to adjust the controls to prepare the airplane to land. Propeller. Torque. Flaps. Gear. All the instruments were in the green where they belonged. A few moments later the wheels touched down and she taxied to the parking apron. As the airplane stopped rolling, she moved the RUN-CRANK-STOP switches to the stop position, turned off the Master Switch, and the engines slowly spun down to a stop. Then, sitting on the ramp in the silence of the airplane, she started shaking.

CHAPTER 28

The Portuguese aviation safety authorities arrived at the airport soon after Danielle landed, having been alerted by the air traffic controllers. They were accompanied by a NATO officer and several national security personnel.

She was sitting in the door opening with her feet on the step below the door. As they walked toward the aircraft she stood up to greet them. The chief of the Portuguese aviation officials was General Domingo Sierra, whom she had met a few years before at the Paris Air Show. He smiled as he recognized her, then bowed and shook her hand. "Miss Simones, I am so distressed to learn that you have experienced difficulty with your aircraft. We were told that there was a flight which landed here after an 'incident,' but they did not tell me who it was." He pronounced her name "see-mo-nays", in the European fashion, rather than "sigh-moans" as most of her friends did.

"Thank you, General Sierra. I don't know what happened to me, but there was some malfunction in my airplane. Would it be possible for me to arrange to put it in your hangar while I examine it?"

"Certainly. Whatever you need." He turned to one of his subordinates and directed that the MU-2 be towed to the government hangar. The official hurried toward the airport office to make the arrangements. The General turned back to her. "I will assign a mechanic to assist you. Do you need someone to work on your aircraft?"

"Not yet. I want to do a thorough inspection first. Then, depending on what I find, I will either want to repair it here or ferry the aircraft to Global Aeronautique in Paris for repairs."

"I will have a ferry permit sent right over. You *will* let me know if you need anything else?"

"Of course. And thank you again for your courtesy."

The entourage of officials, minus the NATO officer, turned and left. The tall, thin officer, an American Air Force Lieutenant Colonel, delayed and stood by the nose of the aircraft as the remainder of the group walked away.

"Can I help you, Colonel?" she asked.

"Well, ma'am, I just wanted to meet you. A while ago I was your left wing-man. I'm Hank Taylor."

"It's nice to meet you, Colonel Taylor. I guess I owe you some thanks. You saved my bacon. I'm Danielle Simones." She shook his hand.

"That's just part of the job, ma'am. It *is* a little unusual to see a rocket like this cruising at 2,000 feet and 300 miles an hour."

"Believe me, it's a little unusual for me too," she laughed. "I'm glad you were there when I woke up otherwise I might have found those mountains the hard way."

"Who are you going to have work on the airplane?"

"I do some of the work myself, when I have time. It depends on what it needs today."

As they spoke, a tractor with an aircraft tow-bar roared up to them. The operator hooked the tow-bar onto the nose wheel of the MU-2 and began towing it slowly to the government hangar, with Danielle – and the tall American – walking behind the plane. As they crossed the tarmac, she walked from one side of the aircraft to the other, examining as much of it as she could see for anything out of the ordinary. It looked fine.

When the MU-2 was in the hangar and the wheels had been chocked securely, she re-entered the plane and returned to the cockpit. The American sat in the co-pilot seat next to her as the checkout continued. She carefully rechecked each item. Everything seemed to be working properly. She went to the rear of the aircraft, opened a few inspection panels, and examined systems located inside the tailcone. Everything appeared just as it should.

"Perhaps I'll need to run the engines to check other systems, but that'll require towing back out onto the ramp. I want to check inside the engine cowlings while we're still out of the sun. Do you think you could find a work-light?"

"Sure thing. I'll be right back."

He was, and by the time he returned, Danielle had found a short stepladder near the hangar wall and had the engine cowlings open. If there was something wrong with the plane, the first place to look for it was in the air-conditioning system.

The air-conditioning system and cabin pressurization system both operate on 'bleed air,' a relatively small amount of high-pressure air taken from the compressor stage of the aircraft's turbine engines. The air in the compressor stage of the engine is hot as a result of the compression to which it is subjected in preparation for injection of fuel in the engine's burner section.

For air-conditioning, clean, highly compressed bleed air from the engines is first cooled to the outside air temperature by going through a heat exchanger, and then is allowed to expand, which further cools it. From the heat exchanger and expansion chamber, it is conducted to the cabin in the form of cool air for the comfort of the passengers. A regulator system controls the amount and temperature of the air entering the cabin. The cooling feature of the air-conditioning normally is used only at lower altitudes. At higher cruising altitudes, normal outside air temperatures are so low that cooling is virtually never needed, and the system functions as a heater instead. The air-conditioning system automatically controls the temperature of air entering the cabin, keeping the cabin at a comfortable temperature selected by the pilot.

At very high altitudes, because the thin air has too little oxygen for breathing, compressed bleed air is taken from both engines' compressor stages, but only slightly cooled. The air-conditioning system provides compressed and heated air to the cabin, mixed with cooled air, thus keeping the internal oxygen pressure and temperature in the aircraft at a safe and comfortable level. An exhaust valve in the cabin controls the interior pressure by releasing air at a rate that maintains the pressure in the aircraft cabin.

Danielle carefully examined the bleed air shutoff valves on the port engine. Instead of the usual air conditioning duct from the compressor stage of the turbine to the shutoff valve, where it gets clean fresh air ahead of the burners, there was a duct from the exhaust section, after the burners. The shutoff valve had a strange additional controller attached to it, equipped with a barometer-like bellows. The outlet in the compressor stage, from which bleed air should have been taken, had a plug in it. The system had been rigged to carry exhaust gases directly to the cabin as soon as the aircraft reached a certain altitude. She didn't say anything, but was mad as hell. This was no accident or mechanical failure. Someone had deliberately rigged her airplane to divert exhaust gas into the cabin when she reached a high altitude.

She walked around the nose of the aircraft and peered into the open cowling of the starboard engine. The duct from the compressor stage was in its usual place. The airplane had been sabotaged to let her get to high altitude before she would be overcome by the exhaust gas fumes in the cockpit. The air conditioning had worked, because the first engine she started in Marrakech had not been tampered with. She closed the starboard cowling, carefully fastening each screw holding it shut and then returned to the port engine and repeated the process.

The American was leaning against the nose of the airplane watching her perform the inspection. She turned to him. "Colonel, I have to take this plane to Paris. The mechanics at my old employer's company are familiar with it, and I'll have them fix it. General Sierra said he would have a ferry permit for me. Can you find out where it is and get it for me?"

"No problem, ma'am. I'll find it and bring it here." He hurried off toward the airport administration office.

While he was gone, Danielle found a telephone and placed a call to her London office. Carolyn, her London secretary, answered.

"Carolyn, it's Danielle. I can't take time to explain right now but I want you to call Eric Savage and tell him to implement security plan Alpha immediately. I'm at Lisbon Airport and will be flying directly to Paris. I'll get a commercial flight to Guernsey from there." She hung up and began looking for the aircraft tug and its driver.

When she found the tug driver, she instructed him to pull the aircraft from the hangar. By the time it was outside on the ramp and was being refueled, the American officer was crossing the parking area from the administration office with the ferry permit in his hand.

"Where're you assigned, Colonel?" she inquired as she supervised the refueling.

"Ramstein and here on TDY this week. But I'm transferring next week to The Hague for two months, then I'm retiring. I've put in my twenty, and it isn't fun any more. There isn't the adventure there used to be, and there's too much 'Mickey Mouse'", he said, referring to the explosive growth of bureaucratic requirements for himself and other pilots.

"Are you married?"

He chuckled, "Are you interested?"

Danielle smiled and shook her head. "No, but I'm wondering if you would be available for a potentially dangerous job, and I don't want to be responsible for making any widows out of wives."

"That depends on the job, and no, I'm not married. Divorced, no kids."

"How would you like a job flying the fastest and largest aircraft in the world?"

"I don't follow you. The fastest aircraft in the world is the SR-71 but it isn't the largest. And the largest certainly isn't the fastest. What are you proposing?"

"A company with which I'm associated is building a new airplane. It'll be several times as fast as the SR-71. I'm not sure exactly how fast, but over 17,000 miles per hour, somewhere around Mach 25. And I'm not sure what its ultimate gross weight will be, but it will certainly be more than the Antonov 126, which is currently the largest. If you pass our skills tests and physical tests, you'd start as a test pilot, and then move on to being a line pilot hauling cargo in that plane. It might be the fastest truck in history. I know it won't have the same zip as an F-5, but it will be considerably faster, and no one, I repeat, *no one* has ever done it before. We're going to have about two dozen flight crews. Are you interested?"

"I'm not troubled by hauling cargo in the airplane you describe. I've had a few tours in C-5s, C-17s, C-130s and 141s. But the plane you're describing certainly doesn't sound like any cargo plane I've ever heard of before."

"It isn't."

"But over 17,000 miles per hour! WOW! You could go into orbit going that fast."

"You catch on quick. Are you interested?"

"Yes, Ma'am!! You bet! I sure am!"

"Will I be able to locate you through NATO HQ? I might be able to use your talents very soon."

"Sure. I'll make sure the NATO G-1 has my address and phone number. Give me a shout if I can be of service."

"Thanks again for keeping me in one piece," she said. "I'd better get on my way. I want to make Paris while it's still light, in case I have to land to refuel. This beast really sucks down the kerosene below 15,000 feet. The problem's in the pressurization system so I'll have to fly below 10,000 feet and unpressurized. By the way, don't mention the job to anyone, okay?"

"Roger that. Good luck." He stuck out his hand and shook hers. She stepped into the airplane, pulled the door closed, and sat down in the pilot seat. After starting the engines, she completed the pre-takeoff checklist then taxied the MU-2 to the active runway and took off into the afternoon sky.

The flight to Paris was uneventful. When she landed at Orly, she taxied directly to the Global maintenance hangar and sought out Jacques Belmont, a maintenance crew chief who was fiercely loyal to her.

"Jacques, I passed out while flying this airplane at 23,000 feet this morning and I'm lucky to be alive. I want a careful inspection, of every part if necessary, to know why. Start with the cabin pressure regulator on the Number One engine. It has been sabotaged to route exhaust gas to the cabin and I have no idea who did it. But I passed out too fast for that to be the only cause, and I wouldn't have wakened again if it had been just that. This is scary and I *must* know what is going on." She started to tremble again realizing how close she had come to dying. She related in detail all she could remember from the near-disaster.

Her faithful crew chief nodded and his face became very unpleasant. It was plain that the fact someone had tried to kill her had made him madder than she was.

"I'll call you as soon as I finish, Miss. Where can I reach you?"

"I'm going home on a commercial flight. This whole thing has worn me out. You have my number."

CHAPTER 29

At 10 the following morning the phone rang. It was Jacques Belmont from Global Aeronautique. "Miss, I checked everything on the airplane. The only thing out of order was that hose and extra regulator on the Number 1 engine. I removed it and replaced the hose with a new hose."

"Thank you, Jacques. I really appreciate it. Tell the company to send me a bill."

"You're welcome, Miss. And no one here will send you anything. We charged the time to maintenance on our new boss's plane. He'll never notice. Why don't you come back and work here with us again? The whole crew misses you. *We* wouldn't let your plane get monkeyed-around with like that." Danielle was still unsure whether Jacques' loyalty was romantic or fatherly, but she knew from years of working with him that his concern for her was sincere.

"You are very sweet, Jacques. And tell the men and women in the shop I miss them too, but I have a new project and it just makes coming back impossible. But, Jacques, there is something else."

"What is that, Miss?"

"I have been thinking about my experience yesterday. There has to be more to it. If I had been knocked out by the exhaust coming into the cabin, I should have stayed out longer than I did, or even died, but I regained consciousness quite rapidly. There must have been another factor. Are you sure you checked everything?"

"Yes, Miss. We even checked the oxygen system, and it was getting a good flow to your oxygen mask."

"Well, check it again. Look for anything that could be made to look right when it's really wrong. You know I check out everything on an aircraft before I fly it, and I didn't find any discrepancy during my preflight checklists. I blame myself for not finding the tampered-with air-conditioning. I should have looked more carefully inside the cowlings. There must be something else."

He knew how precise and thorough she was in her flying.

"Yes, Miss. I will call you back as soon as we check everything again."

Sweet Jacques. She made a mental note to transfer enough to Global to pay for the work on the MU-2. Jacques would be very surprised if he knew she, through several intermediate corporations, actually owned Global.

She returned to her work and worked through the evening. It was 9:30 the next morning when the phone rang again. It was Jacques.

"Miss, we found the problem."

"Well, what was it?"

"Everything mechanical checked out perfectly on the airplane, but we couldn't explain why you passed out so quickly, then regained consciousness again so rapidly after you reached a lower altitude, so I rechecked the oxygen system. It all seemed just as it should be, so, just on a hunch, I had the guys in the lab check the oxygen cylinders themselves. Miss, they were filled with pure nitrogen. There was no oxygen at all in them. If your oxygen mask hadn't fallen off, you would have been dead in minutes."

Danielle thanked him and hung up. Some one wanted her dead. If they had succeeded, her plane and she would now either be on the bottom of the Atlantic in thousands of feet of water a hundred miles west of Gibraltar or plastered on some European mountainside.

She began to realize other ways someone could kill her, if that was their intent. She had driven from the airport to the house two nights before and her car, which was always locked in the hangar during her trips, had been parked in front of the house since she returned, because she had been too exhausted to open the garage door. She thought about what had happened to the airplane. It must have been sabotaged while it was parked on the apron in Marrakech during her visit to the antenna site. Someone wanted her out of the way. Why? Who? It could only be related to the power project. If they knew where and how to sabotage her airplane, the car would not be safe to drive either.

She decided to call the St. Andrew parish police.

"Constable Smythe? This is Danielle Simones. Yes, at Ousley Manor. I need your assistance. Someone is trying to kill me. My airplane was deliberately sabotaged and two days ago I nearly was killed in it as a result. Whoever it was knew where I was, and how to arrange a sophisticated job of sabotage. I just learned of the extent of their effort a few minutes ago.

"Now I suspect that my car, which I left outside for the last two nights, might also be booby-trapped somehow. I need to get to London, and don't want to drive my car to the airport because it also may be booby-trapped, so I'm taking a taxi.

"But I don't want to leave the car here if it poses a risk to anyone. Could you have someone check it out for me, and if it's all right, lock it in my garage? I don't know what form any tampering might take. It could be anything from cut brake lines to a bomb, or it might be nothing.

"I'm sorry I can't be more certain, but I don't want to take any chances. Yes, it's a silver Aston Martin. It's parked in the drive in front of the house. I'll leave the keys with my housekeeper, Mrs. Benson. And Constable, please be careful."

The Constable said he would get a bomb squad in from Scotland Yard to check the car for explosives, and meanwhile would place a guard on it to insure that no one came near it. If there were no bombs, he would have his mechanics give it a good going-over and, if it was safe to drive, they would lock it in the garage as she had requested. He knew she was a sensible person, not prone to hysteria. If she said be careful, he would be.

Her secretary in the London office answered on the first ring. "Carolyn, this is Danielle. Has anything unusual occurred there during the last week? Do I have any mail?"

Carolyn said there were some packages, but they hadn't brought them up yet from the mail room. She told Carolyn to have Security check them out, and treat them as suspected explosives, as well as any other still-unopened packages in the building. Also, to have a 24-hour guard placed on the house in Guernsey and to give the guards the special password to identify themselves to the personnel at the house.

The taxi was waiting outside in front of the house. Danielle put some clean clothes in a bag and went into the kitchen. Mrs. Benson was there, rearranging the contents of cabinets under the counter.

"Ellen, you need to be especially careful around here. Someone tried to kill me yesterday, and I don't know how far they're willing to go. I've asked the police to come and check out my car for bombs or other tampering. They're going to have a guard on it until they finish checking it out. When they get here, call Constable Smythe at the parish police station and verify the identity of the policemen. If they are who they claim to be, give them the keys to the car. They're supposed to lock it in the garage when they're done. Meanwhile, tell Alfred to stay away from it, and to keep his eyes open for any strangers or other possible dangers. I don't know what form it might take, but whoever it is, they might try anything. Also, I'm sending a security force to guard the house around the clock. They will have our special code for you to identify them. Alfred should not let them in either, until they give you our secret code. Understand?"

The housekeeper, awed by the sudden imposition of security measures and fearing undefined threats to her and her husband's safety, nodded her head. She was frightened almost speechless. "Miss Danielle,..." she finally said, "are Albert and I in danger?"

"I hope not. I think they're only trying to get me. If I see any sign that they're after my associates, including you, we'll close up the house, and you'll take a paid vacation for a while, and we'll put the animals in a kennel. I don't want anything to happen to you." Danielle smiled her warmest smile. "Good cooks are too hard to find." They both laughed, the housekeeper a little nervously, and Danielle purely for show. She was very scared, but tried to hide it as she walked out the kitchen door, around the house, and got into the taxi.

At the island airport, she bought a one-way ticket to Heathrow, and started considering the situation all over again. Who was it? What would they try next? Where? Was she the only target?

As she walked into the building housing the London office, a guard at the door stopped her.

"Identification, please."

She pulled out her company identification card, inserted it into a slot, and placed her right thumb on a scanner at the guard's desk. It verified her identity.

"Hello, Ollie," she said. "How is the missus?"

"She's fine, Miss Simones. Thanks for asking. Sorry about the hold-up here, but the Chief said to give everyone the formal treatment, and he's watching for sure on the TV." He jerked his thumb over his shoulder at the concealed TV camera.

"Good work, Ollie. You did exactly the right thing. I want everyone to furnish full ID, even the Chief and myself, and he knows it. And please tell your wife I want to visit her and see that new baby sometime soon. Okay?"

"Yes, Ma'am. Thank you, Ma'am." He turned to another visitor who was just arriving at the building entrance. "Identification, please."

Danielle went to her office and picked up the secure phone to Belau. Her secretary at the spaceport answered.

"Bill, get in touch with the department heads immediately. I'll be there in twenty-four hours and want a full staff meeting one-half hour after I arrive. Andy Brown should be in Seattle visiting Boeing, but it will be the middle of the night there, so have him on a speakerphone with a scrambler. Tell everyone to be sharp about security." She signed off.

An hour later, she arrived back at Heathrow, paid cash for a ticket to Tokyo, via Bangkok, and boarded the plane. As the airliner climbed eastward over Europe, she opened her computer and began setting out additional measures to protect the project against whomever it was that was trying to stop it.

Item one: No advance travel booking. All tickets to be paid cash. That meant additional drawing accounts for all of the top personnel to provide them sufficient funds.

Item two: Limit travel, as much as possible, to cities where we have offices, and always use our own people to pick up our traveling personnel. No taxis. No advance reservations for limos. If someone has the ability to access airline reservations, they could be waiting for our personnel when they reach their destinations. Have each company convert two offices into executive apartments. No more hotels for our VIPs.

Item three: Security and personnel must start rechecking the background information on every employee who has not previously been completely vetted.

Item four: Quality Control must be ratcheted up several notches to be sure to catch any intentional defects that might be slipped through as part of someone's efforts to sabotage the project. She recalled the preflight of her MU-2 two days before. It seemed as if two weeks had passed since then. She had looked carefully into the Number 1 engine cowling at that time and had not spotted the hose from the wrong turbine section. It was just another hose. And no visual inspection could have discovered that there was nitrogen in the oxygen bottles. Even Jacques had missed it the first time around. She simply had to anticipate any possible sabotage and prevent it.

Item five: All transport equipment must be re-inspected. This means cars, trucks, ships, planes, trains; anything our supplies travel on must be inspected for possible sabotage.

Item six: All transportation must, wherever possible, be made redundant. That is, split shipments so they go on more than one carrier or means of conveyance. Ship half by plane and half by ship, or on two different airlines or two different shipping companies. That way, if a plane crashes or a ship sinks, we will lose only half a shipment.

Item seven: Be planning how to implement our own complete transportation system, on which we can provide our own security and maintenance.

As she wrote, she realized that the costs would go out of sight if she had to implement all of these measures. She was defining an unlimited range of possibilities to guard against. Somewhere the security measures had to be limited. Transportation alone could cost more than the manufacture of the space plane. Yet she had to satisfy herself that not only was she not endangering the staff and shipments of materials for the project, but also that she was not subjecting the public to risk of sabotage of, for example, a commercial airliner. She remembered the American National Airlines jet that had been blown up over France by terrorists. She had been on the investigation board and still had nightmares about it.

By the time the jet landed in Bangkok, she had completed an outline of the additional security measures she planned to give the staff at the meeting. She deplaned and told the station agent she was ill (a lie) and could not continue to fly on to Tokyo without a day in bed (another lie). She didn't want anyone who might be tracking her to know what flight she was on. She was getting more paranoid by the minute. After going through customs, she took the first taxi in the queue and went directly to the charter aircraft terminal where she hired a Learjet to fly directly to Belau. She was there four hours later, having slept poorly for the last leg.

CHAPTER 30

September 10

Danielle was anxious to start the meeting. Maurice d'Orleans was there, with Bill Townsend, Jean Claude Lebec, Cliff Kelly and Bob MacDonald.

"Uncle Bob," she exclaimed, "I didn't know you would be here. You sure have marvelous timing."

"I hadn't seen my favorite girl in too long, so I came on out. What's all the excitement?" he asked.

"Trouble. That's what we're all here for." She turned to Bill Townsend. "Have we reached Andy?"

"Over here!" came the voice from the speakerphone. Bill nodded.

"Andy, have you been introduced around?"

"No, I just rang in a few minutes ago and was talking to the engine shop. I asked Bill to cut in when you arrived. Who's there?"

"All right. Here with me are Maurice, Bill, Cliff, Jean Claude and Bob MacDonald. Eric is out-of-touch in England, and I'll call him later. It's the middle of the night there right now. Bill, record this meeting and transmit it to London so Eric'll have it when he gets to work.

"All of you may know I went to Morocco last week to visit the Atlas Mountains site. I was there for two days and then started back for Guernsey in my plane. I almost didn't make it. While I was in Morocco, someone did a complex job of sabotage on my airplane, and it was only dumb luck that I'm here today. This was *not* an amateur job. It was so well carried out that I'm convinced all our operations are in danger.

"There are a number of things we have to do, and I want them implemented immediately. First, no more advance travel reservations for our key personnel. We must assume that if they know me, they know who our people are. If someone has access to a computer reservation system, they might be able to booby-trap our flights. Instead, we buy our tickets with cash at the terminal when we're ready to fly, and only buy one leg of the trip at a time. It's going to be a pain in the butt and expensive, but until we know more, I don't want to endanger the public who might be flying with us. Get with accounting and establish petty cash funds in each office for the managers to draw from if they have to travel. When any key employee leaves their base, I want them to have 5,000 dollars in cash on their person as travel money. Work out security arrangements to help them carry it safely. Minor employees can still be booked through Neverland Travel, but we need a security check on all of their personnel, and see if there's a way to disguise our accounts there to conceal the fact that it's our personnel who are traveling.

"Second, try to limit travel to cities where we have offices. If we have to meet with someone, have them come to our subsidiary, and we'll meet them there. Each company is to convert two offices into apartments and have a car and driver available to pick up our people when they come into town. Our key people can't use public conveyances, particularly taxis or limos where they might be isolated and attacked or kidnapped.

"Third, security and personnel have to review all of our personnel records, particularly in critical positions, and insure that their backgrounds have been carefully and thoroughly screened. If there's someone who could sabotage us from the inside, I want to know about it. Take no action against the employee but let me know."

"Fourth, every company has to redouble its Quality Control measures, whether we're manufacturing the item ourselves, or buying from a vendor. Everything must be checked and double checked. Whoever tried to get me in Morocco diverted exhaust gas into the cockpit. When I smelled it, I automatically grabbed for my oxygen mask, as they must have known I would. But they'd also changed the gas in my oxygen cylinder for nitrogen, which is odorless, so I didn't smell anything strange, I just passed out. If I'd taken time to put the strap over my head before I lost consciousness, I wouldn't be here now. We're dealing with someone who knows the details about how we work and where we're vulnerable. If we're to counter any future attempts, we have to anticipate how they can try again. Every bulk shipment must be tested for the purity of its contents. That means check each shipment of fuels for our vehicles and generators as well as jet fuel, all gases and lubricants. We may need to expand the Quality Control Lab.

"Fifth, any commercial carrier hauling our cargoes must be carefully examined to insure against sabotage. We have to avoid shipping cargoes on passenger aircraft. I couldn't stand for a jetliner to be bombed just because it had some of our cargo on it. That's part of the reason for not using advance reservations. That brings me to number six.

"From now on, when we make a shipment, split it among carriers whenever possible. If one shipment is lost or delayed, we'll still have half the delivery.

"Seven. Security must send a team to Marrakech and interview the airport officials to try to determine who sabotaged my plane. Maybe we can get an idea of who they are; maybe we can figure out their next move and how to stop them. I doubt if we'll learn anything there, but we know that's where they've struck once. I'll talk to Eric about that and have him try to figure out who could be behind the sabotage.

"Eight. Alert all the antenna sites to be aware of anything unusual and to report it to us as soon as possible. Ask also if there's been anything strange before now. We may have to ask our host-countries to beef up their security too.

"Does anyone have any other initial suggestions?" There were no responses. "Okay, where do we go from here? Speak up."

"Suppose we take all these security measures and nothing else happens? What then?" Jean Claude wondered.

"Then nothing happens," she answered. "That's the ideal situation. It will mean our security measures have paid off."

"Well, then!" said Maurice, "that should solve it."

"It isn't that easy," Danielle growled. "Every additional step we have to take costs us money, and slows us down. Whoever it is, we have to assume that they know we're on a tight budget and that our investors are anxious about us meeting our projected schedules. If we run out of money before we finish phase one, additional investment may be impossible to raise. We'll have created the most expensive space junk in the history of mankind."

Bill spoke. "Suppose we do all this investigation and find out who's behind it. What good does that do us? We have no police force or army. Do we go out and ask them to stop, or what?"

"I don't know. Any ideas?"

Maurice was staring into a video image of the Belau forest on the wall with a sour expression on his face. "It could be anyone. It could be the nature-lovers, or ... maybe the oil companies?"

Bill had a notepad on his lap. He looked up. "What if our adversary is a country, rather than a group? Our actions put a crimp into the space plans of several countries, even if they did agree to it. It's possible they never expected us to actually get this far."

Andy's voice piped up from the speakerphone on the desk. "I think we would do better to focus on our current activities. The first plane's cargo doors are almost finished at Gulfstream and the second plane's components are nearing completion at factories around the world. I'm concerned about seeing that they're done, done right, and protected at every step. We'll need extra personnel to inspect each of the components before they leave the manufacturers and to ride with them enroute to Belau. And these can't be clerks. They have to be trained security personnel."

"We haven't really addressed security in this context before," Danielle said, "other than to set up security plan Alpha procedures as a contingency to protect our plants, but how far can we go to protect the parts? If someone tries to damage a part, can our guards shoot them?"

Kelly looked grim. "We don't have any police power anywhere, not even here in Belau. If we find a trespasser, or even catch a saboteur in the act, the most we can do with him is turn him over to local authorities. I suppose we could contact Interpol, but I'm doubtful about their willingness to assist, particularly since we can't show any crime yet."

"What about what they did to my plane?"

"What about it?" asked Kelly. "Did it crash? ... No. I'll bet it isn't even still sabotaged. You did have it repaired immediately, didn't you?"

She nodded silently.

Kelly continued. "So there's no evidence of what you say happened. No fingerprints. No body. No nothing."

"Yes. I wasn't thinking. I just wanted to find out how I'd failed in my pre-flight inspection."

"It doesn't matter," Kelly said. "The point is, if we authorize our guard personnel to use deadly force to protect our property, we have to be able to justify it, to ourselves and to others. We can't have our guards locked up in some prison just because they were doing what we told them to. We haven't hired a bunch of double-O-sevens. These are just ordinary men and women with a little extra training and a badge and a gun; more than anything else the gun is to protect themselves from bad guys who might try to get past them."

"I want a step-by-step breakdown of the final production activities and the delivery steps for each component," she said. "Then I want a special team of engineering, transportation and security personnel to evaluate those breakdowns to determine where we are weak. Got that, Maurice?"

Maurice signaled his agreement. She went on. "Jean Claude, is security plan Alpha up and running at the subsidiaries?"

"Yes'm. The last to get with the program went to full security twelve hours after you called. It was late at night there, in Oregon, when they got the word and they were a little slow. We don't think anyone outside this room knows it's one of our subsidiaries."

"Make sure they respond more rapidly next time. We need all our subsidiaries and suppliers to notify their local police and ask for extra patrols. Give them some top-secret mumbo-jumbo and suggest international terrorists have struck a related company in another part of the world. Don't be specific, don't say where. Just ask for extra patrols.

"Next, Maurice: get with the Belau Minister in charge of public safety. Have him deputize all of our security personnel as police officers. And you have to re-examine the perimeter security and protection plan to insure that intruders can't get onto this installation.

"Cliff, we need the ability to use deadly force here at the base if necessary to protect this project. Have the Belau laws examined for any necessary changes and, if changes are required, I want the draft language on my desk in 48 hours. I'll handle it with the President. Okay?"

Kelly nodded. Danielle turned and looked at MacDonald. "Uncle Bob, you've been pretty quiet. What do you think?"

He didn't speak for a long time. Finally, he looked around the room and his voice was nearly a whisper. "This is as much a psychological situation as a physical one. Whoever it was that sabotaged your plane thought they could stop the project by getting rid of you, Danielle. If we do anything overt, and they're monitoring our activities, they'll know we're sensitive to the pressure they're applying. We mustn't give them that reward for their efforts. If they sabotage us and succeed next time, we have to absorb it and never give a sign that we've been hurt. They may be as interested in making us look like we're failing, as they are in actually making us fail. Everything we do as a result of the attempt to make your plane crash must look like our routine business. For that reason, I think it's a bad idea to ask local police to run extra patrols. If someone is watching, but not part of our staff, they might not notice the implementation of security plan Alpha, but they *would* notice extra police. They might even be inside the police. We need to be the world's best poker players right now, and never give a hint of what kind of hand we're holding. Otherwise, anything negative will surely be used against us." He paused. "And we have to assume that you, personally, are still the prime target." Danielle could see in his eyes that he didn't like that thought, and neither did she.

She looked around. "Anyone else agree with that?" Heads around the room nodded affirmatively. "All right. Scrub the police notification. But internal plant security must be as tight as it can be. The photocell factory and the three antenna contractors are major points of weakness. We must insure that there are no hostile acts directed at them. Jean Claude, could, for instance, a truck full of explosives be driven close enough to any of those four plants to put it out of commission, as was done to the US Embassy in Lebanon?"

"I don't think so," he replied. "All four have large properties with remote receiving buildings far from the production and storage buildings. I'd be surprised if an outside vehicle could penetrate to either production or storage. They could lose their receiving buildings though. The main photocell production is in the old Naval Ordnance Facility in Indianapolis that was built for high security to build NORDEN bombsights during World War II. It should still be all right."

"Andy," Danielle continued, "get me a list of aerospace plants building our components and how many more "inspectors" we need for security and real inspection at each site. Can you have it by tomorrow evening, say thirty-six hours from now?"

"That's a little tight, but I'll have a couple of the project managers work it out for you ASAP. Maybe we can do it faster."

"Good."

Jean Claude suddenly became agitated. "Oh, my God! Food. Water. We have to protect the food supply! We have a planeload of food shipped in here from the States each week, and buy more on the local economy. How do we prevent someone from poisoning the food or water?"

"We won't worry about water," she said. "Everyone is drinking bottled water, I think. The de-sal plant for wash water is inside the perimeter, and we're pumping from our own wells. But have the lab test the water periodically, just for insurance. With regard to the food and drinking water, what's the procedure for buying it? Are we doing anything to insure it isn't tampered with?"

"It never occurred to me that we needed to be concerned about it. We have commercial provisioning companies in Los Angeles send us regular orders each week for the commissary, just as if we were another grocery store in L.A., except the shipping containers of food are delivered to Los Angeles International Airport and loaded directly on a C-5. The same for the bottled water and bulk drinking water."

"Would there be a benefit to letting the managers of the provisioning companies in on our security concerns?"

Maurice shook his head. "I don't think they'd believe us, and they might prefer to lose our business than deal with our problems. It would require explaining what we're doing, and telling that to anyone who doesn't need to know is bad policy. Anyway, our food is pulled from huge food inventories which serve all of the L.A. area. That entire stock would have to be sabotaged to get us. It seems like a long way for someone to go to get at us. There should be more direct ways."

"Okay. We keep on as before with the food. But at this end, I want random testing of all fresh produce, and alert all of our people using the commissary and the commissary staff to be on the look-out for any signs of tampering with packaging; to immediately notify their superiors if they spot anything suspicious; and particularly not to eat it. And I want the bio-med team to analyze biological warfare agents, and get together a plan for response if anyone tries to spring some kind of disease organism on us. We may need a stock of antidotes, anti-toxins, something like that. Ask them, then do it.

"Let's review. No advance travel bookings for our VIPs. Bill, you handle that.

"Set up VIP apartments at each of our subsidiaries' offices. Recheck our personnel backgrounds. Jean Claude, those two are yours.

"Upgrade Quality Control. Andy, you and Maurice work together on that one.

"Security checks for aircraft and other transport carrying our cargoes, and split shipments to reduce the risk of loss. Maurice, you work with Jean Claude and Eric Savage on those two.

"Security to check out Marrakech to try to determine what happened to my plane. I'll coordinate that with Eric Savage in London.

"Alert antenna sites. Bill, you notify the site supervisors.

"Extra inspectors and guards to protect the aircraft components. Analysis of our weaknesses in the space plane production. Andy, you and Maurice work out the details of that.

"We'll skip the additional local police at the contractors' plants right now, but we'll get our security people deputized here in Belau. Bill and I will handle that, and Cliff, you're going to get me the text of any revisions to the Belau statutes which we need to enable us to proceed.

"Maurice, you're going to review our perimeter security with Eric. If we need a completely new security plan, don't hesitate to say so.

"Increased security at the antenna and photovoltaic plants. Jean Claude, that's yours and Eric's.

"Additional lab testing of supplies, water and produce brought in, and look for package tampering. Maurice, you gear up the lab to test everything we buy in bulk and random samples of produce. Bill, get a memo out to the manager of the commissary about the foodstuffs.

"This has to be communicated to the employees here. Maurice, how many are on-site right now?"

"A little over six thousand."

"Okay," she said. "Two levels of notices. One for department heads and plant managers, advising them of increased security measures. No exceptions to plan Alpha, plus the other things we've discussed here today. Then a second general but very important memo to all employees and dependents on-site. It needs to say, "Because we will soon be assembling the space plane, we're increasing the security level of this installation. Be conscious of what is happening around you when you're in town. Don't discuss company business. Watch for any sign of tampering with packaging." Bill, you write up the general employee memo and a generic department head memo. Send the department head memo to the people in this meeting for them to tailor to their own area of responsibility. Also, you coordinate with the bio-med personnel about possible biological agents, and be sure to implement the countermeasures.

"There sure are a lot of new procedures here that we all could have lived without. I guess if whoever it was thought they could get my panties in a twist by working over my airplane, they were right, weren't they?" She chuckled, then became serious again.

"This experience with my plane has made me think a lot about this team and how important you are to me. I'm intensely proud of each of you and how you've managed the project so far. If they should succeed in getting me, I want you to carry on, okay? We have The Plan. Maurice succeeds me, then Jean Claude, then Andy, then Cliff. Once I'm gone, you'll have to figure things out as you see them, but there *is* The Plan, and I wish you luck."

"Don't quit yet, boss." Maurice shook his finger at her. "We're not going to let anything happen to you, so you can't lay this burden on us. You'll have to finish it yourself." There was a nervous laugh around the room in agreement.

Danielle continued, "Is there anything else anyone needs to bring up? If not, let's get back to our "normal" work. Andy, do you have a status report for me on the components?"

"It's already been sent, and the final wing-fuselage assembly is progressing smoothly in the main hangar."

Bill interjected, "It's waiting for you on your desk."

"Great. Okay, Andy. By the way, I think I found us another pilot. U.S. Air Force, experienced in fighters, B-1, and jet transports. He should be with us soon. Keep me advised as things develop on production."

She turned off the speakerphone as Maurice, Jean Claude, Cliff and Bill left the office. Only MacDonald remained.

"I know why you're here," she said, and smiled, "I thought I'd miss it too, and had expected to still be in Europe. But here I am, so let's go down to the hangar and watch."

They walked out of her office, past Bill's desk, which was empty. The entire building was virtually unoccupied. As they walked across the open area between the office building and the immense hangar, they could see the crowd overflowing out of the doors on the hangar's side.

"Let's go in the back way and avoid the mob," she suggested.

They went to the rear and entered by a small door at the corner. Inside, a metal stairway led upward to an elevator to the service area for the bridge cranes a hundred feet above the hangar floor. There was, in effect, a balcony several hundred feet long across the width of Hangar Bay 1, above the upper tracks for the hangar doors. From that vantage point, they had an unobstructed view of the entire hangar bay. The fuselage and wing components had been collected in the main hangar and assembled into two huge parts. Many of the project's employees were now gathered in the hangar below to watch the most significant step to date in the project – the mating of the wings to the fuselage. As the final fastenings were test-installed, albeit temporarily, there was a great cheer from the crowd. Their baby finally looked like an airplane, sort of, minus a lot of peripheral parts. It took a lot of imagination to visualize the nose, wingtips, rudders and other missing pieces.

Uncle Bob and Danielle exchanged a celebratory hug then began to retrace the route back down to the ground level. At the base of the stairs, they turned, and instead of leaving the building, opened a door onto the hangar floor.

The cheers had barely died down when a voice announced over the public address system that three aircraft were now in the airport traffic pattern with the first parts for Low Earth Orbit Station Alpha, or "LEO-A."

They crossed the hangar floor toward the enormous structure that would be the first space plane. Part of the remaining empty space in the hangar was for test assembly of the low earth orbit satellites. It was waiting for the arrival of those components, just beyond the area where the 12 huge engines for the first three space planes were stored, in their shipping containers, under plastic covers. Those engines had been delivered a month earlier, had been test run, and were ready for installation in the aircraft. They towered over Danielle and Bob as they walked past them.

They climbed a rolling service stair to a rear hatch into the half-assembled fuselage. The hydraulic systems had been finished, but the inside of the fuselage seemed to be a rat's nest of wire. The wiring was only half completed, even as the wings were being installed. As they climbed from the cargo floor into the cockpit, Uncle Bob saw the empty spaces where the many instrument panels would eventually be located. The avionics, radios and other navigation equipment that had arrived months earlier, still were stored in the receiving area of the office building, but could not be installed until both the wiring and hydraulics were complete. All the electricians were down on the hangar floor, celebrating with the rest of the workers.

"It certainly is complex-looking," he said, noticing wires hanging from every opening and wondering how anyone could tell one wire from another.

She laughed. "It will be a lot neater when it's ready to fly. The big concerns now are making everything come together on schedule. The project managers continue to find things to worry about: tires are being delayed by Michelin's concern about the tires' ability to withstand the high weight and speed of take-off. The plane's gross weight will be around 2.5 million pounds, and lift-off is supposed to occur at 240 knots. They have no facility to test the tires under those conditions, so they think we're going to test them here the hard way, and if we're wrong in our confidence in the tires, we'll have a 2.5-million-pound, four-billion-dollar sled sliding down the runway on a couple dozen of their flat tires. Actually, I arranged with NASA to use their tire testing facility, and the tires passed, but I haven't been able to tell that to Michelin because of NASA's security requirements.

"The cargo doors and control surfaces haven't arrived yet, and the people I pay to worry for me are worrying that they won't fit. We'll see. Come on."

They went back down to the hangar floor. Standing beneath the broad nose of the plane, it seemed bigger than any plane could possibly be and still get off the ground. She had work to do and started back for the office.

As they walked, she said, "Uncle Bob, I met a pilot in Portugal and need to get him for this plane. He's retiring soon from the U.S. Air Force, and is currently assigned to NATO. His name is Hank Taylor. Who do we have to reach to get him retired right away and sent to work for us?"

"I'll call a friend at the Pentagon and see what they can do. Hank Taylor, you say. Is there some romance here?" he asked jokingly.

Danielle blushed. "Ha. Ha. Sorry," she said. "He was part of the team that kept me from becoming a statistic a couple of days ago. I want to check out his record and his flying, but my sense is that he has what we need to be one of our pilots. We have twenty-nine others already in training in Lakeland, Florida. FlightSafety there has developed what the engineers believe is a very accurate simulator program for the space plane flight profile, and our flight crews are there now. If Hank Taylor is available, I want him sent directly to FlightSafety, to give us ten full crews. Carolyn in the London office can get his travel arrangements for him. I'll meet him in Lakeland and give him a flight check to verify his proficiency, but I'm confident he'll pass."

"I'll make some calls and as soon as I hear from the Air Force, I'll let you know." he said.

"I'm going to call Hank today and re-confirm his willingness to be part of the program. He said he was interested three days ago, but he might have been just looking for a date. Plus, our accelerated pace may catch him off-guard, and if he's as good a pilot as he looks I don't want to scare him away."

Uncle Bob changed the subject and said, "This has been a busy morning for me. I think I'll go to my apartment and take a nap. You forget I'm an old man."

Danielle put her arm around him, and gave him a hug. "I don't forget, and I need a nap too. I've been on the run since I left Marrakech. Tell you what, you have your nap, then meet me at my quarters for dinner. The cook does a wonderful baked fish in a wine sauce, served over wild rice. You'll love it. If I ate it very often, I'd weigh three hundred pounds. I have to go back upstairs now and dictate a few letters, and order our fish caught, then go have a lie-down, and meet you for dinner at, say about 7:30?"

Danielle paused and looked him in the eyes. "Things are moving ahead, and I'm still alive. What more could a girl ask?"

"What a girl," he replied. "If you weren't my god-daughter, I'd marry you and let you bring your cook with you."

"Ha. Dirty old man. All you want is my cook. Have a nice nap." They parted and he walked slowly down the sidewalk toward the visitors' apartments as she opened the door and entered the office building.

CHAPTER 31

That evening after dinner, she was back in her office. She turned on the computer and selected Eric Savage from the telephone directory. A moment later the computer was connected to Savage's London office via the secure line. She picked up the handset and said, "This is Danielle Simones, calling for Mr. Savage." Savage's secretary put her through immediately.

"Savage here."

"Eric, it's Danielle. How's the security situation there? Anything unusual?"

"No ma'am. Nothing out of the ordinary, except we're handling all packages as if they could be bombs, and every person entering your building has to be a properly identified employee or vouched-in according to the security plan. I received the recording of your meeting this morning from Bill Townsend and have reviewed it."

"I'm sorry I didn't have time to fill you in on the reason for security plan Alpha before I left London, but you need to know, and I need you to do some special investigating for the company. When my plane was in Morocco someone sabotaged it, and I'm only here by dumb luck." She outlined to him the events of her flight and what she had been told by Jacques Belmont.

"I want you to send investigators to Marrakech to find out what they can about when and how my airplane was sabotaged. It might help them if they go first to see Jacques Belmont at Global Aeronautique Internationale. Learn everything they can from Jacques and his crew, if necessary, about the condition of the plane when they fixed it. It's still there, if they want to examine it. I need a full report.

"Next, I want a comprehensive security analysis of each of the corporations with which we are doing business, and all of the subcontractors. I want to know where the project can be hit by someone who would like to slow or stop it.

"But I don't want the contractors or subs to know we're doing a security check. They're already on plan Alpha, and I don't want to be raising unnecessary worries on their part. If you find anything particularly alarming, of course I want you to call me immediately, otherwise just have it in a report in say, three weeks. I'll arrange for your personnel to have free access to the contractors' facilities, under the guise of being 'efficiency experts.' If they run into any interference, get names and let me know, and I'll take care of it. Any questions?"

"No, ma'am. I know the major corporations by heart, and I'll get a list of all the subs from the files. We'll get started right away."

"I'm sorry, it's been a long day. I meant to tell you, I'm having Bill send you a new list of the person to contact at each location. Remember, your personnel are 'efficiency experts' and I'm not telling even the managers of the companies otherwise. Understand?"

She hung up the phone and turned out the lights in the office as she went into her apartment, which adjoined her office. She got into bed, pulled the covers up around her neck, and tried to sleep, but nightmares kept waking her up.

Chapter 32

September 13

The sky was deep blue over Greece, with only a few high cirrus clouds. The Ad Hoc Committee met in a villa high on a mountainside overlooking the Aegean Sea near Athens. The last member to arrive, from Iran, was in high spirits. His mood didn't last long.

As he sat down at the table, the Libyan sitting to his right frowned and said, "What are you so jolly about?"

"We don't have to concern ourselves with that woman anymore. That's cause for celebration."

"You haven't heard?" said the Iraqi.

"Heard what?"

"It didn't work. She was seen by our agent in London entering her office two days after she left Morocco."

"Damn. What happened? Who screwed up?"

The Venezuelan volunteered, "We don't know. The expert said it was a sure thing."

"Some expert. So what do we do now?"

The Libyan answered. "That's why we're meeting today. We need to rethink our plans."

"We need to know why it didn't work," said the Iranian. "Are we still going after the woman, or are we trying to stop the project?"

At that the Peruvian across the table jumped into the conversation. "The woman IS the project. Stop her and the project will stop."

The chairman, from Syria, frowned. "How do you know that? I was skeptical about going after the woman all along. Let's stop this chatter and get down to business. Who wants to start?"

The Venezuelan opened his note pad and started making a list. "We have to do all we can to prevent this project from moving forward. Do we all agree on that?"

Heads nodded around the table. He continued, "Then we have to analyze where the weak spots in their operation are, and hit them there. The woman is a good target, but we can't rely on eliminating just one person to stop the momentum of the project."

The Peruvian leaned back, puffed on the well-chewed end of his cigar, and looked at the Venezuelan. "I want to know what went wrong with the plan to get the woman. What did the expert say? How was the plan to get her supposed to work?"

"I don't want to know," said the chairman. "All we need to know is it didn't work."

"How much did we pay the expert?" the Peruvian demanded. "Too much, I'll bet."

The chairman nodded. "The expert had a very large budget. He made some significant payments to the customs director in Marrakech, and I understand the woman's plane was being stored in the customs hangar. I was told it was easy to insure that she had an 'accident.'"

"Obviously, this expert didn't know what he was talking about. Where do we go from here?" It was the Libyan speaking.

"You're right," the chairman said, addressing the Venezuelan, "we have to decide how to stop this thing."

"We know they're building at least three antennas," said the Venezuelan. "One in Morocco, one in Kenya, and one in Namibia. We should be able to do *something* to block their progress."

The Iraqi spoke up, "All of them except Morocco are miles from anywhere in the middle of deserts. They fly in materials to runways they've built near the construction sites. We can't get near them. Morocco is almost as bad. The supplies get unloaded at the Marrakech airport, and are trucked by road into the Atlas Mountains, but the roads through the mountains are so isolated that we couldn't get people in or out without being discovered. We don't dare do anything that can be traced back to us. Plus, simply hitting a truck or even a whole convoy won't slow them down measurably, because the project is so damn BIG! Each antenna will have probably 10,000 truckloads of materials, maybe more."

The Libyan looked up from his notes. "Back up another notch. Break down the project into its component parts. There are the antennas; there are the satellites; there are the space planes; there are the photovoltaic cells. There are a lot of components and each component has a long list of weak points. All we need to do is find out what they are."

The Iranian added, "Maybe there is a more abstract way to look at their weaknesses. There are materials, people and money. Can we interfere with the flow of any of those?"

"Well, she already has the money," said the Libyan. "We estimate she collected at least 55 billion, so far, and we think that's enough for her to do what she plans. But no one is certain where it is being kept. All the investors that we have been able to investigate show their money cleared through one of several banks in Switzerland, but we can't trace it after that. We think money is paid out of other banks."

"What about the materials? asked the Peruvian. "She has to be buying all kinds of materials. How can we block that flow? What materials is she using? What are they? Where do they come from?"

The chairman tapped his pen on the table. "The personnel have to be critical to this operation. What would ruin their morale? If we can slow them down, we may not need to interrupt the flow of either materials or money. It would be very expensive for her to keep paying all those salaries if she was behind schedule."

"So what does it take to demoralize them?" asked the Peruvian. "There are so many subcontractors that it is impossible to be sure which are working on her project. If we hit one of the subs we know are working on the project, it still doesn't point to the project, because virtually all of those aerospace manufacturers are also making products for other buyers. The other area of weakness is their transportation system. They have to move everything from where it is made to where they use it. Most of that is by air, but they're using ocean shipment for some parts. We know that ships are bringing the poles for the Kenya antenna into port in Mombasa."

The chairman answered, "We haven't seen any poles arriving in any port that could serve the Namibia or Morocco sites."

The Peruvian suggested, "It may be that they're flying in the poles to Namibia and Morocco and we haven't been able to see them because our observers have been in the wrong place at the wrong time."

"Maybe they just haven't started shipping them to Namibia or Morocco yet?" said the chairman. "That's as likely as the theory that they're flying them in."

The Saudi, who had been mostly watching the others argue, finally spoke, "Perhaps there are ways to get the locals in these areas to oppose the antennas. I think we should enlist the help of the local community in stopping these plants. It's critical that we remember this woman does not have unlimited funds, and if we can just slow down work on the program, she may run out of cash and fold up."

The discussion continued for hours without resolution. Eventually, after the committee agreed to continue gathering information and to have another meeting in a month, the members departed.

CHAPTER 33

CONFIDENTIAL MEMORANDUM:
TO: *Savage Security Services*
FROM: *Ronald Fredricks, Investigator*
SUBJECT: *REPORT ON INCIDENT INVOLVING MITSUBISHI MU-2X*
AIRCRAFT, BRITISH REGISTRATION G-L-O-B-E

       The subject aircraft arrived in Marrakech on September 3 at approximately 10 AM local time. It was checked through customs at 10:15, refueled, and tied down on the parking apron in front of the airport administration office. The pilot, Danielle Simones, paid hangar fees for three days in advance and departed from the airport in a private limousine with several unidentified male subjects.

       At approximately 1:30 PM the aircraft was towed into the customs hangar for storage then chocked and locked. The keys were delivered by the ramp attendant to the customs office.

       At approximately 6:40 PM two unidentified male subjects, wearing blue coveralls, arrived at the customs hangar in a white Toyota mini-van with the Global Aeronautique Internationale logo on the doors. The mini-van is believed to have had French registration tags; however, no one was able to recall the numbers. The occupants produced identification as employees of Global Aeronautique Internationale and informed the night manager that they had been sent to perform routine maintenance on the aircraft. No one made any record of the names of the subjects. They were in the hangar for three hours, more or less, then departed.

       Interviews with car rental agencies in Casablanca disclosed that a white Toyota mini-van generally matching the description of the van seen in Marrakech was rented to one Jorge Castillo, a Spanish citizen, at 11:30 AM on September 3. Castillo left a large cash deposit and paid for the rental in Moroccan currency. The vehicle was returned at 8 AM on September 6. The odometer indicated the distance driven was twenty-five kilometers more than twice the distance to Marrakech. The rental agency attendant described the renter as a white male, approximately 180 cm. and 85 kilos, with black hair and a moustache, who spoke Spanish with an unusual accent. The rental agent was unable to identify the accent, but believed it not to be French. The subject left the car rental agency in an unidentified local taxi. Check in Spain reveals that the address given by Castillo on the rental form does not exist.

       Interviews with ticket agents at Casablanca airport indicated that several subjects fitting the description had arrived and departed from Morocco during the relevant periods, but it was not possible to identify those persons from airport records.

       The subject aircraft departed Marrakech at approximately 10 AM September 6. It made a precautionary landing in Lisbon, Portugal, at approximately Noon. Portuguese aviation authorities confirmed the information that was initially furnished this office, but were unable to provide any additional information.

Personnel at Global Aeronautique Internationale's Orly maintenance facility were interviewed. Supervisor Jacques Belmont furnished all relevant information. Pilot Danielle Simones delivered the subject aircraft to Belmont at approximately 5 PM on September 6 and reported difficulties with the cabin pressurization system. Inspection disclosed an unauthorized connection between the turbine exhaust section, at an Exhaust Pressure Ratio (E.P.R.) fitting. The Exhaust Pressure Ratio sensor had been connected to a tee-type fitting so that it would continue to operate, but a section of high temperature/high pressure hose had been connected between the exhaust section of the turbine and the cabin air-conditioning system. This hose was connected in the location where a bleed-air hose normally connected at the bleed-air shutoff valves. The bleed-air hose was missing and the fitting on the compressor assembly had been plugged. An aneroid barometer device had been attached to the bleed-air shutoff valve to keep the valve closed until the aircraft was above twenty thousand feet of altitude.

Supervisor Belmont produced for our investigator's inspection the remains of the unauthorized hose, which Global Aeronautique International mechanics had removed from the aircraft. The hose was 164 cm in length, manufactured by 'Aeroquip' and bore part number 489-09-8433926 and date 08-14-90. The hose was nearly burned through. The bleed-air shut off valve and a check valve and pressure regulating valve were also damaged by the high-temperature exhaust gases to which they were subjected and all had to be replaced. Belmont stated that the hose was not of a type intended for applications having the temperature of the exhaust section of the turbine engine. All the fittings where connections were made have unusual threads and sizes and required special connections to be obtained prior to the tampering.

Supervisor Belmont stated that this factor was particularly important because the owner of this aircraft had special high performance engines installed, which are very different from the standard engines for this model and type of aircraft. The bleed-air fittings for the standard engine are also different from the engines installed in the subject aircraft.

Interview with manufacturer of the hose indicates that the subject part is made for General Electric JT9-D turbojet engines. It was not disclosed what the application is on that engine. The particular hose was sold to Miami Aircraft Supplies and Parts and appears to have been sold to the final purchaser approximately two weeks prior to the subject incident. The Miami parts firm was unable to identify the purchaser, who paid cash. An employee of the Miami firm stated he believed the purchaser was Latin, and had furnished the part number, but this is a common part and the transaction was in no way unusual.

Supervisor Belmont stated that his second inspection of the aircraft revealed that the pilot's oxygen bottles had been tampered with, by being filled with nitrogen instead of oxygen. Belmont stated that there was no possibility that the oxygen bottles could have been accidentally refilled with nitrogen, because the fittings on such bottles are deliberately made with different genders and thread sizes for different types of gases, to prevent such mix-ups. Because the gases are kept at pressures of approximately 200 atmospheres, in order to have refilled the oxygen bottles with nitrogen, it first would have first been necessary to fabricate a special adapter. Belmont stated that any person with the facilities to fabricate the adapter could have filled the oxygen cylinders with nitrogen.

Conclusions:

1.   The persons who tampered with the aircraft had been planning the action for several weeks prior to the actual tampering.

2.   The persons who tampered with the aircraft had access to detailed technical information regarding this particular aircraft model and engine model.

3.   The persons who tampered with the aircraft knew there were special engines installed in the aircraft. It is believed they obtained the information by examining the aircraft when it was parked at another airport during a prior trip.

4.   The persons who tampered with the aircraft knew the aircraft would be coming to Marrakech and would be stored there long enough for them to work on the aircraft. The best hypothesis for how they obtained this information is that they monitored air traffic control clearances and that they had informants within the Marrakech airport authorities.

5.   The persons who tampered with the aircraft intentionally provided at least two methods to cause the aircraft to crash; 1) through asphyxiation of the pilot by exhaust gases, or 2) by producing the same effect by causing the pilot to breath the nitrogen in the oxygen cylinders.

6.   The persons who tampered with the aircraft had inadvertently provided a third method to cause the aircraft to crash, which nearly was effective, in that the unauthorized hose was almost burned through, and would almost certainly have caused an engine fire if the hose had failed in flight.

7.   The target of the action was the pilot of the aircraft.

CHAPTER 34

September 20
Uncle Bob and Danielle again toured the space plane in the hangar. The inside of the fuselage was now neat and orderly. All the wiring was complete, and all the circuits were in the process of being tested for continuity. Final wiring installation in the wings was underway. Four very large cargo aircraft arrived that afternoon with the control surfaces for the first space plane and components for its cargo compartment door. The cargo compartment door was so large that each of the cargo planes could carry only one-quarter of one door, in two pieces, with the cargo door's one-half width positioned diagonally in each giant cargo bay. The eight pieces of the door would undergo final assembly on the aircraft into a single hundred-meter-long, ten-meter-wide door. The elevators, flaps, ailerons, elevons and other control surfaces had to be loaded in the spaces between the cargo door components and the walls of the planes' cargo compartments. The control surfaces themselves were very large and it was a tight squeeze, but everything did just fit. The parts were eventually unloaded into the main hangar, where they were suspended from the roof trusses of the hangar to keep them out of the way of other work in progress. Electronics technicians were beginning to install the flight instruments in the cockpit of the plane.
Danielle received daily reports from Maurice on the assembly of the low earth satellite. She didn't want to bother the workmen but went to the balcony above the hangar doors for a few minutes each day to watch them working. The crew doing the test assembly of the low earth orbit station discovered that the designers' provisions to provide ease of assembly in space had paid off. The designers had planned the assembly to take a month in space, with zero-gravity to help in moving components for assembly. Despite the handicap of Earth gravity, the test assembly teams had been able to completely assemble LEO-A in only 10 days, in one bay of the hangar, to the point where it would have been habitable in space, with the help of the large bridge crane inside the hangar. The satellite technicians were now running test programs to discover, isolate, and correct any design defects or weaknesses.

September 26
The space plane was on schedule, but Danielle needed to go to London to review tax documents for several of her corporations. The trip from Belau to England was uneventful and she was able to get some paperwork done during the long flight from Manila to Bombay, and tried to get some sleep during the flight from Bombay to Heathrow, which arrived at dawn. She went directly to her office.
The London office was just as she had left it a month earlier. Carolyn had Danielle's in-box full of documents awaiting her examination. She spent an hour thumbing through the stack, scanning their contents and sorting the groups of papers into her own categories. The result was the same sequence as Carolyn had given them to her. Personnel were beginning to arrive at the office and Carolyn stepped in to offer a cup of coffee.

Danielle declined, then said, "Could you get Jeffrey Sorachi on the line for me? He should be in Marrakech." A few minutes later the phone buzzed. It was Sorachi.

"Jeff. Good morning. I'm back in London today and remembered your suggestion about dinner. I want to thank you for helping smooth out the situation with the Moroccan authorities in July, and, since I'm going to be here for a day or two, I thought perhaps we could have dinner, but I want to treat you."

"Thank you, Miss Simones. I would be delighted to dine with you, but I insist that you be my guest. I did invite you, remember?"

"Okay, Jeff. This time can be on you, next time is mine. Would you mind if we make it a foursome? I'd like you to meet our chief legal eagle, Cliff Kelly, and I think you have already met Helen Overmeyer."

"I would be delighted to see Mrs. Overmeyer again, and look forward to meeting Mr. Kelly. Would tonight be agreeable to you, about 8:30? Where can I meet you?"

"We'll be here at my office. Do you know how to find it?"

"Yes. I'll make the reservations and be at your door at 8:30. Goodbye."

Danielle called Cliff Kelly and told him about the dinner engagement, then went back to her paperwork. The day passed rapidly and before she knew it, it was 6:30 and Carolyn stepped in to announce that she was leaving for the day. Danielle pushed back from the desk, went into the small apartment adjoining the office space, and began dressing for dinner.

Promptly at 8:15 she left the apartment and started out of the office and down the hall for the elevator. Cliff Kelly and Helen Overmeyer were talking in the anteroom outside the office. The three rode the elevator together to the lobby and checked out through security. A stretched limousine was waiting at the curb with Jeffrey Sorachi inside. He stepped quickly out of the door held open by the driver.

"Miss Simones, it is such a pleasure to see you again." He hadn't actually seen her since the briefing in Bangkok over a year earlier. "And Mrs. Overmeyer. How nice to see you again." He took Helen's hand and ceremoniously raised it to his lips, bowing simultaneously. Helen blushed.

Danielle said, "Jeff, allow me to introduce you to our chief counsel, Clifford Kelly. Cliff, Jeff Sorachi." The men shook hands.

Sorachi said, "Miss Simones, I was beginning to believe you were just a voice on the telephone. I am so glad you decided to accept my invitation."

"Please, call me Danielle. And it's my pleasure to accept, because I intend to pick your brain for information tonight while we are having dinner. So be warned." She laughed.

Sorachi and Helen soon began a conversation that started in English, changed to French, and then moved again to Arabic. Cliff and Danielle relaxed and rode silently as the conversation progressed. Danielle knew French well, and a little Arabic, so she knew their French conversation had not been about the project, and she suspected from the few words of Arabic which she could catch that they did not seem to be talking in Arabic about the project, either. Helen was smiling and her eyes had an unusual sparkle.

Sorachi suddenly realized that only one of his guests was talking, and switched back to English. "Please forgive me. I have been telling Helen about the beauty of my country. I am pleasantly surprised to learn that she has done quite a great deal of research on the government and economy of North Africa, and has visited my own country several times. But I am greatly distressed to learn that her husband died while doing scientific research in Algeria. Please, let us discuss something more pleasant. Has anyone seen the latest film from the United States? I understand it is very entertaining."

The conversation continued for a few minutes more, then the car stopped before a large Victorian building with an awning over the entrance. The restaurant was elegant and Sorachi was a perfect host. The staff at the restaurant obviously knew him. In one corner of the dining room, a small musical group was playing romantic dance music. Cliff and Danielle were discussing a new legal theory for international corporations when she realized that Jeff and Helen had spent most of the evening dancing together.

During a lull in the music, while Jeff and Helen were seated at the table, Danielle said, "Jeff, you have a big stake in the project. Can you give me some feedback about our information program? Are we providing our investors enough information on developments in the project? Do we need to give more detail, or less, or is there some other view, which we might provide to help maintain investor confidence? My concern is that a lot of people like yourself have large investments, and it will still be quite a few more years yet before they start seeing any cash-flow back to them. Any suggestions?"

"You and the company are doing a great job," he said. "I know that and I have proof of it in the desert outside Marrakech. I have full confidence that the other parts of the project are going equally smoothly. I'm already getting a positive cash flow in my local investments because of the big increase in Moroccan employment due to the antenna construction. But investors whose countries are not receiving such benefits right now may have less reason to be confident. Perhaps you need to have some 'event' in which those investors can participate. Think along those lines. These people want to be participants, not just investors. You have denied them the usual board of directors' positions to which they are accustomed, so you need to give them something else. I don't know exactly what that might be, but something."

"We expect to have the first space plane flying soon," She said. "It's just about on schedule and perhaps we could work in something involving the plane."

"That would be perfect. Perhaps a party for the first flight?"

"I'll think about it. Thanks for your suggestions. Are you going to ask me to dance? Or are you going to wear out poor Helen dancing only with her?" Helen blushed. The band began playing again.

"How inconsiderate of me. May I have this next dance?"

They walked onto the dance floor, followed by Cliff and Helen. Danielle was dancing automatically, thinking about the space plane, when she realized Jeff was speaking to her. "You seem to be a thousand miles away, Danielle. Did I say something wrong?"

"No. Of course not. You started me thinking about the space plane. The crew at Belau has become so wrapped up in it that we have perhaps neglected the people who have made it possible, the investors who are paying the bills.

"I was trying to figure out when and where would be the best place for an investor party. I want to be able to fly the plane relatively free from publicity until I'm sure we have any bugs worked out. There are always some little problems that develop, and I want to make the best possible impression for the investors. That means they won't get to see any rough spots.

"I can tell *you* that, because you know that I do report our difficulties as we go. Each one is a learning event for us, and advances the project. I just want to do that learning without the investors on the scene."

"Sure. I understand. I'm certain you'll come up with some appropriate event. I can't wait to see what it is."

"You and Helen seem to be having a good time together this evening," she observed.

"Is it that obvious?" Sorachi asked. "She's very unusual. I have never met a woman, a foreigner yet, who knows so much about my country and North Africa generally, and speaks my language as well as she does. Even when I was in college in the States, I met many women who were intelligent, but they all thought they were somehow superior to all men and to me in particular, and they knew nothing about Africa. Helen acts like an equal, and is so well educated."

"When we hired her," Danielle said, "one of the skills we recognized was her knowledge of North Africa. It's been of great benefit to us, and will be of equal benefit to Morocco as a result of the power station, when it comes on-line. We're lucky we found her."

The music stopped and they returned to the table.

When the limousine stopped again in front of the office, Jeff offered to drive Helen home. She resisted, but he was charmingly persistent, and she finally agreed. The driver opened the door and Cliff and Danielle went into the building, checked through security and went back to her office. She sat back on a couch and put her feet up on a hassock. "I think Cupid may have struck tonight. There seemed to be arrows flying everywhere. What do you think?"

Cliff laughed. "I haven't seen two people so wrapped up in each other on a first meeting since high school. They have met before, but I didn't have any signs then of any chemistry like tonight."

"Can her interest in Jeff cause us any problems?" she asked seriously. "Conflicts of interest, *et cetera*? I don't want true love, or even false love, to compromise the project."

"I'll talk to her about it," Cliff answered. "She's a top-notch lawyer for someone so fresh out of law school, and if something comes up that needs another lawyer to prevent a conflict situation, I feel confident she'll let us know."

Danielle stood up. "I have to turn in. I've been awake now for the better part of about twenty-four hours, and I'm starting to fade." She started toward the door to her apartment.

Cliff opened the office door, turned around, then said, "We have a 10:30 meeting tomorrow with the tax people from Lone Star Financial. They have some new tax-saving strategies they want to outline to you. I've told them that you are my legal consultant most familiar with the U.S. tax code. In a way, that's true, but they still think their big boss is Jean Claude."

"You're going to chair the meeting?" she asked.

"Yes."

"I'll try to make appropriate noises from time to time, and if I see anything I don't like I'll really speak up. Okay?"

"Yes, boss." He smiled, "Now, since you are my consultant, and we've agreed on that, I order you to get some sleep and to sleep late in the morning. I don't want you around here until 10:15 at the earliest. I'll have someone bring in some breakfast for you. Got that?"

"Yes, boss," she said. They both laughed and Cliff left.

She walked to her desk, wrote a note to remind herself to make reservations for the space plane party, then turned out the lights and went into her apartment.

CHAPTER 35

On October 15, three Antonov aircraft carrying components for the second space plane's fuselage arrived early in the morning. The first space plane's hydraulics and electrical systems had just passed their final tests, and the exterior finish, a combination of high-tech paints and ceramic coatings, had been applied. A shipment of 100 tires arrived from Michelin. The first plane, which until then had been supported on metal assembly carriages, was fitted with dozens of new tires and rolled into the sunlight. Assembly and wiring of the second fuselage began immediately, while the first airframe was moved to another hangar for installation of the four primary turbojet engines.

On November 10, the second space plane's wing center-section arrived. The first plane's engines, now installed in their airframe, had been retested, and the first space plane, complete except for final testing, began taxi tests, the last step before flying.

On November 18, with every employee standing where they could watch, the first space plane thundered down the runway toward the lagoon and took to the air. The noise was deafening, despite the hearing protectors that everyone was wearing, and the sound pressed them back from the runway. Fiery gases pulsated in the wake of the airplane, making bizarre diamond-striped patterns in the afterburner exhausts behind its four engines. Engineers watched anxiously to see how much of the six-kilometer-long runway was required for the aircraft to lift off. They had carefully computed its take-off weight, and aerodynamic lift factors, but no one had ever built an aircraft with this airfoil before, or this large, or this strange. It lifted off a few meters before they had calculated it would and they breathed a collective sigh of relief as it climbed rapidly out of sight, then they went back to work. LEO-B had been delivered and was waiting to be test-assembled and checked out.

The space plane turned East, then North, then Northwest toward Manila, avoiding the radar of the American air base on Guam to the Northeast. In the cockpit the test pilot, Hank Taylor, was busy monitoring instrument readouts as the aircraft flew through a carefully planned series of maneuvers. The computer was actually flying the airplane, but the computer program had never before been tested in a real-world situation. Hank's hand was poised over the computer cut-off switch, ready to take over in case anything went wrong. The memory of the XB-70 Valkyrie plummeting to Earth on a test flight was firmly imprinted in his mind, even though he had only seen it in a film.

The plan was for the plane to climb to an altitude of 10,000 meters and accelerate to a speed of Mach .82 over the Pacific Ocean between Belau and Manila, then circle back and land while simultaneously performing a series of tests. The speed was comparable to the top speed of conventional jetliners.

In Manila, radar controllers were expecting a jet transport aircraft to be taking off from Belau and flying to Manila. They saw a blip identified as the transport appear on the margins of their radar screen on schedule. After a few minutes on the screen, the aircraft crew called the air traffic controllers in Manila and reported that they were returning to Belau to pick up another passenger. In fact, the real transport was sitting on the ground in Belau, while its transponder codes were being transmitted from the space plane. After the first flight, most future flights would be southeastward over the Pacific, between the Caroline Islands and New Guinea, where there were fewer radar observers. But there were also no airports where the space plane could land in an emergency.

Hank knew he would not try any stalls this or any other time. The engineers had told him that when empty the aircraft would stall at 160 knots. A test stall in the simulator had resulted in a crash of the simulated aircraft. He would not take any chances. He told himself the plane would never get below 200 knots with him at the controls, while it was off the ground.

The flight testing program proceeded swiftly, with many flights in a few days. By ten days after the first flight, on November 28, there had been 17 flights with four different crews. The space plane had flown to an altitude of 57,000 meters, approximately 180,000 feet, and a speed of Mach 7.6, breaking all known altitude and speed records for aircraft. On the ground, work was continuing on the second plane, and on testing LEO-B.

Danielle reviewed the flight-test data piled on her desk. Her confidence in the design team had been well placed and they had built an excellent aircraft. She pushed the button to summon her secretary. It was time for a party.

The invitations to the investors told them to plan to attend a celebration for the new aircraft they had made possible, to plan on being gone for several days, and to wear clothes appropriate for the tropics. Danielle chartered three Boeing 747s to land in a number of cities to pick up investors on their way to Belau. The company's own personnel would be back-up for the charter aircraft crews.

Every room in the small tourist hotels in Belau was booked and the VIP quarters on the installation were prepared for extra-special guests, the syndicate leaders. The local hotels sadly informed guests with prior reservations that a plumbing emergency required their reservations to be cancelled for that period, but they could have reservations another time, at no charge. Maurice chartered the local dive boats that had lost their reservations, for the use of the visitors. Maurice ordered five hundred extra sets of noise-canceling headphones.

A week later, on December 3, during its twenty-sixth flight, the space plane reached orbit carrying its first cargo, LEO-A, minus the satellite's maintenance bay and large storage tanks. The LEO satellites were planned to be the heaviest cargoes the space plane would ever be required to lift. The plane delivered the LEO payload at an altitude of 450 kilometers, about 300 miles above the Earth's surface. Re-entry was smoothly according to plan. The huge aircraft used its rocket engines for braking before finally plunging into the atmosphere for the long glide to air dense enough to restart the turbine engines. In the hangar, the LEO crew completed testing of LEO-B. Boeing delivered the first two of ten passenger pods, each complete and ready for occupation by up to 200 persons for up to a month at a time. The pace of activities at the Belau Space Port was picking up rapidly, and money was flowing outward at an unprecedented rate.

On December 17, the anniversary of the Wright brothers' first powered flight in 1903, the Belau Department of Aviation issued Airworthiness Certificate 001 to Belau Aviation Industries Model 1 in a ceremony for all of the investors at the entrance to the Belau Aviation main hangar. The aircraft carried registration number BA-1. There were many foreign visitors.

A tiny Belauan girl about four years old came forward with a bottle of champagne. Along with a workman who held her hand, she was lifted twenty feet above the hangar floor by a fork lift truck, on a platform covered in crepe paper, flowers and brightly colored ribbons, to the middle of the nose-wheel strut. The workman helped her break the champagne bottle to christen the plane. In a tiny voice, amplified by the public address system, she announced the name of the plane, "I christen this plane '*Polaris*.'"

The band played. The President of Belau made a speech. There was a very large lunch banquet under the half-finished second space plane in the hangar. Then *Polaris* was towed out into the sunshine to a place on the parking apron far from the crowd, where its engines were started. Even at idle, its engines were extremely loud. Appearing to move slowly because of its enormous size, but actually traveling at fifty miles per hour, the plane taxied two miles to the southwest end of the field, and turned onto the runway.

The public address system made an announcement, in several languages, "Ladies and gentlemen, please put on your hearing protection now. Failure to protect your ears can result in permanent hearing loss."

The crowd saw the space plane six kilometers away begin to roll, and after a few seconds the sound of the engines at full throttle, followed by the concussion of the afterburners igniting, caused the distant observers to stagger backwards. Everyone in the crowd rechecked their hearing protectors. The plane accelerated ever faster toward the crowd near the lagoon end of the runway. One-third of the way down the runway, the nose wheel lifted from the ground, followed immediately by the main wheels, the gear doors snapped open, and all the landing gear disappeared into the bottom of the plane. The airplane continued to grow larger and louder as it approached, climbing slowly. It passed the three parked 747s on the apron and the crowd in front of the hangar at an altitude of 1,000 feet and 400 miles per hour. The crowd was stunned, then broke into loud applause and cheers.

Maurice d'Orleans stepped to the microphone. Though diminishing rapidly in size and climbing swiftly, *Polaris* still could be heard, its crackly exhaust rattling the peaceful island calm. He waited until everyone was listening again and announced, "The space plane that you have just seen take off is on its way to our first satellite. It is the key to our project, because of its ability quickly to get to low earth orbit, turn around, and return rapidly for another load. Two weeks ago today, as part of the space plane test program, it delivered our first supply transfer satellite to low earth orbit. It will begin to unload its cargo at the satellite in a few minutes. Tonight, at dinnertime, we will gather as the guests of the President of Belau for a special celebration and the pilots of *Polaris* will join us. Tomorrow morning, *Polaris* will again carry another load of materials into space.

"Behind me you see the fuselage and wing of our second space plane already joined together and soon to join *Polaris* in this important project. We have just received word from our air traffic controllers that the major components of the fuselage and wing for the third space plane are now about one hour away, in six large cargo planes bringing them here from the contractors who built them for us.

"This is the beginning of a new era for aviation, and for mankind. We, the employees of Belau Aviation who have the privilege of being a part of this historic event, thank each of you for making it possible. You made a commitment to this project, and so have we – the space plane proves the progress, on schedule, toward meeting our end of the bargain.

"Now, if you will return to your transportation, we will take everyone back to their hotels. Enjoy the beach for the rest of the day, and we will see you at sundown, that's 6 o'clock, on the beach at the end of Main Street for a wonderful Belauan dinner."

Danielle stood at one side of the hangar, watching expressions on the faces of the investors. Uncle Bob was sitting near her, watching her expression. She liked what she saw in the visitors' faces, because they plainly liked what they were seeing. This event had been worth all the headaches it had caused.

The fuselage and wing components for the third space plane arrived that afternoon. A week later the first two Station Supply Shuttles, the 'space tugs,' were delivered to Belau in pieces. Unlike the space station and construction shacks, which would be assembled in one of the hangar bays to check fits and to train crews, then be disassembled for shipment to orbit, the tugs would be delivered to orbit in one piece, to avoid the need for complex assembly of the rocket engines in zero gravity. The newly arrived pieces of the tugs were immediately taken to the assembly area.

On January 15, *Polaris* placed LEO-B into orbit 180 degrees from LEO-A. Flights for the next month carried tanks for the LEO satellites and construction personnel. *Polaris* waited on-station with the construction crews while they installed the tanks, with the construction crews' passenger pod securely installed within the plane's cargo bay, then returned the crews safely to Belau.

General Motors had completed its part of the living quarters for solar collector satellite construction crews and delivered it in pieces to Belau on January 18. The Daimler-Benz part of the construction crew quarters was delivered four days later.

On February 1, operating on charter to NASA, *Polaris* carried a repair crew into orbit to fix a damaged American Earth-sensing satellite. Because the flight was also carrying supplies for the Web, NASA's cost for the charter was less than the cost of one NASA Space Shuttle Solid-Fuel Booster. The NASA repair crew, which had ridden in the cockpit of the space plane, was amazed to see the amount of material unloaded from the space plane. Subsequent flights during February focused on carrying water to fill the tanks, and other supplies for the LEO satellites.

On March 1, *Polaris* carried the first Station Supply Shuttle, SSS-1, to LEO-A. During March, more supplies were carried to both LEO satellites.

On April 2, the second space plane flew, passed all its tests, was registered BA-2 and named *Sirius*. It immediately began lifting supplies into orbit.

On May 30, the third space plane flew and was named *Ariadne*. SSS-1 began a test flight from LEO-A to LEO-B. *Sirius* carried SSS-2 to LEO-A.

Space plane production was continuing. Parts for planes number 4 through 10 were in various stages of completion in plants all over the world. Although the first plane had cost over three billion dollars, including the design work, manufacturing, and production and assembly tooling, the average cost per plane was dropping, and by plane 10, the actual cost would be less than 750 million dollars each, with the average cost per plane, including design and tooling costs, just under a billion each for all ten planes.

On June 1, a reporter from <u>Aviation Week and Space Technology</u> contacted the Belau Aviation office, and asked for specifications on the plane. Realizing that she could no longer conceal the flights into space, which were averaging more than two a day, Danielle furnished a press release to the magazine, to be published over Maurice's name. The following issue contained a news item which read:

"PACIFIC FIRM ANNOUNCES RADICAL NEW AIRCRAFT.
Officials of Belau Aviation Company on the tiny Pacific island of Belau this week announced the successful flight of a new aircraft design. The aircraft is a delta-wing lifting-body configuration, capable of very high speeds at extreme altitudes.
The company intends to use the aircraft to place satellites in orbit and to service existing earth-sensing and navigational satellites for countries and corporations having satellites requiring maintenance.
The aircraft is reported to have a gross weight of over 2.5 million pounds (1,200,000 kg.). Officials state the cost of chartering the aircraft is highly competitive and much less expensive than current American or Russian shuttle launch technology.
The company reportedly has no plans to produce the aircraft for sale."

The flow of materials to the LEO satellites continued. Each space plane, except when being serviced, was flying a full daily load of supplies into orbit. Materials for the solar collector satellite construction crew quarters were accumulating at the LEO satellites, and they were beginning to be referred to by the space plane crews as "the junk yards." The materials at the LEO satellites were clearly visible with the naked eye from Earth's surface. Amateur sky watchers and professional astronomers were equally unable to explain the purpose of the strangely shaped objects they saw, and conjecture abounded. Military observers made no moves to interfere. They were already using the inexpensive services of the space plane to launch their satellites.

LEO-A and LEO-B were now staffed with crews rotated on a weekly shift, seven days in orbit, then return to the ground for two weeks. The function of the low earth satellites consisted mainly of operating the hydrolysis system that converted distilled Pacific seawater into hydrogen and oxygen gases to fuel the space tugs. The tanks of high-pressure gases at the satellites were rapidly being filled. The hydrolysis section of the satellite was designed with the hydrogen tank outboard of one water tank, and the oxygen tank outboard of another water tank, with the living quarters between the water tanks, so that if there ever were an explosion of a gas storage tank, the water tanks would theoretically shield the satellite from debris ejected by the force of the explosion, rather than damaging the living quarters of the satellite. LEO-A also now included a repair bay for the tugs, a huge room which could be sealed and pressurized to enable workers to repair the tugs in a shirt-sleeve environment, a major luxury compared to the task of replacing damaged or worn-out parts in open space while wearing a pressure suit, and far more functionally efficient.

The crews of SSS-1 and SSS-2 were busily moving materials from "the junk yards" to a location in geosynchronous orbit at zero degrees North and thirty degrees East, in an orbit 22,400 miles directly above Uganda, just West of Lake

Victoria. There, another "junk yard," consisting of construction materials for the construction crew quarters for Web 1, as well as materials for Web 1 itself, was accumulating. Hundreds of tons of materials were cabled together, awaiting a crew to begin the assembly. Because of the long duration of the trip to geosynchronous orbit and back, the tug crews made only two trips between rotations back to Earth. Still, both space tugs were actively trying just to keep even with the flow of materials to the LEO satellites produced by the three space planes. Despite their busy schedule, the tugs were slowly falling behind as materials accumulated at low earth orbit.

The corporation was busily recruiting and training more pilots for both the space planes and the space tugs, because both the space plane crews and space tug crews were either already being over-worked, or soon would be. Two tugs were already in operation and eight more were on order and expected to be delivered very soon, while the mechanics in the main hangar were busily assembling several space planes.

Meanwhile, Omega Personnel Services was screening its job application files for potential space construction workers. Candidates had to be able to work for long hours in the confines of a pressure suit and in a zero-gravity environment. Only a small percentage of the total who thought themselves qualified for construction work actually *were* capable of performing any useful work under these conditions. Of particular interest were those with spelunking and SCUBA diving experience, because of the similar claustrophobic character of the space suits to cave exploring and the similarity of dependence on the space suit's piped-in air supply to diving underwater. Assembly of the solar power satellites would require a construction force numbering in the thousands, due to the sheer size of the structure and the requirement for frequent personnel rotations Earthside. The 30-kilometer-across solar collector array would require at least five years to complete, even with the many automated assembly features being utilized in its construction.

By August 1, the life support materials at Web 1 were sufficient to enable construction of the crew quarters to begin and the first load of construction workers arrived.

During construction of the crew quarters, 400 construction workers lived in two passenger pods, tethered together with the two space tugs, until the crew quarters were completely assembled and had been pressure tested. This assembly process, which the workers had practiced at the Belau spaceport hangar, using the same components they actually assembled in space, was completed in only ten weeks, thanks to the extensive prefabrication incorporated in the design. Because of their already extended stay in space, the workers who completed the crew quarters were taken back to the surface after only four days in their new facilities. During those days they completed final interior details and hook-ups, and some of them, having special artistic talents, provided paintings and other impromptu and highly unauthorized decorations on the walls to entertain the next crew.

The crew quarters was a large flat cylinder, approximately 100 meters across and thirty meters deep. Because it rotates slowly, centrifugal force produces an effect similar to gravity at the outer rim. The small radius of the cylinder requires a slow rotation in order to prevent disorientation, so the "artificial gravity" can be only a small fraction of Earth-normal.

Still, for those not working outside in space, there was some sensation of "down," and it was very useful, particularly at meal-times and bath-time. The long batons on either side of the cylinder provided stronger simulated gravity and were used as a day-room and exercise room, but were too small to serve as sleeping quarters for the many personnel assigned there.

Two space tugs returned to the LEO satellites, one with the two passenger pods in which the workers were riding, and one with its cargo racks empty. When the tug with the passenger pods reached LEO-A, *Polaris* and *Ariadne* were waiting empty, having carried up two more passenger pods that had been unloaded from their cargo bays and were operating on LEO-A's life support system. The Earth-bound pods and their cargo of workers were loaded into *Polaris* and *Ariadne*, and departed the station for re-entry into the atmosphere. The tug refueled, changed crews, loaded up all but two of its cargo racks with materials for the hub of Web 1, and hooked the two waiting passenger pods onto the remaining cargo racks. It then began the maneuver which would carry it back to rendezvous with the Web 1 site. The tug rendezvousing with LEO-B picked up six bundles of materials for the Web, changed crews, refueled and headed back to Web 1. The old crew would be picked up by *Sirius*, which was already climbing into orbit with another tank of distilled water for LEO-B to convert to hydrogen and oxygen fuel for the tugs.

PART III - SPACE

CHAPTER 36

The Web 1 satellite grew rapidly. After assembling the hub at the center of the structure, workers began building the central vertical column, an aluminum tube one hundred meters in diameter and thirty kilometers long, parallel to the Earth's axis. They also began to build the 'axle,' a similar two-kilometer-long aluminum tube intersecting the vertical column at the hub but pointed directly at the Sun. Most of the assembly work was done by several automated machines which bolted a 100 meter-long panel in place, moved sideways one panel, and installed another panel, until it had completed forming a 100 meter-long section, then climbed to the outer end of that section, and bolted another panel in place, repeating the process over and over. Each spoke required 160 hundred-meter-long sections, each section made of 32 aluminum panels around its circumference. Each crew worked three weeks before being replaced by another crew. Eventually, a rotation was established with a passenger pod arriving every week, and 500 workers on the station at a time.

When the axle was completed, a cable was strung from the center of the axle end away from the Sun to the center of the construction crew quarters, which rotated slowly in the shade of the satellite's hub and axle. The satellite's structure thereby provided a measure of protection for the crew quarters against some of the Sun's radiation.

Once the vertical shaft was a few hundred meters long, other automated machines began assembling the four diagonal spokes of the satellite. When these arms became a few hundred meters long, workers began installing the diagonal braces onto which the solar collector panels would be attached between the four side spokes and the two vertical spoke sections. When the spokes were all complete, the spokes would each be ten miles, 16 kilometers, long and cables would be required from the ends of the axle to the ends of the spokes, to prevent flexing of the satellite. At that time, it was planned that the spiders would be brought to the satellite and begin their job of installing the solar collector cells.

On November 4, Web 1, which had been observed by astronomers since the first materials began to accumulate, was announced publicly by the astronomers and became the top news story around the world. For some, the satellite was a mere curiosity, but for others it was a cause of great concern.

Headlines in newspapers around the world all echoed a common theme –

"Giant Structure Found in Space."
"Two Bavarian astronomers reported yesterday the discovery of a new object in space. Initial reports indicate that the object is actually some kind of large hexagonal satellite. Information is lacking on the purpose of the satellite, but early speculation is that it may be a communication facility. The discoverers state that the satellite appears to be in geosynchronous orbit above Africa."

Scientists and space experts around the world rapidly concluded that the new satellite was a solar power collector.

146

In Belau, Danielle was conferring with Maurice d'Orleans, Jean Claude LeBec and Uncle Bob. They decided it was time to go public. She touched a button on her desk. "Bill, get Kenneth Morgan on the phone please." It was 9 AM in Belau and 7 PM in New York.

Bill quickly called back. "They're closed for the evening. I have the answering service on the line."

"I'll talk to them. Put them on and stay on the line." There was a pause and a new voice on the line.

"Hello, Morgan, Friedman and Tinker. This is the answering service."

"My name is Danielle Simones. I'm a client of Morgan, Friedman and Tinker and I need to speak to Mr. Kenneth Morgan immediately."

"Is this an emergency?" the operator asked.

"Yes. I need him to call me back as soon as possible. Can you call him on another line while we hold?"

"No, Ma'am. I can have him return your call as soon as I reach him."

"All right. My secretary is on the line and will give you our number. But if you don't reach him immediately, you must call his partners, and get a person from the firm to call me back in the next few minutes. Do you understand?"

"Yes, Ma'am. I'll relay your message."

Danielle waited thirty minutes. There was no return call. Bill buzzed her. "Nothing from New York. Do you want to call back?"

"No. Call London. I hate to wake Cliff but I guess he won't mind too much." It was half past midnight in London.

The night operator answered. "Simones Associates."

"This is Danielle Simones. Please connect me to Clifford Kelly."

"Yes, Ma'am. One moment please." There was a brief delay while the operator called Kelly's home. A sleepy voice answered.

"... Hello ...?"

"Cliff, its Danielle. I'm sorry to wake you."

"That's all right. What's up?"

"I want to have a teleconference in thirteen and a half hours regarding the Power Satellite. That's 9 AM, New York time. I want Kenneth Morgan in New York to set it up and I want all the big newspapers and wire services around the world to participate. Maurice will make the presentation from here. I'm sorry to wake you but I haven't been able to get through to Kenneth Morgan. Can you reach him?"

"I have his home number, and the numbers for the rest of the firm too. I'll find him if he's there."

"Thanks, Cliff. And I apologize again for waking you."

"No problem, boss. You always keep things interesting for me."

Danielle hung up. Minutes passed and Morgan called. She quickly outlined her plan to him. He said he would take care of the arrangements.

By 10 PM, Belau time, the teleconference was set up. Three video monitors were in her office displaying the rooms in New York, London and Tokyo where reporters were assembling for the briefing. Each of them was a room full of empty chairs, with an occasional person walking through the room for some unknown purpose. The technician had turned down the audio as she didn't need to be able to hear what was happening. The monitors were only back-ups in case the

147

main switching system broke down, as sometimes happened. If all went as planned, the teleconference operator would have Maurice's image displayed in each of the briefing rooms once she turned on the camera in the Belau office. In turn, during the question-and-answer session after the briefing, the operator would switch the video feed to the large television screen on Danielle's office wall to display the image of the reporter asking the questions.

At 11 PM everything was ready. The reporters were in their seats and a large number of them were at each location. Danielle had rechecked the audio from each monitor and satisfied herself that she and Maurice would be able to hear any questions. She switched on the video camera and Maurice began.

"How do you do, ladies and gentlemen. I hope you can all see me clearly. My name is Maurice d'Orleans, and this is a briefing for you regarding the new satellite that has been in the news for the last day or so. I'm speaking to you from the Island of Belau, in the Western Pacific. I'm the President of Belau Aviation, which is located here.

"During the past several years, Belau Aviation has been developing a new kind of aircraft. It has the ability to fly above the Earth's atmosphere. Last year, the first of these aircraft completed its first flight. The unique feature of this aircraft is that it can reach altitudes where many satellites are located, and then can rendezvous with those satellites.

"Because of this ability, Belau Aviation has already assisted some governments by carrying repair crews to damaged weather and navigation satellites. Belau Aviation is now under contract to carry materials into orbit for the construction of the satellite that you have recently observed.

"The company building the new satellite is Charlotte Space Development Corporation. It expects that the new satellite will take about five years to complete. When it is finished, it will be the largest photovoltaic array ever assembled.

"At the same time the satellite is being built, another company, Stellar Power Corporation, is building a system of antennas in Africa. These antennas will receive electrical power transmitted by microwave energy from the new satellite. The solar power received by these antennas will enable African countries to develop new, non-polluting industries. It will also free those countries from the adverse environmental impacts from petroleum and nuclear sources of energy.

"Perhaps I should take some questions now. If you will please come to the microphone at the front of your rooms, I'll be able to see and hear you clearly. Yes, the gentleman from New York."

The speaker from New York paused and consulted his notes. "You said that the solar energy from the satellite would be transmitted to Earth by microwave energy. I don't understand how that works. How does the energy get transmitted?"

"At the satellite, there is a device which converts the electricity produced by photovoltaic solar cells into a microwave signal, which is focused into a narrow beam and directed to the receiving antenna on Earth. This is similar to the signal by which radar antennas operate, although our antennas are physically much larger, both at the transmitting and receiving ends. At the receiving antenna the microwave radio energy is received by billions of small antenna elements, and generates a weak electric alternating current in each small antenna. The current from a single element is rectified to direct current, combined with the current from other antenna elements and transmitted as electric power in wires. Next question, from Tokyo."

"How large are the antennas used to transmit and receive the energy?"

"The transmitting antenna arrays on the satellite will be approximately one kilometer in diameter. The receiving antenna arrays are approximately ten kilometers in diameter. That's a little more than six miles. Next question from London."

"How much power will the satellite produce?"

"We're not sure exactly what the peak power output will be, but the theoretical amount of solar energy striking the satellite is 1.39 kilowatts times the area of the satellite in square meters, which is about 706 million square meters. The satellite will be approximately 30 kilometers in diameter when completed. So the absolute maximum, at 100% efficiency, would be 982 billion watts of electric power. However, for planning purposes, the designers are assuming that the efficiency will be about ten percent, which makes the power output around 100 billion watts, or 100 gigawatts. This is about the power output of 100 to 130 average-size nuclear power plants. Next question, from New York."

"We all know how microwave energy cooks food in our kitchens. What happens if a bird or an airplane flies through this beam you are going to point at the Earth? I don't want to be turned into a french-fry if my pilot makes an error in navigation."

"Nothing happens if you fly through the beam," Maurice answered. "The energy flux level of the beam is approximately one-tenth that of sunlight. It is low because the energy is transmitted over a very large area, and because the transmission frequency used is selected specifically to not create those kinds of problems. If you fly through the beam with an airplane, the paint will completely shield you from the beam. Actually, the energy of the beam at the Earth's surface is so low that a person could live directly under it with no adverse effect. We expect workers to be working within the antenna on a regular basis with no harm. Next question from Tokyo."

"Where will the receiving antenna be located? How will so much power be carried from one location to the consumers?"

"That's two questions," said Maurice, "and the rules for this meeting were only one to a customer." Laughter was heard in all three locations. "But your questions are valid and I can answer both of them with one answer. There are a number of antennas now under construction in Africa. The satellite will have many transmitting antennas, each one targeting a specific receiving antenna, so all the power will *not* be going to one location. Next question from London."

"Will people working around the receiving antenna be subjected to a higher than normal risk of disease because of radiation?"

"There is no ionizing radiation associated with the energy beam from the satellite to Earth," Maurice said, "that is, the kind of radiation you think of with regard to a nuclear explosions or x-rays. What we are developing is similar to the radiation you get when you stand between the transmitter for your local television station and rabbit ears on your home TV set, or use your cell phone, only of course it is somewhat stronger. It would have to be many times stronger to present a danger to people. Where were we? I think the next questioner is from New York."

The questions went on for another half-hour. Finally, Maurice said, "I appreciate your interest, but you all have deadlines, I'm sure. It's after midnight here and I'm worn out. If you have more questions, please send them to us through our representatives who are there in the room with you. And please call us if you would like a tour of the Belau Space Port or one of the receiving antenna sites. We can't handle drop-in visitors, but we'd be glad to arrange a tour for a group, although there isn't much to see, just a big airport in Belau and a forest of supporting poles at the antennas. If a group of you would like a tour of one of our space planes, we'll be glad to set it up. Thank you for coming."

Danielle switched off the camera in her office and Maurice relaxed.

"Whew! Glad that's over," he said.

"We may have to do it more often now. But your presentation was perfect. Give yourself a gold star."

YEAR FOUR

CHAPTER 37

March 13

Kenyan environmentalists were in turmoil. The government, they said, in cooperation with a foreign company, was building a monster power plant in the middle of the Chalbi Desert and was planning another near Lake Magadi. Demonstrators had arrived at the Interior Ministry at 8 o'clock that morning. Their number was increasing and they were getting louder. The leaders were threatening a march on the Presidential Palace, and the President was becoming worried.

The crowd in front of the Interior Ministry had formed a circle, effectively blocking the front entrance to the ministry. The signs were all in opposition to the power plant and chanting could be heard blocks away. "Save Our Country! No Power Plant! Save Our Country! No Power Plant!" Near the center of the circle, a young woman with a portable loudspeaker urged on the demonstrators.

Interior Minister Joseph Kotali nervously tapped his fingers on his desk. He couldn't concentrate because of the noise outside. When he arrived earlier that morning, his driver had asked if he wanted to turn back. But he had decided to go on through the crowd, and had proceeded slowly into the Ministry grounds without any damage to the car. Later that morning, he was told, some visitors to the ministry had been unwilling to push through the mob. Perhaps the crowd had grown since then. It was certainly louder.

His phone rang. It was the President's office. One of the President's assistants was on the line. "Mr. Kotali," the assistant had said, "you must do something about those demonstrators. The President is very upset. He wants them to stop."

"So do I. But I haven't figured out how to make that happen. I thought about asking the police to break it up, but that risks a violent confrontation and, if any of the demonstrators were hurt, we could have the whole country demonstrating."

"Well, the President was very clear. He wants *you* to handle it. Goodbye."

Kotali was perspiring profusely, despite the cold air conditioning. There was no alternative. Now was the time to act to defuse the situation, before the demonstrators became violent. He knew that the police would take any violence as a signal to respond with their full force, and he certainly didn't want that.

He called his secretary. "Get me the Chief of Police."

In a few minutes the Chief was on the phone. "Good morning Mr. Minister. What can I do for you?"

"Good morning, Chief. You *are* aware of the demonstration in front of the Interior Ministry this morning, I suppose?"

"Certainly. My men are keeping it under surveillance."

"That's good, Chief. Look, I don't want to have any violence from the police in this situation. The demonstrators are peaceful so far, and I don't want to provoke them or the general population by having the police come in with force." The noise outside was getting louder.

"Chief, what I do need is a few officers as a sort of bodyguard. I intend to go out and talk to the leaders of the demonstrators, and I don't want to be unprotected. But I reemphasize, I don't want any violence, even if the demonstrators were to hit me or throw rocks, I just want the police officers to be sure to get me away from the violence."

"Are you sure about that, Mr. Minister?"

"You have to speak up, Chief. The noise here is pretty loud and I'm having a hard time hearing you."

"Mr. Minister," the Chief yelled into his telephone, "are you sure you don't want my men to use stronger measures?"

"I'm sure, Chief. We can allow the demonstrators to do a little physical damage to the street signs, or the structures along the street, so long as there is some chance we can turn around the situation through negotiation. I want to avoid injury to any of the demonstrators if at all possible. We don't want to have a Tiananmen Square here. I'm sure the media are covering this event, and I expect the demonstrators to have someone with a video camera recording the whole thing."

"Okay, Sir, I'll have a half-dozen of my best officers over there in fifteen minutes to be your bodyguard."

"Thanks, Chief. Have them come to the freight entrance at the rear of the building. One of my staff will let them in. That way, they won't have to fight their way through the crowd in front. We might prevent an incident if we use our heads. And Chief, I need a bull-horn so I can talk to the crowd and be heard."

"I'll have the men bring one with them, Sir. Anything else?"

"No, Chief. Just get them here as soon as you can. Goodbye." He signaled for his secretary, who stepped in the door. "Have Sydney go to the rear door to the loading dock. The police are going to send some men to protect me while I talk with the demonstrators." The secretary nodded and left.

Kotali started making notes of what he wanted to say. His hand shook. He could hardly hold the pen. He signaled his secretary again. She opened the door and he said, "Get me Stellar Power Corporation. Now!"

The secretary called him in a minute. "Sir, their office said all of the officials are out at the construction site this morning. Do you want me to call London?"

"Yes. Thank you."

She was back on the intercom in a moment. "The London office has not opened yet, and I got an answering service. They want to know if it is an emergency?"

"Hell, yes, it's an emergency! I need to talk to someone there, and I need them RIGHT NOW!" The secretary hung up and a few minutes later Kotali's phone rang again. It was Stellar Power's duty officer.

"Mr. Minister, this is Steve Schwartz. I understand you have a problem. Can you describe the situation there for me?"

Kotali described the demonstration and asked what the company was going to do about it. Schwartz's voice was calm. 'But,' Kotali thought, 'he isn't here either.'

"Mr. Minister, we've anticipated these kinds of reactions, and there are ways to deal with them. Have you spoken yet to the leaders of the demonstrators?"

"No. I'm about to do that, but I wanted to talk to your people first. I don't want to say the wrong thing, and make the situation worse. Can you speak a little louder, please?"

Schwartz spoke louder. "That's very perceptive of you, Mr. Minister. What we'd like you to do is ask a half-dozen leaders of the group to attend a special meeting to discuss their concerns and let us explain the details of the power station to them. We want to learn what really bothers them about our plant, so that we can do as much as possible to address the problems they see with the plant. After we meet with their leaders, we'll hold one or more public hearings to inform the entire community about the project. But we need their initial group to be small enough so that we can have a meaningful discussion which involves each of them.

"We've studied the psychology of such groups and found that what most of them want is to be listened to and treated with respect. If we do that, they should be receptive to what we have to say, and we can find ways to gain their support for our project. We'll have someone from the company down there in a few days. You're acquainted with John Williams, I believe, are you not?"

Kotali answered, "Yes. Mr. Williams was the first person I met from your company."

"I'll call John as soon as I hang up, Mr. Minister. I'm sure this can all be taken care of easily once he gets there. In the meanwhile, you must convince the leaders of the group that you're seriously interested in their fears concerning the project. Can you do that?"

'Of course I can do that,' Kotali thought to himself. 'What kind of fool do you think I am?'

What he said though, was "No problem, Mr. Schwartz. I'll call your office later today and advise you how things worked out in my meeting this morning with the demonstrators."

"When you call back, ask for Mr. Williams. He'll be glad to handle it from here on, and I'll have briefed him on this conversation. Call me back if you need any more information before then."

"Okay. Thank you for your advice." Kotali hung up. His secretary stepped into his office.

"The police are here."

"Send them in." Six large officers came lumbering into his office. They *were* impressive. One of them was carrying a white bullhorn, a portable public address system equipped with a strap that allowed it to be hung from the user's shoulder, and a microphone on a coiled cord. Kotali outlined his plan to them and reemphasized the need to avoid violence at all costs. They were only to get him safely out of the crowd if anyone tried to injure him seriously. They had to be willing to sustain minor insults, both verbal and physical, as there could always be someone in the crowd with eggs or vegetables or even rocks to throw. He was only interested in speaking to the leaders of the crowd.

The policemen all understood and agreed to follow those instructions, plus any he might give while in the street.

Kotali took a deep breath. "We might as well get to it."

The Sun was already blistering hot outside the Ministry. The crowd was still chanting, but Kotali could see the demonstrators were suffering from their exertions. The police formed a cordon around him and began moving from the

Ministry's front steps down the driveway toward the crowd. His approach caused sudden excitement in the crowd. The guard at the gate was surprised to see the Minister himself walking toward this mob. Kotali motioned for the guard to open the gate.

The crowd outside the gate withdrew slightly as the policemen and their protected charge walked through the gate and approached them. The chanting diminished near the wall of the compound, as those nearest could see something was happening, but the people in the rear of the demonstration were still shouting and waving their signs.

A small pickup truck was parked near the gate. The Minister stepped into the bed of the pickup and asked for the bullhorn. He blew tentatively into the microphone and began to speak to the crowd.

"May I have your attention? Please!" A hush passed through the crowd. "May I have your attention! I am Joseph Kotali, the Interior Minister. I appreciate the concerns that have caused you to come here today, and I want to thank you for being so concerned about our country. I worry about our country too. I want to try, as best I can, to learn your reasons for opposing the power plant, and take whatever steps I can to address them.

"Is there someone here who is a leader of this group, or maybe several leaders? We need to talk! Please come forward. I promise there will be no action taken against you. Is there someone here with whom I can discuss your concerns?"

Through the crowd a slender young woman with intense brown eyes and an angry expression pushed her way toward the truck and the Minister. Hanging by a strap over her shoulder was her own bullhorn. As she approached, people who saw her coming moved out of her way. As she touched them, people who had not seen her coming jumped aside when they recognized her.

She reached the truck and looked up at the Minister. "What do you want?" she demanded.

Kotali put on his best ministerial smile and said, "I think the question is 'what do you want?' Maybe we should be introduced." He climbed down from the back of the truck and directed the policemen to allow her into the circle of their protection. She looked suspiciously at them before stepping into the circle.

Kotali stuck out his hand. "How do you do. I am Joseph Kotali." He waited. She hesitated. He said, "You do have a name, don't you?" and he smiled again, he hoped not too much.

She shook his hand. "I'm Wairimu Kwirikia. Hello."

"Well, Miss Kwirikia, are you the only leader here today, or are there others to whom I should be talking?

"There are several others. But they've asked me to speak for them. What do you want?"

"Ahem." Kotali tried to think how to present this proposal. "Well, first, I want you to believe me when I say I share your concerns." He looked into her eyes. She didn't look as if she believed him. He was right. She didn't.

"Second, I want to set up a process for you to meet with me and representatives of the power company. I want you to tell us all about your concerns regarding the power project. And, I want you to listen to the representatives from the power company and their experts so you will have better information about what they are doing."

She almost spat at him. "Lies! Why should we want to hear more lies from developers and their experts? We all know those experts. They will say whatever the person paying them wants them to say. They call themselves 'scientists.' We know what they really are! 'Biostitutes'!" She paused to take a breath and Kotali responded calmly.

"Perhaps. But I am only asking you to listen to them, not to believe them. You have to make that decision for yourself. And I want you to bring a few other leaders who share your worries or who may have other concerns that need to be addressed. I promise to give you a fair hearing, and I just ask you to give us a fair hearing. When we're done, we can compare notes and, if you're not satisfied, I'll keep going until either you are satisfied, or you and I agree that there is no way we can meet your demands. How does that sound?"

Wairimu was caught off guard. She hadn't expected such openness from the enemy. She was very skeptical. What was his hidden agenda? She couldn't refuse to talk, or she'd never be able to change this terrible situation.

"I guess we could meet with you. When?"

"I talked with the power company people this morning. They can be here next week, and we can meet then. Could you do that?"

"Yes. But we want some neutral observers present. We don't want you to misrepresent what we say at the meeting."

"Of course. I have no problem at all with that; I just want the meeting small enough that we can have time to talk out the issues, about a half-dozen of your people, me, and a few people from the power company. How about next Tuesday morning, at about 9:30?"

"It can't be Tuesday morning. I have classes. But Wednesday would be all right."

"Fine. Wednesday morning it is. At 9:30. Now, there's one more thing we have to do."

Her suspicions flamed again. "What?" she demanded.

"I think it would be good if we let these friends of yours go home. I'm sure that you realize there is some potential for a crowd this big to get out of hand or to be manipulated by other people who want to generally discredit the government. I particularly don't want the police to think they have some kind of disturbance that they have to use force against. I don't want anyone to be hurt. Can we send them home? I promise if we can't reach agreement through our discussion, they can come back here again then. Will you speak to them?"

Wairimu considered what he had said, then agreed. "All right. But if this is a trick, next time we'll be back with twice as many people and we'll be at the Presidential Palace." Kotali again stepped up into the bed of the pick-up and assisted her up to stand next to him. He cringed at the thought of what she might say, but started to hand her the microphone for his bullhorn anyway. She refused it, almost as if it was contaminated by his contact with it. He took it back, clutching it tightly in worried expectation of the next words from her mouth. He didn't realize he was squeezing the talk-switch. Wairimu used her own bullhorn, and began speaking to the crowd. "I ....." The two bullhorns, both turned on at the same time, began feeding back into one another and an ear-splitting shriek came from them.

One of the police officers, as if he had the same problem every day, reached up to the Minister's bullhorn, and switched it off. The shrill noise ceased as suddenly as it had begun. She started again. "My friends."

Kotali had been afraid she was going to say 'comrades'.

"My friends! Your hard work is paying off already! The Minister of the Interior is going to meet with us and hear our issues! We are winning! Our leaders are going to meet with him next week! We will have more meetings with you as soon as we hear what they have to say! And if they don't start being responsible with our country, WE WILL BE BACK!"

The crowd cheered. She continued. "Now we have to go back and get prepared for our meeting. Go home and your leaders will contact you with more information. Thank you for coming here today! Your being here makes all the difference! Thank you! Thank you!" She climbed down from the truck and started to leave.

"Miss. Wait!" the minister shouted. She turned. "I don't know how to reach you – about the meeting."

"*You* don't *need* to reach me, Mr. Minister. I'll be here next Wednesday morning at 9:30 with the other leaders and some observers. And don't try any tricks. We know them all." She turned and disappeared into the crowd.

CHAPTER 38

March 20

The following Wednesday morning it was raining heavily in Nairobi. At 9:15, a rusty and faded blue Honda pulled up to the gate at the entrance to the Interior Ministry and a small female figure in a business suit emerged from the passenger door before the car sped away. She dashed through the rain to the gate where she exchanged a few words with the guard, who opened the gate to admit her. She ran on from the gate to the covered portico where steps led to the minister's office.

John (Jomo) Williams had been in Nairobi for several days. The first day, Sunday, he had visited the Chalbi site to review progress with the construction superintendent. The next two days had been spent with the Interior Minister and his staff, in preparation for the meeting with the environmental leaders opposed to the power plant.

Wairimu Kwirikia stepped into the Minister's waiting room, the first environmental leader to arrive for the meeting. The receptionist took her name and asked her if she would like a cup of coffee. Wairimu really didn't want to accept anything from these people, but she was wet and the air conditioning was making her very cold. A cup of hot coffee would be great and she told the woman so. The receptionist seemed to enjoy getting the coffee for her, at least she was friendly, and she made Wairimu feel a little more comfortable and a little less nervous.

The receptionist asked if she wanted to be announced to the Minister, but Wairimu asked her to wait. The others still had not arrived. Wairimu didn't want to sit on the furniture until she dried out a little, so she walked around the perimeter of the room, which had numerous displays of Kenyan tribal art and artifacts.

Her coffee was only half gone when she heard voices and a group of her friends entered the waiting room. There were leaders of four other groups besides her own, and a reporter for the Nairobi Standard who usually wrote the environmental stories for the paper. She had seen the reporter's stories about her own work for many years, and knew from experience that she could trust him to be straight with the facts. Wairimu greeted them. Two still had doubts about meeting with the opposition, but she chided them for their timidity, then asked the receptionist to tell the Minister that everyone had arrived. The door to the Minister's office opened after a few minutes and the Minister himself emerged, smiling warmly, and invited them to follow him into his office. Already there were two other men, a tall, blue-eyed blond, and a young black man. The Minister introduced the two men respectively as Ivan Roberts, an engineer for the power company, and John Williams, one of the company's lawyers.

Wairimu introduced each of the people accompanying her, then the reporter and then herself to the Minister and men from the power company, although she was certain the Minister already knew the reporter.

At one side of the Minister's office was a seating area with couches and chairs arranged in a circle. He invited them all to sit down and asked if any of them would care for coffee or tea, then punched a button next to his chair and told the receptionist, who quickly appeared with the appropriate beverages for each guest.

The Minister waited while everyone had a sip, then began quietly. He had met for the past several days with Jomo Williams and Ivan Roberts, reviewing potential questions and the answers they would give. "Thank you for coming here today. I want you to know, the Ministry and the government shares your concern for the health of our natural resources. Much of what we are in this country is directly the result of our natural resources, and because of what we have lost in the past, it is even more important that we protect what is left. One of the reasons I have supported the power plant project as enthusiastically as I have, is because I believe it presents a significant opportunity to help us *protect* our environment.

"What I want to do today is, first, allow Mr. Williams and Mr. Roberts to give you a briefing on the power plant project. Then I have set up a tour for all of us to visit the Chalbi plant construction site, so that you can see exactly what is going on out there for yourselves. Then I'd like to have you explain to them and to me your concerns about the impacts of the plant and finally, for us to have an opportunity for the power company representatives to try to address your issues. We can discuss what you've seen, and answer any questions, or hear any suggestions that occur to you then.

"When we're done, it's my hope that your concerns will have been alleviated, either through our convincing you that we already have made adequate provisions to protect the environment, or through us implementing changes as a result of your suggestions.

"Either way, I hope that we can resolve your concerns, because I know that you are trying to protect our country, and I appreciate your efforts in that regard.

"I *will* insure that we have a real dialogue today and that this meeting does not end up completely one-sided, although I'm sure you realize much of our time will be spent today learning about the plant. Furthermore, if we don't finish today - if there are still unresolved issues at the end of the day - we're committed to meet again, at your convenience, to address those issues.

"If there's any one message I want you to take home with you at the end of today's meeting, it is that we need to have an open line of communication, so that you can come to me if there is *any* issue, maybe some other issue in the future, which you think will hurt our environment. Please keep that idea in your minds.

"Perhaps, before we go into the conference room, some or all of you would care to make a statement regarding your positions on the issue of the power plant. Does anyone wish to say anything about these issues before we begin?"

There were no responses. The environmental leaders didn't know whether there was any advantage for them to make a statement, and didn't want to restrict their maneuvering positions by committing themselves to anything at this early stage. The Minister realized no one was going to say anything.

"If there aren't any questions just now, we can go into the conference room and let these gentlemen begin their portion of the briefing." The Minister got to his feet and led the group through doors at the side of the office into a large, luxurious room. Wairimu and her friends were awed by the furnishings. There was an enormous varnished mahogany table in the center, surrounded by large, authentic-looking Persian rugs and high-backed swivel chairs. The walls were paneled in hardwoods polished to a high luster. Along the walls were elegant leather and wood armchairs for observers and staff members to occupy during meetings of important committees. On the walls were paintings of all the prior Kenyan Interior Ministers and the colonial interior officers through the years of British rule. At the end of the room a large television set and some computer equipment were on another table.

The Minister again introduced John Williams who began the briefing. "Good morning. As Minister Kotali said, my name is John Williams. Please don't call me Mr. Williams. That's my father. Call me John, if you like, or my nickname, "Jomo," which is what all my friends call me. I'm an attorney with Stellar Power Corporation, the company building the power stations.

"I know, and I want you to understand that my employer knows also, that the opposition that you were expressing last week was sincere and motivated by your desire to protect this fragile land.

"Please don't think I'm patronizing you, because I'm not, but the company and I share those same desires, not only about Kenya or Africa, but about the entire world. Because of my concerns for nature, my participation in this project has been a source of great satisfaction for me, and I hope by the end of our meeting, you'll understand why.

"I think the fact that you're here, and we're here from the company, and we're sitting around this table talking calmly about your worries and our different perceptions of what's happening regarding the power project, signifies a major positive step. I hope today we can continue our meeting on the same positive tone with which we have started. If, at any time today, we find ourselves shouting at one another – which sometimes happens – I promise and ask you also to promise to back up and start over, without raised voices. If we're to thoroughly understand one another, and make the most of this opportunity to resolve our differences, we need to be calm and logical. And, even though I know you have powerful feelings about these issues, the issues are too important to let emotion disable our discussion.

"I'm glad to be able to meet with leaders of the local environmental community, because I personally believe this project has the potential to be the greatest force for good I've ever seen, both for the environment, and by that I mean the wildlife and natural systems of Kenya and East Africa generally, but also for the *people* of Kenya and East Africa. If, at the end of the day, you don't understand why I feel that way, please say so, and I'll try again to explain.

"As we talk today, I'm not asking you to abandon your principles, ideals or goals. What I *am* asking you to do is to listen carefully to the information we will present, then make up your own minds as to what the long-term impacts will be on this land.

Environmental causes can't afford to focus on today, or this week, or even this year. We need to ask ourselves, 'Will a particular action be good for our grandchildren, and for their grandchildren?' 'Will this action help our grandchildren's grandchildren to know and understand the land as we know it today, or will this action cause the land to be changed beyond recognition?' For me, that's the ultimate environmental test of any proposed action. Perhaps you have a different test, and if so, I'd like to hear it."

Williams signaled to Roberts, who reached down and turned on the computer equipment. The logo of Stellar Power Corporation appeared on the television screen, a sun with a bolt of lightning coming from it,

Williams continued, "The antennas being constructed in Kenya are a part of a system to bring abundant energy to Africa from the Sun." A map appeared on the screen showing the locations of the Chalbi antenna and the power distribution grid from it to cities up and down the coast.

"During the past two hundred years, mankind has progressed from an agricultural economy, through the age of steam, the industrial revolution, the development of our petroleum-based energy economy, including the automobile and airplane, and the beginning of the conversion from petroleum to nuclear fuel as the basis of our energy generation. During this period the pollution from man's activities has doubled and redoubled, over and over.

"We've gone from times when the only serious pollution was left by horses in the streets, to now when we have radioactive wastes being generated by the tonne each day in nuclear plants all over the world. Those wastes have half-lives longer than humans have been on this Earth, and yet our hunger for energy has driven countries around the world to accept, almost without question, the apparently insurmountable problems of disposing of those wastes. To date, no country has figured out what to do with either high-level or low-level nuclear wastes, and they continue to produce more every day, because they want the electricity.

"Air, water and land pollution occur as a result of the inability of people to wisely use available resources, often because they lack the energy, or the ability, to reclaim their own inventories from their waste stream. Our present electrical generating plants, both fossil fueled and nuclear, are some of the worst pollution sources in the country. And the need for wood, just for cooking charcoal here in Kenya, is causing major damage to your forests.

"Beyond the damage being caused here in Kenya, power generation and, more broadly, the use of fossil fuels for transportation and other industries around the world is often blamed for a host of other kinds of pollution, including oil spills, global warming and damage to the ozone layer.

"My employer believes that, if there is not a fundamental change in the primary sources of energy used by mankind, as petroleum sources become scarcer, people who need energy to cook with, to warm their homes, and for other uses, will begin stripping the earth of essential parts of the environment, like trees, and will begin strip-mining for buried coal and other mineral deposits, with no regard, in their desperation, for the environmental consequences of their actions. With inexpensive reliable electric power, the destruction of the land to meet these energy needs can be prevented.

"The existing scenario is even more disturbing, because my employer realized that the Earth has enormous untapped resources, including energy, which can be accessed with much less drastic consequences. The resource with which we are concerned is energy, and we have an inexhaustible source of clean energy available to us ... the Sun.

"The Sun constantly bathes the Earth in energy. That energy occurs in many forms from heating waves in the infrared spectrum, to light, to radio waves. The new power station under construction is actually a huge radio antenna to receive microwave radio energy beamed to it from Space, and we're unaware of any pollution generated by that energy. That means no carbon dioxide, no oxides of sulphur, no oxides of nitrogen, no oil spills, no nuclear by-products or wastes, no radioactive gases. We think that's a big improvement.

160

"One of the fundamental purposes of this electrical generating system is to replace all of the fossil-fueled and nuclear-powered generating plants. Our agreement with the government of Kenya, and with Kenya Power, provides that after our plants are on-line and producing reliable power, we'll purchase and dismantle the existing, pollution-causing power plants.

"As more of our power plants come on line around Africa, we will meet the demand by feeding the large amounts of power generated by them to the entire continent through our power grid extending across international boundaries." A map showing proposed future plant locations and the future power grid in Africa appeared on the screen.

"The agreements, between Kenya, other countries, and my employer, also provide for the exchange of power from one country to another whenever a power station in one country is out of service for any reason, so that we can assure a reliable flow of power to all electricity users. These agreements will make African countries interdependent in ways they never have been before, and will be the strongest influence yet conceived for the preservation of peaceful relations between countries.

"Enough about the *benefits* of the plants for now. Let me tell you about the plants themselves. You know they are large. I want to give you a complete picture of the plants. They are *very* large. Each plant consists of an antenna array approximately ten kilometers in diameter.

"Every effort has been made to minimize their impact on Kenya's environment and I'll go into those efforts in a moment. But first, I need to acknowledge the one impact that we have not been able to overcome – the antenna arrays are visible.

"We consider the most significant negative impact of these plants to be their very large size and the visual impact they have on the casual observer. The company has made every effort to reduce this visual impact. We've done this through several actions.

"First, we've attempted to locate the plants in areas which are less often frequented by the tourists on which Kenya depends so much, and which are not frequently or intensively used by Kenya's people.

"Second, we've carefully considered animal breeding, feeding and migration areas in the siting decisions. Every effort has been taken to minimize impacts on the wild animals of Kenya.

"Third, the company has incorporated camouflage into the design of the plant, to make it less visible than it would be otherwise. From near the plant, it resembles a forest of poles, holding a horizontal web of fencing high in the air, about fifteen meters off the ground. The entire plant, and now I am referring to the Chalbi desert site, is to be painted with earth-tone paint to make it virtually invisible from a distance. It will be most visible at night, because we are required to place red flashing lights on and around the antenna array to prevent aircraft from accidentally making emergency landings on the antenna at night. Those lights, because of the huge size of the antenna, will look to an observer like a line of elevated red lights curving into the distance. Aside from these lights, the antenna would look as black and vacant at night as any other uninhabited piece of the desert.

"Again, those lights are not supposed to be visible from the ground, although a person with elevation above the antenna will be able to see them.

161

Because the Chalbi site is somewhat irregular, even people on the ground at some higher parts of the site will be able to look down on the top of the antenna at other parts of the site and see the lights, although those farther-away parts could be as much as ten kilometers distant. We cannot avoid this visibility and still maintain the safety standards to which we are committed.

"Although we have a 45-kilometer-long fence around the site as a security measure right now, we're hopeful that as the plant becomes well-known and accepted by the Kenyan people, including groups like those you represent, we'll be able to remove the fences and allow unrestricted natural movement of wildlife through the site, that is, under the antenna, even though we selected the site to have minimum impacts on animal movements.

"That's a security consideration which only time can resolve. The existing fence is to protect wildlife from dangers associated with the construction going on there right now, and to prevent unauthorized entrance to the site. As you may understand, we have a very large investment in materials at the site, and the possibility of theft during construction concerns us, as many construction materials are stored inside the site.

"The antenna itself consists of thousands of tall poles, or masts, onto which the antenna elements are attached. Between the masts is a network of metal supports, each of which is designed to support a grid of tiny metal T-shaped antenna elements. This one I have here is a sample. Each antenna element will receive a tiny amount of radio energy that will be converted into electricity by the antenna, then electronically rectified into direct current that flows from the antenna. By connecting about a billion of these elements together, the final output of the plant is produced. Each element will produce about five watts of power and therefore the entire antenna can produce up to five billion watts of clean power. This one antenna will meet the needs of Kenya for clean electric power for many years.

"The construction of this antenna is expected to take about five years. When it's done, we'll begin a period of testing. Then there will be a period of transition from the present polluting power plants to this new clean source of electricity. Now, I'd like to take you to the antenna site."

The group, including the Interior Minister, went into the plaza behind the Ministry, where a large helicopter was waiting. They were soon on their way to visit the antenna site. On arrival, they were shown the measures being taken to protect the site from unnecessary damage. Some were impressed and some, who had cautiously refrained from speaking all day, were still skeptical.

Returning to the Ministry, the group again gathered in the Minister's conference room, and some asked questions which Jomo and Ivan attempted to answer until each was apparently satisfied. The environmentalists agreed to go home and review what they had seen, and to come back later with any remaining questions. Jomo and Ivan Roberts returned to the V.I.P. quarters at the company's Nairobi office.

CHAPTER 39

March 21

Wairimu Kwirikia was busily washing laboratory glassware in the back of the chemistry lab, as she did every Thursday after her morning classes, when her attention was diverted by a rattle at the door. She could see through the glass pane in the door's upper half that Jomo Williams was standing in the hall. He looked puzzled, then again tried the door, which was kept locked. It still was locked, of course. Finally, she could see that he was actually looking through the glass and into the lab. When his gaze reached the rear of the lab, he saw her standing there, watching him. He waved.

Wairimu had a sudden and strange feeling of apprehension. She waved back, then after drying her hands, she walked to the front of the lab and stood inside the door, looking at Jomo through the glass. She said, "What do you want?"

Jomo seemed unable to find the right words. He stammered, "Uh ... Um.... Well, I uh...." His voice was muffled by the intervening closed door.

Wairimu wondered if this could be the same self-assured attorney who had made the presentation for the power company the day before. He hadn't missed a single word yesterday.

He tried again. "I ... uh ... I just wanted to talk to you."

"About what?"

"Well, uh ... ah, I mean, well, just talk."

"Go ahead. Talk."

"Can I come in?"

"Why?"

"I feel sort of funny talking through the door, and I would be embarrassed if anyone came along and saw me talking to a closed door. Can I come in? Please?"

Wairimu decided to risk it, unlocked the door, and pulled it open. Jomo stepped into the lab. She saw that he was perspiring despite the air-conditioning in the building, which was set entirely too cold for her own comfort. He appeared to be very nervous.

"Well, talk!" It was more of a command than a statement.

Jomo seemed to back up under the force of her words. He said, "I wanted to talk to you privately. I didn't feel ... I didn't want to ... I... All your friends were there yesterday and I didn't feel comfortable to ..." His sentence, such as it was, trailed off.

"What is it you are trying to say, Mr. Williams?"

Jomo blurted it out. "Would you like to... I mean would you... have dinner with me?"

Wairimu laughed out loud. Jomo looked stricken. She couldn't resist the opportunity to make him even more uncomfortable. She assumed her most outraged expression. "What!? You want me to have dinner with the lawyer for the enemy? You waltz right in here and bold as brass announce you want me to have dinner with you? Is that right?"

Jomo could see he had made a big, major-league, industrial-strength mistake. He started backing up. "Well ... uh ... yes, ... sort of... ." He looked as if he would die on the spot.

Wairimu continued her stern expression and said, "Okay."

Jomo stared in disbelief. "Wh ... What? What did you say?"

"Okay."

"You mean okay to dinner?"

"Yes. That was the question wasn't it?"

"Well yes, of course. Yes. That was the question."

"Well, I said 'okay.' Where did you plan to take me? Not to your apartment, I hope?"

Jomo was really flustered now. His thoughts about Wairimu actually had included the possibility that some time in the future they might end up at his apartment, if he had an apartment some time in the future, except that his present apartment was in London, and they were in Nairobi. He struggled for an answer, and finally said, "I thought we might go to some nice local restaurant. I'd like to know you better." He had begun to breathe almost normally again.

"So we're not going to your apartment, where would you like to go?"

"I'm pretty much a stranger in town. When I'm here it always seems that I end up eating at the hotel, and I'm not a fan of the hotel's cooking."

Wairimu laughed. "Me neither. I ate there once, and once was enough. Do you like Chinese?"

Jomo hadn't expected to be eating Chinese food in Nairobi, but he agreed immediately. He did, in fact, love Chinese food. "I love Chinese. If you know a good place."

"I know a great place. Can you pick me up this evening at about seven?"

"Sure. But I don't know where you live. I had a hard time finding you here. All I knew was that the Minister told me you said you had classes on Tuesdays. I hoped you would be going to the University."

Wairimu's alarms were going off again. Maybe he only was looking to find out where she lived so he could ..., could what? She looked at the nervous young man before her and somehow knew his intentions were not to cause her any harm. "You might have trouble finding my place." she said. "Better you pick me up here at the University. At seven. Okay?"

"Sure," he said, "How about in front of the Science Building, I mean, this building?"

"That's fine. I'll see you at seven. Now I have to get back to work or I'll lose my job. Goodbye."

"'Bye." Jomo backed out the door. "See you at seven. Here. Tonight." He was still muttering to himself as he walked down the hall. He started to smile and thought to himself, "Tonight."

Wairimu closed and locked the door and returned to her washing. She thought to herself, "Seven," and smiled.

At 6:30 that evening Jomo found a parking space along the curb a half block from the Science Building and parked his white Toyota rental car. The broad steps at the entrance to the building were flanked by large, elevated planting-beds with asparagus ferns overflowing down their sides. At the top of the steps were large glass doors, and the glass continued all the way around the building's first

164

floor, with windows from the floor to the overhanging second floor above. He wondered about the energy wasted to air-condition this glass heat-collector. The building was built on an elevated area, and the first floor extended beyond the windows, forming a two-meter wide walkway around the building.

Jomo looked into the lobby of the building through the glass doors, and having confirmed that the lobby was empty, sat down on the top step with his back against one of the planting boxes.

He hadn't been there very long when there was a noise behind him. He twisted around to look and discovered Wairimu standing on the walk around the building, watching him.

"Hi." he said.

"Hello."

"I'm hungry for some of that great Chinese food. How about you?" he asked.

"Sounds good to me. Do you have a car somewhere nearby?"

"Just down the street. How far away is the restaurant?"

"A few minutes' drive, but too far to walk."

They rode to the restaurant in relative silence. Neither said much, other than Wairimu's directions: 'turn left,' 'turn right.' He parked on a side street. The restaurant was very small, and not pretentious, but the food was very good. They ate and talked about the weather and the food.

Finally, Jomo said, "What did you think of the meeting yesterday?"

"What do you mean?"

"Was it helpful to you? Did you learn anything that changed your opinions about the project?"

Wairimu wondered how to respond. She still was concerned about the intrusion of the massive antenna into the pristine landscape of the Chalbi Desert. The presentation *had* been convincing, but there was still something. She couldn't put her finger on exactly what it was that still bothered her, beside the sheer mass of the thing. "Well, your presentation was very informative. But I'm still not satisfied."

"You may not believe me, but I think I understand."

"You do?" *'How can he understand when I don't?'* she thought,

Jomo went on, "You're Maasai, aren't you?"

Wairimu's jaw dropped, but she quickly recovered her composure. "How did you know?"

"I didn't. It was just a hunch. But you are, aren't you?"

"Yes."

"How did you get to Nairobi and the University?"

"I wanted more. I wanted to do something to help my people. My parents let me go to the English school, and I decided I wanted to be a biologist.

"My people just keep on doing what they have done in the past," she continued. "Living in the same ways, with their herds, and moving. But things are changing, and I worried that one day there wouldn't be a place for Maasai. We already can't use the national parks. Tsavo and Amboseli used to be important pasture for our cattle, now we can't go there. The same is true of other areas."

"Do the Maasai graze cattle in the Chalbi Desert?"

"No. We don't go there. The cattle can't survive. There is little vegetation and no water."

165

"But it still bothers you, doesn't it? The antenna being there, I mean."

"Yes. I'm not sure why though."

"Maybe it's because you feel it as another intrusion into your country, another area taken away?"

"Yes. Maybe you're right."

"Well, you're correct. It is."

Wairimu was surprised at his concession. "I guess that's at least part of the problem I have with your power station, since you put it that way. I don't want to give up another square centimeter of Africa to the white man's ways and developments. This power station is another big bite out of my land. Eighty square kilometers ... My God!"

"You're right of course," he admitted. "It is a huge amount of land to give up. I hope in time we'll be able to find a way to use the land under the antenna in a positive way. But it's a compromise – we give up one thing to have something else we value more, or in this case to protect something we value more. We do it all the time."

"I don't believe in compromise. I won't compromise my principles."

"You will. And you do, all the time."

She sat straight upright in her chair and glared at him. "No! I don't. If you're going to insult me, I'll walk back alone."

"Please. Let me explain," he protested. "I don't mean to insult you. I only want you to understand."

Wairimu relaxed a little and Jomo continued, "You love your people, I assume?"

"Yes."

"And their way of life?"

"Yes."

"And you would rather be with them than here in a crowded city?"

"Yes."

"Yet you're here. Because you want to do something for your people. You compromised your desire to be with your family and friends because there was some other way you thought you might be able to help them. Isn't that right?"

"Well ... Yes. I guess, if you put it that way."

"How about the work you were doing when I saw you today? How does that help your people?"

"It doesn't really, except it's how I pay my way, or at least part of how I pay my way. I don't wash lab equipment all the time. My job is really lab assistant to the head biology professor at the university, but I also wash equipment in the chem lab. It lets me learn about the things I am really interested in, and it pays my tuition."

"What else are you doing there? Beside washing equipment?"

"I'm working on my PhD in biology. I have an experiment going right now on the effects of oil spills on marine organisms. We're determining the LD50s of new oil dispersants. But my real interest is in the ecosystems of the interior of Kenya."

"The Ld-whats?"

"LD50s. That's the concentration of a substance that causes a fifty percent mortality of the organism. It's a lethal dose to fifty percent of the test organisms.

And fifty percent survive. Knowing that number means that if some day someone has to use a chemical dispersant on an oil spill they should be able to use the least toxic chemical and keep the concentration down to a level with the least impact on the marine environment."

"So if they use that concentration, they would only kill half of the organisms, is that what it means?"

"Well, I guess that's one way to look at it. Yes."

"Its sort of like the glass of water being half full or half empty, isn't it?"

"Yes, I guess it is."

"How would you like to be able to never be concerned about the effects of oil spills on the environment, marine or otherwise? Wouldn't that be worthwhile?"

"Yes. I guess so."

"There is a price though. You have to make a compromise. It is going to cost eighty square kilometers of the Chalbi Desert."

"I don't know. It isn't mine to give up. Neither the marine environment, nor the inland deserts are mine. I can't make that compromise."

"Let me ask another question. When your village is out on the plains, how do you protect yourselves from wild animals?"

"We find brush and build a *boma* around the village. You already knew that, didn't you?"

"Yes. I knew. But I need you to work through this with me. When you cook how do you heat things? Do you make fires?"

She nodded. "Uh-huh. Yes."

"What do you make the fires with? Is it different from the material you use to build a boma?"

"No. It's the same. So what?"

"How many Maasai and other tribes are using that brush for their cooking fires and bomas?"

"I don't know. A lot."

"Are their numbers constant, or declining?"

"No. Their numbers are increasing."

"Why?"

"Well, we have improved medical care. There are clinics, and medical teams which meet us out there and give the children vaccinations and treat injuries, and counsel pregnant women and do lots of things they didn't do before. People live longer."

"What's happening to the populations of Nairobi and the other cities? Is it declining?"

"No, it's growing. What are you getting at?"

"I think you'll understand in a minute. What about the open land where your tribe grazes its cattle and finds the scrub for the fires and *bomas*? Is there as much of it today as there was last year?"

"No. The farms around the cities are expanding rapidly. There's a lot of desire to export crops among the farming communities.

"So you have a decreasing amount of land and scrub to support an increasing population. When does the demand exceed the supply? It takes scrub to grow more scrub, and there must be a point at which the annual growth rate is less than the annual consumption. Where do those curves intersect on the supply and demand graph? You're a scientist. Do you know?"

"No. I assume they are getting closer, but there is a lot of land left."

"Wairimu, my company knows. We looked at that situation and a lot of others before deciding to locate the first antenna in Kenya. Those curves intersect in between ten and fifteen years from now. Then there will be a dramatic collapse in the populations of all the tribal groups, including the Maasai. Famine, drought; cattle starve, people starve. But there are ways to prevent it. Deny your people, and others, the medical care that has allowed their populations to grow. Let them die from disease and accidents."

Wairimu's face was grim. "No." It was a whisper.

Jomo went on, "If the current energy situation continues, the increasing cost of energy will begin to further polarize Kenya's economy and society. Soon the government will simply be unable to provide those medical teams, because it will need those funds to provide services for the upper class in the cities.

"Wairimu, *you* do not have to deny medical care to your people, all you have to do is continue with present energy sources and the economic marketplace will soon do it for you. How soon? We can't be sure, but we think in about six years, maybe ten at the outside. But even if it's a lot longer, it'll still happen eventually ... unless there's a change in the energy situation. It *is* a compromise. Either you make it, or it's made for you.

"There's more," he went on. "The same situation exists all over Africa. Without a reliable and affordable source of energy, virtually every country will experience the same upheaval. Many countries will be so unable to compete in world energy markets that they'll have effectively no access to adequate supplies of fossil fuels, either oil or nuclear. The Chalbi Desert power station will help prevent that effect in many countries in addition to Kenya."

Wairimu didn't say anything. She absentmindedly stirred the remaining grains in her rice bowl with her chopsticks. She was thinking of her parents and her younger brother and sister and her friends in the village. She thought about the sacrifices her parents had made to enable her to leave the village and come to Nairobi. They were revolutionaries in their own way and had rejected the old ways many times to enable her to be where she was now. She was thinking about famines and dead cattle. Tears ran down her cheeks.

"How do you know so much about my people," she asked quietly.

"*I lived for two years with the Maasai, a few years ago.*"

Wairimu's eyes snapped wide open and she dropped her chopsticks. He had said this in her language. Jomo went on, in English, gently, "I really care what happens to the Maasai, and all of Africa, Wairimu. I really do. The power stations are not the total solution, but I believe they'll help."

"Maybe. Maybe you're right."

"Just think about it. I have some studies you might like to read that discuss the long term economic and sociological impacts of having the power station versus not having the power station. I'll send them to you."

"I'll look at them. I don't know. I don't know what to think."

"Don't try to decide until you read them over. Then check out their facts and their logic. If you find anything that doesn't check out, call me. Call me collect.

Here's my business card and I'll write my home number on the back. Call me anytime."

Wairimu took the card, glanced at it, and put it in her purse. "Thank you for dinner."

"We're not done yet."

"No?"

"No. There's something else I want to talk to you about, which I just thought of as we were talking. I don't want to offend you, or make you think I'm trying to buy your support for the project. It's very delicate… " He paused.

"Wairimu, can I see you again? I mean, would you like to go out again some time, like a date. I mean, well ... I didn't ask if you have a husband or a boyfriend, or...." His words trailed off.

"I don't have a husband or a boyfriend, at least nothing serious." She smiled a little. "But you live a little far away don't you, London, I believe it said on your card?"

Jomo laughed, "Yes. London. But I might find more reasons to come to Kenya more often if there was someone here to eat Chinese food with. Seriously, though, beside wanting to see you again, I want to make a proposal to you, and I don't want you to misunderstand. I already like you a lot, and I especially don't want you to misunderstand what I am about to say."

"What?"

"The Chalbi power station is the very first one under construction anywhere in the world. It is several months ahead of the one in Morocco, and even farther ahead of the one in the Namib. We need to know how it is impacting the environment, both during construction and after it begins operating. The company is sincere about wanting to minimize the impacts of the power station on the environment, but we need base-line information and continuing data to enable those evaluations to be made. We're not satisfied with the existing base-line information.

"I haven't discussed this idea with anyone else. It just came to me as we were talking, and I'll have to get clearance for it from the company, but... would you be interested in being part of a research effort to measure the impacts of the power station on its surroundings?"

"I .... " She hesitated, then continued curtly, "Your offer is very interesting, Mr. Williams, but I have dealt with biostitutes for developers before, and I don't want to be one. My opinions are not for sale."

Jomo noted that she had dropped back from "Jomo" to "Mr. Williams" and mentally kicked himself, but pressed on. "I'm not asking you to be a biostitute, Wairimu. I wouldn't do that. If I can get approval for this concept, and I think I can, here are the main points:

"One, whatever you find will be reported, and if you think the company has not fully and accurately reported your findings, you'll be free to publish those findings yourself, without interference from the company.

"Two, the company will pay all of your expenses plus a comfortable salary.

"Three, we'll attempt to get you a position here at the University, so that you have access to a lab, research library, etc., or, if that doesn't work out, we'll set up a lab. You may want to work as part of a team, maybe with a senior biologist as a mentor, or independently, if you wish.

"Four, I assume you have some student loans or other liabilities incurred before now. We'll pay those off, so you don't have to be worried about them."

"What about my environmental organization? I have a position of leadership there which I value." Wairimu amazed herself as she realized that she was even considering the offer.

"Keep your leadership position. I'm not suggesting you would sell your soul. We won't put restraints on your freedom to speak the truth as you see it. If you feel good about the project, the company will benefit in eyes of the environmental community. Conversely, if you find a problem, we'll do all we can to overcome it or take some action to mitigate its adverse impacts. Either way, we want community support, and we have to earn that with honest disclosure of the facts about our project.

"Does this sound like a possibility to you?" he asked.

"I'll consider it. I have to think about it though."

"Do that. If there are any other conditions necessary to make it acceptable, let me know. You have my card. Meanwhile, don't make any announcement yet about it. I don't really have any authority to invent jobs like this, but I know we need the research and have it in the budget, and I think I can get approval for you to do it. I'll write it up so the terms are in writing and you don't have to worry about my reneging or denying what I've said.

"Also, I'd like to see you again. Maybe for a movie or dancing. Would you be okay with that?" He smiled.

Wairimu smiled too. "Yes, Jomo, I'd like that." She took a scrap of paper from her purse and scribbled on it. "Here's my home address and phone number. The phone number is at the lab. I don't have a phone at home, but you can call me at the lab and leave a message if I'm not there. There's always a secretary or answering service on this number."

Jomo felt better. Wairimu had not said 'Mr. Williams' again. The dinner had taken longer than either of them realized. The restaurant staff was sitting in the far corner of the dining room, waiting for them to leave so they could lock up. The waiter, seeing them finally ready to leave, brought the bill and two fortune cookies. Wairimu took the first one and opened it. It read 'Opportunity comes at the strangest times; be ready for it.'

Jomo opened his fortune cookie, and read the inscription on the slip of paper, 'Exciting adventures lie ahead.' He hoped so.

Jomo paid the bill and he and Wairimu left the restaurant.

The car thief had found the white Toyota parked at the curb around the corner from the restaurant. He was a specialist in stealing Toyotas. The hood was almost cold and it appeared the owner was not coming back for it that evening. Quickly opening the door, he slid behind the wheel and reached under the dashboard for the wires to the ignition. He pulled them down from the rear of the ignition lock, broke the steering lock, and began to connect the jumpers to start the car.

Jomo and Wairimu were walking slowly, looking into each other's eyes, and wondering what this other person was really like. Jomo was telling Wairimu about his mother in Indiana. As they turned the corner, the Toyota exploded in a fireball that illuminated the entire block. Pieces of the hood, roof, windows and car thief rained down. Windows were blown out of buildings along the street and the cars parked near where the Toyota had been were incinerated by the intense heat.

Jomo grabbed Wairimu's hand and literally dragged her back around the corner. He ran, towing her in his wake, as fast as he could, away from the wreckage of the Toyota. Wairimu struggled to keep from falling. She had never run so fast before.

Jomo pushed her into a doorway and ran into the street to flag down an approaching taxicab. He told the driver to wait, ran back and grabbed Wairimu, and they both jumped into the taxi.

Wairimu was crying. Jomo held her against him. "We have to get you home. Which way should we tell the driver to go?"

"My car is at the University. I have to get it."

"Your car may not be safe. Here's some money." He thrust a handful of bills into her hand. "I'll have your car checked out, if you'll show it to me. Meanwhile, you take taxis everywhere! If you run through this, call my office here in Nairobi, and I'll arrange to get you more money until your car's inspected. Driver! Nairobi University!"

"What happened?" she asked.

"I'm not sure, but I think someone besides you doesn't want the power station, and that was a message to the company. If we had been a few minutes earlier, we wouldn't be here to talk about it. I have to get you home, then report in ... no, I better report in first." Jomo took out his mobile phone and called the Nairobi office. The duty officer answered.

Jomo said, "This is John Williams. Call the London office and tell them I'm okay but someone just blew up my rental car. Ask them what I'm supposed to do now. I'll call back in thirty minutes."

He again told the driver to go to the university. When they arrived, Wairimu showed the driver the way to where she had parked her car. Jomo wrote down its description and license number, and turned to her. "You are *not* to go near that car until my office checks to see it is safe. Do you understand me!?"

"Yes, Jomo. But all my books and papers are in it and I need them for class tomorrow."

"Wairimu! Someone just tried to kill us. They don't care about you, or your books and papers. If you touch that car it may explode and kill you, so STAY AWAY FROM IT!! Understand??"

"Yes." She was very quiet.

"Now, give the driver the directions to your place, and we'll get you home. I'm going to walk from here. Call me at the Nairobi office in the morning, Okay?"

"Yes, Jomo." She was starting to cry again. He put his arms around her and kissed her. She clung fiercely to him and kissed him back. She was terrified of being left alone. Jomo got out of the taxicab and watched as it drove out of sight into the darkness.

CHAPTER 40

March 22

It was 5 AM in Belau. Maurice, Andy and Jean Claude were in Maurice's office. Each had come directly from their quarters after the duty officer had awakened him. Danielle was in the United States, but they didn't know just where, as she was on a plane between offices. Cliff was at home in London, and was present in the office via the speakerphone. Kelly spoke first. "The preliminary report is that a car rented by John Williams was blown up less than a half-hour ago in Nairobi. Williams wasn't in it. He is calling back in a few minutes for instructions. What do we tell him? Any suggestions? Oh, by the way, I just called Eric Savage, and expect him on the line soon."

Andy warned, "Remember the discussion the day Danielle got here after her plane was sabotaged? Bob warned us to be poker players. I think he was right, and we still should follow his advice."

"Okay, so we don't acknowledge the attack was directed at us," Cliff said. "Then what?"

Jean Claude started to speak, but was interrupted by Cliff.

"Eric is on the line. Hold on while I hook him into the conversation."

There was a pause and then Eric's voice, "Hello, Maurice, can you hear me?"

Maurice responded, "Clear as a bell, Eric. Did you get a briefing on the current situation?"

"I hear someone's car was blown up. I didn't hear any status report on the employee."

Cliff cut in. "He's okay, but he wants to know what to do next. I expect him to call back in a few minutes."

Eric said, "This is the kind of personnel attack we worried about. The contingency plan is pretty clear. All key people are to go to their local offices. Travel from here on is to be only in company vehicles, with a company driver, and the vehicle is never to be left unattended outside our compounds. This policy applies only to top personnel, and we interpret that to include all of our official representatives in foreign countries. Business as usual for lesser employees, clerks, laborers, etc. When your man calls back, ... Who was it?"

Kelly answered, "Jomo."

"Hmmm, that means our adversary is now in Kenya --- Jomo's smart. He will get back to the local office. He has to be assumed vulnerable if he's out by himself. His protection is dependent on getting back to the office. We're assuming the office is safe, because we've had Plan Alpha in operation for over six months. Tell him to get some sleep and I'll talk to him in the morning. He'll be all right.

"The real concern is the other sites," Eric continued. "Call the site supervisors at Morocco and Namibia and advise them that one of our key reps has been the subject of an attack. They must implement the contingency plan immediately - tonight. Find all their top people and get them in. Right Now!

"One more thing. We know this kind of personnel attack has no effect on the completion of the project. It's intended for a different purpose, to demoralize, and to throw us off our pace. But whoever it is, we have to assume they know this won't stop the project. Their object has to be to stop the project. That's confirmed by the fact that this attack is in a different country from the preceding attack. This means we should be expecting an attack against something more directly linked to project progress, either one of the sites, or more likely, the Belau facility or the space plane itself. My greatest fear is that someone might get into Belau with a heat-seeking or TOW missile. The space plane is vulnerable in that area on the ground and right after take-off. It could be shot down by a fighter aircraft if our adversaries can obtain one, but we should be able to avoid that threat by rescheduling our takeoffs only when there are no other aircraft within radar range. If we can get a space plane off the ground when there isn't another plane flying close by, I don't think any other plane could catch it."

Andy interrupted, "We can't reschedule the takeoffs. The space plane has to lift off and accelerate into orbit exactly on schedule in order to intercept a satellite. It can take off a few seconds early and fly a serpentine course to slightly delay it, and we actually use that technique to adjust for better-than-predicted performance as a result of high altitude winds, but we can't delay much or the plane will miss the satellite, and if the flight is too long, the plane may run out of fuel before it finishes its mission."

"Then scrub the takeoffs."

"We can't do that either." Maurice protested, "Every load is required to stay on schedule. There has to be another way."

"Let the plane stay on schedule and risk the plane, or change the schedule and risk the project – is that the only choice?" asked Eric.

"Wait a minute ...," interjected Jean Claude. "We're flying each plane once a day, except when it's down for maintenance, right?"

Andy answered, "Right, what're you thinking, Jean?."

"We've been sending each plane up almost like clockwork, every day, and the future schedule calls for one flight per plane every eight hours. We did that to distribute the workload equally among our employees' work shifts. But we don't have to. We have satellites in orbit where a plane launching could intercept one every forty minutes. We could launch planes as close together as three in a two-hour period, and still rendezvous with their satellites. I'll check with the ballistic technicians and see how random the launches can be made to appear. We can keep the loading crews on schedule, but launch on a staggered schedule by keeping some planes loaded in the hangar for a longer time, and launching others immediately after they're loaded."

"Perhaps, using the serpentine maneuver, we could launch all three planes during the same window, with one leaving right on schedule and the other two a little earlier or later," Andy observed.

Cliff's voice came from the intercom. "I think we're forgetting something. Andy, you're the expert at this, and I'm just a simple country lawyer, but I don't think we have any of those limitations, if we view the problem correctly. Please correct me if I'm wrong, but as I understand it, only the flights carrying personnel, fuels, expendable liquids, supplies for a low earth satellite have to be delivered to a satellite. Couldn't a plane, if it is carrying parts or supplies for the Web, simply reach an orbital altitude and unload its cargo, with no satellite to receive it? I mean just leave it there in space, and let a tug come and pick it up. That would let you launch a plane any time."

Maurice said, "Of course! How obvious. We've been suffering from a lack of imagination. Cliff, you're almost right, but we don't even have to unload fuels and expendable liquids at a satellite. They're all contained in tanks, which we've been unloading at the low earth orbit satellite and hauling on out to the Web. The only time we need the space plane to rendezvous with the satellite itself, is if a *passenger* pod has to wait for transfer from a shuttle to the space plane, or vice-versa. That's because the pod needs to have the backup life-support built into the satellite, or to deliver water or supplies for the low earth orbit satellites. If we can time the shuttle tugs to rendezvous with the plane, we can effectively use the tugs themselves as low earth orbit satellites. It'll require some extra personnel on the space plane to assist in the transfer, but it's very do-able, and will free us completely from the schedule we've been using!!"

Eric cut in, "I still think our greatest weakness now is the space plane. It's a huge and vulnerable target if someone has an appropriate weapon. We need to see what can be done to erect barriers to block the public view of the plane on the ground, and we need to recheck and test our security measures, both within the installation as well as our security agreement with the Belauan government."

Jean Claude said, "We'll check each of those items at dawn today, but we haven't located Danielle. She's supposed to be enroute to Houston from Seattle, but we can't be sure. Our no-advance-reservation security system unfortunately means we don't know which airline or flight she took. There's a call in to Lone Star, where she was headed. They have a car waiting for her at Houston Hobby Airport and will call here as soon as they have her. I'll notify everyone as soon as we confirm she's all right."

Maurice asked, "Does anyone have anything else? If not, you two in London take care of alerting Africa and our European suppliers, and we'll notify the corporations in Asia and the Americas from here."

Eric came on again. "The attack on Jomo suggests to me that all of the families of top personnel should be assigned guard details and brought in."

Maurice said, "Okay, Eric, do it and let us know when everyone's secure." No one had any further issues to discuss, so Cliff and Eric signed off. Maurice turned to Jean Claude and Andy. "I'm nervous about having the boss out of touch when she's traveling. Maybe we can work out something. Be thinking about it."

Jomo walked across the University campus to a main street into Nairobi's downtown section. He soon flagged down a taxi and within a few minutes, was at the entrance to the Nairobi office. He produced his identification and was admitted. It was midnight.

He immediately called London on the secure line and was connected to Eric Savage. He related as accurately as possible everything that had transpired that evening. Eric took the information regarding Wairimu's car and promised to have a team check it out in the morning.

Jomo went to the visiting officers' apartment in the lower level of the office and went to bed. He couldn't sleep. Every time he started to doze off, he turned the corner again in his memory and saw the explosion, then he remembered

Wairimu's arms around him. Sometime during the night, exhaustion overtook his defense mechanisms and he dozed off, despite his worries.

When he awoke the following morning, he called Kelly on the secure line and outlined the research proposal he had made to Wairimu during dinner the preceding evening. Kelly agreed that it sounded like a good idea, both because they needed the research and because it would give them a contact within the local environmental community.

Kelly, however, was more concerned about the danger to which being associated with the project could subject Wairimu. He told Jomo he'd get approval for the expenditures from Stellar Power headquarters, and send funding down to Nairobi through regular channels. They'd have to work out many details to insure her security and, until then, she couldn't establish any identifiable connection with the company. Jomo was to call her and explain this. Jomo said he would, but realized he couldn't call her from the office. There was no way to know if the office phones were tapped.

CHAPTER 41

March 21

At 3:30 PM, Houston time, Danielle arrived at Lone Star Financial and was given a report on the bombing that had occurred in Nairobi two hours earlier. She immediately called Belau on the secure line. Maurice assured her that everything they could think of was being done, while maintaining the external appearance of imperturbability. She called Cliff. He related the conversations with Jomo and Eric Savage. She was satisfied they were doing all they could under the circumstances, but something else was bothering her.

"Cliff, we have a new problem developing here in the States. The American intelligence-gathering and law enforcement agencies, the CIA and FBI, have been agitating again in Congress for unprecedented power to monitor private communications. They're arguing that they need that ability in order to fight crime, but it looks to me as if it's just agencies trying to prove their own importance to themselves. Our people here are very concerned. If the proposals being put forward are adopted, our secure lines would become illegal, along with our encoded communications between Belau and the subsidiaries and subcontractors in the States. It's an intolerable prospect.

"They were doing this several years ago, Danielle, but it faded into the background noise around Washington, D.C., and I thought it was dead. It obviously isn't."

"You say the CIA and FBI are behind it? Do they have enough political clout to pull it off?" Cliff asked.

"They seem to be only part of the problem," she said. "Recently they've received a boost from other federal agencies. Both the Department of Justice and Treasury now seem to be convinced that they need to be able to monitor private communications in order to protect the government against tax fraud, among other things. Anyway, Congress hasn't approved anything like monitoring of private communications, but Lone Star thinks someone is already trying to eavesdrop on our electronic data exchange. During just the last month, there have been seventeen transmissions from Belau to Lone Star that were garbled during transmission and had to be re-sent. The computer experts here think it's due to someone intercepting or attempting to intercept our messages."

"There are important Constitutional aspects to this concept of monitoring private communication," said Cliff, "but I can't believe the ACLU is standing idly by, while this is going on, is it?"

"No, they're not. But the experts here think the Feds are proceeding to conduct these wire-taps despite the lack of legal or constitutional authority. Cliff, Boeing has been having the same kind of problems with our communications and with communications with their other customers. It appears to affect only data communications, and only those which are encrypted. The messages transmitted in the clear are uncorrupted, but they have had many coded messages with serious defects on the receiving end, yet the sender claims the data-stream was clean when sent."

176

"I want to cut this off at the source," she went on. "We can't afford to let our schedules, costs, delivery dates, and internal bookkeeping become government knowledge or otherwise get out of our control. We can't wait while the political process grinds on, knowing that there is now daily tampering with our communications. I want a meeting with the President of the United States to explain our need for freedom from this intrusion. I'll go as an attorney for Belau Aviation. Can you set it up or should I get Uncle Bob to do it?"

Kelly answered, "I could set it up, given time, but there would have to be a lot of explanations. If I do it, it would have to be as an 'issue-oriented' meeting to discuss government policy, and would have to be justified to a lot of the President's flappers at lower levels, any one of whom potentially could block us. It would be better, and quicker, if Bob sets it up as a political meeting, through his political connections. I think Bob's a better approach, and much faster, too."

"All right. Keep on top of the situation in Kenya, and tell all of the site superintendents to stay on their toes. Another attack directed at the antenna sites themselves could occur anytime. Have them increase their perimeter guards to insure that no one gets through the fences around the sites. I'm calling Bob. Out, here."

Moments later she was on the telephone with Bob MacDonald. She told him that she wanted a meeting with the President, and he said he would see what he could do. He immediately called one of his friends inside the administration and asked him to set up a meeting for her. She went back to reviewing reports and projections with the Lone Star staff. An hour later, Uncle Bob called back.

"You have an appointment with the President, at the White House, at 7:30 tomorrow morning. Use the East entrance. He agreed to give you ten minutes. Is that long enough?"

"That's plenty. If he gives me five minutes, he'll listen for an hour if that's what it takes. Thanks, Uncle Bob. Give my girl an extra carrot for me." Miss Pattycake, her mare, was still in MacDonald's stable. She added, "Could you also arrange me a room at the Willard Hotel tonight? That's just down the street from the White House."

"Sure will, honey," he said. "Why don't you come out and ride a little with me when you get a break? We all miss you here."

"Miss you too, and I *will* come as soon as I can work it in. Love you. Bye." She hung up.

A moment later she was on the phone to Eric Savage. "Eric, I have an appointment with the President of the United States tomorrow morning. I'm going to arrive at Washington National Airport some time this evening and want a security team to meet me there with a limo. I'll be traveling under the name Elizabeth Stevens. We need a large enough team to guard the limo and my hotel room all night and get me to the White House in the morning, then get me back to Washington National. Can that be arranged?"

"Yes, ma'am. I'll have the limo standing by at the airport when you arrive. Call me as soon as you have an arrival time. We'll pull a team of top security personnel from the photovoltaic plants in Indianapolis. I've personally checked them out and they're all good men."

Danielle hung up and called her mother. "Mom, I'm going to Washington, D.C. this afternoon, and need to use your credit card to make an airplane reservation. I'll pay you back." She carefully copied down the card number and expiration date. "Yes, Mother. I'm fine. No, Mother. I don't have a boyfriend. Yes, Mother. I'll wear a warm coat. I know it can be cold in Washington. Thank you, Mother. Love you. Bye." Her mother thought Danielle was short of funds. If only she knew.

She called Neverland Travel. "Marilyn, it's Danielle. How are you? How's business?"

"Oh, Dee. I'm fine, but we haven't seen one another in so long. Why don't you take a break and come to Miami for a holiday? And business is thriving, thanks to a bunch of mystery corporations. Do they have anything to do with you?"

"Ha. You'd be surprised. I can't come to Miami just now, but maybe you could get away for a week or so. Let that office manager I sent you run things. How'd you like a South Seas Island vacation? Beautiful beaches, palm trees, awesome snorkeling and a chance to visit at my office and see what your work has been helping to make possible?"

"I'd love that, and I'll come whenever you say. So what can I do for you today?"

"I want a reservation for a friend to fly from Houston Hobby to Washington, D.C. this evening departing after 8:30, to Washington National, not Dulles. The reservation is for Elizabeth Stevens. Charge the ticket to this credit card." Danielle read her Mother's number and the expiration date. "Then a ticket from Washington National to Oakland tomorrow afternoon. Then from Oakland to San Diego a day later, to arrive in San Diego about 8 PM. Got that?"

'You bet. Hobby to National this evening after 8:30. National to Oakland tomorrow afternoon. Oakland to San Diego the following evening to arrive at 8 PM. Anything else? Hotels? Transportation?"

"Nope. I'm sure Mrs. Stevens will appreciate your efficient service. I'll call back in a little while to see when the flight leaves Hobby."

"I can tell you right now." Marilyn was sitting at her reservations computer. "It's American 634, departing at 8:45 PM from Hobby. She can pick up her tickets at the Omnisphere counter in the terminal. They'll be waiting."

"I'm going to pick them up for her. Can you arrange that without having to identify myself?"

"It's unusual. Hmmm ... I know one of the people there. I'll ask him to put the ticket in an envelope and hand it to you. What are you going to be wearing?"

"I'm wearing a blue business suit, an off-white silk blouse and have a small pin on the left lapel, sort of a sun design."

"Okay. His name is Mark Johnson. He'll have everything you need. Thanks for the business."

"Thank you. And you have to come see me, OK?"

"Okay. Bye."

Danielle hung up and summoned the office's receptionist. "Mr. Felix O'Brian at the Transco Tower. Get him on the phone for me, please."

A few minutes later the intercom buzzed, and the receptionist's voice said, "Mr. O'Brian on line two."

She picked up the phone and punched line two. "Mr. O'Brian. It's Danielle Simones. I'm in Houston for the afternoon and thought you might be able to join me for dinner. Perhaps that cute Italian place across from the Galleria, what was it called? Cafe Italiano?" She knew the restaurant was only a block or so from the Transco Tower and the Houston Beltway and therefore within easy reach of the airport.

"Great idea. I'd love to have dinner with you. What time?"

"I have to be at the airport at quarter past eight, so we should make it early. How about six? Is that too early for you?"

"No. Six is fine with me. Where shall I meet you?"

"I'll be at the restaurant. Can you run me to the airport afterward?"

"My pleasure. See you at six."

The afternoon passed rapidly and 6 PM found her in a car with a Lone Star Financial officer in the parking lot in front of Cafe Italiano. As Felix O'Brian walked from his car toward the restaurant, she left the car and said goodbye to its driver, then walked over to meet O'Brian. It was still hot and humid, although the Sun was low in the West.

The air-conditioning was a welcome change from the heat of the sidewalk outside, and the maitre'd seemed genuinely glad to see them.

"Good evening, Mr. O'Brian. Welcome. Your usual table?"

"Yes, thank you, Tony."

They were escorted to a table in a quiet corner of the dining room, and the waiter held her chair as Danielle sat down.

"Haven't seen you since Bangkok," O'Brian said. "I hope everything's going all right." It was a statement, but the question was clear.

"Yes. It's going very well. It's been only about three years since you and I met, and three space planes are making almost daily trips to orbit carrying materials for various satellites and the solar collector. And we should have two more space planes flying in a matter of a few months. That reminds me, I didn't see you at our celebration for the first space plane. We missed you."

"My daughter's birthday party was the same week-end, and there were big preparations already made. Daddy had to be there. Sorry about missing your wing-ding."

"If you'd like to visit some time, please call the London office, and we'll arrange a special tour for you. You *are* a special investor, you know."

"Oh? How is that?"

"Beside being a syndicate head, you're the first potential investor I talked to after I ran the ad in the Wall Street Journal and other papers. I knew you understood the energy industry, so I went first to you. I knew that one key to selling this program was the need for participation by the current owners of energy companies. What we actually have are the most energy-aware investors in the world, and a large percentage of the investors have wealth that is energy-related, including those in your syndicate.

"What I really wanted to talk to you about, though, is whether you and your syndicate are satisfied with our progress to date. Have you had any feedback from the investors in your group?"

"Nothing negative. The Houston syndicate is very comfortable with your reports, they seem to track very closely with the projections, and in some cases are better than the projections."

Danielle laughed. "I hope they remember *that* when we have some things that run behind the projections. But I *am* very pleased with the way things are progressing. We have an outstanding design and production team, and their hard work has been paying off. I'm glad that your group is comfortable as well with our progress. I had a chance to see some of them at the celebration, but that brief meeting, well ..., trying to entertain several hundred people, there was not enough time to measure their individual reactions."

"All those I have talked to here in Houston were very impressed with the space plane. Whatever you did really wowed 'em. Since I couldn't attend, I asked several of them for a full report, and they were all glowingly positive."

"That's good, Felix. Of course, that was the response we were hoping for, but I wasn't sure we succeeded as well as we wanted. From what you say, it sounds as if we were right on the money. Now, I need some more information from you - you have very good intelligence in the energy community. I need to know if anyone in the global energy community feels we represent a threat to their economic welfare. If they do, I may want to offer them an opportunity to participate as investors. We aren't here to make enemies, and don't see our efforts as a threat, provided we have a chance to educate any person or group who might perceive us that way. Can you keep your eyes and ears open, as a personal favor for me, and let me know if anything turns up? Please?" She smiled her sweetest smile.

O'Brian couldn't say no. He had 200 million invested, and was considering more. "Sure. Be glad to. How's your Primavera?"

O'Brian dropped her at the departures area at Hobby Airport. She picked up Elizabeth Stevens's ticket and was soon headed for Washington, D.C. The plane arrived at midnight and she was met just outside the terminal building by two of the guards from Norden Photovoltaics. Four more were waiting in the car. All were wearing professional-looking business suits. She knew each of them also was wearing body armor and a major arsenal of several kinds of weapons. Eric Savage knew how to select security personnel.

At 7:15 the following morning, she presented herself at the East Visitors' Gate to the White House grounds, and was promptly admitted, walked through a metal detector, and escorted to the President's Oval Office.

President Johnathan DeWitt was well-known for his friendly manner, and even at 7:30 in the morning he lived up to his reputation. He shook her hand warmly.

"Miss Simones, I'm pleased to meet you. What's on your mind so early in the morning?" He indicated a chair for her in front of his desk, then sat in a matching chair nearby.

It was exciting to meet this powerful leader, but her voice was cold as ice. "Mr. President, I represent an international group of companies engaged in a very large, high-tech development program. Much of our industrial effort is located here in the United States and our business is responsible for many billions of dollars of the US Gross National Product. I'm sure you understand that those dollars represent thousands, maybe millions, of jobs. The money we spend here in the United States comes from all over the world, and represents a significant part of the positive side of the United States' balance of trade.

"We're building a system to collect solar power and beam it to Earth. It involves unbelievable amounts of material and capital. For example, our first solar collector satellite will have more photovoltaic surface than all of the photovoltaic cells ever produced in the world before our project. It's going to revolutionize

Earth's energy situation. In the long term, it will replace existing power sources with a clean, reliable, and inexhaustible supply of electric power, which will allow unprecedented economic growth. In the short term, it will make the supplies of fossil energy available to the United States much less expensive than they would be otherwise, by increasing the worldwide supply of energy, and thereby reducing the competition for limited supplies of fossil fuels.

"We have a problem though, Mr. President. Your intelligence and law enforcement agencies have recently been urging Congress to allow them to place wiretaps or other surveillance methods on communications between private parties. They have introduced legislation to make encrypted messages illegal, as well as to require computers to contain features that would allow those agencies to poke around within our very computer files, without our knowledge, and perhaps without a search warrant.

"Our business information is encrypted as a security necessity, both to prevent any potential competitors from obtaining our trade secrets, but also to protect us from hostile acts of those who are jealous of our program. We must have secure communications in order to operate.

"Recently, our subcontractors here in the U.S. have discovered extensive and determined efforts to intercept our electronic communications. Mr. President, someone is already eavesdropping on our communications and we don't like it even a little bit. We believe it's some agency of your government, and we want it to stop, immediately and permanently. We want the push in Congress to invade people's private communications to end.

"I'm sure you're over-reacting, Ms. Simones. Our efforts are only to deter crime and protect our national security. The legislation for the government's investigative agencies to have the 'key' to private computers requires court approval."

"Mr. President, they, your investigators, are using something like that technology, right now, on the private communications of my clients. If your investigators can't be trusted now, without the legislation, how can we trust them in the future? My purpose for coming here today was to go directly to the top on this matter. If there is someone around here with more authority than yourself, I'd like to speak to him, or her. If not, the ball is in your court.

"If we continue to find attempts to intercept our communications, or if the effort in Congress to legislate away our right to privacy continues, my clients will have no alternative but to move their business to another country where they can be free of this government intrusion, and we expect other multinational companies to do the same. I think it would be an economic disaster for the United States. For us, this is a simple business decision. Our business is not secure if we can't communicate in complete privacy with our subordinates and sub-contractors and that means our communications have to be encrypted.

"Nothing we make here in the United States is unique. We can, and do, buy virtually every U.S.-built component in other parts of the world as well, but the U.S. is a major supplier for us because of its good supply lines and resources, both material and personnel. But we can and will drop every single U.S. source if we can't operate in a secure environment.

"Check me out, Mr. President. I don't bluff. I'm not a bluffer. But my clients must and will protect their business interests. During the past two years, at

Boeing alone, we spent over two billion dollars and we have contracts with them for four billion more. Other American subcontractors will account for another ten billion in orders in less than two years. I don't think the U.S. can afford to turn its back on my clients. Or the many other companies who won't accept this intrusion. Thank you, Mr. President. I appreciate your time." She was ready to leave.

The President leaned back in his chair, then stood up. Danielle started to stand, but the President motioned for her to remain seated. He went to his desk, picked up a file, and opened it. He walked back to his chair and sat down again.

"I know you aren't a bluffer, Miss Simones. I know very well who you are, and a great deal about your 'clients' project." He held up the file. "People don't get into this office at 7:30 in the morning without a very good reason, and even though your friend Robert MacDonald is an old business acquaintance and party supporter, even he would not have been able to get you in here this morning, on only twelve hours notice, without your own rather remarkable background. You got in here because I wanted to meet you. I admire what you're doing, and hope you succeed.

"But what you are proposing is not realistic. Congress and law-enforcement agencies are clamoring for *more* authority to prevent drug traffic and other organized crime, as well as various forms of industrial crime. ... Can you stay here for a few hours today? I want you to speak with some of my advisors on this subject, and they're due here at 8:30."

Danielle said she could stay for a while. A soldier appeared at the door and escorted her to a drawing room carefully decorated in lovely antiques and paintings of former Presidents and First Ladies. A small fire was burning in the fireplace. She checked. It was a real fire, which somehow surprised her. She sat in a relatively comfortable chair and considered what the President's advisors might say.

At about fifteen minutes before nine, the President came into the drawing room and invited her to join him in his conference room. He led the way to another part of the building, into a large room that looked to her like a room where the Cabinet would meet, which it was. She was introduced to the Secretary of Defense, the Attorney General, the Secretary of the Treasury and the Chiefs of the Central Intelligence Agency and the Federal Bureau of Investigation. They all had read her dossier and had been told by the President of her earlier conversation with him.

The President began. "I asked you all to meet with me this morning to hear first-hand what this rather remarkable woman has to say. As I have already told you, I spoke with her earlier, and I believe there is a lot of merit in what she's asking. I'd like each of you to consider her arguments, and advise me whether they're sufficient for us to reconsider our position on the Electronic Information Security Bill we're proposing to Congress." He turned to Danielle and said, "Miss Simones, perhaps you could summarize your position to these folks."

She began, retracing the same points she had outlined to the President. They waited until she finished, then all tried to speak at once. She waited until one member of the group had overpowered the others. He said, "You're basically asking us to abdicate our responsibility to maintain order in this country. We need the access which the proposed legislation would give us in order to prevent crime."

Danielle responded, "Mr. Attorney General, there are two ways to prevent crime. One is to apprehend those who commit crimes, and the other is to make ordinary acts criminal then arrest everyone who commits ordinary acts. My clients encrypt their data communications, and all of their domestic and international voice communications are encrypted and therefore secure.

"These are ordinary acts, taken to protect our trade secrets, to insure the security of our personnel, and to enable our business to proceed without interruption by our competitors. We have a multi-billion dollar project underway. Even a minuscule percentage increase in cost of a component can be devastating to our overall budget.

"We're building what amounts to the largest public works project of all time, but we're doing it as a private venture, with no, I emphasize NO, public capital, in the finest traditions of free enterprise. Our project dwarfs the pyramids, or anything else, in its scope. Think of it: one solar collector satellite with an area of photocells over three hundred square miles. This one satellite will produce enough electricity to power at least one, maybe two, continents.

"At the same time we've designed, built and flown, in less than three years, an aircraft with performance only dreamed about in the past, and have already assisted your space agency in delivering repair personnel to many of the U.S.'s own ailing satellites.

"We're doing what America became great doing - design and innovation - but we're doing it on an international scale, with U.S. companies and workers as full participants. In order to continue to operate in the United States, we feel it's essential to have freedom to act responsibly, and to maintain our privacy, and our trade secrets, free from government intrusion. We comply in every way with many volumes of federal, state and local regulations. We have entire departments whose sole function is to insure that we're in compliance with the various regulatory requirements, but we *will not* give up our privacy. Like our bedrooms, the internal communications of our companies are no one's business but our own. If we violate your laws in dealings with others, prosecute us. But if you make our business operation, which requires secure communication for its continued existence, illegal *per se*, then we simply can no longer do business in this country. We'll not knowingly become criminals, and if you give us only that choice, *we must leave!*

"If it was only our company," she continued, "perhaps the government of the United States could dismiss us. We will represent only about sixty billion dollars in revenue, world-wide, over a ten-year period, without economic multipliers. But we're not alone. Many businesses today are international or multinational, perhaps most very large businesses are. All of them could easily move their corporate headquarters to foreign countries where a more favorable business environment exists. I don't think you could afford that. It would make the U.S. into truly a poor relative, suitable only for minor offices and branch dealers, not the major manufacturing sites for those enterprises. If and when our business moves to other countries, we will leave behind the thousands of U.S. employees, unemployed, and the factories, which we are now utilizing, vacant. Our technology is multi-national and transferable, our products are simple, as are many formerly American-made products which now are made elsewhere and sold in the U.S. - with the enormously inflated profits going to overseas producers."

She saw several skeptical faces, so she continued. "You think I'm exaggerating? How much do you think the remaining American companies can take? Many of the classic American products have been steadily moving into production abroad. When I was a child, my gym shoes were always labelled 'US

Keds.' Have any of you seen any Keds recently? What do you suppose their market share is? Where are they made? I'll tell you what you see; Reebok, Nike, Adidas, and a hundred other brands, most of which are made in Singapore, Taiwan, Hong Kong, China, Japan, the Philippines - and maybe a few Keds. I don't even know if U.S. Keds are still made in the United States.

"The Western Electric plant, in Indianapolis, for many years made the best telephones in the world for Americans. Where do your telephones come from today? Those same other places! The Western Electric building was just a rust-belt empty shell two years ago, but it is now a vibrant company, building photovoltaic cells for this project.

When I was a kid, I always wore Levi's blue jeans, 'Made in the U.S.A.'. Where are they made today? I don't know, but I'll bet it's not in the U.S.A.

"You still think I'm exaggerating? Try me! How many companies who could have moved, and have already been pressed to the wall by incompetent regulators badly administering thousands of well-intentioned regulations, and who already are competing against products made abroad by workers earning one-tenth or less of what the domestic American worker earns ... how many of those companies will be pushed over the edge by another unwarranted government intrusion into their private businesses?"

"But what we're proposing is only to prevent companies from hiding their illegal acts behind a veil of encoded data." It was the Director of the FBI speaking. "If they're doing nothing illegal, they have nothing to hide."

She shot back, "Mr. Director, that same argument was used to justify unrestricted police searches of people's homes. It's well-established that there has to be a crime before you can obtain a warrant, then search a home. What you are proposing is equivalent to making it illegal for the homeowner simply to lock his door or do anything else to prevent the police from walking through his home any time they like. We're unfortunately moving in that direction in this country, but there's still hope that we will not fall back to being a 'police state.'"

"You exaggerate the seriousness of what's being proposed, Miss Simones," the FBI Director responded. "It will obviously impact only businesses, and when a company begins doing business, it waives its right to freedom from government regulation. It's clearly different from the warrantless search of a person's home. In a home situation, the search threatens the most basic rights of people, but that isn't true with a corporation."

"Isn't it? Let me take your points one at a time, Mr. Director.

"First, you claim it would impact only businesses. That disregards the fact that the law you have been proposing would apply equally to the computers which millions of individual Americans have in their homes.

"Second, I challenge your thesis that a business, a corporate 'person,' as it were, gives up its rights or has fewer rights than a natural person, simply by becoming a business entity or by operating in a business environment. There is no basis for such an argument.

"Third, intrusion into a business's secret operations is arguably much worse than intrusion into a person's home. It sets up the paradox as to whether the needs of the many outweigh the needs of the few, as popularly postulated between Captain James T. Kirk and his Vulcan First Officer. The answer of course, is *neither*. A corporation involves the privacy and safety of several or several hundred or several thousand persons. If release of a secret threatens their safety, it can be much more dangerous than an intrusion into a single home. The companies which I represent employ many thousands of persons, and unauthorized release of even the most trivial information can put any or all of them in jeopardy. Big companies, doing big things, irritate people. Our project will make many people very wealthy, and will make others much less wealthy than they are today. We are changing the world, and some people don't like it.

"During the past six months, there have been at least two attempts to kill people working on our project, one of which occurred less than twenty-four hours ago. The responsible officers of my clients will not risk the lives of those employees to coddle the paranoia of law enforcement and intelligence officers like yourselves who think someone *might* be doing something they disapprove of. We don't know what other steps anyone who intends us harm might try, but if we can't encrypt our communications, their task will be much easier.

"I don't want to see our companies move their operations out of the United States, and my purpose for coming here today is not to 'threaten.' But we are at a cusp, and a decision must be made and made right away. If we don't see an immediate, public and dramatic reversal of the policy supporting the intrusion of government into our private business, we have no alternative but to leave. This administration is well-known for its concern for the long-term welfare of Americans and America, and we felt it was necessary and appropriate to let the administration know of the pendency of this decision of ours, to enable you to prevent this move if possible."

The President looked at the Secretary of Defense, "George, where does this policy impact Defense? Do we need the electronic eavesdropping capability to protect our defense posture?"

The Secretary of Defense, a well-known authority on defense-related policy long before nomination to his current post, looked as if he had stepped in something smelly. "Mr. President, it's pretty well known that I've *opposed* this policy since it was first proposed several years ago, when technology was beginning to make it possible. There's no moral or constitutional justification for the Department of Defense to spy on its citizens. It sounds to me more like the tactics of the old Soviet Union's GRU than anything that would fit in any way within our American ethical framework. Still, this lady's particular enterprise does suggest military potential. I'm concerned about the military uses of the satellite that her clients are building. It is just possible that having the ability to oversee their internal communications may enable us to detect military actions before they occur."

Danielle looked at the Defense Secretary and said, "Mr. Secretary, let me say first that I've read many of your law review articles and admired and enjoyed them. You suggest that our satellite 'might' be used in a military way. I'll acknowledge that such a use is theoretically possible, although it would run the cost far beyond our limited budget. But I want to ask you if it isn't as likely – and probably a lot more likely – that our satellite will be used as a force for peace? ... Think about it. Our business is the sale of electric power. Our investors expect a return on their investment. That return depends on *use* of our power in the countries where it is received. Each contract with the countries where our receiving antennas are located effectively requires the country, as a condition to receiving the power, to maintain peaceful relations with its neighbors. The country receives a royalty for each unit of power transmitted from its antenna to users in its country, and to other countries. If it fights with its neighbors, it can lose its royalty payment, and even its power supply. If the neighbors fight with it, they can have their electric power cut off. These are powerful incentives, included deliberately to induce each country to find peaceful ways to resolve differences with its neighbors. Instead of creating a resource which can be 'seized' by a military force, without the power beamed from the solar satellite our antennas are just a lot of junk metal.

"If there's a military threat to the United States from our satellite, I haven't been able to identify it, and believe me I've thought about this program as much as anyone. In order to be a military force, there would have to be a foreign government with affluence comparable to the United States, and the resources necessary to divert enough assets from other activities to create a full military force with enough personnel to occupy an adversary's territory. Such a force might someday exist, but it won't be in your lifetime or mine.

"Anyway, Mr. Secretary, don't you think it's a little disingenuous for the United States to worry about my clients building satellites when the U.S. has so dramatically abandoned its own space program? We've never concealed the fact that our satellite is a concept borrowed directly from NASA, and that much of the technology we're using was developed by NASA. We've made the technology we've developed available to the United States, and we intend in the future to build very large space stations at which the United States will be welcome to be a tenant, along with any other country that can pay the rent for the 'space.' Our investors have spent a lot of money - only after the U.S. backed out. Now you want to put us in a box, like an insect, to watch carefully in case we should try to do something of which you don't approve. We won't be put in that box."

"Isn't that a little over-dramatic? ... "

He didn't have a chance to continue. She shot back, "Not a bit! We've raised billions of dollars to make this project a reality. What you're proposing, by your outrageous intrusion into the private business affairs of your citizens and residents, is for you to risk the entire investment of those forward-looking people, as well as the lives of the many employees who're risking their lives each day working in space, flying the space plane, or just going to work in cities around the globe. The man they tried to kill last night was a very bright young lawyer from Indiana, minding his own business.

"You may risk the lives of your soldiers every day, Mr. Secretary, and never think a thing about it, but I guarantee you, Sir, *you will not* risk the lives of *our employees!* Not while I am still alive and breathing, and I think not while any of the officers of the various corporations I represent are still kicking."

The President broke into this heated exchange. "Let's take a break for a few minutes. Would anyone care for a cup of coffee, or a soft drink, or something?" He called an attendant who was standing just outside the door and requested him to bring refreshments. After a break, the President continued, "Miss Simones, I'm very troubled by the issues you've raised, and I'm going to direct that a careful analysis be made of each of them immediately. General," he said, looking at the Attorney General, "you are directed to withdraw the bill from the Congress, until we have the opportunity to give these issues another look."

"But, Mr. President," the Attorney General protested, "if we withdraw the legislation, the Republicans will eat our lunch. They'll say we don't know what we want, *et cetera*."

"Well, General, maybe they'd be right. But the big law-and-order push for this bill is coming from the Right anyway. We have to be thinking about how we'd look if a whole bunch of American businesses called a press conference and said they were firing thousands of American workers and moving overseas because of the bill *we* pushed. I think Miss Simones has done us a big favor by coming to us in person and privately. There may be some situations in which secure and private communications are better. Like now.

"Miss Simones," the President continued, "I don't know where we're going with this, but we *will* pull the bill, at least for now. I'll have a review and a final decision within as short a time as possible."

Turning back to the Attorney General he went on, "I want a thorough analysis, and I want you to bring in those Constitutional experts from Harvard, Michigan and elsewhere, and I want their opinions, uncut, for my examination. And if we decide not to go with the bill, as I suspect we might, I want a clean break from it, and public disclaimer of its objectives. I don't want some clique in Justice, or Treasury, trying to sneak it back in some other disguise; be sure all your personnel understand that.

He turned back to Danielle. "Miss Simones, I want to give you my personal thanks for coming here today. Few business leaders are so forthright, and willing to duke it out with our resident pack of mad dogs." He swept his hand around the room, gesturing at the others present, then continued, "I guarantee we'll give this question our full consideration. Frankly, I'm surprised," he said, looking again around the room, "that these issues weren't raised the *first* time this legislation was proposed and discussed in this room. You've done us a great service."

Six hours later Danielle was sipping an iced tea on Uncle Bob's terrace in Santa Cruz.

CHAPTER 42

November 18

A buzzer on Danielle's desk sounded quietly.

"Yes, Bill?"

"Mr. Oribati is asking for you."

"Please, put him on."

Across the large office from the desk was a 2-meter by 3-meter window looking into the tropical forest of Babeldaob. It was in fact a video display, and it changed to project the face of an agitated man. Tom Oribati was one of the wealthiest men on the planet. He had put four billion dollars of his own money into the project so far, and had assembled investors who had raised another six billion, making the Japanese-Australian group the second largest consortium in the project, close behind the South Africans. He was also the designer of the satellite's electrical control system.

"Hello, Tom. What's on your mind?"

"Your latest report has the investors from Hokkaido very upset, Danielle. They want me to find out what is going on and why we're behind schedule." His florid features seemed to become more inflamed as he spoke.

Danielle didn't say it, but she too was upset by the figures. For the first time, the production figures were behind the projected schedule, mostly in the satellite assembly. "I'm glad you called, Tom. It *is* important that we keep our investors' confidence levels high, and I want to be sure both you and they understand my desire to do just that.

"One of the most important things I have to do, to maintain their confidence and yours, is to protect my credibility, and that means giving them complete information on status of construction operations at the station, even when it's not as favorable as we'd like to see." She continued, "It *is* true that we slipped a few days behind schedule last month, but our overall program is still within its projections. I'm sure they'll be pleased with the next annual report. You know we did anticipate that there would be an occasional unplanned delay, and the master schedule factors that in. I want you to be sure to convey to Mr. Kobayashi - it is he who is so concerned, is it not? - that I share his concern with every aspect of the schedule, and I'm giving it my personal attention. Do you think that will placate him for a while?"

"I suppose so, but he was pretty upset."

"We all have a big stake in this project, Tom, so it is not hard to understand that he would be concerned. But Tom, I need you to handle as much of this as you can without bringing it to me in the future. I frankly don't have time to address every investor's individual concerns. You know there are over five hundred investors and they're each important to the project, but if I have to talk to each of them, I won't have time to work on the project. Can you please try to deflect as much of these questions from your group as possible?"

"I'll sure try, Dee, but some of these folks are pretty concerned."

188

"I know they are, Tom. Please remind them that we have a staff with the sole function of providing personal briefings to our investors and answering their questions. All they have to do to get an updated briefing is call. You're a dear, and I do appreciate your efforts. I recognize that you have more at stake here than any other single investor, so you understand how critical it is that I be able to focus on the job at hand. Got to go now. Out here." She switched off the phone. The face on the screen faded and the forest reappeared.

She spoke into the intercom. "Bill, have the helicopter meet me at the chopper pad in ten minutes and notify the airfield that I want a seat on tonight's flight. I'm going up to the Web."

"Yes, Ma'am."

The construction and project management reports were printed in neatly bound volumes on the corner of her desk. Their message was not promising. There had been a series of delays and accidents, and the project could not stand much more without seriously damaging the confidence of the investors. She tossed a few notes into the briefcase on the desk and stepped into the adjoining apartment to pick up her small travel bag, then walked out the rear door of the office and down the hall to the elevator to the roof.

The Sun was setting over the lagoon inside the coral reef west of Babeldaob. From the rooftop, the view of palm trees and breakers on the far coral reefs was beautiful, but she hardly noticed. Her attention was on the airfield on the other side of the building. Several of the corporation's giant space planes were parked there, in a perfectly straight formation. She knew one of them, *Polaris*, had just completed loading cargo and fuel for a trip to a low earth orbit satellite. All cargo and passengers bound for the Web had to be unloaded and reloaded there onto the station shuttle. She would be the only passenger this trip.

The helicopter was waiting on the pad, with its engine idling and rotors turning slowly when she opened the door from the elevator lobby. The crew chief opened the chopper's starboard door and jumped to the pavement to hold it open for her. The helicopter's engine began to pick up speed and the rotors revolved faster. As she approached, the crew chief came stiffly to attention. She nodded and said "Thank you, Alec," and stepped into the rear compartment

The crew chief watched her carefully to verify that her lap belt and shoulder harness were properly secured, then passed her a headset. She admired the professional performance of this crew, like all the crews who worked for the company. She pulled the microphone to her mouth and said, "Straight to the dispatcher's office, Jerry."

"Yes, Ma'am. Dispatcher's." The helicopter lifted smoothly from the pad and rotated toward the airfield as it climbed. Moments later it hovered before the operations building then gently touched down on its designated parking spot.

The airfield apron was oppressively hot in the afternoon sun. Danielle walked to the office and handed both her briefcase and clothes bag to the station manager, who would weigh them and adjust the trim of the giant aircraft accordingly. He already knew her weight because Bill had provided it when he made the reservation. She walked back onto the ramp to *Polaris*, and began her own careful pre-flight inspection. As she approached the captain, she said, "Hello, Hank. I'm your passenger this trip."

The captain smiled and nodded. He was in the process of conducting his own inspection, and she joined him as he carefully peered into the port wheel well, then moved on to examine the wing, engines and tail surfaces, then on to the starboard side where the process was repeated. She knew the first officer had already completed the same inspection, and was now in the process of carrying out numerous preflight checks in the cockpit. "Our takeoff is set for 1730 hours, Ma'am," Hank said. "We should be getting aboard."

"Very well, Captain. Please advise the First Officer that I'll be riding in the jump seat and to plan his weight and balance accordingly."

"Yes'm." He lifted his wrist to his mouth and spoke softly. "Ms. Simones riding in the cockpit tonight, Jake." He knew his copilot had already made the necessary adjustments in their flight plan. His call merely confirmed it.

"Roger," came back a voice from the small radio.

Walking to the nose of the aircraft, the captain and Danielle entered the elevator, which lifted them to the cockpit high above the pavement. He opened the door to the airlock, motioned her in and then crowded in himself. It was quite cozy. As the airlock cycled to match the pressure of the interior, she thought about this man who had saved her life over the Atlantic Ocean west of Portugal. He said it had all been part of his job. Hank Taylor was an excellent pilot, modest and intelligent, and the Air Force had lost a good officer when he retired. The project was fortunate, in a strange way, that she met him at just the right time, out over the Atlantic. Some day perhaps she should arrange to have dinner with him and see what might develop. The inner door opened and they stepped onto the flight deck. She found her seat and strapped in, noting that her briefcase and travel bag already had been placed in front of the seat. Her own pressure suit had also been stowed in the locker with the crew's own space suits. After fastening the seat belt and shoulder harnesses, she proceeded to immerse herself in reviewing construction schedules and reports, while the flight crew completed its pre-flight checks.

The captain turned to her as the first officer began the engine starting sequence. "Are you securely belted in, Ma'am?"

"Yes. Thank you, Captain." She gave the belts an extra tug and stowed the computer and bags in the compartment next to her seat.

The engineer and first officer were busily completing checklists as Captain Taylor released the brakes. "Rocket One ready to taxi," he radioed. The call came rapidly back, "Rocket One cleared to runway 3; cleared for takeoff as scheduled." The giant plane began to roll toward the taxiway. There was a detailed flight plan in the computers of the Operations office and of the aircraft itself. Once activated, the ship would take on a life of its own, following the flight plan in every respect.

As the plane taxied into takeoff position at the end of the runway, the captain and first officer exchanged glances and activated the on-board flight computer. The digital display showed the time remaining as the computer counted down to the moment of launch; the throttles, controlled by the computer, seemed to move themselves forward, first to 100% power, then to the first - 10% - afterburner position as the brakes released and the plane began to accelerate down the six-kilometer-long runway. A third of the way down the runway, as the afterburner went to 20, then 30%, the nose wheel of the plane lifted from the pavement and the main wheels were airborne a second later.

The gear doors snapped open, the wheels were swallowed into the bottom of the aircraft and just as rapidly, the gear doors closed. The throttle began to advance again in afterburner, now 40%, 60%, 70%, as the airspeed rapidly climbed into Mach numbers and the altitude passed 20 kilometers. Through the cockpit windows Danielle could see the skin of the aircraft begin to glow a dull red from air friction. Beneath the plane, the scramjet doors slid open and air molecules captured in the giant scoop on the underside of the plane and compressed by the plane's forward motion were mixed with hydrogen fuel and ignited in the scramjet engines, adding their thrust to the turbine engines already running at full power. The plane leaped forward in another burst of acceleration, pressing her harder against the seatback.

As the altitude indicator passed 50 kilometers, blue sky was far below. Surrounded by the blackness of space, the throttles moved all the way forward and the plane's engines went from turbine mode into full scramjet mode, with every increment in speed increasing the efficiency of the engines. In the intake on the underside of the plane, molecules of oxygen in the thin air, compressed by the enormous speed of the plane, glowed bright red-hot. A titanium panel, extending all the way across the rear underside of the plane, began sliding forward, revealing a series of nozzles from which hydrogen fuel sprayed. The fuel, ignited in the red-hot air, exploded violently, creating a rocket-like flame from the rear of the plane, which again accelerated forward in response. As the amount of oxygen available to the engine from the rapidly thinning atmosphere began to decrease with altitude, other nozzles began to spray liquid oxygen into the combustion area, converting the rear of the plane into the nozzle of a rocket engine and giving the plane its final acceleration into orbit.

Now free from the air that had provided its lift into space, the plane coasted silently toward its rendezvous with the LEO-B satellite. The speed of the plane, carefully planned, carried it upward and outward to the orbit of the satellite. There, with a brief blast from maneuvering thrusters, the plane matched orbits with the satellite, 285 miles above the surface of the earth.

CHAPTER 43

November 25
    The faint line swept across the radar screen and back again as the station's radar scanned the approaching ship. Ginny Robinson, the approach controller, watched carefully for any deviation from the approved track. The tiny blip on her screen marking the ship, with its accompanying coded information block, remained within acceptable course limits.
    Ginny nodded her head in approval. This pilot was all right. The ship's track was only 21.3 kilometers above the station's orbit and was just a few meters ahead of the pre-calculated optimum track. The ship was still over 10,000 kilometers away, and slowing as it braked to rendezvous with the station. It would be many hours before the ship would be visible to the naked eye from one of the station's viewports. By that time, it would already have been in the orbit-matching maneuver for some time, firing its main engine to change its vector. Failure to correctly match these orbits would mean coasting past into a long orbit in space.
    Such events rarely happened these days, as the single rocket engine with which the tugs first were equipped had been supplemented almost immediately with a group of smaller maneuvering thrusters with a combined thrust greater than the tug's main engine. The supplemental thrusters were there as a spare engine, insurance in case of main engine failure.
    The few ships that had ever missed the station had been rounded up by the emergency repair boat, which carried a crew of mechanics and complete spare parts for the main and supplemental drive engines. If the ship failed to match orbits, it would take the repair boat several hours to match orbit with it. The two vessels would then stay locked together, imperceptibly slowing because of the gravitational pull of Earth, until repairs were finished. At that time, the two ships, still together, would begin a maneuvering sequence and set a new course to intercept the station.
    Ginny knew that the greater danger was a collision between the ship and the station. It was for this reason that the standard approach course was over twenty kilometers to the North of the station's orbit until the final adjustments were made.
    There was nothing more to be done at this time. The emergency crew would take their stations in the repair boat when the approaching ship was about an hour out. By that time the ship should be well into its braking sequence and would have adjusted its trajectory to intercept the satellite. If all went well, they would be off-duty again a few minutes after the ship was secured in the landing dock on the back of the crew quarters.
    Ginny unsnapped her belt harness from the console's command chair and slowly drifted away from it. With one toe, she gave a gentle push toward the hatch to the living quarters. "I'm getting spoiled," she thought to herself. With simulated "gravity" in the living area, she greatly preferred it to the zero-gee area of the docking center. Also, positive gee was where her "family" was. Her family was a white, long-haired cat named 'Snowy'.
    "Gravity" had arrived at the base when spin had been applied to the great cylinder of the station's living quarters. Ginny had been part of one of the crews that

assembled the crew quarters and she had lived there for a while when the entire station was under construction. Of course, the centrifugal force produced by the structure's slow spin was not real gravity and it was less than one-twelfth Earth's gravity even now, but it made so many things about life much more bearable. For example, cooking could be accomplished without a sealed container, although lids were still required. Ginny, like all the other workers, had access to the station's galley if she wanted to prepare something different from the crew meals. During construction, it had been necessary to "vacuum pack" food in plastic bags, by taking the food into an un-pressurized part of the station and loading it there into the bags, before placing them in a radiant energy cooker, to prevent them from exploding all over the living space. Now, vegetables could be placed in a pan, in water, and boiled with only a cover to prevent spray from the bursting bubbles. To Ginny it was wonderful!

Pseudo-gravity also simplified many aspects of personal hygiene, such as taking a bath, and made it possible for Ginny to have a cat, because of the essential cat pan. Snowy was the pet for the entire construction crew and got lots of attention. He loved the low gravity and could leap improbable distances, tracing strange paths through the air as a result of the Coriolis effect. He even ventured often into the zero-gee areas at the center of the station where much of the base's supplies were stored. There he cruised around the cargo, floating from one item to the next, searching for bugs and exploring as any self-respecting cat would do. His one experience at trying his standard plumbing arrangements in the zero-gee area, however, had convinced him to always return to the safety of his litter pan in the pseudo-gravity area for those functions.

Ginny walked through the base Operations office, and sat in a chair on the far side. The "day" shift was in control. Three crews were responsible for construction operations. One shift, called the "morning" shift, was on duty from 2400 hours until 0800 hours, Greenwich time. The "day" shift was on from 0800 to 1600, and the "night" shift from 1600 to 2400. Each crew member spent two months on a given shift, then rotated to the next shift. Several extra crew members "floated" from position to position to insure that everyone had adequate time off, and each crew member had sixty days each year Earthside, usually in 20-day vacations several months apart. These vacations were not only necessary to avoid something similar to 'cabin fever', they were also essential to provide necessary exercise for the crew members at Earth gravity. Each crew member also spent a week Earthside for training at the beginning of his or her three-month tour. When a crew member returned from training, he or she began working on the appropriate shift. In between training and vacations, every crew member worked out two hours each day in the fitness center located in the 'baton,' a capsule on the end of a long arm, with higher artificial gravity, extending from the station's rotating cylinder. Another arm, extending in the opposite direction, contained the day room and counter-balanced the personnel working out in the gym. The station's computer automatically allowed water, which served as balancing mass, to flow from tanks near the center of the station out to tanks in the appropriate baton to offset the mass of the personnel in the gym or day room, as needed. When the personnel moved back into the main part of the station, the water was pumped outward so as to keep the station turning smoothly. It was an inexpensive but effective system that operated automatically to keep the slowly turning station in balance.

193

November 26

The supply tug made its last maneuvering adjustments and matched orbits with the satellite, hovering motionless a few meters away, its docking ring precisely aligned with the receiving ring attached to the crew quarters. A worker in a pressure suit floated near the docking ring of the satellite, with a heaving line. The line, which had no 'weight' in free-fall, was attached on one end to the satellite and on the other end to a small permanent magnet which, not surprisingly, had no weight either. But the magnet did have a larger mass than the line and would carry the line out to the tug without snarling. If the worker's aim was good, the magnet would contact a steel plate on the nose of the tug, put there just for that purpose, and would stick there, enabling the worker to go hand-over-hand across the line from the crew quarters to the tug. With a handhold on the tug, the gentlest of pulls on the line to the satellite would begin the tug and its cargo, together weighing hundreds of tonnes, moving toward the docking ring. The original procedure had been for the tug to dock under power, but too much fuel had been wasted and someone finally realized it was faster and cheaper to have a skilled worker manage the final docking by hand once the tug was aligned with the docking ring.

The tug had been an object of interest for several hours, because an order had arrived from Earth Base for all three shift supervisors, the three construction supervisors and the project superintendent to meet with someone arriving on this trip.

As the tug's docking adapter engaged the station's docking ring, there was a faint 'click', and the docking ring lights on the control board all turned green. The pressure in the airlock between the docking ring and the hatch into the station began to build, and when it reached the same pressure as the ship's interior and the station's interior, another panel lit up with rows of green lights. Ginny pressed a switch to release the electric latches on the airlock hatch, and a moment later, two men in pressure suits emerged from the lock, helmet visors open, followed by a smaller figure, Danielle, also in a pressure suit. Unlike the suits of the crew, however, Danielle's suit looked new, as if she never wore it. 'It's easy to tell someone who hasn't been here before,' Ginny thought, 'she won't be able to navigate and I'll probably have to hold her hand to ease her fears of weightlessness.'

The pilot of the shuttle was Gus Irving. He turned and said, "Ginny, I want you to meet Danielle Simones. Danielle, Ginny Robinson." After shaking hands, Danielle had failed to hang on to anything and began drifting across the compartment. Gus reached out and grabbed her foot as it passed him. "Sorry, Danielle. I should have reminded you."

Ginny said, "I understand you want to meet with some of our honchos?"

"Yes. Are they here?"

"Fat chance. Well, they're sort of here, but not here in the center of the station. They're all spoiled by the station's artificial gravity, so they're waiting for you in the Operations office. I'll show you how to get there. Just a minute." Ginny looked through a viewport at the tug and could see that the tanks that had been attached to the sides of the tug were in the process of being removed. Empties, already floating nearby, were ready to replace the full ones. These, she knew from the fittings on their sides, were water tanks. They provided, through hydrolysis, the hydrogen and oxygen to fuel the tug's motor on return runs from the power satellite to the low earth orbit satellites, for the maneuvering thrusters on the construction workers' suits, and for the satellite's station-keeping thrusters, as well as oxygen to make up for minor losses in the recycling system that produced oxygen for the occupants to breathe. Hydrolysis units to produce oxygen and hydrogen circled the exterior of the hub of the power satellite. The tug Danielle had arrived in, with its nose secured in the center of the station, seemed to be rotating slowly outside the viewport. The docking ring holding the nose of the ship slid silently on sealed bearings. Actually, the crew quarters was rotating and the tug was stationary. Ginny turned to the pilot and copilot of the ship. "Are you guys going to be with us for a few days?" she asked innocently.

"Not that long," said Gus. "We have to head back as soon as Miss Simones finishes her tour and meetings. I expect about 24 hours."

"Enough time for one of my home-cooked meals, I hope?" she said, looking at Gus. The co-pilot, Garth Steiner, could not contain his smile. He elbowed the pilot in the ribs and winked. The pilot, caught off-guard, blushed as he sailed across the compartment. Danielle had spent the last few days in the shuttle with these two men, and she laughed at Gus's embarrassment. He had told her there was someone on the station with whom he had a special relationship, but Danielle hadn't expected to meet her so soon.

"Follow me," Ginny said, as she shut down and locked the power to her console and dived for the hatch leading to the outer levels of the station. "Be sure to grab something and hang on so you can swing your feet outboard as we drop down, then slow your motion with your hands on the outside rails of the steps. Coriolis will pull you away from the steps. Nobody actually uses the steps that I know of, someone could have saved some boost weight there. Bend your knees before you hit the bottom."

Danielle landed as instructed. She bent her knees, but was unprepared for how little one-twelfth Earth-normal gravity really was. She bounced into the air, and only the alert pilot next to her saved her from hitting the overhead, by simply reaching over and pushing down on her head. He in turn would have bounced into the air, but for his still-firm grip with his other hand on the stair rail.

They continued with Ginny leading. The corridor curved 'upward' out of sight straight ahead. As they approached the Operations office, the sound of several voices could be heard. "Here we are, Compartment A-6," said Ginny. "Let me know if you need anything else. I'm in Compartment C-46. That's two levels up and on the other side of the station. Once you get your space-legs, it's a lot easier to go up to C Deck, then go around to number 46. Bye." Ginny glided easily down the hallway, arm-in-arm with Gus. Garth had disappeared into another compartment to remove his pressure suit.

Danielle stepped into the doorless compartment and found five men and two women waiting there. They were the three operations supervisors, the three construction supervisors and the satellite superintendent. A lively discussion was underway regarding the Power Ball Lottery Earthside. One man was in mid-sentence when she swung around the corner into the room. He stopped so fast Danielle thought he might have bitten his tongue. Laurie Steinberg, the satellite superintendent, introduced Danielle to the rest of the group as a representative of the company, then suggested a break for Danielle to get out of her pressure suit. She said, "You folks entertain yourselves for a few minutes while I take Danielle to her quarters so she can change and freshen up. Danielle, if you like, you can come with me."

The two women stepped into the hall and walked to the nearest stairwell. Danielle tilted her head back and looked up. From the bottom, it looked like an endless extension ladder going up 50 meters in a very tall closet. She hadn't realized how high it was when she came down a few minutes earlier. She turned to Laurie, "How high do we have to climb?"

Laurie laughed, then said, "Don't worry about it. We don't have to climb at all, so long as we stay in shape. Your quarters are on B Deck, right across from mine. All you have to do is give a little jump, and grab the ladder when you're at your floor. If you jump a little too hard, just grab the rail of the ladder to stop rising and start falling – remember, you are actually moving in a circle all the time – then you can step onto your floor when it comes by again. Just don't jump too hard, or you'll end up back at the center of the station. Do this." With that, she gave a little hop, and floated to the next level above. Danielle followed, and it was *fun*.

Laurie stopped at Compartment B-2, pulled aside the curtain over the door opening, and motioned Danielle inside. "Here we are, home sweet home for you during your visit. I'm right across the hall in B-1. Here's the bunk." She folded the bed down from the wall, then replaced it in the stowed position. "And here's your desk." She pressed a button and the desk opened up from a flat wall, then she reached to the wall beside the desk and touched another button. "And here is the chair for the desk." She laughed, "It doesn't have any padding but at less than one-twelfth gee, you don't really need it, and if you're like me, ... well, I have enough padding that I don't need it even at Earth-normal gravity."

Danielle didn't tell her that she already knew where everything was because she had worked on it with the design team. She enjoyed seeing how it really worked in space.

Laurie continued, "Across the hall, there's a shower in Compartment B-9. All the girls on this level share it. The 'necessary room' is in B-10, across from the shower. We usually only wear a towel going to the shower as B-1 through B-50 are the women's quarters, as are C-1 through C-50, and D-1 through D-25. We don't have any married quarters yet, but there are some romances brewing, and the company should be thinking about making provisions for couples.

"Let me help you out of your suit," she said, reaching to unfasten the neck clip. "On the station, almost everyone has a regular partner who helps them suit up and get out of the damned thing. You need to get your designers thinking about better suits, so that a person can put it on and get out of it by herself. The low gravity helps, but it's still a pain in the neck."

Danielle thanked her for her assistance, then looked around and saw that her briefcase and traveling bag had been placed in the corner of the cubicle. She looked back at Laurie, "Where can I find a towel? Sorry. I didn't bring one; I'm too used to going to hotels."

"Don't you worry about it. I made sure there were clean towels in the linen closet before you arrived." She opened a concealed door in the wall and pointed out the towels. When you're done with them, drop them, along with your dirty clothing, into the laundry chute between B-10 and B-12. You do have your name in your uniforms, don't you? The laundry department will have them clean and folded back here in about eight hours, and you have plenty of towels, so don't worry about scrimping. If you happen to run out, help yourself to mine."

"Thanks. I do need a scrub-down. That space suit is really stinky."

Laurie laughed again, "Yours looks brand new. You should see how stinky they get when you've been working in them eight hours a day for several months. That's another thing, someone might figure out how to make them easier to clean and disinfect inside. Workers occasionally have 'accidents' in them, and even the best adult diaper doesn't keep the suit entirely clean. We aren't dealing with military astronauts here, these are just working men and women in pressure suits. We can't ask them to use catheters. And it's impossible to use catheters on a daily basis anyway. People aren't made to be subjected to that every day."

Danielle tried to imagine, shuddered, then said, "I'll be quick, then I'll come right back to your office, okay? Oh, and by the way, when I get back to Earth Base, I'll get a team of designers working on both a suit that's easier to get on and off, and easy to clean, *and* a more accessible bathroom arrangement for workers during their work shifts. I guess a big part of the problem with the suit might be that it's so hard to get on and off."

"Thanks a lot! See you in a little while in my office."

Fifteen minutes later, she had finished her shower and put on a clean jumpsuit. She came to the drop tube, hesitated, then stepped off the edge. Slowly she began to descend to the floor below, and caught herself without bouncing, she thought, or at least not much.

As she approached the door to the superintendent's office, a group of male workers passed her and whistled.

"Ignore them," Laurie said loudly from inside the office. "They get like that whenever a new female arrives on the station. They can't help themselves; it's in their genes. Come on in and have a seat."

Danielle stepped into the small office, and saw that the group was standing in a circle in front of their chairs, waiting for her, with one extra chair next to Laurie's. The room was too small for a table and all the chairs, so the desk had been folded away.

"Please, be seated," Danielle said, taking the empty chair. "Thank you for your courtesy. Let's get down to the reasons I'm here. The assembly of the Web has been going on for several months, and I wanted to see how work was progressing; I want to try to get a feel for the morale of the work force; and I need to discuss with you, who are actually on the job-site, an idea that has been circulating at Earth Base. We'll take the last item first, then I would like a tour of the satellite.

"You each know the construction sequence that was originally planned: hub, then axle, then spokes, then diagonals, then reinforcing cables, then antennas, then wiring, then spiders, then collector panels. Most of these steps overlap, but that's the general sequence they were planned to start in. Just so we understand each other, let me review the nomenclature we use at my office to describe the Web:

"We have six spokes, separated by sections of solar panels. The spokes are numbered using the degrees, divided by ten, from the North spoke; 6, 12, 18, 24, 30, and 36. Each section feeds its power to the spoke clockwise from it, viewed from the Sun. That is, section 1, the first sixty degrees of the Web, transmits its power down the spoke we call number 6 to the center of the satellite, section 2 transmits its power down spoke 12, and so on. The power from spokes 6, 30 and 36 was originally planned to feed the top antenna array, on spoke 36, with power from spokes 12, 18 and 24 feeding the bottom antennas on the end of spoke 18. The design team always thought the Web would be nearly completed before we would start beaming power down to the receiving antennas.

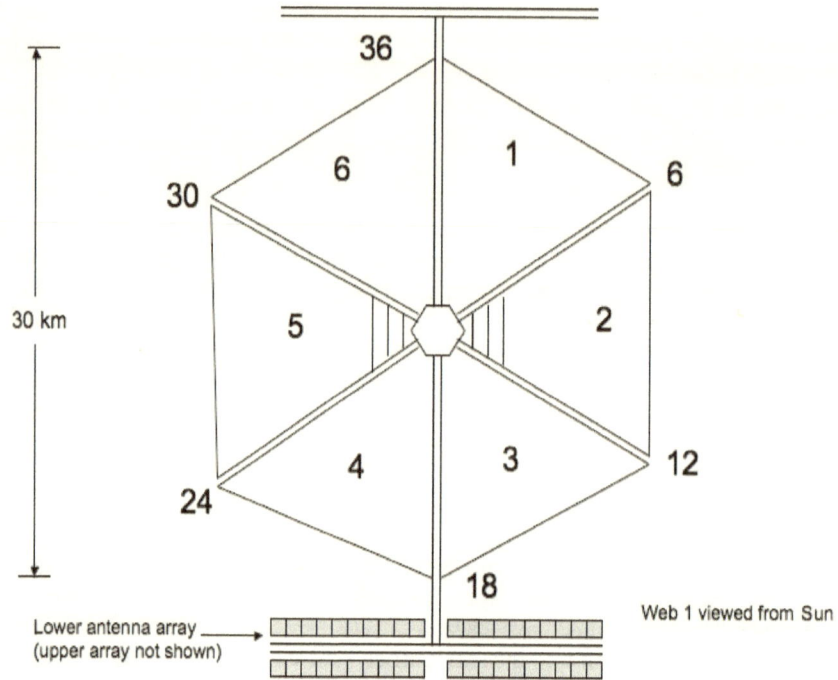

Web 1 viewed from Sun

Lower antenna array
(upper array not shown)

"Recently, some of the engineers have been discussing a way to power up parts of the Web prior to finishing the construction work on other parts. It would involve some scheduling changes. Overall, the work should go on about the same as now, but it would mean working with live power cables running internally in spokes 12, 18, and 30, feeding power from section 2 and 5, which we call the 'bow-tie,' to the antennas on spoke 18. Spokes 6, 24, and 36 would not be energized until their connections were fully completed, but in spokes 12, 18, and 30, power would be phased on and off as construction progressed. If the phased work can be accomplished safely, we might apply the process to the entire station. But we don't want to take any chances with safety.

"As you know, we planned to build both the upper and lower antenna structures simultaneously, and spin them up together. Each of them has to rotate around the satellite's vertical axis once every twenty-four hours to keep its antennas constantly pointed at the receiving antennas on Earth. Now, the design people say the structure will be strong enough to run the antenna rotators independently, so what we are considering is finishing one antenna assembly entirely, on the end of spoke 18, then running all the wiring for spokes 18, 12 and 30 to the hub, running the power from spoke 30 through the hub to spoke 18 to the lower antenna array, rather than to the array on spoke 36, and then powering up the bow-tie elements of the Web, sections 2 and 5. The amended concept includes loading the spiders on the bow-tie as soon as possible and installing solar panels as fast as there are diagonals for them to be attached to.

"The big uncertainty is whether our personnel can work safely in spoke 18 while it's carrying the power to the antenna array at the end. Our engineers and design people feel it can be done, in theory, but we're *not* comfortable assuming it can be done *safely*, because none of the designers have ever had to actually work in space, or in the confined quarters of the interior of Spoke 18 with a lot of hot electrical cables.

"So you please tell me. Can it be done and can it be done safely?"

There were seven solemn faces looking at her. They all knew how dangerous working with live electrical cables inside the spokes would be. The operating voltage would be higher than any Earthside power plant had ever used.

Finally, the third woman in the room spoke. "It isn't safe to work in 18 while there are hot wires there. In zero gravity, if you lose your grip, you just keep coasting until you hit something, even inside. Our workers don't have suit jets, unless they're working outside, because they make the suit so bulky. Working in 18 with hot wires, that's *too* dangerous. But, there's a way, ... ," she began, "if we do all the wiring in 18 first, ... ," she thought some more, then continued, "and if we have all the wiring for section 3 installed at the same time, then we could exclude workers from 18 entirely." She paused. "However, that still means section 4 has to be wired across the hub to 36 while section 5 is hot and running power across the hub to 18. Section 4 was supposed to feed the antennas on spoke 18. Having the power running across the hub, if we have to run power from 30 to 18, ... No, I'm wrong. The hub would still be hot, and the wires have to cross. I don't see any way to accept that."

Danielle asked, "Suppose we wire spoke 18 first, including the wiring for Section 3, then wire spokes 12 and 30, so we can power them up, then run the wire for section 6. It goes to spoke 36, which will be cold. Then in spoke 24 we run the wire almost, but not quite to the hub, and when we are ready to connect spoke 24, we shut down section 5 entirely, and make the cross."

Harry Elbertson, one of the shift supervisors, cut in, obviously very irritated, "What's the purpose of this amended concept? Margie's right! The power from sections 1, 5 and 6 should go to spoke 36, and from sections 2, 3 and 4 to spoke 18. It's the only sensible arrangement!

"There must be something driving this proposal you haven't told us. It worries me because we've always considered the center of the hub as a safe zone; this way it's not only unsafe, but we lose the ability to shut down one end of the satellite and work on it in comfort while we still serve the receiving antennas. It means we can't neutralize one end of the satellite and work safely in the hub without taking the entire satellite off-line. And if we someday decide to rewire section 5 to feed spoke 36, we still have to shut down the entire satellite's output."

Danielle thought for a moment, then said, "Harry, you're right. There *is* a reason. We need to bring some power-receiving stations on-line as soon as we can. If we can put part of the Web on-line, we can begin our test program much sooner, even if we don't have full output."

Harry looked at her, then around the room looking for confirmation from the others, and said, "We can produce the power you need, Miss Simones, without the problem Margie was describing. We only need one section, section 2. We wire up spokes 12, 18 and 24 as originally planned, with the dead zone in the middle of the hub. And spokes 6, 30 and 36 feed spoke 36. That's the original arrangement, and you can have limited power too." There were nods of agreement from the others.

"But what about balance?" Danielle asked. "We were thinking about using only one section, but couldn't produce any plan besides the bow-tie that wouldn't produce an unbalanced solar pressure condition. If we only run section 2, the asymmetrical pressure of sunlight hitting that right side will rotate the Web so that it's no longer facing the Sun. We never planned the station-keeping thrusters to impart rotational moments of that magnitude on the Web. They're all primarily set up to move the Web straight toward the Sun. We envisioned running both section 2 and section 5 to avoid the problem of rotation."

Harry responded, "You don't need to produce power to balance the solar pressure on the solar cells, you only need the cells installed. We can go ahead and have the spiders install the solar cells in section 5, but don't turn the cells on. We can install the wiring in spoke 18 first, then 12, then 24. We'll install the feeder lines for spokes 12 and 30, on the diagonals, but not the main power conductors in spoke 30. As soon as the diagonal wiring in sections 2 and 5 is installed, the spiders can begin installing cells. It would be desirable to install the diagonal wiring on sections 3 and 4 before turning on section 2, so that the wiring is all completed in sections 3 and 4. We shouldn't have to work on that wiring once spoke 18 has hot wires in it. All cells are installed turned-off anyway, so we can install the main conductors in 30 later, feeding power to the antenna on spoke 36, according to the schedule, but meanwhile all the connections to spoke 18 will be complete, and all you need to produce power is to turn on the cells in section 2.

"I was hoping to have the redundancy of either side of the bow-tie," Danielle said, "but I see the problem, and understand how the proposal to run power from spoke 30 to spoke 18 creates an unacceptable risk. Harry, your proposal solves most of the problem, and anything it doesn't solve, doesn't need solving. The working conditions on this job are already dangerous enough. I realize that. But I had to be sure. If any of you, or any of your crewmembers, come up with an idea that will enable us to make the working conditions safer or will speed up the process, please send it up the line. If we can save money, or time, there'll be financial rewards for whoever comes up with the idea and everyone in the chain-of-command. Meanwhile, I'll take your ideas back to Earth Base and see what changes in work schedules will be needed. Now, when would be a good time for me to take a tour of the satellite?"

Everyone else in the room cringed inwardly, thinking of having a novice in free-fall evaluating their work. They'd seen new workers arrive and go through hell for the first few days of zero gravity. It was a lot like the seasickness that new sailors were reputed to experience. Fortunately, after a day or so, it went away, but, despite the best air-conditioning, the whole station often had a sour smell as a result of new workers who spent more time throwing up than anything else. If that happened to Danielle, an official from the company, how would it effect her attitude toward the construction supervisors and their progress on the satellite?

Laurie turned to Danielle, smiled and said, "Now's as good a time as any, if you're game. Come on, I'll help you suit up." She turned to the others, and said, "See you at the air lock." She and Danielle ducked out of the office and hopped up to the next level. The other six began to move toward their quarters to get their pressure suits.

Twenty minutes later, Laurie and Danielle were in pressure suits at the construction pressure lock, in zero gravity at the center of the station, at the end of the crew quarters opposite the lock where the shuttle was docked. The others were waiting in their pressure suits, gripping handholds to maintain their positions. All eight went in together, and there was a great deal of room remaining. The pressure lock was designed to lock fifty workers, packed in like sardines, in or out at a time. They waited a long time for the extra air in the compartment to be evacuated by the recovery pumps. Finally, the pressure gauge reached zero, and the lights at the door to the outside changed from red to green. One of the suited figures pressed a button near the door, and it slowly swung inward. The hatch to the outside was wide open.

From a swivel attached to a fitting near the airlock, a thin cable extended across what seemed to be several hundred meters to a round aluminum disk, into which there were many hatches or openings. The aluminum disk was suspended, and seemed to be rotating slowly, almost as if it were hanging at the end of the cable, surrounded by the blackness of space, and uncountable millions of brilliant stars, which were also slowly rotating. At six points around the circular aluminum disk, there were very large spools, each of which Danielle knew contained nearly sixteen thousand meters of cable, waiting for the completion of the spokes, to which the cables would stretch from the end of the axle. That axle end was the aluminum disk she was viewing end-on from the crew quarters.

The leader of the group tapped his helmet, indicating he was using his suit radio. Danielle reached up to the chest pad on her suit and tapped her radio switch to the 'on' position. The volume was too loud and she turned it down. The man leading the group spoke, and turned out to be Margie. "Okay, Miss Simones, can you hear me?"

Danielle answered, "Yes, thank you. Call me Danielle."

"We're going to go across to the satellite now. Your cable slide will snap onto the cable. Hang on to your cable slide, and keep with the group. If you have any problem, speak up. Just do what we do." Each suit was equipped with a piece of narrow webbing attached to the waist of the suit with a single, large snap-swivel on the free end. It looked more than anything else like the leash for a dog. Danielle remembered the selection and acquisition process for this strap. NASA's equivalent item cost nearly $500 each and was built to government specifications. NASA bought them eight at a time. The power project's equivalent item was a horse lead bought from a harness maker. Danielle decided if it was strong enough to control an angry 1,000 pound horse, it would do to restrain a 200 pound person in a space suit. It cost $1.75 and she bought two thousand of them for less than NASA paid for eight. They were regularly inspected for deterioration, but so far had been holding up very well.

The first four members of the group snapped onto the cable and pushed off from the station toward the aluminum wall. The ones who pushed harder than those in front of them rapidly caught up and were soon moving along the cable holding onto the person ahead. They put Danielle in the middle of the group. She grasped a handhold on the side of the exit, then reached out with her other hand and snapped onto the cable. She jumped into space, and suddenly was overwhelmed by the star-filled expanse of it. She loved the sensation of zero gravity. It was like flying inverted, or even outside-g maneuvers in a fighter, only better.

As she moved away from the crew quarters, she looked back at the slowly turning structure. Behind it she could see the accumulation of supplies for the construction of the satellite, awaiting incorporation into the structures. There were rows upon rows of banded-together aluminum panels in various shapes, and numerous tanks she knew contained water, hydrogen, oxygen, nitrogen and air. A few workers with jet-equipped suits were moving about among the stockpiled materials.

Continuing to slide across the cable, she realized it was much longer than she had initially estimated. She recalled that it was a kilometer long. The actual size of the aluminum wall began to be apparent. She knew well that it was 100 meters in diameter, but until she reached it, that number did not have real significance for her; its diameter was the same as the length of a football field, including the end zones. The people ahead of her, already at the wall, had the appearance of tiny insects on an enormous aluminum garbage-can lid.

Eventually she reached the aluminum wall herself, and discovered it was crossed by rows of handholds, along which her companions were travelling, moving hand-over-hand toward the edge of the wall. She unclipped from the cable and followed them. She was followed by the other supervisors.

When they reached the edge of the round surface they stopped and again snapped their waist straps to a nearby handhold. Danielle caught up and came alongside. Margie's voice came over the radio, "I thought you might enjoy this view." Danielle held on and peered over the edge. It was magnificent. The kilometer-long aluminum axle of the satellite receded into the distance, then seemed to mushroom into a large hexagonal box. She knew it was the hub of the station, and from each of its sides, there was a growing projection. A machine was moving on each of the spoke stubs a short distance from the end, attaching the aluminum panels from which the satellite was constructed. One machine was leaving the line of attachments it had just completed, and was moving out one panel-length to the very end of the unfinished spoke. A mechanical arm on the side of the machine reached onto its back and secured another huge panel, 10 meters wide and 100 meters long, which it extended ahead of the machine. The machine began its task of making another series of fastenings along the bottom and side of the new panel. Between the short spokes, a few diagonal segments were already installed. They seemed close together from Danielle's distant viewpoint, but she knew they were one hundred meters apart, more or less, and many were already in place. Calculating from the number of diagonals, she concluded that the spokes were already nearly two kilometers long.

Margie's voice came over the radio. "Earth seems to be most beautiful from this view."

Danielle looked around and suddenly noticed that Earth was behind her. It was nearly noon in Africa, and although her perspective was upside down, and Antarctica was 'up', she could not mistake the places she knew so well. The islands of England and Ireland, and her precious little isle of Guernsey, were near the bottom right as she looked at Earth's lovely disk.

"Miss Simones, ... Danielle, ... we can't stay here all day." It was Margie's voice.

"Yes, ... Yes. We have a lot to see, I'm sure." Danielle didn't want to leave that scene, but took one final glance, then turned back to the group. "It's so beautiful."

"I know. Come on. There's more to see."

"Where're we going?"

"Inside. It's where most of the work is, and we're less likely to lose you there." Over the radio in her helmet she heard chuckles from the others.

The group clambered along the aluminum face until they reached one of the hatch openings she had seen from the crew quarters. Margie's voice came over the radio. "There's another cable inside. Be sure to hook up."

The hatch opening turned out to be not far from the edge of the axle's end disk and about ten meters across. Danielle followed the example of the person in the spacesuit ahead of her and reached into the hatch. A cable stretched from the edge of the hatch into the distance inside. She grabbed it and hooked on. The inside of the axle was lit by many very long strings of fluorescent lights, extending to the center of the satellite. In their glow she could see the shiny interior of the aluminum tube, and realized that many workers were inside. They were busily assembling sections of the satellite's diagonal supports into long subassemblies. While she watched, a group began moving one diagonal beam toward her. The nearest end, secured by several lines, was guided toward another of the hatches, similar to the one through which she had just entered. The part nearest, with wire ends dangling from it, passed through the hatch, angling across the inside of the axle so as not to hit the crew quarters moored beyond the axle. As the long beam continued to slide by, almost like a very long one-car train at a grade crossing, Danielle asked, "How long is it?"

Harry's voice came back over the radio, "Just a kilometer, about 3,280 feet. We make up one-kilometer-long modules inside the axle, complete with the associated wiring, because the working conditions are better, and our personnel are less likely to get lost. Outside crews join the one-kilometer sections into whatever length they need for the particular element they're working on at the moment. The diagonal sections are coded, so that the wiring is sized properly to carry the current produced by previous sections. A number 1 section always starts the diagonal, where the wiring is smallest at the beginning end, then the numbers, and wire size, increase to the end where the wiring attaches to the spoke. We also have three shorter section-lengths for the intermediate diagonals, which are added to the starting end. They don't produce enough power to make a difference in the wire size. Because all the stations on the spokes are numbered, we can immediately tell how many sections each diagonal requires. For example, the outermost diagonal, number 150, at the perimeter of the web, will have 15 one-kilometer sections. The one immediately before it, at station 14.9, will have 14 one-kilometer sections, one 500-meter section, and two 200-meter sections."

"What else is going on inside here?" Danielle asked.

Laurie's voice answered, "In the other end of the axle we're assembling cables for the wiring in the spokes. There are six teams, each one joining conductors and the switching sub-assemblies into ready-to-install cable assemblies for one spoke. You prefabricate the cables Earthside and we just have to hook them together. Inside the spokes themselves, crews are moving in behind the automated panel installers where segments have been completed and are installing the insulators and other incidental wiring devices required to control the switching systems. We'll start wiring-up the control systems as soon as the panel installers finish building the spokes. That's also when we start installing the stabilizing cables to the ends of the axle."

The little group continued along the cable toward the hub. At the connection between the hub and the axle, she looked into the great hexagonal room created by the hub, and saw many workers, floating freely from place to place, almost like fish in an aquarium. They seemed to be working on a large framework in the center of the hub a little toward the sun-side axle. A lattice-work of small cables crossed the space, and workers were using those cables to move from place to place.

"Harry, what are they doing?" she asked.

Margie's voice came back on the radio. "I get to explain this part, Danielle. It's my baby. These people are assembling the fixture for assembly of the magnetic bearings for the antenna bases. The antenna arrays that will revolve on the ends of both spoke 18 and spoke 36 will each be held in place by a magnetic bearing, which will prevent any physical contact between the revolving antenna array and the satellite itself and also will monitor and regulate the rotational speed. When spokes 18 and 36 are almost done, the bearing assemblies will be moved out to the end, down the inside of the spokes, guided by cables of course, so they don't hit anything on the way.

"We don't have the parts for the magnetic bearings yet, but as soon as they arrive, we'll begin assembly. For now, we're getting ready by building the assembly fixtures."

They had been out in space for almost two hours, and Danielle began to wonder how long before they might run out of air or heat for the suits. She was sure it was cold inside the satellite although her suit was insulated. She asked, "How long can we stay out here without running out of air? Don't we need to recharge our batteries or something?"

Laurie replied and pointed, "Don't worry. If you'll look at that side of the axle, you'll notice there are stations every hundred meters, with an attendant to change oxygen bottles. The gauges in your helmet show the time remaining in your primary and backup O_2 cylinders"

Danielle looked carefully along the sides of the station and saw the O2 stations, and realized that there were many cables stretched the length of the axle, parallel to the one along which she and her group were travelling.

"Your suit automatically removes excess CO_2," Laurie continued, "and maintains your oxygen at the correct percentage and pressure. If either varies ten percent from the standard, you'll know it, there's a warning system with a beeper and flashing lights inside the helmet, and then you rush to the nearest station and get two refills. Plus every worker carries an extra oxygen bottle and CO_2 removal cartridge, for himself or a buddy if they need it. Your suit has extras too, although since you need to reach over your shoulder to touch them, you may not have realized they were there. There's an emergency connection in the center of the chest in front. Each bottle is good for about an hour and a half, so each worker has three hours of oxygen hooked up, plus an hour and a half in his reserve bottle, even though we change the two main bottles at two-hour intervals.

"As for battery power, we change the suit-heater batteries at four-hour intervals. The radio batteries will theoretically last forty-eight hours, although we change them every shift."

"Well," Danielle said, "I've seen more than I ever dreamed possible a few years ago. You and all your crews are doing an excellent job. I'm very pleased with the way work is progressing, but now I think I should be getting back to the crew quarters. I should check in with Earth Base."

The leader pointed the way back to the nearest cable and the small group made its way back through the work area of the hollow satellite to the crew quarters. In her bunkroom, Laurie and Danielle helped each other remove their pressure suits, then headed for the showers. As they stood under the spray and scrubbed, Laurie hesitated, then said, "Danielle, the three supervisors and I think we know what your relationship is to the solar power project. We're glad you've come here, and we hope you'll join us for dinner. As far as I know, no one else here knows who you are."

Danielle was suddenly alarmed, but said. "Thank you. I'd love to have dinner with you, but I have to leave immediately after dinner. I can't miss my shuttle."

"Don't worry about it. The shuttle crew is sure to be eating with us too. I doubt you'd leave without them."

"I guess not," she replied, and they both laughed.

Laurie said, "It'll be about two hours 'til dinner. Get some rest 'til then. *I'm* going to. This is about the middle of the night for my internal clock because I'm usually on a different shift. I'll have someone wake us in an hour and a half."

Danielle returned to her cubicle, made a few notes on her observations at the satellite, then lay down to rest. She started to wonder why Laurie would be having someone wake her if it was her 'middle of the night,' then was asleep and dreaming of Earth, viewed from space. She woke to Ginny speaking to her from the door.

"Miss Simones. Psst. Miss Simones!"

"Yes?"

"Thirty minutes to dinner. The boss said to wake you."

"Is she up yet?"

"She's already down in her office."

"Thank you. I'll be right down." As she spoke, she realized the air was full of delicious smells. Hurriedly, she put on a jumpsuit, brushed her hair, and fixed her makeup.

She dropped to the lower level and went to Laurie's office, but it was empty. Then she heard the sound of many voices coming from farther along the hall. Proceeding around the station, she remembered the large dining room was directly ahead. In it were hundreds of people, sitting at two parallel rows of tables, waiting. As Danielle walked in, the assembled workers all stood, and applauded. She was caught completely off-guard, stunned.

"Ladies and Gentlemen," announced Laurie, "it is my privilege to be able to introduce Miss Danielle Simones, who is here from the company to share Thanksgiving dinner with us, and I want to personally give thanks for her being here."

Laurie turned to Danielle and said, quietly, "We, who were with you today, want to thank you for letting us be part of your project." Danielle wondered how they had found out. She had tried carefully to keep her position in the company a secret from all lower-level employees, to promote candor in conversations with them about the project.

Someone yelled, "Speech!" but she held up her hand.

"Please," she said, then raised her voice so as to be heard over the general hubbub. "Please! I'm very happy and excited to be visiting with you today. Thank you for your hard work on this project. I think we have a great team, and each of you is an important part of it. Thank you again." She sat down at a space with a name-card, a piece of paper with her name handwritten on it, in front of the silverware.

Laurie turned to her, "Danielle, everyone here thanks Someone for the food we receive every day. Thanksgiving is a special holiday for Americans, and we hope also for the other nationalities working on this project. We don't know who at Earth Base to thank for the Thanksgiving turkeys you sent us recently, but I want to thank you personally for remembering us up here. Happy Thanksgiving! And please pass the cranberries."

Danielle thought that despite the metal trays and informal atmosphere, it was probably the best Thanksgiving dinner she had ever had. Across the table from her, Gus Irving sat next to Ginny Robinson, with whom he was having a very friendly conversation. She was obviously very happy. Danielle said, "Excuse me, Gus."

Gus looked across the table and smiled. "Yes, ma'am?"

"What's our departure schedule? I don't want to hold you up."

Gus said, "We're scheduled to blast back to LEO-A at 0930, that's fourteen hours from right now." He looked back at Ginny, and she blushed.

Danielle didn't ask any more questions. She knew the low Earth satellites were always in a favorable position for the return trip, with appropriate course adjustments. "I'll be suited up and at the command center at 0900, if that will be okay?"

"Yes, ma'am. That'll be fine. We will be in the shuttle running checklists." He looked back at Ginny, who had wrapped her right arm around his left arm, and was gazing into his eyes.

After dinner, Danielle jumped up to the command center and sent several routine messages to Earth Base. They had to relay through a satellite dish in London, as Belau was over the horizon and out of direct line-of-sight. She thought back to a solar power conference she had attended in Paris a few years earlier, made a mental note to start a team on a power reflector, a giant mirror in space to enable them to reflect the microwave beam from this station to spots out of sight over the horizon, particularly Belau, and then she dropped back to B deck. Being twenty-two thousand miles above the surface of the Earth really changed the way she thought about things. She could have Belau on solar power before they even had a solar power satellite over the Pacific.

As she prepared for bed, she fastened the light-weight straps intended to prevent her from falling out of bed if she rolled over suddenly. She wondered if it was possible to be hurt falling a half-meter at less than one-twelfth gee, then decided she didn't want to be the guinea pig. She pulled a blanket over herself and went to sleep.

A few days later she was back in her office in Belau.

CHAPTER 44

December 5

At 0700, the morning sun was shining brightly as Danielle walked from the assembly hangar to the Belau office building. A fresh breeze was blowing from the Northeast and frigate birds, albatrosses and seagulls were soaring on the thermals. It was a beautiful Pacific morning, but somehow she still missed the fog the sea breeze brings off the Atlantic in the Channel Islands.

She stopped at Bill's desk and said, "Good morning, Bill. Get the CEO of World Express on the phone for me, will you please?"

She continued into her office, and as she touched a button on the console next to the desk, the video view into the forest dissolved into a view of the main hangar, from the catwalk above the doors. She had been spending too much time walking out to the hangar, she had decided, so remotely controlled television cameras were now mounted high in the rafters of the hangar, enabling her to observe everything happening there, without leaving the office.

The cameras swiveled on both a vertical axis and a horizontal axis, and had a special zoom lens, so she could actually read the print on documents being used anywhere on the hangar work-floor.

The phone rang. Bill said, "Mr. Hatcher is on line two."

Danielle said, "Hello, Mr. Hatcher. This is Danielle Simones. I hope I'm not calling at an inconvenient time?"

"No," Hatcher answered, "... No, indeed, Miss Simones, although I am surprised to be receiving a call from you. Let me say how pleased I am to be able to speak to you. I've admired your work for many years, and have read a number of the articles you've written. To what do I owe the pleasure of your call?"

"Thank you. I'm glad you enjoyed the articles. Seriously now, the reason I called you was to make you a business proposal. Are you interested?"

Hatcher said, "I'm always interested if there's a way to make a little profit for the company. What's your proposal?"

"Your company has set the industry standard for overnight service in the United States for many years now, isn't that right?"

"We like to think so."

She said, "I've been watching the air express business for many years, as part of my general interest in all aspects of the aviation industry. From my perspective, the express business has a severe shortcoming. For many years, Asian and Western Pacific customers have been unable to enjoy the same level of service that your company has provided in the States and Europe. It sometimes takes a week or longer to get a letter from New York to Manila, for example. I've noticed that your company hasn't made much effort to compete in the international express market to the Western Pacific. I was wondering if you'd given any thought to getting into that market."

Hatcher replied, "We looked at it a couple of times, but every time we looked we concluded we couldn't provide any measurable improvement in service over our competition. We can get a package to Tokyo or Hong Kong in one day, but by the time we island-hop around the Pacific Ocean, it still would take us a week for a delivery. You see, stateside, we can carry a package all the way across the country, Miami to Seattle, the longest route, in less than six hours. There's no way to do that for the Asian market. If we can't provide better service, there isn't much reason to go into a new market, because the result may be only a division of the existing market into two parts with both competitors losing money. That's bad for us, and bad for our customers, because service deteriorates. For that reason, we usually hire the competition to deliver our packages for us in that area of the world."

"How'd you like to be able to offer overnight service to Asia and Australia, and everything in between, operating from a base located between Manila, Guam, Japan and Australia? Specifically, on a direct line between Tokyo and Darwin, and directly East of Singapore."

"It's not possible," he answered. "We've already looked at it, as I told you. I assure you, my people are very thorough. If they say it can't be done, I believe them."

"I'm sure I'd believe them too, if I were in your position, however there's a new factor in the equation, which perhaps your people didn't consider. Have you heard that the company I am working for, Belau Aviation, has developed a new aircraft?"

"I guess I did see something about that, now that you mention it. But as I recall, it was more space-related than commercial aviation-related. And I think I saw that the company wasn't going to sell the planes and so I dismissed it as another secret government project."

"I assure you it is a very private project, with no government involvement other than as a customer. You *are* correct, though, we don't plan to sell the aircraft. However, we *can* offer very attractive charter or leasing arrangements to the right customer, if we can work out a few logistical details. Our planes can fly from Europe or the United States to our airport in the Western Pacific in about an hour, because we fly at almost orbital altitudes and speeds, where there's no atmospheric resistance. Are you interested?"

"I'm very interested, but it doesn't sound economically feasible. Where's the catch?"

"The catch is logistics, Mr. Hatcher. Right now, there's only one landing strip in the world designed for this aircraft. It's here in Belau, and it's 18,000 feet long. In order to fly out of other locations, similar facilities would have to exist. We do have a crosswind limitation of 20 knots, but that isn't a problem in most locations. The only other significant requirement is to have a local government that will permit the noise levels this aircraft generates when it takes off. It's very loud, ten decibels louder than the Concorde. The ideal site for an airport would be in a relatively deserted location, away from all habitation. The NASA shuttle runway at Cape Canaveral would do, but it isn't a commercial airport, and is probably too remote from your usual customers. The same thing is true of the runway at Area 51 in Nevada. The Belau government is friendly, or we couldn't get away with it."

Hatcher said, "I know of a few present or ex-military air bases with very long runways, and some of them are in remote areas. I'd have to check them out, but I'd bet there are a few in Europe and North America that fit that description. There are some other considerations, though, such as the lease cost. That could be prohibitive."

Danielle said, "Let me give you the bottom line. If we *were* to sell this aircraft, and I re-emphasize that we are most definitely *not* going to sell it, the price would be in the neighborhood of two billion dollars a copy. That may seem a lot, but ours is a unique airplane, of significant capability and very bluntly, is probably worth more than that. What we would propose, eventually, is a lease arrangement, whereby we provide the plane, crew and maintenance, and a terminal at our airport here in Belau, and you provide the landing facilities at the other end of the line, cargo loading and unloading equipment and fuel. Your cost to lease the plane would be in line with any other lease for two billion dollars worth of equipment. And it would let you carry, overnight, *all* the freight bound for the Western Pacific for your competition. That ability alone might pay for the cost of leasing the plane."

Hatcher asked, "You said, 'eventually'. What did you mean?"

"I mean, I'm looking ahead. Today, I have seven of these aircraft flying. I need ten for our present commitments, and components for the other three are already under construction and scheduled to be completed within the next few months. The manufacturers of the components will then start laying off the workers who make these parts for us. If that happens, we again run into large start-up costs, what with retraining and other overhead, but if I can continue the production for a few more units, it's an opportunity for this company, and for other companies which can use the unusual capabilities of this aircraft, to make some serious money. But, even right now, our present seven aircraft are under-utilized. They each fly one flight a day, which takes up about six hours of their time, and they often return here empty, then sit on the ramp for another 18 hours before they go again.

"Our maintenance schedule leaves significant uncommitted time on these aircraft, and I'd like to expand their workload. I envision our aircraft stopping in Europe or North America, or South America, or Africa, on their way back here, to pick up cargoes of express packages, and bring them here for trans-shipment to their destinations in the Pacific Rim. Conversely, one of our aircraft might come here and pick up a cargo for you and take it to an airport on one of those continents, from which the cargo would be transshipped to the addressee."

Hatcher was full of question. "What's the capacity of the airplane? Does it require special equipment to load? Will it handle regular cargo compartment containers?"

She laughed at his burst of questions. "Slow down. Yes, it will handle regular airline cargo compartment containers, either regular or wide-body, but it will also hold the cargo containers used on ships. We have a pressurized insert that we use to carry passengers. The plane has a cargo door, so that should be no problem, as there's lots of room. Our aircraft loads cargo from the top, like a toy chest. Here in Belau, we load it with a bridge crane which spans 300 feet, so we tow an aircraft under it and just load the cargo directly in the top, then tow it on through, with plenty of room on either side. The aircraft has a cargo capacity, that is, payload capacity, of 100 metric tonnes. In fact, we could put an entire 747 fuselage in our cargo compartment, and still have almost 100 feet of empty space at the end. Oh, and we have a drop-in conversion to a 400-passenger configuration, in case you hear of anyone who might be in the market for high-speed international travel. I doubt you could fill one up with all the Pacific-bound packages for any 12-hour period."

"Actually," Hatcher said, "we envisioned trying to ship out one load every six hours, but we'd have to reconsider that, with this increased capacity. 100 metric tonnes, that's more than the gross weight of many of the airplanes we use."

"If you're interested enough in this proposal to talk some more with me about it in detail, I'll have our staff here work up some numbers on what it would cost for you to charter one flight daily each way. That's two flights a day, as a temporary measure, then I'll have them figure out what the cost of leasing one aircraft for your own routes would be. Then I'll come to Little Rock and meet with you face to face to discuss those numbers. How does that sound?"

"Sounds good to me," he said. "You'll call when you get the figures together?"

"Yes, indeed, sir. I expect it'll take a couple of weeks. I want to go home for the holidays anyway, and if I can meet with you right before Christmas, it would get me going the right direction. Thanks for your time."

YEAR FIVE

CHAPTER 45

January 16

Maurice called early in the morning. Danielle punched the speaker-phone button. "Yes?"

"It's Maurice. Do you have plans this evening? We're organizing a flight crew party on the beach tonight, and I thought you might like to attend."

"Sure I would, Maurice. What's the occasion?"

"One of the pilots' girlfriends is having a birthday, and it's supposed to be a surprise party. All the flight crews who aren't on duty or going on duty within eight hours will be there. I thought you might like to join us."

"Should I bring a gift?" Danielle wondered where in Belau she would find an appropriate birthday present on short notice.

"Not necessary. Save your present for the bridal shower. I suspect that will be pretty soon, if I've sized up the situation correctly."

"Who's the pilot and who's the girl?"

"The pilot is Jake Boesinger, the first officer on Crew 8, and she's a local girl who's the assistant manager in the commissary. She's real sweet and very bright. They've been going together for almost a year."

Danielle thought about the policy of hiring only single pilots. Well, she couldn't prevent love, no matter what the company policy was.

"Are you sure they won't be put off if a stranger, me, I mean, comes to their party?"

"Heck no! They'd be glad to have you there. Everyone at Earth Base knows you work here, but none of them know what your real position is. As far as anyone knows, *I'm* the head of Belau Aviation, Jean Claude is the head of Charlotte Space Development Corporation, and you're some kind of an engineering management consultant who doesn't talk much. That's how you wanted it."

"Yes, but I think the word is getting out somehow. I had a strange conversation with the superintendent on the Web at Thanksgiving. She told me she knew who I was and my relationship to the project, and thanked me for letting them be part of it. I didn't tell her anything or confirm anything, but I sure do wish I knew what she really knows! I'm always concerned that I might not get candid information if they know I'm in charge."

"I don't think it's productive to be concerned about what you can't control, Danielle. If they know, they know. I'll pick you up at the building entrance at about 1800 hours, OK?"

"Sure. I'll look forward to the evening." She turned off the phone and went back to her paperwork.

At six that evening she was waiting in front of the building. Wearing matching luau shirts, Maurice and Sophie drove up in a Jeep. Danielle climbed into the back seat, and they drove out through the security checkpoint at the entrance to the Base.

The beach party was already in full swing when they arrived at the pavilion in the company's recreation area. Some of the guests were chattering in small groups at picnic tables; others were dancing to the band playing under the palm trees. As Sophie and Danielle were discussing the problems of keeping long hair in place while riding in an open Jeep, Danielle saw a tall man in bare feet, a blue swimsuit and a bright print shirt come striding toward her.

"Danielle!" he called.

She paused, then realized it was Hank Taylor. "Hi, Hank. How's the party going?"

"Great! Can I get you a drink, or a beer, or a soda?"

"What're you having?"

"Well, ... I'm having a soda, but don't let that stop you from something stronger. I have a flight in the morning. The company has us flying so much that with our 24-hour no-alcohol rule, we drink a lot of soft drinks these days.

"What rule is that? 24 hours?" Danielle knew that the company's rule was 16 hours, double the American Federal Aviation Administration's rule of eight hours. She had written it.

"Actually, it isn't really official," he said. "The company says we can fly 16 hours after we've been drinking, but all the pilots have agreed on a 24-hour minimum. Most of us are flying 20 days a month, and that doesn't leave much time to drink and feel comfortable doing it. Also, occasionally someone gets sick and one of us will be called to substitute for them on a flight. So we never really know when our next flight is, even if we don't have one scheduled for a couple of days. I don't miss alcohol; I never was much for the sauce."

"Well, thanks for the offer. I'll have a soda, if there's a cold one somewhere."

Hank left and returned promptly with another soft drink, and they walked slowly down to the beach. The small waves of the lagoon lapped gently at the edge of the sand. Little sand crabs scuttled aside as they approached. Tiny seashells littered the edge of the beach.

"Do you know the birthday girl?" she asked.

"That's Terry. She's Jake's girl and a real sweetheart. You'll have to meet her. You know that Jake's my copilot, don't you?"

"No," she said.. "I hadn't made the connection. I don't have many opportunities to socialize with the pilots and hadn't kept track of who was on which crew."

"You mean you haven't met all the flight crews? I'd better introduce you. Most of them are here tonight."

She answered, "I did meet all of the pilots when they were interviewed before being hired. I think there were a couple who Maurice interviewed without me, but I did check all their records."

"Did you give them all the same flight check-ride you gave me?" Hank asked. "You're one of the toughest check-pilots I've ever ridden with."

"No. Maurice hired many of them based on check-rides given by other check-pilots, but all six of the check-pilots had check-rides with me. I made sure they were equally thorough. I probably would have made you a check-pilot as well, except I felt you would be the best to do the initial test hops in *Polaris*. Was I wrong?"

Hank smiled. "Nope. I enjoyed that first flight and the first orbital flight as well. Thanks."

"Did anyone tell you we submitted that first orbit to the FAI, the world aviation record-keeping organization?"

"You what?"

"Yes," she said. "I'm sorry, I guess that news got lost in the rush. You're now in the record books for first of a whole lot of things: first aircraft to break a whole string of Mach numbers, first to fly from the surface to orbit in a single-stage vehicle, several like that. We were so busy with the press corps and putting materials into orbit that it slipped my mind. When we get an appropriate occasion, I'd like to see them presented to you formally, but they're actually yours personally, and if you want to pick them up, you can get them anytime from my secretary, Bill Townsend. Just come up to the office."

"That's all right," he said. "You keep them for me. The whole company earned them. Maybe the company could build a display case downstairs in the office building and put them on display. Are they certificates or medals or what?"

"Both, actually. There are several certificates, as well as a medal and a plaque for your own "I love me" wall with each certificate. One thing, though: if you have a shadow-box with your military stuff in it, as I know many military types do, none of the F.A.I. awards will fit, and there are several of them, so you'd need a big display case."

"You keep them for me. I'll claim them when I retire, OK?"

"As you wish," she said. "Hey, look who's here!" Danielle stepped forward to greet Bertram Allen. "Bert! How good to see you! Let me introduce you to Hank Taylor. Hank, this is Bertram Allen, the President of Belau." Hank and the President shook hands.

"What brings you to the party, Bert?" she asked, then hastily added, "Not that I'm not glad to see you."

"Of course. It's a birthday party, you know, and the birthday girl is my cousin. Our whole family is here." Danielle looked up from the beach to the area where the band was playing. There did seem to be more people than just the company's flight crews.

"Well, how nice. I didn't know. I hope I'll get a chance to meet some of them, and to meet the birthday girl as well."

"Count on it. Now, if you'll excuse me, I have to get out and shake some hands. Politician's work, you know, even if lots of them are my own family."

Hank and Danielle walked back to the party area and Hank introduced her to some of the flight crew members and to Terry Orsa, whose birthday it was.

The Sun was beginning to set; the scene was bathed in brilliant reds and yellows. At the center of the crowd was Terry, a very attractive young girl, wearing more flower necklaces than the others were and smiling broadly. Around the crowd, tiki torches on tall sticks cast flickering light on the crowd as the Sun disappeared into the sea.

Broiled fish, roasted pig, fresh fruits, and delicious salads were piled high on long tables. Everyone ate more than they should, then gathered around the birthday girl. Maurice, holding a very large birthday cake with what seemed to Danielle to be a very small number of candles, stepped into the crowd. There were choruses of "Happy Birthday" and Terry blew out the candles, cut the cake into many small pieces, and distributed them to all the guests.

After a few minutes of birthday congratulations, Jake Boesinger stood up and called for quiet. "Excuse me! Friends! Can I have your attention?" The crowd slowly quieted and Jake spoke again, "I, ... that is, ... We, ... that is, ... Terry and I, um ... have an announcement."

Terry's patience couldn't stand the waiting. She stood up on the seat of a chair and cried out happily, "We're going to get married!"

Everyone cheered, shouted, shook Jake's hand and kissed the bride-to-be. The band began to play romantic dance music, and the couples gathered on a piece of beach that was serving as a dance floor. Couples danced barefooted on the sand, holding their partners close, and speaking words meant only for one another.

Hank turned to Danielle and held out his hand. "Dance?"

She didn't answer but reached a hand out to him and let him pull her up from her place on the sand. The music was soft and pleasant. She could smell Hank's skin through his shirt, and it smelled, well, interesting. He held her close to him, and although the evening was warm, she wasn't uncomfortable. His nose was in her hair, and his warm breath was moving the small hairs behind her ear. She liked his arms around her. Some of the tiki torches had run out of fuel, and parts of the beach were quite dark. Many couples had disappeared from the dance area into the shadows. As they danced, Hank looked down at her. She turned her face up to his. He kissed her gently, and her knees weakened as she held him closer and kissed him back. She felt all warm and tingly. Then she pulled back.

"No, I can't. Please, Hank."

Hank didn't quite understand her reluctance, but he wasn't one to be pushy. He stopped kissing, and resumed dancing.

"Did I do something wrong?" he asked.

"No, it's not that. I just can't get involved. I ... I promised some people I'd give the project my complete attention, and I can't let them down." She didn't say she was afraid of becoming one of those widows she had tried to avoid creating.

"Okay. But I really do care about you," he said. "I think you realize that, don't you."

"Yes, I do. And I appreciate it, but I just can't give the commitment a relationship requires right now. Please try to understand, Hank."

Hank didn't answer.

They continued dancing for a long time afterward. At about 1 AM Hank drove her back to the Base and dropped her off at the office building. He still had no idea what she did for the company. She let herself into the darkened building and rode the elevator alone upstairs to her apartment.

Later that night the commander of the Earth Base security guard contingent was carefully checking on the guard posts around the Base's perimeter. There were thirty-six posts around the Base, not including the main gate and the auxiliary gate. Along most of the perimeter, the posts were located a half kilometer apart. It was too far to walk, and he always drove around the Base in his Land Rover. As a result, the guards always knew when he was coming. The Land Rover's straight-cut lower gears whined loudly as the truck slowly negotiated the sandy road inside the high chain-link fence. At guard-post 34, the two guards on duty were responsible for overseeing 500 meters of fence near the main hangar. They both had been up late that evening, at the beach party with everyone else, and could barely keep their eyes open. The Land Rover, with its lights off, ground slowly along the sandy road toward guard-post 34. One of the guards elbowed the other, "Psst. Wake up. Look alert. Here comes the Captain." Both guards tried to give their best impression of alertness.

The Guard Captain stopped the jeep for the next-to-last time on that circuit of the Base, and got out. He walked over to the guards and asked the standard question, "Anything unusual?"

The answer also was the standard one, "No, sir. Everything quiet."

"Very well. Carry on." The Captain got back in the Land Rover and drove on to the next post.

One guard picked up a pair of night-vision binoculars for a quick scan of the fence, and the jungle beyond in their sector of responsibility. It looked exactly as it always had. Nothing. He put the binoculars down and leaned back in the small "foxhole" which was guard-post 34. His eyelids were very heavy. So were his partner's. It wasn't that important anyway, they would always hear that noisy gear-train in the Captain's Land Rover.

The perimeter of the Base was the same almost all the way around. The access road ran along the inside of the fence, about 25 meters from the fence. The fence itself was four meters high, and topped with concertina razor wire. Within the fence, several thin wires were strung to warn of any attempt to break through the fence. Such an attempt was expected to break the fine wires, which would interrupt the electric current in the wires and set off an alarm at the main guard post. Every 500 meters and just inside the fence was a 'foxhole,' a shallow excavation occupied by security guards, which could be used as a protected firing position in the case of an armed attack. Outside the fence, the ground had been cleared for another 50 meters to the edge of the jungle. Anyone attempting to break into the Base would be very exposed to observation as they crossed the fifty-meter clear-zone.

Just inside the edge of the jungle, eyes peered into another pair of night-vision binoculars, watching the occupants of guard-post 34, as they had for several nights. They were also watching guard-post 33, because the area between those posts was the weakest point near the main hangar. Not only was there a small dip in the ground between those two posts, but there was also a significant structure near the fence, the desalination plant, about 50 meters inside the fence midway between the guard-posts, and the high-pressure pumps running constantly in that building were noisy enough to mask small sounds.

The watcher observed the occupants of guard-post 34 for some minutes, then turned to his accomplice. "They both appear to be asleep. One looked this way five minutes ago, but hasn't moved since then. The other one has his chin folded down on his chest, and has to be asleep. No one would sit like that if they were awake. What's the status of your two guys?"

The accomplice answered, "They seem to be talking. It looks like a big discussion of some kind. Wait, ... they've turned away from us. Now's our chance!"

Quickly and quietly, the two black-clothed men moved rapidly across the clear-zone outside the fence and lay on the ground, in the dip and parallel to the fence. One of them carefully located the fine alarm wires woven in the fence fabric, then took from his pocket several other wires with tiny alligator clips on each end. After fastening the jumpers to the alarm wires in the fence on either side of the spot where he intended to cut the fence, he clipped the original wire in the middle and waited.

In the main guard house, there was a momentary fluctuation in the meters indicating the current in the wire. The guard on duty saw it happen and watched the continuity meter intently. No, it was stable again and the needle was in about the same place as it had been last time he looked. He made a note to ask the chief about such fluctuations. Some animal probably tried to climb over the fence, he surmised.

The watcher and his accomplice held their breaths. There was no alarm. The new jumper wires had bypassed the break. Now they had to cut through the chain link itself. From his pocket the accomplice produced a small pair of bolt cutters. Unlike side-cutting pliers, the bolt cutter's jaws could be moved together as slowly as the operator wanted. He would not allow the jaws to snap together and reveal his presence and his partner's. He was very, very careful. A half-meter up the fence and along its bottom, the accomplice made a series of cuts horizontally along the fence, cutting every vertical wire in a half-meter-long section of fence. Then he cut the last wire at the bottom and top, and twisted it from the fence fabric. A small opening in the fence appeared. Moving quickly and quietly, the two men crawled through the hole. After checking again on the guard-posts, and wiring the flap shut so that it would not be noticed by a casual observer, the two men rapidly moved to the shadows around the desalination plant.

From the desalination plant, they crept to the large gas-turbine generator that provided power for the Base. They passed it and moved through the shadow of the main hangar to where the space planes were parked in a long row. Most of the planes were brightly lighted, however one, "Aldebaran", BA-4, was partly shaded, parked beneath the enormous bridge crane, and many men were working on top of it, loading long aluminum girders, diagonals for the satellite, into the plane's cargo hold. The plane's open cargo hatch, hinged along its right edge, cast a dark shadow on the entire right side of the plane. Each man quickly removed his black outer garment, and turned it inside out, exposing the blue inside. They now looked just like the blue coveralls of the workmen loading the space plane.

The two men strode confidently across the parking ramp to the space plane and walked beneath the trailing edge of its massive right wing. If any of the loading crew saw them, there was no reason, without a close inspection, to think the two were not company mechanics. After taking a tool from his pocket, one of them opened an inspection cover in the engine nacelle and attached something to one of the engines inside. Then he closed the cover, pocketed the tool, and walked away from the space plane, talking and gesturing with his partner in an animated conversation. Fifteen minutes later, they were back in the jungle.

At 0900, maintenance crews began the final maintenance checks on the space plane. Everything checked out fine. The small shaped-charge that had been placed on top of the number three scramjet turbine engine was virtually invisible, a dull aluminum color similar to the engine, and connected to an atmospheric-pressure-activated timer-detonator. It was set to explode a certain length of time after the space plane reached a very high altitude. The mechanics opened the one inspection cover where they could see the explosive but failed to recognize it as a foreign object and reclosed the cover.

At 1000 hours, Hank and his flight crew arrived at the space plane and began their preflight checklists. Their launch time was 1100 hours. Everything checked out, and they didn't see the explosive. They were ready to go.

Engine start-up and taxi to the runway were just like every other flight. The pilot engaged the space plane's computer and at eleven hours, zero minutes and zero seconds in the morning, Belau time, the throttles advanced and the brakes released. The giant plane hurled itself down the runway toward the lagoon, lifted its nosewheel and leaped into the air. With the wheels tucked away, the plane climbed rapidly, and the computer progressively advanced the throttle as the altitude increased.

At the 50-kilometer altitude, with the engines just beginning to operate in scramjet mode and the plane's turbine engines in full afterburner, an explosion suddenly ripped a large hole in the first compressor section of engine number three, just behind the air intakes. Pieces of metal were driven by the force of the explosion into the rapidly rotating turbine blades and blades began breaking off, moving into turbine wheels farther aft and breaking off more blades. The damaged three-meter diameter turbine wheels, now impossibly out of balance, but still spinning at nearly 50,000 revolutions per minute, simply exploded, unable to withstand the huge imbalance to which they were subjected. Pieces of the turbine wheels, turbine blades, stator blades, parts of the turbine housing, accessories from the exterior of the engine, and burning fuel were blown down out of the engine nacelle, and upward into the wing, tearing jagged holes in the upper and lower surfaces of the wing and the tanks in that wing containing jet fuel.

The crew was frantically trying to regain control of the plane. Cockpit lights flickered as the alternator on the number three engine failed, then automatic switches transferred the load to alternators on the number two engine, the inboard engine on the port side. The plane, which before the explosion already had accelerated to Mach 10, was rolling to the left, out of control at one revolution every five seconds. Hank Taylor knew if he didn't do something immediately, he would lose the plane. It would simply disintegrate as it fell into denser air below. He hit the autopilot disconnect switch and called to Jake Boesinger, the first officer, "Zero thrust." The four 200,000-pound-thrust turbine engines had to be throttled down to idle speed, and the scramjets had to be shut down. What little atmosphere there was at their altitude howled past damaged metal.

Marion Douglas, the flight engineer yelled, "Fire in number three."

Hank wondered how there could be a fire at 30 miles above the Earth's surface, with almost no oxygen to burn anything. Jake began the engine fire procedures. The plane was still out of control, rolling rapidly, and now it was pointed down toward the Pacific Ocean far below. Hank moved the control yoke in the direction opposite the roll and nothing happened. He needed hydraulic power to move enormous control surfaces designed to provide aerodynamic control in air so thin that it was almost non-existent.

"What's the condition of one and four?" he called out to the flight engineer.

"One and four appear normal," was the reply. They were at flight idle, running at about 60% of their full-power RPM. The flow of hydrogen fuel to the scramjets had been shut down, and the scramjet air inlet doors were closed.

"Bring one and four to 90%, and monitor their condition," Hank ordered.

Jake reached down to the throttle quadrant between the seats, and advanced the two outboard throttles until the engine power meters showed ninety percent power. The hydraulic pumps on the engines began to produce pressure in the system and the oversized ailerons slowly began to have an effect on the roll rate, which slowed, then stopped. The space plane was now pointed almost straight down, traveling over Mach 12, and accelerating. The noise of hypersonic air tearing at the holes in the engine nacelle caused by the explosion was becoming even louder. Hank began pulling back on the control yoke, and slowly the nose of the plane began to come up. The skin of the plane glowed red-hot. Skin temperature gauges were at the upper limit red line. 'Jesus, Mary and Joseph,' Hank thought. It was about as close as he got to swearing, but another line from someone else's religion kept repeating in the back of his head, 'Pray for us sinners now and at the hour of our death.'

The space plane was designed to fly relatively slowly in the thick lower atmosphere, accelerating gradually in the thin upper layers and increasing its speed as the air thinned. He had to slow it down now, before it descended into the dense lower air, or it would simply burn up in the dense air like a shooting star. Only one way - trade airspeed for altitude. He pulled the nose further up and started the plane into a climb. The outside of the plane glowed brighter. "Reduce power to 85%," he told Jake. He knew if he slowed the engines too much, he would lose hydraulic pressure again and lose all control, but he had to stop accelerating now.

The plane was climbing a little more slowly now, and speed was down to Mach 9. "What's our stall speed at this altitude?" he asked the flight engineer.

Marion checked the altimeter and a chart in a large binder and said, "Mach eight point six."

Hank pushed the nose over again, and held the speed constant at Mach 10, 1.15 times the stall speed. The plane was now descending and in its gyrations had turned westward. Hank scanned the panel and said to Jake "Call Base, tell them our situation. Maybe we can make it back."

Jake pushed the transmit button on the control yoke. "Earth Base. Rocket Four."

Technicians at Earth Base had observed the sudden change in the plane's course and speed on their telemetry readouts. Their response was immediate. "Earth Base. Go ahead Rocket Four."

"We have a big problem up here. Something happened a minute ago in the number three engine, and we had to shut it down. The fire light was on, but fire control seems to have worked. We are running engines one and four at 85% to maintain hydraulic pressure, and are attempting to return to Base. Number two is running at idle. Request emergency landing clearance."

"Roger, Rocket Four. Understand emergency return to Base. You are cleared to land. Say your position, course and speed."

"Rocket Four is at four zero kilometers altitude, airspeed Mach ten, one five hundred kilometers south southeast of Base, course, ... wait one, ... course two eight five degrees."

The control tower was an exercise in organized chaos. Several people were on the telephone alerting crash trucks and emergency personnel, ordering the airfield cleared of unnecessary vehicles, and alerting medical personnel to be prepared to handle any casualties. The plane was still a thousand miles away.

"Stand by Rocket Four." There was a long pause, then the voice on the radio said, "Rocket Four, all emergency equipment is on alert. What is condition of aircraft?" The ground controllers knew the ability of the plane to reach Belau would depend on how much damage it had sustained.

Jake touched the transmit button again. "Earth Base, Rocket Four is descending at two kilometers per minute, maintaining Mach 10, altitude three eight point five kilometers, course two niner zero degrees. Starboard fuel dropping rapidly. Three engines running on port tanks."

In the office building, Danielle's phone buzzed. She pushed the speakerphone button. It was Maurice. "Rocket Four has an emergency and is coming back to Base. I don't know what's happened, but there was something about a big engine problem."

"I'll come right down to Ops." She hung up the phone and ran out of the office, stopping for the keys to one of the several vehicles parked in front of the Engineering building. She jumped in and sped away toward the Operations building. Screeching to a stop by the entrance, she jumped out and raced through the front doors. Everyone in Operations was anxiously watching the speaker on the office wall as if it were a television set. Maurice was there ahead of her. "What's the situation?" she snapped.

Maurice answered, "They're trying to get back here, but they're still 300 miles out and over 100,000 feet high. And Danielle, they are coming in very hot. The last message showed them still at Mach 5. That should have them here in only a few minutes."

"Are the helicopters up? If they don't make the field, we need to be able to attempt a rescue, ... if there's anything left to rescue. If they go in the ocean, we'll need rescue personnel in SCUBA gear."

"We already thought of that," he gently reminded her. It was all in the Emergency Operating Procedures. "All the choppers are up. There are SCUBA personnel in three of the six choppers. The others have fire suppression equipment and firefighters aboard. If we can get to them, we'll, ... well, we'll do all we can." His lack of optimism was evident. The plane was still loaded with kerosene and liquid hydrogen and oxygen, a deadly explosive mixture.

The speaker on the wall suddenly crackled with Jake's voice, "Rocket Four is descending through flight level five zero zero. 100 miles out. Mach 3." The plane had passed 50,000 feet in its descent.

Maurice turned to Danielle. "Come on. We can see what's going on better from the tower." He led the way down the hall to an elevator and pushed the top button. The elevator surged upward, then stopped and the door opened at the top floor. They had to climb from there.

They left the elevator and started up a spiral staircase. After three turns, they came into the cab of the control tower. The slanted glass of the windows shielded them from the noonday Sun. One of the air traffic controllers, with binoculars to his eyes, shouted, "There they are!" and pointed to the southeast. Squinting, Danielle saw a small dark spot high in the sky. It was far away, but she could see with her naked eyes that there was a trail of smoke behind it. The tower shook as the double explosion of the sonic boom from the plane hit it.

"Oh my God!" someone cried, "They're on fire."

The plane rapidly approached the island from the southeast. It was apparent it would have to land from the southwest, and that it would be too high to land on its first pass. A 25-knot northeast wind was blowing straight down the runway. The plane seemed to alter course to the south, turning slightly to the left of the island to swing around it. It was still approximately 10,000 feet high as it began a large descending spiral around the island, streaming smoke from the rear of the airplane. As it came closer, the observers on the ground could see flames in the trail of the plane, where raw kerosene fuel was still spraying from the right wing tanks into the exhaust of the number four engine. As it circled to the northeast of the island, it continued to descend. It was now at only about 6,000 feet, and the fire seemed worse than before in the increasingly oxygen-rich atmosphere.

In the cockpit, Hank was fighting for control of the huge plane. The plane wanted to roll to the left, because of the full left wing tank and empty right wing tank, but he had to make it circle to the right. He feared that if he began a left turn, it would simply continue rolling, drop its nose and plunge nose-first into the Pacific below. The plane had circled back to the south side of the island, and was at 3,000 feet, making a final turn to line up with the runway. The noise of air screaming past the damaged skin where the engine had exploded seemed less since they had slowed. "Ten degree flaps," he called to Jake.

Jake moved the flap handle to the first notch and watched the flap indicator to verify the proper flap deployment. Nothing happened. "Negative flaps, Captain," Jake said. Marion, the flight engineer, was busily trying to restore functionality to the flap system.

"Try 20 degrees," Hank said.

Jake did. Still nothing. "Negative flaps."

"Advise the tower we're coming in hot."

Jake touched the transmit button. "Base, we have negative flaps. We'll be landing hot."

The tower controller acknowledged the message without comment.

As the giant plane swung around to the southwest and began to line up with the runway, the occupants of the tower cab could see the landing gear appear from the underside of the plane.

In the cockpit, the gear deployment unexpectedly slowed the plane below 200 knots. Hank called for the number two engine to be brought up to 100%, and began feeding in left rudder to offset the asymmetrical thrust of the two engines on the left side pushing against the one remaining engine on the right side. Soon he was pushing as hard as he could with his left foot to keep the big plane flying straight. The airplane continued to slow, and Hank called for 100% percent on engines one and four. The plane was entirely too slow now, and began to 'dutch roll,' a slow rocking to the left and right, at a high angle of attack, with its nose much higher than it should have been. There was no way to get the nose down. The plane was behind the power curve. There wasn't enough power to climb and not enough altitude to trade for airspeed. If he pushed forward on the control yoke, the giant plane, still full of liquid hydrogen and oxygen and balanced between the thrust of its engines and the enormous column of air in front of and under its wings, would sink immediately to the ground, or water, short of the runway, and roll itself into a ball of fire. He had no more power. The throttles were all the way forward. The plane was still three miles from the runway and had descended to fifteen hundred feet.

They were committed to land, and he would try to make the best of it. But he needed more altitude. The plane was descending at 2,000 feet per minute, and at that rate would not make the runway.

Hank had an inspiration. He didn't know if it would work, but it was worth a try. If he could reduce the drag, the lift would improve. He called out to Jake, "Gear up!"

Quickly, Jake reached down and lifted up the gear lever. The gear pulled back up into the underside of the plane, and the plane's sink rate decreased by half; at least they still had hydraulic power to the gear!

The plane was now a mile and a half from the runway, at an altitude of 1,000 feet. The nose was still impossibly high. It was almost standing on its tail and dancing toward the end of the runway, still oscillating left and right, like a stop sign in a high wind. The instruments told Hank he was centered on the runway's centerline, but he couldn't see anything directly ahead. He could only see out the cockpit window on his side, and all he was seeing was water. Suddenly, the shoreline passed beneath the cockpit's side window and he knew the plane was within a quarter mile of the end of the runway. They were still 500 feet above the ground. That is, the cockpit where the altitude instrument was located was 500 feet above the ground, but Hank knew the tail of the 700-foot-long plane must be almost touching the ground.

He yelled to Jake, "Gear down, then idle power!" Jake quickly shoved the gear lever to its bottom position and pulled the power levers for engines one, two and four to the idle position. The green lights, showing the gear locked up, went out. Red lights indicating the gear in transit came on. The sound of the huge engines began to diminish. Then the tail of the plane struck the ground, bending the trailing edge of the fuselage into a jagged curl, and tripping the giant 'air dancer.' The plane fell and rotated forward onto its landing gear, bounced back into the air, rolled left again and the left wing struck the ground. Pieces of the wing-tip broke and ground off as the tip was crushed. The plane rolled back to the right and again was erect on its landing gear. 3,000 feet of runway lay behind them, cluttered with pieces broken and shaken from the airframe, which was still moving 150 miles an hour toward the far end, 15,000 feet away.

Hank called to Jake, "Reverse!" and Jake moved the engine controls from their normal position into the reverse thrust position. Nothing happened. Hank had both feet standing on the brakes, but the plane continued down the runway unchecked. Hank had no way to know the first explosion in the number three engine had also severed the hydraulic lines to the brakes on the landing gear as well as the controls for the thrust reversers. Hank shouted, "Get on the brakes with me!" Jake pressed with all his might on the brake pedals above the rudder pedals, but it made no difference. The huge plane was still traveling at 150 miles per hour toward the far end of the runway, 10,000 feet away.

"Tell them we're going off the end," Hank said.

Jake touched the transmit button on the yoke. "Tower, we can't stop this beast. It looks like we're going off the end."

"Fuel off, engines off, master switch off, everything off," called Hank as he struggled to keep the plane centered on the runway with just the rudders. Jake and the flight engineer worked desperately to shut down all of the plane's systems in the seconds remaining before the plane ran off the end of the runway, still a mile away.

In the control tower, Danielle and Maurice watched the plane speed down the runway, with no sign of slowing. Two million pounds of airplane and cargo and people headed for the perimeter fence, with the lagoon beyond. Emergency ground crews with aluminum fire suits stood helplessly watching as the plane rolled swiftly past them and their crash trucks at 150 miles per hour, strangely silent as it rushed to its destruction.

The crew in the plane could see the end of the runway fast approaching. They felt the jolt as the nose wheel rolled off the reinforced concrete surface and began to bury itself in the sand. The plane began to slow. The rear of the airplane dropped off the pavement as the plane continued toward the beach. There was another, almost imperceptible jolt as it struck the perimeter fence and continued on, with a tattered chain-link streamer on either side of the nose gear.

The structural loads on the nose gear climbed rapidly as it buried itself deeper and deeper in the sand of the beach. As the nose wheel entered the water at the shoreline, the fittings, on which the nose gear strut was designed to pivot inside the nose landing gear well, failed. The nose gear, trailing severed hydraulic and electrical lines, was ripped from the underside of the airframe and, imbedded in the sand, it scratched along the bottom of the plane as the fuselage continued over it and into the water. The nose of the airplane, deprived of its support, fell violently the forty-five feet from its normal height to the water surface, making a terrific splash. The forward fuselage, already weakened by the wrenching-away of the nose gear, began to collapse.

Now travelling only 100 miles an hour, the plane entered the water and drove the nose of the airplane, diving downward, under water along the bottom of the lagoon. The great plane, pushed by the kinetic energy of two million pounds of plane, fuel and cargo, traveled 600 feet more, until the nose struck a massive brain coral. On impact, the broad nose folded up and Jake screamed. The plane stopped.

Inside, water poured in from the forward bulkhead below the cracked windshield frame on the right side of the cockpit. A spray of saltwater covered the crewmembers. Through the windows it was apparent that the plane was under water, as the murky silt stirred up by the crash obscured everything. Flashing rays of sunlight reflecting through the surface waves showed they were near the surface.

Hank unfastened his seat belt and shoulder harness and asked, "Everybody okay?"

"I'm fine," said the flight engineer, "just a tiny bit shook up."

"Jake, you okay?"

"Boss, I think I've got a problem," said Jake. "My feet seem to be caught." There were tears running down his cheeks.

Hank tried to look under the instrument panel to see the rudders and Jake's feet, but could only see the rising water in the cockpit, which had already risen almost to Jake's knees. He dived headfirst into the space between Jake and the center power console, and reached into the water with his right arm. Halfway down Jake's legs, he felt a twisted aluminum panel. The floor had buckled upwards behind Jake's legs, and the forward cockpit bulkhead had moved aft to clamp Jake's legs in a giant vise. The water was above Jake's knees.

Hank searched the cockpit for a lever or anything he could pry with. There was nothing. "Jake, we've got to pull your feet out of there," he said. "Let me have your left leg." Jake leaned to the right, and Hank grabbed Jake's left leg just above the knee. The water was up to Jake's waist. Hank pulled as hard as he could, but couldn't budge Jake's left foot. Jake screamed again. Hank switched to the right, and tried again. Still he was unable to free his stuck first officer. The water was up to Jake's chest. Divers appeared at the window and were trying to get in.

"Boss, give Terry a message for me, will you?"

"You'll have to give it to her yourself! Don't quit on me now." Hank looked wildly around the cockpit for anything that would enable him to free his friend. There was nothing. He thought, 'I have to have more time to work, and the water is rising so quickly!'

Hank sloshed through the waist-deep-water, which was now up to Jake's shoulders, over to the galley and storage area just inside the inner airlock door. He knew there was something there he could use, what was it? It hit him like a bolt of lightning. Space suits. He grabbed the nearest suit and dragged it back to Jake's seat.

"Jake, you got to figure out fast how to wear this thing without putting it on over your legs." Hank held the suit in front of himself. The wearer had to crawl in it like a sleeping bag, legs first, then fasten up the front, fasten the neck clip at the rear, and put on the helmet. It was impossible to get over Jake's legs.

The air did not actually go into the helmet, but into the shoulders instead, and the emergency air tank supplied a fitting at the ribcage in front. The water was up to Jake's neck.

Marion saw the anguish and frustration on Hank's face. "Hank, here, let me! Do you have a pocket knife?"

"Yes. Why?"

"Give it to me! Quick!"

Working swiftly, Marion cut the space suit in half at the waist. She took the top half over to Jake and helped him put it on. He was forced by the tanks on the back to lean forward, but they got it on him. Then Marion snapped the neck clip, and installed the helmet. "Keep your arms down or it may float off of you." she warned. "Boss, we better get into our own suits, unless you have gills."

Hank and Marion quickly put on their space suits. The water was over Jake's head, but he was still alive, trying to smile inside his helmet, despite his pain. They helped each other into their suits, and were about to put on their helmets when a banging came from the airlock. The view port showed the lock to be full of water with a diver inside. Hank opened the inner door, and the diver was washed into the cockpit like a goldfish spilled from its bowl. The water level was now chest-high and Jake was completely under water. The diver said, "What's your condition, sir?"

Hank answered, "Two of us are okay, but our copilot has his feet caught by some metal damaged by the crash. We need to get him out as soon as possible. I don't know what other injuries he may have."

The diver looked around. There were plainly only two people standing by him. Hank pointed downward at the oil-slick covered water at the right front of the cockpit. "I don't know how long the air in that suit will last. Can we get a medic in here to help him, and a lot of extra air bottles?"

"Yes, sir. Will you close the inner airlock door so I can exit the airlock, sir? I had a hell of a time getting in."

"That shouldn't be necessary. The pressures on both sides should be equal now. I think you can open it and have both doors open at the same time. If the electrical safety systems haven't failed yet, they should soon with all this salt water. Get us some air and a medic!"

"Yes sir! On my way." The diver reentered the air lock, and soon the sunlight coming through the water from the air lock indicated both air lock doors were open. The water rose again a few inches, then stabilized, about even with the top of the airlock door. Hank could still remove his helmet without getting more water in, but Marion's helmet was half under water. Hank leaned over and tapped on her helmet. "Can you hear me?" She nodded. He said, "I don't know how deep we are here, but I think we should stay here until we find out. You could be hurt if we're very deep and you pop to the surface in this suit." Hank realized that they hadn't been in the water long enough for the bends to be a problem, but sudden decompression could cause serious hemorrhages as well as air embolisms if they were very far under the surface and came up suddenly. She nodded again, just as two divers came through the airlock.

They started to speak, but were interrupted by Hank. "How deep are we here?"

"About three feet below the surface, sir. The top of the cockpit is just awash."

"Good." Hank indicated Marion. "Take her to the surface, and get her ashore, but bring the air bottles from her suit back to me. And I need a real SCUBA rig, so I can get rid of this space suit." The water was comfortably warm, and the suit was full of water anyway. Hank needed to be able to work on getting Jake freed. One of the divers pointed to the airlock, then followed Marion out.

The other diver turned to Hank. "What's the situation with your co-pilot, sir? I'm a medic and they said you needed me."

"He's right here, with a partial space suit on, but I'm worried about him. We need to free him and get him to the surface."

The diver ducked under water, checked on Jake and resurfaced. "He's conscious, but I don't know what else is wrong with him. I can't get a clear pulse with that suit on. I'm going to get another SCUBA rig for him in case we need it. I'll be right back."

"Get one for me too," Hank added as the diver headed for the airlock.

A moment later the medic was back with two sets of SCUBA equipment, and four more divers. They shined intense lights into the area below the instrument panel where Jake's legs were pinned. Other divers could be seen moving about outside the cockpit. Finally one diver came up, took off his mask and spoke to Hank. "Sir, with all respect, you're in the way. We need to tear out much of the floor under this cockpit to get your man out, and we can't do it with you here. We'll take good care of him, sir, I promise."

Hank didn't want to leave. He wanted Jake to come out with him. But the divers were right. He had done all he could, and it was up to them now. He put on his helmet and ducked into the airlock. The buoyancy of the helmet made it bounce against the ceiling of the airlock, but then he was outside of the plane and on the surface. Several hands pulled him into a boat anchored next to the hulk of the plane. His helmet was fogged and covered with hundreds of water droplets and he couldn't see, so he took it off and saw Danielle waiting there.

"What's Jake's status?" she asked.

"His feet are caught by some bent metal around the rudder pedals. Marion and I put a space suit and helmet over his head so he can breathe, but I don't know if he has any other injuries, and I'm not sure how well our jury-rigged space suit will work for more than a few minutes."

"Is there any air in the cockpit?"

"Yes, there's a bubble near the roof, but Jake's head is about a foot underwater."

Danielle turned to the operator of the boat, "How deep is the water here?"

The operator looked at the boat's depth sounder. He turned back and said, "It shows about 45 feet right under us."

Danielle looked back toward the runway. The furrows dug by the main gear ran across the overrun, down the beach and into the water. In the shallows the severed nose gear strut poked out of the water at an angle. Several hundred feet from the beach, the twin vertical tails of the plane and the bent trailing edge of the wing rose above the water at the rear of the airplane. Air bubbles were still coming in a steady stream from the starboard wing. Small oil sheens were appearing from leaks in the port wing. She turned to Maurice, who was overseeing the rescue operation.

"Maurice, what's the status of the main gear?"

Maurice didn't know. His attention had been focused on the trapped pilot.

She quickly outlined her idea, "If the main gear are not completely buried in the bottom, we might be able to rig a sling under the nose and tip the plane back, lifting the nose out of the water. We can use two of the empty water tanks from the de-sal plant and float them on either side of the nose. Cable them together, running the cables under the fuselage as far forward as we can. Then we sink the tanks, take up the slack in the cables and refloat the tanks with compressed air. Use the big loaders we use to move the empty tanks to carry them down here and put them in the water. Empty, they should float like corks."

The reinforced fiberglass tanks were six meters in diameter and thirty meters long and each normally held two hundred thousand liters of water. They were designed to fit into the cargo bay of the plane, and had many fastening points all over their exterior surfaces.

Danielle checked to insure that Hank and Marion were being taken ashore for a physical exam and when she learned they were, she turned her attention back to Jake's predicament.

Maurice grabbed an unoccupied diver and instructed him to check out the conditions under the plane. The diver fell backward over the side of the boat, and swam out of sight below the leading edge of the wing, about 15 feet below the surface. A minute later he surfaced on the far side of the airplane and swam back toward the boat. Maurice leaned over the side while the diver took off his mask and explained what he had seen.

The main gear were buried only to the axles in the bottom. The plane's forward momentum and the huge wing had either created enough lift to keep the wheels from digging in or the sea bottom was harder than the beach, the diver couldn't be sure which. There was a space below the plane about 10 feet high at the gear, and there was a clear space big enough for a cable to slide all the way up to below the cockpit. The long nose of the airplane was bent upward, relative to the remainder of the airplane, and was lying flat on the bottom, while most of the fuselage was tilted downward toward the nose. The water under the airplane's tail was at least 20 feet deep.

Maurice picked up a portable radio and instructed the ground crew personnel to bring two of the water tanks, cable, and compressed air to the accident site. Minutes later, two large loaders could be seen far down the runway, each holding a tank aloft and moving slowly from the desalination plant toward the beach. A truck loaded with cable, cable clamps and compressed-air bottles was also on its way.

Maurice had one of the rescue boats meet each tank at the beach, and tow it to the wrecked plane. Other boats shifted toward the nose of the wreckage while the boats towing the tanks dragged them slowly from the beach, around the submerged wings, to the side of the fuselage just ahead of the leading edge of the wings. The plane had been in the water for only fifteen minutes. After attaching cables to one tank, divers dropped the cables to the bottom, and led them under the aircraft. The cables were then hauled back to the surface and attached to the second tank. On command of the crew leader, several valves on each tank were opened, and the tanks sank rapidly as they filled with sea-water. Workers standing on the fuselage held ropes to position the sinking tanks, as did rescue boats holding positions away from the wings. The tanks were almost standing on end before they slipped under water. Air bubbles still emerging from the openings on the top marked their locations.

On the bottom, divers armed with wrenches loosened the cable clamps and took the slack out of the cables. The cables were tightened until they were straight between the attach points on the two tanks. Another diver fastened a loop of cable around the middle of the cables linking the tanks and secured it to the forward main landing-gear struts. Now, the cables between the two tanks could not slide forward out from under the nose of the wrecked plane.

When all the cables were secure, divers closed the valves on top of the tanks, then connected several hoses from compressed air cylinders in boats on the surface to fittings on the bottom of the tanks.

After a few minutes, the tanks began to float free from the bottom. Now they were held down by the cables passing beneath the plane. More air flowed into the tanks.

In the flooded cockpit, four divers were working to free Jake, while another diver, a medic, monitored his condition. The medic was not happy with what he saw. Even though the water seemed relatively warm, the victim was not as warm as the medic would have liked, and he appeared to be getting shocky, alternately slipping into and out of consciousness. The medic could no longer see Jake's face, as the inside of the space suit's helmet had fogged over, and Jake's pulse, at his left knee, seemed to be weaker. Air bubbled up constantly around Jake's waist where the suit was cut in half. It had been forty minutes since the plane ran off the end of the runway, and Jake's condition was looking worse by the minute, despite changing his air tank twice, each time the bubbles stopped.

The divers removed the floor of the cockpit behind Jake's seat. Beneath the cockpit floor was the electronics compartment, filled with racks of power supplies and 'black boxes' connected to the instruments, radios and other displays in the instrument panel. The floor panels came up easily until they reached the panel immediately behind Jake's seat. It was wedged in place by the distortion of the cockpit structure. Finally, in desperation, one of the divers gave an extra heave, and the panel broke free. The condition of the space below the last panel was not encouraging. Radios and other electronic equipment there had been crushed backward and upward, making it impossible to get at the underside of the floor beneath Jake's seat. The plan had been to remove the seat, then remove the bent floor panel behind his feet. Unfortunately, the seat was through-bolted to the floor, and they needed to get to the underside of the floor to remove the copilot's seat. Also, they were very worried that when the seat was removed, there would be no support for his body, and his legs and ankles could be further damaged or that his makeshift breathing apparatus would slip or float off. Every few minutes, the divers would surface, remove their masks and confer on their progress and the next step. Trying to disassemble a smashed-up airplane underwater was enormously difficult. It was awkward, everyone was in everyone else's way, and there was no way to hammer anything because water resistance prevented the divers from moving the hammer fast enough to make more than a light tap.

Outside the cockpit, sharks were beginning to gather around the plane in the disturbed water. All the divers, except the ones actually inside the plane, had returned to their boats. Compressed air continued to fill the tanks alongside the fuselage. Suddenly, the fuselage began to move. The long shovel-shaped nose, which had driven itself into a coral reef, now scratched along the side of the massive brain coral head, then broke free. The fuselage bobbed to the surface, one of the large cylindrical tanks lying close to each side of the fuselage. The port-side tank, however, had come to rest against the outer door of the airlock. There was now no way to get in or out of the cockpit. An hour had passed since the crash.

Inside the cockpit, the occupants had been sloshed around by the sudden movement of the fuselage. The light became much brighter as the cockpit windows emerged from the water, and water began to recede out the open airlock door. One of the divers looked out the window and saw the shoulder of one of the de-sal tanks. The same scene was repeated on the other side. He went to the airlock, and discovered it was blocked by the tank outside. The water level continued to drop and for the first time in an hour, Jake's head was above water. The medic removed the space suit and shook Jake's shoulders, but there was no response. Jake's pulse was irregular and weak. He was still alive, but unconscious and very pale. The medic wrapped a blood pressure cuff around Jake's left biceps. The blood pressure was 80 over 40. He called out to the people on the tank outside, "Get me an IV down here, and a bunch of blood." Grabbing Jake's shirt, he tore it open, and pulled out Jake's dog-tags. "Make that 'A Positive,' and hurry it up."

"Guys," he said to the other divers, "we've got to get this fly-boy out of here. He doesn't look good. We could still lose him."

Someone handed an IV kit through the small space between the tank and the door, along with several bags of whole blood, plasma, and saline solution.

The divers attacked the problem with renewed vigor. One of them went to the airlock and called out, "Hey! Up there! We need a hydraulic jack." The diver quickly discussed the situation with someone out of sight on top of the tank. What they really needed was the 'jaws of life,' a hydraulically opened wedge used by fire departments and rescue squads to remove accident victims from mangled cars, but there wasn't one on the entire island. There were many hydraulic jacks, however, and within a few minutes a helicopter was hovering above the wreckage with a dozen hydraulic jacks of all sizes.

Maurice directed workers on top of the wreckage to take fire axes and cut through the top of the fuselage. The titanium-carbon-carbon-graphite composite skin was tough and the work went slowly. When the hole was large enough, several jacks were passed down to the divers in the cockpit, who continued trying to free Jake while others enlarged the hole in the fuselage.

The largest jack weighed several hundred pounds and was three feet long compressed and almost six feet long extended. The next-smaller one was only 18 inches long compressed. Quickly they placed the 18-inch jack on the floor next to Jake's left leg, with its top against the underside of the instrument panel, and began careful pumping.

Slowly the panel began to distort, and suddenly tore free from the center console of the plane. The pressure also forced down the floor panel which had trapped Jake's legs. The medic tried to reach through the gap to pull free Jake's feet. The opening was large enough to put his hand in, but he couldn't move the feet in their boots. The other pieces of wreckage still had Jake's feet trapped. The medic pulled his hand back and it was covered in red liquid. Blood. How much had this guy lost during the hour he was underwater? Was that why sharks were circling the wreck?

The workers now had long pry-bars as well as the jacks. They inserted the bars into the space between the floor and front cockpit bulkhead, carefully avoiding Jake's feet, and pried downward against the bulge in the floor. The force of the prying enlarged the gap. They repeated the process and gained a little more space. Again the medic reached into the space, and this time he was able to move Jake's left foot. He carefully felt above, below and all around the foot, then turned it clockwise and lifted it from the opening. The boot was severely lacerated. Blood was oozing from several cuts in the leather. The medic cursed softly to himself, put a tourniquet on the left thigh, and reached back into the space, trying to free the right foot.

The medic thought the right foot should be easier to free. However, that foot was twisted impossibly far to the right already. Again he surveyed the position of the foot, and tried to move it, but it would not move. His hand touched a piece of metal which had penetrated the right boot sole, and apparently the foot as well.

He backed out of the space under the instrument panel, and turned to the other workers. "His right foot is pierced by a piece of metal. I think it's part of the rudder pedals. See if you can get that metal free from the airplane. If we can't, we may have to amputate his foot." Quickly, he put a tourniquet on Jake's right thigh.

The workers again tried to increase their working room. Shifting Jake's unconscious form to the left, they pried along the right side of the cockpit where the floor panel joined the cockpit side panel. The space they created was enough to insert the smallest jack which, compressed, was only about six-inches-high. After pumping the jack for a few seconds, something failed in the structure in the front cockpit bulkhead, allowing it to collapse forward and away from Jake's feet.

Shining a light into the space, the medic could see that a jagged piece of metal angle was protruding from the top of Jake's boot, which was twisted at more than 90-degrees from its normal position. Something was broken for sure. The metal angle was protruding through a hole in the floor aft of the bulkhead.

The medic turned to the workers near him. "I have to pull that metal angle out of his foot to release him. He'll probably lose a lot more blood when it comes out. Call up and make sure there's a chopper ready to take him aboard."

"They're ready now," came the answer. The roar of a hovering helicopter could be heard from above. Just then there was a lurch and a grinding sound as the fuselage slipped on the supporting cables, then caught again.

The medic quickly reached for the trapped foot. "Hurry!" he urged. He lifted the foot gently, and it would not move. He had to try to avoid any further damage wherever the break was, but he couldn't tell where. He closed his eyes, said a quick prayer and forcefully lifted the foot straight up and off the metal. A few drops, then a solid flow of blood came out of the boot, top and bottom. "Damn!" he swore softly. He tightened the tourniquet around Jake's right thigh, then said "Quickly now, take him out."

The other workers carefully lifted Jake's limp form from the copilot's seat and raised it toward the jagged hole cut in the overhead. Arms reached down through the hole, grabbed Jake's arms and lifted him through the opening. A few moments later, the sound of the helicopter changed and then began to fade until it could no longer be heard. An hour and a half had passed since the crash.

The five men leaned against the bulkheads in the wrecked cockpit, rested a moment, then helped one another climb out through the jagged hole in the top of the fuselage.

CHAPTER 46

January 17

Maurice and Danielle watched the helicopter carrying Jake climb away from the wreckage, swing around toward the Base's buildings, then land in front of Operations. Small waves in the lagoon were washing up against the fuselage where it emerged from the water as if it were another island.

Maurice directed the boat's operator to return to shore. There they took one of the company vehicles from the many gathered on the beach at the gaping hole in the fence and drove back to the Operations Building.

At Operations, the emergency medical team had carried Jake to the dispensary, where fresh units of blood were connected to the intravenous tubes in his arms, and his clothing was cut away. The tourniquets were loosened momentarily, and blood again poured from both boots. The tourniquets were retightened.

The medics quickly cut the laces from Jake's boots, then, with great difficulty, cut the leather down from the bottom of the laces to the sole, allowing the boots to be removed. The left boot was easiest to remove because it was severely lacerated, and the medics had only to cut to a convenient laceration in the boot's upper material. The sock underneath was thoroughly blood-soaked and was soon cut away. The left foot had four major wounds. It was obvious that if any two of the cuts had been much longer, most of the foot would have been completely severed. As it was, the foot still might be saved, if they could stabilize the patient.

The right foot was much worse because of the ankle injury. There was an L-shaped opening in the bottom and top of the foot, where the structural metal angle had penetrated. Quickly, they packed the wounds and turned their attention to that ankle. It was swelling ominously, and it was impossible to determine what damage had been done, except that the right foot was now pointed more backward than forward. Possibly the entire ankle was destroyed, or the bones in the lower leg might have been broken and twisted off. Whatever it was, it was obvious the injuries were beyond the capabilities of the Base's few medical personnel.

The left foot was rapidly bandaged together and packed with gauze. They needed to loosen the tourniquets from time to time to insure circulation. When the left tourniquet was taken off, the foot seeped blood steadily, but at least the blood was getting there. The toes rapidly regained a healthy pink color.

Removing the right tourniquet was more uncertain, the bleeding appeared to be stopped by the packing in the wound, but the ankle was continuing to swell, and it appeared that the swelling of the ankle might be interfering with the circulation to the foot. The color of the right toes did not look nearly as promising as the left toes. At least the medics had stopped the bleeding, and Jake's blood pressure was up to 110 over 65.

There was another problem. Jake still had not regained consciousness. As soon as the bleeding was under control, the chief medical officer instructed the medics to prepare Jake for transport.

When Rocket Four had gone into the water, Jean Claude had called Manila and ordered a Learjet ambulance from Dustoff Air Ambulance Services. It was due to arrive at the Base any minute. The Operations Office radio operator was calling the Learjet. "Dustoff, Dustoff, Belau Aviation calling Dustoff."

The speaker on the wall came to life. "Belau Aviation this is Dustoff. We're about 25 miles out, and will be entering the pattern in about five minutes."

"Roger Dustoff, understand five minutes, we're standing by."

"He's on his way in," said Maurice to the chief medic. "A few minutes."

As they were speaking, a frantic Terry Orsa came bursting through the doors of the Operations Office, tears streaming down her cheeks. She was virtually incoherent.

"Where is he? Where's my Jake? Oh, my God! Where is he?"

Danielle reached for her but she pulled away.

"Don't touch me! Let me see him! I MUST see Jake!"

Maurice signaled for help and enveloped her in his arms. Another man helped hold Terry until she stopped resisting.

"Terry. Cherie.... Come with me."

She now clung to him, tears still running down her face.

"Oh, Morrie! ...," she cried. "I'm *so* scared. Where is he? How is he? I've got to see him."

"I know. I know. It's going to be all right," he said. He hoped earnestly it was true, but he didn't have any idea what Jake's status was and was saying it as much for himself as for Terry.

Still holding her, he turned to the radio operator. "Call Dustoff and get a status report."

The radio operator picked up the microphone and said, "Dustoff, this is Belau Aviation, what's your status?"

"Belau Aviation, we are on base for runway Nine."

"Nine!" shouted Maurice. "He's at the wrong airport! He's at Belau International! Get him on the horn and tell him to abort his landing."

"Dustoff!" called the radio operator, "You're at the wrong airport. Abort your landing! Abort your landing! We are seven miles northwest of your present position, on the northwest side of the big island. Active runway is Zero Three. Wind is ... what's the wind?" He looked around at the anemometer and wind direction gauges. "Dust Off, wind is zero four zero at two zero."

"Roger Belau Aviation, Dustoff is aborting landing at Belau International. We'll find you. ... Oh, wow, ... We have the runway in sight. Dustoff is on long final for straight-in approach to your runway."

There was a pause, then the radio speaker was active again. This time it was the controllers in the tower cab speaking.

"Dustoff, this is Earth Base Tower. We have you in sight. Cleared to land."

"Belau Aviation, this is Dustoff. We're going to need to refuel. Hope you have some Jet-A." The pilot needed to refuel his aircraft with aviation kerosene.

"Roger, Dustoff. Will have Jet-A standing by for you."

Maurice led Terry out of the Operations office and down the hall toward the Medical Clinic. As they neared the Clinic, Hank and Marion came into the hall in front of them. Terry started crying loudly again. Hank and Marion wrapped their arms around her.

"Hank. Wh ... Where is he? I've *got* to see him. Please, Hank! *Please!*"

Hank looked behind him into the Clinic. Jake's unconscious form was lying on the examining table. Someone was just putting a sheet over his legs. He motioned to the medic. "This is his fiancée. Can we let her see him for a minute?"

The medic nodded. Jake turned back to Terry.

"Come in here. Jake's right here."

Terry caught her breath, then hesitated. She thought to herself 'for better or worse, in sickness and in health ... 'til death us do part', and turned the corner into the office.

Jake was lying on a table in the middle of the room. On either side was a rack with an IV bottle dumping whole blood into him. Wires ran from his body to several monitors. On each side of him was a medic, looking like an honor guard. Actually they were there to keep her from inadvertently injuring him, but she didn't realize that. He was covered with a sheet from his waist down, and his upper body, the body of the man she loved so much, was bare. His face was covered with an oxygen mask and his eyes were closed. At first she thought he was dead. She started to say something, then, through her tears she saw his stomach rise as he took a breath. Her heart jumped.

"Is he ..., Is he all right?" she asked.

"We don't know yet. His foot ... ," the medic paused.

Terry looked at Jake's feet, and for the first time noticed that only one foot was holding up the sheet. Tears flooded her eyes again. His foot. He had lost his foot. She knew it, and knew it would kill him if he couldn't fly again.

"Will he ... have to have an artificial foot?" she asked hesitantly.

"I hope not," the medic said. "His right foot appears to have a broken ankle, and he has a lot of cuts to both feet, but I hope he will keep the foot." He thought about the impact of that statement, then revised it and said, "I think he will keep it." He didn't mention Jake's unconsciousness.

"Why isn't someone fixing him?" Terry asked.

"We're going to take him to the trauma center in Manila. They can give him the best possible treatment. The plane should be here any minute."

On the runway, the Learjet had just touched down, but was far from the parking apron. The tower called them. "Dustoff, make good time to parking apron. Aircraft in pattern behind you. Confirm."

"Tower, this is Dustoff. Say again."

"Dustoff, make good time to parking area and exit runway. Heavy aircraft on final behind you needs the runway."

"Yes, sir." The Learjet jumped forward as the pilot advanced the throttle to produce a maximum taxi speed. He wondered idly why there weren't any turn-offs from this huge runway onto the parallel taxiway.

The Learjet reached the parking area and turned from the runway. The pilot taxied a short distance further, then, following directions from the tower, turned the small jet toward the Operations building. As the jet turned, the rumble of another aircraft's engines attracted his attention. He looked to his left, and nearly fainted when a huge space plane, which had just landed behind him, rolled past, still taxiing at nearly 80 miles per hour. He stood hard on the brakes, and the Learjet stopped. Watching the big jet, the Lear's pilot nearly forgot to breathe as the huge plane slowed and turned off of the runway. He watched dumbly as it taxied to a spot in front of the main hanger, where the doors were already opening. He had never seen such a large plane; it was at least twice as big as any plane he had ever seen.

"Dustoff," said the Tower. "Do you have a problem?"

"No. ... It's just so *big*!"

"Roger that, Dustoff. It's big all right. Now, your fuel and your passenger are waiting, if you're ready."

"Roger. Where should I go?"

"Taxi to the large building on your left, directly under the tower. We'll insure that you get here."

Inside, there was an announcement over the P.A. system. "Dustoff is in front of Ops. Refueling will be completed in approximately ten minutes."

The chief medic turned to her assistants. "Get a stretcher and get him on it. Bring a half-dozen units of Type A."

"Can I go with him, Morrie?" asked Terry.

"Sure, Honey. Sure you can. And I'll go with you."

Outside, the Learjet pilot exited his plane to supervise the refueling. Looking back at the main hangar, he was surprised to realize that the giant plane he had seen taxiing had disappeared and the hangar doors were closed again. As he watched, another door began to open, and a jet looking identical to the one that had landed behind him was being towed from the hangar.

"Is this satisfactory, Sir?" the fuel truck driver asked.

"Huh? Oh, Yes," the pilot said, looking into the tank filler opening. Then his attention was drawn back to the building from which a group of people with a body on a stretcher was approaching. He called to his co-pilot and instructed him to help load the patient while he supervised the refueling.

Re-entering the plane, he completed his checklists and double-checked that all his passengers were securely belted in. The Learjet taxied rapidly to the far end of the long runway and turned into the wind. As the Learjet began its takeoff roll, the pilot realized that the space plane had been right behind him on the taxiway. The Learjet was rapidly airborne, climbed to 1,500 feet, and turned back downwind, on instructions from the tower. As the pilot watched, the space plane on the runway far below him began its own take-off roll and then climbed rapidly out of sight. He could hear the sound of its engines over the noises of his own airplane. The Learjet, now several miles South of the long runway, turned West for Manila and began its climb to cruise altitude.

An hour later, it touched down in Manila and the group was met by a chartered helicopter, which carried Jake and the other passengers directly to the trauma center's helicopter pad.

CHAPTER 47

January 17

    The Learjet pilot had not been eager to have the extra passengers come along. His plane left Belau overloaded and crowded, because all the passengers had insisted on coming. The man in charge had made it clear to both him and his copilot that they were *all* going, and that one of the passengers would fly the plane and leave both Learjet pilots standing on the runway if they didn't cooperate.

    They cooperated. Besides the patient, the passengers consisted of the two medics from the patient's company; an older man who was obviously in charge; a man and a woman in some kind of uniforms, who looked as if they had been swimming in their clothes, they were a mess; and an hysterical young woman who seemed to be related to the patient. The pilot resolved he would file a complaint with his company about these people threatening his authority.

    When the group arrived at the trauma center in Manila, the medics rapidly conferred with the hospital's medical staff and turned their patient over to them. It was 2:30 in the afternoon. All six people sat in the waiting area outside the operating room. After a few minutes, a person wearing a surgical gown came out and looked around the room. Seeing Terry in tears, he said, "Are you Mrs. Boesinger?"

    Terry paused, then said, "No." and started crying again.

    The surgeon, somewhat confused, asked, "Is there someone here who is the next of kin of the patient?"

    Maurice stepped forward. "I'm the company representative and he has designated the company to act as his next of kin in this kind of situation. But we're all his family. What do you need?"

    "We need some papers signed. There will be a nurse who will talk with you about them."

    "Can you tell us anything about his condition?" asked Hank.

    "He seems stable. But his right leg is really messed up. We've called for an orthopedic specialist from Hong Kong. She should be here in about two hours. We'll know more then."

    "Is he conscious?" asked one of the medics.

    "No. We'll let you know when we know anything else."

    There were several forms to be signed. Consent forms. Payment forms. Other forms with no apparent purpose. Maurice signed them all.

    And they waited.

    And waited.

    Eight hours later, a short, plump Chinese woman in a white surgical gown came out of the operating room. She walked into the waiting area and found Maurice and Terry. Maurice was looking at a magazine, wishing he was somewhere else, and Terry was staring glassy-eyed at the opposite wall.

    "Hello," the woman said. "I'm Dr. Li, from Hong Kong." She paused, then continued, looking at Terry, "I'm sorry ..."

Terry's heart sank. She choked and started to cry again, but the doctor continued, "I'm afraid Mr. Boesinger won't be able to dance at your wedding. He's going to have to stay off both feet for quite a while."

Terry leaped to her feet and embraced the woman, tears of joy flooding her face. The doctor hugged her back.

"How is he?" Terry asked.

"He'll be okay. But he's going to have a lot of pain for a while, and then he'll probably have to learn how to walk all over again. His left foot was a mess. There were seven broken bones in it. The right foot only had one broken bone in the foot itself, but the ankle was completely dislocated, and the tibia was broken in four places. We had to pin it back together. From now on, he won't be able to go through any metal detectors without an explanation."

Terry's happiness flooded the room. "Can I see him?" she asked.

"Not right now. He's sleeping." The doctor, seeing the impact of that denial on Terry's face, relented. "Oh, all right. But just you. You *are* Terry, aren't you?"

Terry nodded.

"He was conscious and talking to me for a few minutes and all he wanted was to see you, but we sedated him and he's asleep now. Come with me. He won't know you're there, but you can see him. The rest of you will have to wait until he wakes up."

The doctor led Terry away down the hall.

Maurice turned to Hank and Marion. "Thanks for your quick thinking in the plane after the crash, both of you. I'm going back to the island now. You two stay here with Terry. Check all of you into a hotel and charge it to the company."

He handed Hank several credit cards, then turned to the medics. "You guys come with me, we've got a business to run." Maurice and the two medics walked out of the room.

As he passed the nurses' station, he stopped and told the nurse, "Anything Jake Boesinger needs, see to it that he gets it. If you need any approvals, Hank Taylor there ...," he gestured back toward the waiting area, "has the authority to approve it. Do you need anything else? No? Good. Let's go, guys."

Two hours later Maurice was back at Earth Base.

CHAPTER 48

January 18

Danielle stood at her office window, looking out at the end of the runway. It was over a mile, too far away for her to see the tracks from the concrete to the water, but she could see the tail and fuselage of the wrecked space plane half-submerged in the lagoon. Around the plane, she could just make out the two yellow oil-spill retention booms encircling the wreckage to contain any fuel still leaking into the water. A barge was floating low in the water inside the booms, off-loading the jet fuel from the port wing tank. The starboard wing tank had leaked out all of its fuel, either during the emergency descent to the Earth Base, or in the lagoon after it crashed. The hydrogen fuel and oxygen from the fuselage tanks had been pumped out as soon as possible after the crash. Also within the booms was an oil skimmer, borrowed the day before from the island's refinery. It was collecting any jet fuel that spilled into the water during the de-fueling process.

Maurice and Jean Claude were sitting behind Danielle at the conference table. She turned around and sat down at the table.

"What happened?" Her voice was a whisper. Neither of these men, two of her best friends, had ever seen her so mad.

Maurice was the first to speak. "We found the break-in point when the perimeter was checked after the accident."

"It *wasn't* an accident," she corrected him.

"No. You're right, of course. We don't know just how they did it, but I believe we will when we get the plane out of the water."

"We have two issues at least to discuss," she said. "First, how to prevent future occurrences? I *thought* we had already had that meeting. Second, what does this do to our schedule? Let's talk about security again," she continued. "Does anyone have any ideas?"

Maurice spoke. "Jean Claude is still confident that the manufacturing plants are secure. We thought we had this place secure too, but we learned otherwise yesterday. We followed tracks of two persons from a hole in the fence. They led through the jungle to the beach. There was an indication that an inflatable boat had been pulled ashore and concealed. It was gone when we got there. It couldn't have been earlier than noon on the 16th or later than 6 AM on the 17th. We think it occurred during the night because it's almost certain they'd have been seen during daylight."

"Where did it come from?" Danielle asked. "We're a small dot in the middle of the ocean. How did they get here? Can you identify a mother-ship?"

"We've scanned the ocean and all the traffic which has left the island since noon on the 16th. There were only three vessels. All of them have been checked out and we're confident that none of them were involved. We think the boat must have been dropped and picked up by a submarine."

"A submarine?" She was surprised by the idea.

"Yes. It's the only possibility that makes any sense. We obviously misjudged the determination of whoever is behind this. I spoke to Eric last night and we're developing a new security plan for the Base. It'll be a full order of magnitude more secure than before. I wish I could be sure it will be enough."

She was making doodles on her note pad, and didn't say anything for several minutes. Finally, she spoke again to Maurice. "What's our flight schedule? Review it for me, please." She knew it as well as he did, and he knew that, but he had worked with her for long enough that he knew when she asked the obvious, there was a good reason.

"We have, ... *had* ... eight planes. Now we have seven. We've been flying each airplane one flight a day. The next two planes are in the main hangar and should be completed within the next four months. Your order for four more planes last month will put us into those additional planes in about 18 months. The components have a 12-month completion time and we need about five to six months after delivery here for us to finish them out."

Danielle nodded. "So we now have seven planes available for our use. What's each plane's schedule?"

"Typically, a plane will launch from here, rendezvous with a satellite or tug, and be back here within six hours. That time consists of about one hour to boost to orbit, an hour and a half to return, and three and a half hours to unload and turn around, including reloading empties at the satellite. It then goes into maintenance for a condition inspection and refueling, which is averaging about three hours. Anything the inspection turns up is fixed and the plane is then put on the line, where it sits until it's loaded. Loading is usually pretty fast, less than an hour for the actual loading and post-load checks, then the plane sits again until about an hour before launch, when the pre-flight is performed."

She had been writing several columns of figures on her pad. "We're taking three hours for maintenance, one hour for loading, and an hour for preflight. Is that right?"

"Right."

"And take-off, climb to orbit and landing require two and a half hours?"

"Yes. Give or take a few minutes."

"And turn-around at orbit requires three hours and a half?"

"Yes. Actually the average has been three hours and 12 minutes."

"When one plane takes off, there is one about to return from orbit?"

"Yes. The average is one flight about every three-and-a-half hours, not considering periodic maintenance down-time, when we do more complex checks and preventive maintenance. It was one every three hours before we lost Rocket Four. And add an average of a half hour for the periodic maintenance."

"Can we modify the flight decks to carry three more people?" she asked. The cockpits already had seats for five.

"I think we could, but I'd have to check with the engineers. It seems to me that we should be able to modify the galley area to provide room for three more seats, if we made the galley L-shaped rather than like a closet, as it is now."

"Do it. If they can figure out how to do it, go ahead and modify the planes. You'll need to be rescheduling all the crew times. There's a billion dollars worth of the most sophisticated airplane in the world out there in the drink and I'm unwilling to risk any more damage to our planes. We've been assigning a crew to one plane for a round trip to the satellite. I don't want to do that any more. That system has left us with six planes sitting on the ramp here between flights, just waiting for their turn to fly. Or for someone to blow them up.

"From here on," she went on, "I'd like to store our planes in a safe place between flights - *in orbit*. I want a report as soon as you can get it to me on the pros and cons of doing just that. If we can get a favorable projection, we'll start as soon as you can get all planes modified to carry an extra crew back."

"How's that going to work?" asked Maurice.

"We send a plane," she said, "with its cargo, into orbit to either LEO-A or -B, and start unloading it. By the time the next plane comes up with its cargo, the first plane is ready to return, picks up the second crew and carries both crews back. Over a week or so, we could have all the planes, which are not being loaded or serviced, parked at one station or the other. We leave half the fleet at each satellite. Each of them would have fuel on board sufficient for reentry and return, plus the normal reserves. When the next plane arrives at the station, it is parked, the crew switches to a plane already unloaded and ready to go and leaves orbit returning here. The crew doesn't have to wait for unloading, so their flight can be completed in three or three-and-a-half hours less than it takes now. The station crew at LEO is responsible for unloading and reloading anyway, so it might enable them to schedule their work more efficiently as well. There *is* a safety issue: we may be unable to preflight the plane while it's in orbit in the same way we do here. It will have to be one preflight per cycle, still done here. I want a careful safety review of the concept and any problems that it might generate.

"Also, I want to know if we can make a stop in Europe, or the U.S., provided there's an adequate runway available. Last month we reviewed the economics of working some charter flights into the operation, and World Express wants to pursue the Asian delivery market. Maybe we could turn the planes carrying cargoes to orbit as fast as we are right now, and also make a revenue run for the express companies at the same time. We already have the crew on duty, and the express company would pay for the fuel for the extra legs. So have a feasibility study prepared on the impacts it will have on our operations.

"Also, get me a report on any deterioration we can expect as a result of storing the planes in space, due to radiation, vacuum, whatever, compared to the deterioration we're seeing here in Belau from the salt air. I know we're getting a lot of salt-air corrosion here. Perhaps that can be reduced by parking in space. At least there should be less oxidation, since there's so little oxygen there. We don't want to find out the hard way that some component is falling apart because of prolonged exposure to space conditions. My hunch is that we'd identify those conditions during the condition inspections each day, but I don't want the safety of our personnel dependent on my hunches.

"Oh, and while you're at it, have some of our engineers draw up a proposal for a commercial 'materials-in-space' testing facility. Maybe we can market that to someone, and the information will certainly be useful to us as we move into later phases."

"Okay. How soon?"

"Have a preliminary discussion on the viability of space storage to me in a week, and the final study in three. Meanwhile, begin working on the extra seats in the plane. We can try the space storage for a while and develop some empirical data to assist the writers of the storage report. I'm confident there won't be any catastrophic failures over the short term. Be sure though, that we have a refueling capability at both LEOs. The materials testing plan should be done within the month, say by the end of February. Okay?"

"You've got it. Any other security-related issues?"

"No, Maurice. You and Jean Claude and Eric handle it. Just one thing. Tell Eric I want him to develop a program to try constantly to infiltrate our security here, and at our major manufacturing facilities, as a way of improving the security provisions. We've become complacent about security. If he has any questions, have him call me, or we'll have a conference call with you, whatever you like. ... Next, I want to know how the loss of number Four will crimp our schedule."

Maurice said, "Boss, you never cease to amaze me. Before I came in here this morning, I was going to say we would lose a trip a day. But if we use your plan and store our planes in space, I think we can maintain the current schedule. I'm not sure and won't be until I have a number-cruncher check it out, but it looks that way. When we get the last two planes assembled and flying, we may be able to exceed the prior delivery schedule projections. If your plan doesn't work out, we'll be one plane down unless we accelerate the loading schedule.

"For putting materials in low earth orbit, the limiting factor for the foreseeable future is the rate we can perform condition inspections and other maintenance on the planes. But, if we increase our maintenance and loading capability, we could theoretically get two or even three flights a day from each plane, and then the limiting factor would be our ability to move materials out to the Web, and we would be short of space tugs. If we solve that one, then we don't have the human work-force at the Web to assemble the materials at the rate materials would be arriving. You can see, our production is based on a balance of manufacturing, delivery, and assembly."

"What you're telling me is stop pushing so hard, isn't it, Maurice?" She smiled.

"You could put it that way, Danielle, but I understand why you're so concerned after yesterday, and that concern is fully justified. What I want to talk about, though, is something else. I would like to either appropriate one bay in the main hangar or build another hangar."

"What for?"

"I believe we can significantly improve our maintenance time, and I need more protected room for condition inspections, but the main reason is I want to rebuild Rocket Four."

Danielle's eyes popped wide open. "*You what?*"

"I think the main structure of number Four may be rebuildable. We can order new parts to replace anything damaged, provided, and this is a big "IF," if the center of the fuselage and center-section of the wing are intact. The other parts have a much shorter lead-time, and are already in process, due to your order for four more planes. We can easily change that to five more sets of parts. If, and I reemphasize if, the basic parts are reusable, we might be able to rebuild number 4 and have it flying again ahead of number 10. Otherwise, we can increase our order from four more planes to five."

"How long will it take you to know if you can rebuild it?"

"We have to get it out of the water, rinse it off, and tear it down to the undamaged sections. We'll see then. I expect it will take us a week or two to get it ashore. The fuel is coming out today, and I don't want to risk a spill. Tomorrow we have a barge and a crane arriving to unload the cargo. The condition of the cargo is uncertain, but Hank did an incredible job of getting the plane back on the ground. He didn't even blow out any tires, so I think the main gear and attachments should be OK. The nose gear is sitting there on the beach with two intact tires on it, despite all it went through, but it will probably not be worth salvaging. I suspect parts of it were over-stressed when it was torn out of the fuselage.

"If the diagonals for the Web that were secured in the cargo-bay are undamaged, we'll still have to rinse them down, and do whatever's necessary for corrosion protection before we can use them although, as you said, there probably isn't much opportunity for oxidation in space. We have a standard for everything we ship up, and I won't compromise it. But we should be able to ship them out within a few days, assuming they're undamaged.

"The starboard wing tank is being resealed right now. It should be done, patched at least, today. After we get the fuel out of the port tank, we'll pump both of them full of air, add inflatable rubber bridge floats under the wings, lift the plane off the bottom, turn it around, and tow it to shore. I have an Australian Army tank-hauler coming to carry the nose ashore on, so we'll be able to back it into the water, put the front of the plane on it, drag it onto the runway and tow it to the hangar. We're starting this afternoon to rebuild the overrun with crushed rock so it can support the plane rolling back from the beach. There's a barge of crushed rock at Koror, which I bought a couple hours ago, and we're borrowing 100,000 square feet of pierced-steel plank runway material from the Australian Army Engineers, along with the inflatable bridge floats. Also, we're working closely with the biologists from the Belau government to minimize damage to the lagoon. They've been a big help in locating local resources. Oh, by the way, I think we should rebuild the overruns, to prevent gear damage if we have any more go off the end some day. If we hadn't lost that nose gear, we could probably have rebuilt Number 4 with just one new engine, three rebuilt engines, some repairs to nose and tail and wingtips and a rewire."

Danielle felt as if she would cry. "Maurice, I love you! Have I told you that recently?" Then she smiled and added, "Don't tell Sophie."

Maurice ignored her and went on, "We may be able to rebuild three of the engines too. No guarantees, but they were shut down and just coasting when the plane hit the water. Maybe just new bearings and new accessories, who knows. We might be able to keep the cost to less than half of a new ship."

"Sounds great to me," Danielle said. "If you need anything, let me know. What else do we need to discuss? Nothing? That's good. You two are a terrific team. Maurice, go ahead on a second hangar. Make it a duplicate of the first, so we don't have any design delays, unless you must have a change. By the way, how are the employees handling the crash?"

"They seem to be suffering from shock, seeing their work damaged and sitting there like that. Otherwise, they're all right."

"Maybe you could ask for volunteers to be on the rebuild crew? That's just a suggestion - it's your show - but it might get them back into a positive state of mind.

"Also, I want you to put out a Press Release about the crash. Word it something like this: 'Belau Aviation experienced damage to one of its fleet of aerospace planes on January 17, when the aircraft overran the runway, following, ... no, *during* an emergency landing after an engine problem. Management credits crew proficiency and structural design excellence for the limited damage to the plane. The plane's cargo of satellite parts was undamaged and will be shipped on a subsequent flight.' Fax it to Aviation Week, New York Times, Wall Street Journal, and the international news services. We'll show them they can't hurt us, whoever they are. But," she emphasized, "I don't want any more security breaches."

Maurice said, "We've already doubled the number of guard-posts, and Eric and I are planning another fence with additional security features. We're not sure whether we'll have dogs or laser beams or what, but it'll be a lot more difficult to defeat."

"Your conclusion that our saboteurs departed by submarine worries me," she said. "That could mean a <u>country</u> is behind this, rather than individuals. If they have missiles as well, and are intent on getting us, they could conceivably destroy one or more of our satellites. And if that's the case, I don't see how we can defend against it. I think we have to assume they don't have that capability and focus our efforts on trying to identify the person or persons behind the attacks. Perhaps we can figure out whose submarine it was." She paused. "You're sure it was a submarine??"

"We've ruled out everything else."

"Anything else you want to discuss?" she asked.

There was nothing more, so the two men left the office. Danielle walked back to the window and watched as another space plane thundered down the runway and into the air, climbing to several thousand feet before it passed over the salvage operation in the water at the end of the runway. Then it turned eastward and began the climb to orbit. She went to her desk, and pushed the intercom button.

"Bill, call the President of the United States for me. Tell them it's a personal call from me to him. Ask him to call me back at his convenience." It was after 8 PM in Washington, D.C..

241

CHAPTER 49

January 18, 10 AM

The intercom buzzed and Bill's voice said, "The White House is on line one."

"Thanks, Bill." She picked up the phone. "This is Danielle Simones."

"This is the President's Office in Washington, D.C.," said a female voice. "Miss Simones, we received a message that you needed to speak to the President. I'm sure you realize it is very unusual for individuals to be able to call the President directly?"

"Of course, but I must speak with him. It *is* very important."

"What do you need to speak to him about?"

"I'm sorry, but I can't give you the details, but I need a favor, and he's the only person who can do it."

"I really must determine the nature of your call before I can forward it."

"I'm sorry, miss, but I can't discuss it with you. If the President doesn't wish to speak with me, so be it, but I can only discuss it with the President. Frankly, I'm reluctant to discuss it with him at all on a non-secure line. This line isn't secure, is it?"

"No ma'am, it is not," the secretary answered. "The nearest secure line to your location is at the U.S. Embassy in Koror."

Danielle said, "I realize it's quite late in the evening there. If the President wishes to speak with me, I can be at the U.S. Embassy in half an hour. Please consult with him and call me back and either tell me he won't take my call, or tell me when I can call him from the U.S. Embassy. I don't believe this situation is so time-critical that I need to speak to him this minute, and I could call him early tomorrow morning, Washington time, and it will just be late evening here. I'll wait for your call." She disconnected without giving the secretary the opportunity to answer.

A few minutes later, Bill announced another phone call. "It's the White House again."

"This is Danielle Simones."

"Miss Simones, this is the President's Office again. I'm sorry, we seemed to be cut off before. I spoke with the President's secretary and he does want to speak with you. He can call you two hours from now at the U.S. Embassy if you can be there.

"I can be there. It would be helpful to have authorization to land my helicopter on the Embassy's helicopter pad, if that can be arranged. I may be able to arrange it myself, but a call from your office would certainly open the door for me."

"I don't know, but I'll check. The President did say he'd call you at the Embassy at noon, Koror time. So you should do whatever you need to do to be there."

"Thank you. I'll be there. Goodbye." She hung up and pushed the intercom button.

"Bill, get me a helicopter here right away. I need to fly to Koror. And call the U.S. Embassy. I want to land there, and need their prior approval. I've asked the President's office to authorize it. Get the radio frequency for the Embassy too, and we'll stay in touch with you by radio, in case they can't get an approval or frequency for us to use. If we can't land at the Embassy, I'll have the chopper drop me on the beach near downtown, and I'll walk to the Embassy. I must be there before noon."

An hour and a half later, she was seated in the Communications Center of the Embassy. The Ambassador was attempting to be a good host, but was intensely curious about the reason an obscure lawyer from the space plane company was receiving a phone call from the President of the United States. After a few minutes, the telephone rang. A technician answered, switched on some electronic equipment, and handed the telephone to Danielle. "It's the President's Office," he said.

She took the phone and said, "This is Danielle Simones."

"Miss Simones, this is the President's Office. Please hold."

She waited, then heard, "Miss Simones, this is John DeWitt. What do you need from me?" She recognized his voice.

She answered, "Excuse me, Mr. President, but I need to speak to you privately. Is this phone secure at your end?"

"Yes, certainly."

She turned to the technician and the Ambassador. "I need to be alone here. Please wait outside, and don't try to eavesdrop on this conversation." She was confident the conversation would be recorded at the White House end and probably at the Belau end also. She continued, "Mr. President, I'm sorry for the delay here but I didn't want to publicize the reason for my call.

"Sir, the fact that you have called me back tells me you remember our earlier visit – when I was in your office last March?"

"Yes, you saved me some serious embarrassment."

"So I suspected and I'm glad. But now I need a favor, and I believe it *is* in the interest of the United States to do it. Mr. President, last March I described to you our space project. If I was successful in explaining it properly to you, you should realize it will be a powerful force for peace as it begins to produce power for developing countries.

"Our first satellite is nearing the time when we will start transmitting power to Earth, although it is only partially completed. Unfortunately, yesterday one of our space planes was sabotaged and its crew nearly killed in the ensuing crash. We believe the saboteurs were picked up from our island base within the last 48 hours by a submarine. I would like to know whose submarine it was, and I believe the United States has the capability to locate all the submarines in the world, and determine which one could have been here between noon two days ago and dawn yesterday, local time.

"If it was a major national power attempting to stop our program, I believe it's also in the national interest of the United States to know who it is, because it threatens the future peace of the world.

"On the other hand, if it's a minor country which may have been financially motivated to drop some individual's or group's operatives here in Belau, I need to know who it was so I can try to reach whomever is behind it and sell them on joining me, rather than fighting this program. I thought you might give this question to your Navy as an exercise in submarine location. Maybe you can't arrange it, but I'd like to know if you can help with this."

"Thank you for the information," the President replied. "I'll have my people check it out, and I'll call you and let you know whether we can do what you're asking. I'll call you at your office and advise you of our decision. Anything else you need?"

"No, sir. Thank you."

"Very well. Goodbye."

"Goodbye." She hung up the phone, stood and went to the door. Outside, she found the Ambassador and the technician waiting.

"Thank you, gentlemen, and thank you, Mr. Ambassador for letting me use your phone."

"Any time." The Ambassador was still wondering about the reason for her conversation with the President.

"It's after lunch-time, Mr. Ambassador. How would you and your technician like to join me for lunch? My treat. There is a small bar near here which has excellent fish sandwiches, and I'm in your debt for allowing me to use your equipment."

The Ambassador debated the propriety of eating with one of his subordinates, and of accepting lunch from Danielle, but he didn't want to appear rude to her as she obviously had important connections. He accepted. The technician was equally nervous about accepting an invitation for lunch that included his top boss on the island, but Danielle's warm invitation was not to be denied.

Together, the three walked to the bar that she had visited during her first trip to Belau almost five years earlier. Lunch was still as good as she remembered, and afterwards, they walked back to the Embassy where her helicopter was still waiting. She thanked the technician and Ambassador again, and climbed into the helicopter. The Ambassador and technician backed away from the helicopter as it revved its engine and rotor, lifted off from the pad, rose into the air, and disappeared into the distance.

CHAPTER 50

January 17, 11 PM Washington, D.C.

The President of the United States sat in the Oval Office wearing his bathrobe. He had been about to go to bed when Danielle called. He pushed a button to summon a duty officer. The door joining his office with his secretary's opened and an aide entered. "Yes, sir?"

"Two memos. One to Defense. I want to know the identity of any submarine that has been in the waters off the islands of Palau, ... they were part of the Pacific Trust Territories until a few years ago ... during the last forty-eight hours. I want that report ASAP. Second memo, to the Director of the National Security Agency. First, tell me who's likely to be behind an attack on the space project in Palau. And arrange a secure line between here and a company called Belau Aviation, also located in Palau, and have the Director call me first thing tomorrow morning. And call Miss Danielle Simones at Belau Aviation, and tell her we're working on her request. Just that, nothing more. That's all. Good night."

"Good night, sir." The aide left and closed the door behind him. The President went back to his bedroom.

**

January 19 Belau

American Naval Intelligence had been busy. The morning after her call to the White House, the American Ambassador's limousine arrived at the front gate to the Base.

The security guard called the main office for instructions. Maurice said to ask the Ambassador to wait and to give hearing protectors to the Ambassador and anyone with him. Then he went to the gate to escort the Ambassador to the executive office.

The Ambassador knew Maurice was the CEO, and was surprised to be met personally by the top officer of the company. The Ambassador's aide was left waiting at the gatehouse.

As Maurice and the Ambassador rode across the Base in Maurice's Jeep, the Ambassador commented on changes which had occurred since the last time he had been there, when the very first space plane had been christened two years earlier. The landscaping was now lush, and grass was everywhere, he noted. Maurice nodded.

"How's the salvage coming?" the Ambassador asked awkwardly. The disaster of a few days earlier was still too fresh in everyone's memory and he was hesitant to refer to it because it was well known that Belau Aviation had suffered an enormous loss.

Maurice was almost casual. "Coming right along, actually. We should have it back on land in a few days." Then he changed the subject. "Wish these trucks weren't so slow," he said, referring to the vehicle carrying the long fabricated aluminum beams ahead of them. They were creeping along at less than ten miles per hour. The truck with its long articulated trailer, which was coming from a cargo ship being unloaded at the dock, was plainly headed to a paved area near the airplane parking apron where row on row of the same items were already stored on supports, awaiting shipment into space.

End on, the ½ meter-wide W-shaped beams seemed perfect for nesting one within the next. But as they began to round a curve, the actual length of the beams became apparent to the Ambassador. "Say!" he exclaimed, "those things are really *long*!"

"Actually," said Maurice, "they're each a hundred meters long. That's longer than an American football field and is just the length of the cargo bay in the space plane. The plane carries the equivalent of four of these truck-loads on each flight; that's about 110 tons."

"What're they for?"

"They're diagonal supports for the solar cells on the satellite we're building. When it's done there'll be many miles of them out there. They hold the wiring that conducts the electricity from the solar panels. If you look at the sides of the beams, you can see fittings where the solar panel frames and wiring attach to the beams."

"They certainly *look* substantial. Why are they built so heavy, if they're going to be out in space? You wouldn't think you'd need such a large support without gravity."

"If they only had to contain the solar panels, they could be really thin, just as you say, and early conceptual designs had that kind of structure. But the designers of this satellite realized there would be more need for strength. For example, the longest assemblies of such beams will be 15 kilometers long; that's about 10 miles long. Even so, if they only had to carry the solar panels, they still could be feather-light, but there are meteoroids flying around in space, mostly little ones the size of a grain of sand or so. The meteoroids will be constantly damaging the solar panels, so a bunch of repair machines will be constantly moving around on the satellite removing and replacing damaged panels with new ones.

"The beam is designed to carry the loads of the repair machines moving around on the satellite. The center web of the 'W' is actually the track for the repair machine, which, although it has virtually no weight in space, will have a considerable mass, so the beams on which it moves have to be quite stiff, relatively speaking."

"How long before the satellite begins operation?" the Ambassador asked.

"Well, ..." Maurice hesitated, "that isn't quite certain yet, but the project is on schedule, and the early schedules called for power production to begin in about a year." He looked at his watch. "You need to put on your hearing protector," he said, as he reached for his own.

The Ambassador put the oversize plastic earmuffs with the soft ear-seals on his head, and looked around expectantly. Maurice pointed to his watch, and counted down the last five seconds, holding his hand out with four fingers and a thumb extended and folding in one digit as each second passed down to ... something? The Ambassador was puzzled. Nothing had happened. He looked around, then it hit him, the concussion he recognized as the ignition of the afterburners of a space plane. It was much fainter, of course, from the Embassy in Koror, but he could hear that sound every time one of the space planes took off. From his office, it sounded a little like distant thunder. Here, the rumble of the accelerating plane was very loud, even with the ear protectors, then it lifted above the earthen mound which paralleled the runway and the full impact of its exhaust noise hit them. He realized the delay in the sound was due to the long distance from the plane's starting point at the far end of the runway, nearly two miles away. Maurice had been timing to the actual second of afterburner ignition.

Maurice interrupted the Ambassador's thoughts by pointing at the distant aircraft, already only a small dot in the sky, as he removed his hearing protectors and the Ambassador took off his own. The rapidly receding dot was still producing a rasping, rattling grumble. "Here we are," said Maurice, as they arrived at the office building.

Maurice punched a code in the keypad at the door, and pushed. Inside was a security guard, backed up by television cameras in all corners of the foyer. The guard recognized Maurice, who signed for the Ambassador. The guard reached under his desk, pressed a button and the elevator door opened.

As they rode up, the Ambassador said, rather nervously, "Mr. d'Orleans, I was told to see Miss Simones, but perhaps I should be speaking to you instead?"

"No," replied Maurice, "Miss Simones is my most valuable staff member. I always include her in discussions. Sometimes I even let her handle things by herself. She's very capable."

"Well, ... if you say so."

Maurice repressed a laugh.

The elevator stopped and they walked to Danielle's office. Bill Townsend announced them, and they went in.

She was standing at the window, waiting for them. "Good morning, Mr. Ambassador. What brings you here this morning?"

"Miss Simones, a message arrived at our communication center during the night. I was told to personally bring it directly to you, to not discuss it with anyone, and to wait to see if you had any message to send back." He looked around nervously, suddenly realizing that his instructions had not mentioned Maurice, with whom he had been discussing the message, and who was standing right behind him.

"If you're worried about Mr. d'Orleans, don't. But you were correct to bring it straight to me. Thank you. Please ... have a seat." She gestured to the several chairs in front of the desk. "Can I get you something to drink?"

The Ambassador and Maurice declined. Both were intensely interested to know what the message contained.

Carefully, she opened the envelope, then removed and read its contents. She looked up at the Ambassador and asked, "Are there any other copies of this message?"

"No."

"Good. Well, Mr. Ambassador, you've accomplished your mission. There is no reply right now. If we need to send one later, I can fly over to the Embassy. Thank you for bringing this to me. Perhaps Mr. d'Orleans can show you around a little while you're here, if you're interested?"

"I'd enjoy that very much. Thank you."

She looked at the clock, then out of the window. "Have you seen one of our planes land, Mr. Ambassador? Here's your chance. Come over to the window. There's one in the pattern now." From the window she could see the Sun glint from the fuselage and wings of the giant plane, still at high altitude, making its final turn to line up with the runway. It descended steadily toward the runway. Almost at the last instant, the nose rose a little, and the main gear touched the pavement,

247

generating a cloud of smoke as the tires spun up to runway speed. The nose landing-gear settled gently to the concrete, making another smaller puff of smoke, and the plane began to slow rapidly. Inside the well-insulated office, it was just possible to hear a hint of the four huge engines roaring in reverse thrust. Then the sound diminished, and the plane turned from the runway onto the taxiway, having used less than half the runway's 18,000-foot length to land, slow and then turn off. It taxied to the parking area, and stopped.

The Ambassador didn't know quite what to say. He didn't know an aileron from a turbine blade. "Very impressive," he finally managed.

Maurice gestured toward the door. "Mr. Ambassador, come with me and I'll show you our design department." The two men went out and closed the door behind them, chatting amiably.

Danielle looked again at the contents of the envelope: three items. One was a letter from the President, one was a copy of a heavily censored report from US Navy Intelligence and the third was a report from the US National Security Agency.

The President's letter invited her to establish a secure direct line between the Belau Aviation office and the White House and offered the resources of the United States to assist in identifying and locating the persons responsible for actions against the solar power program. It was a tempting offer.

The second enclosure, one page, described the number of submarines various countries had in service, and their general locations. Those numbers referring to the United States and the Commonwealth of Independent States were blacked through. The other countries with submarines were listed, and most of them were confirmed as being in their home ports during the period during which information was sought. Others had been positively identified far from Belau at a time which would have precluded them from being anywhere near Belau on January 16 or 17. There was only one submarine which could have been in Belau waters, the Peruvian "Albacora".

The NSA memorandum listed the members of ICEPIC, the major private, energy-related international organization, and identified the members most likely to be involved in clandestine attacks against the space project. The persons identified by the report as potentially involved in the attack were all on Danielle's original 'hot list' of potential investors, but none had invested. All the other named ICEPIC members were investors, including Felix O'Brian. The report also stated that American agents in Peru had observed obviously non-naval personnel boarding the Peruvian submarine Albacora just prior to its departure from its home port weeks earlier.

CHAPTER 51

THE WHITE HOUSE
Dear Miss Simones,
        Following your call last evening, I have asked our intelligence agencies to prepare two reports for you. The first identifies possible ships that could have been used to transport the persons who sabotaged your airplane, and the second discusses persons possibly behind the sabotage.
        Your conclusions regarding the importance of the space project to the United States and the rest of the world mirror my own. I sincerely appreciate your call and the opportunity for the United States to assist in resolving this situation. If you need any further assistance from the United States, please call me.
        To facilitate future communications between your office and the White House, I have requested the National Security Agency to make available to you secure communications equipment whereby you can call this office without the necessity for you to travel to the U.S. Embassy in Koror. I hope you will accept this offer.
        Please feel free to contact me if I can be of further assistance.
Sincerely,
(Johnathon)

January 18
Miss Danielle Simones
Belau Aviation
Republic of Belau
****
MEMORANDUM
SUBJECT: *Identification of vessels near Belau*
FROM: *DEPNAVBUINT*
TO: *JCS*

1.   *Reference your inquiry, subject same as this memorandum.*
2.   *Negative military surface vessels in subject vicinity on January 16 or January 17.*
3.   *Analysis of potential submarine traffic follows:*
a.   *Global submarine population is (deleted).*
b.   *United States submarines in two classes, (deleted) guided missile and (deleted) attack submarines.*
c.   *Commonwealth of Independent States (frmr SOVUN) submarines in two classes, (deleted) guided missile and (deleted) attack submarines.*
d.   *No US or CIS submarines reported in subject area.*
e.   *Remaining submarines belong to 42 other countries and total 103 submarines, all diesel electric.*
f.   *Of the 103 other submarines, 74 were in their home ports during the subject period. Of the remaining 29 submarines, 28 were identified in locations and*

at times which would preclude being in the subject area at the designated time, due to their cruising speed limitations.

g.   The only potential submarine remaining is the Peruvian submarine "ALBACORA", positively identified 0030Z 18Jan at 143 degrees East and 4 degrees North, proceeding East at 21 knots.

****

MEMORANDUM
SUBJECT: Sabotage of Palau Space Project   (AKA Prometheus)
FROM: NSA
TO: Office of the President
DATE: January 18
1.   Reference your request dated January 17.
2.   Persons most likely to be involved in attack are members of the organization called International Council of Energy Producing Industries and Countries (ICEPIC). ICEPIC members have previously acted independently to influence their competition, often dramatically and adversely.
3.   At this time, however, it is the opinion of this office that a majority of the members of ICEPIC are participants in the Palau Project, and therefore ICEPIC is unlikely to be directly involved in any attempt to damage or delay the Palau Project.
4.   ICEPIC membership is believed to be 45 members, some of whom are unknown, because they represent countries who frequently change their delegate to ICEPIC.
5.   Key members of ICEPIC are as follows:
*Chairman: Gilbert Smith, President of Inter-Nuclear Technologies
Carlos Hernandez-Guerra, Venezuela
Ali Ibn Faud, Saudi Arabia
*Dieter Juergens, Daimler-Benz
*Felix O'Brian, Texas-American Oil and Gas, Inc.
Alberto Molino, Electricidad Peruviano
* Denotes known investors in Palau space project.
6.   Best estimate is that a minority group of ICEPIC members is involved, either directly or indirectly, in the action against the Palau Project.

CHAPTER 52

Eric Savage was on the phone.

Danielle said, "There's a lot of work coming up for you, Eric, in addition to the new security measures here. For starters, I want to know all you can find out about the Peruvian Navy, particularly a submarine called the *Albacora,* and a person in Peru named Alberto Molino. I want to know all his connections, and where to find him when I want him. Additionally, I expect to be getting a list to you of other people, and I will want a tail on each of them so that I know where each is at all times. Get the necessary agents together, and have them standing by. I don't know where they will have to go, but I'll advise you as soon as I know. We're going to get to the bottom of these attacks and stop them."

"How soon do you need this?" Eric asked.

"Give me all you can get in 24 hours, and we'll see where we go from there."

"You got it. Anything else?"

"Not now. Goodbye."

Bill buzzed her with Felix O'Brian on the other line. She began, "Hello, Felix."

"Hello, Danielle. What can I do for you?"

"We had a setback day before yesterday. One of our planes crashed."

"I saw the notice in the <u>Journal</u>. What happened? Or do you not want to talk about it?"

"No, it's all right and you need to know anyway. It was sabotaged and an engine blew up when it was at about 150,000 feet. The pilots managed to get back here, but had so much damage they couldn't stop on the runway and the plane ended up in the lagoon. What really bothers me is a crewmember has been seriously injured. I'm tired of my people being put at risk by outsiders, and I need some information from you."

"From me?"

"Yes."

"What kind of information?"

"You're a member of ICEPIC."

"I am?"

"Don't play games with me Felix!" she snapped. "There are thousands of lives and billions of dollars at risk on this project and I don't have to tell you that several hundred million of those dollars are yours, and your syndicate has over three billion dollars in the project. We both have responsibilities to those investors who have placed their confidence in us. So don't give me any more of that 'who me?' crap!"

"I'm sorry. I just didn't realize you knew about ICEPIC or that I was a member, but you're right, I am. What information do you need?"

"I need a list of all the members. And I need it right now."

"Can I put you on hold for a minute?"

"Yes."

She waited tensely for several minutes. In Houston, Felix was rifling his files for a list of members. All he had were notes from meetings. He came back on the line. "Danielle?"

"I'm still here."

"I don't have a single list, but I have some notes from meetings. The organization has avoided printing a list to help keep the membership confidential, but I think I can assemble the list from my notes and memory. Are you ready to copy?"

"Go ahead."

Felix began reading names, and adding ones that weren't in his notes, as he thought of them. When he finished, there were forty-three names on Danielle's note pad.

"That's only forty-three," she said. "There are more."

"You're right. There should be forty-five. Look, I need to go through this file, and I'll call you right back, OK?"

"Do that. I'll be waiting."

An hour later, Felix called back with the two missing names. She called Eric Savage.

CHAPTER 53

Eric Savage's report on Alberto Molino was in her hands four hours later. Senor Molino was the fourth wealthiest man in Peru, and had significant influence with the Peruvian government. He had been considered as a candidate for Vice-President, but had declined, presumably because he already had the power he wanted. His cousin was the Peruvian Defense Minister, and his son-in-law was Captain of the *Albacora*. Molino also was the majority investor in the one nuclear power plant under construction in Peru.

During the time required for the Peruvian submarine to cross the Pacific Ocean to Peru, Eric Savage's operatives fanned out around the world. All 45 members of ICEPIC were being watched. Their actions appeared relatively unremarkable until just after February first, when, almost simultaneously, seven of them departed for South America.

Eric believed he knew where they were going, and sent agents to Lima to intercept and follow them. The seven ICEPIC members arrived just as Eric had expected, and went to the hacienda of Alberto Molino near Cienguilla. The hacienda already was under round-the-clock observation by many of Eric's agents prior to the arrival of the ICEPIC members and, with their arrival, the initial surveillance was reinforced.

Simultaneously many of Eric's security personnel arrived in Peru, most of them in the guise of tourists or businessmen. Within hours, they would not have been recognized as foreigners, unless they were required to speak Spanish, which some of them could not do. Each agent was equipped with a radio furnished by the United States government which linked them via satellite directly to Belau, to Danielle, to Eric and, not accidentally, to the American intelligence services.

CHAPTER 54

While the submarine rapidly cruised back to its home port, its progress was carefully observed both by the United States government using highly sophisticated military satellites, and by Eric's agents using a small fleet of aircraft which simply circled high above the submarine as it cruised along the surface oblivious of the watchers above. When it was within a day's travel of its homeport, Danielle was notified.

February 16

The two saboteurs departed the submarine in high spirits. They had succeeded in their mission, and the space plane was sitting on the bottom of the ocean, or so they thought. Rocket Four was actually sitting in the main hangar with around-the-clock crews stripping it down to its basic components.

As the two entered a taxi and proceeded to an estancia outside of the town, they were unaware of the car following them, or of the armed guards stationed strategically along their route. The estancia was the center of a vast rancho near the Peruvian coast and, although the entrance gates were equipped with cattle guards to prevent straying livestock, there were no security guards. A peasant's broken-down pickup truck was near the gate, its disheveled driver standing in front of it peering intently into the open engine compartment. The two men went directly to the main house, where several others already were waiting for them.

The Ad Hoc Committee, waiting anxiously at the rancho, began at once to question the two saboteurs. Everyone asked questions at once and in the confusion no one was getting any answers.

Another large group arrived in several cars less than a minute behind the taxi. They followed the same path taken earlier by the saboteurs, and met several bodyguards waiting outside the library where the meeting was in progress. The bodyguards, out-numbered and out-maneuvered, were told by the visitors that they were expected at the meeting. The conversation inside the library was clearly audible through the door.

There was a knock on the library door and one of the members of the Ad Hoc Committee went to open it. Eric Savage walked in.

"Who are you?" asked the committee member.

"It doesn't matter who I am," Eric answered. Two large men walked in and took up positions behind the two saboteurs. They looked around apprehensively.

Eric continued, "There is someone here you need to meet." He stepped aside, and Danielle walked into the library.

"You!!" sputtered one of the members.

"Good morning, gentlemen," she said. "Don't you think it's time we talked?" She pulled out a chair and sat down. Behind her came Molino's three bodyguards from outside the library, with their escorts who had made it clear that their cooperation was essential to their continued good health. The two men behind the chairs snapped handcuffs on the saboteurs and pulled them away from the table.

The majority of the committee members were still sputtering, unable to complete a sentence. One finally blurted out, "What are *you* doing here?"

"You gentlemen have been playing rough with my operations, and I'm not happy about it. I think it's time you stopped. So we're here this morning to talk about it."

"I'm leaving!" said one of the members.

One of Eric's men, lacking any vestige of gentleness, pushed the man back down in his chair.

"Please sit down, and don't try to leave," Danielle said. "That's better. Now, let's talk."

She explained to them that she knew who they were, and knew why they had attempted to disrupt the project. She described each of their holdings in rough detail and their relationships to others, particularly to the investors in Project Prometheus.

She explained that she could build planes faster than they could blow them up, and that even if they were so successful as to exterminate her personally, she had an endless list of successors who would continue the operation, just as if she were there. She explained that any more of their inept attempts to interrupt her operations would be cause for response against each of them, in a similar manner to those attempted against her. She explained that her agents had instructions to carry out their orders regarding the committee members if anything happened to her.

Finally, she let them know that if any more incidents were directed at the project, or if they did not cooperate fully with her, she would publicly identify each of them to the investors in the project, some of whom were much better organized than their pathetic committee, and some of whom had much less patience than she did, and even less reluctance to use violence against those persons in the library facing her. She reminded the committee members that it was those investors' investments that their group was actually threatening.

The committee members began to realize how precarious their situation had become. Finally one spoke. "Look, Miss Simones, we certainly never meant you any personal harm, I'm sure you realize that, don't you?"

"You must be joking!" she replied, remembering her flight to Lisbon. "You don't have many choices now. I think there are only two. Here they are. It costs 100 million dollars apiece to be part of this project. You can be part of it by buying a share. Your alternative is to be on the outside looking in. I told you I know all about each of you. I knew everything about each of you four years ago when I first started recruiting investors and invited you to join, but you weren't smart enough to get in then. This is your second *and last* chance. The minimum ante is 100 million and if you don't take it, I will personally see to it that you are financially wiped out. I can almost guarantee that all the current investors in the project will help, if they haven't already eliminated you by then.

"So, ... What will it be? Are you part of the project, or do I announce who's behind the sabotage we've experienced?"

"Even if we put in our money," asked one, "how do we know you will do what you have said you will do?"

"You have the same assurances as the people who have put 60 billion dollars into this project already - *my word*. Take your choice.

"Here's my card. Let me know within a week by delivering your check for at least 100 million US dollars to my office in London. If you want a bigger piece, there's no upper limit on how much you can invest. Each of you can put in many times the 100 million, and never miss it, and I know it.

"If I don't have your checks by a week from tomorrow, you can start looking for a place to hide, but I'll tell you right now, there is no place to hide where I can't find you."

She stood, took one last look at the committee members, still cringing in their chairs around the table, and turned to her own bodyguards. "Let's get out of here."

Eric Savage looked out the library door, signaled the way was clear, and led the group back to the car with their driver waiting. The saboteurs were dragged along too, and thrown into the back of the pickup truck that previously had been seen broken down on the road in front of the hacienda. The trip to the airport seemed dull.

CHAPTER 55

A chartered jetliner was waiting at the Lima airport when the scraggly motorcade arrived. The many agents who had been stationed around the estancia and along the route between there and the seaport had inconspicuously joined the convoy to the airport. The motley collection of cars and trucks acquired for the operation were parked together at the edge of the airfield. One of Eric's South American operatives would arrange to dispose of them. Many of the agents headed for the terminal to board planes back to their normal duty stations.

Danielle went into the cockpit while Eric and the security guards, leading the two saboteurs, went to the passenger section. The saboteurs, in handcuffs and leg-irons, were terrified. They had no idea where they were being taken. Separated by several rows of seats, they were unable to converse either with each other or with their captors. Attempts to speak to their guards had been met with either silence or physical abuse.

The plane took off and flew for hours. After a while, someone began to prepare meals for the passengers, and when the agents around them were served food trays, the captives were brought identical trays. The meal was typical airline food, dull, but enough to take the edge off an appetite. In their predicament, the saboteurs were too scared to be hungry, but ate anyway, because it was obviously expected of them.

When the prisoners had finished and the trays had been cleared away, they were told to get up and move to the rear of the plane. They obeyed, not that they had any choice in the matter. A guard directed them to sit down, one on either side of the aisle, in the last row of seats, with their backs against the bulkhead that formed the forward wall of the aft galley. One of their guards stood behind them in the airplane's aft galley, while the rest of the guards returned to seats more toward the front of the plane. There were at least eight rows of empty seats ahead of the prisoners.

After a few minutes, Danielle came to the rear of the plane. She sat sideways on the right-hand aisle seat one row forward of where they were seated, with her legs in the aisle, and looked at them. She looked up at the agent standing behind the handcuffed men and said, "Go forward. I want to speak to these men alone."

After the agent was gone, she looked again at one then the other. "Which one of you is the boss?" she asked. They were silent.

"Perhaps you don't understand your situation," she said, "but I am in charge here. Do you speak English? Habla Espanol?" She also tried French, German, Japanese and Arabic. They still said nothing. She was out of languages.

She turned and motioned to Eric who came to the rear of the plane and stood next to her between the seats in the third row forward from the galley. She gestured at the prisoners and told Eric, "I'll have the pilot slow down the plane and depressurize. Throw them out the door when I give you the signal." She got up to walk back to the cockpit.

The response of the captives was immediate. "Wait!" one said.

She turned back to them, "So you do speak English." It was no longer a question. She sat back down. Eric looked at her inquiringly. "Do you still need me?"

"Wait one, and we'll find out." Again she turned to the two men. "Are you going to answer my questions now, or do you want to continue playing games?"

"What do you want to know?" one asked.

"That's better. Which one of you is the boss?" One pointed to the other. The other, obviously startled, began to sputter in denial.

She looked closely at them again and, in a voice that made clear her irritation with their continued lack of honesty, said, "If you can't give me straight answers, I have no further use for you - either of you. What is it going to be?"

The one who had pointed first at the other, said resignedly, "I'm the boss."

Danielle turned to Eric, who was still standing by her right shoulder. "Go back to your seat. I'll call you if I need you again." Eric turned and walked forward several rows and sat back down. He continued to watch the proceedings at the rear of the plane from his more distant seat.

"Let's begin again," she said. "You're the leader, is that correct?" The leader nodded in confirmation. "What's your name?" He started to speak, but she interrupted, "Don't give me any more crap, because whatever you say will be checked out, and if it's not true, I still can do anything I want with you."

"I want a lawyer," the leader said.

"A *WHAT?*" She laughed, then turned to the front of the plane and raised her voice to Eric. "He wants a lawyer!" Eric and the men sitting forward of him laughed loudly. She turned back to the men.

"Okay. *I'm* a lawyer. What else do you want?"

"I mean I want my own lawyer," the man insisted.

"You just don't understand, do you? A lawyer won't do you any good here. I am THE LAW. There is no judge, no jury, no appeal. I'm what you've got to deal with. Whether you live or die is up to me, unless you'd like me to put it to a vote of the rest of the plane?"

The men looked forward at the other occupants of the plane, most of whom still looked like very rough Peruvian peasants. The prisoners realized their prospects with the men in the front of the plane could be a lot uglier than their present interrogator, who was at least asking them civil questions. They had experienced some very harsh treatment between the rancho and their arrival at the airport, and it was clear the agents had no sympathy.

"All right," the leader said. "We'll talk."

"Good. Now, what are your names? You first," she said, indicating the leader.

"Jose Hernandez," was the reply.

'Now we're getting somewhere,' she thought. "Where do you live?"

Bit by bit, the two captives spelled out their history and their involvement in the sabotage of her MU-2, the bombing of the car in Nairobi, and the bombing of the space plane. The interrogation continued for several hours. She wrote down the key points. When she was done, she motioned to Eric, who had the men moved back to their original seats. Back in the cockpit, she was soon on a secure satellite link talking to Cliff Kelly in Belau. She passed on all she had been told and instructed him to check it out, through Eric's office in London.

After refueling in the middle of the Pacific Ocean at Fatu Hiva, the plane took off again, still heading westward along the Equator. A while later, it overflew the Earth Port at Belau, made its approach to land on runway 3 and was soon parked in front of the Operations Building.

As soon as the two captives left the plane, they recognized their location as the site of their attack on the space plane. Danielle was among the last to leave the plane, along with Eric. As she stood in the door of the airplane at the top of the air stair, with the two prisoners held between two very large agents on the parking apron between the plane and the Operations building, Eric turned to her and said, "What do you want to do with them?"

She looked at the two men, who by now had realized the hopelessness of their position. "Find some place that can serve as cells, and put them in it. Lock them up separately. Keep a guard on them around the clock. I don't want them escaping. I'm sure they couldn't get back to 'the World,' but I don't want to have to hunt them down in the jungle either. I'll figure out what to do with them later. I don't think I want to impose them on Belau's simple prison population. Most of the Belauan prisoners are just drunks who get stored overnight while they sober up. There would be too much opportunity for these bad guys to escape into Koror. Just lock them up here and I'll decide later what to do with them."

Danielle walked away from the plane and caught a ride to the office building. In the office, she went to her apartment, took a shower, and went to bed. She was exhausted and felt dirty from her proximity to the two saboteurs and their bosses.

The following morning, she called Cliff Kelly into the office. "I need to know what my authority is to deal with these bastards. They've admitted their guilt and told me the details of their operation. Now I have to figure out what do with them."

Kelly said, "The Belau government has passed laws making you a regional governor. Your powers are virtually unlimited. If you want to execute these two, you can do so perfectly legally. Their crime under Belau law is a capital offense. Or, you can empanel a jury to hear their case, and you can assume the role of an appellate court, to weigh the propriety of the jury's decision, but you don't have to. And if you make the decision alone, there is no statutory right of appeal."

Danielle was pensive for a few minutes, making doodles on a note-pad. Then she looked back at Kelly. "Can we set up a courtroom in a conference-room downstairs?"

"Sure. What do you have in mind?"

"We're going to give them a trial, ... of sorts. You're the only person here with any judicial experience so you'll be the judge, Sam Thompson can defend them, and I'll be the prosecutor. We'll see what a jury decides."

"Where are you going to get a jury?" Kelly asked.

She replied, "I'll appoint one."

"I've never been a criminal trial judge before, and Sam's not a criminal defense attorney," Kelly protested.

"Don't let that bother you," she responded, "I've never been a prosecutor either, and when it's done, I'm going to be the appellate court, but I'm not going to let these technical niceties prevent these two men from having a trial. Let's convene the trial in the morning. That will give you and Sam a day to prepare. Get Maurice to set up the courtroom."

"Okay, boss," he replied reluctantly. "I'll tell Sam." He left the office.

The next morning the prisoners were brought to the main conference room on the third floor of the office building. Still in leg-irons and handcuffs, they looked around apprehensively. The hallway passed between offices and larger open areas filled with individual cubicles where designers and engineers were busily working at their computers on refinements for the satellites and other new equipment for the project.

The guards escorting the prisoners stopped at a closed door and said, "In here," then opened the door.

An elevated desk on one side of the room faced two tables. At one, Danielle sat. At the other table, to her right, sat Sam Thompson. To the right of Sam's table, but at right angles to it, was another table with four chairs. The two captives were seated in the middle chairs with a guard on either side of them. Other guards sat behind them.

A guard at the door called out loudly, "All rise!"

Everyone in the room jumped to their feet. Judge Clifford Kelly walked into the room, sat at the chair behind the desk, and said, "Please be seated." Everyone sat.

Kelly rapped a machinist's hammer on the desk. It was as close as they could find to a gavel on short notice. The prisoners jumped at the sharp noise. Everyone looked at the judge, who said, "This is the regional court for the Island of Babeldaob, Republic of Belau. My name is Clifford Kelly and I have been appointed by the regional governor to serve as judge for this trial. The attorney for the prosecution is Danielle Simones. The attorney for the defense is Samuel Thompson. An audio and video recording of this proceeding is being made. Please bring in the jury."

The door at the far end of the conference room opened and six people came in, five walking and one on a hospital gurney. The jury consisted of Marion Douglas, Hank Taylor, Jake Boesinger, Terry Orsa, Maurice d'Orleans, and Bill Townsend. Judge Kelly realized that Danielle had picked a totally impartial jury. They took their seats at the end of the courtroom, facing the defendants. Bill and Maurice were rolling the gurney on which Jake was lying into the room, and Hank and Marion were restraining Terry. It was clear to all present that if Terry were free to do as she wished, there would be no need for a trial. Her eyes were blazing and she appeared to have been crying recently. Every few seconds either Hank or Marion would grab Terry's wrist and try to calm her. The effort seemed to make her even more agitated.

The judge said, "Will the prosecutor please read the charges."

Danielle stood and faced the defendants. "The defendants are Jose Hernandez and Alberto Marin. They are charged with trespassing; destruction of private property; sabotage of an aircraft, two counts; six counts of attempted murder; and one count of first degree murder." She sat down.

The judge said, "Under Belau law, the maximum penalty for sabotage of an aircraft, attempted murder, or murder, if convicted, is death. Do the defendants have any questions regarding the charges?"

Sam Thompson stood up and said, "The defendants have been informed of the charges and have no questions." He remained standing.

Kelly looked at the prisoners. "How do you plead to the charges?"

Thompson responded, "The defendants plead guilty to all of the charges and specifications."

"Then we are holding a trial merely on the question of the sentence to be pronounced against these defendants. Does either side have any opening statement?"

Danielle stood and faced Kelly. "Your honor, the defendants have committed at least three related crimes. The first was the deliberate sabotage of an aircraft in Morocco, with intent to kill the pilot of the aircraft. The second was a car-bombing in Nairobi, Kenya, during which an unidentified person was actually killed. The third was the deliberate sabotage of an aircraft here in Belau. The crimes which these defendants have admitted committing are the most serious sort, that of intentionally and premeditatedly attempting to cause the death of another person. In one instance, in Nairobi, Kenya, these defendants were successful in killing one person although the victim was not their intended target. In another event, the three persons who were the targets of the defendants' criminal action were only able to survive an attack committed against them here in Belau, through a combination of luck and their uncommon skill and quick thinking. In a third instance, the intended target of their attack in Marrakech, Morocco, escaped serious injury only through good fortune, after the sabotage of an aircraft. These attacks have left one person dead and another seriously and permanently injured."

Facing her, the prisoners, fearing the worst, suppressed their desires to attempt an escape. Their fears had turned to total terror, visible in their eyes. In the jury area, realizing the hopelessness of the prisoners' situation, Terry smiled.

Danielle continued. "These men are both legal residents of the United States of America and reside in Miami, Florida. They are Cuban exiles, who have obtained American citizenship by naturalization. They are also members of a Cuban counter-revolutionary organization called "Alpha Sixty-Six". They have been training as mercenaries for the past twenty years, since they arrived in the United States after leaving Cuba. They are both trained hit-men, and have used their training to attack the various persons as set forth in the charges. The prosecution requests the most severe sentence, ... Death." She sat down.

Sam Thompson stood, looked at the defendants, then at the jury, then at the judge and said, "Your honor, the defense would like to call witnesses to show the character and background of these defendants."

Kelly considered the defense request, then asked, "What would such testimony show? Do you wish to make a proffer?"

Sam said, "Your honor, the witnesses whom the defense would call would testify that both of the defendants are family men, good parents, and are active in community and civic organizations, in addition to Alpha Sixty-Six. Jose Hernandez is a trained machinist, has four daughters, ages four through sixteen, and a wife to whom he has been married for eighteen years. He is a leader of his church. Alberto Marin is the father of two boys and a girl, ages seven through eleven. He is an aviation parts specialist, and coaches Little League baseball. The witnesses would show that prior to the three acts of which they are accused here, and to which they have entered their guilty pleas, the defendants have never previously engaged in any

261

other acts of this sort, or any acts of violence at all, for that matter. An investigation conducted in Miami during the last forty-eight hours regarding these men will support this testimony.

"Additionally, your honor, the testimony will show that the defendants were informed by the persons who engaged them that the Mitsubishi aircraft in Marrakech, the Toyota in Nairobi, and the space plane here in Belau were engaged in activities in support of the Cuban government of Fidel Castro. Their actions were intended as an attempt to impede the Castro government rather than as an attack on this project. That is our proffer."

The judge looked at Danielle. "Does the prosecution have any comment on the proffer?" he asked.

Danielle stood, looked at the defendants, then turned to the judge and said, "The prosecution stipulates to the facts alleged in the proffer."

The defendants leaned across the table to Thompson. Their guards eyed them suspiciously, alert for any sudden move. The prisoners whispered hoarsely, "What does that mean?"

Sam held his hand out to them, palm downward, then shushed them with his finger to his lips. He leaned over to their table and said, "It means we won't get to bring in your witnesses. The prosecutor has accepted as true all the things we were going to prove. Is there anything else you want to present to the court in your own behalf?"

The defendants were lost and confused. They didn't have any idea what would have helped them, and thought it was possible that nothing would have.

"Mr. Thompson," asked the judge, "do you have anything else?"

"No, your honor. The defense rests."

The judge looked at Danielle. "Does the prosecution have any witnesses?"

"No, your honor," she said, "the prosecution rests."

Cliff Kelly looked at the jurors. "Ladies and gentlemen of the jury, the defendants before you have plead guilty to the charges. It is now your duty to make a determination and recommendation to this court for the appropriate sentence to impose on the defendants for their acts. You are to consider each defendant and each charge separately, and recommend the appropriate punishment. The defense's proffer regarding the background and character of the defendants is to be accepted by you as true as stated by the attorney for the defense and considered in your deliberations. Your choices for the punishment for each defendant and for each charge can range from no punishment to death. Is that clear?"

The jurors all indicated they understood their duties.

Kelly again addressed the jurors. "You will now be taken to a nearby room where you are to consider the charges and the evidence, and reach a verdict regarding the punishment. Please signal the guard outside your conference room when you have reached a verdict."

The six jury members were taken from the courtroom. The defendants looked nervously at the judge, the prosecutor, and the guards around them. One leaned toward the defense attorney and said, "What happens now?"

"We wait," the young lawyer said.

"How long?"

"I don't know. As long as it takes."

The wait wasn't long. Twenty-five minutes later, the guard came into the room and informed the judge the jurors had reached a verdict. Kelly said, "Bring them in."

The six jurors, five walking and Jake on his gurney, reentered the courtroom. Those who could sat down. Jake's head was turned to enable him to see the defendants.

Kelly said, "Who is the foreman?"

Marion stood and said, "I am, your honor."

Kelly said, "The defendants will stand and face the jury."

The defendants stood.

"Please give the verdict to me," said Kelly. Marion handed him a piece of paper which he read and then handed back to her.

Kelly said, "Please read the verdict."

Marion read, in a clear voice, "We the members of the jury, having considered the charges and the confessions of the defendants, and after considering the evidence regarding the character and the background of the defendants, recommend to this court the following punishments: For both defendants, and on all charges, death. So say we all."

Kelly then interrogated each member of the jury, and verified that he or she agreed with each of the verdicts for each defendant. They all agreed.

He turned to the defendants. "Jose Hernandez and Alberto Marin, you have pleaded guilty to the charges. Your sentence has been considered by a jury, and the jury has recommended that you be executed. Do you have anything to say?"

The two defendants didn't know what to say, overwhelmed by the speed with which they had been captured, tried, convicted and sentenced, and remained silent.

Kelly waited a minute then said, "Upon recommendation of the jury, I hereby sentence you to death. You will be taken from this courtroom to a place of confinement, and then to the place of your execution. While you are being held awaiting execution, your defense attorney may wish to register an appeal with the regional governor, who is the appellate authority. That is all. Guards, take the prisoners away." He pounded the hammer on the table and left the room. The guards grabbed each man by the arms and led them back to the empty storerooms that were being used as cells.

Sam Thompson gathered his papers and went to meet again with his clients to discuss preparing an appeal. Danielle left the courtroom. Terry was holding Jake's hand and crying. Marion and Hank were by her side. Bill Townsend and Maurice had returned to their offices.

Danielle walked from the elevator into her office, where Cliff Kelly was waiting for her. "What kind of jury was that?" he demanded.

She smiled. "That was a jury I randomly selected from the personnel here at the Base. Particularly, I selected them because the four, Hank, Jake, Marion and Terry, had been victims, and needed to feel they had some effect on the outcome of this process. I still haven't yet figured out what I'm going to do with our two saboteurs, but I have an idea. I presume Sam will be filing an appeal?"

"I'm sure he will."

"Good. We'll have an appeal hearing. I'll bet the prisoners will faint when they learn who the regional governor is. Now I need your advice."

"On what?" Kelly was obviously irritated at the lack of anything in the trial resembling American due process.

"Well, for starters, I can't simply execute those two men. I don't believe in the death penalty, particularly for people who are so gullible, and so I have to figure out an alternative. The men who hired them, who are much more guilty in my book - I have offered them a chance to invest in the project, and they each stand to make a very sizeable fortune if all goes according to plan. If I let the primary bad guys off, I can't impose a different standard on their triggermen. But I can't just let them go, either. We don't have the facilities to imprison them here, and I won't ask the Belauan government to hold them."

"What else did you have in mind?" he asked.

"These two have cost us a bunch of money. How long do you suppose it would take them to work it off, if we put them to work?"

"Forever."

"Exactly. So that's what I think we'll do. The damage to property is somewhere over half a billion. That's 250 million dollars each. If we paid each of them 50,000 a year, they would only need 5,000 years to work off the debt.

"Actually, the new group of Peruvian investors, who I can honestly say were somewhat reluctant to become investors, are going to be surcharged for the damage they caused the project. Their payments from the project will be far below those to other investors, when it eventually starts."

"How do you propose to put the convicts to work?"

"I don't know. I haven't figured out that part, but it has to be a part of their sentence. Let's allow them to stew for a few weeks before we decide whether to consider their appeal. In the meanwhile, I'll look for ways to put them to work. And Cliff..."

"Yes?"

"I know you're not delighted with that farce of a trial. I apologize for surprising you that way. Thanks for going along with it."

"I almost didn't when I saw that jury you picked."

"I know," she said. "But you know I won't treat anyone unjustly, don't you?"

"Power corrupts," he said.

"And absolute power corrupts absolutely. I know. Sometimes I worry about that. Will you do something for me?"

"What?"

"I want you to review the appeal proceeding that I'm going to have for these men, as if you were an appellate judge reviewing the lower court for *fairness*, nothing else. Then I want you to tell me if I have been unduly harsh with our two prisoners. I want you present when I eventually get around to meeting with them, OK?"

"OK. It's a little unorthodox, but here - well - here there aren't any laws covering this situation, and you have virtually unlimited authority, thanks to the laws we drafted for the Belau Assembly to adopt. I'm beginning to have second thoughts about the wisdom of those laws."

"I understand your worry, Cliff. And I'll try not to let you down. I know your cooperation this far has only been due to your personal loyalty to me. I do appreciate it."

"It's more than loyalty. I have confidence in your integrity. I've watched you work on this project for five years, and I've never seen you take an unfair advantage in a business situation. I've hoped that would carry over into this current legal morass, and so far, although the procedure's been, ah ... unconventional, the results have been acceptable. That still bothers me though, for two reasons."

"What two reasons?" she asked.

"One," he replied, "is that I have had, for a long time, a philosophy that you can't justify a bad process with desirable end results."

"I feel the same way," she said. "I know this legal situation isn't desirable, but I've been focused on getting the project underway, and my greatest fear is that we could get bogged down in some legal entanglement. We have *so much* going on at the same time, all over the world. It scares me that we could still fail if everything doesn't stay on schedule. Maybe you can prepare a study paper on ways to restructure the Belau laws so we aren`t putting the results ahead of the process. I'd like to see that."

"I guess so," he said, a little skeptically. There's a lot going on right now for the legal staff too."

"What was the second thing that bothered you?" she asked.

"Having so much responsibility attached to your position makes me worry because you will die someday," he said. "I don't know who would replace you."

"I hope most of that is covered by having much of my authority from the Belau government personal to me. It doesn't transfer automatically to my successor. I know we included that in our drafts which were sent for approval by the Belauan Assembly."

"That's true enough, but I can't be sure... I don't have any reason to have confidence, if something did happen to you, that your successor couldn't persuade the Assembly to pass on equivalent powers to him, whoever he - or she - might be. You could be the effective start of a very powerful ruling dynasty."

"Do you really think that could happen?"

"It isn't beyond the realm of possibility."

She studied his expression, his usually good-natured face clearly showing worry about the potential for upsetting the rule of law. "Cliff," she said, "work out a plan to revise the Belau laws that trouble you. I want us to review it together. I won't promise to make any changes immediately, but I want to see what you think needs changing, and work out a way to make the changes as we can. Is that good enough?"

"Sure." he said, somewhat unenthusiastically. "I just wish we had approached this whole legal situation differently from the beginning. I guess we can't change the past." He brightened. "I'll start working on it as the other things on my agenda slow down a little. I appreciate your willingness to discuss change."

She looked him levelly in the eyes. "Cliff, you know I built the best possible team to accomplish this project. I wanted you because I admired the quality of your legal thinking and your integrity. Now, we've worked together for five years, and nothing about you has caused me to question my original decision to have you as our chief legal advisor. If you think something needs to be changed, that tells me there's a situation I need to be giving a lot of consideration to changing. Thank you for your dedication to the project."

"Sure, ... sure." he said. "You're welcome. And I'm glad to be here. I know you know that. ... I have to get back to London soon, though. The missus will be worrying about me."

"I want you here when we hear the appeals on the sentences," she said, "but that shouldn't be for several weeks. I want them to stew awhile. You can either go back to London until then, or ask your wife to come out here. We can put you and her up in the VIP guest quarters. Think it over."

"I'll talk to her and see how she feels about it. Thanks for hearing my worries."

"That's what I'm here for," she said, suddenly realizing it was true.

Three weeks later, the prisoners, whose activity during that time had been limited to exercise sessions walking around the outside of the main hangar, were brought back to the main office building. The time scheduled for their appeal hearing before the regional governor had arrived.

Again wearing the handcuffs and leg-irons which they had worn at their trial, they were escorted by their guards into the foyer of the office building, where they were met by Sam Thompson and Maurice d'Orleans, who authorized their entry into the building.

Instead of going to the makeshift courtroom on the third floor, however, Maurice selected the top floor. They exited the elevator into a wide, carpeted hallway lined with engineering cubicles. Maurice let the way, followed by Sam Thompson, with the two prisoners and their guards bringing up the rear.

Maurice stopped at Bill Townsend's desk. "Is she ready?"

"Yes. You can go on in."

Maurice opened the door to Danielle's office, and the group entered the office, with Bill Townsend following. Bill went into the adjoining room, then came back out and said, "The regional governor will be right with you." He turned and walked out of the room. The two prisoners were surprised to see Cliff Kelly, the judge from their trial, already occupying one of the chairs at the large conference table. Maurice directed everyone except the guards to be seated at various places around the table. The guards remained standing behind the prisoners. A space plane took off, the rumble of its afterburners penetrating even the well-soundproofed building. A moment later Danielle walked into the room. Maurice jumped to his feet, and so did Kelly and Sam Thompson. Seeing everyone else stand up, the prisoners did the same. Then they recognized who the regional governor was: the prosecutor from their trial and the woman who had questioned them on the plane. Their expectations for any favorable result fell to zero.

Danielle was relaxed and feeling fine. "Please sit down, everyone. Sit down." She sat at the opposite end of the table from the prisoners. For several minutes she watched the prisoners fidget. The only sound in the room was the occasional clinking of the chains connecting their handcuffs and leg-irons.

She considered the guards, then the prisoners. Addressing the prisoners, she said, "Your situation is pretty hopeless, isn't it?"

One of the prisoners nodded his head. The other, apparently coached to be cooperative and agreeable said, "Yes, ma'am."

She turned to Maurice. "Have the guards remove the handcuffs and leg-irons." Looking at the prisoners, she said, "You can't get away from here. I'm sure you've already realized that. We know who and where your families are. I'm sure

266

you have already realized that also. Don't try anything cute. Just sit there and speak when spoken to. All right?"

The men nodded their agreement. The guards removed the restraints.

She motioned to the guards, who left the room.

"You men have caused me a lot of headaches, and worse. Now you've been sentenced to death by a judge after a jury heard your confessions and the facts regarding your personal backgrounds and characters. If I understand correctly, you're appealing your sentences. Is that right?"

Sam Thompson started to speak, but she interrupted him. "Sam, is there anything else about these men that I need to know or that wasn't brought out in the courtroom that bears on their sentence?"

"Yes, ma'am. They are very sorry for what they've done. They realize they were misled into thinking the project was related to Castro's Cuba."

"Okay. Thank you. I'll consider that. But now I'd like to talk to the prisoners. Is that all right with you?"

Sam hesitated. He didn't expect that she would ask him for permission to speak to his convicted clients, for obviously she didn't need his permission. It was a formality. He said, "Certainly. Please do."

Again she looked at the two Cuban-Americans. "Your present sentence is death. What do you think it should be instead? Mr. Hernandez?"

Hernandez was obviously unprepared for this question. He thought and thought, but couldn't decide what to say. In the end, he said nothing.

She turned to Marin. "Mr. Marin, what is the appropriate sentence?" Marin was equally unprepared for the question.

"Let me ask you another way," she said. "Suppose someone was sitting in front of you. They had tried to kill you. They had tried to kill another plane-load of people. They had actually killed one person with a car-bomb. And they had done millions of dollars worth of damage. What *is* a fair sentence for a murderer? How about death?"

Hernandez and Marin hung their heads and said nothing.

"I have a proposal to make you," she said, "and it seems to me that you don't have much negotiating room. Are you willing to work for this company?"

The men, who had been looking at the table, looked up. "What do you mean?" asked Marin.

"Just what I said. Are you willing to work for this company? Jose, you're a machinist, and Alberto, you're an aircraft parts man, isn't that right?" The men nodded in affirmation.

"We have here, in case you haven't noticed," she continued, "a large aviation operation. I can put both of you to work, either here or at our satellite assembly site, and hold your death sentence in abeyance. What I can't do, is let you go, or hold you in prison. This isn't a prison facility. We don't have and don't want to have the staff to operate a prison. So we can't confine you to a cell. We can, however, restrict you to this island or to our satellite assembly site.

"I'm prepared to offer you a deal. You will remain with this company for ten years. We hold your death sentence in abeyance. You do not leave our premises and you will have a place to eat and sleep. You will go only where we send you. You will not visit your families. You will not cause us any trouble, of any kind whatsoever, while you are here. If you do all of these things, at the end of the ten years, we'll tear up your death sentences and you'll be free to go wherever you wish.

"On the other hand," she went on, "if you screw up even once, give anyone any lip, or cause any kind of trouble, if you are here on the Earth Base, I will personally take you out on a ship and throw you overboard with your legs chained to a heavy weight. If you are at the satellite assembly site - by the way, did I explain that it's 22,000 miles out in space? - and you screw up or give anyone a hard time, I will have you dumped into space without a space suit. I think you know I mean what I say.

"Well," she asked, "are you agreeable to that arrangement? Take your time. Do you want to talk it over or discuss this proposal with your counsel?"

The men conferred quietly about the proposal. They leaned over and talked with Sam Thompson, who advised them to take the offer.

The men straightened up in their chairs. Hernandez said, "I accept."

Marin followed rapidly, "Me too." Then he added, "Why are you willing to do this for us?"

Danielle leaned back in her chair. The entire demeanor of the two men had changed. When they had come into the office, they had been hopeless cases, clearly beaten by the circumstances into which they had placed themselves. Now they had some hope in their eyes, with the immediacy of their execution lifted. "I would have had a hard time executing you two right off, even though you tried to kill me, and did kill a person who had the misfortune to be in a car you booby-trapped. You are so pathetically stupid and gullible."

"What do you mean?" asked Hernandez.

"You were told we were working with Castro, and that you were going to hurt Castro by hurting us, isn't that about right?"

"Yes."

"You, and the thousands like you who hate someone like Castro, never realize that what it is you are up against is not a person, or in our case this project, but an *idea*. You don't understand that. The fools who hired you don't understand that.

"Your argument, that is, the argument of the leaders of the Cuban community in South Florida, is not against Castro, it is against the *idea* of Castro`s version of communism. Those bumblers in Peru who hired you were not smart enough to realize that their effort couldn't succeed in damaging us, because the threat to them was the *idea* of our project, not the project itself.

"An idea can't be killed. You can't shoot it or blow it up. The only defense against one idea is a better idea. Castro's weapon against Batista was an *ideology*, it was an *idea* that things could be better. If the population of Cuba hadn't accepted Castro's idea, there never would have been a Cuban revolution. The only way to get rid of Castro's communism is to sell the Cuban people on a *better* idea, but the Cuban community in Miami has spent 40 years isolating itself and the rest of the free world from Communist Cuba so thoroughly that the people within Cuba can't learn about the better ideas that are waiting to replace Castro's faulty ones.

"The best ally Castro has had in hanging onto his communist government has been the anti-Castro leaders in Miami, who have kept the Cuban people from learning about freedom. It's the same attitude that caused the Batista government to fall 40 years ago. Except for the isolation of Cuba, free expression of ideas would have brought down Castro years ago, as it did the Soviet Union.

"The only reason the Cuban exile leaders have been keeping Castro isolated is that they want to force a confrontation to enable them to get the land back, the property they abandoned to Castro. They don't care about the ordinary Cubans, either on the island, or among the other exiles. The power structure in the exile community is the same people who kept the ordinary Cubans under their thumb during the time before Castro came to power. Put them back in Cuba, back in power, and the situation of people like you would be just as it was before Castro. The sad thing is that the exile community in South Florida apparently hasn't a clue about what real democracy is. Their attitude is still to attack anyone who has ideas contrary to their own. Many of the young Cuban-Americans *do* understand, but they won't be going back to Cuba.

"If Castro falls, there will simply be another Latin American dictatorship in his place, masquerading as a democracy, and trying the keep the idea of democracy from the ordinary people. Unfortunately, that won't work either, because when the ideas about real democracy reach the people in Cuba, they won't accept the dictatorship of the rich.

"The crowd from Peru didn't understand about ideas either; maybe it's because they have a political tradition based on military control of the government, as do many other Latin American countries. If they had succeeded in stopping our project, all that would have happened is that someone else would have picked up our idea and continued with it. It's too good an *idea* to let go.

"Now, do you have any questions? If not, let me remind you this is no joke. I have your execution order already signed here in my office. You perform and produce and act just like everyone else working for the company. There will be an order to our employees to treat you as if all your actions had never happened. Your families will receive some money from the company each month to insure that they don't become your victims as well, and you can write to them. Just don't try to leave here. You may have noticed that we were waiting for you when you landed in Peru. We have agents everywhere and most of the governments in the world are working to help us in any way they can, so even if you were able to get off this island, we would still find you. We know who all your family members are, and have the ability to monitor all of them, if we have to. If you should try to leave, we can find you.

"And," she emphasized, "if you leave here, and I have to send someone to find you, their instructions will simply be to kill you where they find you. Have I made myself clear? Mr. Hernandez?"

Hernandez nodded. She looked at Marin, who also nodded.

"That's it then," she said and stood up. "Gentlemen, shake hands with Mr. Maurice d'Orleans, who runs this place. Maurice, find quarters for these men and get them some identification. If they give you any trouble, let me know, and I'll arrange a one-way boat trip for them. Now all of you get out of my office and let me get back to work." She turned away from the conference table and looked out the window. Another space plane was just landing. She turned back and looked at the group who were leaving. "Cliff, please stay here for a minute."

The others left and closed the door after them. "What did you think of this appeal hearing?"

Kelly smiled. "Danielle, with you, nothing surprises me anymore. I think you handled it just fine. But I'm still going to review the legal framework here in Belau for procedural due process."

"That's good, Cliff. That's what I want you to do. And let me see it when you're done. Thanks for your help." Kelly left the office.

CHAPTER 56

March 10

The phone on Danielle's desk buzzed. It was Laurie Steinberg. She was downstairs at Earth Base, and wanted to meet to discuss activating the bow-tie. Danielle invited her to come up, and called Jean Claude to join them, asking him to bring along the chief of the antenna design team, Aaron Parrish. A few minutes later, Bill notified her that there were three visitors waiting to see her. She welcomed them as they all sat down around one end of the conference table.

"Do you all know one another?" Seeing affirmative responses she continued, "Last November I visited the Web and outlined to Laurie and the shift supervisors my desire to bring the satellite partially on line, using the bow-tie configuration. We had a very good discussion of the pros and cons of the bow-tie plan, and worked out an alternative plan that would avoid safety problems, and would make one-half of the bow-tie available. We reviewed and approved those plan changes the first week of December, and they've been implemented since then.

"This morning Laurie called me asking to talk about the bow-tie, and I thought it would be good if we could all discuss it together. So," she asked, turning to Laurie, "how has the amended work-plan been going?"

"It's fine, Miss Simones, ..."

"Please, call me Danielle. We're all on a first name basis here, unless we have company. This is Jean Claude and Aaron, OK?"

"Sure, ... Danielle, ... ah, what I was going to say is that the work has been proceeding very smoothly, but I felt a little more acceleration might be possible, if we can take some short-cuts. I just don't know enough about the engineering of the Web to feel confident that we wouldn't hurt ourselves down the line.

"Let me put it this way," she continued, "you know the original plan was to connect the wiring from the spokes after the antennas were installed. Under the amended work-plan, we're deferring construction of the top antenna array until after spokes 18, 12 and 24 are wired, which we're doing concurrently with the construction of the lower antenna array, in order to let us put section 2 of the satellite on line as soon as possible. Is that accurate? I think so."

Aaron nodded and said, "That's the amendment we approved, with basically all personnel working to complete those portions of the job first, before returning to work on wiring for spokes 6, 30, and 36, and the top antenna."

Laurie continued, "We, - by that I mean the crew shift supervisors and myself - think there is a way to further accelerate the time when the Web can begin producing limited power. But we don't know how it would impact the structural integrity of the Web.

"Right now, construction on the spokes is continuing. The spoke builders are about half-way to the ends on all six spokes, that is, about seven and a half klicks is assembled on each spoke. As the spokes become longer, we install sections of diagonals to fill in the spaces. Up to now we are about two or three klicks behind the spoke builders, partly because we got a head start by building diagonals in one part of the axle, and even in free orbit before the hub and axle were finished. It's obvious to us that as the spokes get longer, our ability to keep up with the spoke builders will fall far behind, because construction of the spokes progresses on a linear basis, while the requirement for diagonals increases geometrically with the length of the spokes. We have to assemble 6,750,000 meters of diagonals, while the spoke builders are building only 90,000 meters of spokes. They're machines, we're not. So we're at somewhat of a disadvantage as we have to build 75 times as much length as they.

"For that reason, and because our present plan involves completing all the diagonals before wiring the cables inside the spokes and loading the spiders and solar panels on sections 2 and 5, installation of the diagonals becomes a controlling activity for the time when 2 and 5 can be loaded with solar panels.

"So far, we're out to about the five kilometer mark on each spoke with diagonals, but that represents only 750 kilometers of total diagonals, after six months of diagonal assembly. We have to assemble six thousand more kilometers of diagonals to finish the job. That's eight times what we've done so far, and at our present rate will require four more years to complete. We think that's longer than necessary to begin producing power, if you approve another change." She looked expectantly at the others, then continued.

"If we leave out the diagonals in sections 1, 3, 4 and 6, we can, we think, have section 2 producing power in less than a year, provided the transmitting antenna assembly goes on schedule. The problem is, we don't know how dependent for its structural integrity the Web is on the interconnection between spokes 6 and 36, 12 and 18, 18 and 24 and 30 and 36. If we leave out those diagonals, can spoke 18, for example, handle the loads imposed when the antenna spins up, or when thrust is applied to spoke 18 to counteract the solar wind on the transmitting antenna assembly?

"Also, we're concerned that if we install all of the diagonals in the bow-tie first, we may not be able to make the diagonals fit in the empty sections later."

"These are not minor concerns, as we've concluded that failure of spoke 18 while the antenna is rotating, for example in the event of a magnetic bearing failure, would destroy the entire satellite. That concerns us not only because we want the project to be successful, but also because we'll be working inside of the satellite while the rotator on spoke 18 is running. But it does offer a way to cut the time for limited power production, from four years to one."

Aaron had been taking notes. "I'm not sure, ... that is, I can't say for certain whether there's any significant difference in the strength of the satellite with the diagonals or without them. If the antenna bearing fails, the torsional loads would probably severely damage at least spoke 18, in either case.

"Several provisions in the design should prevent such damage, but realistically they may only limit it. First, the magnetic bearing includes sensors to give a warning of any impending failure. In that case, power transmission to the antenna is automatically terminated, both by pulling the connection to the antenna's power supply, and also by knocking off-line any power panels that are connected at the time. Second, you're aware rockets are built into the antenna base to spin it up. Remember, other rocket units are also to be installed there to de-spin it, either for maintenance, or in the case of emergency. Their effective time of action, however, is too slow to prevent damage if the bearing were to seize suddenly, which is the reason the bearing also contains actual teflon bearing surfaces as an emergency measure. They will never make actual contact - in normal operation."

Aaron went on, "I think you've hit on a good strategy, Laurie, but I want to run the figures through the computer. As far as the ability to install diagonals in the empty sections later, I wouldn't be concerned about that. You already have diagonals installed out to number 50, that's five kilometers, and they are five kilometers long at that point. From there out they are very flexible because of their length. However, I *do* believe, with your proposed change, that we should install supplemental cables across the tops of all the spokes from one to the next, to prevent any radial or angular movement. Combined with the cables from the ends of the axles to the ends of the spokes, this should insure the structural integrity of the satellite. I'd suggest building the last few diagonals for all the sections and installing them right away, as soon as the spokes are complete. Then install the cables to the axle, plus the cables I just added, then fill in the diagonals in sections 2 and 5. I'll run the numbers, but I think that'll work."

"Was there anything else you wanted to talk about?" asked Jean Claude.

Laurie answered, "No, that was all."

"Well," he said, "this certainly could be a boon to us. Even if we can't have full power, to have one section in operation in a year would be great!"

"Not so fast, Jean Claude," Aaron interrupted. "There are still some problems."

Jean Claude's face fell. "Oh," he said unenthusiastically, "what problems?"

Aaron replied, "The antenna assembly is necessary in order to transmit power. Our schedule for the antenna assemblies, including all 18 arrays on the lower antenna assembly, was scheduled for completion on the order of the four years Laurie was originally talking about. We will have to move antenna materials to orbit and assemble the antenna assembly four times as fast in order to be ready to transmit power in just one year. Also, you need to have the spiders and solar panel assemblies ready to install, then begin installation on a schedule that completes the installation on both sections 2 and 5 at the end of the year. But the spiders haven't even been delivered yet. The first 24 are sitting in storage at Daimler and GM plants; Those contracts anticipate having 120 completed by three years from now. Their production schedule is 20 per year each for the next 12 years, under the current contracts for the first three webs."

"I don't understand what that means," said Jean Claude.

Aaron continued, "Each section of the Web has 221 million solar cells, so for one spider to load the solar cells, it would take, lets see, hmmm, ..." He fussed with his pocket calculator for a minute, then said, "Each spider would have to install 420 solar cells a minute. That's about 70 times faster than they are designed to operate, not counting reloading time. So it can't be done in a year. To load one section in a year, at six cells a minute, you need 70 spiders. And you have to load both sections 2 and 5, so you need twice as long. To load two sections you need 140 spiders, but you won't have that many, under the present contract, even in four years."

Danielle broke in. "How much of the two sections could we load in a year with the 24 existing spiders?"

"Theoretically, Danielle," he answered, "each spider can load 3,135,600 solar cells per year. Twelve would be able to install 37.5 million cells."

"How much power can we expect to produce from that many cells?" she asked.

"About, let's see, ..." Aaron hunched over the calculator and entered more numbers, "well, that's about 16 million square meters, and at a nominal 10% power ..."

"We'll do better than that," objected Jean Claude.

"I think we will too," said Aaron, "based on the reports from the manufacturers, but for a conservative figure, I'm using ten percent. That's just over two billion watts. Actually about 2.2 gigawatts."

"That's great!" Danielle said. "We don't need any more than that to test the ground stations."

"Yes, it's great, but it can't happen," said Aaron.

"What do you mean?"

"As I said, the spiders are sitting in warehouses in Stuttgart and Detroit. The solar panel frames aren't installed, so even if the spiders were at the satellite, they can't be put to work. The solar panels are still accumulating in warehouses in the United States, waiting until the satellite is ready to receive them, so even if the solar panel frames were in place, the spiders don't have any solar cells to install. All the delivery schedules have been based on four-year completion."

"Well, that pretty well explains it," Danielle said with less enthusiasm. "Jean Claude, how's the supply of solar cells and the solar panel frames? Do we have a year's supply on hand?"

"No, but we have enough to start, and we'll be ahead constantly, because our production capacity exceeds the installation rate for all the projected spiders. We expect to have all the solar cells for Web 1, over 1.4 billion, completed within the next three years. We keep finding ways to speed the production, and our photovoltaic efficiency is improving also."

"Okay, you and Aaron work out the details and come up with a revised work schedule. How long do you expect it to take?"

Aaron answered, "About a week. We can have a completely revised work plan by then."

"There are some other considerations." she added. "We have to begin Web 3 and Web 2 as soon as possible, to serve India, Bangladesh, Pakistan and China, but also to get back-up coverage for eclipses. I need a time-line and flow-chart for the delivery of materials to the Web 3 and Web 2 sites, at 90 degrees East and 60 degrees East. As soon as the panel installers are finished with Web 1, we need to move them to Web 3, get the Web 3 hub built and start building the axle and spokes. We also must start building the Web 3 crew quarters. The acceleration of work at Web 1 will dramatically affect our ability to put materials and crews into orbit for Web 3. And then we need to get started on Web 2.

"Then we need to deliver spiders and frames and solar cells to Web 1, and we need crew work schedules for assembly of the panels and solar cells at Web 1. The design we have for prefabricating the solar panel frames, and simply unfolding them at the satellite, still should enable the panel installation crews to stay ahead of the spiders. But, recall that we originally planned for each spider to return to the hub for reloading its solar cell rack. We should work out a procedure to take full loads of solar cells to the spiders, and reload the spider's racks while they're in place on the Web, without having to stop them and make a round-trip to the hub. Look over the time and personnel required. If we need more hours of labor, we need to know whether the existing crew can work overtime without compromising safety, or if we need to make provisions for more workers at the station. If we have to send more workers, there's an entire logistical train which results, and we need to see if we can support it with our existing facilities.

"Laurie, when I was at the station, Harry Elbertson asked me why we were pushing the schedule with the bow-tie scheme. I didn't answer him very well, but the biggest reason is I need to show our investors that the project is actually a money-maker. With the bow-tie, or even with just section 2, we can feed the receiving antennas which are partially completed, and begin selling electricity in Africa. When that begins, we slow the rate at which our bank account is being drained for the construction of the satellite. And for future satellites, for that matter.

"But we have to have all the pieces in place before we start transmitting, and there is a risk, because with only one antenna array, there is no back up if we have a failure there. There will be some unavoidable black-outs each year with eclipses. At least we know when they're going to occur. The old plan, to power-up both antenna arrays at once, would have given us a back-up transmitting antenna for every receiving antenna, but still wouldn't avoid eclipses, of course."

"I understand why you're so eager to speed up the schedule. We'll do all we can at the station," Laurie said. "Consistent with safety," she added.

"Maybe Laurie could help us work out the details," said Aaron. "She's more familiar with conditions on the satellite than anyone here."

"That sounds like a good idea," Danielle said. "While you're at it, work up an amended schedule for shipment and assembly of the lower antenna array, including all 18 antennas. Laurie, are you available to help on this?"

"Sure," Laurie answered, "... well, I'm actually on vacation, but I'll be glad to work on this anyway."

"What did you have planned for your vacation?"

"I was going visit my parents' home," Laurie said, "but I can call them. They'll understand if I'm a little late in arriving and cut it a little short."

Danielle looked at Jean Claude and asked, "Do you think the company could move Laurie's vacation back a week and pay her for her help here?"

"I don't see why not. Sure, Laurie, I'll have finance make an appropriate notation. I guess that's about it, unless you have something else. Danielle?"

"Nope. Glad to see you again, Laurie, and thanks a lot for your suggestions. Let me know if you need anything. Jean Claude, wait here a minute. Aaron, please take Laurie down to personnel and get her an ID card for access to engineering, then show her around. I'll call right now and approve it." The engineer and the project manager left the office.

Danielle turned to Jean Claude, "We have to measure the profit we make between the time the station first comes on line and four years from now. You figure out the details. Then Laurie, the shift supervisors and the work crews on the stations are to get a fair percentage of the additional profits they make possible by this change. I want a large part of it to go to Laurie and the supervisors. Figure out what the correct percentage and distribution is, and bring it to me for approval. Thanks."

Jean Claude left, as Danielle called the Personnel Department and authorized Laurie's new ID card, then went back to her paperwork.

CHAPTER 57

April 3

Houston was hot and sticky already, even though it was only April. Danielle was having lunch with Felix O'Brian at their favorite Italian restaurant across the street from the Galleria Mall.

"How's the project coming?" he asked. "... Really."

She wondered about his question. "I'm not sure what you mean. You've received our most-recent quarterly status report on the satellite and the receiving antennas, haven't you?"

"Yes, but there *are* some unanswered questions. For example, your report told about the sabotage of the space plane, and the improved security measures."

"Yes. We thought we'd given a full report. What do you think we left out?"

"Your report was fine as far as it went, but it left me wondering how we can stay on schedule if we're short one airplane? Also, it didn't say how much we'd drop behind without that one aircraft. Those are two sides of the same coin, but they *are* important, particularly since we investors are deferring income from our investments for about ten years. Any delay potentially extends that wait."

She smiled. Felix wondered why she was so jolly, in the face of a serious setback. "You don't seem very perturbed," he said, puzzled.

"Felix, I'm sorry you were so concerned. I have been playing my poker hand close to my vest for so long that it's very difficult for me to give out all of the facts, even to my best friends, or ... to my first investors.

"There's been a lot more happening than what appears in our quarterly reports. If we wrote it all up, it would require a truck to deliver each report. Also, the sabotage made me a lot more conscious of our vulnerability. I suppose limiting the amount of information was a subconscious reaction to the crash, to some degree, but part of it *was* intentional.

"What else happened - that wasn't in the report - is that we thoroughly reviewed our security measures, *and* our entire operational concept, and then we made some changes. We discovered a way - an unconventional way - to reschedule the flights. It will allow us to fly as many flights as we were flying with the eight completed planes, but with just the seven planes still flying after the crash. So the answer to your first question is that the crash hasn't set us back."

"Well, *that's* reassuring!"

"That's not all," Danielle continued. "After reviewing the revised operation schedule for the planes, we ended up with an improved delivery schedule, at least from Earth to low earth orbit. Then we discovered that we have unbalanced the production schedule, and we now don't have enough tugs to take materials to the satellite as rapidly as we can put them in orbit."

"Maybe you need more tugs?"

"That won't make any significant change, either, unless we put more workers on the satellite, and even then the limiting factor is the number of machines which install the solar cells in the satellite. But we've figured out a way to get power production from the satellite, in a limited way, much sooner than was originally predicted."

"How can that be?"

"Our personnel on the satellite devised a way to produce partial power from one small section of the satellite, and to increase the power production as additional areas of the satellite are completed. So we can produce some power without the satellite being fully complete. It won't give us a fail-safe power supply, but it will enable us to verify the operation of the receiving antennas and begin selling power on a limited basis to the grid in about a year, instead of four. That will partially offset some of our expenses."

"That's good. I'm glad to hear it."

"There's more. A month *before* the crash, I had ordered four more airframes from our suppliers, and an appropriate number of additional engines. So we'll have an enhanced fleet of planes."

"Why more planes?" he asked. "I thought we were building enough planes to do the job."

"You're right, of course, but I decided to make the operation produce some revenue. So I've cut a deal with World Express to carry its cargoes from Europe and North America to Belau. From there they can provide overnight service to the Far East and Central Asia. They are, in effect, chartering one airplane, but we'll fly the missions to Belau with whatever airplane is returning to Belau from space, and missions from Belau will require one extra round trip, about two extra hours of flying time. We can do it without changing the regular crew schedule, because our pilots' schedules have them under-utilized, and while we could fly them for eight hours right now, all we have been able to use them for so far is about a six-hour round trip. We furnish the planes, the crews and the maintenance, all of which we're already paying; World Express furnishes the fuel, the other landing sites, everything else, and they pay a whopping big charge to the company, as if they were leasing a two-billion-dollar airplane. The most it will cost us, at least in the short term, is for tire and brake wear. Over the next four years, the World Express lease will pay for at least one extra airplane, and those revenues might make it possible to start paying back our investors significantly earlier than planned.

"I promised we'd spin off the space plane as a revenue-producer. That's what we're beginning to do, but a lot earlier than we expected. It will let our lessee borrow two billion dollars from an international bank for each aircraft leased, in effect enabling us to purchase a plane from ourselves at a significant profit, allowing us to invest much of those funds in more satellite equipment. We underwrite the loan, but don't have to come up with any cash. The lessee pays the payments to the bank for the plane, which covers the principal and interest on the loan, and gives us a positive net return as well. I'm also actively looking for airlines interested in starting high-speed international passenger service. That will allow additional planes to be 'financed,' but that service will require actual dedication of the planes, because the passenger configuration has to be specially set up, and will eventually require us to build the plane in a pressurized version. The airlines will, at least initially, use the World Express landing facilities, so World Express is going to benefit, not only from improved express service, but from landing fees and terminal revenues from those other airlines."

"Sounds like a good time to buy World Express stock."

"Could be," she said, with a face so expressionless that it confirmed his statement.

"Finally, one other item which I omitted from the quarterly report, because it was not confirmed at the time: Number Four, that is, *Aldebaran*, the plane that crashed, is in the main hangar at Belau, and is, as we speak, being rebuilt. All the damaged parts have been removed and the remaining parts are being treated to counteract their salt-water bath, and will be reassembled into a new Number Four. Because I had already ordered four more aircraft, we'll have the necessary parts available before the reassembly is ready for them, as well as the parts for the new production. Since the crash, I've notified the parts manufacturers to build an extra set of the parts that were damaged. The extra set will replace the ones we borrow to rebuild Number Four.

O'Brian said, "That's very reassuring. You've certainly been busy."

"We're also working on establishing a testing facility for materials in Space. It should be available in about three months. We see a market there from the companies to whom we are going to sell space launch services."

"I thought you had a monopoly on Space," O'Brian said.

"Well, I do," she answered, "... sort of ..., but Space is too useful not to be used, and our little satellite-power company isn't wealthy enough to produce all of the products which are Space-related. For example, many communications companies *must* have satellites. We're making big money putting them in orbit, but we don't charge anyone for the privilege of having their satellites in Space. Several countries still want to have military or military-related satellites in orbit, such as the American Global Positioning System Satellites or their spy satellites. We're still providing launch capability for all those countries, because they simply can't justify spending the cost of using their own obsolete launch equipment when ours is available and so inexpensive.

"But Felix, we don't really *have* any ability to evict someone from Space, if they really want to be there and are willing to spend the money. Our ownership is mostly 'in name only,' even though we have all the legal documents we could think of at the time."

"That doesn't sound very encouraging. Why are you so optimistic?"

"Because no one has any reason to challenge us. We're providing all the launch capability the world can use right now. And no country, to the best of my knowledge, is moving toward building a plane like ours, which is the logical direction they'd go if they had in mind challenging our position.

"And the only effort, so far, to stop us, which was comically inept, has been terminated, thanks - in part - to your help to us in finding the location of their meeting place."

"Don't mention it." he said. "Particularly, don't mention it to them."

"Don't worry. No one knows what you told me besides you and me. And I won't tell."

"That's good. So what are you going to do with them, now that you've found them?" he asked. "How do you know they won't do it again."

"There's no incentive for them to interfere any longer. First, I told them if they didn't cooperate, I'd expose their sabotage efforts to the other investors. Then, I told them they had to invest in the project. And they have. How'd you like to have them in your own syndicate?"

Felix answered quickly, "No, thanks! I'm glad you're on *my* side."

She smiled, "I couldn't have done it without you. Your support since the beginning has been very important to our progress so far. So thanks again, from me particularly. But, all this talk makes me hungry, Felix. What's for dessert?"

"What about your girlish figure?" he laughed.

She laughed back, "What about it? Last time I saw it was several years ago. Maybe it got launched into orbit. I don't know about your girlish figure, but mine's having dessert."

The dessert was delicious, and they left the restaurant in high spirits, but she had something nagging at the back of her mind. She couldn't figure out just what it was. It would come to her eventually.

She went back to the offices of Lone Star Financial Consultants, Inc. and resumed work examining the project's financial projections. The money was running down; nearly 30 billion dollars were already committed, and there were thousands of employees on the payroll at sites from Africa to Belau, and in Space. There were several more satellites and many more receiving antennas to build. The projections said it would work.

She hoped they were right.

CHAPTER 58

April 9

Her return trip to Belau from the United States was via the Base's grocery flight from Los Angeles. It took many hours, and she was unable to sleep during the entire flight. When she finally arrived at the Earth Base, she hurried to her office. It was only 2300 hours but she was exhausted, and it was more than just 'jet lag'.

She called Bill at his quarters. "I just arrived. Are the others here already?"

"They're at their quarters waiting for your call. Shall I have them come up?"

"No. I'm too tired to meet with them tonight. Tell them to come up here at eight o'clock in the morning. I have to go to bed. See you in the morning."

"Okay. Good night."

She hung up the phone and leaned back at the desk. She closed her eyes and pressed her fingertips to her temples. She had to get some sleep. It was a welcome relief to be back in her own place. The apartment at the Earth Base had become so familiar, she seldom saw Guernsey any more. She turned the air-conditioning down, crawled into bed, and pulled the covers up to her neck. She was immediately asleep, but didn't sleep well. She had the same recurrent nightmare she had first had in Houston a few days earlier. Someone was trying to take away the project.

At 6 AM, the cook came in as usual. By 7, breakfast was finished, and Danielle was in the office reviewing her notes. Bill stuck his head in the door and said cheerfully, "Good morning!"

She tried to respond in kind. "Good morning, Bill. Anything unusual today? Besides the meeting this morning, I mean."

"Nope. It gets real quiet around here when you're gone."

"I bet. Call me when anyone arrives, ... wait, ... no, just send them right in."

By 8, everyone who was supposed to be there had arrived. She buzzed Bill, who answered immediately.

"Yes Ma'am?"

"Have someone cover your desk and come on in. I want you to be in on this meeting."

In her office were Cliff, Maurice, Eric, Jean Claude, Andy and Bill. All were seated in chairs in front of the desk. She got up, came around in front of the desk herself, and sat down.

She pulled a note pad from the desk behind her. "I don't know quite how to start. While I was in Houston, celebrating our defeat of the group behind our sabotage, it occurred to me that there's another threat to the project. What is it that we are doing here?"

"Building solar power satellites?" said Maurice.

"And space planes," volunteered Andy.

"And what is it that no country in the world had been able to do before we did it?"

"Exactly what we're doing." said Maurice.

"That's right," she said. "I'm worried how long we can continue before one of the countries we finessed out of the Space business will try to take it away from us."

"Do you think that's a possibility?" asked Cliff.

"I do. But I can't figure out who, or when, or how. I need your help."

"What makes you think we can help?" asked Jean Claude.

"We're all we've got. If we can't figure it out together, we can plan on losing the project, sooner or later."

"But, what makes you so sure?"

"Jean Claude, I just feel it, and I know it's true. Maybe I'm paranoid, but I know I'm right."

Eric spoke up. "You're right on both counts."

"I am?"

"Yes," he said. "'The fact you're paranoid doesn't mean they're not out to get you'. It's an old proverb. We should have realized it earlier. As we progress with the project, the likelihood of an attempt to take it over increases. Think about it. When we started, the only risk was that we might lose our investors' money. As we approach having a successful project, we begin to represent a real threat ... to someone. And we *are* in danger. We've been preoccupied with protecting our factories and aircraft, but what we really have that needs protecting, we've been assuming was safe."

"I don't understand," she said, puzzled.

"Neither do I," said Maurice.

Eric said, "What do we have, or will we have, that someone might want? ... The satellite. It's the source of our power. Without it we have nothing."

She stared at him, "But who? Who would do that?"

"I think the question is, 'who *could* do that?'" Eric answered. "Who has the ability? It would require a force able to take control of the Earth Base, and our satellite, or satellites if we have more than one when they make their move. It would also require a country able to face down the rest of the world. There aren't many countries with that much clout."

"Which countries?" asked Maurice.

"Figure it out for yourself," Eric continued. "We know the U.S. had the ability to put people in space before they abandoned their space program. The Russians had the remains of the Soviet program. The French had their launch vehicles, although of limited capacity. The Chinese were just starting their space program. The Japanese were beginning to talk of space projects, and had a limited launch capability, but didn't have their own shuttle. They were mostly using American launch equipment. But they did put up some experimental solar power satellites, tiny, but on the same track, and they had a plan to establish a system providing a third of the world's energy by the year 2040. And then there're the Chinese: they could have a completely developed launch capability and even if the great military powers are aware of it, we might know nothing of it. We haven't spent a cent monitoring anyone else's space activities. Any one of them could mobilize the necessary forces to take over this Base, for example. But which of them could take over the satellite? And get away with it?

"When we're trying to identify a potential criminal," he went on, "we look for motive and ability. We've already talked about motive. But ability? That has to include both the military ability to occupy the terrain, which in this case means the ability to get to space, as well as the ability to stand up to the other countries in the world to hang onto the prize after it is in-hand.

"I believe there are a few other countries which *could* have the ability to seize this Base with a surprise attack, and they might have the motive in addition to the ones I just mentioned, such as Germany and Brazil, for instance. But most of them have no real space launch ability. And I can't see the rest of the countries in the world standing by and letting them get away with it. The same goes for France. So we're back to the U.S., Russia, China, and Japan, and maybe India and Brazil, as potential threat nations."

"But, which one?" she asked.

"All of them, ... potentially," Eric replied. "But I think the more important questions than 'who?' at least at this stage, are 'where?' and 'how?'."

"Okay," she said. "'Where?' What does that mean? We're all over the world. There are a hundred places they could hit us."

"Yes, but not decisively," Eric answered. "That was the problem those bozos had with their attempts at sabotage. By the time they started on us, we were so spread out that none of their attacks was enough to cripple us. They might have really hurt us with their attack on your airplane if they had succeeded, but we were lucky and they failed.

"What we're talking about now is entirely different, or at least that's how I interpret it. No one else has the launch capacity of the space plane. Now we're discussing what an adversary would have to do to take over our operation and use it to their own purposes. In order for any force to do that, they have to control the launch capability, which is our space planes, and that also means both the Earth Base and the low earth orbit satellites, and they have to control the power satellite."

"Not all at the same time," interjected Andy. "All they have to control initially is the Earth Base. That control amounts to a blockade or siege on the satellite, because the satellite is so dependent on Earth Base for its life-support. If they control the flow of materials to the satellite, and cut off that flow, how long can the satellite hold out without resupply?"

Maurice and Jean Claude compared notes, made some rapid calculations, then Maurice looked back to the others. "We calculate they could survive with their existing stores for about a month, before cannibalism began, provided they were alerted to begin conservation immediately when the crisis began. They have an ample supply of nitrogen, and water. Their oxygen and hydrogen are recycled, and there is ample oxygen in the spare water loads that are on-site for producing fuel for the tugs. If they need to replenish the oxygen in the station, they can use some of the shuttle-fuel oxygen. They don't have the facilities to set up hydroponics, particularly on short notice."

"And if they don't get a warning?" asked Cliff.

"About two weeks, maybe a little longer."

Danielle was writing on the pad on her lap. "We have 18 people on each low earth orbit satellite, and 10 two-man crews in the tugs, and 480 people at the satellite site. That's 536. What happens to them if Earth Base is taken over by a hostile force? They're dependent on us for air, water and food, plus transport back to Earth. We have an obligation to them. We can't let them die!"

"Calm down, Danielle," Eric said. "There's no reason to expect any move against the project until it's almost done. *If* someone did want to push us out, they'd want us to do as much as possible before they moved, and they'd want as much time as possible to prepare their action against us. But we *do* need to prepare."

"Calm down, you say! How in the hell can I calm down? I've had almost no sleep since I realized, or thought I realized there was a threat. Now you say I'm right, and you want me to calm down!"

"Please," Eric was speaking gently. "Please, Danielle. Don't be too hasty throwing in the towel. What we need is a careful analysis of the threat, and a plan to address it. Let's focus on the plan, and then see where we are afterwards. The first thing we have to do is figure out where, and how, we can be hit, and then figure out how to prevent it, or how to defeat it if we can't prevent it."

"You're right, of course," she said. "Let's begin. Where can we be hit? And how? And ..., we have the potential for a crew of more than 500 people to be abandoned, starving to death in the vacuum of space after a two-week wait. We need to implement a plan to prevent that."

"Agreed," said Maurice. The others nodded their heads in agreement. "But we have to figure out what kind of plan that is."

Danielle made some notes. "We don't have to decide that right this minute. We'll work on the details later, but we will take some steps to insure that no crew can be abandoned at the Web. Where else are we vulnerable?"

"When we started discussing this," said Eric, "I was thinking we could be subject to damage in Europe or North America at the freight stops, but as I think about it, it seems less likely that any major power would do that. The space planes are major resources of the project, and if someone wants to take over, they're unlikely to destroy any of them."

He paused, then continued, "It's a little like the normal military policy regarding dams, large bridges, etc., in the theater of combat. These major public works projects are often protected from damage even though they are under the control of the enemy, because the cost of rebuilding them is so great, and the winner's ability to use the territory may depend on having them intact. So, despite what you see in the movies, it's very unusual for a military force to blow up a big bridge or a dam or any other particularly important economic resource. They'll fight an entire war all around such a structure, and maybe destroy the easily replaceable infrastructure which serves it, such as roads, approaches, wiring, railroad tracks, culverts, etc., but will leave the big structures intact.

"I think we have to make some assumptions, and the first one is that our launch capability, the space planes, while they *can* be reproduced, are nevertheless a very valuable asset, and one which a force with designs on our project would gain a great advantage by capturing intact. So we assume they won't try to destroy the space planes. That, we can call 'assumption number 1'. The opposite assumption, 'number 2' is that they will try to destroy the space planes they can reach, and we have to protect the project, and the construction crew, even if they succeed."

Andy shot back, "And just how do we do that?"

"I don't know yet," Eric admitted.

"Danielle," asked Bill, "how many planes could they reach at one time? We're still keeping many of the planes based at LEO-A or LEO-B."

"Actually," Andy volunteered, "at any given time, there is probably one plane in maintenance, one being loaded, one enroute to LEO, and one enroute to Earth from LEO. That leaves three of our seven flying planes sitting at LEO, and one on the way there. When the World Express program begins there will also be, at any given time, the possibility of one plane enroute from here to the cargo pick-up points or from there back here."

Maurice corrected him. "Andy, number 9 is coming off the final inspection line tomorrow. We should have it in service by the end of the week, if all the testing checks out, which I expect it to.

"Okay, so we figure we'll have eight planes flying within a week, and that at any time after that we'll have four parked in orbit and one headed for LEO. Where does that leave us?" asked Andy.

"One thing it means," Danielle said, "is that we have the potential to rescue the crew of the satellite, *if* there's always a tug and two empty passenger pods at the power satellite site, and *if* there is always a space plane and a flight crew at LEO."

"That means we always have to keep a crew on standby at each LEO," said Andy.

"No," she replied. "It means we always have to have a crew on standby at *one* LEO, because a tug pilot coming in from the Web can select his approach to rendezvous with either LEO satellite. But I think it may be a good idea to have one on standby at each LEO anyway, as a safety factor. Suppose for example, a crew were to depart from here for LEO with some of *your* coffee, Andy, and they all drank some of it during the flight. They could be incapacitated for *days*!"

They all laughed at Danielle's feeble attempt at humor. But they also agreed on the concept. A crew could become disabled on their way to either LEO. A relief crew would then either have to be sent up from Earth or would need to be standing by at LEO when the disabled crew arrived. And if they had to be sent from Earth, the delay before they arrived could be many hours, depending on the condition of available aircraft.

"I think," said Maurice, looking to Andy for confirmation, "that we can work out a schedule that rotates a flight crew to each LEO every six hours, and insures that in the event of a crew emergency, or the attempt to take-over the project, there would be a crew available to carry the evacuees back here. I'll work it up with Andy. It'll mean we'll need more flight crews."

"All right," Danielle said. "While you're at it, work out a schedule to insure a tug, a crew and two passenger pods are always at the Web. You can do that by carrying two empty pods up with the next crew change, in addition to the pods with the new crew. Be sure the empty pods are each fully equipped with non-perishable rations for two hundred fifty people for two weeks. If they have to evacuate, it will take at least a week for them to get back to LEO. The space plane crew will have to sit tight until they arrive. They can't bug out and leave the evacuees without a pilot back to Earth. I don't think a tug jockey could fly one of the space planes back here safely. Not that it's hard; it's not, but they would have to know how to fly it to be certain of getting back on the ground in one piece."

Eric said, "So that sort of takes care of the construction crew. At least they shouldn't end up marooned in space. There are a lot of details to fill in, but we have at least defined the rescue mechanism."

"I hope I don't have to be this blunt," Danielle said, "but we have to make these contingency plans seem like routine safety precautions, with no mention of the possibility of a hostile take-over." She continued, "There's more we have to look at. We need to prevent anyone from moving in and taking over this Base. I have an idea. I don't know if it will work, but it may be worth a try. Do any of you know about the history of Thailand?" There were puzzled expressions around the room. Obviously no one knew what she was talking about.

"During the nineteenth century," she went on, "the European powers were busy colonizing Asia. The British had their Raj in India, the Dutch were moving into Indonesia, the French were consolidating their forces in Indochina. China was free from colonization because of its enormous size, although the British made an attempt in Hong Kong, and the Portuguese set up shop in Macau. The Japanese had a policy of total exclusion of Europeans, which wasn't broken until the American fleet sailed into Japanese waters in force.

"Thailand - it was Siam then - was a small yet independent country. Its ruler was wise enough to realize that, if he allowed any European government to become dominant in its influence on his country's government, that European power could swallow up Siam as a colony.

"To prevent the consolidation of influence by any European power, the King of Siam negotiated agreements with several foreign governments simultaneously. As a result, one country seeking a favorable relationship helped build roads, another helped build canals, another helped with some other element of the local infrastructure.

"Then, when any one of these European ambassadors came to the King seeking more influence, the King could politely decline, citing his need to avoid offending the others with whom he had obligations as a result of their help. It worked, and Thailand is the only country in Southeast Asia that *never* was a European colony. It did have a puppet government under the Japanese in World War II, but the Thai government was like rubber: it yielded to the Japanese force as long as it had to, then snapped back immediately after the war.

"I think maybe we can negotiate an arrangement similar to that Thai king's, and hold all of the threat powers at bay. If it works, perhaps it will give the others a reason to intervene on our side if any one of them tries to take over the project."

"What if it doesn't work?" asked Eric.

"What if it doesn't? Do you have any better ideas? I'm open to any suggestion anyone has. ... Well?"

There were no other suggestions. She continued, "My evaluation of our security forces here at the Base is that if any one individual or small group were to try to infiltrate our perimeter, we are now able detect and stop them. Is that an accurate statement of the situation, Eric?"

"Yes, I think so," he answered.

"My evaluation," she said, "is also that if a determined and well-organized military force were to lay siege to this island with the intent of taking control of the Base, our forces wouldn't stand a snowball's chance in Hell. Am I correct?"

"Yes," Eric replied calmly.

She said, "Then we can't let that happen. Eric, you and Cliff and Maurice work out the details of a system to give us the maximum warning time of an approaching force. We have a LEO satellite passing overhead every forty minutes or so, don't we?"

"Actually," Maurice said, "because of the inclination and rotation of the Earth, one goes overhead, or nearly so, only about once every six hours, and half of those are during the night, in case you were thinking of watching for an approaching attack force from LEO."

"Well, that was something like what I was thinking of. I'm wondering if there was any way to pick up such a force on radar from the LEO satellites."

"Maybe so, if it was a naval armada, but I don't think that's what we'd experience," said Andy. "I believe if anyone tried the kind of takeover we're discussing, it would be an airborne attack, with large numbers of planes landing on our own runway and overwhelming our security forces from the interior of the base. Also, even if it were possible to see such a force from the satellite, we can't afford the hardware.

"We could, however, detect such an aerial force with our own existing radar, here at the Base, but I don't know how early that warning could occur. The range of the radar is theoretically 250 miles, but that's at fairly high altitude, because it's intended to allow us to track our planes departing for or returning from Space, and also because we simply can't see below the horizon."

Danielle replied, "Okay, well, we need a plan to respond if such a force is detected. How much warning could we get?"

"About an hour," Andy said, "assuming the planes were typical military turboprop cargo planes, flying at under 300 miles per hour. Or about half an hour, if they were C-5 type turbojet aircraft flying at about 500 miles per hour. That's an outside number, assuming they come in high, and not right down on the deck. They would have an incentive to be high, at least until they get pretty close, because we're so far from any place from which they could take off, and because the fuel consumption of turbine engines is very high at low altitudes."

Danielle looked at her notes and said, "I want a set of contingency plans, to define our possible responses to an attempt to take over the Base. Where we can't define a potential response, I want a comprehensive list of the issues to be considered. Maurice, you handle that. Any questions?"

"No," said Maurice.

"Bill, check outside. I want to be sure no one's in the outer office."

Bill looked out of the office door, then returned to his chair. "No one is there, Danielle. Maurice's secretary is answering my calls at her desk down the hall."

"Very well," she said. "I want what I am about to say kept in the strictest confidence. Any discussion must occur in this office and only in this office, unless we decide it can be handled another way. Does everyone agree?" They all were baffled by her new insistence on confidence, but all nodded their agreement.

"Maurice," she continued. "how tight a beam can the antennas on the Web send out?"

"It depends on how the computer is programmed," he answered. "The normal spread of the beam requires a beam about six minutes wide. That is about one-tenth of a degree. That gives a beam with a nominal width of about ten kilometers at the surface of the Earth. We can expand it to fit as closely as possible to the exact size and shape of a receiving antenna on the surface, all of which are currently ten kilometers in diameter. However, the ability to tighten the beam width increases as the size of the antenna increases. This is the same principle as is used in very large radio telescopes, to obtain very fine resolution on their observations. As I recall, the absolute minimum resolution of one of the standard one-kilometer-diameter phased arrays on the Web is on the order of point zero one seconds. That would give a beam width, at the Earth's surface, of about one and one-half meters. Call it five feet." His expression was grim, and Cliff, Eric and Jean Claude were equally disturbed by the five-foot number. Bill looked puzzled.

"Maurice, are you sure?"

"I'm quite confident of the number, plus or minus about five percent," he replied.

"Bill, do you understand what that means?" she asked.

Bill was unsure what she meant. "No, I guess not. I guess you need to explain."

"Bill, one of our antennas is designed to transmit one-eighteenth of the power produced by half of the Web. Right?"

"Right."

"And that is one-sixth of the power produced by one section of the Web. Isn't that correct?"

"Yes."

"Maurice, how much power is that?"

Maurice said, "The entire Web has a theoretical output of 90 GigaWatts, at an efficiency of ten percent, so one-sixth of that, one section, is fifteen GigaWatts, and one-sixth of that is two and a half GigaWatts."

Bill still didn't understand. "What are you saying?" he asked.

Danielle answered him, "Bill, don't you see? Two and a half GigaWatts - two and a half billion watts - is a hell of a lot of power. If all that energy is *focused* on a five-foot diameter circle on the Earth's surface, it isn't just power transmission, it's a *weapon*.

CHAPTER 59

The men in her office were silent. Finally, Bill spoke. "We've built a weapon?"

"No. We're building a power satellite," she answered quietly. "It's just that one of the ways the power satellite can be applied is as a weapon. I never want to have to use it that way."

"Oh." Bill was obviously shocked.

"But I will if I must to protect the project. Bill, we have the legal right to be where we are, in Space. If I can manage it, no one will ever consider attacking us. But if the project has to be defended, and if we can't find a friendly country to intercede on our behalf, then we'll have to defend it ourselves. Does that bother you?"

"Yes."

"Do you want to quit? I know I've promised everyone, including you, that our project is a peaceful one, and I won't expect anyone to be part of anything different from what I promised without their full agreement."

"No. I want to stay. I'm just sorry that it has come to this, that's all.

"So am I. And I sincerely hope that we never have to use the satellite as a weapon. I really do."

"I know. We've been a team for a long time." He had started as Danielle's secretary eight years earlier at Global Aeronautique.

"Yes, we have. Remember this though, Bill. Any new technology can be a weapon if someone wants to use it that way. The first person to discover fire could have used it to burn down someone else's shelter. A car could be a weapon, if someone used it to run over someone else. Our space plane could be a formidable weapon, if it were used to deliver bombs onto enemy targets. It's all in the application, and whoever controls it controls how it will be used. Alfred Nobel invented dynamite for mining. It was immediately used for warfare. If someone takes the power satellite from us, there's no reason to think *they* won't use it as a weapon, if that suits their purposes."

Maurice spoke. "If we have this great weapon, how can we make the most of it?"

"The fact that we recognize this capability presents us with new kinds of problems," Danielle said. "We need to redouble our efforts to prevent having to use it, but we also have to perfect its potential, so that if we do have to use it, it'll do exactly what we want it to do, and no more, exactly when we want it to do it. Let's take it a step at a time.

"The most important mission for this use of the satellite is the defense of the Earth Base. And that's beyond its ability, because we're over the horizon from Web 1. We have to build Web 3, at 90 degrees East, and do it as fast as possible, in order to protect ourselves."

"What do we do in the meantime?" asked Jean Claude.

288

She answered, "We have to do all we can, to work out every available capability of the existing satellite. Maurice, you said the antenna beam-width is controlled by the computer. Which computer?"

Maurice hesitated, "There are actually hundreds of computers. The satellite is equipped with two independent sets of computers, one for each end of the main axis, and each antenna on each end has a full set of computers. There are several functions, and each function for each antenna is controlled by a set of three computers, operating in parallel, and constantly cross-checking each other. If any one of them fails to agree with the other two, it is overruled and the two that agree with one another control the function. The third computer is dropped off-line for servicing. If, after that, the remaining two ever fail to agree, the entire antenna or antenna segment is dropped off-line and its job is transferred to its back-up antenna or segment.

"The original concept has been for the back-up to be provided by another satellite, when one is available. We know a back-up satellite is necessary to prevent loss of power to the ground stations when the satellite passes through the Earth's shadow. Until there's a second satellite on-station, the back-up is to be provided by an antenna on the other pole of the satellite, but of course that won't prevent loss of power during an eclipse. Even while the North end of the satellite is still being completed, pairs of antennas on the South end of the satellite are being used to back-up one another.

"There are three main functions the computers control: the first is alignment, which uses a signal sent from the receiving antenna and provides adjustment of the orientation of the antenna. Each antenna array is physically rotated left and right and up and down to point most accurately at the receiving antenna. This is a very coarse alignment we do when the antenna is first installed. Once it points in the correct direction, we don't expect to have to change it unless we decide to target an entirely different receiving antenna, because our electronic aiming capability is so flexible.

"The second function is control of the number of photocells connected to the antenna. This is also done by a signal from the receiving station, which is constantly measuring the current in the electrical transmission grid and relaying that information to the solar power satellite. As the power in the grid fluctuates, feedback to computers at the satellite automatically turns photocell panels on the satellite on or off. That's the component you incorporated to keep the system from being just a base-load system.

"The third function focuses the beam to coincide with the external dimensions of the receiving antenna. Optimum efficiency of transmission requires all of the energy transmitted to Earth to strike the receiving antenna, and for the energy to be evenly distributed to all of the receiving elements. So the receiving antenna measures the flux density across the antenna surface and broadcasts a signal to the satellite that the computers at the satellite use to adjust the beam strength at different points on the antenna. The transmitting antennas are special phased arrays to enable the signal to be precisely spread over the exact surface of the receiving antenna. It's all designed to happen automatically.

"Each of these functions has a trio of computers for each antenna. Then there are other computers used for station-keeping. They're set up to fire various thrusters on the station-keeping tug, as well as on the spokes of the satellite, to

289

compensate for the effects of the solar wind. We don't yet know how often or how much the station-keeping thrusters will be required.

"We're using the United States' Global Positioning System for determining the precise location of the satellite. There are eight GPS sensors, one on the end of each spoke, and one on the end of each axle, which together tell the location and attitude of the satellite. Right now it is moving toward the final desired position at 12 centimeters per hour, but it is still many kilometers from that location.

"We'll set a conditional final position of the satellite as soon as the South antenna is ready to spin up, and begin determining base-line data from that position, which will be carefully measured and recorded from the first spin-up of the South antenna array, until the first station-keeping adjustment is required."

Danielle interrupted. "All right. I already know most of that. What do we need to be able to do to redirect a transmitting antenna? For example, if one of our theoretical adversaries were to launch a missile at the satellite, how could we divert the beam from a receiving antenna in Africa, and point it at the approaching missile, while simultaneously focusing the beam down to its minimum width?"

Maurice answered, "I'm confident it can be done, but we can't do it without involving others not in this room. We need to have a new missile-tracking radar on the satellite, and an interface with the computer. It will require the efforts of many technicians and engineers to make it work."

"Buy a missile-tracking radar pointed away from Earth as well," she said. "I don't want a missile coming at us from the rear. If it takes two separate systems, we must have them. Perhaps a second system as a back-up would be a good idea anyway, even if one system can cover the entire sphere."

"Global had several suppliers for top quality missile-tracking radar," said Maurice. "We can order them through one of the offshore subsidiaries. They're cheap compared to our budget and I think we should order two of them right away."

"Good. Do it. Get two for each Web."

"The difficult part will be finding an appropriate location, or locations, on the satellite, and designing the interface," Maurice continued. "The obvious approach for the interface is to substitute data defining the location of the approaching missile for the data from the receiving antenna, and to substitute the minimum focus coordinates for the antenna perimeter data, and fool the transmitter into thinking it's adjusting its signal to the receiving antenna. The big question is how to trigger the change-over away from genuine receiving antenna data over to the fictional data from the missile-tracking radar. Some of our electronics whizzes will know how. And coverage of the side away from Earth will require at least one transmitting antenna directed that way. You can't spin something as big as those antennas one hundred eighty degrees rapidly enough to respond in time."

"There's something else," Danielle said. "We want to be able to bring more than one transmitter to bear on a target, or be able to track multiple targets with different transmitters, if necessary, and when they're in this mode, we need full power from the solar cells. Also, be sure it has some kind of 'Identification, Friend or Foe' programming in it, and equip all of our shuttles with an IFF transponder. It must be encoded so no one can reproduce our friendly transponder codes. We don't want a screw-up like the one a few years ago that resulted in the United States' shooting down an Iranian jetliner. The tracking radar has to be connected to a computer capable of computing an approaching missile's trajectory, and determining whether it is actually approaching the station. There must be a provision for a human, here at Earth Base and maybe at the station as well, to verify and override the computer's decision-making. For purpose of defense, let's use within five degrees of the satellite as the criteria for whether the target is approaching the station. Work on that basis, and let me know if you decide a different criteria is better."

"Who can we let in on the secret?" asked Maurice.

"Work it out with Eric, and bring me a logical system for vetting the personnel who will know about the defense program. They'll have to be assigned some kind of security clearance, or reassigned if they aren't qualified for a clearance."

"Cliff," she continued, "you've been very quiet."

Cliff leaned back in his chair, and ran his fingers through his hair, squeezing the back of his neck to relieve stiffness that had developed from the tension in the meeting. "We have a lot of work to do. I think, if we ever have to use this weapon we're building, we will have sealed our own demise. I can't imagine the world powers standing still for our holding such power. I don't know what their reaction would be, but I can't believe they wouldn't react."

"Probably so," she agreed. "That makes our job, yours and mine, all that much more important. I want you to stay after the rest leave, and we'll start working on the legal and political angles."

Cliff nodded his assent.

"Maurice," she said, "when Web 3 is even partially operational, we need to have your computer interface able to accept coordinates from our air traffic control radar here, to direct the beam against any attacking aircraft. Work on that."

"Okay," he said. "At least there's some lead time there."

"All right," she asked. "I think we've got our work cut out for us, but does anyone else have any ideas about ways to protect the project? Jean Claude? Andy?" They were silent.

"Get on it, then. Let me know if any questions come up that you can't resolve without me." Their team had worked together for a long time, and they all knew what was expected from them. Bill opened the door and left the office, followed by Maurice, Andy and Jean Claude. Cliff moved over into the chair next to Danielle.

"I'm sorry to call you all the way here from London," she said.

"That's no problem, Danielle. This issue needs the entire team to work on it. I understand now why you were so urgent about this meeting. We've come a long way since we first met, haven't we?" he said, recalling their first lunch in Tallahassee. "And the job ahead is enormous. Where do you think we should start?"

"I've been running the problems around in the back of my head, and they seem to be in two categories; things we have to do with our relations with the several potential adversary countries, and the things we have to persuade the government of Belau to do. We need to re-define our relationship with the government of Belau. We need to find ways to draw in the Americans, Russians, Chinese, Japanese and maybe the Indians. In January, the President of the United States offered us a secure line to the White House. I accepted, but the American line terminates in a building near the Embassy in Koror, not here. We have a secure link, which we control, to that building from here, so I can call the White House without leaving this office. But I'm not satisfied that we've created enough of an American interest to protect us from the other big powers. And we need to find something we can request from Russia, China, Japan and India as well."

"Where would you like me to begin?"

"Suppose you review the international agreements Belau has with the big powers. Maybe we were a bit hasty in getting rid of the American presence here. Let's see if it's possible to strengthen the obligations of several countries to defend Belau against foreign interference, then insure those obligations include protecting us. I also want to re-examine the rights we have under Belau law and its Constitution, and the privileges we have been granted by the Belau government. Take that in any order you find appropriate. Let me know if there are any other issues you see fit to pursue. How many attorneys do we have on the payroll now?"

"Still the same six we started with as direct employees. Many others working indirectly for subsidiaries."

"What're ours doing?"

"They're each working quite closely with the project managers on the receiving antenna installations. Jomo Williams and Helen Overmeyer are spending a lot of time in Africa. Elizabeth Mayhew is overseeing the Namibian site, but basically operates from London. Phil Eckhart and Sam Thompson have been coordinating the agreements and construction of the direct current power grid from Morocco to South Africa. Steve Schwartz is working with me, helping to keep track of progress across the continent. And all of them have secondary and tertiary projects underway which will begin construction soon."

"Can we shift one of them onto the defense problem?"

"Yes, I think so. Phil can pick up Sam's duties in North Africa. It will leave us pretty thin in that part of the project, but we can live with it."

"Do it. I want you to be looking forward to the time when the African grid is complete, and we can divert these people to setting up other receiving antenna sites. We need to start looking, very soon, at central and southern Asia. We may need to hire some more attorneys."

"I'll do that. Meanwhile I'll get Sam to come here, and we'll put a full-court press on the Belau legal situation. That'll leave you free to work on political and economic manipulations to insulate the project against any nation moving against us."

She said, "Speak to Bill and he'll arrange for you to be assigned living quarters. Ask him to set up a place for Sam, too. Do you want some time to return to London and wrap up anything there?"

"No. I'm here, and I'll get right to work. We have the legal system set up with everyone cross-trained, so if we lose any member, someone else can pick up that load. Steve Schwartz will carry on my function in London until I can get back there."

"Cliff, if you decide you need to meet with any representatives of the Belau government, from the President on down, let me know, because I want to set up any such meeting personally. Any questions?"

"No."

"If you need anything here, call me.

"Thanks," Cliff said, then he stood and left the office.

She closed her eyes and tried to relax. She was *so* tired. She got up from the chair and walked out of the office, down the hall, and into the library. Taking the encyclopedia from the shelf, she began to read about China. She had to learn all she could about these countries, if she was going to play them off against one another. Her admiration for that Thai king was growing rapidly.

April, May, June and July passed rapidly. It was full summer in the northern hemisphere, but seven degrees above the Equator, with the perpetual breeze from the lagoon, it seemed to be summer all year round. Perfect days, one after another, in Paradise. Or so it seemed.

The spoke builders completed their work at Web 1, and tugs were shaping new courses to the site of Webs 2 and 3, where materials were beginning to accumulate. The spoke builders soon were in place at the Web 3 site, ready to begin spoke construction as soon as the Web 3 hub could be completed.

Space planes delivered the twenty-four existing spiders to orbit, along with 70 million solar cells, which the spiders soon were busily installing as rapidly as solar panel frames could be set up to receive them. Each panel contained 9,967 solar cells, and the construction crew was busy unfolding and attaching the nearly 10,000 solar panels required to hold the cells. 70 million solar cells would only partially fill the bow tie, but there was a year's work for the spiders installing them, and the construction crews were very busy, delivering solar cells to the spiders' good-cell racks, and unfolding solar panels.

There were nine space planes flying now, the first pieces for Plane Number 11 had arrived in Belau and Number 4 was nearing completion of its rebuild. Parts began to arrive for Number 12. Most of the launch capacity of the space plane fleet was now required to carry materials for the south antenna array. The magnetic bearing for the rotator on spoke 18 had been delivered in pieces, and was being assembled in the center of the hub. The pieces of the antenna base assembly, onto which the ten kilometer-across antennas would be attached, were also being assembled. The base assembly was another tubular structure, shaped like an upside-down letter T, 22 kilometers long across the crossbar of the tee, with antennas, 20 above and 20 below, spaced every 1,000 meters along its length.

The transmitter antennas were delivered to the Earth Base from manufacturers in several countries, in container ships, necessary because of the 100-meter length of the antenna segments. Each portion of the antenna was accordion-folded into a long ten-meter-wide rectangular prism which, when unfolded in Space, would be 1,000 meters long and 100 meters wide. 10 of these together formed one transmitter antenna, then were attached to the waveguides and bases required for their operation. Each antenna section was one space plane load, and it took almost six weeks, 400 trips, to get all 40 antennas into orbit. The final pieces to make the satellite operational were beginning to arrive at Web 1.

Occasionally, the space plane carried a load up to LEO for Web 2 and 3, mostly pieces for the construction crew quarters. With the increased number of planes, and materials to be carried to both Web 1 and Webs 2 and 3, the number of tugs would soon become the bottleneck in the system, so Danielle ordered more tugs.

Negotiations were ready to begin with India and China. India was *really* hungry for energy. Its nuclear energy program had been enthusiastically pursued for years, and there had been several major accidents. The public clamored for more energy, and simultaneously for protection from the dangers of nuclear power. The Indian government was a bureaucracy patterned after the British Raj model, and it made the governments of most African countries look like one-man businesses by comparison. Cliff's staff spent four months examining the Indian government, the political parties, and the potential for damage or loss of the receiving antenna site. Then there was the problem of identifying a suitable site. There just weren't any suitable locations that weren't crowded with people or set aside as nature preserves. The siting problems in India seemed insoluble.

August 8

Danielle conferred with Cliff, who reviewed the problems of locating any antennas in India, confirming her own analysis. She reviewed all the information again, then fell back on the most reliable form of contact, and telephoned the largest investor from India.

Mrs. Kavita Raghupati was the widow of one of the wealthiest men in India, and a leader in the Conservative Party. She had invested several hundred million dollars, and was the head of the largest Indian investors' syndicate. Danielle received a call back from Mrs. Raghupati on the second day.

"Mrs. Raghupati," she said, "I'm sure you remember when we met in Bangkok, four years ago? I'm calling about the solar power project."

"Yes, my dear, of course I do. Can I help you in some way, or is there anything wrong?"

Mrs. Raghupati was graciously polite, she noticed.

"No, ma'am, nothing's wrong. In fact things are going quite well. I was hoping I could come to India and meet with you to discuss ways that we could begin looking at siting some power stations in India. Do you think that would be possible?"

"Of course, when would you like to come, dear?"

"As soon as possible, if it can be arranged. Whenever you have time to meet with me."

"How much time do we need?" Mrs. Raghupati asked.

"I can describe the situation to you in about an hour, but I think we might want several hours after that to discuss related matters."

Mrs. Raghupati said, "Would you be able to come here on Friday? I'd like to talk with you on Friday afternoon, then you can plan on staying here at my home Friday evening and if we need the weekend for more discussions we will have it available. How does that sound?"

"I wouldn't want to impose on your hospitality."

"Dear, have you ever been in Bulandshahr?"

"No."

"Well, I won't hear of your staying anywhere but with me, because I want you to tell me all about the project."

"You *have* been receiving our quarterly investor reports, haven't you?" Danielle inquired, a little concerned about her curiosity.

"Yes, but I know how those reports are cleaned up before they are sent out, and I want the full story."

"Mrs. Raghupati, I assure you we are giving you complete reports."

"Yes, dear. And please call me Kavita. Do you mind if I call you Danielle?"

"No, I don't mind. All my friends call me that. I'm just worried that you think we're not being honest with you, and we've only met once, four years ago in Bangkok. Meanwhile, I have several hundred million of your dollars, which I'm spending on the project."

"Danielle, dear, don't worry about my not believing you. I've been watching your progress carefully, believe me, and I'm confident you're being honest with the investors. But, I've written a few annual reports myself over the years, and I know how much one has to leave out. I want to know all the little details. You're making history, dear. And I'm a part of it, and it's *exciting*. I want to know about all of it while I'm alive to savor the excitement." Then she laughed. "I can't wait to meet you again."

Danielle hesitated, then thought, 'what the hell' and said, "Okay, Mrs. ... I mean, 'Kavita,' I'll be there on Friday. I'll aim to get there at noon. I'll take a taxi to your home and then you can fit me into your schedule anytime in the afternoon. Okay?"

"I have a better idea," Kavita offered. "If you come here, you have to fly into Delhi, then hire a car and find your way here. Chances are the driver of the car will drive three times as far to get you here, just to run up a big fare. Let's do this instead: when you get your reservations, let my office know what your flight is, and I'll have someone meet you and bring you directly here. How does that sound?"

"Wonderful! I'll call back as soon as I have my reservation. See you Friday."

"Very well. Goodbye."

"Goodbye."

Neverland Travel had the reservations two hours later and Bill relayed the information to Kavita's office. It was the middle of the afternoon when the phone rang again. It was Hank.

"Pick you up at five thirty?" he said.

"Oh, my gosh!" Danielle exclaimed. "I'm late." It was already four thirty. "Okay. Five thirty. See you then, in front of the building. Bye."

She dropped what she was doing and went into the apartment. In the living room, she had spread out her dress for this evening. Usually she just wore casual clothes, blue jeans, or whatever suited her and was comfortable. Tonight, she was going to be wearing a new dress, nice but not too nice, and she still had to get cleaned up and dressed, and there was only an hour. She went through the apartment looking for the housekeeper. Mrs. Tor was in the utility room, ironing sheets and watching videotapes of soap operas from the United States.

"Mrs. Tor, I need you to help me with my hair. I'm late and have to hurry." Her Thai housekeeper turned off the iron and the TV set and followed her into the bath.

"You take bath. I take care of everything." Mrs. Tor started setting out the various tools required to make Danielle's hair look socially acceptable. She always thought that without Mrs. Tor's care, her hair would look like the Reverend Henry Ward Beecher's beard, which reportedly had several animals living in it. She turned on the water in the tub.

An hour later, Danielle was standing inside the front doors of the office building, head wrapped in a scarf to protect her hair from the relentless breeze from the lagoon. Hank drove up in a company sedan, came to the front door and gave her a peck on the cheek. "You smell yummy," he said. He was dressed in a formal tuxedo.

"Don't start that now, you wolf."

"I'll try to restrain myself." They went out and got into the car, which Hank then drove south across Babeldaob and over the bridge to Koror.

Eventually they arrived. Everyone was dressed in their best clothes. Danielle realized how removed she was from the business she was responsible for. As she looked around she knew most of the guests were company employees, but realized she knew relatively few of the people there. At Global, she had known almost everyone in the Paris plant. Of course, there, she reminded herself, it was not a secret that she was the boss. The crowd was centered on a large pavilion a few hundred feet from the beach, right in the heart of town. There were hundreds of folding chairs set up under the pavilion and outside on the sand. There were hundreds of additional people, for whom there were no chairs, standing outside the rows of chairs on the sand.

The chairs had brightly colored paper decorations and the pavilion itself was a veritable flower shop with festoons of tropical blossoms on every column, and along the rows of chairs. It smelled like a perfume factory. She didn't think she had ever seen so many flowers in one place at the same time.

Then she saw Maurice and Sophie. They were with Jean Claude and his wife, plus Bill, Andy and his wife, Cliff and his wife and the American Ambassador and his wife, plus many other people whom she recognized from the Base, and a few whom she recognized from the town.

Her chair was next to Maurice. She sat down and removed her scarf. Hank had disappeared. After a few minutes, music began to play, and the crowd became silent. From the side of the pavilion at the front, Hank and Jake came in and stood tall. Jake was still on crutches, and Hank helped him onto the raised platform in the front of the pavilion.

As the music played, several very pretty women in formal dresses walked ceremoniously down the center aisle toward the raised platform, some of them strewing the aisle with flower petals and took their appointed places. Danielle noticed one who looked particularly familiar, then suddenly realized it was Marion Douglas, the flight engineer on Hank's crew.

There was a brief pause, and the familiar strains of Mendelssohn began. Everyone twisted around in their chair to catch a glimpse of the beautiful bride. Terry was radiating so much happiness that it was almost impossible to see her father, who was escorting her.

When she reached the platform, Jake hobbled out to take her hand and help her onto the platform. They stood side by side, her tiny figure next to his tall form, his height accentuated by the crutches under his arms.

Then the minister stood and came toward the couple. Danielle hadn't noticed him before, but it was Bertram Allen, the President of Belau! She hadn't known that he was a minister.

The ceremony didn't last long. The couple exchanged their vows, and rings, and a kiss, although Hank had to hold one of the crutches to allow Jake to bend down to kiss Terry. There wasn't a dry eye in the whole place. The music played again, as Terry and Jake Boesinger walked, and limped, back down the aisle to the rear of the gathering, into the warm welcome and equally warm good wishes of all of their friends and family members.

The celebration went on for hours, and many celebrants simply went to sleep on the beach. Hank and Danielle were guests that night, along with Maurice and Sophie, at the President's home. The next morning, they drove back to the Base.

Three days later, Danielle left for Delhi.

CHAPTER 61

August 11

Danielle took a commuter flight from Belau to Manila, then an Air India flight to Delhi.

As she departed the aircraft at Delhi, most of the other passengers had already left ahead of her. She thanked the flight attendants for their efforts. The captain was standing in the cockpit doorway. The approach had been turbulent, and the plane had bounced on landing. "Nice landings," she said. "I thought the second one was the best, but the first and third ones were pretty good too." Then she smiled, and he knew she was kidding him.

"The union won't allow us to make more than three on any one airport, without the company paying us overtime." He was laughing.

"That's what I thought," she replied, trying to keep a straight face, and went on up the jetway into the terminal. The airport terminal was chaotic, stifling hot, packed with people. The heat was almost overpowering. There was an unusual smell. She resolved to put it out of her mind, then remembered she had a thirty- or forty-mile drive yet before she reached her hostess's home.

As she cleared customs, she saw a large youngish man in a uniform, holding a sign which said "*DONIL SIMON*". He looked more like a football player than a chauffer. She concluded the sign was intended to refer to her and approached the man.

"Are you Mrs. Raghupati's driver?"

"Yes, Miss," the driver said in clipped very British English with a distinct Indian accent.

"I'm Danielle Simones. She said someone would meet me."

"Do you have any checked baggage, Miss?" he asked.

"No. This is all."

"Yes, Miss. Veddy good. I am carrying your bag, Miss. Please follow me."

The driver seized her bag and proceeded through the crowd like a bulldozer. There were actually few collisions, as most people saw him coming and moved out of his way, but he never slowed.

Danielle had to almost run to keep up with him, and to avoid being trapped in the crowd that surged back together after he passed. Somehow, she managed to stay in the wake directly behind him, and avoided collisions, or almost avoided them. The man suddenly stopped, and she ran into him. He was more embarrassed than she was, but she told him it was her fault. She had expected that he would be heading for one of the doors to the outside, but he had halted before an elevator.

"Aren't we going outside?"

"Yes, Miss. Please come with me."

The elevator door opened and the driver hit the top button. She realized as the elevator began moving upward that the building contained a parking garage. The car must be in the garage. The elevator stopped, and the door opened again, with blinding sunlight streaming in. They were on the roof of the parking garage, and sitting in the middle of the roof, with its rotors turning slowly, was an Aerospatiale

Gazelle helicopter. Three guards armed with M-16 rifles were stationed around it, keeping any cars from entering the roof, and providing security. Danielle hesitated.

"Come with me, Miss." The driver walked casually to the helicopter and tossed her bag into the back seat, then turned to her. "Would you like to sit in front, Miss?" he asked.

This was an unexpected opportunity. She smiled. "Yes, I'd like that a lot."

He helped her into the left seat, checked the seat belts and shoulder harness, handed her a headset and climbed into the right seat. He revved the engine, and when the RPM was correct, he signaled the three guards, who ran to the helicopter and jumped into the back seat.

The driver/pilot turned to her and said into his microphone, "Would you like to fly, Miss?"

Danielle thought a half-second, then said, "No, thanks, I'm not current in helicopters." Then, as an afterthought, added, "Maybe I could follow you on the controls, for review. I promise to let go if anything happens."

"Veddy good, Miss."

The pilot reached over his head, switched on and adjusted the radios, and called the airport's control tower for permission to take off.

Danielle placed her right hand on the cyclic stick between her knees, and her left hand on the collective lever next to the seat. Her feet rested lightly on the rudder pedals. The throttle was advanced another notch as the collective was lifted a little. The pilot began delicately adjusting the cyclic and applying rudder, to correct for the torque of the main rotor, as the helicopter began to hover just above the concrete.

As the collective came up more, the helicopter began to climb, and the cyclic moved ever so slightly forward in its tiny oscillations. The helicopter answered the controls by tilting its nose downward, moving forward and climbing high above the parking garage and the masses of humanity below.

As they climbed, Danielle simultaneously scanned the instrument panel, searched the sky for air traffic, sensed the movements of the controls, and watched the city pass beneath. Buildings were packed together, and the streets teemed with people. At their altitude, 600 feet higher than when they took off from the rooftop, according to the altimeter, they still could smell the city. As the city passed beneath them at 100 miles per hour, she was glad Kavita had offered to provide transportation rather than allowing her to take a taxi. She couldn't imagine how long it would have taken a taxi to move through a city that seemed to be one huge traffic jam.

"Would Miss like to fly by herself?" the pilot asked.

"Are you sure it's all right?"

"Yes, Miss. I'll take over if I need to."

"Our course is 120 degrees?"

"118, Miss."

"Roger. Let me know when we get close to our destination."

"Yes, Miss."

Danielle flew the helicopter for another twenty minutes. Dense urban development continued uninterrupted as the miles passed below. She knew from her study of the geography of India that they had passed over several cities. After a while, the congested urban scene slowly changed into one of increasing greenery, trees and farms. Then the man in the right seat pointed ahead. Another city was there, and in the midst of the drab poverty, like the Emerald City in the middle of Oz, there was a green island. Danielle flew the helicopter in a circle around the property, and the pilot indicated a helicopter pad near the main buildings. She slowed the helicopter and set up the approach, thinking that the pilot would take over the controls for the landing. The helicopter descended smoothly until it was a few feet above the pad, and she held it there at a hover. She looked over at the pilot, who seemed completely unconcerned that she was flying this very expensive helicopter, at a stationary hover, three feet above the ground, sitting with his arms folded.

Finally, seeing no interest on his part in landing the helicopter, she eased down the collective, and lowered the helicopter slowly to the ground. It touched gently, bumped once, and settled its weight onto its skids. She remembered her conversation earlier that day with the Air India pilot, and was glad her landing had been smooth.

The pilot began the procedure to shut down the helicopter's engine as the guards exited the helicopter and disappeared from view. Danielle watched with interest as he ran through the shut-down checklist. He was quite thorough, although she still wondered how many strangers she would allow to hover *her* helicopter.

Finally, the engine was silent and the rotors coasted to a stop. "Thanks for letting me fly," she said.

"You fly pretty good, Miss."

"Thank you." As she spoke, she saw a small woman wearing a simple sari coming toward the helicopter from the imposing building that had to be the main house. She came directly to Danielle's door and welcomed her as Danielle unsnapped the seat belts and shoulder harnesses, and stepped down from the helicopter.

"Danielle?" asked the woman.

"Kavita?" she said. It had been several years since they last met in Bangkok.

They both nodded and shook hands, then Kavita tossed out her British-trained reserve and gave Danielle a hug and a peck on the cheek.

"Welcome to India. I hope Vijay has given you a smooth flight."

"Vijay? Oh, you mean your pilot? Sure, he gave me a perfect flight." The pilot was standing by the front of the helicopter, watching the conversation.

"My pilot? He's not my pilot. Well, he *is* A pilot and he flies this helicopter, but he's not *my* pilot. It's not even my helicopter, it's his helicopter. He's my son."

The woman turned to her son and said, "Vijay! You haven't been giving Miss Simones that 'Yes, Memsab' punkawalla routine again, have you?"

The young man didn't answer, but Danielle saw the slightest hint of a smile at the corners of his mouth.

Kavita said, "Both of you might as well come inside and have a cool drink." She led the way back to the house, and was as casual and hospitable as her son had been brusque and formal storming through the airport. As they walked, Danielle expressed her admiration of the elegant formal gardens around the house. Kavita thanked her, then admitted it was difficult to keep such gardens, knowing the conditions outside of the compound, an obvious reference to the area which the helicopter had over-flown.

Kavita, Vijay and Danielle went into the kitchen, where an elderly cook was busily making something in a bowl. Kavita stopped and put her arm around the woman. "Danielle, this is Fiona. She's part of the family. She has raised all of my children as much as I have. Fiona, this is Danielle and she'll be with us for a few days. If she needs anything, you get it for her, will you, please?"

Kavita went to a large and ancient-looking refrigerator, opened the door and looked in. Then she turned back to Vijay and Danielle and said, "It appears that we have iced tea or lemonade. Can I get you either one? Or would you prefer something stronger? Or water?"

"I'd love a glass of lemonade."

"Oh, my!" Kavita turned suddenly, "I'll bet you haven't had any lunch, have you?"

"Well, I had a snack on the plane a few hours ago. But I could eat a little more," Danielle said, but thought 'like three big sandwiches'.

"Fiona will make up something for us. I haven't had lunch either, and I do hate to discuss business on an empty stomach, don't you?"

Danielle agreed that a bite to eat would be good. Kavita poured three giant lemonades and led the way into a drawing room, which appeared not to have changed for a hundred years, except now it was air-conditioned. A few minutes later Fiona announced lunch.

After lunch was finished, Kavita led them back to the drawing room. Vijay was still with them. Kavita began the discussion. "Danielle, you called me last week, so I think we should have you begin and tell us why."

Danielle hesitated. " Kavita, is it all right to talk about this with Vijay here?"

Kavita laughed. "Sure. I gave you 300 million but 50 million of that was his. I hope you don't mind?"

"No. Of course not. The reason I called was that I need your help and expertise about India. You know that our project is targeting Africa as the first receiving continent for solar power. We began installing receiving antennas there in the summer, in July, three years ago. Those antennas are under construction as we speak, and will begin receiving power - although both the power satellites and receiving antennas will be only partially completed - in a little less than a year. Full completion of the first power satellite and receiving antennas will take about three more years.

"Meanwhile, we have started the second and third solar power satellites. The first satellite is located directly above 30 degrees East latitude, which is over East Africa. Its primary coverage area is the African continent.

"The second satellite, which is Number 3, will be located at 90 degrees East latitude, which is just Southeast of India. Its primary coverage area will be India, East Asia, and Indonesia.

"The third satellite, which is Number 2, will be halfway between the first two, at 60 degrees East latitude, which is about halfway between the Southern tip of India and Nairobi, or just Northeast of the Seychelles. The third satellite will provide primary coverage to countries along the Arabian Sea, but more importantly, it will enable us to eliminate the occasional power outages, for most of the primary coverage area of Satellites 1 and 3, which will occur when one of them passes through the Earth's shadow. Eventually the numbers will go 1-2-3-4 … all the way around the world, so they seem out of sequence now.

"As I explained at the briefing in Bangkok, our initial program is targeted primarily at providing electricity to Africa. That's where we are expending most of our funds. But the biggest cost is in building the power satellites, and we have to have redundancy, which means multiple satellites.

"The key is that in order for the satellites to be most efficient, they need to be producing power that we are *selling*, not just providing back-up, and we need to sell all the power they can produce. So we need to sell power in the primary areas of Satellites 2 and 3.

"One of the most obvious markets for power is India. India has a very large population, and a high energy demand. It has attempted to meet that demand with nuclear power and conventional power sources, but has not been able to keep up with the demand, and therefore still needs more power.

"So we started a study, looking for potential receiving antenna sites in India, using the same criteria we used in Africa. In Africa, we looked for deserts or other large, flat areas with low population densities, and dry climates. Then we asked the governments of those countries to furnish those sites to us, in perpetuity, and we're building the antennas at our expense. All of the countries with the best sites have agreed.

"We have been unable to find any acceptable site in India, mostly because of the high population densities, but also because of the present political instability. We don't feel it's responsible for us to put our investors' money, *your* money that is, in an area where we can't have confidence in the government's ability to prevent damage to the receiving antennas."

Vijay started to protest. "But India is not so unstable, ..."

Danielle interrupted, "Vijay, please hear me out. We aren't giving up on India. If we had a suitable site, we would probably try at least one antenna. But we haven't found any sites, and one site isn't enough for India. There are a billion people here. It needs at least several sites, just for starters. And it needs a source of clean energy that doesn't pollute its land.

"We can't afford the cost of the land in India. We can't deal with the problems of trying to move the populations that would be necessary to make a site available. Remember our receiving antennas are 10 kilometers in diameter. That's about 80 square kilometers for each antenna. Additionally, we require a two kilometer clear zone around the antenna, which makes the required area 14 kilometers across. Is that a fair trade for two to five gigawatts of power? That's equivalent to two to eight nuclear power plants. I think it's worth it, but the people whose homes would be displaced might not agree, and we aren't equipped to deal with them.

"That's why I'm here. I think with proper encouragement, the government of India could see fit to provide suitable sites, and provide funding for the construction of the receiving antennas, on our terms, which would be to the great advantage of India and its people. We need to know whom to approach, and how to convince them that they should participate.

"We would treat India sites in an identical manner as we have the Africa sites, except that we need the government of India to loan us the money for construction, on which we will pay them back principal and interest, in addition to the royalty on the electricity produced. They would have to bear the cost of moving people from the site and site preparation, which involves removing existing structures. They would then turn over the sites to us in perpetuity, just as the governments in Africa have done, *and* accept the risk of loss if the population gets out of control and damages or destroys one or more receiving antennas.

"I'm here because I believe you may know persons who can help us persuade the Indian government to participate."

Danielle paused. Her suggestion had obviously gotten Kavita and Vijay thinking.

"Well?" she said, "What do you think of this proposal? I guess that's the first question... The second question is, 'will you help?'"

Kavita looked her in the eyes. "What would be your terms?"

Danielle knew well the standard terms. She had written the first draft of most of them.

"First, the government provides us a site which we select. We can work with them on the selection process.

"Second, they give us the site, permanently and irrevocably.

"Third, the government guarantees to protect the site from any hostile activity by people, while we provide security inside the site. It must guarantee, on penalty of forfeiting its investment in the antenna, that the antenna will be protected. And it must loan us the funds for the construction cost of the antenna. This condition is different than we used in Africa, where we provided the funds to build the antennas.

"Fourth, the antenna is built by our employees, to our standards, using our materials, which we bring into the country with no duties or other charges on our materials, tools, equipment, personnel, anything and everything, and no taxes on our property, profits or revenues, ever.

"Fifth, the government agrees to do absolutely nothing that interferes with our operation of the antenna and sale of the power it produces. We control production of power from the antenna and transfer of power on the international grid.

"Sixth, we pay the government a 15 percent royalty on all the power we produce from that receiving antenna, and none on electricity which is imported, regardless of its source.

"Seventh, we have the unlimited right to transfer power into or out of the country to meet demand. Electricity that is produced by the antenna, or transferred in from our system in another country, can be sold to the local utilities at the customary rate, which right now is about one-tenth of a US dollar per kilowatt-hour.

"Eight, if the government fails to comply with the agreement, we reserve the right to turn off the power from the antenna and from other countries.

"Ninth, after we prove the sufficiency of our system to provide the necessary electricity, the government or the existing utilities may, if they like, sell us, at a very low price, the old power plants, which will be disassembled. If they are nuclear plants, the government must dismantle them and provide final disposal sites for all of the nuclear waste and pieces from the nuclear plants that are dismantled.

"Tenth, the terms are not negotiable. If the government doesn't wish to participate, that's fine, we'll sell our power elsewhere.

"Those are the terms. We believe they're fair, considering what we're offering, which is clean, inexpensive electric power, a commodity which is only approached with hydroelectric power plants, of which India has only a relative few.

"So what do you think? Are our terms unfair?"

Both Kavita and Vijay had been taking notes, and Vijay began. "Isn't it sort of unreasonable for the government to have to provide your company a site? Most companies planning to build an industry have to buy their own sites."

Danielle explained. "No other industry will come in and install a facility which will solve so many problems at one time. In fact, many of the others cause many problems. Plus, if a company offers to come into most countries - and the policy here in India has not been consistent - governments often provide low cost financing through Industrial Development Bonds, which are really subsidies from the country's taxpayers, or by tax breaks, or by providing development sites, or by combinations of these or other inducements. Whether India does these things or not really doesn't matter. It's competing for new industries with other countries, which _are_ giving these incentives, so the desirability of locating anywhere must consider that possibility. Our power will also make other environmentally-friendly industries more attractive. And finally, we're giving the government a 15 percent royalty, off the top, so to speak. Taken as a whole, we think all of these advantages offset each of the costs associated with our terms. And of course, we're not insisting that any country participate. They can continue to generate their own power in any way they find appropriate, or buy power from another country that has one or more of our antennas. For example, if India chooses not to participate, it may end up buying our power from Bangladesh, Pakistan or China, assuming they elect to participate, and India would be buying our power indirectly, and not receiving the 15 percent. Of course, the only effect is to put 15 percent of the cost of this country's electricity into another country's treasury. Frankly, we can't see ANY advantage for a country NOT to participate in our program. From our perspective, it's all positive for the country, and there's an advantage for a country to get into the project as early as possible, because of delays in antenna construction for late joiners.

"I'm sorry to be so long-winded, but your question is one which is often asked."

Kavita said, "We're investors. We have a big stake in the company. How is it to our own advantage for India to be involved?"

Danielle admired the woman. She got right to the point, not like her son's excursion into the relatively irrelevant issue of the land. She explained, "The ability of our project to start paying profits to its investors, and the amount of the profits, is dependent on maximizing revenues, first to enable us to build out Phase 1, which is the construction of the first three satellites, but also because it shortens the time which elapses before we have enough revenue to begin paying the investors. I know the investors with whom I have discussed this issue would like to see as much money flowing their way as fast as possible. It _is_ exciting, Kavita, as you said when we spoke earlier this week, but it is also a business and if we can't make a profit, it won't be a successful business. We need sales in order for the business to be successful. We have a certain production capacity, and need to sell as much as possible of our capacity. If that happens, we reinvest and build more capacity, and expand our markets.

"So in answer to your question, it's in your interest as an investor, because you will get your investment back faster, and receive profits sooner if we increase our sales of electricity; India is the most obvious customer."

Kavita looked at Vijay and shrugged. "That seems reasonable to me. I think we should introduce Danielle to your uncle." She turned to Danielle, "My brother-in-law is very well connected in the government. If you can persuade him, he can get the Indian government to participate. I think you need to talk to him."

"Kavita," Danielle said, "I came to you because I trust you. You pointed out yourself that you have a stake in the business, and I've found that our best salespeople are our investors. If you say that I need to speak to - What did you say his name is?"

"Ramesh Mehta."

"Okay. If you say I need to speak to Ramesh Mehta, I'll speak with him. How do I manage that?"

"Leave it to me. You *are* going to stay here for a day or two? Is your weekend free?"

"Yes. You and I were going to discuss the details of progress on the project. I don't have to be back in Belau until Monday."

"Good. We'll invite Ramesh for dinner tomorrow evening, and for a business meeting beforehand. I'll warn him to be expecting some interesting information. Excuse me, I have to make some quick invitations."

Kavita left the room and Danielle turned to Vijay.

"Well, Vijay, suppose you come clean with me."

"I beg your pardon?"

"I want the truth, about our little flight this morning."

"What do you mean?"

"You know what I mean. You gave me the controls of your helicopter, and then sat there, with your arms folded, by God, while I flew almost the entire flight, including about a minute and a half hovering three feet off the ground. What in God's name inspired you to do that? I could have turned your lovely Gazelle upside-down in a second. Why did you do it?"

"I wanted to see if it was true."

"If what was true?"

"That you knew how to fly a helicopter."

"How did I do?"

"Perfect. But that wasn't the only reason."

"What?!"

"I said it wasn't the only reason."

"I heard that. What was the other reason?"

"I never flew before with a MIG-29 instructor pilot."

"How did you find out about that?"

"Is it true?"

"Well, ... Yes, but it's been a long time since then. How did you find out?"

"You know Felix O'Brian?"

"Yes."

"Felix and I went to college together. I was at our tenth class reunion last year and we started talking and discovered we were both investors in your project. He told me what an unusual person you were, and sent me a copy of a report he had

306

on you. When I learned you were coming here, I had to check you out. Are you mad at me?"

"No, I guess not. I really enjoyed flying your helicopter. I've been spending too much time flying a desk since the project started, and enjoyed the stick time."

"I'm glad you did. You're welcome to fly it any time. You don't need me to guard the controls, and I knew that as soon as I watched you set up the approach. But I'm real quick at grabbing the controls. I found that out when I let my girlfriend hold them once. Never again." He laughed.

"Well, thanks anyway."

Just then Kavita returned to the room.

"I reached Uncle Ramesh," she said, "and he will definitely be here. He may bring some of the other government officers with him. I hope that's all right?"

"I guess so. I can sell this project to one person or a thousand just as easily. But I hope the number won't distract the key people from my message."

"I'm sure it won't. You're very persuasive, Danielle."

"Thanks for the compliment, I think."

"Yes, well, the guests are invited, and I've advised Fiona, and we have the menu set up. Now, tell me about the project."

CHAPTER 62

August 12

Kavita and Danielle spent the afternoon and evening recounting their experiences. Danielle began with a few details about the progress of the project which, for lack of space, had been omitted from the quarterly investors' reports. Kavita was more interested in the people working on the various parts of the project than in the hardware. After a couple hours, Kavita began telling about the adventures of growing up in colonial India as the protected only child of a wealthy Indian family. She went on at great length about the severe difficulties of the transition to independence for the great nation. She continued to explain her own awakening as an intelligent, self-actualizing woman in a society with difficulty accepting any formal female independence. Her experiences while she turned the family's ancestral wealth into a spectacular fortune during the past 50 years were fascinating. When Kavita tired of talking about herself, she persuaded Danielle to tell about her own childhood, education and development into an industrial manager. Their conversation continued through dinner and into the late evening.

Finally, Danielle admitted she was tired, and Kavita showed her to her room. She thought it was more like a wing of a palace. It was, in fact, exactly like a wing of a palace because that was what it was.

The following morning after breakfast, Kavita invited her for a tour of the district around the palace. It was just as she had seen from the helicopter the day before, except close up it was orders of magnitude worse. Poverty was matched by filthy conditions, and Danielle wondered how the population could avoid constant epidemics, then suddenly realized maybe they didn't, but it didn't make any difference in the numbers because there were always more to fill the vacancies left by disease. The thought caused a chill down her back, despite the oppressive heat. As they drove on through the teeming community, Kavita pointed out historic and cultural landmarks and talked about the people and their businesses, their families and their traditions.

Slowly, as the morning passed, Danielle began to see beyond the wretched living conditions and really to look at the people. The recognition came, bit by bit, that these were proud and hard-working people, struggling to survive in a situation beyond their control, but they were trying anyway, and in a few places, they were pushing back the squalor and living lives of dignity and relative prosperity. Her prejudices and preconceptions, acquired through decades of magazines and biased news reports, gradually slipped away and her admiration of them grew. She admired their perseverance, their ingenuity, and their dedication to their beliefs, even though those same beliefs were, she believed, part of the obstacle in their way. She was beginning to see them through Kavita 's eyes, although she wasn't yet aware of it.

They returned to the palace and were ready to meet Kavita 's guests by 3 PM. The visitors arrived in several large limousines, and as the doors opened, she realized the cars were armored, as the window glass was very thick, probably bullet-proof. A group of other cars around the limousines formed a motorcade, and as the passengers exited the cars, the occupants of the escorting vehicles formed a perimeter guard around the visitors.

She was certain there had been at least this much security around the President when she visited the White House, but it had not been visible. She wasn't sure why, but it made her nervous.

Kavita was the perfect hostess. Her servants opened doors before her and her guests as they made their way into the formal living room of the enormous home. Kavita made sure each guest was comfortable, then introduced Danielle and explained that she felt they should hear what Danielle had to say.

Danielle got straight to the point and explained about the power project. She described the satellite at 30 degrees East, and the space plane, then told about The Plan for providing power to the African continent. The men listening to her were interested and impressed. It showed in their eyes. Then she told them about the satellite to be constructed at 90 degrees East, and the satellite to be constructed at 60 degrees East, and saw the light of understanding beginning to shine in those eyes. Finally, she described her desire to sell power to India, and the inability of her engineers, planners and political advisers to devise a plan for the company to install its antennas on the Indian sub-continent.

Kavita's brother was obviously the most animated of the guests and interrupted with questions several times. Several others didn't say anything during the entire afternoon, but they *were* paying close attention. After describing her perception of the problems of putting receiving antennas in India, Danielle paused for a glass of water.

Ramesh looked at Danielle and asked, "How much does one of these receiving antennas cost to build?"

"About two billion dollars, at current prices. There are delays, of course, in the process, and as a result the costs tend to creep up with time. But the antennas are reasonably durable and won't require much in the way of repairs, unless someone deliberately damages one. The operating costs are quite small as they basically have no moving parts."

"Two billion dollars is a lot of money. If I understand my sister-in-law correctly, you want us to pay for the antennas, isn't that correct?"

"That is substantially correct, but I think you need to reexamine just how much the cost is, and what you would gain for your investment.

"Each antenna costs about two billion dollars and that antenna has a maximum output of about 5 GigaWatts. That is more than the output of six typical 800 MegaWatt light-water nuclear plants. The cost of building one such nuclear plant is on the order of two and a half to three billion dollars today, assuming you can find a suitable site, and assuming you can resolve the public concerns about nuclear power, and assuming you can locate a suitable source of fuel. In fact, the Americans' only new nuclear plant has cost them over ten billion dollars so far.

"Or you might have a breeder reactor somewhere, and fuel might not be a problem." As she said it, there was a change in the expressions and the eyes of the men in the room and Danielle knew it was true.

"But if you do, then waste disposal is an equally serious problem," she continued. "I know India has an ongoing nuclear power program, in an attempt to keep up with the growing energy demand in your country, so you are obviously addressing the problems I've mentioned with nuclear power in some fashion.

"However, the two and a half to three billion dollars you spend to build a nuclear plant is only the beginning. There are a whole set of additional costs which you don't usually consider; for example, the cost of maintaining the plant. For example, the cost of disposing of low- and high-level nuclear waste generated by the plant. For example, the loss of fisheries in the rivers and coastal waters you use to cool the plants. I'm sure you realize you throw away two-thirds of the energy produced by your conventional steam-operated nuclear or fossil-fueled plants just because of the fundamental inefficiencies of steam power involving the laws of thermodynamics. That factor is imposing large and un-quantified costs on your country. You pay them, but they don't appear on anyone's ledger books because of defective accounting used by most energy experts.

"Our plants are an order of magnitude less expensive than your modern nuclear plants. What costs us two billion to produce with one of our plants would cost your nuclear industry between 14 and 80 billion, just for the plant, then a whole lot more for operation and maintenance over the life of the plant. From my perspective, it's simple economics. If I were in your shoes, I'd be doing all I could to get out of nuclear and into the power supply I could afford."

"Are you proposing that India build these plants for you?" asked another man.

"Absolutely not. The only arrangement that we will agree to is for us to build and own the plants. We are proposing that India provide the sites and loan us the funds to build the plants."

"So you want us to loan you two billion dollars?"

"Yes, times however many power stations you would like to see here producing power. From my own point of view, it would make sense for you to completely change over to satellite power, but those are decisions your government has to make in its own way. I can only assure you that, in the long run, our power will be far less expensive than any other kind available to you today."

"Two billion dollars per plant, then," the same man continued, "and what kind of collateral do we have for our money? Are you going to give us a mortgage on the plant our money builds?"

"No, we're not. In fact, in strict terms, there would be no collateral on your loans. What you would receive in return for your money would in effect be a promissory note from me. Just a personal note, promising to repay your loan with interest over a given period of time. Before you object, let me tell you that a large number of private citizens already have made a similar commitment of large amounts of money. That money has gone to build the power satellites and the African power network. They have an equally insecure arrangement, but they can see the promise in the project and have been forward-thinking enough to make a commitment to it. All they have is my promise of repayment.

"As far as India is concerned, I think your interest is different and greater than the private investors. They are only looking to maximize the long-term return on their capital. Many investors are too short-sighted to commit their funds to a project they can only see with a telescope, then wait for perhaps ten years before they begin to see any return at all. It takes foresight and courage to make this kind of an investment.

"But for India, the question is not one of *raising* the funds. You are raising, and spending, that amount and more, ... about ten times more ... constantly, to build and operate more and more nuclear plants. So the money is there. What will you do when electric power is available to you by purchase from across the border in Pakistan or from Bangladesh or China for a fraction of the cost of your nuclear-generated power? Which one will you use? Again, that's a political decision that your government has to make for itself, but if I were your government in that situation, I'd be buying power from across the border.

"We expect to be generating that power with our plants in those countries. And for every kilowatt generated, the host country will receive 15% of the amount we charge to the utility. If you own the utility and the plant is in this country, we'll charge you for the power, then rebate the 15% royalty to the Indian government, because the antenna generating the power is in India.

"That may not sound like much, but consider this. Our five gigawatt plant could produce 43,800 gigawatts of power in a year's time. One gigawatt will cost the utility 100,000 dollars, at current rates. The royalty on one gigawatt at that rate is 15,000 dollars. Over one year, if one plant ran at full output, which we frankly don't expect, the royalty would be over 600 million dollars, 657 million, actually.

"If India decided to make it possible for us to locate one or more plants here, we could be making a significant positive impact on your national treasury in six years.

"Take this hypothetical situation. Assume the plant runs at 50% of capacity. It produces a royalty of 328.5 million dollars to the host government. If you buy that power from a plant located in a neighbor country, that neighboring government receives the royalty instead of you. If they buy the power *from* you, *you* receive it."

"Here is the situation I'm in. My company needs to sell power to make a profit for its investors. Your country needs more power than it has available to it, and more than it can afford to provide using current methods, if my analysis is correct. Your people need more power to enable them to improve their economy. I'm proposing a solution which requires you to trust me.

"If you don't trust me, well, I leave and you continue doing what you have been doing. If you *do* trust me, on the other hand, getting onto the schedule for antenna installation as soon as possible will insure that as few as possible other antennas are installed *before* yours. It takes about five years to build one of our antennas, because they are so large, about the same time it takes to build a nuclear plant if everything occurs on schedule, not considering the permitting delays in most countries.

"Oh, one more thing. I think you need to understand that the reason we haven't chosen to build an antenna in India at our own expense is the problem of obtaining a clear site. We require the government to provide each site for us, secure and clear of people and buildings. Our antennas require a clear area fourteen kilometers in diameter. That's about nine miles. We think only the government in India can deal with the problems of clearing such a large site of people.

"That's all I have to say. I want to thank all you gentlemen for being so attentive. If you have any more questions, I'd be glad to answer them or, if you think of some later, please feel free to contact me through Mrs. Raghupati's office."

The men were quiet for a few minutes and several of them were conferring quietly in a corner. Then one of the conferees turned and said, "How soon could such an antenna site begin receiving power?"

"About three to four years after we receive the site, plus or minus a year, at limited levels," Danielle answered. "The construction time on a satellite or antenna is about five years, but we can begin producing electricity at a reduced level before the antenna is entirely complete, by using only a part of the antenna as it is completed. We'll provide power to antennas in the order they are contracted for, assuming their construction has progressed to a satisfactory stage. The construction on the primary satellite that will provide power for this part of Asia is just beginning now, and we estimate three to four years before it will be ready to begin power transmission. When that time comes, the receiving antennas have to be at least partially ready. We'll soon be transmitting power to a small section of our first African antenna, even though the total construction of that antenna is only about half done. Does that answer your question?"

"Yes. Thank you." The man turned back to his companions, and they resumed their animated discussion.

Dinner was delicious, and Ramesh Metah was a charming dinner companion seated on Danielle's right. After dinner, the entire group returned to the drawing room and Ramesh said, "I think I can speak for all of us when I say we enjoyed your presentation, Miss Simones. I'm sure we will be pursuing the opportunity you have presented; however, as you are aware, there are some political considerations. To clear a site of the size you have outlined will require relocating several million people. I can't see any way to do that rapidly."

"That is the same problem my experts identified, Mr. Metah, and why I'm here. Perhaps an equally important consideration will be the selection of the site or sites for the antenna. If you decide to proceed, please contact me, and I will have our experts consult with yours. Perhaps we can locate some satisfactory sites where the population problem is less difficult. We want to help in any way we can."

Ramesh thanked her and the guests reboarded their limousines and departed. Kavita and Danielle talked and compared notes on the reactions of the men for hours after the meeting. The following morning Danielle began the trip back to Belau.

CHAPTER 63

August 13

The plane from Delhi landed in Manila on Sunday afternoon. Danielle checked through customs and took a taxi to her hotel. The following morning, she was waiting at the Chinese Embassy when it opened. After being interrogated by several minor functionaries, a clerk led her to the office of the Ambassador. Her Chinese vocabulary was limited to a few formal expressions, which were quickly used up. The Ambassador smiled politely and said, "Miss Simones, perhaps you would feel more comfortable with English?"

She laughed, "Yes, thank you. I'm afraid I don't know any more Chinese. That might limit our discussion."

"Yes, it might," agreed the Ambassador. "What brings you here this morning?"

"Sir, you may have heard about the solar power program which is underway for Africa. I'm working with the companies carrying out that program."

"Yes," he replied, "I have read several news releases about the program. How is it progressing?"

"Very well, actually. The satellite over Africa is well on its way to being completed, and we have two more satellites in early phases of construction. That's why I'm here. When the second and third satellite become operational, which should be within the next five years, we'll be able to beam power to the nations of Asia and the Western Pacific. We've identified China as a potential customer for our power production, and I'm here to begin a process for the discussion of that possibility."

"How much power would you be able to deliver to China?"

"I can't say exactly, for several reasons which I'm sure you will understand. We've made similar offers to other countries, and don't know yet what the demand will be from those countries. The efficiency of the satellite is constantly increasing as improvements occur in photovoltaic cell technology. These two factors make it impossible for me to say with certainty just what our available capacity will be when the satellites are finished, but I can confidently say it will be quite large.

"Each of the satellites will be receiving nearly a thousand gigawatts of energy from the Sun. At the present time, we are using a 10% efficiency factor for planning purposes, but we expect to exceed that, even in the first satellite. That means we would have the ability to transmit about 100 gigawatts from each satellite to the surface of the Earth, at relative high efficiency. If we assume a typical large nuclear power plant produces 1,000 megawatts, that is, one gigawatt, our satellite will produce power equal to 100 large nuclear power plants. We don't believe any one country has that much operating nuclear power capacity, although our information on China is a little sketchy."

"Hmmm. That's very interesting. What do you expect from me?"

"I'd like to begin a dialogue with the Chinese government for the purpose of placing one or more of our receiving antennas in China. We need markets for the power we produce, and China is an obvious market. We think it will be in the long-term interest of the people of China to be using this form of power, rather than more traditional power sources."

"Why do you say that? We, I mean China, has been able to do very well with its existing sources of power. Why should we change?"

"Sir, the present sources of heat energy all around the world, fall into three main categories: nuclear, which is mineral energy; petroleum, which includes coal, natural gas and oil, - I think of all these sources as 'fossil energy'; - and wood. Then there is hydropower, but the sites available limit that. Each of these energy sources involves significant pollution and is potentially limited by various factors, such as the amount that is available. We have examined the costs associated with each of these sources of energy and concluded that they are not viable in the long term. Either they are consumed and you run out of them, in the case of wood and petroleum or, if you decide to go with nuclear power, even if you use a breeder reactor ... " Danielle hesitated, "are you familiar with the concept of using a breeder reactor to produce nuclear fuel?"

"Yes, please go on."

"If you use that technology, the result is a continuing, unending accumulation of low- and high-level radioactive nuclear waste for which there is no currently available technology to neutralize the radiation. And it is very expensive, not only in the waste disposal, storage, or other consequential costs, but also in the simple operational costs of the power plants. From our point of view, the choice to use our power can be justified merely on an economic basis. Our power will be less expensive than any other source of power for the foreseeable future.

"I'm here because I need to meet with the appropriate Chinese decision-makers to present our program to them for consideration. We need the Chinese energy market, and we believe that China, as it grows and develops, will need the power that we can provide. It's a mutually beneficial arrangement." She paused, then smiled and added, "Which is the best kind."

The Ambassador also smiled and said, "I agree. It *is* the best kind. I will contact my government and relay your request. How can I contact you?"

Danielle gave him her business card, with the London telephone numbers, thanked him and left.

A few days later, she received a call from Ramesh Mehta.

"Miss Simones," he said, "I was very impressed by your claims, but frankly, some of them were a little hard to believe. I want to come to Belau to see the Earth Port for myself."

Danielle considered his request. Normally, a request from a non-investor would be rejected. But this request could easily lead to another sixty billion dollars worth of capital for constructing antennas and satellites. The answer took about a tenth of a second.

"We'd be delighted to show you around, Mr. Mehta. How long can you set aside to see our operation? I have a one-day tour, a one-week tour, and a three-week tour."

Mehta was confused. "I'm sorry, Miss Simones. I'm afraid I don't understand. I thought your operation was in Belau. I don't see how it could take three weeks to see it." He was embarrassingly formal and she hurriedly explained.

"I'm sorry to have confused you, sir. I should give you a little more explanation. If you only can spend a day, if you can come here, I can show you our

314

spaceport, the main hangar in which we assemble and maintain the space planes, and take you on a six-hour flight into Space."

There was a nervous cough at the other end of the line. "Did you say ... 'Space'?" he asked.

"Yes, sir. We fly many flights each day into Space, hauling materials for our satellites. I'm sure I told you about the several satellites which are under construction, didn't I?"

"Yes, ... harumph..., of course, I just hadn't considered the possibility that you would, um, be taking visitors into Space."

"Yes, sir, I understand your surprise. Ordinarily we wouldn't take a visitor into Space. A few of our most important investors have had the trip, but we don't do it for everyone. It is still quite expensive, and every pound we boost into orbit costs us a lot of money. However, the potential of having an Indian element in the project, ... well, that would be worth the expense, although I can only provide that trip to one person. I am assuming you would be the best candidate. If there is someone else who should go in your place, I'd like to know."

"No. Certainly not. I mean, there isn't someone else who should go. No. And I am sure the trip would be very informative."

"Good, I'd love to show you, and if you have longer, say a week, we could meet in Nairobi, Kenya, and I will show you the antenna site there - it is the most accessible - then we'll come back here for the last day. That is basically three days in Kenya, two days for traveling, and a day here."

"But you also said there was a three-week trip. What is that?"

"Ah, yes," she replied. "The three-week trip would include a visit to the solar collector satellite. It takes a week each way out and back. It's 22,000 miles out in space."

"I've seen it through a telescope. It's actually quite pretty that way."

"I think it's rather pretty viewed close-up, also," she said. "If you'll check your schedule and tell me how long you can spend, and when, I'll make the arrangements."

"Miss Simones, I hadn't expected you to make special arrangements for me," he protested.

"It's no trouble, I assure you. The only arrangement required is for the flight you take into space, we have to be sure we carry a space suit to fit you, and adjust our fuel and cargo calculations for the additional mass. Many flights launch from here every day and I'll just have our managers make the necessary adjustments in the one aircraft we are taking."

Mehta asked, "Would next week be too soon?"

"No, that would be just fine. I'll accompany you, of course, so I can answer your questions and introduce you to some of our key staff people. We don't have anyone on the satellites escorting visitors, and the staff there have more than enough work to keep themselves busy all the time, so I don't ask them to do any tour guiding." Danielle paused, then said, "By the way, do you get seasick?"

"No, not that I recall. Why do you ask?"

"Some people are not comfortable in free-fall. The trip to the power satellite and back is almost uninterrupted free-fall. I wouldn't want you to be sick the entire time. It would spoil your tour, I can assure you."

"You said 'almost uninterrupted.' What did you mean?"

"Sorry. There I go again, leaving out details. There are a lot of details in our project - too many really to explain them all - but the free-fall is broken by acceleration and braking maneuvers on the way out and back. We do have a simulated gravity condition in the living quarters of the satellite, although it is quite different from Earth-normal gravity."

Mehta hesitated, "Well, ... I'd certainly like to see the entire operation, and I will make a three-week space on my calendar. I hope I don't embarrass myself by getting sick."

"I wouldn't want you to worry about that, there are anti-nausea medications available which are quite effective. Here's what we can do: We'll go to Africa first. If you'll meet me there, in Nairobi, we'll tour the receiving antenna site and I'll introduce you to some of our personnel in the ground operation who can describe the system for connection to the commercial power distribution grid. Then we'll come back and tour the base here, then go to the low earth orbit satellite. Once we reach the LEO satellite, we can determine how comfortable your insides are with free-fall. If you are handling it okay, we'll go on for the next two-week part of the trip, but if you're nauseated, we'll cancel the trip to the power satellite and come right back here. How does that sound?"

"I trust your judgment, Miss Simones. When should I be in Nairobi?"

"Let's see. Can you leave Delhi on Sunday night?"

"Yes."

"I'll have my travel agent book you a seat for Nairobi, leaving Delhi Sunday night or as soon thereafter as there is a flight. She'll call you with the flight information. I'll be in Nairobi to meet your flight when you arrive, and that should take care of it. Any questions?"

"No. I'll be waiting to hear from your travel person."

"Very well, I'll see you in Nairobi on Monday. Goodbye."

"Goodbye." Mehta clicked off. Danielle hung up the phone and began making arrangements for the tour.

YEAR SIX

CHAPTER 64

March 28

The final connections had been completed to enable section 2 of Web 1 to begin producing power. The receiving antenna in Kenya was also ready, incomplete but partially set up to receive the microwave signal from the satellite. An area of the receiving antenna five kilometers in diameter, but only about 18 square kilometers of the antenna's total area of 80 square kilometers, was connected to the Kenya Power distribution grid.

At noon, Kenya time, all of the final alignment checks were done, the circuitry which converted the electrical output of a small portion of section 2 into microwaves was turned on at a very low level, and microwave energy began to flow steadily from Space to the Earth's surface. Aside from very low-power tests conducted earlier by the Japanese and a few other national space programs, this was the first such power transmitted. The power transferred to Kenya Power was measured and Kenya Power was charged for the energy received, making it the first commercial power transmission from Space. Danielle received the news in London and instructed Carolyn to issue an already-prepared news release announcing this historic event. The Wall Street Journal for April 1 included the following item:

'FIRST COMMERCIAL POWER FROM SPACE
SATELLITE BEAMS POWER TO EARTH
London, England
            Officials of Stellar Power Corporation announced yesterday the first transmission of commercially produced power from space. The transmitting facility is a solar photovoltaic collector satellite located 22,000 miles in space directly above East Africa. The receiving facility is an antenna that covers nearly 100 square kilometers in Northwest Kenya. Company representatives said only a small fraction of the capacity of either facility was used for the initial transmission.
            Power was transmitted using microwave radio signals in the 2.45 GigaHertz band. The company is building a network of receiving antennas and a direct-current power-transmission grid that extends across Africa from Morocco to the Union of South Africa. The first power was sold to Kenya Power, Ltd., which distributed it to its customers in Kenya, primarily in the Nairobi area. When asked if Kenya Power had any plans to abandon its network of conventional power-generating plants, spokesmen said they would be conducting reliability and capacity tests of the new power source before making any decisions.
            According to a Stellar Power Corporation spokesman, the solar power project is the product of efforts by a group of private corporations, but Stellar Power Corporation did not respond to questions regarding details of the organization. The company said that at least two more satellites are under construction, but did not provide details.'
            ***

A year later, The Wall Street Journal again reported on the project.

317

  Stellar Power Corporation, a multi-national company based in London, announced yesterday the partial activation of the second of its solar power satellites, located 22,000 miles above the Indian Ocean, Southeast of India. A company representative said the satellite is expected to have a capacity similar to the company's first satellite, located over Africa, which has a design capacity of approximately 100,000 million watts. The second satellite is intended to serve electrical utilities in Eastern Asia, Malaysia, Indonesia and Australia.

  Representatives of the Indian government stated that a network of receiving antennas was under construction across the Indian sub-continent. Massive relocations of populations have been reported during the last several years in several Indian states, and it now appears that these areas are the construction sites for receiving antennas, although government sources refused to confirm these reports.

  Stellar Power Corporation spokesperson Robert Scott said the third such satellite is under construction over the Western Indian Ocean, at sixty degrees east longitude. The first and second satellites are located at thirty and ninety degrees east longitude respectively, according to Scott. The satellites are visible to the naked eye for observers in Europe, Asia, and Africa, but cannot be viewed from the Western Hemisphere. When asked about plans for additional satellites, Scott did not have any comment. Several astronomers described unidentified assemblages of materials above Western South America, but Scott had no comment on the astronomers' observations.'

  In Belau, there were significant changes as a result of the activation of Web 3. The large photovoltaic array behind the main hangar, which had provided electricity to produce hydrogen and oxygen fuel for the space planes, was disconnected. A small antenna array receiving beamed power from Web 3 was furnishing power in its place, as well as providing power for the entire Earth Base, the remainder of Babeldaob and neighboring Koror. The gas turbine generators were shut down and provided power for the base only when Web 3 was eclipsed in the middle of the night for a few days during equinox. They were tested monthly and could be restarted in an emergency, but were no longer necessary for routine daytime operations.

  In Kenya, construction was underway on Stellar Power's hydrogen production facility. Hydrogen produced there would be shipped in converted LNG tankers to distribution centers around the world. At the same time, new plants to build fuel cells that would use that hydrogen to power transportation, business and industry were being built in several parts of the world.

YEAR EIGHT

CHAPTER 65

March 29

Danielle left the London office for the airport in a company car with one of the regular drivers. Neither she nor the driver noticed the car following them. It was simply another of the ubiquitous London taxicabs in downtown traffic and on the highway to Heathrow. The man standing behind her at the ticket counter observed which flight she was taking and purchased a ticket for the same flight.

The Delta flight was nonstop to Miami, then continued to Houston International Airport. During the long hours across the Atlantic, Danielle worked on strategies for expansion of the project into the Western Hemisphere. Several particularly depressed countries in Central America were being considered for the first western-hemisphere participants. The man seated a few rows ahead of her was just another unknown traveler.

At Houston, the plane pulled up to the gate, the jetway was connected, and passengers began deplaning. As usual, some of the passengers in the rear of the plane were in a hurry and crowded their way ahead of those sitting in front who were slower preparing to leave the aircraft. She waited for the aisle to clear, as was her habit, then stepped into the aisle and walked forward. As she passed the man, he stepped into the aisle behind her and followed her off the plane.

The corridor from the Delta gate to the main terminal was long, and she had just begun walking in that direction when the man came from behind her to a position next to her, and said, "Miss Danielle Simones?"

Surprised, she responded, "Yes?"

"I'm a federal process server, and I'm serving this summons and complaint on you," he said. "Will you be so kind as to sign this receipt?"

Danielle signed, accepted an envelope of papers that he handed to her, and stuck them in her purse.

Upon arriving at Lone Star Financial, she went directly to the office they kept for her use and opened the envelope. It contained a summons from the Federal District Court for the Southern District of Florida and a complaint naming Danielle as a defendant, along with Stellar Power Corporation, Belau Aviation, Neverland Travel and Marilyn vanDuser. The summons purported to serve both Stellar Power Corporation and Belau Aviation by the service on Danielle, and alleged that they and all of the other defendants were '*alter egos*' of herself. The plaintiffs were Felix O'Brian and several of the investors from his syndicate.

As she read the complaint she became more and more angry. The investors in Felix's syndicate were demanding control of the project, and alleging that Danielle had misrepresented its scope. The complaint went on to state that she had falsified documents and furnished the investors with reports incorrectly describing the status of the project.

Danielle called in a secretary and handed her all the papers. "Make two copies of this. Transmit a copy to Carolyn at my office in London, with instructions to deliver it immediately to Clifford Kelly. Tell Carolyn to have Kelly call me as soon as he receives it. Then bring the original and both copies back to me." The secretary took the papers and went out, closing the door behind her.

Danielle picked up the telephone and told Lone Star's receptionist, "Please get Felix O'Brian on the telephone for me."

A moment later, the receptionist called back, "Mr. O'Brian is on line three."

She hesitated, looking at the telephone in a way which would have melted the phone if looks could do that, then composed herself and stabbed the button for line three with her index finger. She spoke into the telephone with sugary sweetness, "This is Danielle Simones."

O'Brian answered, "Hello, Danielle. You called me. What's up?" There was no trace of suspicion in his voice.

"Hi, Felix. I just got into town and thought we might do lunch. Cafe Italiano?"

"Why sure, Danielle," he said, cheerfully. "What time would be good for you?"

"How about one o'clock?"

They agreed to meet at the restaurant. The secretary returned and delivered the original and both copies of the documents to her. She put one of the copies into a new envelope and shoved it into her purse. The original and the other copy went into her briefcase. Then she went back to work. A few minutes later, the phone rang again. It was Cliff Kelly. She said, "Hello, Cliff. Did you receive my message?"

He said he had the O'Brian complaint.

She said, "What do you think of it on first reading? ... Yes, that's what I thought too. ... Who? Bailey? ... Yes, they'd be good. ... Call them and set it up. I'll go there tomorrow from here. I'm going to have lunch with Felix O'Brian today and blow him away. ... Yes. Yes. ... I know. Call me back when you have the time for my appointment with the attorneys."

Kelly had suggested that they should retain a prominent Washington, D.C., law firm that specialized in federal civil litigation. He had also cautioned about meeting with the opposing party. Danielle smiled her first real smile since she had read the complaint and went back to work.

Shortly thereafter, she called Marilyn vanDuser at Neverland in Miami, who hadn't been served with the papers yet. Apparently the plaintiffs' lawyers didn't want Danielle to have any advance warning about the suit, so would serve Neverland and Marilyn after their service on Danielle was confirmed. She told Marilyn to just accept the papers and forward them to the London office by Global Express. Cliff would handle all the arrangements for the defense and not to worry.

At 12:30 she put her work down and prepared for lunch.

Felix was waiting for her at the entrance of Cafe Italiano. The rat smiled and stuck out his hand to greet her. She took it, returned her best smile, and told him how glad she was to see him. She was, but he didn't suspect why. They walked into the restaurant and were seated at his usual table.

Lunch was, as usual, delicious. They were half-finished when Danielle said casually, "I got your love note today."

O'Brian, who had just put a forkful of pasta in his mouth, responded, "Hmmm?"

She reached into her purse, removed the copy of the complaint from the envelope and tossed it on the table next to his plate. "This note."

O'Brian choked on his pasta.

She smiled at his discomfort. "I thought you might like to tell me what you think you're going to gain from this exercise?"

O'Brian was still trying to compose himself. Finally, he swallowed and said, "What do you mean?"

"I mean what I said. Have you ever known me not to mean what I say, Felix? I said, 'What do you think you're going to gain?' Do you understand the question?"

He responded, "I don't think I should discuss it. My lawyers said not to."

"Okay, Felix. Don't say anything if you don't want to. I'll do all the talking. You just listen. You know this is a good deal for the investors the way I set it up, don't you? ... No, don't answer, just listen. I already know the answers. I set up this project to give a bunch of intelligent investors the chance to make a lot of money, and they will, Felix, even you, you ..." She didn't call him the name she had in mind.

"But, I have an obligation to all of the investors to protect their investments and a commitment to focus my attention on the project. I've given up a lot to meet that commitment, Felix, but I gave my word, and I'm going to do it.

"This farce of a lawsuit you've created, is not going to work, Felix. I set up this project to prevent this kind of foolishness and I won't be manipulated in this way, and I won't let the project be delayed. But I'll tell you what I *am* going to do, Felix. I'm going to charge you and the other plaintiffs for every cent of the costs that I have to spend defending against this lawsuit. Not just for the lawyers we have to hire to represent me, but for all of the staff time that has to be committed to working on the defense. Every plane ticket we have to buy. Every telephone call we have to make. And all of *my* time, Felix. How much do you think *my* time is worth, Felix? A thousand dollars an hour? Ten thousand dollars an hour? A million dollars an hour? What do you think, Felix, how much shall I charge you and your little group of pals to fight this thing?

"You can't win this way, Felix, because I set it up so that you would only win if you played by the rules we agreed to at the beginning of the game. Oh, you'll still make a profit, but it'll be a lot less than it would be otherwise, because you'll be charged for our expenses as they occur, Felix, and it'll be charged against your own two hundred million. I'll bet the retainer for the law firm I'm hiring to defend me will run at least a million, Felix. That doesn't consider *my* time or the time of the project's staff. Your money is effectively earning compound interest, right now, because you aren't getting any payments yet, probably not for another five or six years, but your balance at the end of that time will be a lot less than everyone else's, Felix, because every expense we incur will be deducted from your and your cohorts' principal as it occurs.

"Pass that message on to your co-plaintiffs, Felix. This project is bigger and more important than either of us, and I won't let anyone stop it. Not you, not *anyone*. Understand?"

Danielle signaled the waiter, who came right over. "Tony, here's my credit card. Lunch is on me." Then she turned to O'Brian, who was still in his chair. "But *you'll* be paying for it anyway, Felix. Remember that." She signed the charge slip, walked out and got into the waiting car, which drove her back to Lone Star Financial.

March 30

She left Houston for Washington, D.C. and went straight to the company's litigation lawyers' office and conferred with them for the next two days. When she left, the firm had filed a motion to dismiss the lawsuit, and a request for a hearing at the earliest possible date.

May 12

The large courtroom in the Federal Courthouse in Miami was brightly illuminated by tropical sunlight streaming in through windows near the high ceiling at the back of the room. Behind and above the judge's bench, the wall was covered with a brilliant mural depicting the conquest of Florida by the Spaniards.

The judge looked down at the attorneys from his elevated position, and said, "We're here this morning, Mr. Bailey, to hear your motion to dismiss the complaint in this case. Please proceed."

Benjamin Bailey stood and addressed the judge. "Your honor, I'm here this morning representing all the defendants named in this lawsuit. For Stellar Power Corporation and Belau Aviation, I am only making a limited appearance to challenge the jurisdiction of this court. This is because the complaint alleges that service on defendant Danielle Simones constitutes service on the two corporations. However, Miss Simones is neither an officer nor a director of either of those corporations, and thus service on her cannot constitute service on either of them. We move to quash the subpoena and complaint and offer Ms. Simones' affidavit regarding the fact that she is not an officer or director of either of these entities.

"Additionally, because both of those corporations are off-shore corporations, there are special requirements under the law of the countries in which they are incorporated, which the plaintiffs must meet in order to obtain jurisdiction over them. There is also the question of establishing a legal basis in the United States for jurisdiction over these two corporations, which normally requires at least an allegation that the defendant corporation is doing business in the United States. The plaintiffs have neither met the requirements of the countries of incorporation nor have they alleged the corporations are doing business in the United States, and the court therefore does not have *in personam* jurisdiction over these two corporate defendants.

"Nor does the complaint establish a basis for *in rem* jurisdiction, as it fails to allege any property is owned by these defendants within the jurisdictional limits of this District, or, for that matter, anywhere in the United States. Accordingly, we are requesting the court to dismiss the lawsuit as to Stellar Power Corporation and Belau Aviation, for failure to serve any proper representative of either company, under the law applicable to either company or its country of registration or to allege a basis for the court to maintain jurisdiction.

"Secondly, the lawsuit names Neverland Travel and Marilyn vanDuser as defendants, and claims they are defendant Danielle Simones' '*alter ego*.' Ms. vanDuser is in the courtroom this morning, as is Ms. Simones, and we invite the court to take judicial notice that Ms. Simones and Ms. vanDuser are completely different persons, and neither is the *alter ego* of the other." They both stood up.

"You will notice that Ms. vanDuser is a beautiful blonde and Ms. Simones is a lovely brunette." Both of the women blushed. Bailey continued, "We therefore ask that the lawsuit be dismissed as to Marilyn vanDuser, since it fails to state a justiciable claim regarding her, the only allegation connecting her being the claim that she is Ms. Simones '*alter ego*.'

"With regard to Neverland Travel, the lawsuit is deficient on its face to support any connection with Ms. Simones. The lawsuit alleges that Neverland Travel is also an *alter ego* of Ms. Simones, and that she created it as a conduit for the investment funds of the plaintiffs. However, the complaint also alleges that Ms. Simones met with plaintiffs seven years ago and induced them to contribute the investment funds. We have an affidavit from the office of the Florida Secretary of State indicating that Neverland Travel was created ten years ago by Marilyn vanDuser, who is the sole officer and director, over three years prior to the alleged meeting between Ms. Simones and the plaintiffs. We have affidavits from both Marilyn vanDuser and Danielle Simones which state that Ms. Simones has no ownership interest in Neverland Travel and never has, and that Neverland Travel is now and always has been 100% owned by Ms. vanDuser.

"Your Honor, Neverland Travel acknowledges that it handles travel arrangements for Ms. Simones on occasion, as it does for hundreds or thousands of other customers, but without more, which has not been alleged, that cannot be grounds for this lawsuit, and we therefore ask that the lawsuit be dismissed as to Neverland Travel. Our reading of this lawsuit is that Neverland Travel and Ms. vanDuser - as Florida residents - are included only to give the plaintiffs an opportunity to meet the jurisdictional requirements of this federal court."

The judge interrupted, "Mr. Bailey, if I understand you correctly, you are asking me to dismiss the three named corporations and Ms. vanDuser as defendants in this action, is that correct?"

"Yes it is, Your Honor."

"What about Ms. Simones? Aren't you seeking a dismissal of her also?"

"Yes, Your Honor, I was just getting to that."

"All right, please continue."

"Your Honor, Ms. Simones was properly served, as an individual, by the process server. We acknowledge that. However, the actions for which she is being sued are either not actionable, or are not within the jurisdiction of this court."

The judge looked up. "I hope you have an explanation for that."

"I do, sir. The complaint alleges that Ms. Simones, individually, approached the plaintiffs, and invited them to invest in a project. It further states that she misrepresented the scope of the project, although there are no specific allegations regarding the nature of that misrepresentation. We request that as to the allegation of misrepresentation, the complaint be dismissed as to Ms. Simones, because the complaint lacks the specificity necessary for Ms. Simones to frame a response to the allegations.

"The complaint continues to state that Ms. Simones has failed to accurately report the status of the project. Again it fails to state in what way the status of the project has been incorrectly reported, and we request dismissal for lack of specificity in that regard also. But there is yet another basis on which the complaint must be dismissed.

"The lawsuit names Ms. Simones, *in her individual capacity*, as a defendant, but her capacity in the handling of the money of investors, possibly including the plaintiffs, is in the capacity of a *trustee*. The complaint fails to recognize her trusteeship, nor to claim that the plaintiffs have any relationship to the trust, nor to claim that she has acted contrary to her obligation as trustee. As a trustee, Ms. Simones can only be called to answer for her actions in clearly prescribed ways. The plaintiffs, if they wish to question her actions as trustee, must follow the procedures required for actions against trustees under the laws of the jurisdiction of the trust, which they have not done. Therefore, the lawsuit against Ms. Simones, in her individual capacity, must be dismissed." Bailey sat down.

The judge looked at the attorney for the plaintiffs, who immediately stood. "Mr. Goldman, do you have any response?"

Adrian Goldman, the plaintiffs' attorney, answered, "Yes, Your Honor, we do. My esteemed opposing counsel has given the court an amazingly contrived view of this situation. The plaintiffs would like to call a witness to clear this up for the court, if we may, Your Honor?"

"Proceed."

Goldman said to the bailiff, "Please call Danielle Simones."

The judge said, "Miss Simones, please take the stand."

Danielle walked to the witness stand and the bailiff swore her to tell the truth, the whole truth and nothing but the truth. She sat down.

"Miss Simones," said Mr. Goldman, "please state your name and address."

"Danielle Marie Elizabeth Margaret Simones. Ousley Manor, St. Andrew, Guernsey, Channel Islands."

"Are you the head of the space project?"

"I beg your pardon?"

"Are you the head of the space project?"

"What space project?"

"The project to collect power from the Sun and beam it to Earth?"

"Oh, you mean the Solar Satellite Power System. There are many heads of different elements of that project. My position is more of an overall coordinator or consultant."

"But it was your idea?"

"No. It wasn't my idea. The idea was published by NASA in the mid-1970s, but it wasn't NASA's idea either. I think most of the credit has to go to Dr. Peter Glaser, who works for a think-tank in Cambridge, Massachussets. He has been a primary proponent of this source of energy."

"Did you have any influence on the development of the project?"

"Yes."

"What was that influence?"

"I thought of a way to build the aircraft that makes it possible to move materials into orbit inexpensively. But the aircraft was actually designed by a design team."

"Is that all?"

"Basically. Oh, and I invited a number of people to invest in it."

'Aha,' thought the attorney, 'now we're getting somewhere.'

"Miss Simones, did you place an advertisement in the Wall Street Journal and other newspapers in March seven years ago?"

"I don't know. Was it March? I thought it was April. Whatever, I did place an ad there sometime in that Spring."

"And thereafter, did you meet with the plaintiffs in Texas?"

"No."

"No?!!" Goldman was hot on her apparent error. "DIDN'T you meet with Mr. Felix O'Brian in his office?"

"Yes. But I met *only* with Felix O'Brian - he is one of the plaintiffs, is he not? - in Texas."

"You met with Mr. O'Brian?" he repeated.

"Yes."

"Who met with the others?"

"I presume Mr. O'Brian did," she answered.

"And you asked Mr. O'Brian to invest in the ... " Goldman hastily looked back at his notes. "In the Solar Satellite Power System?"

"No."

The attorney obviously was surprised at her answer. "No?"

"No. Not at that time."

"What did you ask him to invest in?"

"Mr. Goldman, I never said I asked him to invest in anything. I told him of the idea to collect solar power from Space and beam it to Earth. And I offered him a chance to attend a briefing on how that power collection and beaming would be accomplished."

"And did he take you up on your offer?"

"He did."

"Was the briefing held?"

"Yes. And Mr. O'Brian attended."

"Where was the briefing held?"

"In Bangkok, Thailand."

"And at that briefing did you invite Mr. O'Brian and other plaintiffs to invest in the Solar Satellite Power System Project?"

"Well ..."

Ben Bailey jumped to his feet. "Objection, Your Honor. The question is irrelevant, as any actions taken in Bangkok, Thailand are beyond the jurisdiction of this court."

The judge thought about Bailey's objection for a moment, then said to her, "Answer the question, Miss Simones."

Danielle looked at the judge and the plaintiffs' attorney, then answered, "After the end of the briefing, I invited everyone who was in attendance to participate in the project as an investor. Mr. O'Brian was there, but not the other plaintiffs."

"And did the plaintiffs invest in the project?" Goldman asked.

She looked again at the attorney asking the question, then at the judge, and said, "I'm sorry, Mr. Goldman, but that gets into my actions as trustee, and I'm precluded from answering any questions about the trusteeship. I'm sure you understand."

The attorney was furious. "Your honor, will the court please direct the witness to answer?"

"Miss Simones," the judge said, "can you please be more specific?"

She turned to face the judge. "Your Honor, I have been sued as an individual, not as the trustee of this trust. I am bound by my fiduciary obligations to keep all matters pertinent to the trust absolutely confidential. Therefore I cannot answer Mr. Goldman's question."

The judge looked at Goldman. "Mr. Goldman, have you attempted to serve Ms. Simones as trustee?"

Goldman was embarrassed. "Your Honor, we haven't been able to find out where the trust is established. Until we do that, we won't be able to determine what the requirements are to serve the witness in her capacity as trustee."

"It looks," the judge said, "as if you haven't done your homework, doesn't it, counsel? It also looks to me as if you're trying to do discovery in my courtroom, which I don't appreciate. You should have deposed her if you wanted to ask her these questions." Goldman looked mortified and didn't say anything. The judge continued, "The court dismisses this complaint as to Neverland Travel and Marilyn vanDuser. Plaintiffs have 30 days to amend their complaint as to Danielle Simones, Stellar Power Corporation and Belau Aviation, and to obtain service of process on Stellar Power Corporation and Belau Aviation, as well as to state a cause of action for which this court has jurisdiction. Plaintiffs shall have 30 days as well to obtain service on Danielle Simones as Trustee of this Trust. Plaintiffs may depose Danielle Simones regarding her personal actions, but may not inquire into the details of the trusteeship until this court has ruled on its jurisdiction. Good luck in locating the trust, Mr. Goldman. Court is adjourned." He banged his gavel and stood up.

Everyone in the room stood while the judge left the courtroom. The court reporter began packing up her stenotype machine. Danielle placed her left hand on Bailey's right forearm, and turned to the plaintiffs' attorney. "Mr. Goldman, can I speak with you for a few minutes?"

Bailey protested, "Danielle, you shouldn't talk to him!"

"Take it easy, Ben. You just wait right here. I can't say to him what I want to say with you around. I'll be back in a few minutes."

Bailey continued to object, "Danielle! He can't talk to you without your lawyer present. It's a lawyer-ethics thing."

"I know, I know. Oh well, if you must, come along then." She stepped from behind the defendants' table and walked over to Goldman. "Mr. Goldman, let's step outside."

Danielle led him from the courtroom, down a hall and into a garden with numerous trees and flowers, and several stone benches, in an atrium of the building. The old coral courthouse had Spanish-style colonnades along both sides of the garden with distinctly Moorish columns separating the walkways from the garden. A small fountain splashed in the corner of the garden. The midday Miami heat was oppressive, reflecting from the coral walls, but in the shade of the trees in the garden it seemed cooler.

She found a stone bench and sat down. "Please, Mr. Goldman, have a seat. I won't bite you." With her left hand, she patted the bench. Finally Goldman sat at her left side, and Bailey sat at her right.

Goldman was very hesitant about having a tete-a-tete with the defendant. In fact, he knew he was on uncertain ground; he was still smarting from his humiliation in the courtroom. He knew he should not have tried to conduct discovery in open court and that he should have known better.

Danielle said, "Mr. Goldman, please relax. I know you're trying to represent your clients' interest as best you can, isn't that true?"

"Hmmm, sure," Goldman responded, reluctantly.

"How much do you know about me?" she said, then retracted the question, "No, don't answer that. I'm sure Mr. O'Brian has given you a copy of the research he did on me. So I guess you do know I used to teach law school, don't you?"

Goldman acknowledged he did.

"Do you remember the ethics course you had in the first year of law school?"

Goldman nodded. He remembered he had taken ethics, although he would have had a hard time to recall the specifics of the course.

"Let me give you a little law school hypothetical situation. As an attorney, what is your obligation to a client who informs you that he has committed a crime?"

"Miss Simones, I didn't come out here to discuss law school," said Goldman, more than a little irritated.

"Of course not, but humor me. I assure you it will help you in your representation of your clients. You understand, you and I both represent your clients, you as their attorney, and I as their trustee, so we both have a duty to look out for their best interests, although in different ways, wouldn't you agree to that, Mr. Goldman?" She turned to Bailey, "Ben, doesn't that pretty well describe our situation?" Bailey nodded. "Do you concur, Mr. Goldman?"

"Yes. I guess so."

"Then we need to have this discussion. Tell me, what do you do if your client comes to you and says he has committed a crime? Hypothetically speaking, of course."

"He has a right to the best defense possible," Goldman said. "There may be any number of mitigating circumstances which constitute defenses, such as diminished capacity, for example."

"Okay," she said, "now suppose your client, still speaking hypothetically, comes to you and informs you that he intends to commit a crime at some time in the future. What is your duty then? Suppose your client tells you he intends to perjure himself by lying under oath."

"Well, if the crime he intended to commit were serious enough, I might have to warn the authorities, or else become an accessory to his crime .... or if, as you suggest, he were going to perjure himself, I might have to withdraw from his representation. Where is this going?" he demanded.

She didn't answer his question, but said, "Bear with me. Now suppose you learn, during your representation of a client, that actions he has taken, or may be planning to take in the future, may - I emphasize, MAY - be against the law. What is your duty to your client there?"

"I'd have a duty to counsel my client to obey the law."

"And if he didn't indicate any intention to change his plans, despite your warnings?"

"I'd have to decide, then. It would depend on the situation."

"Suppose this planned action of your client's, which you had discovered in the course of your representation, would be certain to be publicly disclosed by your continued representation of that client, at least along the present course you were taking?"

Goldman answered, "I'd probably have to withdraw, and I might have to advise the authorities."

"Mr. Goldman, you know being an attorney isn't easy," she said. "Sometimes things our clients do aren't all black or white, right or wrong. Sometimes they don't tell us everything we need to know to properly represent them. I want to give you one more hypothetical, then let you think about it.

"Suppose a group of very wealthy people put big hunks of money into an investment, hypothetically speaking. They won't recover any dividends for many years, but when they do get those dividends, there will be very large sums, tens of millions of dollars each year, coming back to them, or to their heirs. Those dividends, however, will not be paid necessarily in the country where the hypothetical investor resides, hypothetically speaking, but somewhere else, where there is no income tax on the dividends. Suppose you learn that one of your hypothetical clients is set up to receive such hypothetical future dividends. Suppose that you don't know whether receipt of those dividends will be a violation of the United States' tax laws at whatever time in the future they are paid, but you know that your continued prosecution of your client's case will reveal the existence and pendency of this future income, in the hypothetical public records of the Federal District Court. And exposure of your client's planned receipt of those dividends could provide an opportunity for the client's government to make changes in tax laws which might make those future receipts illegal or otherwise dramatically harm your client's interests.

"What is your duty to your client then, in that situation? You don't have any way of knowing whether that action will or won't be illegal in the future, because the laws are constantly changing. It might not even be illegal now. But it might be, too.

Goldman took a breath and started to speak, but she stopped him.

"No, don't answer, Mr. Goldman. This is a law school test question. A paragraph with a hypothetical situation, and they give you ten pages to discuss the issues, which isn't enough, because there are four hundred issues in that simple paragraph. I want you to think about this hypothetical, Mr. Goldman, and then we'll continue with this lawsuit. Just remember that your clients may be rich, stupid and greedy, but they're still your clients and you do have duties to protect their interests. That's all, Mr. Goldman. Did you have anything you wanted to say to me? Any questions you want to ask me? One free one, off the record?" She turned to Bailey, "Ben, you aren't hearing this." Bailey was obviously very uncomfortable.

Goldman replied, "Just one. How does one become an investor in your project?"

"That's easy. You need a hundred million dollars in cash. And ask Felix O'Brian to recommend you. Felix and I are really very good friends. Did he tell you that too? I'd venture to guess not." She stood and pulled her companions to their feet.

The two lawyers and Danielle walked back into the almost empty courtroom. Goldman was wondering what to think of her. Marilyn was still waiting, so Danielle invited her and Bailey to lunch. As they walked together to the small Cuban restaurant on the corner, Danielle again invited Marilyn to take a break from the travel agency and come visit her on the island.

CHAPTER 66

That afternoon, Bailey's office received a notice of taking Danielle's deposition. Goldman wanted her to appear in his office in Miami to enable him to ask her questions about her involvement with the plaintiffs and the project. Bailey immediately filed an objection to the deposition, demanding that Goldman take her deposition at her office, and asked for a hearing before the judge on the location of the deposition. The hearing, held two days later, was over in two minutes. Goldman was to take Danielle's deposition at her office, not his own. Bailey called the London office, and Carolyn immediately connected him to Belau.

Danielle had arrived a few hours earlier from the United States. "Hello, Ben. What's up."

"Danielle, I just left a hearing before Judge Parker. He denied the plaintiffs' request to take your deposition in Miami. They have to come to your office."

"Good work, Ben. When's the deposition date?"

"A week from today. I thought my wife and I could get a flight to London a day or two early and have some vacation time in Scotland while I'm there."

"That may cause a little problem, Ben. Did the judge actually say the deposition was to be in London?"

"No. Why? I thought your office was in London. Yes. I'm sure I dialed London."

She laughed. "You did, Ben. Our system is a little confusing to outsiders. The problem is that I'm not in London, and I don't particularly want to go to London next week. Tell me, was there any specific mention made of London, or England, in the hearing?"

"No. There wasn't. I told the judge your office was out of the country and it would be an inconvenience for you to come to Miami. I've been communicating with Cliff Kelly and I was sure I called him in London too."

"That's true enough. Ben, I have several offices, but the main one is here at the Earth Port. Cliff is here most of the time as well these days, although sometimes he does travel back to London. We've really mixed you up, and I apologize. Let me straighten it out for you.

"The Earth Port is in Belau, which is a small island nation in the western Pacific. We have a direct telephone connection, via satellite, to London, which is how you're speaking to me now. To get here, you have to first fly to Manila, in the Philippines, or to Guam. We are about an hour or two from there by air. Be sure you give our address to Mr. Goldman. It is Belau Aviation, Babeldaob, ... that's *B-A-B-E-L-D-A-O-B*, Republic of Belau. Some people may still refer to it as P-A-L-A-U, which is an incorrect spelling previously imposed by the American government." Danielle suppressed a laugh, thinking of Goldman's likely reaction.

"Now that you know that, was there anything in the judge's order or the discussions during the hearing which would preclude having the deposition here?"

"No, I guess not. I'm drafting the order right now for the judge to sign and I'll insure that it spells out your office in the Republic of Belau. Then I'll see what I have to do to get there."

"Don't even start. Just call Marilyn's staff at Neverland and say you want to come here, and when. You can recommend Neverland to Goldman too. They know all the flights and will save you a lot of headaches. I'm sorry about Scotland, Ben."

"So am I. My wife was looking forward to seeing the Hebrides. I'll just have to tell her we'll go another time."

"Ben, why don't you bring her with you? Can you both get away for a week?"

"I guess so. We'll have to put the dogs in a kennel, but we were going to do that anyway. What do you have in mind?"

"Tell your wife you're taking her to a tropical paradise. That's actually what this is. We have the most beautiful coral reefs in the world, and the place has a rich history. Some of the bloodiest battles of World War II were fought here. And the little village that passes for the national capital is simply enchanting. I'm sure she'll love it, and you can take her to Scotland another time. It will be a vacation she'll never forget." She had another thought. "Ben, do either you or your wife get seasick?"

"No. I guess we better not if we're going to go diving on the coral reefs."

"Actually, I had something else in mind. Since we're competing with Scotland here, I thought you and she might like to see something that even Scotland doesn't have. How do you and she like airplanes?"

"We love them. My wife used to fly in amateur aerobatic competitions and occasionally she takes me flying with her."

"My kind of people! Plan on leaving Washington three days before the deposition, and returning four days afterward. We'll work in the diving, deposition, local color and a very special plane ride for both of you. Can you work out your schedule to accommodate that?"

"You're the boss. We'll be there when Marilyn gets us there. At least, I know we'll be there a week from today for the deposition. I'll call back if there are any changes, otherwise I suppose we'll get there when we arrive."

"You won't be dealing with Marilyn herself. She's here right now and will still be here next week. She's relaxing in the Sun and catching up on her reading. I'm sure her staff will take good care of you though. Oh! One more thing; I need your height, weight, and clothes sizes. You know, what size suits do you and your wife wear?"

"I'm a forty regular, five-eleven, a hundred and eighty pounds, but I'm switched if I know what Beth wears. Why do you need that information?"

"It's a surprise. Maybe we want to have custom wet-suits for you; maybe it's something else. Just get me the information, okay?"

"Okay. Whatever you say. I'll call home right now and call back."

"Don't do that. Put us on hold and call home on another line. We're paying for the call, aren't we, in the long run?"

"Yes, I guess you are."

"Well, then I'll have my secretary wait on the line while you check. When you come back on, give him the sizes and he'll take care of the details. All right?"

"Sure. See you in a few days."

"Fine. We'll be waiting for you. Bill Townsend will be waiting for you on the line when you come back on. Bye."

"Goodbye."

Danielle called Bill and told him to hold on the London line, to get Mr. and Mrs. Bailey's space suit sizes, to alert Operations and to prepare the VIP quarters.

May 18

Four days later, Danielle met Ben and Beth Bailey at the Belau Airport. She led them to the Belau Aviation helicopter and gave them each a special noise-canceling headset. She explained that with the headphones on, they would be able to hear her over the noise of the helicopter's engine and rotors. The helicopter lifted off and began its flight to the nearby Earth Port. The pilot, in constant contact with the Earth Port control tower, altered his flight path, staying to the East of the long runway on Babeldaob. As the helicopter passed over the airport perimeter, a space plane descended past them on its final approach to the runway. Beth Bailey was delighted. She had never seen or even imagined such an aircraft before. She asked, "Miss Simones, would it be possible for me to see one close up?"

Recognizing her excitement, Danielle said, "I'll have our chief pilot give you a guided tour. How's that?"

Beth was so excited she was fidgeting in her seat in the helicopter. The helicopter crossed the runway at mid-field and turned on approach to the pad in front of the Operations office. As it touched down, Beth reached up to take off her headset. Danielle stopped her.

"Don't take off the headset until we're inside the Operations Building. It's also a hearing protector, and you'll need it." She had seen another space plane waiting to take off at the end of the runway as they passed it. The passengers had not noticed it because their attention had been distracted by the arriving plane. As they stepped from the helicopter to the pavement, the departing plane's afterburners ignited and the two visitors pressed their headsets tighter to their ears, to block out the noise. Danielle led them into the Operations office, and demonstrated by example that it was all right to remove their headsets.

"I see what you meant about the headsets," Beth said, "those are really loud planes. I've never seen any like them before. Are they military?"

"Nope, they're all ours."

"Where do they fly to?" Beth was very curious about the huge planes.

"Space. That's what we do here."

"Space...," her voice trailed off. She looked again at the space plane that was taxiing toward the main hangar.

Danielle said, "It's lunch-time. Would you like to join us for lunch in the cafeteria? It's not fancy, but the food is good."

Bailey and his wife exchanged glances. "Why certainly, we'd love to," said Beth.

"The bus is due in a minute," Danielle said. "They run mostly between takeoffs, but keep your headsets with you. The Operations people will deliver your luggage to your quarters."

The shuttle bus was soon joined by several others, which had discharged their passengers outside the main engineering office building. Danielle led the visitors into the building, and down the hall to the company cafeteria. Several hundred people were eating lunch, and the room was only partially occupied. She looked around the room and spotted Hank, Jake and Marion sitting in their usual spot. She waved and they waved back.

"Here's the food line," she announced. "Have whatever you like."

Bailey asked, "Who do we pay?"

She smiled. "You don't."

"I'm not sure I feel comfortable with that, Miss Simones," he answered, stiffly.

Danielle put her arm around him and gave him a little hug and a smile. "Get used to it, Ben. You're our lawyer, and that makes you part of the family. No one pays for meals in this cafeteria. If you look around, you'll notice there's no place to pay. ... And while you're here, it's 'Danielle'."

"How do you handle the bookkeeping? It must be very difficult to keep track of who receives the meals."

She shrugged. "We don't keep track. The kitchen prepares more or less the same amount each day, and it all works out. The line is open around the clock, 24 hours a day. I guess sometimes we get leftovers, but no one complains."

Ben couldn't easily accept the idea of hundreds, maybe thousands of people getting free meals, and asked, "Don't you have to report the meals as part of the employees' pay?"

"Report? To whom?" she asked.

"To the IRS. On the income tax reports."

"This is Belau, Ben," she said. "Our employees don't pay income tax here, and what they do for their home countries is up to them. We do furnish them a statement showing what their theoretical income is, which they can use to file income tax returns, if they still have to pay them where they came from, but most of them have been here long enough that they aren't liable for income taxes at home. In any case, these meals aren't part of their pay. They don't have to eat here; for our part, it's a gift to them. If they get their groceries at the commissary, they don't pay there either."

He persisted. "Doesn't the government here require an income tax report?"

"Nope. One of the benefits of a small government is it doesn't require a lot of money to operate. There are fewer than twenty-five thousand Belauan citizens and the rent we pay for this site more than covers the cost of running the country."

Beth asked, "How do you determine who eats here and who doesn't? Some people might abuse the privilege. Doesn't that ever occur?"

"We don't keep track," Danielle answered, "and it doesn't matter if they want to eat every meal here or none. Some of the employees with families here on the island have their families join them for meals. Look. There." She pointed across the room. "There's a woman sitting right there with her husband and two children. They aren't in school today, because it's a vacation day. The father teaches in the school, the mother is an engineer in our space manufacturing design department."

"How can you afford that?" he asked. "It must run your costs up a great deal."

"Our cost of this operation, to feed everyone, is only a tiny fraction of our operating cost. We import huge amounts of food from other countries, and the cost of that food is millions of dollars each year. Some of it we provide to our employees in the commissary; other parts of it are consumed here, and some of it we ship up to the crews working on the satellites. But we're spending billions of dollars here on this project and our food cost is insignificant. 'Do not bind the mouths of the kine who tread the grain.' I read that in a Robert Heinlein book once. I think it originally came from the Bible." She paused. "You're part of this project now, Ben, and you're welcome to eat here anytime you wish during your visit. We will however, be having some meals at my quarters, and with friends, and at a few special restaurants, ... well ..., they aren't exactly restaurants. 'Eating places' would be a better term, in Koror. There's a bridge across the small channel between the islands, and the local cooking is delicious. I'm sure you're going to enjoy it. Now let's eat."

They went through the line and joined Hank, Jake and Marion in the dining room. Danielle introduced the visitors. "Beth and Ben, this is Hank Taylor, our chief pilot, and his crew; Jake Boesinger, co-pilot, and Marion Douglas, flight engineer. This is Beth Bailey, who I understand has had some aerobatic experience, and her husband Ben, who's representing us in some legal matters."

She turned to Ben and gestured apologetically, "Sorry, Ben. Here anything to do with airplanes gets priority over legal matters."

Ben shrugged back. "That's no change from our house, so I feel right at home." Everyone laughed.

Danielle winked at Hank and said, "Hank, Beth wanted to see one of the space planes. Can you arrange a tour of one for her?"

"Sure," Hank said. "Beth, would you like the regular tour or the deluxe tour?"

Beth looked puzzled. "I don't know. What's the difference?"

"With deluxe you get egg rolls," Marion quipped.

"Ignore her," said Hank. "With the deluxe tour, you get the aerial demonstration."

"You mean you'd fly the plane?" asked Beth.

"That's it," said Marion.

"But where would you fly to?" Beth asked.

"We only fly to one place, Ma'am," said Jake, who had been silent until then.

"But Danielle said your planes went into Space?" It was more of a question than a statement.

"Yup," said Jake.

"Yup. Uh huh," said Marion.

"That's what we do, ma'am," said Hank. "Want to come along?"

""Do I? DO I? Eeyow! Of course I do!" Beth's answer didn't leave much room for doubt.

"Will Ben be coming along?" Hank asked.

Beth's enthusiasm was suddenly dampened. "Uh, I don't know." She turned to Ben inquiringly, who in turn looked to Danielle.

Danielle said, "Let's all go. Okay?" She looked to Ben for confirmation. Ben nodded. "Okay, that's it," she said. "We're *all* going. When do we leave, Captain?"

Hank looked at his watch, then said, "We leave in an hour and a half. 'Blast off,' as it were. If you like, Beth, you can meet me on the flight line to do the preflight with me. That's a half an hour from now.

Beth suddenly looked frantically at Ben. "Only a half-hour! I'm not dressed properly, and I don't know where our bags are."

Danielle touched Beth's arm. "Don't worry. After lunch, you and Ben go back to Operations on the bus. Tell them your names and they'll give you your flight suits and show you where to change. Don't forget your headsets. I'll meet you on the flight line in an hour. Your space suits already will be loaded in the plane.

The flight was routine, at least it was routine for Hank, Jake and Marion. For their two visiting passengers, Ben and Beth, it was a once-in-a-lifetime experience. For Danielle it was a refreshing escape from the office.

When the space plane reached orbit, the guests were informed that they had to change planes, and were shown their space suits, which had been placed aboard during the time they were eating in the cafeteria. As the plane closed on LEO-A, Beth was surprised to see many other space planes parked in orbit near the station, some of which were being unloaded. She watched the station crew begin the process of unloading the cargo from the plane they had just arrived in, and was disappointed that she couldn't stay to watch.

The space plane crew helped their visitors suit up, then escorted them through the airlock into the openness of space, with Earth so nearby, yet so far below.

After the excitement of the climb to orbit, a space-walk, and the tour of the LEO satellite, the trip back to Earth Base in a different space plane was almost anti-climactic, but Beth knew, and Ben was pretty sure, that few other humans had experienced this, and both of them savored it.

Three and a half hours after they had taken off from the Earth Port, the two visitors were climbing out of the airlock back at the Earth Port. Danielle escorted them to the VIP quarters, showed them where everything was located, and asked them to be ready for dinner at eight.

At nine thirty on the morning of May 21, a disheveled Adrian Goldman arrived at the Earth Base's main gate, accompanied by a court reporter he'd brought with him all the way from Miami. They were provided hearing protectors and told to wait. After ten minutes, a car pulled up to the gate, and the driver instructed them to get in. The attorney and his court reporter were delivered to the main office building, where Goldman produced his identification, for about the tenth time it seemed. The pair was directed to take the elevator to the top floor of the building, then turn right and go to the end of the hall. They eventually were standing before Bill Townsend's desk.

"I'm Adrian Goldman, to see Miss Simones. I have an appointment for ten o'clock."

Bill said, "Good morning, Mr. Goldman. Miss Simones is expecting you and will be right with you. Please have a seat in the lounge. May I get you a cup of coffee or a soft drink?" He turned to the court reporter and smiled, "What about you, Miss? May I get you something? You're probably thirsty after your trip."

The reporter accepted a cup of coffee. As she was taking her second sip, Danielle stepped into the lounge.

"Mr. Goldman, so nice to see you." She reached out and shook his hand, then turned to the court reporter. "I'm Danielle Simones. I hope you have been made welcome. Has anyone shown you where the restrooms are?" Seeing the negative response, she said, "I thought not."

Goldman started to protest, "Our appointment is for ten ...."

Danielle interrupted, "Mr. Goldman, you've come halfway around the world with this lady. Won't you allow her the opportunity to powder her nose before

334

your urgent deposition? Please?" She smiled at him, and his gruff behavior disappeared. He realized he wanted to powder his nose too.

Ten minutes later, Bill showed Goldman and Deborah Winters, the court reporter, into Danielle's office.

"Would you like to proceed at my conference table, or in a more relaxed chair, Mr. Goldman?" Danielle asked.

Goldman motioned toward the table. Danielle sat down at the head of the table, in her usual chair, and invited Goldman to sit at the chair next to her. She spoke to the court reporter, "Would you like to set up here at the corner of the table, between Mr. Goldman and myself, Miss Winters?"

"Where's your attorney?" asked Goldman.

"Oh, he'll be here in a minute. Let me know when you're ready to begin, and I'll get him."

"I'm ready now," said Goldman, a little irritated.

"Very well. Bill, have Mr. Bailey come in, please."

Bailey emerged a moment later through the rear entrance to the office, removing his hearing protector. He had been on the roof watching the planes land and take off. He ran his hand across his head, simulating a comb and returning his wild hair to approximately its correct location.

"May I begin now?" asked Goldman, a little exasperated.

"Of course, Mr. Goldman. Please begin," Danielle said.

"Please state your name." The court reporter's fingers pressed several buttons on the stenographic machine.

"Danielle Marie Elizabeth Margaret Simones."

"What is your residence address?"

"Ousley Manor, St. Andrew, Guernsey, Channel Islands, United Kingdom."

"If that's your residence, why is your office thousands of miles away?"

"Objection to the form of the question. Failure to lay a proper predicate," said Bailey.

"I'll rephrase the question. Miss Simones, where is your office located?"

"Right now it's here."

"Is it other places at other times?"

"Yes."

"Where?"

"London, Paris, Tokyo, New York, several other places."

"Why do you use those other locations?"

"Because they suit my purposes at the time."

"But you're here now?"

"Objection, repetitive," said Bailey. "You're badgering the witness."

Goldman gave Bailey a particularly pained look.

Bailey looked over at Danielle and said, "Well, I do have to make it look like I'm earning my fee, don't I?"

Danielle said, "Let's continue."

Goldman said, "Miss Simones, why is your office here right now, rather than in London, Tokyo, New York or Paris?"

"Because this is where my work is now. I have my office where my work is."

"What is the work you are doing now?"

"I'm a consultant to the several corporations involved in the satellite solar power system project."

"On what subject do you consult?"

"Quite a number, actually. Would you like me to list some of them?"

"Yes," he said, then added. "But I'm asking the questions."

"Certainly," she agreed. "I'm consulting in the areas of law, business management, engineering, mechanics, economics, marketing, ..., I guess that touches the high points."

Goldman was busily writing. He looked back at her, "In the area of law, what is your ..., what are your duties with regard to the project."

"Which project?"

"I mean the satellite solar power system project. Isn't that what we are talking about?"

"Are we? I don't know. What part of the project are you asking about, Mr. Goldman?"

"What part? What do you mean? How many parts are there?"

"Mr. Goldman, I really must ask that you ask your questions one at a time, won't you please? That's a dear." She smiled as sweetly as she could.

Goldman was becoming very irritated. "Miss Simones," he said. "Please tell the court reporter how many different parts the project has."

"Many. It seems there are more parts every time we look, Mr. Goldman."

"Please be specific, if you can."

"I'll try. First, there is the part involved in the design of the space plane. Then there is the part involved in the manufacture of the space plane components. Then there is the part involved in the assembly of the space plane components. Then there is the part involving training the space plane crews. Then there is the part involving the testing of the space plane. Then there is the part involving the maintenance of the space plane. Then there is the part involving flying the space plane. Then there is the part involving loading the space plane. Then there is the part involving unloading the space plane. Then there is the part involving providing fuels and supplies for the space plane. Then there is the part involving certification of the space plane. Then there is the part ..."

Goldman interrupted. His note-taking was falling far behind the listing of the parts of the space plane program. "Miss Simones, aren't you going to talk about anything else than the space plane?"

"Well, Mr. Goldman, you said you wanted to know all the parts of the project. You said 'be specific,' and I interpreted that to mean you wanted to know all the different parts of the project."

"Perhaps I should have asked you to speak more generally, then to gradually get more specific. I need some background."

"Mr. Goldman, I only want you to fully satisfy yourself about these questions of yours. Should I assume that you would like a broad description of the parts of the project, rather than specifics?"

"Please."

"Well, as you have undoubtedly gathered already, the space plane is one part of the project, speaking generally. I mentioned it first because it is the part that makes the rest possible. The other major parts are the satellites and the receiving antennas. Then the antennas are connected by a distribution network, and the satellites are supported by a system to move supplies from one point in space to another. Then there is a financial aspect, which involves billing for the electricity delivered and paying the expenses of the project. And of course there is the design effort, which is an ongoing effort to move forward from wherever the project is at any given time."

"So there are seven main parts of the project, is that correct?"

"Not exactly. The project can be divided into many different segments, depending on how one chooses to look at it."

"Can you please explain that?"

"For example," she said, "each satellite could be considered as a separate part of the project, but they are actually interdependent, because of the peculiarities of nature."

Goldman paused, "I beg your pardon?"

"I said the satellites are interdependent because of the peculiarities of nature," she repeated.

"I heard that, but I don't understand what you mean. Will you please explain?"

"Certainly. The power supplied to a receiving antenna should be uninterrupted, because there is always demand on the system. Street lights, lights in homes, cooking, televisions, etc. There are demands for electricity around the clock."

"I understand that," Goldman said. "What does that have to do with interdependency?"

"What it means is that the power satellites have to fill in for each other, so to speak, once each day, for several weeks each year during the equinoxes. Because at midnight, each satellite stops producing power for a few minutes as it passes through the Earth's shadow. We call that an 'eclipse.'"

"What do you mean 'fill in for each other?'"

"I mean that, for the power to flow without interruption, as it is eclipsed, the satellite which is producing the power has to have another satellite, not eclipsed, ready to beam power to the first satellite's receiving antennas. We do that by having a transmitting antenna on each of *two* satellites aimed at each receiving antenna. A few minutes before an eclipse, the satellite which is going to be eclipsed starts to shut down, and an adjacent satellite begins to bring up its microwave signal strength. It's all computer-controlled, so the users on the ground never are aware that the hand-off has occurred. Then a few minutes later, we hand-off back to the original satellite, because the shadow will soon hit the second satellite. At this point transmitting antennas on the first satellite begin to beam power to the second satellite's receiving antennas. This happens once each day for each satellite, when that satellite is directly opposite the Sun. Do you understand now?"

"Yes. Thank you. But what I'm really interested in is the money. My motto is 'Follow the money.' One of my old law-school teachers from the University of Chicago, Miss Johnson, taught that to me."

"But you haven't asked me about the money, Mr. Goldman."

"I'm about to. Can you tell me how much ... " Goldman was interrupted by the rumble of a space plane taking off. "Can you tell me how much one of your space planes costs to build?"

"I can tell you very accurately how much it cost to build the first one. Three point two billion U.S. dollars. That included the design work and manufacturing all of the tooling at all of the contractors. Subsequent planes have been significantly less expensive. The last one to fly cost, this is just an approximation, about three-quarters of a billion dollars."

"How many space planes are there?" he asked.

"Fourteen are flying now. We finished the last one about two years ago."

Goldman was busily adding and multiplying on his legal pad.

"Then you have about fourteen billion dollars of the investors' money in the space planes?"

"No."

"No?" He looked up from his note pad.

"I didn't say the space planes were built with investors' money, Mr. Goldman."

"Whose money were they built with?"

"If I understand your question, you're asking where the companies that built the space plane got the money to build the space plane, aren't you?"

"Yes. That's what I'm asking."

"You'll have to ask those companies."

"What are the names of the companies?"

"Which companies?" she asked, innocently. She knew he'd never unravel all the companies, at least not during only one deposition. The Liechtenstein trust had initially formed several very independent banks, in various countries, to which Danielle had made loans. The banks had loaned money to many corporations, which had contracted with intermediate corporations to hire aerospace companies around the world to build different components of the space plane. The completed components for each plane had been sold to other corporations, then delivered to Belau Aviation, which had completed the assembly under contract. Meanwhile, each complete plane had been sold to yet another corporation, which leased it to another corporation, which subleased it to another corporation, which chartered it to another corporation, which hired another corporation to fly the plane. All that corporation did was pay the crewmembers, each of whom was a private contractor. Belau Aviation was contracted to provide maintenance and other separate corporations were contracted to load the planes and to unload the planes in orbit, different corporations being used at each LEO satellite. Goldman would never get to the bottom of it, which of course was that Danielle owned everything through the Liechtenstein trust. And the satellites were owned by her through similarly entangled, but different arrangements.

"The companies which built the space plane! Isn't that a clear enough question?" he demanded.

"No," she said simply.

"What?!" He was confused by her answer.

"No," she said,

"No, what??"

"No, that's not a clear enough question."

Goldman turned to the court reporter. "Please read back the question."

Deborah looked back at her stenotype machine tape. She read back the last several questions and answers. She didn't understand Goldman's question either.

Goldman looked back at Danielle, then at his legal pad, then at Danielle again. "Miss Simones, what is the name of the company which built the fourteen space planes you have now?"

"Mr. Goldman, you must understand, the space planes are not built by any one company."

"Well, which companies then?"

"Let's see, there's Global Aeronautique International in Paris, Lockheed in Burbank, Boeing in Seattle, Messerschmidt in Frankfurt, and a bunch of others, including Belau Aviation here."

"But who paid for them?"

"Who paid whom for them, Mr. Goldman?"

"Who paid the companies who built them for them?"

"I think you should ask the companies and not me. I would think they could tell you who paid them."

"Do you know who paid them?"

"I don't know who paid for any particular plane, except that the last four were financed with a large international bank."

"Which bank?"

"The Bank of China."

"Who arranged the financing?" he asked.

"I did."

Goldman said, "With whom at the Bank of China did you make the arrangement?"

"The person with whom I initially spoke was ..."

Danielle was interrupted by the intercom on her desk. Bill was shouting. "Danielle! There are three unidentified aircraft 250 miles out."

"Excuse me, Mr. Goldman, we have to stop for a while."

"But I'm not done," he protested.

"You're done for now!" she snapped. "Now get out of my office and do what my secretary tells you. Your life may depend on it."

"But...." he sputtered.

"Out!" She turned to Deborah. "I'm afraid you'll have to leave for a while, dear. Mr. Townsend outside will show you where to go. Hurry!" The court reporter reached for her dictation equipment.

"Leave the machine," Danielle said. "It'll be safe here. Go quickly." Deborah hurried out, following Goldman and Bailey. Goldman was still protesting as Maurice came in and closed the office door behind him.

Danielle punched a button on the desk and the video forest scene changed to a view of the Operations office. "What's going on?" she asked on the intercom.

The faces turned to the video camera, and one of them said, "We have three bogeys 225 miles out and have been hailing them on all the usual frequencies. They don't answer. We estimate their arrival in 30 minutes. They've been descending, apparently trying to stay below our radar, but they didn't start down soon enough and we spotted them."

"How many planes do we have on the ground?" she asked.

"Two space planes, a Learjet, and a 727, plus the usual helicopters."

"How many of them can we get off the ground in half an hour?"

"One space plane and the Boeing are fueled and ready to go. The Learjet is ready but its crew is in Koror. The other space plane just landed and hasn't been through maintenance." Maurice stepped into her office.

Danielle turned to Maurice. "You'd better get to Operations and handle things from there. I'll monitor the video. Get crews and fly out the three planes with fuel. Someone will know how to fly the Lear and the Boeing. Send the 727 to Manila. I want the Lear vectored to the bogeys and a report on who and what they are. Warn the Learjet crew to keep a sharp lookout for any fighter cover, and we need to know if there are any ships heading this way. Put two crews on the ready space plane and have them park it at a satellite and lay-over there. If we lose this base, they're to pick up all the crews from the satellites and tugs, then land at Edwards Air Force Base in California, the Area 51 airstrip in Nevada, or the shuttle strip at Cape Canaveral. If there are any planes ready to come back from orbit, be sure they stay put. See if you can get crews to refuel and replace the necessary stores on the remaining space plane in a hurry, but skip any maintenance you can. If we have to, we'll do maintenance in orbit. I want both of them out of here before the bogeys arrive." Maurice left the office at a run.

Fifteen minutes later, cruising thousands of feet above the bogeys, the Learjet turned and began a descent that ended with a close pass behind them. It radioed back to Earth Base that the aircraft were C-130-type military cargo aircraft, in camouflage paint, with no discernible national markings or registration numbers. It also reported a small force of naval vessels much closer to Belau, only about ten miles away and headed toward the island. There were three very large ships and four more about three-fourths the size. The pilot didn't know much about ships, but he could see that they were big navy ships. There was no fighter escort.

One space plane departed for orbit as Danielle called Maurice. "Are you in touch with Laurie?"

"Yes. I alerted her as soon as the bogeys were reported to me. She says she's ready with Web 3."

"I hope so. Send all employees to their shelters or defensive positions."

"I gave a warning order ten minutes ago and the air-raid sirens have been on since then. Everyone is standing by for an execute order and will be in position in minutes after they get it."

"Tell them to do it right now. What's the location of the bogeys?"

"60 miles northwest, at 2,000 feet. By now they must know we're onto them. We've been calling them constantly. Their formation has spread out. Our message says 'Identify yourself immediately. Approach within 10 nautical miles of Belau will be considered a hostile act. Identify yourself immediately.'"

"They haven't tipped their hand yet, though, have they?"

"No. Not a peep."

"We'll wait for some sign. Do you have computer control of the satellite?"

"Yes. And Angelina Perez is running the fire control computer. She's our best operator."

"The test spot in the lagoon. Can she hit it?"

"Two keystrokes to begin the burst, and one to stop it, I think. I wish we had been able to test this," Maurice said.

"Too late for that now. Give me a two-second burst at that test spot." Danielle watched the lagoon through binoculars from the window next to the conference table. Suddenly, a huge cloud appeared over the lagoon as a portion of it turned to steam. It was more like an explosion than just hot water. As she watched, the normally calm surface of the lagoon became full of waves. She suspected the column of water had vaporized all the way to the bottom from the satellite's beam and that the water from the lagoon had rushed in to fill the empty space. She wished she knew for sure.

"Maurice, did you lock the radar system tracking the blips to the fire control computer? If we have to, I want you to be able to down all of those planes with one signal."

"We already did that. I wish I knew who it was."

"We'll find out. You have a lower burn-level beam available too, don't you?"

"Yes. I'm not sure how accurately we'll be able to direct it."

"Be ready to drop back to your alternate location if Operations is jeopardized."

"Roger. Ten minutes to arrival. It doesn't look as if the other space plane will make it off the ground. Sorry, Boss."

"Don't give up. Tell the refuelers to get at it, but keep the hangar doors closed until they're ready for engine start. They can start the engines in the hangar, with just the intakes outside if they want. Have some fire control teams standing by."

Maurice didn't come back to the camera for a minute. "I've passed on that word, but I don't like it a bit. The refueling crew is still working and there's a crew aboard ready to start. I sure hope they don't attack the hangar first thing." The space plane's main tanks were filled with highly explosive hydrogen slush fuel and liquid oxygen for the scramjets, while the wing tanks were filled with kerosene for the turbine engines. Refueling was normally only done far from the hangar, a safe distance considering the explosive nature of the fuel. It was very dangerous to refuel the plane in the confined space of the hangar, where any leaking hydrogen gas could collect, and much too dangerous to then start the space plane's engines in that space where any stray hydrogen would ignite explosively, taking the whole hangar and the space plane up with it.

Danielle was suddenly very afraid. "Maurice," she said quietly, "I don't want to start a war with anyone."

"I know, Boss."

"We have to hold our fire until there's a definitely hostile act."

"If they land here," Maurice said, "I think I can hit their planes as they turn off the runway onto the apron. The computer has a built-in protected area for the runway and for each building or personnel shelter, and it shouldn't fire at any of those spots, but there's a designated target area between the runway and the Operations building, and we can sweep that with the beam if we need to."

"I'm worried about 'sweeping' any place we need to operate. I don't think we'll have an apron left if the beam sweeps it. Try to just use short bursts, Maurice."

"I'll try. The bogeys just busted the ten-mile boundary, Danielle."

"Hold your fire, Maurice. We have to see a definite hostile act."

"One of the planes seems to be setting up to land. The others are circling."

"Are you tracking all of them?"

"Yes. Still tracking. The one landing is turning base for Runway 3."

"I can see it from here. Don't fire until there is some verification of an attack." She was standing at the window, watching the approaching aircraft with binoculars.

The C-130 flew slowly down the long runway, a few feet above the runway surface. As it neared the parking apron, it touched down and turned onto the apron toward the tower and stopped just off the runway near the Operations building.

"Danielle," Maurice said, "someone has to confront whoever this is. I guess I'm elected. I'll take the mobile radio with me, and keep it turned on so you, and the computer operators, can monitor what's going on."

"Maurice, ..., be careful."

"Don't say it. I don't know how to be careful in this situation. Wait 'til I see what's up."

Maurice's figure came out of the door of the Operations building and got into a white Jeep that had 'FOLLOW ME' signs on the back. The Jeep drove from the Operations building, across the pavement, toward the military aircraft. It stopped 50 feet from the aircraft's nose. Maurice got out of the Jeep and walked toward the door on the left side of the big plane, just ahead of the wing. The number 2 propeller, next to the door, was stopped, and the other propellers seemed to be coasting to a stop. Apparently the visitors were planning to stay a while. Danielle could see one of the two other C-130s circling the field at an altitude of about 1,500 feet. The third one was probably circling behind the administration building on the opposite side of the installation from the one she could see.

Danielle listened intently on the monitor to the sound from Maurice's portable radio. The whine of the large plane's engines and gear-reduction drives for the propellers spinning down was clearly audible. As she watched, the door on the airplane swung open, and a person stepped out, in a military uniform.

"Hello." It was Maurice's voice, a little tinny over the radio. "Can we help you?"

"Are you in charge here?" The voice had a distinct accent.

"I'm the airport manager." Maurice's statement, while true, was hardly complete. "What can I do for you?"

The strange voice spoke again. "I am Colonel Zhang of the Chinese People's Liberation Army. The government of China has declared this facility to be its property. You are required to surrender the facility to me."

Maurice protested, "Sir, this is a private operation. We're not connected with any government. There must be some mistake."

The Chinese voice was sharp. "No mistake. You must surrender now."

"I see," said Maurice. "You understand, I'm only the airfield manager. I have to get authorization from my superiors. I'll have to call them from our Operations building." Danielle saw Maurice gesture toward the Ops building. "Would you like to come with me? Please?" Maurice gestured toward his Jeep.

The Chinese officer turned back to the aircraft and motioned to someone inside. The tail ramp began to open, and a large number of troops in combat gear, at least a hundred, exited at a run from the rear of the aircraft and set up a defensive perimeter around the plane. The soldiers all had rifles, and looked ready to use them. The officer turned back to Maurice and followed him to the Jeep, signaling to one of the soldiers, who joined him with Maurice. The three men got into the Jeep and Maurice drove slowly back to the Operations building. They got out and went into the office. Maurice still had his microphone turned on, and Danielle could overhear his conversation. She watched from her window as they entered the Operations office. She switched the monitor in her office to view the interior of the Operations office.

"Colonel, this is our Operations office," said Maurice. "I must call my superior and inform her of your action." Danielle's phone rang almost immediately and she answered it.

"Miss Simones, there is a Chinese Colonel Zhang here who has informed me that the base is being taken over by the Chinese."

"Maurice," she said, "put me on the speakerphone."

"Okay, you're on the speaker."

"Colonel, can you hear me?"

"Yes, I can hear you."

"I certainly appreciate the civilized way you are handling this matter, sir. I would appreciate it if you would come up to my office, so we can make the necessary arrangements. Would that be possible?"

The Chinese officer considered this offer, then agreed. He was amazed that the civilians were completely defenseless. This was like taking candy from a baby, he thought. He decided it was a sign of western decadence. He and the soldier with him got back into the Jeep with Maurice, who drove to the main office building.

A few minutes later, Bill announced that Maurice and the Colonel had arrived at Danielle's office. She went to the door and invited them in. The soldier, with his rifle ready, carefully checked the office and then indicated to the officer that it was clear. The officer walked in. The tropical forest scene dominated one wall.

Danielle formally greeted the Chinese officer with her small vocabulary of Mandarin.

He bowed in return with military formality.

"Colonel, please come in. I've been watching your arrival. As you can see, I have an excellent view of the flight line from this window."

The officer looked out the window at the parking apron, runway, buildings and his aircraft, surrounded by soldiers. One of his airborne C-130s was flying its elongated oval pattern in the near distance. He turned back to her. "Are you in charge here?"

"Yes, I'm the coordinator."

"Then I must inform you that the government of China has annexed this facility. You are to turn it over to me immediately."

"Can you tell me what the authority of the Chinese government is to 'annex' our facility, Colonel? I have been under the impression that this island was part of the independent Republic of Belau."

"That is a political question which I must refer to my higher headquarters, but it is irrelevant to my job, which is to take control of this facility. I have heard something about this group of islands having been properly due to the Chinese government after the Great War."

"I certainly understand your position, Colonel, but tell me, what would happen if we were to resist your takeover?"

"Miss Simones, ... it is Miss Simones, isn't it?"

"Yes."

"We have an overwhelming force here, Miss Simones. And you have no defenses. I am afraid you have no choice. There are over one hundred highly trained soldiers with my plane, and an equal number in each of the planes circling overhead. Additionally, - are you familiar with the Vietnam War, Miss Simones?"

"A little."

"Our aircraft overhead are equipped with rapid-firing cannons, often called 'Gatling guns,' which they can direct against any point of resistance on your base. These weapons could level all the buildings on your base in minutes. Then we have a large occupation force on several ships which will be landing in a short time."

"You certainly seem to have come well-prepared for any contingency, Colonel. I want you to understand how sorry I am that the situation has come to this turn of events. I'm sure you don't want to damage any of the buildings or other property here if you don't have to, do you?"

"No, of course not. These properties are very valuable, as you correctly realize. But it is not necessary for you to apologize for your actions."

"I wasn't apologizing, Colonel, just expressing regret that your government has seen fit to act in this way. I am afraid you have left me with no options."

The officer smiled. "A well-planned military operation is intended to leave the enemy with no options, but surrender."

"Very well," Danielle said, "do you wish to surrender?"

"Me!?" He laughed. "You are quite a kidder, Miss Simones. I received a briefing about you, and it was said you had a sense of humor."

"Yes, Colonel, I guess I do. But I am very serious now. We have a present for you, sir. Would you come over to the window, please?"

The Colonel came to the window and looked out. One of the C-130s was just completing its turn to fly a course parallel to the runway.

Danielle looked at the aircraft on the ground and in the air, then back at Maurice, who was watching from the middle of the office. She drew her index finger across her throat in a clearly recognizable gesture.

"Now?" Maurice asked.

She nodded.

Maurice spoke into the microphone hanging from his lapel. "Now, Angelina."

The C-130 parked on the ramp suddenly exploded in flames, spraying flaming jet fuel over all the soldiers around the wreckage. Those who hadn't been killed by the explosion were running wildly around the aircraft parking area, covered with burning fuel.

Another pulse from the beam vaporized an elongated hole, several feet across, in the right wing of the C-130 visible flying above the jungle on the far side of the airfield, as it flew through the beam. That area included the main wing spar, just outside the fuselage. The wing folded upward, then tore away from the rest of the plane. The flaming wreckage seemed to be falling slowly, with the combination of still-running engines on the remaining wing and the tail surfaces causing the fuselage to spin as it fell. It struck the ground and exploded as the remaining fuel tanks ruptured on impact. A fireball followed by black smoke rose from the jungle where it impacted. The other C-130, not visible from the office window, had a similar fate, but fell into the ocean on the West side of the island. Danielle heard a cheer from the hallway outside of the office.

The soldier who was standing across the room from the window had not seen what happened, and was puzzled by the sounds from outside and by his commander's sudden extreme agitation.

"Sit down, Colonel," Danielle said. "It's all over. Tell your man to put down his rifle. We have many armed personnel in the hall outside this office, and all he can do, if he's stupid, is cause your death and his own needlessly."

The Colonel, seeing that his ace had been trumped, sat down in shock. He told the soldier to put down his rifle. The soldier hesitated and the Colonel got up, took the rifle from him and handed it to Maurice. Maurice opened the door and handed the rifle to Bill. Several company employees armed with M-16s were standing in the hall.

"Colonel," Danielle said, "please direct your soldier to leave my office and to cooperate with the people outside. You and he are going to be our guests for a while."

The Colonel spoke sharply to the soldier, who walked out the door with his hands in the air.

She turned to the desk and selected the view of the Operations office, which replaced the forest scene. "Operations, where are the ships?"

The duty officer in Operations looked at the video camera. "They're now about five miles offshore, - it looks like about 500 yards from the reef - and have turned to the North, into the wind. Four are in Toagel Mlunguni, the bay on the outside of the reef, and the others are north of there, just outside the Aiwakako Passage."

Maurice said, "I think they're preparing to launch landing boats with troops. Either that or they're preparing to fire on us."

Danielle rapidly considered her options. "I think so too. Sink them."

Maurice said, "Fire control, are the ships targeted?"

"Yes, sir," came a very quiet female voice in response, from the Operations office.

"Commence firing. Let me know when they're not floating any longer." Maurice looked out the window. Belau Aviation employees were examining the burned soldiers on the parking apron, looking for any who were still alive, trying to help them if it was still possible.

In the ocean West of Babeldaob, seven ships of the Chinese Navy were preparing to disembark troops. Suddenly, the center of the largest ship disappeared. The sudden concentration of energy in the ship released enormous amounts of heat, exploding the ammunition and fuel stores of the ship. Effectively burned in half, the ship simply folded up and slid below the surface of the sea. The rest of the fleet suffered similar damage. After a few minutes, only one ship remained on the surface, its bow and bridge missing, but its engines still running. It moved forward, with the survivors of its crew and passengers crowded around the stern. Rapidly taking on water, what was left of the front of the vessel sank lower and lower in the water. Fire raged amidships.

After several minutes of aimless circling, the front of the vessel sank so low that the propellers lifted from the water and the ship stopped, its stern rising higher and higher into the air. Survivors had been leaping over the side and swimming away from the ship, which then slowly rolled over until its still-turning propellers were the highest point on the wreckage. Then, very gradually, it slid beneath the waves.

In the Operations office, one of the radar operators looked back to the video camera, and said, "Miss Simones, the radar returns from all the ships have disappeared."

"Thank you. Well done," she said, then switched off the video from Operations. The forest reappeared on the screen.

She turned back to the Colonel and Maurice, who were both still standing in the office. Fewer than ten minutes had elapsed since the Colonel had entered her office. She didn't know what to say. She didn't know what to do. She sat down at her desk and looked at the several piles of papers there, shuffling them aimlessly. Maurice and the Colonel watched as tears filled her eyes, despite her efforts to hold them back. She had failed in her attempt to keep the satellite from being used as a weapon, and she was the one responsible. She sniffed and swiveled around in the chair, turning her back on the two men. "Excuse me," she choked, and stood up. She walked from the room into her apartment, where she ran a basin-full of cold water and dashed it on her face. She dried her face and went back into her office, and sat down again at the desk, still stunned by the results of her own actions.

"Oh, my God," she exclaimed. She punched up Operations again. "Get out the crash helicopters. We have to see if there are any survivors from the ships. And what is the status of our plane in the hangar?"

"It's ready to go, Miss Simones."

"Tow it out and launch it." She turned back to the Colonel and Maurice. "Colonel, do you understand what it was you were to capture today?" She looked out the window as Maurice and the Colonel came to stand beside her. The massive hangar doors were sliding open and the space plane, towed by its usual tractor, began to roll out onto the parking apron. The still-burning remains of the Colonel's C-130 was a few hundred yards from the front of the hangar, a tall pillar of black smoke blowing southwestward from the twisted and scorched metal. The tractor towed the space plane around the downwind side of the wreckage. A moment later the engines were running and the space plane taxied to the end of the runway, paused for a few seconds, then hurled itself as usual into the sky.

"What kind of plane is that?" the Colonel asked.

"It's a very special plane, Colonel," she said wistfully. "One that is changing the future of the Earth. One that many people have died for today. So unnecessary ... So unnecessary. I *am* so sorry, Colonel."

Danielle went to the desk and picked up the phone. "Bill, call the marina and see how many boats can be sent out to look for survivors. If there are any, we need to get them out of the water right away or the sharks will get them. And call the defense minister of Belau and ask him to help. Just tell him that there has been an accident, that some ships exploded West of the big island."

She turned back to the Colonel. "Colonel, you are our guest here for the time being. I expect you to be on your best behavior. You may want to see if there are any survivors from your aircraft, or from the ships. Please organize whatever religious services are appropriate for your dead, and report to me as you proceed. We will provide quarters for you and your men. You will have my assistance however I can give it and, if it will help you, we will release your soldier to assist you. Maurice will show you where to start and assign an assistant to you as liaison between you and our Operations people. And Colonel, please remember, we are *not* your enemies." Maurice and the Colonel left her office.

CHAPTER 67

Danielle called her secretary again. "Bill, we've never used the secure line to Washington, D.C. and it's been several years since it was installed. Do you suppose it still works?"

"I haven't mentioned it because it didn't seem necessary," he answered, "but they call us the first of every month to check it out."

"Call the White House for me. I wonder if they'll remember who we are?"

"Someone will remember. I'll buzz you."

Mechanically, she went back to her paperwork. As she processed the papers, her mind was racing over the implications of the day's events.

The intercom buzzed. "The White House phone is ringing on line two."

She picked up the phone as the White House answered. "Situation Room, Waterman." the voice on the phone said.

"Situation Room?" she asked, "I thought I was calling the White House."

"You have reached the Operations Center at the White House. It's called the Situation Room, This is Mr. Waterman. How can I help you?"

"This is Danielle Simones. I am calling from Belau Aviation in the Republic of Belau. I have a message for President DeWitt. Can you deliver it for me?"

"Yes, ma'am. I'm ready to take your message."

"Tell the President that Chinese military forces have attempted, unsuccessfully, to seize the Earth Port here in Belau. We don't know if there will be another attempt. Many Chinese lives have been lost. That's all we know at this time, but I wanted the President to be informed. The United States has been very supportive of our project."

"Is there any further message?"

"No. The President may call me here if he has any questions."

"I'll relay the message."

"Thank you. Goodbye."

"Goodbye."

She hung up the phone, then picked it back up. "Bill, get Ramesh Mehta for me."

A few minutes later, she had given brief but slightly inaccurate reports of the morning's events to representatives of the Indian, Japanese, and Russian governments. She said that a group of Chinese planes and ships had unexpectedly exploded while visiting the base. She didn't tell any of them that the force was actually attacking the base or how the attack had been foiled. Then she called the Chinese.

The call to the Chinese Prime Minister was answered first by a series of secretaries and assistants. She explained to each of them that she had to speak to the Prime Minister. Fortunately, when she finally reached him, he spoke English fluently.

She began slowly, starting to explain carefully who she was, but it was quickly clear he already knew. "Mr. Prime Minister," she said, "I have the unhappy duty of informing you that a large number of the military forces of China have been killed here in Belau this morning. We observed several ships and aircraft approach our airport, and one airplane landed. Then for some reason, all of them exploded. I'm only certain of two survivors from the aircraft, but I have hope that there may be more survivors from the ships. I have boats and helicopters out in the ocean right now, looking for survivors. It is a great tragedy, sir, and I don't know quite what to say."

The Prime Minister was silent on the other end of the connection.

"Mr. Prime Minister? Did you hear me?" she asked.

"Yes. I heard. ... Who are the survivors?"

"A Colonel Zhang and a soldier who was accompanying him, perhaps his sergeant. He came into my office with a very strange story. He told me he was in charge and that the government of China was 'annexing' our operation here, which I am sure must be untrue. Then, suddenly, his aircraft, which was parked on our airport apron, blew up. It was on the ground, but two others were in-flight and crashed, and - well - there is no possibility of survivors from either of those two planes. I'm not sure about the plane on the ground. Some of the soldiers were outside it when it exploded, so there may have been survivors. I saw our personnel looking for survivors among the bodies."

"This is most unfortunate," the Prime Minister said hesitantly. "I don't know what to say either, Miss Simones."

"Mr. Prime Minister, we owe it to the men who died today to insure that such a thing won't happen again. Sir, I need your help, and we need to work together to prevent any recurrence of today's events. Will you help me?"

"What did you have in mind?" he asked.

"If there is any truth to the story the colonel told me, it means someone in China is seeking to control the solar power project. From my perspective, it seems it might be an appropriate time to begin construction of power stations in China. That way, your nation could share in the benefits of the program. I don't want your countrymen to feel excluded from this energy source."

"That might be an idea worth exploring, Miss Simones. Now, though, I must deal with this sad news you have given me. We will need to send personnel to recover the remains of our military forces."

"I'm sure you will, sir. And you need to send medical personnel to treat the injured. However, you must also insure that the intentions of those personnel are peaceful. We wouldn't want a recurrence of the unfortunate accidents today, would we, sir?"

"I will insure that all personnel visiting your base are peaceful, Miss Simones. And we must meet soon to discuss other matters."

"Yes, I agree. Thank you. Goodbye."

Danielle sat at her desk trying to put together all of the events of the morning. There were so many things she needed to know, but didn't. Was it a mistake to call the White House? Would the Chinese make another attempt to take over the Earth Base? Should she tell all the facts to other governments? Was this really an action of the Chinese government, or just some clique in the military trying to grab power for itself? There were too many variables and possibilities and she didn't have any reliable information on which to base a decision.

She was still trying to sort it all out when the intercom buzzed. Bill said, "White House on line one."

Before she picked up the phone, she said, "Bill, call the Philippine and Australian governments and ask them for some emergency medical teams. If we could get a couple dozen doctors and nurses from each of them fast, today, we would be very grateful." She punched line one and picked up the phone.

"This is Danielle Simones," she said quietly.

"Please hold for the President," said a female voice. Danielle waited.

"Miss Simones, this is John DeWitt."

"Hello, Mr. President."

"I understand you had some trouble there today." It was more of a question than a statement.

"Yes, sir. There were three C-130s and seven ships. But they're gone now."

"Gone? You mean they left?"

"No, sir. They exploded. I'm afraid many lives were lost. My people are out on the ocean looking for survivors."

"Can the United States be of any help to you, Miss Simones?"

She thought for several seconds before answering. "Yes, you can, Mr. President. We need several things right away."

"Tell me what you need, and I'll see what we have to do to get them to you."

"Mr. President, there are many dead soldiers here. We need personnel to manage the bodies, and caskets or body bags ... I don't know how to deal with them. The Chinese commander is here trying to find survivors and to help any who can be helped.

"If there are many wounded survivors from the ships," she continued, "we will need medical support. If you could have a mobile hospital and graves registration unit deploy here, they could begin triage while we try to determine the number of casualties. I just don't know yet, it's been so sudden."

"When did this all occur, Miss Simones?"

"About twenty minutes ago."

"That was when you called my office. I mean, when did the attack occur?"

"It was only about twenty minutes ago, sir. It was all over in a minute." She paused. "Mr. President, there's something else. I don't know if there are more hostile forces coming. Would it be possible to borrow an American AWACS plane, so that we can have some warning if there is another wave of attackers?"

The President said, "I don't know. Can you hold for a minute?" She waited a few moments then the President came back on the line. "We can have one AWACS plane there in three hours, from Guam, but we feel you should have two, so that one can be airborne at all times. The second one will take a day to get there."

Her brain had gone into overdrive. She was beginning to think of problems that a very large American presence could create, and remembering Siam. Her answer was nevertheless calm, "That would be good, Mr. President, for a short-term measure, until I'm confident the threat is past. How many personnel would those two planes require for support? I'm afraid we aren't set up for a lot of aircraft here." It was not quite true as the field had been built to park all of the space-plane fleet, but she didn't want to say so.

"I'm sorry, Miss Simones," he said, "but that's a technical detail I don't have an answer to. I can have someone from Defense call you with the numbers. Meanwhile we'll get working on the medical support people. I think we might be able to send some units from Korea."

"Thank you, Mr. President. Have them call me, and we'll make arrangements here to accommodate your personnel and aircraft. We appreciate your assistance."

"We're glad to help, Miss Simones."

"Mr. President, there is another factor we should discuss."

"Yes?"

"I've already spoken to the Chinese Prime Minister. I told him what had happened, and that I thought it was an unauthorized military action. I wanted to give him an opportunity to save face, sir. I don't want to provoke a confrontation between the solar power project and *any* country. I need China as a customer, not an adversary, so I asked him to send some personnel to assist with the dead and wounded. I'm also asking the Australian and Philippine governments for some assistance, so your people shouldn't be surprised when they arrive and find representatives of other countries here. I'm sure you understand that this project can't afford to be linked too closely to any one country, don't you, Mr. President?"

"Yes. Of course. Do you think you're going to have too many medical people there?"

"I certainly hope so, Mr. President. I sincerely hope that everyone on the ships has survived uninjured, and all the medical personnel will have to do is sit around and talk to each other, but I don't really believe that. Sir, seven navy ships sank. There must be some survivors and many of those will surely be injured. I don't even know how many people there are to pull out of the water, and the sea here is full of sharks. We've sent out boats from our marina, and our crash helicopters, but we're not set up for a situation of this magnitude and I haven't received the first report back yet. If it's all right with you, I'll keep in touch with your office by this line, and advise you as we learn more."

"That'll be fine. Anything else?"

"No, sir. Thank you. I'd better check on the rescue effort."

"Goodbye," said the President, and hung up.

She switched the video monitor to Operations. "Maurice, what's the situation in the ocean?"

"We don't know yet, Danielle. The choppers are just getting there."

"Keep me informed." She looked from the window at the wreckage of the C-130 in front of Operations. Bodies on the pavement around the plane's remains had been hastily covered with tarpaulins. In the jungle across the runway, a column of greasy black smoke marked the spot where one of the C-130s had crashed.

The base's tiny medical staff had divided itself into two teams. One went to the main hangar and began setting up a hospital to receive the injured. The other team loaded a vehicle, jumped in and headed for the marina and beach. There were only six people on each team.

Ben Bailey stuck his head into the office. "Danielle? What's going on? Mr. Goldman and I were in the Library with Miss Winters, and then we heard explosions and shouting and then there were people carrying guns, and now the office is suddenly empty."

Danielle had been monitoring the communications with Operations and the activity there. "Ben, I'm really busy right now, ... No. Wait,...do you or Beth know any first aid?"

"Sure, some."

"Find her and get down to the main hangar and help the medics there. If you can't find her, go there without her. Take Mr. Goldman and Miss Winters with you. If they're willing, I'm sure they'd be a big help. Someone tried to attack us, and there have been a lot of casualties." She turned back to her note pad, which was rapidly filling with a list of things that needed doing immediately or sooner. She didn't look to see if Bailey had left the office.

On the beach, in the Toagel Mlunguni Recreation area, near what she called the Gooney Marina, Marilyn vanDuser had been lying on a large towel under a palm tree, reading and trying to improve her tan without getting directly in the Sun. She had heard a siren a few minutes earlier, but didn't recognize it as meaning anything, and had dozed off. She was suddenly awakened by the sound of an explosion, as the remains of a large aircraft crashed into the water a few hundred feet offshore and a quarter-mile or so up the beach from where she was lying.

She was staring at the smoking wreckage protruding from the water when another explosion diverted her attention to a group of ships in the ocean a mile or so beyond the breakers along the reef. One of them was on fire and as she watched, all the rest blew up with great displays of pyrotechnics as their munitions ignited. A few minutes later, all had disappeared from sight. She was stunned by the sudden noise and destruction occurring before her eyes.

She ran to the main building at the marina, where she asked the marina manager what was going on. He was rushing around the building gathering armloads of life jackets. He turned to her and without answering her question, he snapped, "Why aren't you at your duty station?"

Marilyn protested, "But I'm on vacation. I don't *have* a duty station."

The manager wasn't impressed. "Stay out of the way," he growled, then went on collecting equipment, ignoring her. Marilyn went back outside. Aside from the crumpled wreckage of the C-130 in the water, and the marina manager's bizarre behavior, there was no indication of anything unusual. The ocean breeze was rattling the fronds in the tops of the palm trees. The ocean beyond the reef, where she had seen several ships explode only minutes earlier, was now calm and empty again, or so it appeared from shore. As she considered going back to her visitor's quarters, six cars full of people raced into view on the road from the main base, and slid to a stop in the sand a few feet from where she was standing. The occupants jumped out and ran into the marina office, then down the docks to the base's small fleet of pleasure boats, which they untied and then maneuvered rapidly out the channel through the reef.

Marilyn clutched "The Mists of Avalon" and her towel and waited. There was supposed to be a tram back to the base every half-hour, and she assumed it would be along soon. As she waited, several helicopters flew over the marina toward the ocean, turning slowly toward the North. She walked back out onto the beach to get a clearer view of them.

The ocean west of Babeldaob, viewed from the helicopters, was a mess. The surface of the water in the Toagel Mlunguni, the natural cove in the coral reef near the marina where the color of the water changed from light green to deep blue, was covered with oil slicks. From the helicopters approaching at an altitude of 500 feet, there appeared to be debris floating everywhere. As they came closer and descended, it was clear to the helicopter crews that the debris actually consisted of clusters of bodies, living and dead, drifting in their life jackets on the gentle swells of the calm sea in the lee of the island. One helicopter flew to the North, toward the Aiwakako Passage through the reef. At that location was another area of oil slicks, but there the water was rougher with fewer bodies. The chopper then flew westward to the furthest extent of the debris and bodies, descending to just a hundred feet above the sea. The pilot completed his circle to the South, all the while describing the situation to the air traffic controllers at Operations. The pilot estimated 5,000 people in the water. The co-pilot thought the number was more like 10,000. Either way, there were a lot of bodies out there, and many of them were still alive. Some of them waved for help as the helicopter flew over.

Looking back to the marina inside the reef just east of Toagel Mlunguni, the chopper pilot saw a small fleet of about two dozen boats setting out from the marina and heading for the narrow channel through the coral reef. The pilot realized the inadequacy of those boats to rescue the victims of this disaster. He called back to Operations. "Ops, Crash 3."

"Go ahead, Crash 3."

"There are some boats going out through the reef. It isn't going to work. There are too few boats and too many people in the water. Thousands. We need a ship – maybe several ships – to handle the survivors. But there may not be time for a ship to get here. Some of these folks are in real bad shape. I can see many with what looks like severe burns."

"What do you recommend, Crash 3?"

"We need to get as many vehicles as possible to the beach to use as ambulances. Helicopters can move survivors from Toagel Mlunguni to the beach at Pkulngril. Divert some of the boats to the Aiwakako Passage area. There are fewer survivors there, and the passage is nearer the shore. You'll need vehicles on shore there too, at Ngardmau, to carry survivors to the hospital. Basically, you're going to need all the wheels you can get."

"Roger, Crash 3. Medical crew will be standing by on the beach by the marina to conduct triage. Bring any survivors you pick up there."

The pilots hovered the helicopter at the surface of the water, while two of the three crewmen in the back stood on one skid and hoisted survivors from the water into the rear compartment. The third crewman grabbed a victim and dragged him into the cabin of the helicopter. They left the obviously dead. It was back-breaking work for the crewmen and extremely dangerous for the helicopter. These helicopters weren't made for water operation. There was a long swell running about two feet high, and the helicopter had to be flown upward as the swell passed underneath, then downward into the trough. The pilots knew their tail rotors were precariously close to hitting the water, and if they did, the rotor would shatter and the helicopter would spin out of control and crash into the sea. But the people in the water had to be rescued fast, and that was that.

Marilyn watched curiously as a helicopter approached the beach, then she suddenly realized it was about to land right where she was standing. She backed up into the stand of palm trees at the top of the beach and shielded her face from the blowing sand kicked up by the rotorwash. The helicopter touched down with its skids in the gentle surf and two crewmen jumped from the rear door, turned and began to lift a body from the rear compartment. They carried it up the beach to the area near the palm trees where Marilyn was standing. The pilot, sitting in the right front seat of the helicopter, yelled at the men, "Just get them out of the helicopter, don't carry them up to the trees." No one could hear him over the helicopter's engine and rotor noise.

Marilyn walked over to the man lying on the beach. His clothes had been burned off, as had much of his skin, but he was conscious. He looked up at her and tried to speak. She couldn't understand his words. They weren't English. His head was lying on the sand at an awkward angle so she folded her towel and placed it under his head and wondered what she ought to do.

The helicopter's pilot was leaning out of the door, talking to the crewmen. Another body was pulled from the helicopter and deposited on the sand a few inches above the water, then two more. Then the helicopter took off and flew back out over the ocean. Marilyn ran down to the men lying at the water's edge and found they had burns similar to the man at the top of the beach by the trees. One of them said, "Water."

Marilyn looked around. She was alone on the beach with four horribly burned men. Then she saw more helicopters coming. She ran back to the marina building, but it was deserted. On the side of the building toward the ocean, overlooking the docks, was a small cafe. She let herself behind the counter, and found a pitcher and some glasses. Filling the pitcher with water and ice, she ran back out and down to the beach. Seven more bodies had been dumped on the sand, and she realized there was a steady line of helicopters coming toward the beach to unload their grisly cargoes. The bodies and the exploding ships suddenly made sense. These people must have been on the ships! But where did the airplane come from, and why did all of the ships explode at the same time?

Marilyn went along the beach, giving a mouthful of water to each man. The water in the glass was fresh, sweet water but her tears were as salty as the sea and they ran down her cheeks unnoticed.

After a few minutes, during which more injured men were deposited on the sand and Marilyn was still the only person on the beach able to stand, a truck carrying six medics arrived. The medics found her administering water to the many men surrounding her on the sand. She had lost track of how many were lying there. "Who are you?" the chief medic demanded.

By this time, Marilyn was so upset that she could scarcely speak. "Marilyn...," she choked out.

"Never mind," said the medic abruptly. "Can you drive?"

"Ye ... Yes."

"Okay. Now you're a driver. Come with me!" He led her back to the very large truck in which some of the medics had just arrived. It had a flat cargo bed with no sides. The medics were busily removing supplies that had been piled in the center of the bed.

"Do you know how to get back to the Base from here?" the medic demanded.

"Yes," answered Marilyn, composing herself. "I know the way."

"We're going to load the truck, and you take it back to the main base. Tell the guard at the gate you need to go to the main hangar, and he'll point you in the right direction. Got that? Main Hangar!."

Marilyn nodded. She knew where the main hangar was, and she thought she knew how to get there. Past the marina, past the Pumpkin Egg Roll docks where the big ships unload, into the main gate, then left around the office building, past Operations - she knew. She got into the truck and looked at the gearshift. It wasn't an automatic. She hadn't driven a stick-shift in years, and never a big truck. She lowered her head to the steering wheel and began to sob again.

The medic came back to the driver's door and saw her crying. "What's the matter," he demanded.

"It's not an automatic."

"Well, can you drive it or not?"

"I can do it," she answered. 'I *have* to do it,' she thought. 'It'll be just like the tractor back in Nebraska.' She had driven her uncle's tractor once or twice when she was a teenager, many years before.

She looked behind her and realized the bed of the truck had been loaded with bodies of burn victims, laid alternately with the heads to the left and right. There must have been twenty bodies on the truck, and she didn't know if these bodies were alive or dead. The medic came back to the side of the truck. "Tell them at the hangar we need more trucks. *Lots* more trucks! Now, GO!"

Marilyn pushed the clutch down and shoved the gearshift lever into third gear. She carefully let out the clutch and the engine died. She pushed the clutch back down and turned the key, and the engine came back to life. She tried another gear and this time found second. Gradually releasing the clutch again, and racing the engine, she made the truck slowly begin moving, then it lurched when she removed her foot from the clutch. She ground the gears between second and third, but she *was* going to get these burned men to the main hangar somehow, even though she didn't know what was there for them.

She wiped the tears from her cheeks with the back of her gritty hand and looked back to see if there was anything behind her. She hoped she hadn't dumped anyone off the truck when it lurched. A few minutes later she was at the main gate. She spent most of the day driving the truck back and forth from the beach to the hangar, and by the third trip, she knew where all the gears were and could start without jerking or killing the engine.

Maurice was on the telephone with the Belau authorities. Yes, they had an empty barge in Koror harbor. Yes, they had a tug to move it. Yes, the ferry which usually operated between Koror and the other islands could be sent to help in the rescue effort. Ten minutes after Maurice's call, the barge was on its way across the Komebail Lagoon toward Toagel Mlunguni, but it was a 20-mile trip and the barge was only moving about five miles per hour.

After a harrowing half-hour during which the helicopter crews continued to pull the injured into the helicopters directly from the water, several boats from the marina were rafted together, and other boats began picking up injured soldiers and sailors from the water and bringing them to the small, makeshift raft. From there they were lifted into the helicopters hovering overhead. The new rescuers in the boats were a fortunate arrival for many of the survivors who were rescued, since the exhausted helicopter crewmen could not have lifted many more bodies all the way from the water into the helicopters.

After an hour, the six helicopters had brought 500 survivors to shore. But sharks were beginning to gather in the warm, clear water and across the calm ocean the screams of their victims were briefly heard.

At the Earth Base, three hours into the disaster, radar operators reported six more large aircraft approaching from the Northwest and three from the Northeast. The ones to the Northwest were 250 miles away, and closing the distance from the base at 460 miles per hour. The ones to the Northeast were only 100 miles out. The radar operator couldn't explain why she hadn't seen them earlier. Maurice called Danielle. "We have nine more bogeys. Six Northwest, 250 miles out, 400 knots. And three more Northeast, 90 miles out, also 400 knots."

"Hail them," she ordered. "And have Angelina stand by with the satellite."

Maurice picked up the microphone and nodded to the radio operator who selected the international distress frequency normally monitored by all aircraft. "Aircraft approaching Belau from the Northwest, please identify yourself."

There was a pause, then a voice came back on the speaker on the wall. "Howdy, Earth Base. This here's a U.S. Air Force Mercy Mission. We got us some Doc's and a whole hospital for y'all. What's your control tower frequency? We can't find it on our charts. Over."

Maurice breathed a sigh of relief, which was echoed by everyone listening to the radio. "Air Force, our tower frequency is one twenty-two point four."

"Roger, changing to one two two point four."

The tower radio operator changed its transmitter setting back to the Earth Base tower radio, and Maurice spoke again, "Air Force. Earth Base."

There was a pause then the same voice as before, "Earth Base, this is Air Force."

"Air Force, what's your ETA?"

"Four zero minutes."

"Roger, Air Force. Understand ETA 40 minutes." Maurice suspected the other aircraft, to the Northeast, might have monitored the conversation with the aircraft to the Northwest. He keyed the microphone again and said, "Aircraft to the Northeast of Belau, This is Earth Base. Please identify yourself."

"Earth Base. This is U.S. Air Force Airborne Sentry. We have two support aircraft with us. Over."

"Roger, Sentry. What is your ETA?"

"Earth Base, Sentry will be in your area in 10 minutes. Our support aircraft will be landing in about one five minutes, but we'll be orbiting at 30,000 feet for the next eight hours. Then we'll land for some grub and gas. Over."

"Roger, Sentry. Earth Base standing by."

A few minutes later, air traffic controllers in the tower saw two planes entering the traffic pattern for the airport. The two aircraft, a KC-10 tanker and a C-141 full of technical personnel and equipment, were soon parked on the ramp. The support aircraft for the AWACS plane were just turning off their engines when the tower controllers spotted the flight of C-5 Galaxies approaching from the North. Thirty minutes later the main hangar was a bustle of activity as hundreds of doctors, nurses, medical specialists and technicians hurried to care for the rapidly increasing number of survivors lying on the hangar floor.

Four hours after the rescue effort started, the barge arrived at Toagel Mlunguni from Koror. It was towed through the channel to the outside of the reef, then to the center of the large mass of drifting bodies, but it couldn't be anchored because the water was over a thousand feet deep. Instead, the tug remained attached to the barge by a long line, providing a gentle constant pull to hold the barge stationary against the wind and current. The tug's pilot had to maneuver the large vessel left or right from time to time to avoid running over the floating bodies drifting past. The towline stretched taut as the barge climbed the front of each swell, then sagged and dipped into the water as the swell passed beneath the barge.

Although it also was rising and falling on the swells, the barge at last provided the helicopter pilots a reasonably solid landing pad on which to set down their helicopters while the survivors were loaded for the trip to the beach. More boats had been brought from Koror to pull them from the sea. The ferry from Koror was outside Aiwakako Passage to assist in the rescue operation there, and a fleet of small boats was shuttling survivors from the water outside the Passage to shore.

In the main hangar, teams of Army and Air Force surgeons set up multiple operating rooms and were busily treating burn victims and many victims with other severe wounds. Danielle had requested and received authorization to transfer most of the burn victims to the U.S. Army's Brooke Army Hospital burn treatment center at Fort Sam Houston, Texas. The U.S. Air Force had been notified and was sending several more C-5 and C-17 aircraft to evacuate burn victims. The six planes that had arrived with the hospital unit and personnel were rapidly converted into huge flying ambulances, and as fast as they could be filled with stabilized burn patients, were taking off for the long flight across the Pacific. They would be met and refueled in mid-Pacific by tanker aircraft from Hawaii. Other air ambulance aircraft were on their way to Belau to pick up additional survivors.

On the beach, six exhausted Earth Base medics had been augmented, then relieved, by teams of fresh U.S. Army and Air Force medics, who were conducting triage under the palm trees at the top of the beach. Helicopter pilots were rotating in one-hour shifts to fly the grueling and grisly missions, moving survivors from the sea to the shore.

Near the marina, in the pavilion that had so often been the site of parties, the Army Graves Registration unit was beginning its grim job of preparing the unfortunate victims of the attack who had not survived, for their last flight back to China. Many who made it to the beach alive didn't get any farther, either because they perished there before they could be seen, or because their injuries were so massive that others with a better chance of survival were taken to the makeshift hospital in the hangar ahead of them, under the triage procedures.

Late in the afternoon, Danielle left the office to check the situation on the beach. She had turned on the video camera in the main hangar several times earlier during the day, and had observed the proceedings on the office wall video display, but each time the conditions in the makeshift hospital were so painful to watch that she soon turned it off again. She went to the ground floor, found a sedan and drove to the marina.

Conditions on the beach, she realized as soon as she arrived, were significantly worse than they were in the hangar. Medical personnel with stretchers were running to meet each helicopter as it landed. Other medical personnel on the floating barge had already classified the victims, and as the new arrivals were unloaded from the choppers, the personnel on-shore began treatment. A significant number of victims awaited the trip to the main hangar.

She stood by the side of the road near the marina office, where the stretchers with victims were waiting. A large white truck came around the curve into the recreation area, looped through the parking lot and pulled up next to the queue of injured. The driver, a woman with a dirty tear-stained face and disheveled blonde hair, looked familiar. She suddenly realized it was Marilyn, her travel agent! Uniformed military personnel were busily lifting stretchers with their unfortunate occupants onto the rear of the truck. Marilyn saw Danielle standing at the front of the truck, opened the door to get out, and fell to the ground as she tried to step down from the cab. Danielle ran around the truck to the door and helped Marilyn to her knees. Marilyn was clearly exhausted, and began crying again. Danielle knelt by her and held her in a gentle hug. "You poor dear. How long have you been doing this?"

Marilyn couldn't give a coherent answer. The trauma of the day's events had used up all her energy. The last several trips had been accomplished on will power alone. She couldn't speak or stand. Just then, a soldier ran to the cab and said, "Let's *Go!* Get this truck out of here!" Another truck had pulled up and was being loaded with victims.

Danielle looked up at the soldier and said, "Help me get her into the truck." He paused, and she said, "Do it *NOW!*"

The soldier recognized a command when he heard one. Together, they lifted Marilyn to her feet and around to the passenger side of the truck, where she was helped into the cab.

Danielle climbed into the driver's door, put the truck in gear, and drove out of the recreation area toward the main base. Marilyn had gathered her strength again and tried to direct her to the makeshift receiving area, which medical corpsmen had established in front of the center of the huge hangar. Danielle already knew where it was. She had been watching it all afternoon from her window. The truck was unloaded while she waited and it was then reloaded with empty stretchers. She drove to the Operations office. Just inside the door, Maurice instructed someone to help get Marilyn down from the cab and into the now-vacant Earth Base infirmary. There she found an unoccupied bed and instructed Marilyn to lie down and take a nap. Danielle walked back into the Ops office, and told Maurice, "When she wakes up, be sure she gets to the cafeteria for something to eat. I need someone else to drive this truck, and we still need more trucks to carry survivors from the beach. There's a backlog down there and we may be able to save more of them if we can get them to the hangar faster."

Maurice had set up a pool of personnel, composed of all the mechanics, engineers, housekeepers, secretaries, etc., who were not otherwise occupied on the emergency. They were waiting to relieve other shifts of rescue workers. Their assembly area was inside the employee cafeteria, where they awaited their next job assignments. Maurice picked up his radio and said, "Personnel, I need someone to drive a truck. Have them standing by at the driveway. The truck will be over to get them." He didn't wait for a confirmation.

Danielle drove to the cafeteria entrance of the building, where there was a group of people standing on the sidewalk waiting for their rides to their next job. She yelled out the open passenger window, "Where's that truck driver?"

"Here I am!" came a loud voice. A tall middle-aged man pushed through the group on the sidewalk. It was Adrian Goldman.

"Get in," she said. Goldman opened the passenger door and climbed into the cab. He was startled to realize the driver of the truck was the woman whom he had arrived that morning to depose.

"Miss Simones, what happened?" he asked. "One minute we were taking a deposition and the next minute all Hell broke loose."

"Yes," she said. "That's exactly what happened. Are you okay? Have you had a chance to eat?"

"I'm fine. Deborah knows first-aid and she's working on burn victims in the hangar, but they didn't need me because I don't know anything about first-aid, so I went back to the personnel managers to see what else I can do to help. We had dinner a while ago."

"Can you drive this truck?"

"I guess. If you'll show me the shift pattern."

Danielle demonstrated the shift pattern as she went through the gears driving out the main gate. "Pay attention to the route," she said. "It would be hard to get lost. Just stay on the main road. We go by the docks, and to the recreation area. Loop through the parking lot, and stop where the soldiers have the stretchers waiting. Come back to the big hangar the same way. Can you do it?"

"I've got it."

She stopped the truck and soldiers immediately removed the empty stretchers from the flat bed at the rear and started lifting stretchers loaded with more burned bodies onto the truck. Goldman slid over under the steering wheel and she looked up at him. "Thank you, Mr. Goldman. We appreciate your help. I'll have someone take over for you in a few hours, so you can have a break."

She walked away from the road, back to the beach and surveyed the operation. The six helicopters were still shuttling constantly from the barge that was just visible on the horizon, to the beach and back to the barge. At the end of the beach opposite the marina, there was a growing accumulation of dead men lying in rows along the sand. She watched as two men with a stretcher came down to the beach, loaded a body on the stretcher and carried it back to the pavilion. She followed them to the pavilion, and asked the first soldier she saw to tell her who was in charge. He directed her toward a young female sergeant standing at the entrance of the pavilion. She looked too innocent for such grim work.

"Sergeant," Danielle said, "I'm the base coordinator. Can you give me any idea how many dead there are?"

"No, ma'am," the sergeant answered formally, "but we've already processed three hundred today, and there are at least that many more down on the beach. We don't know how many more are still out there...," she gestured toward the ocean. "We think the rescue people are passing up any who look dead and trying to rescue only the live ones. If that's true, it means the ones here died since they were fished out of the water. I'm sorry, ma'am."

"I understand. Thank you, Sergeant. By the way, have you seen a Chinese officer around? He should have at least two other people with him."

"Yes, ma'am, I saw him several times today, but I don't know where he is now. Sorry, ma'am."

"Yes, thank you," Danielle said. She walked back to her sedan in the parking area, and picked up the radio. It was set on the frequency for ground operations. "Operations, this is Simones."

Maurice's voice came back, "Go ahead, Danielle."

"Maurice, do you know where Colonel Zhang is?"

"No. Wait one, I'll find out." There was a pause and Maurice said, "Jorge, Ops."

Somewhere Jorge Sanchez keyed his microphone and said, "Go ahead, Ops."

"Jorge, where is the Chinese colonel right now?"

"He's with me in bay three of the main hangar."

Maurice's voice said, "Did you copy that, Danielle?"

"Roger, Maurice. Jorge, this is Simones. Please ask the colonel to wait there for me."

"I'll do that, Miss Simones." The radio was silent again.

Danielle drove back to the main hangar. At the rear of bay three, Colonel Zhang was sweaty and disheveled, moving around between the stretchers, stooping and giving encouragement to the injured soldiers. She waited while he finished speaking with a row of soldiers, then stopped him. "Colonel, can you come with me? Please." Her vehicle was parked at the side of the hangar. The Chinese soldier and Jorge Sanchez, whom Maurice had assigned to accompany the colonel and serve as a liaison between the colonel and the base, followed and got into the rear seat of the sedan. She drove the group to the office building and escorted them to the top floor. As they passed the library, she said, "Colonel, please have your man wait here with Mr. Sanchez." The colonel spoke a few words of Chinese to the soldier, and the soldier and Sanchez walked into the library and sat down. She and the colonel walked on down the hall to her office. She stopped at Bill's desk and asked, "Anything?"

Bill shook his head, confirming the absence of a further response from the Chinese government as she opened the office door for the officer, and said, "Please sit down, Colonel. I'm sure you're tired. This has been a very difficult day, for both of us." The colonel found a chair and sat on the edge of the seat, rigidly at attention.

"Please, Colonel, relax. I asked you to come here because I thought you might wish to contact your superiors and report in. I called the Chinese government this morning, right after you left my office, and informed them that their ships and planes had exploded. I also said I expected there would be some wounded personnel and invited them to send medical and other humanitarian support for the injured, as well as to take charge of the remains of those who have been killed.

"Unfortunately, I've had no call back from your government, and I'm becoming concerned that either they didn't believe me, or that they're planning another attack on this base. Also, since this morning, I asked the American military to assist in treating the victims of this disaster - you've seen the American personnel who are working here - and I've sent several plane-loads of your injured men to the United States for treatment of their burns. I did this without consulting you or your government, and perhaps they'll understand better if *you* explain to them about the condition of the men and their need for treatment. I particularly want to insure that there's no repetition of this morning's attempt to take over this facility, as it would only cause more loss of life."

The colonel sat silently for some time. Then he said, "I must report my failure to my superiors."

Danielle looked at the dusty, sweaty man, in his rumpled uniform, proud and authoritative so recently, but now dejected and overwhelmed by the loss of his command, and said, "Colonel, it was not a failure of yours which caused this disaster. You handled this situation with great credit to yourself and to your men. The fundamental error was made by those who sent you to 'annex' this facility. When I asked you this morning, Colonel, if you wanted to surrender, I wasn't making a joke. It was your mistake to think I was, and that faulty conclusion of yours sealed the fate of your men, but that was a minor mistake compared to the decision of those who sent you here. You didn't have a chance to take this base, Colonel, you never did. Unfortunately for your men. Now, to whom would you like to speak? I'll have my secretary call them for you."

The colonel named a senior officer in the Chinese Army, and told where he could probably be found. Danielle relayed the information to Bill, who had the colonel's senior officer on the telephone a few minutes later.

The Chinese officer sat across the room from Danielle as he made his report to his superior. When it appeared the conversation was drawing to a close, she spoke to the colonel, "Remind them we need their medical personnel, as well as personnel to attend to the dead."

The colonel spoke again, briefly, to the person on the telephone and then hung up and looked at her. "They will send medical personnel. They say to dispose of the dead bodies here."

Her response was immediate. "Colonel, I don't operate that way, and I won't have that manner of behavior dictated to me. The bodies of those who have been killed today will be sent home to their families, for a proper funeral. If your superiors won't see to it, I'll have to ask the Chinese government to do so, and if they won't do it either, I'll take care of it myself." She paused to catch her breath, then said, "Hell, I don't even know what the proper rituals are, I guess some of these men would be Buddhist, wouldn't they?"

"Perhaps," the colonel answered.

She went over to her desk and punched the intercom. "Bill, get me the Chinese Prime Minister again." She turned back to the colonel. "Colonel Zhang, may I get you a beverage? Coffee, tea perhaps, ... a soft drink?"

"No, thank you. You are very kind."

A few minutes later, Bill's voice came over the intercom, "Prime Minister, line one."

She touched the button for line one and said, "Hello, Mr. Prime Minister?"

Of course the person on the other end was a secretary and not the Prime Minister. "Please hold for the Prime Minister."

She was determined to be polite but firm. She put the call on the speaker phone and said, "Mr. Prime Minister, I'm calling because I had not heard back from you and need to know what the Chinese government is doing about this situation." She waited for his response.

"Ah, yes, Miss Simones. Since your call this morning I have attempted to verify your story. Unfortunately, our military forces have been unable to reach their commanders, and I am waiting for them to confirm your information. You must agree, it does sound slightly, - how do you say? - hard to believe."

"Mr. Prime Minister, your military can't reach their naval commanders because their ships are lying on the bottom of the ocean in a thousand feet of water. I have sitting in my office the officer who led this misadventure this morning. He can tell you exactly what the situation is. His name is Colonel Zhang. Please say hello to him - but Mr. Prime Minister?" ... she paused.

"Yes?" he asked.

"We all speak English," she said. "Keep your conversation in English, please."

"Of course," the Prime Minister said. "Colonel, can you hear me?"

"Yes, sir."

"What is the situation there? What has happened today?"

"Sir, I arrived here at ten thirty this morning, and informed the personnel in charge of the airfield that I was taking control of the installation, pursuant to my orders. I was then invited to meet with the commander of the installation, to make appropriate arrangements. I was escorted to the office from which I am now speaking, where I informed this woman, Miss Simones, of my orders. She invited me to surrender, and when I did not, she asked me to join her looking from her window at the airfield. As I looked from the window, my command aircraft parked on the airfield apron suddenly exploded, as did another airplane that was providing airborne cover for our ground forces. Our third airplane apparently experienced the same disaster, although I did not observe it explode as I did the other two. I have seen its wreckage, however, which is some distance offshore in the lagoon west of the island. All of the personnel in both of the flying aircraft were surely killed either when those aircraft exploded, or when they hit the ground. There are ... were, six survivors from my own aircraft, myself and my sergeant, and four others who were outside the aircraft when it exploded. One of those has died this afternoon from his injuries. The other three may survive, although they are badly burned. They have been sent by Miss Simones to the United States, to a special hospital for treatment of burn victims."

"What about the ships? Miss Simones spoke of ships."

"Yes, Sir. This task force included three heavy cruisers and four guided-missile frigates. All of them were fully armed and ready for combat. In addition to their crews, they carried 6,000 marines for an amphibious landing. I did not see what happened to them, but I understand they exploded and sank. The civilians on this island have been bringing ashore survivors from the ships all day, and there is a very large hangar full of severely injured personnel from the ships. American military medical forces arrived several hours after the explosions, and they have been treating as many injuries as they can. Many burn victims have been sent to America on large aircraft and others have died. I cannot say how many."

"How many casualties did your forces inflict, Colonel? What damage to the installation?" The Prime Minister couldn't believe his ears.

"None, Sir."

"Which do you mean, no casualties or no damage?"

"I mean both, Sir. We did not fire a single shot. There was no opportunity. One moment everything was under control, and the next moment, the only persons uninjured were my sergeant and myself. We had no opportunity to take any action, and after the loss of all our forces, there would have been no purpose."

"Of course. Who is your commanding officer?"

The colonel gave the Prime Minister the name of his superior and advised the Prime Minister that he had just briefed his commander.

"I will speak with him," said the Prime Minister.

"Mr. Prime Minister," Danielle interrupted, "there is some business to which you must immediately attend. We need your medical personnel here immediately to assist the American medical personnel in treating your injured soldiers and sailors. The American capabilities are limited, and the number of your injured is very large. I estimate we may have 5,000 injured men lying on our hangar floor as we speak and many more are still being pulled from the sea. Many of them will die of their injuries if they are not promptly treated, but the Americans are too few to handle the treatment. We must have Chinese medical personnel and equipment, and lots of it. I re-emphasize, Sir, there are *thousands* of severely injured men here. We could use several hundred doctors, surgeons, plus an equal number of nurses, medics, whatever you call them, and medical supplies.

"In addition, there are many dead, and the Americans are working to prepare the dead for shipment back to China. Their abilities are not equal to the task, Sir. Dead bodies are accumulating on the beach, and those are only the ones who appeared to be alive when they were pulled from the water and expired during the trip to shore. There are many more dead Chinese soldiers and sailors floating in the ocean in their life jackets, and we will recover those bodies, as soon as we believe we have pulled in all of those who are still alive.

"We *must* have immediate Chinese assistance for the American graves registration personnel. That includes equipment and supplies, and they must arrive today, Sir. When Colonel Zhang spoke to his superior a few minutes ago, he was told to leave the dead here. I haven't asked what that would amount to specifically, but in any case, it is not acceptable. Chinese personnel must come here, today, and attend to the injured and prepare the dead for return to their families. Then the Chinese military must transport the dead back to China. I insist on it. Am I making myself clear, Mr. Prime Minister?"

"Well, Miss Simones, you must understand that the disposition of remains of Chinese military personnel is entirely within the authority of the Chinese military leaders. You...."

Danielle was furious and interrupted him again. "Sir, you seriously misunderstand me. I am *not* giving Chinese military leaders any choice, nor am I offering any choice to you, Sir. All of these dead and injured must be treated appropriately according to their condition and returned to China. If your government cannot see its way clear to do so, I will insure that the personnel here do all they can to save as many lives as we can, and I will personally return the dead to their homes. If you fail to act, I will personally contact the families of all of these personnel and inform them of the shameful behavior of your government and military. Attacking an unarmed civilian installation, indeed! It is disgraceful! I assure you, Sir, I am fully capable of making an international incident of this, which will revive the world's memories of Pearl Harbor or Nanking. It will be the kind of situation that topples governments, Sir, if that is what you want. I called you earlier and attempted to describe this situation in a way that would allow your government to save face. I will not do that again. What is it to be? Have I made myself clear?"

"Ah, yes, of course. Please be assured, Miss Simones, that I was only speaking theoretically regarding the authority of our commanders. Of course we will be sending medical and - what did you call them? Grave ...?"

"Graves registration. They prepare the dead for return to their families."

"Yes, of course. We will send those personnel also. How many did you think would be needed?"

"200 graves registration personnel. Assume they have to process 5,000 bodies. And send enough caskets and supplies for that many. By air, and today.

"Then," she continued, "we also need at least 100 surgeons and an equal number of nurses, along with operating room equipment and hospital supplies. Again, by air and today."

"I'm sure they are already preparing to load onto aircraft to bring them there, Miss Simones."

"I'm glad to hear that, Sir. There's just one more thing."

"What would that be?"

"There is a colonel sitting in my office, and a sergeant who has accompanied him. I want your assurances that they will not be held responsible for the disaster which occurred today. I'm sure you realize, because of the suddenness of the loss that occurred here, the ships and planes that exploded were probably sabotaged before they left China. I was standing by the colonel when his aircraft blew up. I vouch for his performance. It was clearly not his fault and he has conducted himself very honorably."

"That will be a decision which must be made by the military."

"I'm sure you can be very persuasive with the military in such a matter, can't you, Sir? I *do* insist on it and I rely on your doing whatever is necessary."

"I'll see what I can do," the Prime Minister said.

"Thank you, Sir," she said. "When should we expect your medical and graves registration personnel to arrive?"

"I will call you back and advise you," he said.

"Thank you, Sir. You may obtain our number from my secretary, so please hold for him." The Chinese Prime Minister was probably not used to being on hold to wait for a secretary.

"Bill," Danielle said into the intercom, "the Prime Minister is holding on line one for our phone number. Be sure to give him the London number." The commercial phone connections from China to London were better than those to Belau. She turned back to the colonel, whose spirits were obviously very low.

"Colonel, that should take care of your government for a while. You and I have people to attend to in the hangar. I'll drive you back. Your helpers are in the library. Get them as we go by. By the way, have you eaten anything today? You *must* eat. Your men need to see you strong and confident. You're their leader. They need your demonstration of confidence to help them pull through their injuries. We'll stop at Operations, get you a jump suit and arrange for your uniform and that of your sergeant to be cleaned and pressed before you go back there. While we're waiting for the uniforms, you and your sergeant, and Mr. Sanchez, will come with me to the cafeteria for some food." The colonel started to protest, but she interrupted him. "Don't argue with me, Colonel. In case you haven't noticed, I *am* in charge here, and you really haven't any choice. That's better." She led the sergeant and Sanchez to the car and the four of them drove to Operations.

CHAPTER 68

May 31

Clean-up work after the attempted takeover was continuing. The first Chinese planes arrived at midnight of May 21 with medical and graves registration personnel. On the second day, more Chinese personnel arrived and began the task of recovering remains from the two crashed aircraft. Danielle received regular status reports from Maurice on the rescue and medical treatment operations. There were only a few less seriously injured men still in the main hangar, awaiting transportation to China. Chinese medical personnel and most of the American medics had departed. All of the coolers at the commissary, which had been hurriedly emptied of food and refilled with corpses, had been cleaned out as the bodies were returned to China. Toagel Mlunguni and the Aiwakako Passage were quiet as before, except for numerous oil slicks on the surface, the result of fuel leaking from the sunken ships.

Danielle sent letters to the American and Belau governments, thanking them for their assistance in responding to the disaster. She knew there would be large bills coming for the cost of the fuel, personnel and supplies used in the operation and wondered how much it was costing for the several thousand burn victims being treated in Texas. Then she made a note to make it a charge against future Chinese royalties from the power system and dismissed it from her mind.

Cliff Kelly had come to Belau from London as soon as he learned of the attack. He was very worried when he arrived at her office, but his calm exterior would have fooled anyone who didn't know him. He sat down on the couch across from the desk, kicked off his shoes, and put his feet on the coffee table. "Well,... you've really done it now," he said.

"I know," she replied, a little depressed. "I didn't want to, but it was either that or hand over the base. I don't know if our employees would have been willing to give up without a fight, and a lot of them might have been injured or killed.... No. It's more than that. *I* wasn't willing to give up without a fight. I thought I could overwhelm them – and I was right." There was something about the way she said it that made Kelly realize that she was trying to rationalize her actions to justify them to herself, despite the fact that thousands of people had been killed.

"What are you going to do now?" he asked.

"I don't know. I'm not sure any more. Things are moving too fast." She had tried to work out all the factors in her mind. The note pad on the desk was full of diagrams, depicting relationships between various parties and how her actions or the project's actions impacted each of them. She could find no coherent rationale for organizing the mess.

"What the Chinese precipitated was probably going to be necessary all along," Cliff said. "We should have seen it and discussed it before now."

"What should we have discussed?" she asked. "I thought we had already discussed all the possibilities."

Kelly didn't answer, but said, "What kind of defensive capability do the satellites have?"

"What do you mean?"

"I mean, if the United States or Russia, or Japan or China, or anyone else starts firing missiles at them, can you stop the missiles before they get close enough to harm a satellite?"

"Maurice says we can," she answered. "Some debris might get through if the missile were on a trajectory heading directly for the satellite when it was hit by our beam. Remember, even with carefully guided navigation in our tugs, it still takes a considerable amount of precise course adjustment to match orbits with the station. It's a big place out there. I've never tried to consider what kind of a course would be required for a simple collision. I guess if someone were trying to blow up a satellite, they'd only have to get a thermonuclear warhead in the vicinity of the satellite. We've been operating on the premise that no one who understands the value of the satellites would intentionally destroy even one of them. Maybe that's not a valid assumption."

Cliff didn't respond to her discussion of the likelihood of a power satellite becoming a target for an attack. Instead he said, "Is it?"

"Is what?"

"Is it a big place out there?" he asked.

"Sure it is. What do you mean? Of course it is! What are you saying?"

"Is it a place? Isn't it just a lot of absence of stuff, the vacuum of Space?"

"It *is* a vacuum. But it's also a place. Of course it's a place! I have a deed to it, don't I? From the U.N. and all the member nations."

"So it *is* a place," Kelly continued. "Do people live there?"

"Yes. Of course. There are over 500 people at each of the satellites still under construction, that's 1,500 people, plus the 40 person operation staff at Web 1, plus the crews on the low earth satellites and the tug crews - over 1,600 hundred people. So what?"

Kelly looked intently at her. "What government are those people under? Who makes their laws and settles their disputes?"

"I do," she answered, "... I guess. I handle personnel problems if Laurie asks me to. Sometimes she's too close to the people involved to side with one or another of them. That's about all the disputes we have. We have some simple rules of conduct to insure that people's privacy is protected. Nothing complicated."

"Then you, I mean *you*, Danielle Marie Elizabeth Margaret Simones, are their government. Who elected you?"

"Me? ... I wasn't elected. I'm just in charge. I mean, someone has to be, don't they?"

"I don't know," said Kelly. "Do they?"

"Of course they do. Without someone in charge, the project wouldn't have any direction. We wouldn't have gotten even Web 1 finished. But I'm not the government."

"I think you are, and trying to deny it won't wash. You are the *de facto* government, and, if your 'deed' is valid, I think you are the *de jure* government as well. *You* own space, through your network of corporations and trusts, and *you* rule it. *You* are its government, and it is *your* 'country.' You have residents, who are at least semi-permanent; you have 'government', which maintains law and order within the governed jurisdiction, even if the government is just you doing what you must to have the project succeed; and you have the ability to defend the Space you control. You have the essential characteristics of an independent nation."

"You're joking."

"No. I wish I were. I thought about it before I left London, and a lot more on the plane on my way here, and I'm convinced it's the only way out of this situation. I wish we had thought of this a week before the attack."

"Thought of what?" she asked. She still hadn't caught on.

"It's time for you to announce the formation of a sovereign state of Space. You have to think of a proper name for it."

"I think you just did. 'The Sovereign State of Space'. How's that sound?" She was still joking.

"Too pompous. Besides, 'Space' is too all encompassing a term. It means anything you define as occupying volume. You need some term which is more specific to exclude anything on the surface of the Earth."

"How about the 'State of Outer Space'?" she asked.

"That's good. That's very good. It can also be abbreviated 'S-O-S', which pretty accurately describes our present situation. So, ... if we have a name for our new country, ... does that sound right? 'Country'? That word - 'country' - implies land. I don't think it fits. We'd better be sure to use the term 'nation' when we talk about this thing, whatever it is."

Danielle was shaking her head in disbelief. "I can't believe you're serious, Cliff. Tell me you're putting me on."

"I'm very serious. It may be the only thing which will prevent you being brought up before the World Court for your unprovoked attack on those innocent Chinese ships."

"What?!" she jumped to her feet. "What unprovoked attack? You know full well they were attacking us!"

"Were they? Can you prove it? Remember the sabotage on your airplane right after the project started? You couldn't prove that either."

"I have tapes of the Colonel demanding the surrender of the base and stating that the ships and planes had soldiers to take over the Earth Base. There was a court reporter in here when the attack started, and she had left the audio recorder portion of her dictation machine running." She sat back down at the desk, stunned.

"That might be enough to get a verdict in your favor, after a long and nasty public trial. I'm hoping, if we move fast enough, we can avoid that eventuality."

"How?"

"If you declare the independent State of Outer Space today, how many countries around the world would recognize you as the legitimate government?"

"I don't know."

"Would Belau?"

"I think so. Bert has helped us a lot, and he understands how important the project is to the future of humanity. ... He's a very concerned person about the problems of society generally. ... And the project has been good to Belau. I think he'd recommend recognition, and the Belau Assembly would ratify it. The countries that are receiving power from us would probably also recognize us."

"Okay. I'll have the legal staff draw up a Declaration of Independence and the recognition papers. We want Earth Base to be the seat of government."

"Can we do that? Doesn't the seat of government have to be in the governed territory?"

"There you go again. 'Territory,' from the Latin word 'terra,' means 'land.' We aren't talking 'territory' here, but 'Space' - 'Outer Space' to be exact. And, to answer your question, no, you don't have to have your seat of government within the governed place. History is replete with governments-in-exile which were recognized by the international community even though they operated from another country. We once had a city called 'Islandia' on a group of islands in Florida, and virtually all the voters lived on the mainland. The elections were held three counties away."

"All right. So what do we have to do?" she asked.

"Call Bert. Ask him to come over here. We'll outline the basics of the plan to him and ask him to support it. His big motivation will be that, without this approach, Belau could continue to be the pawn in a giant chess game, and more lives could be lost here, including those of Belauans. There's been enough war here in the last century. If Belau agrees, we'll begin contacting other countries that have receiving antennas or major contracts building components for the project. They'll have a big incentive to go along with us and recognize this new 'nation.' We'll keep it quiet for as long as we can, then when it can't be continued without becoming public knowledge, we'll petition the U.N. for full membership; perhaps even membership on the Security Council."

"Will it work?"

"I certainly hope so. Our argument is that the Earth Base facility is the 'sovereign territory' of an independent nation, by lease from the Belau government, just as an embassy of one country in another country is the 'sovereign territory' of the foreign country. When the Chinese attacked the Earth Base by landing their plane here and demanding its surrender, it was an attack against the State of Outer Space, which required immediate action to repulse." Kelly stopped, then continued, "Does anyone know why or how the Chinese force was destroyed?"

"We haven't told anyone of this capability, outside of our Operations people, and a few computer programmers and designers. ... Hell, I don't know," she said, "maybe the whole base knows about the military capability of the satellite."

"Satellite? You said '_the_ satellite'? Is Web 3 the only one with this capability?"

"No, I mis-spoke. All the satellites have it. Even the low earth orbit satellites have been fitted with a rudimentary system, but they have neither the photovoltaic area, nor the right size antenna to broadcast a really powerful beam. We hit those ships with a full two-and-a-half gigawatts from Web 3. The LEO satellites would be hard-pressed to come up with a few megawatts of power from their photovoltaic arrays, and when they're eclipsed, which is almost half of the time, they must run on battery or fuel-cell power, which gives them relatively low power, only a few hundred kilowatts. The most we expect from a beam from a small power source like that is to disrupt an attacker's electronics. Of course, they aren't entirely defenseless during all the time they're in eclipse, because they are within view of one or more Webs part of that time as well, so the Web that has them in view can provide some protection. We have to be careful with that though, as well, because a beam fired from one of the Webs at a missile attacking a LEO satellite will continue past its target and burn anything else it touches. As a result, we can only fire on targets around the LEO satellites when the satellite is over water, to avoid inadvertently burning someone on the Earth's surface. Even that isn't risk-free. We might accidentally hit a ship if it happened to be in the path of the beam."

"So, many of the employees know," Cliff said. "What about outsiders? Hasn't your purchase of the radars you need to locate, identify and aim at your targets generated any questions in the global military community?"

"We've tried to avoid that, and think it has worked so far, by buying them through Global Aeronautique Internationale. They are supposed to be for a hush-hush military project for a small nation no one has heard of," she said.

"You're right."

"What?"

"You're right," he said. "You're correct. The small nation no one has heard of is the State of Outer Space."

"We've suggested to China and others that the ships must have been sabotaged before they left to come here, but even so," she said, "once the fact of all the ships and planes blowing up at almost the same time gets out, someone will figure out what we have in the way of a weapon. When that happens, we need to be able to frame an appropriate response."

"We won't answer such conjecture," said Kelly. "It's simple. The State of Outer Space has classified the use and operation of the satellites and no one without a 'need to know' and proper clearance has or will get access to the information. We simply don't acknowledge that there is any defensive or offensive capability. Questions about military uses only get a 'no comment.'"

"Get the documents drafted and I'll look them over," she said. "When they're in final form, I'll call Bert and invite him over to visit my office. How soon can I expect the finals?"

"This afternoon. We aren't writing the Magna Carta. Just a simple Declaration of Independence, and a document giving political recognition to you and your new nation. Congratulations! I think you should pass out cigars, or something."

She put her elbows on her desk and held her head. She didn't want this. She didn't need this. "Cliff, can't we avoid going through this charade?"

"It isn't a charade, Danielle," he answered soberly. "This result was probably unavoidable from the moment your first space plane flew successfully. You – your nation, that is – meets all the criteria for an independent nation. I guess you have one option left. You could turn it all over to some other power to run. How about the United Nations? Remember the Moon being claimed as the 'common heritage of mankind'? I sort of liked the way you finessed them out of that contrived concept, but you *could* give it back. Do you think they'd run it better than you can?"

"My God, NO!" she exclaimed. "The whole world is a mess, except where we have our receiving antennas, or countries using our power. They, that is, each of those countries who receive our power, are required to maintain peaceful conditions within their country in order to continue receiving power. Africa is peaceful for the first time in modern history and is beginning to get both its population and food supply under control. Literacy levels there are up forty percent. It's really amazing to me. And we've only been beaming commercial power to Africa for a few years.

"India, Pakistan, Bangladesh and China are all getting along quite well together too, and I believe it's all because we can now, or will be able to in the future, cut off their power if they don't. In fact, several dictators have turned their governments over to democratically elected assemblies as a result of our refusal to allow them to get on the power grid under their military governments. We couldn't risk the threat of revolutionaries damaging our facilities."

"So they've traded one dictator for another, haven't they?" Cliff asked.

"What do you mean?" she asked. "You mean *me*? I'm not a dictator...," she paused "... am I?"

"If the shoe fits," he answered, "you're it, Cinderella."

"*No!*"

"Yes," Cliff said. "Sorry, but if it makes you feel any better, we're all in it together. We made it happen. The whole team, I mean. I don't want to be telling the newest dictator what to do, but I have a suggestion."

"I might as well listen, I guess," she said reluctantly. "Does it get worse?"

"That all depends on your perspective. My suggestion is that you need to be figuring out how this power you have created is going to be managed when you aren't around to do it any longer."

"Easy," she replied and laughed. "I appoint you as my successor, and I quit."

"Not that easy, I'm afraid. First, I don't want the job, and wouldn't take it if it were handed to me on a silver platter. But more importantly, whatever system you come up with needs to be free from the kind of manipulation that oil cartels used in the past to control prices. And you have a virtually unlimited military power with which an irresponsible person could terrorize the entire globe. You need to guard against that kind of abuse by your successors."

"But how can I protect against that?"

"I don't know," he answered. "I said it wouldn't be easy. But you may have another element to work with before too long. Tell me, how soon can the system begin to provide power to Western Europe?"

"Not for maybe ten years. We're going to power most of Africa and a lot of Asia with the four Webs now either on line or under construction, but the Greenwich Web, at zero degrees, will be the sixth to be built, and it's supposed to be the first one we build with lunar materials. To do that we have to build and test the lunar mining and fabrication facilities. Once they're operating, we'll build Webs 6 through 12 fairly rapidly and begin construction of the city in orbit at the LaGrange location in space known as 'L-5', in the Moon's orbit sixty degrees ahead of the Moon. Western Europe won't have Web power for - this is just a rough guess - at least ten years. That's five years to set up the lunar mining and fabrication facility and five years for Web construction. Why do you ask?"

"This is just a hunch, understand," he said, "but I think your power is going to have another impact you didn't anticipate. How much are you going to charge the European Community for electricity?"

"Same as everyone else pays, ten cents a kilowatt-hour, delivered to their grid as alternating current. So what?"

"The 'so what' is in the 'same as everyone else pays,' Danielle. I think you're on the brink of becoming the world monetary standard. Is there any reason for your price for electricity to increase over time?"

"None that I can think of. Our contracts are locked in for materials through Web 5, and for most of the materials we have to buy for the lunar facility. We make our own fuels from water. We produce our own electric power. When the lunar facility is operating, we won't need Terran materials any longer, or at least most construction materials will be mined on the Moon, which I also own. There may be some metals, such as titanium for more space planes, which we'll have to buy if we can't find them in Space, but that's not a big part of the cost of the power. And our power source is free to us, of course. I don't foresee any need for future increases. No."

"That's what I suspected. So the solar satellite power system will stabilize the global price of energy, at ten kilowatts to the U.S. dollar. I think the whole international monetary system is going to lock into that price. No longer will any commodity, gold, petroleum, or anything else that has to be shipped from one place to another, be able to push the price of local currency higher or lower. If I'm right, you've inadvertently hit on the most stabilizing influence the world has ever seen. I'll bet you that in ten years, if we're both here to see it, we'll find the entire world economy will be as settled as Africa's political structure is becoming right now."

"That would be nice, but how about my Declaration of Independence? I want to call Bert right away."

"Yes, Boss. I'll have the draft to you in a couple of hours. If it's okay, you can call Bert then." Cliff left the office.

Danielle stood and walked to the window. On the pavement in front of Operations, paving crews were busy repairing the area where the C-130 had exploded and burned. Several C-5 transports and the KC-10 and C-141 support aircraft were parked with the off-station AWACS plane. A space plane was turning onto final approach to land at Earth Base. Just another day in Paradise. She went back to her desk and stared into the forest on the wall across from her. Water was dripping from the leaves of giant ferns. It reminded her of Guernsey and the fog from the Atlantic Ocean, and made her homesick.

CHAPTER 69

May 6

Almost two years had passed since the abortive Chinese attack on the Earth Base. Felix O'Brian and his syndicate had dropped their lawsuit. Danielle didn't know if it had anything to do with Adrian Goldman's experience during the Chinese attack, but he never attempted to complete her deposition. John Fitzgerald (Jomo) Williams was now the representative from Outer Space to the United Nations. Helen Overmeyer was Danielle's representative with the World Bank. More receiving antennas were being constructed across Africa, Asia and Australia, and throughout the islands in the Indian and Pacific Oceans. Webs 3 and 4 were fitted with many very small transmitting antennas to serve the many small islands in the Western Pacific. Web 3 was operating at full power following its completion and Webs 2 and 4 were in various stages of construction.

Uncle Bob arrived in Belau and Danielle welcomed him into her office. "Uncle Bob! I thought you'd never get here. I want to tell you about what's been happening. There's been so much progress,...." She stopped. "How'd you like to go for a ride? I want to talk with you about a new idea."

"I'm always ready to listen to your ideas, dear," he said. "You know that. What's your idea this time?"

"I don't want to tell you yet. Can you wait a while?"

"Whenever you're ready. Where're we going?"

"To Space. Are you game?"

"I'm an old man. I'll be 85 this year, you know."

"I know, and we'll have a big party here for your birthday." She turned to the desk and punched the intercom. "Bill, notify Operations that Bob MacDonald and I will be on the flight to LEO-A at fourteen hundred. We'll be going on board the station for an hour or so. Remind them to put suits on the plane for us. We'll drive over."

"I'll tell them."

She turned off the intercom. Operations kept personal pressure suits ready for all of the executives, and one for MacDonald, courtesy of his favorite god-daughter. "We better be getting to Operations if we don't want to miss the plane." She held open the office door as he walked from the office into the hallway. As she passed Bill Townsend she said to him, "Are you two going to come over for dinner tonight? We're having a cook-out and it would be wonderful to have Marion's potato salad."

Bill answered quickly. "I think she'll be agreeable to that. I'll call and make sure. If there's any problem with her schedule, I'll get on the radio to you. She'll probably be glad to get out."

Uncle Bob and Danielle boarded the space plane and were soon nearing the LEO satellite. They donned their pressure suits and transferred into the station, where they removed their helmets and floated weightless in the crew's living area. Hank Taylor, the pilot of the plane, was with them.

Danielle pulled Uncle Bob over to the large viewport and looked down at the Earth, slowly sliding by below.

"It certainly is beautiful, isn't it," he said. "Every time I come up here, I can't believe how beautiful it is. Did you want me to see something in particular?"

"Yes. I knew this orbit would take us over a particular location." She handed him a pair of binoculars. "Look there. There's Florida, and South of it, Cuba, and to the Southeast, Hispanola. I was up here a while back, looking at it like this, and I got an idea. Do you see what's below us now?"

Uncle Bob looked intently at the large island below. "It looks like Hispanola - let me see," he adjusted the binoculars, " - Is that what you wanted me to see?"

"Yes," she answered. "The western part is Haiti and the eastern part is the Dominican Republic. Haiti has been completely stripped for cooking fuel. There's so little vegetation remaining that we can tell the difference in the color from here. With these strong binoculars, Haiti looks like bare earth, although it's easy to see vegetation in the Dominican Republic. And we're only 285 miles up."

"What does it have to do with us? Does it relate to the project or to your new idea?"

"Both, in a way. Web 1 is operating over Africa, and Web 3 over Malaysia, and Web 2 is almost finished over the Seychelles and already producing power. Web 4 is just starting at 150 degrees east. For several years, I've been sending occasional loads of materials for the Web over South America. I'm going to put the fifth Web over the Galapagos, and provide power to Haiti and other countries that are on, or over, the edge of collapse in the Americas. But there's a problem. They can't afford the electricity, so the market isn't good to sell energy to them, unlike it was in Africa. We have to seed them with new industries so they can buy our electricity."

Just then, Hank floated up behind Danielle, put his arms around her, and gave her a hug and a kiss on the back of the neck. "Hello, Gorgeous, what are we doing for dinner this evening?"

She smiled and turned to Uncle Bob, "Isn't he sweet, Uncle Bob? Aren't you sorry you gave me away?" Then she turned to Hank, and said, "I gave the cook the evening off, Sweetheart, and invited Bill and Marion to a cookout. Bill thought Marion would want to come but wasn't certain. You know, she's big as a house, and a little self-conscious. I hope it's a girl. Maybe Jake and Terry would like to come too? By the way," she added, "you're the cook."

"Okay," Hank said, "I'll cook, but you eat it at your own risk. I'll ask Jake. But Terry may have a problem getting a babysitter on short notice."

"See if she can bring the baby. I want her to. The baby's growing up so fast."

Hank argued, "She's only three months old."

"Yes, and her brother is almost two. They'll be grown up before long, and I want to play with both of them some more while they're still little."

"Okay. I'll invite them and try to convince them to come. But I'd better get back and see how the preflight is coming on the ship for our trip Earthside." He left them floating by the viewport.

Danielle turned back to MacDonald. "Uncle Bob, in order to justify a power satellite over the western hemisphere, I have to develop a use for a lot of power. We are producing hydrogen in Mombassa with the surplus power from Web 1, and shipping it to consumers all over the world. Our fuel-cell plants are busy making it possible for folks to power their homes, cars and airplanes with that hydrogen. We need to have a satellite on-station anyway, to meet the demands of the Americas as they begin to develop. We know that need will grow as the supply of conventional energy decreases. But until that need is fully developed, the fifth Web will have a lot of excess power output, and we can't sell it to the general public in competition with the oil companies as long as they think they have an excess supply of oil. So I'm going to move on to something else. The project doesn't need me to run it any longer."

"But the project is your creation! How can you think of leaving it?" he said.

"I'm not necessary any longer. We expect to have an annual average hourly output of 45 gigawatts this year from Web 1. Next year is the first year I have to pay out dividends to the investors at 20% of their original investment. That means I have to come up with 12 billion dollars annually for those payments. The energy we sell this year will bring in just about 39 billion, and that's just from Web 1. We'll pay six billion in royalties. The investors will get 12 billion. Our operating costs will be about five billion. That leaves an operating surplus of about 16 billion from Web 1, most of which we'll spend on design and construction of the Moon Base and the fabrication facilities there and at L-5, which leaves all the revenues from Web 3 for me to use as I like. About half of those revenues I'm putting into building more satellites and receiving antennas. The numbers for Web 3 are higher than Web 1, as India is consuming a lot of power, and that will pay additional profits to the investors. The original investors will be receiving a big dividend on their investments, which will be paid forever by Web 1. The project could probably pay most of them back their principal almost immediately with surplus revenues from the other three satellites, but we aren't scheduled to return their original investments for five more years. After that, they will be receiving a percentage of the profits from all the secondary enterprises that have come from the project. Stellar Power manages the power distribution and the billing between countries and collects the payments. Lone Star's Swiss subsidiary works out the dividends to the investors and pays them and the royalties to the various host countries. Maurice is running the space plane operation and Jean Claude is overseeing the space station program. There's a process in place for determining their line of successors. There are eight more Webs in the design or construction stage, and we're testing parts of the Lunar station, where we'll be building the structural components for Webs 6 through 12, which will be paid for by revenue generated by Webs 2 and 3. The design is well along on the Space City at L-5. The whole process runs itself now, and I'm not needed to run it any longer. I'm still the head of state of the new nation, and I own it, and that's enough for me."

"Well, what are you going to do?" McDonald asked.

"That's what I wanted to talk to you about. Remember your old real estate business?"

"You mean landfills?"

"Yes. You sold out to Waste World."

"That's correct. What about it?"

"How many landfills did they buy?"

374

"About a hundred in the U.S. In addition to several hundred I had previously sold them a few at a time. Why?"

"How many other landfills are there in the United States?"

"Thousands. Managing them is one of the largest problems facing government."

Danielle said, "If you wanted to buy them back from Waste World, how much would they want for the hundred you sold them ... how much did they pay you?"

Uncle Bob hesitated, then said, "They paid me seven and a half billion, but they're all probably filled by now. Hell, they'd probably *pay* a lot to anyone who would take those landfills off their hands."

"Who else owns landfills, ... particularly filled ones?"

"Most are owned by local governments. They spend a fortune on them and they're an environmental nightmare. Rainfall percolates through them and leaches out the worst of the heavy metals and chemical pollutants, despite efforts to have liners and leachate treatment. They're like giant poisonous tea-bags. Leachate and smells are the big problems, but they also generate a lot of methane which usually has to be burned."

"I want to buy some landfills," she said.

"You really are losing it, dear." He started laughing and lost his grip on the railing next to the viewport. He was drifting around the compartment, laughing. Finally, he grabbed a hand-hold and composed himself.

Danielle pretended to be offended by his laughter, but had anticipated this reaction. "I'm serious. I'm going to mine the landfills and recover their contents. Think about it, Uncle Bob. For decades cities all over the world have been putting literally everything they couldn't figure out what else to do with into these mountains of garbage. They represent years of abandoned inventories from manufacturers all over the world. All we have to do is figure out how to sort out and market the contents of these piles."

"But Danielle," he protested, "these places are a witches' brew of chemicals. They all leak and every one is polluting the underground water. The liability for the operator is so huge that no one but government can afford to own one."

"Waste World owns a lot of them, doesn't it?"

"Yes, but they have special exceptions in the liability laws."

"We'll have those kinds of laws too, maybe, but we may not need them. If we can attack one landfill successfully, we should be able to go anywhere we want afterward. Cities will be begging us to take their landfills, maybe paying us to take them. I'm going to build a team of miners, chemists, and engineers to sort the materials on the sites, reclaim the reclaimables, process the solids into reusable materials, neutralize the poisons, and reclaim the chemical constituents. These are the biggest and most concentrated assemblages of resources in the world. Landfills are mountains of money, waiting there for us to shovel them up. It is raining dollar bills, Uncle Bob, and I'm going to turn over my umbrella and collect some. Even if we only do it once, then we'll know how, and we can sell or lease the technology and let someone else do the work. The technology will be fantastically valuable."

"How do you plan on doing this when no one else has been able to? And why?" he asked, skeptically.

"If you recall, that was the same question everyone asked me about the solar power satellites. The answer is because I have access to virtually unlimited amounts of inexpensive energy, which I can buy at 15 percent less than the price we sell it to other utilities, because there's no royalty to pay. And I win no matter what happens, because I own the satellites and will be buying the power from myself. The existing revenues from the *other* satellites will pay for the construction cost of the fifth Web as well as all the other parts of the program. We can focus that Web's transmitting antennas on receiving antennas on the landfills. As each landfill is cleared, we'll have a site ready for installation of a power-receiving antenna, located right in the middle of a major metropolitan energy-consuming area. We've learned a lot from our experience with small receiving stations in the Pacific. When we're ready, we start selling electricity to the local utility at a price less than they can produce it. I don't think they'll be able to resist the economics of the opportunity. Unlike Africa, in the U.S. we'll have a separate marketing company for each site.

"Our objective will be to clean up those sites, cleaner than they were before the first load of trash arrived. We'll pump up that witches' brew of leachate, concentrate it, refine it, sort it out and sell it. And make a lot of money in the process.

"And in the meantime, I'm going to install receiving antennas starting in Haiti and El Salvador, and then we can sell power to their neighbors. The royalties will provide the economies of these depressed countries with a big boost, and we'll also provide technical expertise and financing to help develop energy-related industries to increase their employment and standards of living, while we make money doing it."

He slowly realized she was serious, and began to see the possibilities. 'Here we go again,' he thought, 'Heaven help me, I love it so.'

EPILOGUE

So Danielle is now back in Guernsey more than ten years after it all started. She didn't realize, and never anticipated, that she would be unable to finish the space plane project and move on. That is, however, what has happened.

Like Prometheus, she has ended up chained to Mount Caucasus, except her Mount Caucasus is in Space, or rather it *is* Space. She should have known that the potential for development of the project would be so great that no one could finish it in his or her lifetime.

The design department has completed plans for the Moon base, and contractors are building the equipment for the Lunar mining and refining installation. The overall effort is moving swiftly forward to complete the plans for the Mars colony. Their big discovery is the ease of moving materials in Space. The exploration mission to the asteroid belt will be underway before they get to Mars, and they're hoping to find more materials there that can be used for building the space station and city at L-5.

Meanwhile, Earth's oil is beginning to run out. After a sag in prices when Prometheus began to supply large quantities of electrical energy, the price of other kinds of energy has begun a dramatic climb. There was a small door of opportunity when energy was still relatively cheap, and Danielle successfully stepped through it. If she had waited, she would not have raised the money to build the first Web. She can complete the Web system now and furnish the energy that is no longer available elsewhere because it has become too expensive for Earth's consumers to get it from traditional sources. Mankind, through the Prometheus Project, has broken free of the limitations imposed by Earth's gravity and taken the first baby steps toward the stars. We're on our way.

POST SCRIPT

Dear Reader,
The novel you have just finished is a work of fiction. There is no space plane. There is no solar power satellite. There are no receiving antennas. But the premise of the story is true. Microwave transmission of electricity is a reality and large-scale transmission is a real possibility. The 1977 NASA design study mentioned in this book really exists and proposes a similar system. The X-30 National Aerospace plane was indeed abandoned by the USA in the early 1990s. It was only in 2004 that the USA finally flew Hymat, a model-airplane-sized remote control aircraft designed to test the high-speed scramjet technology proposed for the X-30 and described in this book for the space plane. Scientists at Lawrence Livermore National Laboratories have proposed a space plane-type vehicle, but nothing further seems to have been done. The first draft of this story was written in 1994. It is now 2008 and still no one in the world seems interested in seriously addressing the global energy situation. In 1994, as I was beginning to write this book, the Japanese did in fact announce a plan to produce a large fraction of the world's energy needs with solar satellites by 2040, but by 2001 those plans degenerated to a plan to launch one satellite by 2040. I have heard nothing more about those plans since then. It seems to me that people who are seriously interested in the future of mankind would be asking why that is, and why we haven't started building a space plane or something like it already?

I want to thank some of the people who made this book possible. Above all, my wife, Pamela, who put up with my preoccupation with the book during the long time I spent working on the story.

After that, thanks to my good friend, Marilyn Zatinsky, whose travel business was the inspiration for the Marilyn VanDuser character, and to my sister, Maria, for their encouragement. I thank my high-school chum, Boyce Rensberger, for reading a draft and providing me his excellent critique of it. Thanks also to Wairimu Kwirikia, who really exists, but not as the fictional character in the book. She is in real life an exciting, inspiring young woman I met in Atlanta, Georgia in 1997. She graciously authorized the use of her name for the environmental activist character in Kenya, but the character is fictional. Special thanks to my artist friend, Maggie McClellan, for the cover design.

All the characters in the book are fictional, except Dr. Peter E. Glaser. Thanks, and apologies also, to Dr. Glaser, who was instrumental in the 1977 NASA study. Dr. Glaser was decidedly unhappy with the military application of the satellite in the story. His big criticism of my early draft was that everyone who writes about solar power satellites seems to be caught up with the "death ray" possibilities, and I guess I'm no exception.

Thanks to the folks at FlightSafety, in Lakeland, Florida and Houston, Texas, who provided technical details about the MU-2 air conditioning system and MU-2 checklists. Thanks to the Jeppesen Chart Company, who provided air navigation charts of Lisbon, Portugal. Thanks to the United States Geological Survey for maps of Palau that were instrumental in getting the geography of the islands right.

Thanks to the folks at the Washington, DC office of the Republic of Palau, who helped me with information about the islands. The places described in the book are real, but the topography is fictional. In 1994, the political situation of the islands was similar in reality to the situation described in this book. The large corporations described as participating in the space project, such as General Motors, FlightSafety, Boeing, Daimler-Benz, and Aerospatiale are real, but the events and their participation are fictional. Café Italiano was a real restaurant in Houston that I managed for a short time, but it has been out of business for many years. All the characters with a role in the book are fictional, and all the names are fictional except Dr. Glaser's and Wairimu's.

I hope you enjoyed reading this story as much as I enjoyed writing it and that it made you think about possibilities for the future.

"What if ...?"

Michael F. Chenoweth
Key Largo, Florida

www.ingramcontent.com/pod-product-compliance
Lightning Source LLC
Chambersburg PA
CBHW020934020726
47495CB00002B/485